MERCY

Tuula Costelloe

This paperback edition

First published 31st October 2024

Front cover art by Alena Nikolaeva/Shutterstock.com

Back cover art by Vladimir Mulder/Shutterstock.com

This story is best enjoyed with a hot cocoa and a cyanide pill

Prologue

Erica

Oh mama, I love you, but you've gotta let me go.

It's been ten minutes since he left the cellar, and the keys are still there.
He dropped them as he left.
They lie there, accusing me, that familiar bouquet of silver and black.
They're about three feet from my cage.
And if I could reach those keys, I could see my mother again.
I bounce out from the huddled position I take so easily these days, the only position that keeps me warm, and slide myself towards the cage's bars. My bare thighs collect more specs of porridge and old vomit fills my toes.
I stick my leg through the bar; it's skinny enough, of course. Now extend, just like in the ballet classes you used to do when you could do things, extend alllllll the way, and point that toe.
It comes up just short. A tantalising two inches between my big toe and his keys. Yet another thing to long for; for those two inches to dissolve. Now I have even more reasons to be unsatiated, unsatisfied; now hope has even more tools with which to burn me.
But if I reach those keys, I can see my mother again.
Because they aren't coming for me. No one's coming to save me. Nobody's gonna risk their life to get me out of here. I've learnt this. I've accepted it. Humans aren't here to help each other.
For as long as humans have skin, we're gonna skin each other alive.
And now I've finally accepted that, the opportunity to save myself has pretended itself. My captor has dropped his keys, three feet from my cage.
Come and get me.
I press myself against the bars, and twist my body to its side. I know, because I've tried it so many times before and failed every time, that no matter how much he starves me, the bars are too narrow for my body to fit through. I try again, get lodged at my shoulders this time; I reach out my arms and there's nothing I wish for more in that moment than to be able to dislocate them.
I can sense the footsteps of you all, up above me. You are my ceiling, you are my sky. Walking free. Walking across me. No idea what's below you. No idea how much I want to join you. No idea what I'd do for you once I found you.
I push at the cage. I've never bothered trying to move it forward, because what's the point when I can't get out of it? It would only make him angry. But now things have changed. Now there is two pounds of shiny, jingling temptation that has turned my six by six foot world upside down.
I push the cage again. It is paralysed. It obeys him, like everything else.

It's so cold down here. I swear it gets colder every day. I've become a bloodsicle, a tearsicle, a cauterised corpsicle - a frozen funsicle for his tongue to stick to. Today, this persecuted popsicle is gonna melt, and all its sticky liquid is gonna flow through the cage, seep under the door, and back into my mother's mouth. Then she'll make me solid and I'll walk free with all of you.

But how?

I look around, from my bowl to my cup. I could throw them but they are more likely to push the keys away. Why didn't he leave some of his ropes this time, some of his chains?

I put my leg through again, trusting that the world will let me grow taller if it knows that means I get to see my mother again. Surely the world will let me be longer once it understands how that would feel. He enjoys stretching me anyway, he enjoys putting me on the rack anyway - so stretch me now, stretch me good, stretch me deep - and *let my toes reach the fucking keys.*

And there it is again. Two inches of space. The space that has no idea how much it is oppressing me, how much loneliness it is damning me to.

But I **am** going to see my mother again.

I know what I need to do.

Holding onto the bar, with my leg still through, I bring my hips up and backwards, building momentum.

What is one more moment of pain, after all? What has all this pain been for, if not for now?

I close my eyes, and then I hurl myself; I am a snort, a vomit, a tear, and I catapult my pelvis into the bar.

I hear it, I feel it, I taste it.

Something has cracked.

Not in the cage. Something in me. Not in my heart. In my body. A bone, a ligament, maybe both. I have cracked something and it has made me long and tall and flexible.

And now my toe feels those keys for the first time in eight years.

And it curls around them like a first kiss.

And it is clutching them.

And it is bringing them to me.

And I am going to see my mother.

From the feet, to the hands, here they come. Black and silver. It's happening.

The keys are in my hands. I scuttle like the cockroaches I see sometimes, to where the lock is, my arm at a weird angle. Keys in, and keys round, and keys through. Turn. Turn. Turn. Again.

The cage opens.

My torso pulsates.

I leap through the cage.

Crash to the ground.

Oh my god. Oh my god. I'm outside of my cage. The bars are less rusty on this side. And on this side, I can stand up straight. So I do. Fuck you.
Standing in the space I thought I'd never stand in, in the kaleidoscope of forbidden dreams and the dust and the footsteps I dreaded.There's the hook he hangs the keys on. There's the rack. There's the chair. There's the tank. All the things he used for his experiments. They look so much smaller on this side.
And now there's nothing between me and the planks. The large wooden planks. He nails them across the gap, every time he leaves. Always the same ones.
I've craved this moment so many times. Can't remember life before I craved this. **And from the craving, comes the carving.**
You see? Swap the R with the A and you run your whole damn life again. A girl who can carve is a girl who is strong, a girl who can get the future she wants. So I'm going to carve my way to that door.. Nothing will carve him up like coming back to an empty cage.
Oh god, oh god, is this going to work?
If it does, I get to see my mother again.
I grow a thousand limbs as I run to the planks. I slam into the wood, I'll take all the splinters in the world, for the rest of my life, if this door will just open for me now.
See, these planks have been my friends for eight years, from twenty to twenty eight; we've rotted together. We've watched each other every day. I've seen how weak they've become, how sloppy, how they've died down here without light and without fresh oxygen. He's shamed their texture from solid oak to something like moss, something like crepe, something like dough, and I know as I slam myself into them over and over again they're going to submit for me, come apart sluttily for me, disengage from each other for me. Hail Satan, Hail Splinters, they shower me in their shards, but this is a pact, this is a promise, I know they want this for me - *if it can't be us, then let it be you.* A couple more lunges and they've hatched me through.
I'm past the planks. I'm at The Other Door.
The Iron Door. I would see it just for a second when he takes the planks down. The keys in my hand are only for my cage, not for this door.
This door is bolted. A fresh challenge. But, you see, he designed this place very specifically, with everything in mind. He tore out the whole basement of his house so that he could do this to me. He made it so he could bolt it on this side, so the few times he lifted from my cage and to the tank, there would be a delay in me getting through this door, and he'd catch up to me in time easily. Then he bolted the other side too of course. But, for efficiency, he made it so the bolts were connected. This side controls the other, and vice versa. This symmetry is going to be what lets him down. Six silver rods, slammed to the left, and I'm free.
Top bolt first.
Bish. Bash. Bosh.

Second bolt.
Bish. Bash. Bosh. Let's go.
Middle bolt.
Slash, slash, slash. This is too quick. This is too easy. The bolts aren't even stiff; I guess he uses them all the time.
Bottom bolt. Slash. Bash.
Last one.
There we go. *I've unbolted the fucking door.*
I'm crying thinking it's a trick, but then I push, and the door opens for me oh-so-submissively. It was just a door, all this time. It can't say no. Doors can't give consent.
Now the staircase. I remember this staircase. I remember the day I was thrown down its flight, how many bones I broke on the way. I told it I would come back for it. I told it I would break it before he broke me.
I peer up it. It tries to be ominous, it tries to remind me I am a creature of the underground, that I will never rise up. But what it told me for eight years, my mother told me the opposite for twenty.
You have to be quiet, you can't fuck this up now. But you have to be fast.
I take two at a time, a perfect blend of speed and lightness. For the first time I am glad he gave me no shoes.
A spiral staircase like something out of a fairytale. It smells of popcorn in here. *Watch this. Watch how fast I can run.* I can't wait to eat popcorn with my mother again.
I have reached the hatch.
I look at the keys. This must be what the other one is for. The silver for the cage, the black for the hatch. He's told me, taunted me, about how he locks it when he comes in, just to ensure I'll never escape unless I can get the keys off him first, and he is so much bigger and stronger than me.
I see a tiny hole in the floorboards. Next to it, another little hook for him to hang them on.
And I know what that means. This man is a perfectionist, and he's very, very careful. He's not a loner, I can tell - he has people over. He has business to attend to. He is too careful to leave a pair of suspicious keys lying mysteriously around his house. He locks the hatch when he leaves, but he pushes the keys through this hole and hangs them off this hook. There are no other keys. There are no other barriers. There's nothing on the outside There is nothing else sealing me in.
I plunge the key into the hatches lock. I try it one way; it doesn't move. I try it another; it doesn't move.
Deeper. I need to go deeper.
I force it in. He's taught me well. Turn it to the left.
Eyyy, now we're talking, in I go. Open up, baby. Slut and wood, nothing more.
I've unlocked the hatch. And that's when I feel it.

My body throbs with dread.
Of course, of course. He's too smart to leave the keys to his captive lying around the house, and so he's too smart to leave the hatch she is under uncovered. I may have unlocked the hatch, but there's something above it.
And I'm very, very weak now. It'll be a miracle if I'm strong enough to move it.
But if I am strong enough, then I will get to see my mother again.
The hatch may be heavy in my underfed, underused arms, but it's just light enough that I can wedge it upwards a couple of inches. Sure enough, there is something above it. One hand balancing the hatch, my fingers fight to find it, press into it. Come on, come on, why can't I just swallow it? I'll swallow all the wood in the world, the hatch and all the floorboards too, if it'll just let me through.
As my fingers press into it, I feel it. I test it. It's the bottom of something. A box. A chest, perhaps. I test it again. I feel it again, confirming my suspicions. Thank you, thank you, thank you. Whatever it is is empty. And empty, means light.A full chest would have been heavy. But this. Just. Light. Enough.
And though it is agony to walk it towards me, to stretch my fingers to the end of their nerves, to send hot wires down my arms, to turn my armpit into a crater of sizzling electricity, I've got just enough strength, just enough balance, to walk my fingers across the bottom of the box until they've reached the end of it. I sacrifice my skin to the edge of the hatch and I pull something impossible from the depths of my shoulder and somehow, somehow, I send the chest sliding off the hatch and onto the floorboards around it.
One last push.
One last big brave push.
Both hands now. I push the hatch, and it flips open. I hope it broke its back.
My hands plunge into the floorboards. Hook my nails in and then jump, jump until my ribcage is at one with the floorboards. This is the benefit of being light; it's easy to drag my legs through. I'm an alligator now, belly low to the ground as I roll. I'm out.
I look up and realise I'm beneath a bed, its beams glinting above me. This wasn't here when he first dragged me down; this room wasn't a bedroom before. Turns out he really does sleep above me.
Oh god, what if he's sleeping now?
Gently, I roll, and roll again, edge and edge until I'm out from under the bed. Edge and edge and edge and oh how good it feels to not have something two feet above me and edge and engage and sit up and - he's not in the bed.
And there's a window. There's an actual window. My brain can't process that I'm looking at the outside again and I'm seeing real air again. I think it's mid afternoon, I think it's winter, but it's too much to process - all that matters is that this bedroom is on the ground floor.

As my eyes dance round the room, I see the memorabilia of our life together. The corsets he made me wear. The silk he made me stroke. The glass he made me eat. The mirrors he made me look into.

Shall I look? Shall I see it? Shall I see what he's done to me down here? Shall I see what I look like now?

Too late; as I spin I catch my reflection anyway, blots of me making their way to the fingerprints on the mirror, showing me the truth. That's me.

Look at this. Look at that. Look at me. How do you bring yourself to break the jaw of a butterfly?

I want to count my bruises, I want to explore the split in my lip, but there is no time, Erica. Erica, Erica, is that still my name? There's no time for Erica. There's no time for anyone. I HAVE TO GET OUT OF THIS ROOM.

I hear a car oh god the outside oh god not him not him. Duck down, duck down, what if he sees you through the window. I crawl to the door. *It's not locked.* If I move, I'll be in the hallway. WHAT IS HAPPENING.

Move, Erica. MOVE.

Feels like a joke but it's happening, my legs are moving, my arms are dragging, my body is through, and I'm through, I'm through, I'm out of the room, the room whose floor got to call itself the sky to me for so long.

But I'm about to see the real sky. I'm about to let it touch me. Everything can touch me but him. *GO.*

And I'm back in the hallway I saw all those years ago. He still has that Vase on the mantelpiece, I tried to grab it as he dragged me by the hair. He still has a collection of blue umbrellas. I think the carpet has changed. I can see the front door. It smells like him.

I think he's upstairs.

I think he's watching TV.

Another contraction erupts in me; an unjust ripple of tantalisation and excitement and dread that it's going to go wrong. I've dreamed of this door so many times before - it petrifies me that this might mean this is just yet another one of my freedom dreams, the ones where I wake up more chained up than I was before.

But if it's not a dream, then that means - say it with me now - *that I get to see my mother again.*

See her, feel her, hold her, become a vibrating effigy of mucus and love, create a fifth element with our love - a mumnado, mumcano, mumpocalypse, a natural disaster brewed from the emotion we will feel when we see each other again.

All I have to do is get to the front door.

I think the TV has stopped.

I think I hear footsteps.

I think he's heard me.

But he's up high, on the top floor; he'd have to get down four or five flights of stairs to get to me, and that's if he heard me. I'm six metres from the door. For the first time, I have the advantage.
And there's nothing between me and the door but the air. Am I scared of the air? Nah. I'm not scared of anything.
And so for all the times he's force fed me, now I force feed the air - I plunge my torso down it's trachea til it's coughing, hacking, choking, regurgitating me back up, and, with a gurn and a splutter, sending me straight through the front door.
And that's exactly what it does.
The doors open. I'm on the other side.
I don't even remember how I got the door open - maybe I ran straight through it. All I know is now I'm standing in the fresh air on a residential road.
I think my heart has stopped
And it's just started again.
Now it pops.
Now it crackles.
Now it stops.
Now it starts.
Now it blooms.
Now it howls.
Now it's burst my gut.
Now it's up my spine.
Now it's in my eyes.
Now it's frost.
Now it's fire.
Now it's stolen the sun.
Now it's swallowed the sky.
Oh god, am I really free? Could I really be, the F word, me, could that really be meant for me? No, no, there's too much air out here, I'm not made for this oxygen, I'm not made for this air, I'm not strong enough to carry the sky without a cellar's ceiling to do it for me. *Except maybe I am.*
I've done it.
I'm it, I'm it, I'm the girl who came back.
I'm the girl who made it out, the girl who burst through the earth.
Nobody has ever felt this before.
Freedom's already a concept, freedom's in the dictionary, freedom's been done before. Not this.
They hadn't invented this feeling before now. This is being born again.
No. It's more. This is how it feels to be conceived.
No. It's more. It's more, baby. This is the inception of the universe.
This is the very first moment. This is the first thing ever. This is the big bang. This is the spark of life. All the power that came then, comes to me now.

So why am I still standing outside his front door?
Why haven't I moved yet?
Why am I rooted to the spot, letting him find me?
Why am I giving him the chance to catch me?
Why am I waiting to feel his hands around my neck?
Come on. If I run now, I can see my mother again.
And not just that.
I can lie in the sun again.
I can drink tequila again.
I can ride a rollercoaster again.
I can dance again.
So why haven't I run? Do I still belong to him? If not, then why haven't I run?
Let's be honest. This is wrong, isn't it? Me, escaping, like this, today - it doesn't click, it doesn't fit, it doesn't make sense in my body. I don't belong up here, in the light. I was born to be down there - I was born to be his.
This is gonna upset the balance of the universe.
For one person to go up, another must go down.
For one person to fly, another must sink.
And what if that person is you?
Could you do it? Could you handle what I've handled? Could you take what I've taken? Do you possess that strength? Will you take my place, to satiate him, to placate him, so he doesn't come for me?
Go on. Tell me you would. Give me the strength to escape. Give me the strength to be happy. Give me the strength to let you rot in my place.
After all, deep down, you know that you deserve it. I don't know what you did but I know you did something you can't live with - the moment I met you I could smell your shame.
You need to let it out. You need to tell someone. You need to share the secret. It'll feel so good to finally say it.
Say it and I'll run. Say it and I'm gone. Say it and I'm free.
Tell me.
What did you do?

Part One
The Mistake

Chapter One

Myles

A girl walks down the street. Spring in her step, hope in her heart.
She is barely twenty, the world at her feet. She moves with the kind of warm confidence only a young stunning girl can possess. Her hair tumbles down her back; buttery blonde, long and thick all the way down. Her outfit is simple; slim fitting grey hoodie and tight black jeans; but that body makes any outfit magic. It's a cold morning but the air feels fresh on her skin, diving merrily into her lungs, sparking her eyes awake as she takes in the day. A smile here, a nod there, everybody on her side. Though many moments are like this for her, somewhere inside her she knows it's a moment worth treasuring. Another special second in her special life.
She pulls out her phone to ring her friend, who answers instantly – 'Heyyy Taylor,' – the only question on their soft lips being 'How will we have fun today?'

But this is not the story of the girl walking down the street. Let's turn our attention to thirty feet above her, up, up, up, to the rooftop of the building whose shadow she bathes in. Up to where a nameless man stands at the edge.
About to jump.
If only he knew. If only he knew what'll happen if he doesn't execute the perfect jump. If only he knew that if he leaps too far forward or if he drops down too close to the ledge, a monster will be made. If only he could see what will happen if he doesn't lean back quick enough. If only he knew what he'll do if his fall takes too long.
If only he knew what he's about to do.
If only Taylor knew to move out of the way.
If only we could tell them what they need to know -
If he gets the jump wrong, he will crush her.

15 hours til The Jump

Myles and Gerry met in a hotel bar.
Both were wearing what they said they would be – Myles a blue suit, Gerry a pair of brown overalls.
Above them, The Debate raged on screen. Today was a Thursday, and it was a Thursday that would go down in History.
It was a debate the UK had had to fight to have, now shaking the Houses of Parliament with the passion its topic ignited. *The E Word.* The government had even considered holding a referendum on the issue, until the research had shown

it was almost positive to go through if they did. With the public, this topic played well, hitting a spot nothing else could hit.

The other guests were so transfixed on The Debate - you could hear a cocktail stick glide into an olive with the reverent silence they gave each argument - that they didn't notice Myles and Gerry, even though Myles was the kind of man you usually couldn't to ignore. And yet today, he wanted it this way. Today he was Gerrys, and Gerry his.

They approached each other in silence, shook hands and made their way to the lift.

Myles had already checked into room 505. He slid the key card in and when it sighed open, held the door open for Gerry, who nodded a thank you. They entered, still silent, admiring the subtle class of the suite. As Gerry poured himself a glass of scotch, Myles handed him the envelope for five thousand pounds. Gerry nodded thank you once more. For the first time, he looked into Myles eyes.

They were both big men, over six foot and strong, but Gerry was by far the biggest. A blend of protein and fat, standing tall and girthy in the room. He had a large tongue in a large head, a large chest, large thighs – and his hands. His hands were perfect.

There was a delicacy to those hands as they unlaced Myle's tie, unravelling it to reveal Myles neck, just as they had agreed. He let the tie fall to the floor and then Myles walked over to the bed.

He knelt on it gingerly, before laying facing down. And then he remembered; Gerry wanted to look him in the eye as he did it.

Myles, obeying the conditions of their agreement, rolled over onto his front, just as Gerry finished pulling on black leather gloves. Gerry walked over to the bed, led by the molten, swollen texture between his legs.

He crawled up over him, smelling him. He smelt no nerves, not even a little bit, no particles of sweat waiting to catch those that dripped off Gerry. As calm as though this was meant to be.

He'd never knelt on a more comfortable bed, never felt silkier sheets, never stayed anywhere with this much ambience. Everything was just right. The maids had even left two mint chocolates on the pillows; he'd have both after.

Gerry reached the spot he'd been imagining for so long; himself knelt over another man's chest. Finally he could do it, the act that had danced in the distance of his brain for all those years.

He rolled up his sleeves, placed his hands around Myle's neck – and began to choke him.

14 hours til The Jump

As Myle's neck became a weak, malleable thing between his hands, Gerry became only stronger, thicker, solid as gold.

Choking Myles was giving him the kind of undeniable hardness that no stroke from a hand or a tongue had managed to do, not from a man or woman, not once in all these years. As the blood washed from Myle's face, it swelled Gerry's shaft.

And he knew everybody would judge him, but he didn't care. Everybody had given into their urges at one point. Everybody had cheated on a diet. So how could they be sure they wouldn't do this, if it was murder not chocolate that they craved?

He lifted his thumb from the trachea, watching as he, and only he, allowed a little glimmer of life to spit back into the man between his thighs. Frustration billowed in Myle's eyes but his lungs still succumbed to it, still greedily hoovering in that little bit of air. And then just like that, Gerry shut his thumb down again and forbade him from a breath that was desperate to come.

This was how he liked to do it, how he had been playing with the neck for the past sixty minutes; on, off, on, off, watching it perform perfect pulsations in his paws, watching it glide from shades of violet to lilac to amethyst. Purple had always been his favourite colour, and now he knew why.

Only just now, did he have the perfect grip. It had to come to him naturally, the neck snug in his hands. All he had to do was

keep

applying

pressure

And he would be what he wanted to be. A killer.

13 hours til the Jump

Client and customer. Sinking deeper into the silk.

They'd agreed to this online. Found each other on the dark web. Myles had initiated contact. Gerry was simply fulfilling a desire. A man's desire to die. And he did have that desire, there was no doubt about it - Gerry could see it. He'd expected him to back out until the moment he met him, until the moment he could see the pain on his face. It was all in the swirling brown eyes; rusty red stitches from crying, looking up at him from the bed now, utterly without resistance. As though being choked didn't hurt him at all. Looking up at him, the way a lash fluttering deer looks up at those who have crashed into her on the road: begging them to just do it.

But Gerry hadn't done it yet.

Cos Gerry could not help how good it felt, to stop then start, lift one thumb then the other, basking in the control he had over when and how Myles breathed. Riding that rush of shame all the way to the edge, then reeling it back.

'Gerry,' at last Myles rasped. 'Is there anything I can do? To help?'

Those words were what he needed. How dare his prey speak to him, question him, offer to *help* him! Granite and gravel were injected into Gerry, and he raised his big paw and slapped him in the face.
'That's enough talking,' he sneered. 'That's it for you. You'll never say another word.'
Let's shut him up for good.
Time for the climax.
All the anger in all the world, Gerry squeezed into Myles neck, a thousand particles of fury he tried to combust into that one lonely cylinder, years of tyre flips and steroids fuelling Gerry's obsession with turning that neck from a python to a worm – Myles had been right to tell him to wear gloves, not just for his protection but he would never have had any grip with how much his hands were sweating – and from python to worm it started to happen – the eyes rolling back, the body jerking, *at last* the cries of resistance, and finally Gerry was brave enough to go through all the rules that told you to be good.
He was falling now, into a hazy pleasure, a melancholy soup of shame inviting him to the land of satisfaction, reserved for those who cleansed the earth of its waste.
But
Then
No
Oh, no, no. Uh oh.
He didn't fall into shame. Instead, he became it. He was nothing else.
One flick and it happened. A nausea that could last for eternity, a reptilian retch inside his ribcage, and suddenly everything hurt, everything smelt, everything stung, and he cared for the man beneath him more than he'd ever cared for anything in his life.
Regret poured down his throat – glug glug glug – and he knew in an instant he would never be able to swallow again if he didn't let go of this man's neck.
He leapt from Myles, releasing him, rolling to the end of the bed – agile in a way his bulk had never been
What the hell are you doing, boy!
What were you about to do, boy!
The gloves were ripped off, exposing a sinner's hands, hands he buried his face in to welcome in the blackness. He was breathing so hard anyone would think it was him who'd just been choked. He couldn't look up, couldn't look forward, couldn't look at the other warm presence on the bed, the presence of the life he'd been planning to take.
What, what, what had he just been doing - the debt he was just about to incur - why, boy, why!
His hands singed, flayed open, every molecule wrestling with what it had just done. And he could not hear breath and he could not hear movement and he was

very much aware that it may be too late and he couldn't turn around for fear of what might be there. Or *not* there.
Thankfully, there was then a shuffle. Myles was coming to him. Sure enough, bit by bit, regaining his strength and voice, he rolled to the end of the bed too.
'Gerry? What's wrong?'
Gerry couldn't speak. *Couldn't look.*
'Ok, let's take a break for a second,' Myles's voice was calm. 'Just breathe. Relax. Would you like a glass of water?'
There he went again, this strange and handsome man, offering him the chance to quench a thirst.
Gerry rose from the bed, walked around it, to the window, looking out at the grey sky. He had chosen the hotel, one of the best spots to see the view in London. He had stepped on the control, accidentally turning on the flat screen TV - The Debate blasted into their room, the whines of politicians recentring Gerry for a second.
Myles was still there, the gloves were still on the floor, the 'Do Not Disturb' sign on the door – everything was still in place.
Myles' voice was tender. 'Come to bed. What can we do to make this work?'
He turned back to him, at last meeting his eyes.
'I'm afraid you're going to have to leave,' he said. 'You can take your money.'
Myles stood too, til they were level. A new kind of brown churned in his eyes, spinning on saucers of betrayal.
'Why?' he whispered. More confused than angry.
Then Gerry spoke words he never knew he could speak, never knew he even wanted to speak, and bit by bit, word by word, came a strange feeling.
'I guess …' he laughed as the realisation tumbled through him. 'I guess I don't have it in me. I guess I'm a good person after all.' Glee. This was glee. His heart danced and he couldn't help but chuckle. 'It's not that I can't do this, it's that I don't *want* this.' He was not against the world. He was *with* the world.
He paced the room, processing his new reality. More glee came and scooped him up. 'I am good. I am kind. And I'm not the parasite they told me I was.' Yeah baby. He gave a little spin. 'All this time I felt like nothing. I'm *something*. I'm someone. I don't have to hate myself anymore. I - actually - deserve to be happy. Fuck, I can't believe this is real.' He caught sight of himself in the mirror. A laugh, his first real laugh, popped out of him. 'Tell me, man, what should I do first? Call my brother? Get a dog? Go on a date?' He clasped the shoulders of this strange man he'd met on some dark corner of the internet three days ago. 'Let's open the mini bar!' Serious for a second: 'Thank *you* man.'
Myles stepped backwards and out of his grasp, standing on the control, quelling the TV to silence.
Out of the silence, came a wheeze. A wheeze as Myles sank down to the floor, his knees grinding to the ground. He hunched over, hiding his face.

'Myles?' Gerry knelt next to him. He really did care for him, he realised. 'What is it?'
Myles groaned, thumped on his chest, his hands trying to grab at the carpet. 'It's just - I'm just - I'm so *jealous*.' He laughed bitterly.
'Jealous?' Gerry frowned.
'Yes,' Myles wiped his brow and for the first time Gerry saw him flinch from his own touch. 'Because I wish – I wish I could say the same.' He shivered, recoiling into himself. His next sentence was all gasp, torn from his lungs, twisting as they came. 'I would give anything - *anything* - to be able to say that again.'
Red wires shot through his eyes. 'But I can't. You have no, no idea how lucky you are not to owe someone your life.' He looked into Gerry's eyes as if he was gravity himself. A sadness so intense came over him that Gerry knew he had to get out of the room before it got him too. 'Whatever you do, don't let go of that.'
Gerry nodded, shrivelling inside his overalls. He scrambled to his feet; no, he would not be opening the mini bar for them. He didn't know exactly who he was in this hotel room with, didn't know exactly what Myles was referring to or thinking about; all he knew was he wanted to leave him behind.
So he did. Just as everyone ever had.

12 hours til the Jump

If Gerry wasn't going to murder him, Myles would murder himself.
It would be a considerate suicide.
No delayed metros, no horrified neighbours, no mess upon the pavement. No nooses, no knives, no overturned cars. No roses laid at the point of the tragedy. Nothing but the simple, subtle, silent power of Paracetamol.
Bags throbbing from Tesco to Sainsburys - he'd had to go to several different supermarkets to be allowed to buy enough - he leaned back in the lift that would take him up to his penthouse. A slick and glassy capsule, his penthouse covered the whole top floor of a Skyscraper above the city. You had to be a really gifted events organiser to be able to afford something like this, and Myles was exactly that. He'd been so proud when he bought it, proud it was the profits of his own events company that had made this possible, and it was funny how all that pride amounted to nothing now. How you could make one decision and everything else you'd ever done diffused around it, it and hatred came instead.
The lift chimed. The doors parted straight into his penthouse. A duplex shaped like a heart. A hushed silence hung in its centre.
Good. Good. He would die alone.

11 hours til the Jump

For a man who had sampled the finest cuisine life had to offer, it was a strange irony that his last supper would be a handful of crushed pills.
One week dining in a cliff top restaurant in the tropics, sampling their freshly caught lobster; the next being hosted in a secret gourmet hotspot in Tokyo, savouring their new matcha meringue – everything sprinkled, garnished, seasoned – long meals, heavy meals, feasts, banquets, never knowing how many courses, but knowing no good meal ended before the sun came up. The life of a party planner meant constant sampling, constantly being impressed.
He sat in his lounge, and surveyed the spread in front of him, a world of crushed powder spilling across his glass coffee table. He was reminded of his time as a food critic.
Paracetamol infused Codeine with a Panadol Garnish.
*3****
Slightly sour, with a trace of ink. Not too powdery and ever so easy to swallow. No congestion, no bloating, no difficulty sleeping afterwards. The perfect snack before bed. Disintegrating on the tongue, good for those who aren't good with spice.
Calories: none. Not that that matters any more.
Take with at least 200 ml of water. 2 pills every six hours, so they say. Be aware of the blood in your belly.
Goes down perfectly with a glass of Rose.

10 hours til the Jump

Dear Mum,
I've been sitting in front of my coffee table for two hours, staring at sixteen pounds' worth of ground up painkillers and a bottle of Rose. Trust me; I'm not scared. I want to take it and I will. But I realised what was stopping me; I couldn't take it before I wrote you a letter, before I spoke to you.
Words seem so stupid when you're talking about your mother, when you're trying to do justice to how much you love her – what could I squeeze out of this pen that could ever compare to the way you've rocked my world since the moment I was born? I imagine another life with another mother and I shudder. How boring that would have been.
Mother, mum, mummy, ma – believe me, I know how lucky I am. I'm lucky in a way I can never repay, with a debt so expensive and heavy I was doomed from the moment I came out of your womb. I want to write thank you until there's no ink left in the world – thank you for giving me every moment you could and even the ones you couldn't. You wrapped my world up in love and you rose me up and you made me part of a team. You and me, me and you, the power of two going through this one life together. No matter what people did to me, you could delete the pain, just like that.
But even you, even you couldn't erase what I did to people.

Remember when I was little, really little, like four or five, and you'd pick me up and put me on your chest and tickle me and then I would kick and punch and pummel at you. You'd say, 'you can't hurt me, you're too little, you're not strong enough to ever hurt me,' and I'd growl, 'I am, I am! I'm big and strong!' and you'd say, 'Nope, there's nothing you can do to ever hurt me,' and I'd roar, 'But you're a *girl*! Boys are stronger than girls! Boys are bigger than girls so I'm gonna beat you! I can hurt you! I'll break you! Hahaha!' And I'd drum my fists against you with all my might and kick my little legs at you with all my strength, and you'd laugh and go, 'Ow! What a little monster you are! Help, help!' but you'd let me keep going because it never really hurt you at all.

But it turns out that I was right all along.

I can hurt women.

I am strong and big and powerful, and I am very much capable of breaking a woman in two.

I'm going to try to tell you what I did …

The rage came suddenly one day, leaking through my mind like a first period. Red, unexpected, unfamiliar, globulus, embarrassing, disposable, in need of a mother. I had been in a meeting about launching a new summer event, trying to get my point across to a lazy, misguided group of employees. Suddenly their voices got too much, curling up in me like smoke, hitting a sweet spot of raw meat that couldn't be denied.

Before I knew it I was charred black. I wanted to hurt every single person in that room. They stopped being my colleagues and started being my opponents, vicious fighters who were in the ring to take me down, but I would not let them. No. My rage reached such a climax, so quickly, I could taste the smoke in my lungs as I screamed and roared and lunged for them. *Are you a woman boy?!*

I only knew what I'd done when I came to. They call it 'dissociative fugue.'

A week off and a healthy dollop of embarrassment later, and I thought I was cured. Thought it had just been an 'episode', unprecedented and unjustified, but one I could move on from. The result of not enough sleep and too much caffeine.

But a month later, another Rage came, this time at the supermarket. All I was doing was choosing the freshest looking lettuce and the biggest pot of hummus when the rage poured over me like tar. People were in my way and a tall women was knocking my basket off my elbow and the clerk had looked at me funny and it was all too much for little Myles to deal with, just far too many things to fit into one moment and the only way to make the moment big enough was to scream and hurl a shelf of jars to the floor.

When I came to from that one, I couldn't remember why I was in the supermarket at all.

Glass shards in a mustard-jam-pickle mess wasn't enough to shock the Rages from my body. The tap was unscrewed, and the water was too hot for anyone to get near. Nobody knew why it was happening. Popular, fun, exciting Myles,

Myles with all his money, all his prospects, all his charm, all his ideas, was now utterly at the mercy of his mysterious Rages. They kept coming, unexpected, sudden, each one bigger than the last, and the worst part was, I couldn't reason with them - they had possessed me. They had all the power.

So of course I lost clients, lost friends, but the one thing I managed to hold on to, was Rose. You remember Rose, don't you? I know you only met her once.

And now this next part is the part I've wanted to tell you for so long. Because I want you to tell me that it's ok and I want you to tell me that you will love me anyway.

But I can't.

Like, I actually can't.

Because the truth is I'm living in a fantasy, of a world where you are here to find this letter. You will hold it to your chest and say, 'he was misunderstood' and you will organise the perfect classy funeral for me.

But I'm kidding myself, aren't I?

Because you're not here at all. You can't tell me I still deserve to live. You can't tell me you'll forgive me. You're not here to tell me you want me to be happy – not here to embrace me, not here to reassure me, not here for me to confess to, not even here to make me a cup of tea. You haven't been here for the past year. You died last year and I miss you too much and this letter is probably being read by the cleaner right now. Remember to scrub under the sink.

If only I had you, if I only could hold you, if only you weren't up in the sky or down in the mud, I think I never would have lost control at all.

But you're gone. And it turns out I'm the monster you never thought I could be.

And if you were watching me from the clouds that night, I bet you had to look away.

And there's no point even writing this letter. Cos you can't help me now.

I may as well rip it up and choke on it. I may as well bleed out from the papercuts. I hope I do.

Your son,
Myles.

9 hours til the Jump

He made himself look into the mirror as he took each pill. One by one. Press a button and his flat screen TV revealed his reflection, feeding him the face he had been proud of for so long. Myles' looks were dynamic. He was all charcoal and smoke, all deep eyes and salt and pepper stubble, black hair clipped short in a way only his bone structure could pull off. As the procession of pills made their way to his mouth, he realised how much he'd relished being told he looked like a wolf, like a villain, and how much that disgusted him now. So chew, wolf, chew. Die, wolf, die.

Myles swallowed the pills, every last grain of the powder. He washed back the rose and then he waited. The debate played on his TV in the background; the House of Commons throbbed as the arguments went on. The day was coming to an end, but parliament had no chance of being dismissed - this debate would be going on long into the evening. Myles heard the word 'dignity' and he closed his eyes.
Wherever fate chose to take him, was where he would now go.
Fate chose to make him dream.

8 hours til the Jump

He was a kid again, looking out of his bedroom window. Waiting, waiting, for The Cherry Tomato Van.
He seemed to be the only one who'd seen it – he asked his mother and told his friends but they all made out he was lying, or joking.
Sure enough, as 6am came around, The Cherry Tomato Van came too. It was a giant delivery van, from some supermarket, he was never really sure which, its walls decorated with a summery scene of falling, bouncing red fruits. When the back opened up, inside were hundreds of cherry tomatoes. However they weren't normal sized ones – they were huge, rolling orbs, the size of summer beach balls brought out for children's parties for them to hop on. None were in containers, instead rolling loosely in the van.
There was one container however, empty but large enough to hold them all. Clad in a red net, it was a giant plastic box standing upright at the back.
That morning, the van pulled into a house directly opposite Myles. The driver and his passenger opened up the back, collected the container and knocked on the door. His neighbour Carol answered, smiled and let them in.
Two minutes went by.
Then they emerged, both of them carrying the container. It was stacked with giant cherry tomatoes, but inside it, also, was Carol's husband.
He was screaming, kicking, tearing at the net. Carol followed behind them calmly. They lifted up the door to the back of the van, and for the first time young Myles noticed several containers, each one with a different person inside, flailing to be released from their packets. As they fought and battled, the cherry tomatoes burst, puckering open, both the ones inside the net and the ones rolling free in the van. Each orb split like a stabbed eyeball, filling the van with watery red juice so the containers floated up to be immersed in a yellow-red bath, the nutrient rich juice half bathing half drowning the trapped people, skin from the tomatoes slipping off to seal their screams, the one whole thing a sorry, sloppy mess.
'Carol!' her husband yelled. 'Please, don't do this! I was going to get better! I was going to be strong, for you! I would never have left you or the kids, I swear!' Surely he was not to become one of these sticky people.

Carol came up to the net, causing the men to pause before they loaded him into the van. She looked him in the eyes and hissed as she spoke. 'I *saw* you, tying that rope up.' A juicy sphere gave way with her words, mossy red flesh tumbling out. The fruit washed into his hair as if it was trying to go through him. 'You were willing to put us through the worst grief imaginable. You didn't think we were worth living for. A few months of depression and you snapped. What if one of the boys had walked in on you in the bathroom? So why should I fight for you?'

It all made sense, at last, what the van was for. It was for those who weren't willing to try to live. But the real mystery was, where exactly was it taking them?

'What's going to happen to me?' He cried as he was loaded into the van.

Great big bulbs bobbed towards him. One had opened up, exposing its welted uterus, threatening to consume him in it.

'I don't know. But one thing's for sure,' Carol said. A thick green stalk spun by, prodding him behind the eye. 'I've saved your life today. It'll be a long, long time before my sons have to attend their father's funeral.'

'No! No!' the prisoners of the van screamed at this news, and their throats filled with pith and seeds.

Ripe fruit and rotten people, Myles thought, watching in awe. Or rotten fruit and raw people.

The hinges on the door came down, and the engine revved up. Carol, another customer satisfied, gave the driver the nod. The van oozed calmly out of the neighbourhood, its oozing contents sealed up inside.

They were washed red, in a tease of the blood they would never bleed.

7 hours til the Jump

He saw black. Sweet black.

Am I free? Is it over?

He was inside of a black silk dress, rolling between the fibres, the layers of the fabric. It was slippery in here, and cool, his skin quenched.

So this is how it is. The 'after'. I can accept this.

He was inside of a black moon. There was no gravity, and no sense of space, and worst of all, no sound, but he didn't mind that. He hadn't asked for anything but the black.

Time to drift.

He was inside of a black cat. And the cat was glossy, shiny, stalking through the night, its fur an enviable, perfect, deep black that ink or onyx could never be. He was warm now, could even hear light purring.

Unlucky.

Oh no -

No, stop -

He was inside of a lump of coal - *stop, stop* -
The black silk ripped in half, and the claws of the cat reached through, plucking Myles back into his sprawling living room.
He was on the floor, vomit falling from his lips, each heave a crushing defeat as his cute, easy, edible murderers went back on their promise. He cried out. The rose washed through him to meet the carpet he was clutching. Even his last meal, three days ago, was coming up.
His body wouldn't let him process the pills. His TV still rattled, as The Debate still played - had The Houses Of Parliament ever gone on this late before? A campaigner with watery eyes spoke compellingly to the rest of the chamber. He'd seen the guy speaking everywhere recently; Myles knew that look. A man desperate to get what he wanted. Just like that, he remembered: he wanted the silence.
As a chunk of kale caught on his lip, he let his eyes drift to what was hanging over the chair to his left, what he'd clocked before his chalky feast and knew it might come down to.
His belt. Dior. Limited edition. Black leather.

6 hours til the Jump

See, he'd like to think this was all because he was sad. And of course he was - Myles had gone to a place of sadness that saved its glaze for one man in a century.
But the truth is he was doing this because he was scared. Scared of what they would do to him. When they found out what he'd done.
'They' being everybody because everybody would join in, everybody would want their turn.
Scared of what they'd come up with for him. Scared of how long it would last. Scared of how he'd look after they were done. Scared of the moment it started all over again.
So even though hanging took more balls than pills, he knew he had to get there before they did. Before little bits of him were found in the water.
He tried to get the belt around a beam, but the beams in his flat were too high. He should have remembered from when he'd attached a 'pleasure swing' to the lowest beam, a joke for one of his parties; a guest had broken the beam within the first hour.
And now he couldn't reach. But - no excuses - he *could* reach the curtain rail. All he had to do was tie a knot, just like he'd been taught. Tie a knot and hope for a heart attack and try not to remember what happened three nights ago.
A cardiac arrest would be too easy anyway. What was happening to his heart now was deliberate, nuclear, destroying every cell, changing his DNA.
Hiroshima in his heart. Chernobyl in his chest.
It's Cretin O'Clock.

Time to remember.

5 hours til the Jump

No, on top of no, inside of no, behind no, in front of no, no, it couldn't, couldn't be real. There HAD to be a way to reverse it. There simply had to be a way to go back in time – cold water through him and a thousand hot showers and it had to be over and it had to be a no, a no, a no, over and over, under and under, no no no until it could be taken back.

Despite how much it hurt, he allowed himself to picture her. Rose.

'I think,' she told him once as she straddled him on his boat, smiling laconically, 'Whatever it is *knows* not to hurt me.' She tugged on his lips with her cherry scented mouth, her eyes flickering as he brushed her blonde ringlets from her large almond eyes. 'Because you *are* in control of it. Deep down in there, you're still Myles. MY Myles. You'll always be my Myles. And we're going to beat it. This illness. You hear me?'

Myles nodded, leaning back to let her body fall deeper into his chest. 'Got it, ma'am.'

Rose made it all go away. All the pain, all the shame, all the blame. She made it all better. She was not just beauty, she was not just humour, but she was talent. A gifted make up artist with an eye for artistry, he'd met her when she was making up the fairies for his 'Garden Of Eden' party. A few weeks later he'd managed to pool his connections and get her a job in cinema - she'd just finished work on an arthouse horror that he couldn't wait to see.

He proposed to her on the same boat a month later, and she said yes. He hadn't had a rage in three weeks – perhaps the acupuncture he'd started was working. They'd had a picnic on the boat then jumped into the water naked, then sailed back into town and gone to her favourite club. They'd drunk drinks made of spun sugar and ice, and danced in the VIP area for four hours straight. They went back to Myles office and fucked til it was time for breakfast.

Then he'd hit her, too.

That one he remembered.

She should never have forgiven him. Why had she forgiven him? He'd barely had to ask her twice, and she'd been back in his arms.

Sweet, sweet Rose. Why hadn't she run when she had the chance?

She said it wasn't him, that some beast from the outside had taken away the man she loved and she'd keep fighting til the beast was gone. But the beast ripped the petals off the Rose.

If only she had left him. If only she had listened to her mother. He wouldn't be staring at an empty packet of pills on his coffee table now if she had.

On his 39th birthday, they were happy. He even had the sale of a start-up of his to celebrate. They were on their boat, where Myle's only real friend remained. Jack was now being there for Myles, to pay back for all the times Myles had

been there for him. Where Myles had gone on a path of prosperity, Jack had gone on a path of probation. There was something different about Jack this time, too – a determination to succeed. Myles had got him a job on the arthouse film too, something to do with prosthetics or maybe pyrotechnics, and was the healthiest he'd been in years. This birthday felt safe, and for once, Myles craved that.
'Carry me over the threshold!' Rose whooped, leaping into Myles arms.
He laughed and began spinning her round, pretending to throw her into the Thames
'You've got to walk the plank!' He roared, shaking her from side to side as he mounted the plank.
Rose wiggled her legs nervously, her body slipping around in its grey sheath dress. 'No, no, we'll fall in!'

A scruffy eyed Jack appeared on deck, clutching a Heineken. 'Ahoy!' he hollered. 'Just in time!'
'Captain Jack!' Myles reached Jack. 'Take this treasure!'
He passed a giggling Rose from his arm to Jack's, not letting go til the last moment, seeing that she safely landed on deck. He moved behind her, holding her arms out in a wingspan on the edge of the boat.
'Look, look, we're Jack and Rose!' He laughed, a laugh that could stroke the sun.
'Oh my god, we are!' She threw her body backwards, at one with his chest. 'I'll never let go, Jack!'
Myles pounced over to them and took his place behind Jack, forming a wingspan and becoming the Jack to his Rose. 'Oi oi, don't forget me! I'm the iceberg!' The three of them linked hands and formed a trinity of weird wildness, laughing as they swooned and soared against the highest point of the boat.
It was then that Rose turned around, slipped around, so she was pressed up against the rails and looking into each of their eyes.
'Are you two coming to dance or what?'
Both men knew they were looking at her like water in the desert, and they didn't care. You can bet she didn't either.
She spun back around and walked down the beech wood steps to what was known as the 'recreation' section of the boat. Myles and Jack followed her into it.
Then it was a good night. Rose hit the stereo, selecting a song that had the rumble of reggae and the hedonism of house. Jack was behind the bar, pouring steaming green alcohol into skull shaped jars.
'A toast to Myles,' Jack said. 'For the fight he's shown these past few months.'
Rose nodded, locking eyes with Myles over the bubbling liquid. 'To the fight,' she uttered, her voice hoarse. 'You've got this.'
They clattered their glasses together.

If only they had gone to bed then, bellies and hearts full. If only one of them had got tired. If only Myles had listened to his lust and dragged her away.

As the party had continued, the mood had swung, like it does at all parties. With only one woman, it's natural for the single man to begin to pay her attention. It starts with hands lingering on waists too long or taking part in playful thumb wars, you know the type of thing, the casual looks that have never been indulged before, and you've seen how it builds, how people forget who they are, how bodies brush past each other when they don't need to. Myles almost expected it. The flirting.

He didn't however, expect the kiss.

Ah yes. The kiss. About 2am it happened. One minute they were playing pool and the next they were kissing. Three seconds of contact that changed it all. Rose's mouth, a round marshmallow, belonged to him, and yet its lips were being crushed beneath Jack.

It shocked him so much he didn't see who started it.

'Jack!' Rose shrieked, a nervous laugh catching her. She turned to see Myles, gazing at them on the sofa. 'W-t-f. *Way* too much to drink. Sorry baby.'

'Yoo, sorry mate.' Jack swayed, splashing brandy.

Part of Rose was skipping over to Myles charmingly, trying to win him over. But another part was keeping her back, edging her distance, carving out a circle of safety from him, as she tried to work out his state of mind.

'Babe? Babe, look at me. That was nothing. Babe?'

If only she hadn't been so brave.

Flies. Flies all around him. A brain made of flies. A hive for a brain.

Energy. Thick fists of it, punching at his veins more energy than one human body can fit.

Heat. More than heat, more than red. His insides charred, catching embers, acid washed, crust, mantle, inner core.

This felt fucking good.

The rage. The rage had come. It spiralled to the top of him, making him a diamond. And then he shattered.

The last thing he remembered was throwing the glass at her. Then the rage teleported him to a dimension where only certain people can go.

Drip. Drip. Myles tried to cling to the fugue. He knew he didn't want to come out of it, knew this time it would be bad.

Drip. Drip.

He was yanked from his sleep, yanked from the nest. He begged to stay but his brain let him down.

Maybe you just trashed the place. Maybe you just banged your head against the wall. Maybe it's fine.

The embarrassing blubber of anger began clinging to him, sticking there like food in his throat or weight on his waistline. Just what, oh what, had he done? Hot humiliation seeped over him. What had he burst this time?

The drips were more incessant now, diving to the floor. He wouldn't let himself look at them – because it was water, it was just water, it was booze, it was tears, it was anything but what he knew it was.

'Myles?! Oh my god, what have you done?'

It was blood, all right. The air smelt of it.

Myles had never been looked at like that, and especially not by Jack. 'Myles?! Why mate why?! Myles, shit, call an ambulance!' Myle's eyes were dragged to the source of the blood. Say it with him now; *Rose.*

His Rose. Ground into the floor as though to make a perfume.

She was face down, slumped, unnaturally forced into the wood. Her left leg jutted out at a fierce angle, the strap of her shoe barely clinging to it.

Oh god oh god. Why wasn't she wearing her underwear?

What had he done? What had he done? He was rock and roll, sure, but the other R word? The one that ended with T? The one every boy was always taught not to be? No, no, no. He wouldn't do that. *He would never, ever, ever do that.*

From her head came the blood. Her beautiful hair had caught a lot of it, catching it sticky and thick in the curls, but a healthy well had manage to flow free, blackberry syrup across the boat.

Jack had already reached her. He patted and prodded and checked her, all the while keeping Myles waiting, waiting for the release, the second chance, the tenth chance, the final chance. He'd never touch her again after this – he'd cut off his hands if she'd just wake up one more time.

But it wasn't to be. 'She's … dead.' Jack looked like he couldn't believe his own words. 'She's gone, Myles..'

Myles shook his head. He could find a light in her eyes, a way to wake her up, a chance to resuscitate her, surely? As Jack turned her over, Myles saw it: what happens when beauty becomes death. How could she go this pale? Her lips already blue. Her cheekbone caved. Her mouth forever in a silent O.

But something else was happening, deep down inside him.

The realisation … he'd done it.

All his life he had feared it. Ever since he was a little boy. He'd imagined the horror, of killing someone, of taking a life, of being a murderer. He knew, as soon as you do that, that's it. You're nothing. You give up your right to happiness, there and then. All you deserve, all you should ever be, is pain. You stop being human, or any kind of animal at all. You have to give yourself over, give yourself over to the revenge of the universe. That's it. Boom. Lights out, gone. Doors slammed, keys shut, suck it up buttercup. No sight, no sound, no soul. And any time you start to feel sorry for yourself… you remember. This is just fair. This is one for one. This is science, this is theology, this is written in scripture: you deserve it. Just keep paying your debt. Keep rolling that ball up the hill, only to have it roll down again. Keep knotting together every grain of sand in the world. Keep counting to infinity. You did this. This is all you are.

You had your chance to be one of the happy ones, to value yourself, and you blew it. That's it. Tough.
Myles melted into himself, sliding in a blood streaked shock down the side of the leather sofa. He looked at her again. At a face split, eyes rolling back to meet the moon.
Jack was kneeling before him. 'Myles. Where do you keep the spare anchor?'
Scott gripped his arms. 'Mate. Listen to me. They're gonna come for us. And I'm not getting my probation fucked over for this. I'm just not. So where's the anchor?'
'Under the wheel.' Myles reached for her, grazing her cold fingertips. Trying to swap with her but you can't swap with ice.
It felt like it only took seconds for Jack to leave, and return with the anchor, a large white sheet and a rope. For all the shaking and the swearing, he worked quickly and smoothly as he wrapped the body in the sheet.
'Myles! Myles. Get it together. I need you to help me carry her. I'll do the rest.'
Myles was in a trance as he got up. Was Jack making it go away? If they got rid of the body, would it get rid of the memory?
He howled in horror as his hands touched her feet through the sheet. They were now feet of the past, feet that would never curl again.
'Get it together,' Jack hissed. 'We've just got to get her to the dinghy. Ok? Trust me, Myles, just stay with me until then.'
Dinghy. Such a stupid word.
She'd never been this heavy. What he was once going to spend the rest of his life with was now rolled up like a filo pastry, landing with a slump in the algae and looking like a giant tampon. One last time, he carried her, into the speedboat he couldn't dare step into.
A determined Jack drifted away on the dinghy, quiet as he moored out of the dock with nothing but a torch to cast some light.
On the edge of the boat, his knees pulled under his chest, at one with the cold, Myles stayed in the same position for an hour. Maybe if he held it long enough, he could bring her back.
So he was one of them, one of the people with enough power in his hands to kill another person. What happened to you when you consumed that much? Surely there had to be something – maybe a tumour was starting to grow inside him now. Or perhaps he'd emit a strong scent, constantly give off the pungent smell of the life he'd ingested. Perhaps he'd be able to run faster, powered by the ghost of Rose.
Streaks of grey were streaming into the navy sky, dawn nudging its way through. As it did the dinghy appeared in the distance, drifting back to him. What if she had woken up, on her way out to sea? He hadn't checked for a pulse after all. Jumped up in shock, wrestled her way out of the sheets, screaming in Jack's face? What if she was still alive?

He closed his eyes. He would give anything for that to be the case. He'd have a child he loved more than anything and watch that child die. Just please let her have woken up.

As the boat drifted closer, it was clear only Jack was left. The sheet, anchor and ropes were all gone. Jack's skin was grey. When he reached the boat he didn't bother to tie the dinghy back on. He slithered off it.

As white streaked into the water colour sky, insisting now that the day begin, Jack said with a thick, heavy voice; 'We need to clean the boat.'

Chapter Two

Cupid

A letter to the humans.

Think of vinegar as you read me.
Let's talk about kissing, shall we? After all, is there anything else worth talking about? We all know what a good kiss can do to us, how it can get inside us, change us, brand itself across our brains to be replayed and regurgitated for the rest of our lives. But I don't just want to talk about a good kiss. I want to talk about The Kiss, the one that will change everything. A kiss so good they'll call it the kiss of life.
Or The Kiss Of Death.
You see, some girls can give the kiss of life, revive a man, bring him back to full power through their lips, save life after life on the end of their tongue. But, to me, that's boring. My name is Cupid, and I can give The Kiss Of Death.
In fact, I gave it just the other day. To a woman. I knew she needed it, knew she needed to be put out of her misery before they saw her, before she was cauterised by their ridicule and their distaste. Worse than the fat woman, worse than the frumpy woman, *this was a woman with facial hair*. I didn't want to look at her, at her bristles, at the mossy hormonal mouth where beauty should have been ... so I killed her.
But that's nothing on what I'm about to do now. I'm standing in a hospital wing - I come here often - and I'm looking at a creep. Admit it, you're glad it was him, not you, who gave into your urges. Now watch this.
Don't blink: you're not gonna wanna miss a moment.

Dear Pervert,

My oh my, your face, your lovely face. What have they done ...
They're nothing but parasites. Sucking up your shame and turning it into their pride.
Just stay still for me, don't make any sudden movements, no need to open your eyes. Just listen to my voice. And they think morphine's good, huh? If morphine could hear, it would be jealous of my voice.
Squeeze my hand if you can hear me.
Good.
Don't worry. I'm not here to hurt you. No one is going to hurt you ever again.

I'm not sure what smells stronger; the dried blood or the guilt. I'm looking down at a person shattered into splinters, through bats and fists but most of all through what they call 'justice.'

How could you let them find out what you were?

Things would have been so much easier for you if you could hide it. Your parents would still talk to you. You wouldn't live in fear. You'd have your freedom. Your fingernails wouldn't be hurting now from where they were pulled out. I know. I get it. You wouldn't be having to go back to that place where you are the bait, always wondering what they will do this time, and how many there will be this time, and how long it will be before you go numb.

I know, I know. Calm down. Stay still. I'm not going to make you go back there.

My name is Cupid, and I can grant the kiss of death.

I like to come to this hospital, once or twice a month so the other angels don't get suspicious. I prowl the corridors for hours until I find the person who deserves it.

And today I saw you. Splattered open like a spider, but I know you have more heart and soul than any of those maggots who made you go whip and crack and spill right open. They spilled you out onto the floor and right into my hands.

Look at you. They took all their shame and tried to make it yours, but they failed.

You don't deserve this.

When you die there will be peace – no one will judge what you've done. No one will hate you. They will recognise their own sins and flaws once you're gone. And for you, there will just be peace. Just pleasure, and freedom, and no more hiding who you are.

Then again, there's nothing to hide, is there? Cos you really, really don't deserve this. Like you actually don't.

Cos unlike those prisoners, unlike the mob, unlike your own sister who doesn't believe you, unlike the nurse who I noticed hasn't topped up your water ... I *know* you didn't do it.

I know you were framed.

I know that woman was lying.

You get told you're guilty enough times and you start to believe it yourself. That's why you could barely defend yourself. That's why you're letting them destroy you.

If only they knew they were doing this to an innocent man.

Well I know. I know everything. I saw everything. And I want to be the one to take the pain away.
So what do you say? Squeeze my hands if it's a yes.
Good.
Now kiss me, you pervert.

Yours ever,
Cupid.

Houses of Parliament

Flustered but triumphant, Scott Luther MP threw the letter down onto the table before him.
Or tried to throw it - instead, the letter seemed to *float* down, descending to crown the top of a pile of similar ruby red envelopes with an elegance that suggested it knew its worth, its power. The pile simmered. It was a volcano in the centre of a conference room, a volcano of passion and guts made up of over a hundred of these letters. All from Cupid, all equally shocking.
Howard Pitts MP, united to Scott by his quest, looked at his comrade with bemusement. 'Scott ... mate ... what the Hell are these? Where did you get these?'
Scott shrugged off the question. 'They were sent to my office anonymously. Signed by somebody who calls themselves Cupid.'
'That's it, no return address, no tracking number, nothing?' Howard picked up one of the letters and turned it over in his hand, feeling the quality of the envelope. As his thumb ran across the gold of the seal, he realised it was shaped into a perfect pout.
'Nada. But that's not the important stuff. The important stuff is the words.'
His confused and tired team looked up at him. They would have been naive to expect this break in the debate to be an actual break and not an excuse for more work, but they hadn't expected this. From the spark in the handsome but relentless MP's eyes, they knew he was up to something.
Howard cleared his throat. 'Scott ... you're not suggesting we should actually read these out in The Houses Of Commons?'
Scott's eyes flashed and he picked up the letter again. He was holding a deity in his hand, a piece of paper that had rewired his mind.
'I'm afraid that's exactly what I'm suggesting, H.'
'Scott, please. Be realistic. You're the one who's been snapping at us for wasting time.'
'No debate to win euthanasia has ever been won in this country. When I tell you I want us to think outside the box, these letters are what I mean. They're poignant. They're brave. *And they're fierce.*'

His team, their eyes watery with sleep, gazed at each other. They'd been so naive when they arrived for the debate at 9am this morning, believing the vote would take place at 4pm as promised. Now it was approaching midnight, the vote had been pushed back to 9am tomorrow, and The Houses Of Parliament was still rocking - every single MP wanted to speak on this.
'If we're gonna shake this nation out of conforming to the norm,' Scott was continuing. 'Then they need to listen to this letter.'
Howard sighed heavily. It was down to him to pull Scott back to sanity. 'Scott, we don't need this. We don't need stunts like this or mind-bending words or headline grabbing opinions. We need facts. Statistics. Research.'
Scott tried not to groan. 'Look. We're doing well, but we always do at this stage. You know who else is doing well? The Pro Life campaign. This is the moment where it pulls ahead, where people lose their nerve. The vote is at 8am tomorrow morning. We need more than statistics - we've gotta read these letters.'
'We read this and the chamber will freak! Trust me, Scott. We need to make them feel safe.'
Scott looked longingly at the letter. Deep down, he had known his team wouldn't be ready for it, and maybe the UK wasn't either. He had to move on. But he was gonna give it one last, long try.
'Howard. You know as well as I do we're never gonna make them feel safer than He Who Should Not Be Named. They're never gonna trust us the way they trust him. When he speaks, everything changes.' He Who Should Not Be Named was their Voldemort, a name they didn't like to say in this room, a name they'd even considered scrawling across the centre of a dartboard but had decided against because of the optics.
'Well he won't be speaking. He's in the public gallery. He's not actually an MP.'
'Don't you see that's even worse? He's one of them. The everyman rising up against the MPs who don't value the public's lives.'
The team sighed. Somehow, it was true. Somehow, Eli had eclipsed their campaign.
Eli Jones, a formerly unknown entrepreneur turned Pro-Life campaigner, had ridden into the debate on a wave of emotion and sentiment. Just when Scott felt he was breaking through to more liberal, radical minds, Eli would find a way to pull them back, to warn them about the edge they were staring over.
'I thought we had to worry about the church, but we have to worry about him. Eli.'
The problem with Eli, too, was that he was a hard worker. Despite being well into his fifties, there wasn't a chat morning, morning show, podcast or nightly news segment that he hadn't appeared on, his soulful blue eyes boring into the homes of the nation and telling them not to do this. He was the household name of hope, a pious political rockstar that you didn't want to disappoint.

'He gets people right in the heart of grief, of losing a loved one. That's easier for them to connect with than what we need from them. *We* need to get the people to connect with pain.'
Everything about him seemed to be designed to turn voters against euthanasia: a vibrant picture of health at fifty nine years old. If you looked up GILF in the dictionary, you just might be met with a picture of Eli.
'So we'll take them into the pain of this letter. And then we'll release them from it. What do you say?'
'We. Need. To. Move. On..' The words grinded out of Howard's teeth.
Amanda, advisor to both men, saw the frustration brewing and knew this was the moment to jump in. 'Okay, how about let's run over the counter arguments to theirs again. Let's start with the big one. Our nemesis: the slippery slope.'
'Ah, the slippery slope!' The team rolled their eyes. They had a jar in the room for every time someone had to utter the phrase 'slippery slope', they had to donate a pound, which would then go towards Friday's pub round.
'Hit me with it.' Amanda lay back, her hands summoning their responses.
Mocking, exaggerated voices came back, imitating the arguments of their opposition. 'Oh no, oh my, oh heavens - if murder becomes legal, who's to say this won't spawn an epidemic of murderous children impatient for their inheritance? Or dodgy doctors, who want to test the limits of their new powers? That soggy, slippery, sloppy slope - we can't risk people stepping onto it.'
Scott cleared his throat. He was made for this. He launched into his counter.
'You could use that argument for every innovation ever made in society - you could stretch any argument to its limits until you find a worst case scenario as to why it shouldn't happen. But isn't it interesting how it only happens when the innovation is this: to end pain. Isn't it interesting how that slope only rears it's slimy, slippery head when all we're asking for is for the suffering to stop?
Have you ever thought the slope is inside you? A secret, subconscious slope you're too ashamed to slide down; of the reason why you're fighting so hard, lest it show you the real reason why you want others to suffer.
Slide down it now. Go on. Look inside yourself, and then answer me this - tell me this.
Tell me: are you a saviour, or are you just a sadist?'
He finished triumphantly, looking back at a room of sparkling, satisfied eyes.
'That's the best you've said it.' Amanda nodded, her cheeks flushing. 'It plays. It works. Use that.'
Scott cracked his knuckles. 'Let's get back in there.'

'The suffering of a human being is not meaningless. It does not destroy a person's dignity. It is an intrinsic part of our human journey, a journey embraced by the word of God, Christ Jesus himself. He brings our humanity to its full glory precisely through the gateway of suffering and death.'

Scott rolled his eyes as the MP for Barnes put down his notes. How many more times was he going to have to sit through that kind of speech? He'd heard all this before but it never failed to annoy him, the pious words grating on him a little more every time. The saccharine, optimistic arguments of those who had nothing else to offer.

He watched his opponent, clear his throat, ready to launch into another righteous rant. Howard caught his eye and winked. It was happening as they hoped it would happen; the overload of Pro-Life arguments, late in the evening, was stirring up unease, resentment, and even a bit of rebellion in the chambers. After all, who liked being told what to do, least of all if that thing was suffering? He smiled and gave his opponent the smallest of nods.

Keep going, mate. Give it to them. Show them who you are.

The Barnes MP slumped down into his seat. Scott had to resist the urge to bounce up and try and capture the Speaker's attention himself. As the MP who had introduced the Assisted Dying Bill, Scott had been given ample time to speak on the issue - if he asked for much more, he would be seen as dominating the debate. His team had calculated he had about one more moment to speak, and that moment had to be chosen perfectly.

For now, he could watch, let the debate bounce across the room. There was something kinetic about it; there always was when it came to this issue. The first debate he'd ever had had been on it, way back in a Year 11 after school club, and he'd won it then. Then again for Philosophy A Level, and again at Oxford, winning every time. But he had to win now. *And he would.*

A lot had played in his favour. He loved Thursdays, was often at his best in them - he'd been delighted the debate would take place on a Thursday, not a Monday as others had argued for. The vote on Friday morning; the weekend to celebrate.

The debate was his, but he'd let it go for a moment - if you love something, set it free, right? - let it sift across the room, infuse the air, dance like dust caught in the light, inhaled and exhaled by those who tried to claim it. He could even tune out for a second, let his eyes glaze over, just to see if there was an argument strong enough to pull him back in.

Ah yes, he could hear a new one being broached now. 'New' being a very generous adjective. 'The NHS is supposed to be "cradle to grave" not "cradle to very old". The message being sent here is essentially that "removing yourself from the picture" is what the state wants, and embracing palliative care is not.' The MP for Plymouth was trying to squeeze out a tear, but failing. 'We have excellent palliative care in this country. The focus should be on investing in it, not providing the financially favourable solution of… death.' He finished with a flourish. The argument was decent, but it wasn't distinctive - the people had heard it all before, yet they'd still signed Scott's petition calling for a vote in parliament. If the palliative care was so good, why'd he get all those signatures, eh?

Dismissing her, he found his eyes wandering over to the Speaker of the House, nestled comfortably in his chair. It was an open secret the Speaker had more power than the Prime Minister, able to choose the moment when to call the debate, and he wondered again which side of the coin the elusive Speaker fell on. And was there anything Scott could do to take him where he wanted him to go …

And then he realised who the Speaker was looking at. A chill slipped into his spine as he followed his gaze, up, up, up, to the Public Gallery. There he was. Yet again, Eli was making an entrance, swooping in late as though to save the day. Eli was a man the world moved for, a frisson frothing in the gallery when they realised it was him. Rows parted, seats swapped, as people made sure he could secure his place in the centre of the front row. He slid into it like he owned it. What a suit. What a haircut. Scott loved the confidence.

You could spend all day staring at him, especially as the debate was drilling over the same point about 'those with vulnerable mental health' choosing to prematurely embrace the bill. Stale, stale, stale. Eli was captivating, the room clasped in his claws.

Scott's ears pricked up and away from Eli as he realised a Northern MP was speaking. He had planned this moment with her. The MP was reading a moving letter from one of her constituents, who suffered from a terminal condition he found intolerable, and longed for the chance the bill would give him to escape it. Now *this. This hit a nerve.* He nodded at his comrade, who had barely sat down before the Plymouth MP shot up again, his counter too primed, too premature.

'I respect the words of my honourable friend's brave constituent, but I'd like to ask him: 'I respect my honourable friend's words, but I'd like to ask him. What if, the day after he took his life, the day he reached this 'peace' he speaks of … a cure for his condition was invented? A cure to restore him to optimum health, feeling as good as he did before his affliction. He cannot know an innovation like that isn't coming one day, any day now. Would he still feel the same if he did?'

Scott jumped to his feet, raising his hand to the speaker. His opponent gave way, folding.

'And I'd like to ask my honourable friend, what if you lost your entire family tomorrow? Your wife, your kids, your parents, your brother, all of them gone? You can't know that that's not going to happen.

Can you look me in the eye and tell me you wouldn't want to join them?'

Oh, Scott loved these moments. He lived for these moments, when the room gasped as he struck something new, something they hadn't thought of before.

Play the people. Play their desires. Play into the fantasy.

'Why are we in government if not to give the people what they want? And why can't we have everything we want? Give me one good reason why.'

The Plymouth MP struck back, bouncing up before he'd even yielded. 'This debate is not about people being able to end their lives to 'join their loved ones', and I think my honourable friend should stick to the point.' He looked up to Eli as though seeking approval. In this room, instead of the ceiling, instead of the sky, they had Eli. Casting a shadow, choosing the temperature. Was that a smile Scott saw?
Two bangs of a hammer changed everything. 'This debate is adjourned,' the Speaker declared. 'The house will resume in twenty minutes.'

The break couldn't come soon enough. This time, Scott took it alone.
It was getting really late now. He ascended as high as he could go in The Houses Of Parliament, tucking himself into a small nook so that he could think. So that inspiration could hit.
They were still there. He saw them out the window, a ring around Parliament Square, dipped in the ink of the night. Was he imagining it, or were there more than before? The Protestors. A haunting clot of them; they'd chosen an eerie uniform of doctors scrubs and gas masks, or a handful had gone for humour over fear and amusingly turned up as the Grim Reaper. All day they'd held up their posters:
Caring Not Killing.
Compassion Never Kills.
Not the most innovative slogans. He almost pitied them.
Doctors Against Dying.
There we go, that was an improvement; a bit of alliteration.
EuthaNAZIa.
Oh. Shit. Now that one was good. Credit where it's due.
He flipped open his notebook, scouring the Venn Diagrams, the quotes, the Pros and Cons lists … nothing hit. Nothing was electric. Nothing was undeniable. He took a sip of the hot chocolate he ordered. There was only one slippery slope right now, and that was the one down his throat - he tipped the hot chocolate down it. Luxury and luck as his mouth mastered the moment.
And as that velvet fire glided down his throat, it conjured an image of a different throat altogether.
What if somewhere out there, there was a woman, an older woman, who had just lost the love of her life?
Perhaps that love of her life was her husband, ten years her senior, and theirs was a true love, discovered later in life? They'd both been married before.
Yes, perhaps she was his second wife. Perhaps … it was an affair. A passionate affair, one they had blown up their lives for so they could be together.
And she refused to be alive if alive meant being without him. So now it was her throat Scott saw, but instead of summoning a hot chocolate down it, what was gliding down it was a glass of water and fifteen or so large, chalky, chunky pills. Make that twenty.

And what if she was drinking them down, but she didn't quite get them down quick enough? Didn't get enough of them down her before she passed out? And so later she would wake up even though she didn't want to, wake up to a pumped stomach and her failure of a fate.
And when she woke up, she wouldn't have the same function of her hands, her throat, her stomach or even her speech. She couldn't do the things with her mind and her mouth that had drawn that lover to her in the first place. With the split in her stomach and the sting in her spleen, she wasn't the same woman anymore. But that wasn't the worst bit.
Standing over her was her carer. Scott saw her, clear as day. It was the only person left, the only person around, to help her - her husband and her had been too old to have children by the time they found each other. The only person left, who had some control over his estate, who was still listed on certain papers, who still knew where everything was, was his first wife - the woman he had left for her.
She'd always been hanging around. Some would say watching, waiting, for a moment, though she never thought the moment would come quite like this.
And slowly, our star-crossed lover starts to realise, what is going to happen to her.
That the person who would now feed her, who would now bathe her, who would now change her, who would now move her, who would choose when she slept and when she drank and when she laughed and what she'd see and what she'd hear and what she'd, above all, *feel*, was the woman whose husband, whose life she had stolen, fifteen years ago.
And as the first wife realised she now had autonomy over the safety, the comfort and the groin of the woman who'd stolen her husband, she smirked for the first time in fifteen years and said:
'Things are going to be very different from now on.'
Scott disregarded the cup, angry at it and himself. He got these images all the time, intrusive thoughts that demanded he see them through - no therapist could take them from him. It's why he had first shown an interest in Euthanasia.
He edged the cup towards him again, but as he did, he saw it. The grandfather reaching for the cup he cannot reach, but the cup that will give him peace. And he begs his kind, successful son to move it towards him for him, but the son cannot do it. Or cannot bring himself to do it- he doesn't think it's right and he's scared of what will happen if it is. So he leaves his father there, both howling after each other with the unfairness of it all. But then, from the corner of the room, the son's son emerges. A younger son, only sixteen, with a more liberal mindset, with less years of conformity sunken into his skin, who hates seeing his grandfather suffer. So all he does is leave the pills close enough. That's it. And he helps him hold the water glass in his hand. That's it. And he keeps it steady while he drinks. That's it. And the next day there is peace. But what happens when the confession comes, on a rainy night, from that young heart that

only wanted the best? What happens when you have to look your father in the eye and tell him you took his father from him and wonder if he'll still love you? Or if he'll lock you away. Up to 14 year's imprisonment in the UK.
Scott slammed the cup down. There his mind went again with the images. *That* was why he was doing this.
A mobilising howl came from his mind for him - those people were out there. Suffering. The second wife who longs to join her husband, some version of her was out there. Just like 'The Pervert' in Cupid's letter was probably out there too. People who wanted the peace that could only be found in death. They needed a help they couldn't ask for, a help that wouldn't come. *Scott* was the only one who could make it happen. He couldn't say this out loud - yet - couldn't give his enemies the ammunition of knowing what he truly wanted to do when the vote passed. But one day, if he had his way, suicide would be legal in this country. Real, unfiltered, unadulterated, rock solid, rock and roll suicide, for the old, for the young, for the guilty, for the grieving, for anyone who wanted it, as soon as they wanted it, with no chance of it going wrong
He wouldn't let them down.

'Humans have something called human rights.
Humans have the right to choose. Humans have the right to freedom. Humans have the right to self-determination. But what you want to know is, do humans have the right to death?
I suppose I can't answer that.
And neither can you.
So let's make this easier. Let's make this simpler. Slicker. Tighter. Can anybody in this whole chamber - in fact, let's throw this one out to the public watching at home - can anybody in this house find me one line, one sentence, one clause, in any act, in any bill, in any constitution, in one word of scripture - that says humans have the right to suffer?
When you find me that, we'll suffer. Until then, we'll fight you every day.'
Scott couldn't help but give the MP for Wrexham a little salute as he finished his speech and took his seat. Something had happened in the break. He even popped his feet up on the back of the row, swaggerlicious now, because, baby, it was happening: the tide was swinging in his favour. Maybe it was the late, late hour they were reaching, that the nocturnal animals were surfacing, and a daring streak was coming out.
Screw it. It was time to speak. Seizing the moment's silence, he rose up, gesturing to the speaker, who gave way to him.
'Mr Speaker, they say there's nothing quite like a mother's love. So I'd like to turn your attention to the case of Rhonda Blair. Yes, you're right, that is the 52 year old woman charged with the murder of her son after his accident at a ski resort last February. She calls it a mercy killing, the authorities say she just didn't want the responsibilities of a carer. Even though her son wrote a note

begging for her to do the very thing she did. Rhonda was willing to go to Hell so her son could escape his. Mothers are incredible creatures. They can give the gift of life. So let them give the gift of death.

And make no mistake: *death is a gift.*'

He felt the room drop, cold. He looked to Amanda, who wouldn't meet his eyes. *Dammit.* A misfire.

Why, why, why had he mentioned Rhonda Blair? She was way too controversial; his team had discussed her for hours earlier and all come to the same conclusion that she was a no-go. What had just come over him?

'I will allow one or two more members of the house to speak.'

For the first time, there was a lull in the House. They were getting tired. The public gallery was as full as ever, but it sweated with the longing for sleep. Howard rose to his feet.

Scott nodded. Okay, fine, he wouldn't get the credit for the closing argument, but if anyone could land the plane, it was Howard.

'I know that a debilitating illness can be turned on and off like a tap. I'm not underestimating what the people asking for this law change are going through, least of all those who are eligible for an assisted dying. That's why I'm happy we're having this debate – because I respectfully want them to consider what I'm about to say.' He seemed to find the camera in the room, directing his words to it just for a second.

'You're not just fighters, you're winners. You're fighting for freedom and I want you to win. No matter the body you are in, you deserve to win.'

No, no, no, stop. What was he doing? What the Hell were these words?

'You're fighting for freedom. How about being alive when you experience it?'

Scott tried to catch his old friend's eye. Nothing. He had to get up, rise up, beg the Speaker for one more chance at a close.

'They say 'only God can give life, and only God can take it away.' And then they say, 'but what kind of God would make me suffer like this?' And I agree. If God was truly loving, wouldn't he cure you, save you, make every moment better than the last, make sure you never had to lose anyone again?'

Okay, okay, maybe this was better, maybe this was something. *Look at me Howard, look at me.*

But then he followed Howard's gaze. Inevitably, Howard was looking up, and Scott let his eyes float up too.

Up to the obvious, to the of course, to the omnipotent force he had always known would fuck this up: Eli. Eli's eyes had become the sky, consuming the room - and Eli's mouth had become Howard's.

As Howard spoke, so did Eli, Eli's words always coming just that little bit sooner. *The bastard was mouthing Howard's words for him, spoon feeding each phrase bit by bit, a mother bird cupping its baby's beak, edging in its ideology one crumb at a time.* Maybe it was puppetry, maybe it was voodoo, maybe it was a magic mirror - but whatever it was, it was wrong.

'But God does not do that for us. He does not heal us. He does not save us. So how about something else instead? Listen to this.'
Eli's mouth carved the final few words, radiating wisdom. As Howard came to a close, the room was bathed in a haunting hope.
'*Let's be better than God. Let's work harder than God. Let's love more than God.*'
Fuck. Fuck. Fuck. Grease drained Scott's brain.
'Let's fight harder than God ever could. Let's fight for our health. Not for our death.' Howard swallowed and then pitched his final line:
'Let's do what God can't.'
No. No. No.
They were going to lose the vote.
Just as Scott remembered one of his best arguments, the Speaker banged his hammer. 'Parliament is excused for the evening ... or indeed, the dawn' His voice clipped into action just as Big Ben announced it was 4 in the morning.
'The vote will take place in five hours' time.
I advise you all to get some rest.'

Four hours til the vote. One final chance for the end of pain.
Or.
One final chance for the omniscient Eli, to change things from above. To bend the room to his will without even speaking.
Or one final chance for the country - was this the moment it would choose to be humane?
Scott was alone in the office. The others had tried to persuade him to join them for a sloppy bagel breakfast, but he wouldn't. Not until he'd found the angle, the angle that would change everything.
On their board they had endless plans, statistics, ideas. A large chunk of it taken up by their proposal, for the UK's first version of Dignitas. They had post-it notes littered with things to do, inspiring photographs, quotes, and a long list of significant names who were joining their cause.
In the bottom hand corner, they also had a photo of Eli.
The intern, Felix, had put it there as a joke months ago, and it had stayed. They'd decided against the dart board, but not against the picture. Scribbled with a halo, a pair of buck teeth, and an L on his forehead, it was enjoyable to look at when they needed somewhere to direct their frustration.
Because Eli was *annoying*. Too chiselled for fifty nine, too handsome for his age, too much a picture of health and vitality; the poster boy for his own argument. He had too much of a way with words, delivered with a gentle, regal kind of empathy that got people to trust him. Quite simply, he gave people too much hope, but they didn't realise how much what they were hoping for would hurt.

Scott surveyed the picture now. He really was a good looking man. A Swedish look – bright, tanned skin, fresh blue eyes and clipped salt and pepper hair. A warm smile. And Scott had seen what he'd done up there, what he always did: a simple look at the chambers that made it felt like blasphemy to go against him. Scott could see the way this was going, how it had always gone before.
They believed Eli. They trusted Eli. And they didn't believe Scott.
To get Eli's believers to see it Scott's way, they needed to see Eli fail. Fail at the one thing he said was possible: mastering the misfortune of a terrible, tragic, life altering accident.
You see, try as Scott might, he just wasn't such a skilled, seasoned debater was his rival. If Eli came to the commons at 9am, The Assisted Dying Bill would not pass. It would be a No all over again, despite the years of work it had taken just to get it into the chambers. The ayes wouldn't have it.
But what if Eli wasn't there? What if, quite simply, when 9am came around, he didn't come? What if he *couldn't* come? Couldn't make it, couldn't take it, couldn't bear it.
The eyes wouldn't have it.
He looked away, then back to the picture, three times. Nice eyes.
Really nice eyes.

Eli

London Samaritan's Head Office

'*Eli*? You should be out celebrating. It's practically in the bag.'
Eli slid off his suit jacket. 'Nowhere I'd rather be than here.' He tossed a pile of lilies onto the table in the middle of the room. 'And – can't celebrate just yet. But,' he grinned sleepily, 'No one I'd rather celebrate with than you lot. It was here that we came up with the idea of the counter-campaign, after all. These are for you.' He slammed a velvet box onto the table, chocolates coming down like grenades. Heads poked out of their grey turtle shell booths, smiles cracking open tired faces. Seeing him made their night. They'd always admired him - the entrepreneur who found the time to volunteer - but this week he'd been next level.
Despite the fact he had to be back in the Houses of Parliament in four hours, they weren't surprised to see him here - if there was a life that could be saved, Eli would find the time to save it.
Most of them were in the middle of calls, phones clamped to their ears, but they all betrayed their callers by stopping, smiling, waving, as Eli made his entrance to the office where they had had the idea for their counter campaign.
02077342800. The office may be small, humble and grey, but it was the UK's premiere suicide hotline, and ever since he'd heard of it, he had wanted to be part of it.

Those who were not on their phones stood up to embrace him, the slow, dreamy embrace of people who couldn't quite believe he'd almost pulled it off. 'Course he's here,' beamed Heather, another regular volunteer who put in night shift after night shift. She wrapped her arms around him. 'He never misses a Friday.' He hugged her back. He *had* considered spending the next few hours sleeping, but as soon as the speaker had called the commons to a close, he had been drawn back here, to the grey booth where it had all begun, after one call too many. 'However, we never miss a good deal in the grocery store!' From beneath the table she pulled out two bottles of prosecco. 'Wahey!'

Eli laughed. 'We can't – '

'Drink while on shift, I know, I know, and I know you won't give in – not even a sip. I'm gonna put these in the fridge. They can chill while you're on shift. Then are you gonna go back and watch the vote?'

Eli smiled, knowing that wasn't really a question. They all knew there was no way he was missing the vote, and he would be doing a little bit more than watching it. He nodded subtly, not wanting to tell Heather too much.

'Great. Then, one you're back from your victory – we're popping it open. Deal?'

'*Deal*!'

His eyes darted to his booth. 'Go on,' Heather rolled her eyes. 'Go save another person.' She winked at him.

Settling into his booth, he sighed with relief. The debate, the speeches; all of it was exhilarating, but this was the first time he'd felt content in hours. It just felt right, and it felt like home, down to the old coffee cup in the corner, to be here. To be where it actually mattered, away from the cameras. He fitted his headset on, pressed the red button on his handset, sat back in the chair and listened to the white noise.

Hornets in his ears, broken by a voice, cutting through before he could give the standard greeting he'd been trained to.

'I'm standing on Tower Bridge.' A man's voice. He'd thought it was going to be a woman.

'Ok. And why have you called us today?'

Not two hundred yards from here. He could smell the river air, see the heels adjusting themselves on the rails edge.

'Because I think I should jump.'

'Ok. Would you like to tell me why you think that?' Open communication.

'It's the right decision.'

'And what brought you to that conclusion? Has anything happened recently?'

A pause.

'Things are always happening.'

'Things that upset you, distress you, unsettle you?'

'Yes. All of it.'

'Would you like to tell me more about what these things are? Is it events, people, a memory?' Give options.
He pictured toes, one sliding on top of the other, flirting with balance on the bridge.
'No. It's me.'
'You?'
'I'm sorry.'
'You don't need to apologise. I'm here to listen.' Don't offer advice.
'But I am sorry.'
His friend Matt walked past him, saluting. They silently shook hands.
'You owe me no apologies. Tell me what you mean.'
'I mean it's me. I'm the thing. That's why I should jump. It's the things I do.'
'Sometimes talking about these things can help you to see clearly.' Remember to listen.
'Shut up, bastard!'
'I want you to communicate.' Do not take abuse personally.
'I'm sorry. God, I'm so sorry, I'm so fucking sorry for everything, all of it.'
'Start at the beginning.'
'I'm sorry about all the bodies.'
Eli gulped. No judgement. 'Okay.'
'The world would be a better place without me. I should go. I should jump. It's a quick way to go. I think.'
'Let's keep talking. What makes you think this is the solution?'
'Because I'm dangerous. What if I do it again?'
'There's no reason to think that. Talk me through what's happening now.' Keep it casual. Watch your tone of voice.
'I'm holding onto the rail. Oh god man I'm scared. I can't live with it, I can't say it out loud, I can't jump. But more than I'm scared to jump, I'm scared of myself.'
'And why is that?' Casual, remember, casual.
'I'm dangerous. Bet you'd shake like a chihuahua if you saw me.'
'Maybe I would.' Keep them engaged. 'I think it would be easier to talk if you left the bridge. Why don't you just try it – maybe start with sitting on the ledge instead of standing.' Give options.
'Okay. Okay. I'll try that.'
'Good.'
'I'm sitting. I'm so sorry.'
'That's ok. Why don't you try putting one foot down, behind the railings?'
'Ok.'
Take it slowly. 'Good. And if you'd like to try the other foot too – so you're back standing on the pavement part of the bridge. How's it going?'
'Ok, ok, I've done it. I'm standing.'
'Well done. Where are you going next?' Keep it casual.

'I don't know. I don't understand what I'm doing. I don't understand where I'm going. I'm walking away but it's safer for everybody if I jump.'
'I don't think that's true.'
'You don't get it.'
Don't validate that. 'Why don't you keep walking? Just a little further, back where you can be seen?'
'Okay. Okay. I'm walking. Are you sure this is the right thing?'
'Yes. Take another few steps.'
'Okay. I'm doing it.'
'Good, good, well done. Keep talking to me. Where are you now?'
'I'm walking through the street. Past a bar with leprechauns outside.' Eli knew it; they often went there for drinks after a shift.
'Good. Good. I think you've taken a great first step in being honest with a stranger today.'
'Thank you for believing in me.'
'No problem. Thank you for keeping me company tonight.'
'But, mate, I've got to tell people what I am. They need to know what I'm capable of. I'm so sorry.'
'That's okay. Keep walking, to somewhere where you can be with others, be distracted, okay?' Allow a pause. 'What can you see now?'
'An office building.'
'Good, good, keep moving.' Listen for pauses. Sense the change in the mood.
'A question I am contracted to ask is; do you believe anyone else is in immediate danger, around you?'
'I'm sorry.'
'You don't need to say sorry to me. I am here for you.'
'But I *am* sorry.'
'No need for that. Where are you now?'
'I'm at a door. My hand is on the handle. I'm sorry.'
'You can keep saying that if it'll make you feel better, but I'm gonna tell you again that you don't owe me any kind of apology.'
'But I do.'
Eli rolled his eyes. For the last time.
'And why'd you say that?'
'I'm sorry that I'm behind you. I mean it. I'm truly so very sorry that I'm behind you.
I'm sorry I'm about to blind you.'
He spun his swivel chair round. A dripping wet man faced him, a phone clamped to his ear in one hand, a knife in the other.
That was the final thing he saw. Before two sharp slashes. Before the pain. Before all the colour Eli had known collapsed.
As he saw the last thing he'd see, he gave the first roar of agony he'd ever roared. Once the pain came, it wouldn't end. Once he started, it wouldn't stop.

Chapter Three

4 hours til the Jump

The unbearable boat trip had happened seventy two hours ago. By the second hour, the guilt had doubled, and Myles didn't think it would ever be possible to feel guiltier. But every hour, it doubled again.

Now it was seventy two times strong, and the fact there were more levels to it, new depths waiting to consume him, made him slick with fear.

No one had noticed her missing yet. He knew she had no appointments lined up for the week, and that she lived alone. How long would it take? Before they came for him?

He swallowed and sweated. He pictured the mob. He gulped and glugged. Then with a kick of the chair, he started to swing.

And it was as he swung that he remembered a thought he'd had, on a school trip all the way back in Year 9. For this trip they had taken his class rock climbing - not real rock climbing, the artificial kind in a sports hall or in this case, a shopping mall - but that didn't change how hyped up the trip was, how excited the boys were. And Myles was no different - he could still smell the excitement of the coach ride there, the 'tomfoolery' in the atmosphere In the mall, the walls stretched high, at different angles, some which would have you upside down. Myles was the first to try it – shooting to the top with delight, secretly surprised with his athleticism, waving to the applause below as he hung from a yellow stub. When he reached the bottom, his friend, Leo, wanted to go; and he was asked to belay him.

As the instructor explained what that meant, his face became pale and his mind became brittle. He learnt that there was a technique to it, an exact amount of rope to give and you had to know when to give it and when to stop it, and if you got any of those things wrong, their fall would be your fault. So he had made an excuse to go to the bathroom but when he came back Leo was still waiting for him. So he had refused. He had been called selfish, lazy, a glory seeker, and told that he couldn't come on the next trip, but it didn't matter: all that mattered was not having another person's life in his hands. He knew what that meant, even as a boy.

In fact, it was part of the reason why he became so successful – he'd sworn to himself there and then he would be rich enough to have a driver, someone who could transport him everywhere without him ever worrying about taking his eyes off the road and accidentally harming someone. He was determined not to be someone who'd throw it all away.

Life mattered to him and his conscience mattered more.

So what an unfair irony, what a sick joke, that it was him, not them, not all his carefree friends at school, not one of his less bright, sensitive classmates, not his worst enemy who deserved it, but *him*; him who swung here now, in the body of a murderer.

3 hours til the Jump

If only he hadn't gone back for seconds that time.
If only he had skipped dessert that time.
If only he'd managed to cut the sugar in his coffee.
If only he liked vodka, not champagne.
If only he'd got back into running, not lifting.
If only he'd sweated the weight out in the sauna before this.
If only he'd taken a shit first.
But he hadn't. He hadn't he hadn't he hadn't, and now he really was a man made of regret, a man who'd been swinging for five minutes but for every second of them, hearing the give of the leather, as the belt failed to carry his weight. His muscles crafted in Equinox and fuelled with expensive protein, laughing as all their strength was what was letting this weak man down.
He tried. He tried and he tried to stay in it, just in case, just in case it could pull out his breath in time, but as the belt inevitably split, the curtain rail did too, and this heavy lump of human came crashing to the ground.
He gasped in the air, furious at his failure, furious at his greed, furious at the way he gulped in the debt of breath even now.
Highlights from The Debate churned across his TV. Parliament had finally been excused, but the result was a mere hours away. They kept replaying a moment that had made the whole chamber cry.
His eyes drifted to the open plan kitchen he'd been so proud to help design. There was something in that kitchen. Something sharp. As long as it was still there, it would be enough.

2 hours til the Jump

He had made up his mind. He was one and done. It was over.
He leapt up, striding into the kitchen, grabbing a hunting knife from the drawer. A gift from a birthday spent in South Africa. He nodded, looking at the shark-like blade, making a silent pact with it.
He pressed it to his wrist, but the muscles pushed back, as though he was trying to do the splits. He tried to turn his wrist into a stump but the skin stood strong. He went for a swipe, and found himself grazing through air.
Come ON!
It was time.
He winced, rose up, and slit.
A light scratch appeared, barely deeper than a papercut. It giggled at him. But its arrogance was misplaced - now he knew he could draw blood.
He wanted this. He knew he did. He'd fight this knife.
1…2…3… *SLASH.*

90 minutes til the Jump

He sat in the bath, both palms up, arteries wide at being able to see the world at last. Two newborn cavities as wide as pies, hung open in his wrists, sucking in the water.

The red tumbled out of his body as though it was allergic to him. Billowing crimson clouds, purging from his body, hot water tempting the blood far, far away from Myles veins.

Myles didn't know he could bleed that much.

The water was a potent, pigment red. The white china of the bath had been dyed red. *He* had been dyed red.

Cruel morning light started teasing its way in through the windows. Dreaded sounds of traffic drifted through the glass, people getting up to enjoy their Friday. Next door he heard the sound of breakfast being made. Plates stacking, oil sizzling, toast popping out of toasters. And then a voice; 'Poached egg on avo, baby?'

He looked down at his streaming wrists. They had been bleeding for too long now. Either he'd got the wrong vein, or he hadn't got a vein at all. Or maybe he didn't even have any veins in the first place. All he knew was what had been clear for fifteen hours, and yet only now did he accept it.

This wasn't killing him.

Something was keeping him alive.

1 hour til the Jump

He pulled on a shirt and pants while still wet. He staggered into the lift, and let it take him down.

Fresh, dewy, icy morning air, February air – Myles opened the door of his apartment block and it slapped him in the face.

That's right, gimme some whiplash while you're at it.

The streets were empty, as though hiding from something. Just like that, Myles remembered the deadline for The Debate was this morning. The votes must have been cast by now. Was he waking up in a new UK or the same one as before? He almost wanted to turn back around and turn on his TV, just to join in the camaraderie of the issue that had captivated the country for months; almost wanted to watch the moment when the result was announced. Because what if … what if … just in time for … *no.* There wasn't time. He had to do this before anybody saw him, before anybody stopped him. He had to keep going, and the empty streets sung to him to go now.

Nobody was around to notice his wrists dripping, as he made his way down the pavement. He had chosen the building already. He knew it well; the Bishopsgate Library; how it had a stairwell anyone could access, how there was no security, especially not at this time of morning.

How he'd hosted his first guerrilla event there. 'Library lock-ins.' How he'd snuck women in there, taken them on the stairwell, even one on the rooftop. The jokes he'd cracked.
Time for him to be cracked.
Knowing it was his last hour, he decided to be honest with himself. What was it in him that made him want to hurt women?
Was he jealous of them? Did he want to be one?
No, it wasn't. But surely it couldn't be so simple that it was just *fun*? ... Or was it?
He had reached the library. The door to the stairwell was already ajar. Rose's ghost beckoned him in.

30 minutes til the Jump

HA!
Hahaha, he was up on the roof. HA!
Here he was, up here, up high.
And technically speaking, he could do it. You know, J-U-M-P. Jump.
Hehehehehe. Oh, hohohohohoho. Cackle, cackle, snorty mcsnort, guffaw-faw-faw, haw-haw-haw.
Jump?
Jump, boy? *You*, boy? *You*? Go on then, please; be our guest.
Mwahahahaha. What a hoot and a holler. Sorry not sorry, I'm giddy with glee.
Outrageous. Ostentatious. CANTANKEROUS, I say!
You? You? You? *JUMP*?
You actually think you can? You actually think you can do it? YOU? The ground is thirty feet down! And it's solid, solid rock down there! Nobodies gonna catch ya! Nobodies laying down a cushion for ya! Sorry but you - YOU - actually think you've got it in you?
Who do you think you are? BATMAN? Naa-naa-naa-naa, FLATMAN! WHAT do you think you are? An eagle? A dove? Where's the wings, boy? Where's the momentum? Where's the propeller? You can't fly, ya big ostrich.
It's positively preposterous. It's rude. It's arrogant. Standing on that ledge, acting all big like you're gonna throw yourself over it. Stop it now, stop it, you're giving me a stitch. I'm the pavement, and you're my bitch.
Let me assure you that you will never, ever be man enough to take that step over the edge. You're a cotton wool cretin, and you'll always choose to be safe.
Funny thing is though, the girl this is all for, Rose, right? Rose was never safe, not from the moment she was with you, and she knew it for months, knew how much danger she was in in your bed and yet she - she had the courage to stay. With you. For you. She had more lion in her than you'll ever have.
Ain't that hilarious.

10 minutes til the Jump

He was about to turn around when he heard voices. Female of course.
'The pavement is a woman.'
'The air is a woman.'
'Your mother is waiting for you.'
How could he say no to a woman? Let alone three.
'Jump for us.'
'Just try us.'
'Come to us.'
The sweet, sticky voices in his ear kept him on the ledge, hardening his stomach til the cool air cleared his mind. He lifted his foot. He hovered his toes over the ledge. They weren't wobbling anymore.

5 minutes til the Jump

People were filling the streets now, streaming up and down, beginning the lives that would light up London. He wasn't as alone as he thought. He wasn't going to go as quietly as he thought.
Four days ago Myles would have been planning the parties, the festivals, the surprises, that would be the highlight of these people's lives. A handsome businessman here, a young blonde there, a loved up couple stopping to buy flowers - four days ago he would have relished the chance to be their dreammaker.
Now he would be something else to them entirely. Dreammaker the back breaker.
He squinted as he watched them; there was something in the way they were walking. Sure, everybody was always glued to their phones these days, but there was something about the way they clutched them, the way they double took them, the way they tripped when they saw a certain notification come in, the speed with which their eyes shot up and the distrust with which they looked at each other afterwards. There was something in the way that, now, they kept their distance.
Wow. A truth landed in Myles. There was only reason why they would be looking at each other like that.
The vote must have gone through. The country had changed. *Murder is legal.*

1 minute til the Jump

Both sets of toes had made it over the edge, his reflexes still warning him he might slip. Suddenly the pavement looked warm, like an apple pie for him to dive into and be baked.
He sighed with relief. How kind the human body was.

For three days his mind had been blown by the power of guilt. Guilt, guilt, guilt – nobody talked about it. A chunky spluttering pithy tumour that there was simply no, no way he could be in the world with.
And he didn't have to be. All he had to do was walk; something he'd been doing since he was two. He remembered how proud of him his mother had been when he'd taken his first steps – would she be as proud when he took his last?
Or.
Or he could run. Eyes closed, abandoning himself into the air.
Okay. Okay.
Easy like Sunday morning.
Let's go.

The Jump
3, 2, 1. He ran back from the ledge, he closed his eyes, he sprinted forward, and, just like that, he leapt, letting the air take him.
And then he was free falling
Nothing but him and gravity
Utterly free
All the sky dives and all the rollercoasters and all the rockets of the world rolling through him
If only life could have been like this
As he hit the pavement, he thought his last thought
If only he could feel this, just one more time, before –

CRACK.

Chapter Four

The day after Myles failed to die would be the worst day of his life.

When he was younger he'd had a cat, Sylvester, who was a right little hunter. He remembered one time he'd caught him with a mouse in his mouth – he chased him and scolded him til he let the mouse go. When he saw what tumbled from the cat's jaws, he'd regretted it. The rodent was still alive, but what was left was not for this world; it was something that should be in another place, being digested and excreted. Though he'd felt so bad and even buried the mouse when it finally died, his apology had not been enough. Now the universe was doing the same thing to him. Regurgitating his remains. A mouse's revenge.

There were pillows and there were eyelids and then there was the nurse. Not the old one, or the male one, but Valentina. The one with the soft hands. The one who kept her hair hidden in a bonnet, and her body swamped in overalls, but couldn't hide the kindness in her voice.

'Careful now.'

'Just gonna wrap this up.'

'Think you can manage just one sip?'

And there were more pillows and more eyelids as Myles tried to avoid that dreaded, deadly place named 'Awake', but there was always Valentina. And even as he submerged himself deeper into his hospital bed, his mind screaming because he knew the soldiers of 'Awake' were coming for him, Valentina would calm him. She'd drift by with a glass of orange juice and he'd try to kid himself 'Awake' wouldn't be so bad if Valentina would be there.

He didn't know how long he fought it for. Maybe minutes, maybe hours, maybe exactly twenty four of them. All he knew was between being shamed by morning whiteness to colluding with midnight blackness. He begged his brain to allow him to fall back into dreams, all kinds of dreams, away from the eyelids and the pillows and even Valentina, so he didn't have to wake up.

Eventually, our dreams have had enough of us. They toss us back out into the world like we're the rubble and they're trying to get to the real victims beneath us. And you can close your eyes all you want but you're lying to yourself if you think that strip of yellow can save you; you're awake.

He didn't even open his eyes but he heard it; it came for his ears as he squeezed his lashes tight. The Result. Some nurse had switched it on, even though he'd been pretending to sleep - it was irresistible nectar, the news right now, the froth of outrage and intrigue as the UK digested it.

No matter how hard his fingers fought to find the control and change the channel, every channel penetrated him with the same story. The politicians had made their decision on the Assisted Dying Bill. Despite the battle of a lifetime from the opposition, the government had voted it through, with 399 for Yes to 251 to No, and Myles had woken up in a UK that granted assisted dying.

Euthanasia was legal now. Unnecessary suffering was outlawed. The UK would be opening its own version of Switzerland's Dignitas. Dignity had triumphed over dogmatism.

As tight as he squeezed his eyes, it still came for his ears: the great tease, of a compassion he would never know or deserve, a grace that had come one day too late for him. He squeezed them and squeezed them and willed his tears to become glue. He called to the maggots and begged them to fill his ears instead of this. But nothing worked. On and on a loop, it played.

And then, at some moment, perhaps in the middle of the night or the dull of the afternoon, what he never thought would happen, happened. A peace. A relief. You could even call it Mercy.

They stopped talking about the vote. BBC, ITV, SKY … All of them stopped. All of them moved on.

But how? How? How was that possible? What else could the news want, or need, to cover? What could possibly trump this? How could they want to dissect anything other than the very altering of a nation's soul?

Despite his existential sadness, I guess he was still partial to a bit of gossip. Myles opened his eyes to see what was going on. And it all made sense.

Erica Ash had been found. In fact, not just been found: Erica Ash had escaped. Erica Ash had saved herself.

He remembered when she went missing, eight years ago now. You couldn't forget that face. You couldn't forget that hair. Hate to say it, but you couldn't forget that body. But first, the face: it was one of those faces that had captivated the culture, a face that had driven the country mad trying to work out what had happened to her, why she had been taken from them before they got their hands on her first. The obsession didn't make sense, but it did, because they all shared it - she was just one of those people with It Factor, a certain Je Ne Sais Quoi, a girl born for the spotlight, not for ditches or dungeons or stories or statistics. The potential in her was obvious, potential they'd never got to know. She became a tale of caution, about why girls shouldn't stay out too late or walk home alone, but that never quite sat well with anyone: she wasn't caution, or fear, or trepidation. She was a weapon. Documentaries about her came with a trigger warning. She *was* the trigger. Maybe this was the warning.

Because now she was back, every news bulletin running the headlines and the same grainy video of an impossibly slight girl in a stained grey sweatshirt, running into her mother's arms. *Erica Ash escapes captivity. Woman claiming to be Erica Ash found. The return of Erica Ash.* An ostentatious amount of matted hair swung with her as she ran. How had her hair grown that much in captivity? Her face nestled into her mother, she finally turned her head, just an inch, to look into the camera.

And Myles realised if he didn't deserve empathy, and he didn't deserve mercy, and he didn't deserve kindness, then he certainly didn't deserve to look into that face.

So he shut his eyes again. This time, he slept.

Valentina was sitting right there, adjusting his drip when he finally opened them. She broke into a smile when she saw him, and her eyes broke into pity when he moved.
'Myles,' she said, almost in a whisper, like she knew he wasn't ready for the world. 'You're awake. Hi. I'll be taking care of you. Just try not to move too suddenly. You'll need your strength. Sorry, I – I – I'm rambling.'
Myles looked around the room. A bed all to himself – perhaps he was being segregated. Was Valentina even safe being near him?
'I want you to move very slowly, very gently, because you've clearly had quite a shock.'
Pillows, duvets, eyelashes. 'Make sure your leg stays in place,' she said. 'Very good. Now can you tell me what you see? Is your vision okay?'
'Yes,' he spoke. 'It's perfect.'
The word 'perfect' didn't belong to a man like him, didn't belong to a mouth like his. He was so far removed from anything perfect, he even thought Valentina flinched at the words. She was wandering it too, wasn't she; *why was he still here*?
'Good, good, that's great. You were out for almost three days – no signs of concussion. Have you had your water? Take another sip.'
Another sip, another breath, another night, another sleep.
The whiteness of the room screamed into him; the walls, Valentina's bizarelly baggy uniform, his own skin. He didn't know what he wanted to rip apart first.
'Can I leave?' he asked her suddenly. 'I'm awake, aren't I? You would have told me if something's wrong. Can I just leave? Please. I don't need my things.'
'Your friend Jack bought your things earlier actually,' she said. 'But no, you cannot leave. We'll be monitoring you for a few weeks.'
'I want to leave. You can't stop me, can you?'
'I can't but … the doctor can. He's here now actually.' Valentina turned to the door and held it open, as a strong and tall doctor entered. 'Myles, meet Doctor Harrison.'
Myles went to extend a weak hand, then stopped.
Why was Doctor Harrison looking at him like that?

'Good evening, Myles. I'm your Doctor, Doctor Harrison and I've been treating you and the after effects of your fall, while you've been unconscious.' The brutal expression had gone, replaced with scholarly warm. 'I'm sorry to wake you up but I thought now would be a good time to take you through some of the things you'll be dealing with. Does that sound okay?'
That actually sounded good. Myles was happy just to hear from someone, to get some answers, to find out what had happened since he jumped. He liked the

way the doctor was speaking to him, with a serene calm, with direction.
Valentina exited the humble way nurses like to.
'When you fell, you fell into hell.' Bit blunt. 'Not because of how hard you landed, or the way you landed, or from how high you landed. But because of what you landed on.
Think. What's the worst thing you could land on?'
Myles fumbled inside his brain. What was a surface that could mangle him, yet keep him alive? Or could it be possible there was a surface hard enough to mean death would be coming soon? Is that why this doctor was talking so seriously, why he was taking Myles to the conclusion so slowly?
'Spikes?'
'No.'
'Concrete?'
'No.'
'Ice?'
'No.'
Hurry up. Myles was prepared for whatever it was, whatever his new future held.
'A vat of Acid?' It was getting silly, surreal now,
'No.'
'Well ...what then?!'
'We need to ease you into this. This is one of the worst falls we've seen in forty years. All because of the landing you selected. If it hadn't been for that, you would have been fine.'
'Would have been ...? Will I – can I walk again?'
'Oh yes, you'll be able to walk just fine. Go on, try it. Wiggle your big toe. Try and sit up.'
Myles tried. His toe moved with uneasy ease, his frame slid up to seating without him even thinking about it.
'I can sit. I can lie on my side, too. And I'm - I'm talking. I can think straight, I think. I feel ok – as okay as I can. So what is it? Oh god. Is it my face?'
'Your face?'
'I've ... I've mutilated myself, haven't I' He raised a hand to check out his new form, the splinters and shards he'd divided himself into.
The doctor watched him, smug. 'No, Myles, not your face. You're just as handsome as ever. For now. And you can still walk, talk and eat. For now.'
'For *now*?'
'Want one final guess at what you landed on?'
'Erm, ok. Was it ... a monument? A famous monument?'
He shook his head sombrely. 'No.'
'What was it? Tell me!'
Three more seconds when Myles got to live in a world he could attempt to bare.
And then the doctor spoke.

'*It* was Taylor.'
'What?!'
'Say her name. Taylor.'
'Taylor.'
'She was five foot six. Seven stone ten pounds. Blonde. Twenty years old. Her cushioning broke the impact of your fall and saved your life. But the impact of your *jump* … killed her.'

If you've heard of pain, you've heard of Myles. Thirty feet had seemed so high, but at least that fall had had a landing. The true plummet began now, into layers of pain science hadn't yet uncovered, hadn't yet named.
And they were erogenous, erogenous, everything erogenous.
He was the walls of every womb lining of every menstruating woman while he was the cavity of every rotten tooth of every diseased mouth while he was the twisted nerve in every arthritic finger of every elderly man while he was the open sore of every sore on every promiscuous pouch.
He had killed a second person. In jumping to atone for his crime and to escape his pain, he had failed, kept himself alive, and wiped a young, innocent life full of hope from the world. Again. Why have one when you can have two? That had to be the worst expression in the world.
So there it is; the worst joke in the world. Myle's life.
God, 'life'. That word. Fused to Myles like a lie. All he wanted, was to die. But then again, what if Hell was real? Cos he was definitely going there now.

'Taylor. Do you want to know more about her?
She'd saved up to go travelling. She was planning a Gladiator themed party before she went – she was on the phone, talking about it, that's why she didn't notice the great big lump falling above her. She was an intern at Elle. She loved otters. She had two sisters, one older, one younger.'
The doctor circled his bed.
'I know a lot, don't I? I'm afraid there's one more thing you need to know about why this was the worst possible landing.'
'Go on,' Myles weeped. 'Tell me.'
'Her name wasn't just Taylor. It was Taylor Harrison.'
Myles blinked, confused.
The doctor leaned into him. 'Thought I'd introduced myself?' He whispered. 'Thought I'd told you who I was?'
He reached for his badge, turning it up to catch the light. 'Read it.' He said.
Myles read it, weakly. 'Doctor Harrison.'
'Her father was a doctor.'

Snail skin is nothing like human skin. It's *juicy*. Wet. Lickable. Biteintothepithable.

It's so *tender*. If you peeled off microscopic layer after layer of our skin, I don't think you'd find a single layer so gentle as the first surface on a snail. We are not made of skin you can't wipe your tears into, skin that is exposed and submissive with the promise of succulence.
A pinch of salt and it pops. A dash of heat and it fries. Even just a blunt stone and it splits. Oh, to be a snail, moments from being crushed.

'When you jumped, your condition was extremely critical. You lost an abnormal amount of blood. In fact, abnormal that someone has that much blood in them at all. You must be a very bloody man indeed, Myles, all that sauce running through your veins. I reckon you exercise a lot, don't you? A fit, healthy young man.
The other thing I noticed about your blood was how red it was. So ... vivid. So pigmented. Why is that do you think, Myles? Is it wine? Fan of tomatoes? Eat a lot of berries? No, none of those. Like going down on girls when it's their time of the month do you? *Ah*. That's it. Did you taste my daughter's blood when you woke up in the van, before you were sedated? Believe me, that is the last time you will ever be sedated in my lifetime.'

Two, two, two. Not one but two.
Double trouble.
If only the guilt inside him had doubled, but instead it multiplied, all the way up to infinity – and it wouldn't stop. Contagion, contamination, more, more, more. A new plague, invented there and then.

'You may ask why I'm here. There was a fire in the other part of the borough yesterday. Dozens were hurt. Good people, charity workers, firemen, out to save lives. Most of our leading doctors were deployed to the local hospital up there. I had a bad experience with burns when I was younger, so it's on my notes that it's better for me to take over other duties. I was the only doctor around who could treat a case like yours. Then of course when they bought in Taylor ... I was convinced I could save her. After I couldn't, they said I should go home, said there was no way I should be treating you. But they don't run this hospital. I do.'

Would the mattress swallow him?
Would the light from above fall on him?
Would this man, this father, kill him?
He knew those wishes were too good to be true. There was a reason his fall had been cushioned – he was meant to live. He was meant to suffer.
And finally, through the pain, he felt something else; fear.

'How much do you weigh, Myles? You look strong.'

Myles was too afraid to pause. 'Fourteen stone.'
'Fourteen stone! Ohh! Almost two Taylors. Still I didn't think a weak man like you would be enough to take my daughter from me. A man weak enough to jump from a building on a February morning. It's *almost Valentine's Day,* Myles, don't you have someone to be buying presents for?' He smirked. 'Well, now you're my present.'
He walked across the room, drawing the curtains.
'I run this hospital. The other doctors, the nurses, the aestheticians … they all work for me. They've all known me for years. I reckon you've prayed a bit, in your time here, haven't you? Well here's God. I'm God here, and I'm going to look after you. I'm gonna do everything I can to keep you alive. I can turn away your visitors. I can withhold your meals. But I can do more than that. I picked out a private room for you, way at the bottom of the corridor.
First will come the amputation.
Then the castration.
Then the lobotomy.'
He looked at him, and Myles waited, waited, waited for him to say 'And *then* I will kill you.' But he didn't. Instead he smiled with a rich thick glee, and said;
'Ever had a fly lay eggs in your eye?
Ever have a spider crawl into your ear?
Ever had a wasp sting you on the tongue?'
'No,' Myles tried not to shake.
Him and this doctor understood each other; death was a long way away.
'So innocent. You've experienced nothing. You've felt nothing. Soon you'll know,' Doctor Harrison nodded. 'I'll be back tonight.'

Half an hour went by.
The door opened again.
Myles kept his eyes closed, waiting, waiting for the first touch.
It began with a stroke of the forehead.
'Shh,' she said. 'It's me.'
'Rose?!' his eyes snapped open.
'Rose?' A friendly face looked back. 'No, no. Valentina, your nurse.' She spoke in hushed tones. 'Be quiet. No one knows I'm here. We have to be quick.'
She laid out a tray, and began to assemble equipment.
'Doctor Harrison can't do this to you.' She shook her head. 'He just can't.'
She turned from him again, her uniform now stained.
'It's going to take me a few minutes to set things up.' Her hair was still hidden in the plastic bonnet. 'You just relax. You deserve it.'
Deserve?! I don't deserve anything, I –
But something in her silky voice, made him listen.
She turned to Myles now, a serene smile on her face, and he saw what she was holding; a syringe. *So he was getting his Valentine's wish after all.*

'I can't let Doctor Harrison do anything to you,' she whispered. 'It's not right. It was a mistake. I can't imagine how you're feeling.'
She was fiddling with a small bottle of clear liquid, popping off the lid to a satisfying 'Ahh' sound.
'They shouldn't be letting him in but no one can say no to him.' She poured the liquid into the syringe and screwed the tip back on. 'What happened with Taylor … it's just a tragedy. I know that doesn't mean much but I, at least, can see it for what it is. Trouble is,' she pulled a rubber strap from her bag of equipment. 'I don't see him calming down.'
She turned to Myles, still smiling gently, and moved closer.
'Shh. Hold your arm out, other way.' She deftly tied a rubber strap around his elbow, pulling it tight so his arm was taut. She tapped it, hard, twice. 'Just let me find a vein.'
It was like she had sung those words, created the most beautiful song ever sung, her voice even changed as she said them.
'Myles? Are you ok? I said tense your arm.'
Myles tensed.
'Ok, ok, got one.This shouldn't hurt much, but you may feel a little sharpness.'
'Shit, missed it. Ok, it's fine, let me try the other arm.'
She moved to his other arm quickly, not bothering to unwrap his elbow or disinfect the needle. She tied another strap around it. This time she was rushing. He noticed the blisters of an overworked nurse on her hand.
'I think I've got … no, that one doesn't want to come out. I don't understand what's happening.' She checked the other side of the bed, to where he was attached to an IV. 'Your drip is working, you've been hydrated all day. Let me try a different needle.'
'Fuck!' Myles felt cold. 'Why isn't it working?'
Then came the footsteps. Both their blood drained from their faces. She grabbed her equipment, shoving into a drawer in the bedside cabinet nearby. 'One minute,' she said, disappearing out of the door.
'Hey,' Myles heard her, speaking calmly.
A female voice. 'Hey. Doctor Harrison wants to see the patient.'
'Ok…' Valentina said. 'I was just changing him. Send him down in five minutes?'
Five minutes?
'Yep. Well, I'll check. Maybe he wants to help you change him,' a sarcastic laugh, and the female footsteps went the other way.
'Actually, I'll come with you,' Valentina called out to the voice. 'Double check his instructions.' She poked her head round the curtain, winked at Myles then exited.
Five minutes?
Myles slapped his arm himself. Where were his fucking veins?! He looked around the room. Perhaps there was some oxy …

The door opened.

Valentina stood there, holding a bundle of clothes.
'I'm so sorry, Myles – I don't have time,' she came towards him, sitting him up. 'But we just might have time for this.'
She ripped at his hospital gown. 'These are the clothes you came in. Put them on.'
Myles grabbed at the jeans, the boxers and the shirt, of the man who'd failed to die. He pulled them on, wrestling them desperately over the bandages around his left leg.
'Your friend Jack bought your wallet, your passport and keys. Here you go,' she handed him a plastic bag.
Myles stood – 'Ah!'
His leg! His leg! Shards of it rippled around each other as he started to move. This was what you called 'damaged.'
'Shh,' she said, opening the door to the corridor. She peaked left and right, then she turned, and held out her hand.
Myles took it.

She led him quickly through the dark corridor, through a side door, then another, that brought them to a flight of stairs.
Were they going up? To the roof? Would she push him?
But no. Like everything in the past seventy two hours, they were going down.
Myles hurried down, his leg so sadistic it was practically enjoying it. They moved like butter, holding hands all the way. They crashed through the exit door together, into air that had dropped ten degrees since Myles had tried to die in it.
'Go,' Valentina said. 'Get away from here.'
He turned to the left when he realised – or did he know already – he was still holding her hand.
She smiled, surreptitiously. 'Wherever you're going, I'm not coming with you.'
He knew Doctor Harrison was probably ten feet away. He knew the police were probably looking to question him. He knew he didn't have a friend in this world. And yet he didn't go, not left, not right. He didn't let go of her hand.
'And you don't need to thank me,' she added, looking up at him through her lashes. 'It's just as much for me as it is for you. ***Go.***'
'How can I … how can I keep you safe?' he asked.
Her voice was light, 'I'll be fine. Tell me why you jumped.'
One whisper of the 'R' word and he was back in a world of rosewater tsunamis, petal hurricanes, hail made of thorns and tornado of pollen; he was humbled, crumbled, shrinking before her. Would she have helped him if she knew the truth? Would she go near him? He didn't even know if – no, he couldn't say it – yes, he had to – he didn't even know what he'd done to Rose *before* he killed her.

What if he hurt this nurse now? Threw her into the road, in yet another sudden snap?
He dropped her hand, seeing her face fall, as he turned, and began his new walk; the hobbling half-run of a guilty half-man.

She didn't follow him, and within minutes he had forgotten her, the only thing munching at his mind was the pain in his leg and the compulsion to go faster. He had dropped his keys at some point, but it didn't matter – there was no way he was going home. He knew where had to go.
Crunch.
Crunch.
Don't look down.
No, he thought, look up. Don't look down. Keep walking.
But he had heard it, clear as day, a sound and a series of thoughts many of us have heard in our lives.
Crunch.
Crunch.
Don't look down.
He should keep going. He had to get out of London. And he had to start to deal with the fact that over the past seventy hours, he had killed two people. Two women. Taken two lives. Two women he could never, ever bring back.
Two people. Two women. Two crimes.
Crunch.
Crunch.
He looked down.
NO.
Oh god NO.
It was true, imprinted on his shoe in a righteous tattoo of shell and mucus.
He had done it.
He had stepped on a snail, a snail that should have been stepping on him.
Two people. Two women. Two crimes.
And now the snail too.
He looked down at his shoe, and the longing inside him tripled. The stamp of the dead snail stared back at him. Another debt to pay.
Two women.
One snail.
Three lives.
An infinite debt. Let it begin.

Part Two
The Hands

Chapter Five

Six Weeks Later

One tequila, two tequila, three tequila … FLOOR.
Five tequila, seven tequila, eight tequila … MORE.
Nine tequila, ten tequila, eleven tequila …. WHORE.
Tequila, tequila, MORE, MORE, MORE!

'Okay.' Erica giggled, pulling her mum in closer so she could whisper. 'This is the game. You pick a word, and whisper it, then I have to say it, but a bit louder. Then you go, then I go, getting louder and louder each time. First one to chicken out is the loser. Ok?'

Her mum nodded, biting down on the lime. 'But darling, we're on a *plane*,' she grinned cheekily.

'Oh no, not in public?' Erica said in playful mock-shock. 'Oh we couldn't possibly!'

They both cracked up, even the man in the window seat of their row turning to them with delighted shock at seeing a pair so effervescent.

'Okay, fine.' Her mother said. 'What's the word?'

'You choose. Something to do with tequila.'

'Tequila … tits!' Her mother clapped her hand over her mouth, amazed at her brazenness. The man in the window seat's eyes lit up again.

'Ok, that's the word. You start. Hey, do you wanna play?' Erica asked the man, leaning over her mother. Her mind grinned when she saw the bashful yet intrigued expression on his face.

'Erm… I don't know …'

'Go on!' they said in unison.

'Have some of our tequila!'

'Carpe Diem, babe! You're here! You're alive! You're on your way to *Ha-wa-ii*!' Erica whooped. The air con made her shiver, but it was the good kind of shivering - she knew what real cold, real chills, real temperature torment was, and she didn't have to feel that any more. In contrast, she was about to feel the most sumptuous of suns. 'Hawaii everyone!'

'Woo!' came a few cheers back, mixed with a few disapproving looks.

'Ok,' the man nodded, laughing. 'Let's play.'

'Yay! You going there for business or pleasure?'

'Business.'

'Well then. All the more reason for a game now. We ready? We're gonna play 'Tequila Tits.' Say it as loud as you can. First one to quit loses.'

The three huddled together, guilty grins on their faces. With a coy whisper, keeping her voice low, Erica's mum began.

'Tequila Tits…'

Erica raised her voice just an inch, wincing as she did.

'Tequila Tits…'

Upping the stakes, the man launched his voice a little louder.

'Tequila Tits.'

Reproachful looks were scattered their way. They giggled. It was Erica's mothers turn again.
'TEQUILA Tits...'
'Tequila tits!' Erica squealed.
'Tequila TITS.' The man shouted quickly, clapping his hand over his mouth as more people turned to look at them. He went bright red. Erica, cackling, continued, in a quick sing-song.
'Tequila titsssss.'
'Has to be louder guys ...'
'Tequila tits.'
'No, come on, louder!' Why let a little embarrassment hold you back? Erica knew what it was to be truly held back, to be held down for real. She'd be damned if she ever let anything ever do that to her again. 'TEQUILA TITS!'
'TeQUiLA TITS'
'That's it!'
'TEQUILA TITS!'
'TEQUILA TITSSSS!!!'
'Shhh!'
An air steward marched down the aisle as they scrunched together, burying themselves in their outrageous bubble. It felt like the whole plane was looking now.
Erica grinned. 'Do we give up? Do we yield?'
A wasp's grin lit up her mum's face. 'Never!'
'Go on then.'
'TE-TE-TE-TEQUILA TIIIIIITS!'
Lit up with looseness, Erica screamed too. 'TEQUILA TITS TITS TITS!' Just because she could, because nobody could control her or punish her now.
'WHAT DO WE WANT?'
'TEQUUUIIILAAA TIIITSSSSS!!!' roared the man, the rest of the cabin reverberating from the soundwaves. Try as Erica and her mother might, they couldn't get louder than that. The two girls bounced back in their seats, the wave of mirth rolling through them, as two air hostesses inevitably approached. One of them very stern, bending down. 'Excuse me, I'm sorry, but you can't disturb the other passengers like that.'
The other an amused glint all over her face, her badge saying 'Charlotte'. 'Just *try* to keep it down. It's good to see passengers having fun though. Any more drinks?'
Erica and her mum looked at each other. A brand new feeling - was this spontaneity? - shot through Erica. 'Always. Another round of tequila, please.'
The man reached over. 'This rounds on me. This time we'll do champagne, yes ladies?'
Before her mother could hesitate, Erica nodded an abundant yes. She'd never had champagne on a plane before, but now nobody could deprive her of

anything. 'And we *did* say we'd splash out on duty free. I'd like to buy every perfume in the magazine.'
Charlotte beamed. 'I'll bring the trolley right away.'
Erica stroked the velour of her tracksuit, still marvelling at how it felt to be able to choose her own clothes. Or be clothed at all. 'Thank youuuu!'
Charlotte swept back up the aisle. 'Have fun, you three!'
'Let's make a pact.' Erica, her mother, and the man all clasped hands. They closed their eyes in a parody of a sermon, and waited for Erica to seal their pact. 'To going mile high!'
'*Erica*!' Just when she thought her daughter couldn't surprise her any more, just when she thought any more suppressed spirit couldn't come through. 'Darling, that's outrageous!'
'She sure is,' the man purred back. 'And I'll drink to *that*.' Popping open a packet of peanuts, he tossed them in the air, catching a couple in his mouth.
Erica realised the other air hostess was still standing over them, bearing down with disapproval. 'Listen, I appreciate you're in high spirits, but I do need to ask you to keep it down - '
Her words were sliced away as a shower of spit hit her.
'GALUGH. GAGABLA. UMPHGLEEN!' Three unwelcome sounds came from the window seat. The trio in front of them shot around in unison to see it. A horrible guttural gurning, each grunt building on top of the other.
Each row of seats fell like dominoes, turning over to identify the destructive noise.
Oh Lord. The news hit them all at the same time. *Somebody was choking on the plane.*
Erica's new friend in the window seat, so confident and nonchalant to toss the peanuts in the air a few moments ago, had found one such unfriendly peanut had now lodged itself firmly in his throat.
And that culprit of a peanut now had our man turning purple.
One lone airpod hung from his ear as he rocked, desperately in his seat. A horrific hacking came from his throat, as though it wasn't a throat there at all but something small and angry and frothy. His choking had made the plane a tableaux of shocked, stilted inertia, and who should be most frozen of all but Erica's mother, sitting right next to him but unable to help?
Then everybody started trying to save him at once, and that's when things got even worse. There was the man behind him, smacking him in the spine. There was the man in front of him, forcing his mouth open and plunging his fingers into the drooly drain of his trachea, fighting to find the nut but giving him even less air in the process. There was the wannabe doctor who had climbed over a seat, kicking him in the head as he went, and was struggling to stand him up, to do a Heimlich manoeuvre there wasn't space to do. There was the air hostess running down in the aisle with the first aid kit – the plane bonded in thinking, what the hell is that going to do?

All the while, the man was running out of colours to turn.
Through the sound and the saliva, Erica saw the debilitating distress in his eyes. She didn't know the Heimlich manoeuvre, didn't know how to do anything really, but she knew that look. She reached across her mother who was still stuck in a statue, and ran a hand across his stubble, gentle. 'You're okay.' She whispered. 'You got this.'
There was one giant almighty hack, a sacrilegious sound, and then the nut was summoned back into the stale air of the plane - it came shooting out of his throat with a ricochet. The man gave a hoarse hail, and then, for the first time in two minutes, he took a fresh breath, a breath the whole plane seemed to take with him. Wiping his mouth, not sure where he was, he found he could gloriously, brilliantly *breathe.*
A slimy silence sat across the plane, a flustered feeling still draining the cabin as people tried to figure out if everything was okay. Erica fluttered to her feet, addressing the crowd of bated breaths and clutched Coke cans.
'All good, everybody,' she chimed, smiling at them, taking in their faces - such variety, so many people, so many potential new friends. 'He's fine!' She felt her ponytail swing. 'Enjoy your holiday!' Playful, amused applause scattered back to her. She sat back down.
Her mother pulled her close, and she melted in, her body still wincing with the happy shock that getting a kiss instead of a stomp on the head did to her. 'You look amazing,' she said. 'Just amazing.'
Erica pulled away, leaning across her. 'You okay?' she asked the man.
He wiped his mouth one final time, and nodded. 'Yes. All good.' His eyes flicked up the aisle. 'And there's our champagne's arriving. Just in time.'
Erica picked up her shot glass for a cheers. She lowered her voice, but with a wink said, 'Interesting start to our first day in paradise, right?'
They clinked.
'Cheers. Here's to paradise.'

Hawaii

As Erica stood at the very edge of the shore, trying to understand how the ocean before her was so big, she had only one thought.
'So this is where my tears went this whole time.'
She had cried so many tears over those years she wondered why they didn't drown her. She'd cursed them as they dried, temporary tattoos all across her face. She'd been a dehydrated machine, popping them out one by one; big ones, little ones, each one saltier than the next. She didn't understand why she hadn't run out, why her enflamed tear ducts weren't giving up on her like the rest of her body. But now, now, it all made sense. They'd been coming here, to fill up this ocean, an ocean that would one day get to wash her pain away.

Again she blinked and again the panic splintered in her, because closing her eyes meant she would have to open them and that might mean it would turn out it was all a dream. She couldn't deny how often that had happened, how many dreams she'd had of escape only to wake up and find she was still in His dream, still the non-sentient figment of his imagination that he could do whatever he wished to. But this time, when she opened her eyes, she was looking at something she couldn't have even dreamed. Something she thought she'd made up sometimes to comfort her.

The wide, endless, forgiving expanse of deep, benevolent ocean.

How could it be possible, that she, the underground creature, was standing here right now? With the sun pouring warm caramel down her back and with the powdered sugar sand kissing her toes. With a hazy pink air mixing into the melted vanilla milk that was her blood. With the moment just before sunset tickling all the spaces in between her collarbones, behind her throat, at the small of her back. How was it possible that she, a voodoo doll, had had the pins pulled from her, the rotten cotton emptied out of her, and been stuffed with spun silk and stitched back up without a single needle?

And she hadn't even stepped into the ocean yet.

It was hard to comprehend that she could walk from left, to right, or back to front, and no one would stop her, let alone that she could take three steps forward and be submerged in water that didn't have to end.

It was blue, all shades of gorgeous blue, just like her bruises had been. Her favourite kind of bruise were the spiral ones, the swirl going from aqua to turquoise. She was standing before a patch of water that looked just like that now.

She wondered if there were sea creatures in there, waiting for her. A turtle, for her to touch. A seahorse, she'd always wanted to see one of those. A crab. *Hermit no more, hermit no more.*

With every slap, every bite, every creative new moment of pain, when she was down there, when she was his; the words had been strong in her head – '*I don't deserve this. I don't deserve this. Wah, wah, wah, I may not have been perfect but I – don't - deserve - this.*'

But ... did she deserve *this*?

This much ... Satiation? That was the word, *Satiation*, the glorious resolution to a forty day fast. This much satisfaction, this much relief, this many sensory baths? Could anyone really deserve all this at once? Every cell in her body gaping open lustfully for a delayed gratification others could only dream of. There's a reason blind people have to wear special sunglasses for weeks after their operation, even if they've been able to see before – nothing can prepare them for the light.

Down there, she had wished, so many times, it could be possible to go numb. Permanently numb, so she'd never feel anything physical again. Again and again, it had not worked. But because her feelings, all those naughty nerves and stubborn synapses, had refused to switch off, now it meant she would *feel* the ocean, without gloves, without layers, without anaesthetic. She'd feel it like a lover who had been craving her his whole life, who wouldn't stop til he devoured her.

And it was going to be glorious. But the question was, had it been worth it? Was it worth those years of agony, for this moment of reward now?

Only one way to find out.

'Go on, darling,' her mum said, who had been standing respectfully behind her, for the ten minutes since they'd got to the beach. 'You can do it. Take a step.'

Erica smiled and looked back at the water, a rush rustling through her veins. So much water. Who needed this much cleansing?

'Let's do it together,' suddenly her mother was taking her hand.

Erica was about to take the step - but she couldn't help what happened next. She fell to her knees.

She landed on the sea bed and gasped at more sensations, the sugary sand on her shins, her kneecaps becoming oil in the heat. A white hot feeling in her hands as she gripped at the sand, reeling every time a piece of glass wasn't there.

Maybe the doctors had been right, to advise her to 'go slow', to 'find a routine'. Maybe she should have listened to them when they said she needed to 'take it day by day' and 'settle into society'. Maybe they were onto something when they said her brain wouldn't be ready for this much freedom at once, that it was reckless. Maybe she should be choosing therapy over thrills. Maybe it was too soon for a holiday. They'd all advised her that six weeks after captivity was too soon for this much stimulation - and that her Vitamin D deprived skin may not even be able to take the sun. But she'd ignored them, and her mother had granted her wishes. 'To Hawaii!' she'd roared, and off they'd gone.

Now as she sunk into the sand, for the first time, their words felt real. Maybe this was all too much, all too soon, all too brave.

And maybe. Here came that voice.

Maybe she didn't belong here. Maybe she didn't belong this close to the sun. In fact, she probably didn't belong above the ground. Surely spending that long in a cellar, mould had grown on her. What if everyone could see it? What if she dripped into the ocean and contaminated everything? And salt water should be for tears, not for swimming, not for her.

She should go home. She should hide. She should disappear. She should bury herself again before everyone saw what she really was.

She should 'adjust to her freedom accordingly.'

No. No. Fuck that.

Remember what it was like. Remember.

Every single second down there had spat on her, and leaned in closely and whispered, 'We've got you now, and we can take as long as we want with you, and rub away all the ends and the edges until they're nothing left,' and she'd sworn if she ever got out she would never waste a second up here again, that she would beat every second black until it burst.

And now she was out. And she could do whatever she wished with the seconds in front of her.

'Are you ok?' her mother was next to her in the sand, rubbing her arm. 'It's alright, darling. Let's go get lunch instead.'

For the first time, she didn't need to look at her beautiful mother, for some kind of reassurance.

She stood.

We thought we buried you once.

She stepped forward.

We thought you were being munched by the maggots.

She took another step.

You were one of our sacrifices, presented from us to the Earth. And it gobbled you up.

She halted.

You're a creature of the underground, not a girl of the land. And certainly not a sea creature. No mermaids here; hermit, hermit.

She gulped.

Submit, hermit, submit.

She felt the water wash into her toes.

Submit, hermit, submit.

NO.

Half plunging, half sashaying, she lurched into the sea; she gasped in awe as it took its first bite of her. Cool fresh gums of water were suddenly caressing her ankles, and lilting up around her torso. It warmed her just enough to bake her and cooled her just enough to refresh her -

Do I deserve this?

It was up to her shoulders now – who knew being eaten could feel so divine? It was celestial, luscious, and oh so strange, a thousand gallons of cream and music that brushed her in every direction -

Do I deserve this?

'Mum!' she called out. 'Come in!'

Her mother, smiling, began walking into the water. Erica planted her feet in the sea bed, the sand even nicer here, before she ran to her and jumped into her arms. 'Ahh!' they laughed and then they were submerged, submerged in all the opulent tears Erica had cried for all those years.. As Erica came up for air she saw everyone else in them for the first time. The families, the couples, the friends, all playing volleyball, straddling, kissing, surfing and rolling in her silvery tears. All of them drenched and dripping, unaware that the beads that drizzled down them, that they splashed at their friends and swirled on their tongues, had been made by her for eight years straight. She hoped they were enjoying them, hoped she'd got the temperature just right.

Look at you all. All I had to do was drain my ducts ... and now you get to float.
Is this really what everybody had been doing, all this time, while she'd been down there? While she'd needed them, while she'd cried out for them, while she'd waited for them, had they really been having this much fun? And when he found a new way to humiliate her, to make her lonelier, and make her cry more, were they just happy that it meant they could dive deeper? Were they just pleased that the waves they could ride were bigger? Did not one of them think to ask why the water kept coming?
Yes. Yes. I do deserve this.
If they can deserve this, so can I.
Her eyes flicked from the group playing volleyball, to the couple holding their breath, to the woman swan diving into her tears.
I deserve this more than all of them.

It was as hard to leave the water as it had been to enter it. Her mother left a good half an hour earlier, but once Erica was in, she couldn't quite imagine a world where she wasn't in its liquid love. It was only when the hunger kicked in, and she realised with a thrill she could satisfy it instantly, not wait for him to bring her a tray, that she leapt up and out.
Her shoulders glazed by the heat, she met her mother at the shack they had said to meet at. Her mum was just paying the woman behind the counter. Erica smiled at a man sitting by the till; the son, perhaps? Sympathy swelled in her heart when she noticed he had been in some kind of accident, the bones crushed slightly in hands and face. She looked away.
'Got us two pina coladas,' her mother grinned, handing her a glossy green orb. 'With extra rum.'
'Thank youuu,' Erica grinned, sipping. Oh *yes.* The tang bounced off her tongue. Salty skin, warm hair, and now a coconut cocktail. Her life was a music video.
'Nah, you girls are getting it wrong. You need to try the watermelon vodka boats. *That* blows your head off.'
Erica and her mother turned. Two men. American. Late twenties. Big. Brawny. Grinning. Leaning. Looking.
'Mmm,' Erica said. 'Maybe next time.'
'Maybe tonight,' one of them said. 'Where you staying?'
'This hotel,' Erica smiled. 'You?'
'Same. It's great but ... we can't get a table for dinner. They only accept bookings of four.'
Erica looked at her mother with a giggle. As expected she saw the nerves in her mother's eyes. That this was too soon, too much, that Erica shouldn't be speaking to strangers. Especially men. And most of all, the thing she couldn't shake; why wasn't Erica afraid?
'Mate, I am *so* sunburnt,' the other groaned. 'Rookie error.'

Her mother looked at the ground as Erica reached into her beach bag.
'Whereabouts?' He turned, revealing a volcano's carcass across his upper back.
'Ooh!' she exclaimed.
'I know, I know ...'
Erica was already shaking her sun cream. She looked at his friend. 'Shall you do it, or shall I?'
'You apply it, and we'll take you for dinner later as a thank you.'
Her mother finally looked up, meeting Erica's eyes. A thousand conversations passed between them, a snake pit of debates and arguments, but each one ending in the one thing they had agreed once they'd been reunited. '*Carpe diem.*' Erica was applying the sun cream, ever so gently, onto the strangers back before her mother's smile had even cracked.
'What time's good for you?'
'We'll be taking a while to get ready,' her mother smiled. 'It's our first night so expect the full works.'
'9pm then? The seafood place?'
'Ok... we'll be there. Come on Erica, let's get to our room.'
Erica took her hand.
'My back feels better already by the way,' the man said, with a grin. 'Literally. Nice one.'
Erica winked at him, her mum lacing her arm around her waist. 'That's my daughter,' she said, kissing her cheek. 'Isn't she great? You should see what she can do when the moon comes out.' Erica giggled as the guys gaped.
The mother and daughter duo turned and sauntered back to the hotel.

The day bled gold and Erica did too. She stood in her hotel room, drenched in the sun's blood, getting used to this new feeling that was satisfying yet another appetite of yet another mouth that had puckered open inside her tanned skin. The *after sun, after beach, lazy, hazy* feeling of a triumphant day spent basking – 'basking', a new word she could now use, now she was a lioness. And she looked like one, too. Her skin was tawny, dusky and ever so sexily burnt; her body still thin but she was gaining some compact muscle, evidence of all the frolicking she was doing. 'Frolicking', a new verb bestowed into her life.
Her face had kept the same angular, dexterous carving it had had before she was taken. A fusion of the feminine and the feline, every feature seemed to have been sculpted with a cat's claw, to be small yet sharp yet sweet. Where her nose was tiny, her eyes were saucers, blazing an unnaturally bright blue against the gold of her face. The lips were petite but they pouted.
And then there was her hair.
Ever since I was little, ever since I could remember, I wanted long, long princess hair just like in the Disney films. I remember an exact moment in Year One, when a teacher pointed out this girl 'Lisa's' hair – 'isn't it lovely, look how long? Long enough to sit on,' and that was it, my first ever sin as jealousy

popped open inside me. I ran my fingers through my own hair, my stomach grumbling as my hair confessed to me how it only, inadequately, reached an inch or so below my shoulder blades. I swore there and then my hair would be longer than Lisa's, within the year – hair grows after all.
But it didn't. I begged my mum to never cut it and she obliged. As soon as I reached my teens, I was making a mess in the kitchen, brothing up masks of honey and eggs and anything else I'd heard off. I'd sit in the shower, my eyes stinging as I willed blends of peppermint and pepper to work, kick it into action, give me my dream hair, hair that could make me feel special. I gorged on nuts and avocados, convinced that the nutrients would float up beyond my brain and make me into a princess.
Yet despite seeing other girls who didn't even try, shoot past me with their flowing rivulets, my stubborn strands refused. My collarbone-length curtain became a mocking, infuriating curse.
But, then ...
Down there ...
Down in that cold space, where no one could see it –
It grew. Oh baby did it grow.
Doesn't make any sense, doesn't it? No sunlight. No fresh air. And no, he did not give me any scalp massages.
Neither of us couldn't explain it, but the difference was obvious within the first couple of months. There was a gushing, a flood, a damn finally unblocked from my motivated skull. It was at my waist in under a year. Two years and it was sailing down my back, passing the forbidden tailbone with a mocking laugh. Four years and it had surpassed my bum – now it got to touch my thighs, swaying and swishing, finally a comfortable blanket to sleep on. Six years and I could wrap it around myself. And this was healthy hair, too, shiny and triumphant, soft enough to stroke him and strong enough to choke him.
He loved my hair too. He loved playing with it. Braiding it. Pulling it.
One of my biggest fears was one day he would cut it.. One slash and it would be gone.
But that wasn't really his style. To cut. I worried he would 'pluck' it, with his fingertips. One by one, strand by strand, gasp by gasp.
But to his credit, he didn't. He let me keep it. He let me live out my dream as a Rapunzel, with no window to dangle it out of and no Prince to climb it.
And now, since leaving the cellar, it hasn't grown an inch. I'm eating better, I've got sunlight, I can wash it whenever I want, but it stays the same length. Almost as though it wants something. Almost as though it misses him.
If one more person tells me to 'cut it for a fresh start', I'm gonna scream. They have no idea who they're dealing with.
It will grow again.

Erica swayed in the mirror one last time, admiring the forty five rippling inches of bronze, brandy coloured hair, before turning to apply her body lotion for the evening.
She already smelt like clementine from the rainwater shower she had sat in. She had already lathered herself in a pearl blossom body wash, and scrubbed herself with a macadamia sugar scrub. But she wanted more. More, more, more.
She opened the bathroom cupboard of the suite and surveyed the choices.
Blackcurrant beauty, or sugared rosewater, or cinnamon smoke.
All of them.
She gathered all three bottles and began to lather them on, not stopping between squirting one and applying the other, the rich creams nourishing her.
More, more, more.
She was running a jasmine serum through her hair and dowsing her lips in a plum balm.
More, more, more. All of it.
She tried on her emerald necklace, her gold leaf one, before deciding on both.
She slid on a white dress, spinning.
More, more, more. All of it.
She grabbed a shimmering oil, rose oud and gold leaf, and poured it up her inner thighs. She grabbed a handful of bottles, not even checking the labels, and plucked off their caps. More, more, more.
She only stopped when her mother knocked and entered. 'Come on darling,' she said. 'Dinner time.'

They were called Sam and Mike.
'So,' Sam said with a glint in his eye. 'Are you oyster girls? Lobster girls? Or are you more indulgent – sea bass, miso cod, etc?'
Erica threw her menu down. 'I know what I want.'
'Love it, love it,' Mike said. 'Let me guess …'
'You'll never guess,' Erica grinned. 'Because I want this.'
She pointed to the middle of the menu. The men laughed in shock.
'*What?*'
'You can't!'
'Now?'
'We need starters first!'
Erica shook her head. 'I want it, and I don't want to wait.'

When Erica went missing, she went with a bang.
Bang. Bang. Bang.
Finally everybody knew her name.
She had a perfect face for a missing girl. Beautiful enough to be a loss to the world, unique enough to believe someone would choose to take her and only her. Cute enough to want to be saved, eyes dark enough for them to wonder if it

was somehow her fault. Hair wild enough to look like the kind of girl who might run away, but a smile kind enough to be a girl who would have returned. They hadn't known what they'd been missing until she was no longer there, and they wanted her back.
Had somebody actually found her, they probably just would have taken her for themselves.

They brought it out, sliding across the platter, heads turning in the restaurant to look at it, forks stopping on the way to mouths. Every other morsel shrivelling in shame, every other person thinking, 'Why not me? Why didn't I choose that?'
The Beach Chocolate Supreme. It had won an award when the hotel had invented it, and gone viral since for the infamous things it did with seven different types of chocolate.
Chocolate, chocolate, all those years waiting for chocolate. Who is really melting who?
'That's mine!' Erica called out, her spoon sharp in the air. 'Bring it to me!'
People cheered coyly as the platter was delivered to her. She gave them a wink, a flick of her hair, then licked off the first layer of fudgy lacquer, looking Sam and Mike in the eye the whole time.
Her heart used to hurt so much she was convinced she was having a heart attack. A sore spiciness within her the whole time.
But she was out now, and her heart beat normally. And she was damned if she'd spend another second not being in love. 'Grab a spoon, guys. Let's fall in love with chocolate.'

There should have been a rage in her, when she was taken. Don't they say humans are capable of anything; that there's white hot fire inside all of us, just waiting for the opportunity to explode. And when she was taken, that was her chance; that's when she should have proved how capable of violence she was. How she should have hit him, fought him, gone for the eyes, the ears, the balls, anything to get him off her, to not let him take her.
But the rage hadn't been there. She was too nice to scream.

They all tried it, and they all could have swapped their lives to be a tongue in that moment. Four spoons stuck in the sundae, bonding them between the conversations.
'So, were you guys following the vote back in your country?' Sam asked, opening up a mineral water.
'What debate?'
Sam and Mike exchanged a look. 'Just pretty faces, are we? The one about assisted dying. It was all over the news even over in the US.'

Erica met her mother's eye. The vote had been cast the day after she'd escaped - her mother knew she wouldn't want to talk about that. 'We were - erm - pretty busy around that time.'
'Ah, okay,' Sam poured them each a water. 'But what do you guys think about it? I've always loved debating this. It gets so juicy.'
Erica took her water, throwing him a silky smile as she sipped.
'I find it a bit haunting,' Mike said. 'A bit dystopian. What about you girls?'
Erica sat back, looking at the Chocolate Supreme. For the first time since it had arrived, she didn't want another bite.
'If someone's suffering – in the worst possible place – then they deserve to leave it. They deserve to escape, to get out.' She rested her arm on the table and watched how the moon lit it up, how it highlighted all the shimmer she had applied. 'But ... life is extraordinary. And there's always a chance. Always a chance you can make it. Back to the light. Back to your mother. You just have to be ... strong enough. The question is; who is?'
Mike grinned. 'I bet you are.'
Her mother threw her spoon down, spearing the chocolate. 'I'm too full.'
'Me too.'
'Too full for *anything*?' Sam asked.
'Everything. I need to burn it off. Is there anywhere we can go after this? Continue the night?'
'You kidding me? We're on the *beach*. There's no party like a beach party. Let us take care of the bill and we'll meet you down there.'

Erica had already fallen in love with the beach during her swim. She hadn't been prepared to fall in love with it all over again at night.
There was nothing like it at night time. It felt so surreptitious, so mysterious, illuminati vibes even. The whole landscape had gone black and orange; black for the night, orange from the flames.
She couldn't wait a second longer. She shot down the stone steps, and into the belly of the beach.
Just in time, she remembered to call for her mother. 'Mum! Down here!'
The sand felt even better now it was cooler, a creamy ceremony in between her toes. Tomorrow she'd have her first pedicure - she'd neglected her toes before. Never again. There'd never be a bit of pampering she'd turn down ever again.
Her gorgeous mother reached the bottom of the steps.
'Mum, I've got a question,' she said.
'Go on, honey.'
'The boys made me think about it, going on about that vote. They've got me thinking all about murder.' She laughed, enjoying how outrageous she could be, how she could tear through her inhibitions in a second. 'Is it love or is it murder?'

In the darkness, confusion blazed. She wrapped her arms around her mother, not wanting to worry for her a moment longer. Her mother spoke into her shoulder.
'What do you mean?'
'Can murder be love?' It felt good to say it out loud. 'I'm wondering if I could murder someone and call it love.'
'Wait, what?'
'If I did it, there's only one way I could go through with it. It'd have to be someone who wants it. Even if they don't know it. Someone who is not long for this world, who has someone waiting for them in heaven. Who is just counting down the days til they see them again. I wonder could I do it then?' She wasn't trying to scare her - she was genuinely interested. This was just another question she could now finally ask herself, now an open future lay before her. Could she murder someone? Had she suffered so much that she deserved that one indiscretion?
She pushed the thought away as quick as it came. 'I think I'm drunk on chocolate. Sorry mum. Let's get to the beach.'

Mike took her hand, and Sam took her mothers.
'See,' they said. 'Told you we could set you on fire.'
It blazed in the middle of the beach, a ravenous red statue; surrounded, decorated, by guests and locals alike. Tourist or resident, the fire didn't discriminate. It sparked out and lit up anyone who dared to go near it. The difference here was that, everyone dared.
'Ha! We don't need you to set us on fire,' her mother put her arm around her. 'Our surname is Ash. Us Ash girls have a special gene. We can spontaneously combust.'
'It's true,' Erica wrapped her arm around her waist. 'So watch out.'
'Fair enough,' Mike grinned.
Sam put his arms round the two of them, muscling his way in between. Erica tried not to be annoyed at being denied more moments, more hugs, with her mother. 'No, I think they need to prove it. Girls – ' Her mother squirmed, enjoying the word but not believing she deserved it. Erica swore to herself she would knock that insecurity from her, not let her waste a second. 'Show us your moves.'
Her mother squealed. 'Oh, no, I *never* dance.'
Wasted seconds, grumpy, flared up in Erica. 'Yes you do.'
Accepting her fate, her mouth joined the other three as they skipped, joyfully, to the fire. A band of tribal drummers demanded more, more, from the bodies of the beachgoers. Guests whooped, swayed, untied sarongs. Erica closed her eyes and gave her face to the moon. She let the noise come. Music, too, had been a distant memory, something that sounded too easy, too indulgent. Music let you pretend you were in some kind of movie, instead of embracing what you had. Embracing the silence. Embracing him.

Now her ears were wide open, ready to choke on the beats. And fill them up the beats did. And Erica found her body begin to move, more than she'd ever believed it could. It was night-time but the black sun dripped through her; the beats bounced in her blood, her body finding something primal in the drums. Music forgave the whole crowd for their sins, brought them together in a capsule of cool. She decided now she was free, she would be a great dancer. Her moves would be unique to her and they would open the ocean's mind. A hand wrapped around her hair and somebody was running their tongue up the back of her leg. Or were they. One thing was for sure; as she indulged her feet in cool, creamy sand, somebody came behind her, and whispered:
'Have you seen The Man On The Rock Yet?'

'Have you seen The Man on The Rock yet?'
That was what they called him, everybody who stepped onto Poipu Beach, Hawaii. The nickname had been coined almost straight away, and in the past six weeks he'd become as much a part of the scenery as the grains of sand. It didn't matter if you were the seventy year old setting up his coconut stall at 6am, or a honeymoon drenched couple cavorting in the water at midday, or a group of teenagers pouring beer on the crabs in the small hours of the morning - you had all seen him out of the corner of your eye, perched on one of the charcoal rocks clawing around the coast, as out of place and washed up as a merman. He dressed simply, always stared off into the distance, and never swam, no matter how searing the heat. It was as though he was waiting for something. Like he knew something was going to happen that the rest of us didn't.
He seemed to arrive and leave before anyone could notice, but he wasn't adverse to getting up from the rock, to buy a bottle of water or a papaya. When he did, they noticed he walked with a slight limp. He never made eye contact, only managing to mutter 'Thank you' and shimmy a fake smile up the corner of his mouth.
Despite all this, the boring bastard could not hide the fact he was handsome. Drop your kaftan, accidentally lose your bikini top, will you do my sunscreen kind of handsome. His mysterious, dark aura would not have been out of place in a noir thriller, and his thoroughbred build promised a strength and security you'd be lucky to come across again.
Myles knew of his nickname. He thought about making jokes about it, and making a new friend over it, and sitting on the beach one day instead of on the rocks. But he couldn't bring himself to do so. The thought turned to ash in his mouth.
Myles hadn't meant to end up somewhere as beautiful as Poipu, believe me. When he had arrived at the airport, he'd been in a blur, stricken black by the tar of his adrenaline, pumping through him, telling him to get away, get away, get away. He'd gone to the desk and got on the first flight they had offered him - to Budapest. The entire flight he'd struggled not to tear out his hair. He didn't

remember landing, getting through customs, nothing; he just remembered reaching the ticket desk at the other end of the terminal, the girl behind it flinching from his sweat beads, and demanding to get on the next flight. This time it was in Newark, New Jersey, and when he landed there still the blood pumped through him, telling him to go, go, get away, get away. He had practically crawled to the ticket desk, his whole body itching. And then it was only when he landed again, in Hawaii, that the noise finally stopped. He finally decided he could stay.

Pleasure, joy, merriment, euphoria, and ecstasy. They were all banned feelings, feelings Myles had promised himself he would never step into again. He wished it was easy, that it came naturally, that he could seal himself up like a tap, but oh, oh, it was so difficult. How hard it was not to be human. Hawaii's dopamine waved and nudged at him every second of every day, but he couldn't acknowledge it. He wasn't good enough to feel the sun on his back, he didn't deserve to see the kaleidoscope of palm trees and fruit and ocean, it was a disgrace that he was able to hear the laughter of people around him, or get hit by the atmosphere of a smoky beach bar, heaving with energy and fun. He was sorry he'd ended somewhere so beautiful, and man - he was trying to make it ugly. Forcing himself to make misery out of paradise. Doing anything he could to suffer. He was a dog in a hot car. In fact, being in Hawaii was an exquisite kind of torture - surrounded by such hazy hedonism every day, and not able to enjoy it. What he would give for a dive in the salty ocean, to close his lips around a chilled beer on a hot day, to wear something 'nice', to talk to the interesting people, to take part in the mountain hikes with men his age, to attend a cava drinking ceremony and look into a friends eyes. But no, no, no. Myles had his rules. He had even stopped wearing sunscreen, in the hope that his skin would burn raw.

His only purpose was to wake up, drink some water, get to the beach, and wait on the rock. He would look into the ocean, and a craving burnt deep within him, ulcerating all over his organs. This craving made him weaker, more of a pussy than anything ever had. Even more than throwing yourself off a building without looking at what was beneath.

It just … he didn't … it wasn't meant … if only … maybe … just once … one day … come on. Come *on*. It had to happen sometime, right? It had happened before. It was a busy beach. The sea was rough. People were careless, happy, high on life and tequila. Tequila could be troublesome in these waves. The teenagers were always cavorting, showboating, seeing who could get the furthest out to sea, who could flip off the highest rock. Some afternoons it got so crowded out there, mottled with bodies, limbs like algae twisting in the surface. It couldn't be that much longer. Soon, someday, someone was going to nearly drown.

Nearly – because Myles was going to rescue them.

He'd finally feel the ocean. Finally cool his skin.

He had to do it this way. He had to save someone's life.
And then he'd need to do it again. And again. Three lives for three. Rose, Taylor, and the snail.
And then maybe just maybe he'd be able to not forgive himself, but accept himself. Sleep through the night. Build something out of the little life he had left.
Until then, he would wait.
Until then, he was The Man On The Rock.

Chapter Six

For the first time in her life, Erica woke up on a beach. The sand was better than any bed, and the air was perfect. She probably would have slept for hours if her mother hadn't crawled over, shaking her gently awake.

'Erica darling,' she said. 'Gotta wake up.'

'Mm,' Erica opened. *But it's my choice now when I wake up, and it's my choice when I sleep.* Such realisations sent beads through her brain, mixed molasses into her mind. *Mine. All mine. My life is mine.*

'Remember darling what we said we'd do today …'

'Huh?'

'Don't back out now, babe. We made a pact on the plane.'

'Oh, *damn,* we did!' Erica rolled over, laughing in the sand. 'Oh my god, aren't you even a little bit scared?'

'Terrified! I've spent all morning trying to talk myself out of it. But a dare is a dare. And we need to match.'

She held out her hand and Erica clasped it. 'Shower first?'

'Shower, *then* a big breakfast. The place doesn't open til 11.'

'Which one are you gonna get done?'

'My left is my perkiest.'

'Ok, then I'll get it on my right.'

They grinned at each other, giggling.

Erica's mother pulled her to feet and they strolled languidly across the beach together. 'What happened to the guys?' Erica's mother asked her.

'Think they gave up – aww!'

Erica squealed as a beautiful, but gaunt, teenage cat jumped on the wall next to them. It had a mottled, gorgeous coat, swirls of gold and black. A white muzzle gave its face so much character, the beauty obvious despite the scabs around its jaw. The cat had a regality despite its emaciation.

'Erica, don't touch it!' A mother again.

'Can't we get it some food? Looks like it hasn't eaten in days.'

'On the way back. Come on, I'm dying for that outdoor shower.'

Erica pulled away and gave the cat a little stroke, running her hand along its limber body and damp fur. The puss purred, a grin appearing in its soft feline face. What cheekbones. 'Don't worry little one,' Erica said, and she couldn't resist – she dropped a kiss on its little pink nose. 'It'll get better!'

In no time at all, they found the Tattoo parlour that had been recommended to them last night. A small, cool place consisting of a waiting room and a private piercing room, located along a strip bursting with bars and hippie bikini shops. In keeping with the holiday spirit, their friend from the plane - Big Dave, they had called him - was waiting outside, just like they'd texted him too. 'Oh my god, Big Dave!' Erica dove into his arms. 'You're keeping the pact?'

'Of course.' He swung his arms around both of them. 'I wouldn't let my ladies down. We're not leaving this island til we get our nipples pierced.'

The three of them cackled again with incredulity at what they were doing - it was a pact they had devised during one of their many drinking games. Erica had managed to persuade them to just go for it, that they would only live once, and somehow she'd got through to them. This was the kind of thing her mother never would have given her permission for before she was taken, but everything was different now. She couldn't wait to make her body sparkle even more.
Cool stone on their feet and palm trees tingling their heads, they dived through the door and explained what they wanted.
Big Dave went first. Erica and her mother heard his howl all the way from reception. They felt a bit bad, but that dissipated when they saw him. Oh, how he rocked the ring.
No backing out now. They rose to their feet, gulping as the pact became real.
'Take a seat, ladies. We don't usually allow pairs in at the same time, but as you're early.'
The man who they'd chosen to pierce their nipples was tall, hunky, and German. Erica beamed up at him as he sterilised his needles. 'Can we call you The TermiNiptor? As in Terminator for nips.'
'*Erica*!'
The piercer grinned. 'Call me whatever you like ladies.'
They held hands as they lay on black leather beds next to each other, sweat pooling beneath their lean legs.
'Ok girls, I just need you to take your straps down. Who's going first, by the way?'
'She is!'
'No she is!'
'Save the best til last,' her mother said with a wry smile. 'And do me first. Let me get it over with.'
Erica rolled her eyes. 'Your boobs are great.'
'Imagine what they looked like thirty years ago!' she laugh-groaned.
'So, you first?' The TermiNiptor snapped on his gloves and pulled a needle from a plastic sheath.
'Me first.'
'Ok. Remove your strap please. First I'm just gonna clamp it – '
'Aaah!' Erica fake screamed as her mother got ready. Her mother gestured a kick, grinning at her.
'You ready?'
'Yeah. Ok. Bring it on.'
He came over and adjusted the appendage. 'Ok. Tell me when to go.'
'Let's count him down babe. 1, 2, 3 … GO!'

They were out of the parlour twenty minutes later, both struggling with the pain but more struggling with the urge to show off their new, sparkling jewellery. They held hands, both smirking whenever they walked through a patch of sun, knowing that the light would glint off the tiny new daggers in their chests. They moved now with the confidence of knowing they were daring, with the satisfaction of knowing they were living life to the full. Truth to be told, Erica realised, we'd never have felt this if I hadn't been taken.

'Is that the cat we saw earlier?' Erica's mother pointed, as they came closer to a creature, equally etched in shades of brown and gold.

'Nah,' Erica said. Even if there hadn't been a difference in their bodies – this one was clearly healthy, even flirting with plumpness – the cat had no scabs or scrapes, instead a perfect bloom of shiny white fur around its mouth. Relaxed, languid, indulged and serene, this was a cat without a care in the world 'Just as *ca-ute* though.'

'Meow!' demanded the puss as they went by.

'Erica …'

'Sorry mum,' Erica grinned whimsically and couldn't help but stroke her. It gave her the same big smile as the skinny one earlier. 'Aww. Right, come on. Let's definitely buy a kebab for this one.'

'Girls!'

They turned, still holding hands.

It was Sam and Mike. They were on the other side of the road, on two hired vespers.

'Did you just come out of the tattoo parlour?'

'We did indeed,' they said in unison. They crossed the road casually, their hands swinging between them. Sam and Mike looked at each other, serpentine grins winding up their faces.

'What did you get done?'

'Maybe you'll find out later.' Erica quipped. 'Are you going for a ride? We're going back to our hotel. To the spa.'

'Nope, you're coming with us.' Mike took her arm. Why did his touch not scare her? Why wasn't this too much, too soon, inappropriate, unhealthy, compounding the damage? If anything, it wasn't enough. 'To the top of the mountain.' He pointed at a green mountain, oozing out of the road they stood on.

'Nah, we don't like sight-seeing.'

'This isn't sight-seeing. There's something going on up there.'

'What?'

Sam broke off two long strips of green bamboo from a tree above. He took her mother and began wrapping the vibrant green leaf around her eyes, tying it at the back. 'It's a surprise.' He passed a strip to Mike, who turned Erica round and began blindfolding her too.

'You girls happy to ride on the back of a Vesper blind? It's a windy road to the top. You'll have to hold on tight.'

Erica reached for her mother's hand in the darkness, and connected as her mothers was reaching for hers. She ran her finger over her crystal ring. She heard her mother's voice; 'I'm happy if she is.'
'I'm always happy,' Erica said then hoped they didn't notice the shiver that went through her as a flash of her life underground jumped beneath her blindfold. She changed her tune quickly. 'Happy? Actually I'm bored. I think *we* should be the ones driving.'
She heard the male laughter, smoke in her ears. 'Bored? We can't have that.'
Before she knew it she was swept off her feet, and placed on the back of hot leather, her arms being fastened around a hard torso. 'Last time I'm gonna tell you. Hold on tight!'
And off he zoomed.

Screaming, whirring, whirling, they swerved to the top of the mountain. Sometimes Erica couldn't hear her mother; then sometimes she could hear her screaming for her life.

Blindfolds removed
They had been taken to mud.
Not just any kind of mud. Mud up the walls, mud in the trees. Mud above, mud below.
It was an enclave of jungle within the top of the mountain. The entire jungle floor had been turned mellifluous, no space for trees or plants; nothing but mud, and that meant nothing but play.
In front of them, sixty or so people writhed, all coating and painting themselves in different shades of mud. They were leaping into pits and popping out of pools, rolling in the ink, their bodies dipped in the stuff. Somewhere out of the mud, a giant pair of speakers rose, booming techno beats around the forest until the coconuts fell.
This was a mud party. A daytime mud rave. A mud festival.
And then Erica saw it. What they had all come here for.
The mud slide.
Winding round a tree and coaxing its way up a hill, the slide had to be twenty feet at least. Twenty feet of vertical mud, a tongue that would run you down it and deposit you straight into the stream below.
Yes. Yes. Yes. This.
This is life. *This* is living. This is what I came for. This is why I rose up.
She was running up a slope before she could even find her feet, the playful paint of the mud climbing up her calves, drying in an instant. She couldn't see the entry point of the slide but somehow she knew how to get there - and now she was winding through the queue of hesitant people, barrelling past all of them too afraid to take the drop.

In an enclaved aisle of bamboo trees at the top, there stood a master of ceremonies, a young man with a goatee guarding the mouth of the slide. His eyes widened at the speed with which Erica reached him.
She gasped as she reached the bamboo, her lungs vibrant with air. She was getting fitter and fitter, she realised.
'Do we have our first volunteer?' He said.
From up here she could see her mother, Mike and Sam watching below. 'We do.'
'Behold,' he cheered, bringing her to the edge of the slide so that the crowd could see her, so they could raise their fists to her. 'Today, we crown Our Mud Queen!' The crowd cheered, hailing her. A loop of vines was placed atop her head.
He stood behind her and edged her towards the slide. 'You ready?'
'I - '
'Off you go!'

They did everything they could think of doing in the mud, cavorting, dancing, playing, diving, splashing, sliding down the slide over and over again. They did everything you can do in mud, everything you can do for a good time - well, everything except for *that.* Erica wasn't ready for that, or was she, they said she wasn't but as more and more hands draped her in a smooth brown cloak, she became less and less sure of what all the professionals said and more and more sure of what she felt in herself, about herself, *for* herself: that nothing could scare her.
Sam was picking her up, moving her through more of the souffle sensation pits. 'You sure this is mud?' she beamed at him. 'Feels better than chocolate.'
He didn't answer, just spun her round, and she threw back her head and to her surprise felt something swirl through it; she had forgotten about giddiness, about hyperness, about how it felt to be swept off your feet. If you could melt reggae and pour it into her brain right now, that's what today was doing.
She clawed into his back to hold on. 'Back feels smooth,' she purred. 'Sunburn gone?'
'It actually *has,*' his eyes widened. 'Trust me babe, it was agony! Since yesterday though – '
'So since *I* applied your sunscreen?'
'Exactly!'
'Erica,' her mother's voice cut through. 'Darling? We have to go.'
'Go? Why?'
'We're late for our massage!'
Oh. More pleasure. More sensation. More indulgence. More, more, more. Erica, Erica, Erica. Will it ever stop?

'Ok!' Erica released her legs from Sam's waist, and hoisted herself out of the mud bath. She didn't want to miss this. 'How are we gonna get back down to the hotel?'
'I've ordered us a taxi.' A sensible tone, a serious vibe. The responsible aura of a mother. It felt alien, an echo from the sensible life Erica was denying.
Erica posed above the mud pit, letting Sam ogle her from this angle.
'See you later. Thanks for the mud. And keep applying that suncream!'

If I think really hard, I can just about remember the things he did to me. Half burnt and half-baked memories that are on their way to being forgotten.
But there is one thing I know I'll never forget. I remember the first time he did it. It was when he went down on me.
Three days I had been with him then; for three days I had belonged to him. In every one of those seventy two hours my heart had changed shape. Hell had opened wide for me then, greeted me as its honoured guest. I knew I was kidding myself as I tried to come up with ways to which a girl as talentless as me could get through the cage, and then through the door, and then up the stairs.
Hell opened wider again. Then he walked in and opened the cage door.
What can I tell you? What can I say, but a tongue is still a tongue, and nerve endings are still nerve endings, and they're all collected right in that spot? Let's face it, ladies; we all know it – nothing feels quite like those two coming together.
It didn't matter who he was or what he'd done to me - when he licked it he unleashed a glorious cascade of transgressive tears. Oh, he knew, he knew everything about me, knew exactly how I wanted it, knew how to make me bloom, knew exactly the rhythm to glide his mouth up and down. Of course I still wrestled, writhed, fought to get away, but whatever move I made just let him create more of that sweet friction inside of me.
I could have reached into his pockets, to try and steal his phone. I could have closed my legs around him to try and choke him out. I could have stopped squirming into his stubble and looked for a clue about how the cage worked.
But I didn't. My body floated away and even I couldn't find me.
Sometimes I worry. I worry I'll never feel anything quite like that again.

They called her The Mute Masseuse.
What she lacked in, 'are there any particular areas you'd like me to focus on today?' and 'is that enough pressure for you?' she made up for in her pure and profound intuition for other people's pleasure. She knew about secret patterns, secret messages that lurked under the skin and she knew exactly how and when to reach them.
She was the mute masseuse. Gina.
That was where Jodie came in – Jodie worked at the spa too, but since they'd been able to secure Gina's legendary services, Jodie did very little massaging,

scrubbing, or wrapping and instead worked as her translator, there to gently ask people's preferences and talk them through the process. And worst of all, let them know when time was up and Gina was done.

Erica and her mother had heard about her since the moment they arrived on the island, and it was finally time for their experience. They had booked the 'Bestie's Massage', where both Jodie and Gina would be working on them, swapping over throughout with Jodie doing all the communicating.

They'd been greeted with open palms holding lotus and frangipani, plied with hibiscus tea and cucumber water, and now they'd been lying in a white and gold pit, for who knows how long. Time and touch oozed into one as the two masseuses tricked their bodies into mollusca, vertebra by vertebra. She really was a goddess of touch, pouring amnesia into their skin so they could forget the very first thing that had ever made them tense.

This is why I escaped, Erica thought peacefully. Next time I miss him, I'll remember this.

She heard her mother snoozing gently, lazily throughout the massage. Jodie only bothered them every now and then, with a few short words to make them the centre of the universe – 'Would you like the hot stones again?' 'She can spend more time on your temples if you like.'

The only problem with a massage this good is you spent the whole time dreading it ending.

But when Erica opened up her eyes, she was ready. Ready to jump up and embrace the evening. See, Gina knew how to energise you.

Happily, they got changed, raving with each other about how impressed they were with the massage. After another complimentary drink and buying a few skin masks, they came to reception where the two women were waiting for them.

'Thank you so much,' her mother said, tipping them heavily. Again. 'It was just sensational.'

'Aw, thank you.'

Said Gina.

Not Jodie.

Gina.

Erica's eyes bounced to her mother; her mother's bounced to Jodie's; Jodie's bounced to Gina's and Gina's bounced all around.

'*Shit*,' she squawked, and clapped her hand over her mouth.

Erica's mother looked at her. They couldn't help it – they burst out laughing, kept their tips in their wallets and then ran from the salon, still wearing the towelling slippers.

'What the *fuck*?!' Erica crowed. 'Was she *faking*?!!'

'Must have been – did you hear her voice?! She knows she'd kill the mood!'

They clattered down the road, cackling airily past shacks and shops.

Erica couldn't stop frowning. 'She actually made a condition up?! *Why* would they do that?'
'I guess it's an advertising thing…' her mum said. 'I mean that's how we heard about that particular spa in the first place. Works, doesn't it?'
'It's still pretty… elaborate. Pretty weird. Being tricked like that. Would ya go again?'
Her mum nudged her gleefully in the ribs. '*Hell* yes, and don't say you wouldn't!'
Erica giggled. 'Ok, fine. Same time tomorrow?'
Chuckling, giggling, they laughed every type of laughter and they would have found new ones if her mum hadn't stopped abruptly and pulled her daughter in front of her, clasping her shoulders. She looked into her eyes and pulled her into a hug.
Erica clasped her back. They dropped their bags in the middle of the street.
'I'm so happy,' she said. 'I can't believe I've got you back.'
Erica held her back. Their bodies were similar. Erica's shoulders were still bonier and her legs still more fragile, but she was catching up, able to eat anything now she was free. Maybe tonight; a burger.
She'd have the fattiest one on the menu.

'What's that?' I'd asked him. It had been weeks since I'd seen a plastic bag.
'Vitamins,' he said, starting to unpack, greeting me with that familiar rattle of pills fighting in the bottle. He began listing the names of what he'd bought, as he lay them out in rows. 'Collagen, for your joints. Pantothenic acid, for your brain. Iodine, for thyroid function.' He knelt down between the bars and passed me one green pill. 'I don't want you to become weak down here. I want you to be healthy. I want you to be strong. I want you with me, for as long as you can be.'
I looked at the piles of vitamins surrounding me. Can you be too healthy?
'I'm taking them too,' he announced. 'So I can live a long time, too. So I'll be here for years, to look after you. So we can be together.' He lifted it to her lips.
'Swallow.'

They'd been invited to the beach party again, but why would they do anything twice? Why not make sure to do everything she hadn't been able to do before now?
So she drank wine when she didn't even like it, and ate a whole lobster when she didn't even crave it, and went to a silent disco even though she didn't get the concept, and met a group of guests who insisted on building an afterparty around her. Around 4am Erica and her mother ended up back at the hotel bar, the one that looked over the beach, where they found themselves sitting in a circle of people, swapping stories until one of them fixed Erica with a look and said, clear and robust, 'Tell us a joke.'

Jokes. Only Erica knew how it felt to actually *be* a joke. A tragic one. A controversial one, at that. People'd tried to keep this information from her, but apparently Erica Ash was one of the cards in Cards Of Humanity. Erica had been a sick joke until the day she came back.

Show them what you are.

Tell a joke. She could do it, she could tell one. She liked to joke. Now she was free, she would be funny. Maybe she'd get into stand up comedy.

Tell a joke. A truly hilarious one because what is better than laughter?

And so she told them her favourite joke - though she would never tell them it was the truth – and she watched them laugh.

And when they asked, 'Who told you that?' she would never tell them it was him.

And then she realised she was laughing too. Combustible laughter that replaced her brain with a bath bomb and replaced her thoughts with sparkling water. Her laughter was the richest of all, the one coated in duck fat; they'd get ulcers if they tried to laugh as hard as this. Because imagine laughing when you thought you'd never laugh again.

Imagine laughing knowing you had been made to pay a price for something, something you hadn't even done, but at some point you had overpaid and now everybody owed you instead.

Erica didn't know how long she was going to live for but she knew whether it was two days or two hundred years, she was going to spend them laughing. At them.

These people had frolicked and played in the ocean of her tears for eight years. Now she would give them something else to play in. What was the point of her escaping if she let them all down now? She'd never let them dry out. She would start it tonight, and every night thereafter. Now they would splash and play and leap in the spit and the foam of her laughter. And just when they were about to drown, she'd stop.

'Tell us another joke.'

'Knock, knock.'

'Whose there?'

'The Man On The Rock.'

'The Man On The Rock Who?'

'The Man On The Rock Who Wants You To Drown.' Erica couldn't help it, she just had a feeling; that's what he wanted. Across the bay, she could see him. This time, they didn't laugh.

There are a few things you want to get through your life without seeing. A cat being thrown from a window, a vat of acid coming towards you, a toddler's tragic accident, your dad bursting into tears.

And – worst of all – a man, all alone, on a rock, in the dead of night. A man who knows something. A man who breathes danger.

And - even worse still - for that man to be watching someone.
Watching you.
But he couldn't help it. Erica's aura had been shining all night.
And Myles couldn't take his eyes off her.

Chapter Seven

Let me take you down that long country road, to the guilty kind of gravity only you and I know.

The only thing crueller than guilt, was guilt under the sun. He knew this now. He didn't belong in paradise. He should be somewhere the ice could bite his bones.

Every morning there was a cruel ritual. When the glorious heat forced him away from the sleep he didn't deserve. It went something like this. The moment he remembered.

There.

That's it.

That moment, right there.

It's that sickness, it's that thud, that switch of the world from okay to nausea, that rancid rinsing where your heart and your bowels open all at the same time, that shard of synapse that reminds you who you are and that the only reason you'd ended up in paradise was because they'd chosen to boil you, slowly, instead of freeze you in one go.

I squeezed the hamster.

I dropped the baby.

I invented acne.

For the first few weeks here they had tried to befriend him. He had gone days without talking to anyone, but had had to crack after moving into his bedsit, and going to the local shop to fetch toilet paper.

'Hey, I'm Misty,' said the girl behind the counter. 'You're new here, aren't you? What's your name?'

He didn't want to answer, but he didn't deserve to be rude to anyone, but he had always liked his name, and so he chose to come up with a new one.

'Piles.' He said.

He saw the flicker. 'Piles?'

'Yes,' he nodded, warming to his theme. 'Like the Haemorrhoids.'

And just like that Myles became Piles, slipping into his new, excruciating, cringing skin. 'It suits me,' he had said, placing more change than necessary on the counter, and leaving.

But the next day he returned, allowing himself one more necessity; toothpaste. His hermetic tactics hadn't worked. 'You should come to a party at Tappy Tiki later,' she said. 'They're on every two weeks, and they're awesome.'

'I'm busy, sorry,' he said.

Piles had gone home, and taken a good hard look in the mirror. It hadn't gone right yesterday. It wasn't enough. Somewhere deep within him she still saw Myles, or at least an average boring bloke named Giles. Couldn't they

understand that Myles, Giles, Niles, all of them *had* died in that jump back in London? What was left over was the residue.
Piles. He turned and spun, looking at his unfed body that had already spewed away most of the muscle he'd spent his adult life building. Piles, an abrasion. A secret. How could he show everyone what he was when he had to bend over just to see himself?
The next day he returned to the store. This time he did not buy a necessity; he bought a luxury. A glossy, wet tumbler of fresh orange juice. Squeezed locally from the freshest farms, bursting temptingly from its plastic walls. Misty smiled at him as she buzzed it through the counter. He went outside and he downed it, glug, glug, glug, he could have wept as the tang went through him. Gulp, gulp, one, two, three, it took him under two minutes to succumb to his greed.
Then he walked. Around and around, up and down, layering sunburn on top of sunburn as he strolled through the ramshackle village in which he'd chosen to live.
Humiliation.
After about twenty minutes, he was ready.
He went back into the shop, and he stood in the aisle directly across from Misty's counter. And then he wet himself.
That did the trick. Nobody had been near him since.

If he did look in the mirror, he taunted himself with the following words. The bruise from the jump was still stamped on his ribs; he wasn't giving himself enough nutrients to build the white blood cells that would help it fade.
'How're them ribs doing now?
You killed three people. You should tear them out.'

Now he sat on his rock, waiting. For the three people he would save. For the trio of atonement that would come.
How good a swim would feel. He loved to swim. Beneath the water, he would swim to London and back if he could – but he had sworn to himself he would not grant himself that cool relief, unless, until, it meant he was saving someone's life.
The one thing that stopped him from tying rocks to himself so he never came up was the belief that he would one day, someday soon, do it.
Not one.
Not two.
But three.
The three of them came to him, every time, as he sat on the shards of the rock.

1.) Taylor.

Sometimes he hated Taylor. I mean, at twenty, shouldn't she have had better reflexes? Or at least better eyesight? Shouldn't she have seen him coming, a fourteen stone beast falling from the sky? She'd been distracted, on her phone, like all youngsters these days. And the fact she was crushed by him – seven and a half *stone*? He bet she was on some silly diet, a crash diet to look better than her friends. He hoped she was really arrogant. A bully, even. Oh Taylor, if only you'd moved to the left.

2.) The Snail

The Snail. Was it a male or a female? Did it have a family? What had it been up to, on a London pavement that day? Did it hurt when he broke the snail's back? He was too afraid to google that, too afraid to google anything. He knew snails were innocent. They were herbivores, leaf munching simpletons without a signal carnal drive. Piles chose to model his new life after that snail. Sexless. Unexciting. Squishy. Still. His skin was even going grey. He made sure to rescue every bug he ever saw, floating in the water, in its honour.

3.) Rose

All the time he'd had her, he'd felt she was magic. And it turned out he was right. Rose had transformed into a ghost.

He cried at the luck that he got to see her again, and cursed at the pain that his hand went right through her. Then he slapped his hand for trying to touch her. Every time she appeared on the rock, a body scribbled in red, he asked her the same question. He just wanted, just once, her to say one of these things.

'I forgive you.'

'You didn't mean to do it.'

'I still love you.'

'Go and be happy.'

But she never did.

She sat opposite him, legs folded, head cocked to the side. For minutes it seemed that she was never going to speak at all. Then it would come.

'Love. Love destroyed me.

Did you not think about what I could have become? Before you got your hands on me, before you let the rage take me, did it not occur to you what I could have done with my life? Nobody ever believed in me, but I thought you were the one who did.

Turns out I was wrong. But at least you believe in ghosts now.'

Red is the colour of Anger. Green is the colour of Envy. Purple is the colour of Pride.

But what is the colour of Guilt?

What does Guilt smell like? How does it taste?

Every night was the same, lying there, folding through pointless thoughts. His leg, still damaged from his jump, twitching as the thoughts came.

Always charge your phone with wet hands, just in case. In case you get lucky.

That was one of his little tricks, a little promise he gave himself, flirting with the chance of a quick death. There weren't many things he could do, but there were a few. Such as the fasting.

It had been so much easier than he thought, to go three days without food. It had actually felt *better* than eating, to carve out some part of him and lend it to the universe.

Because he was so puffed up full of pain he thought his stomach might split, so bloated on beastliness his thought his ribs might rip, and the chest can't contain a heart after it's broken into so many pieces, splitting at the seams – he was all digestion, no exhalation, constantly congesting as the night refused to swallow him.

He spent the night navigating the nails beneath him and the thorns above him as he waited for the sleep to come. Breath wouldn't take no for an answer but it took strange and teasing diversions before it actually reached his airways, making his nose and mouth smaller in his wide face, til he was chinny like a Buddha.

Eventually, the sleep would come. But it was a temporary relief - he knew what was coming one day in its place. Listen very hard and you could almost hear them, calling, climbing, out of the waves and up the beach.

The mob. When they found out what he had done to Rose, they would come.

Perhaps he'd been asleep for half an hour, when he remembered something that made him liquid, so that he could be poured on coals and turned into steam.

Oh god, he missed her. *He missed her, he missed her, he missed his mum.*

And he was pregnant with her like she'd been pregnant with him. He felt a womb open up in him, large enough to carry not nine months of his mother, but his mother at seventy seven, the age she had been when she'd left him. And as foetus's go, jeez, this one kicked. Her size five, always pedicured feet were kicking and bucking their way through his torso, cracking his ribs and puckering his intestines – he could never have explained it to anyone around him, before he'd be carted off to NASA to the 'Alien Experimentation' wing, but he didn't care, he was just happy to be full of her. Could he ever carry her as well as she had carried him, nurture him in the way she'd nurtured him? He would refuse to give birth to her; he'd fight every contraction, deny the world the chance to confirm he was the world's first biological pregnant man – he'd keep her safe inside his belly til there was room for nothing more, nothing more than his love for his mother. How're them ribs doing now?

It had all gone wrong the moment he lost her. The moment she'd passed, the rages had come, and he'd made the only mistake she wasn't there to wipe up. Oh god, he needed her, and another well opened up inside him, rich and luscious so that people dipped their fingers in to taste it. The tapenade of longing, of an edible wishing fountain, so delicious people spread it on their bread and marinated their chicken in it. These people were ravenous, and ravage they did, taking all the babaganoush and the guacamole from Pile's scrumptious soul, and he let them. He had so many different ways in which to beg; he'd beg the sky to give her back to him, to drop her out of it in any form – rain, hail, a

stone, a sick bird, a fallen angel, a shard of a broken plane – he would give anything to bring her back, and even more to die to be with her.
Would she still love him if she knew what he did? Or would she turn from him even in Heaven?
We should be taken from them at birth. Separated like the cows and the calves. That's the answer. It came to Piles in a flash. It would save all the complications. The snip of the umbilical cord should be the first and final moment of goodbye. Everything else just leads up to an inevitable cindering of the little bit of that cord that remains, funnelling us with fire that can't be put out. Yes. Yes. Yes. He would suggest it. Separated, tagged, rode off, like the cows and the calves, never meeting, never naming, never knowing about our mothers. He'd make it happen, make it his life's mission before more grief can come for us.
They'd find some other use for the milk, he was sure. Beauty products, perhaps. Medicine, even. Mix it with morphine. Enough of it and you'd sleep forever.
At the words 'sleep forever', every comforting chord in him was played, and he couldn't help but smile.
He hadn't smiled in six weeks, and he had forbidden himself from ever doing so again. So now he had failed, and his debt had doubled. He should rip his lips off, become owner and attacking pet chimp all in one. But he didn't have the strength for that, he could feel himself getting weaker every day, in fact maybe tonight would be the night he would be too weak to wake up - and that thought had him smiling harder.
So now he really had a debt to pay.
How was he going to punish himself?
He knew exactly how. He'd been thinking of doing it for a while, the opportunity obvious, lingering in his mind. An opportunity for humiliation.
His own self-hate wasn't enough. He needed the hate, the horror, of the people of this island. Let it come.

Yoga

'Ok, class, that was excellent. Give yourself a pat on the back because you know what you just did? You just gave yourself the best possible start to your day. Now everything should be in alignment because you made it here and set yourself up for a day full of productivity and inspiration. Now we've got a little bit of time left, so if you'd all like to lie flat on your mats, we've got time for a Shavsana, and a little guided meditation where you can just switch off. That sound good?' Joey, all elephant tattoos and hippie trousers, smiled admiringly at his morning class.
'Yes,' the class echoed back.
'Excellent. Alright everyone, in your own time, get down on to the mat and lie flat on your backs. Feet hip width apart, chest open, palms facing upwards. Eyes

closed. It's just you and the room. Anybody know what this position is called? Nobody. Alright, I'll tell you after. For now, just focus on your breath … *inhale*, and *exhale* … nice … and just allow yourself to forget about anything outside of the room that might be worrying you … right now it's just you and this moment. I want you to focus on becoming as relaxed as possible. Your body is water, your mind is liquid, your toes are liquid, your ankles, your calves, your knees, are liquid, your thighs, your glutes, are liquid, your lower back, your abdominals, your ribcage, is all melting into the floor … your shoulders are made of silk, your neck is made of butter, and your mind, your mind is molten. Okay. Nice. Looking good guys. I'm just going to go prepare your lemon water, and when I come back we will begin the guided meditation. You just centre yourselves.'

He slipped out of the room and Erica allowed herself to fall into the bottomless, sunken sheets he had created for her. One tap on a teacup and she dived into the brew, falling further, each bit of her lightly singing. She only heard the vaguest slither of incense and sliding sandalwood, as he began to talk again.

When he did, his voice had changed, to a kind of nectar that her mind could not resist. Erica began to tingle almost instantly, like tiny shards of sugar were pouring on her at every angle.

'Now, feel how your wrists face the ceiling, how they are turned up towards the sky, towards the light. Feel the sun pouring down on them, warming the skin. Keep the palms flat and the wrists still. I want you to slowly feel them opening up. The skin first. And then the veins. Let your veins open. And focus on the feeling of your wrists emptying. Feel all that energy pour out of them, in a cloud of red, flow out of them and up to the sky.'

The class listened, entranced.

'Feel the blood drain – not just coming from the wrists, the wrists should be almost empty now. Feel it come from all the corners of your body, coming, coming, coming to that source of light at the vein you have opened. Allow that blood to release and find its way out of your wrists. From the shoulders, from the stomach, from the brain, let it go.'

The group could not deny that his speech, though strange, was speaking to some part of them, some section of their souls where it made sense.

'And once you feel completely empty, you can now focus on your heart. Open your chest out, as wide as it can go. I want you to offer up your heart, out of your chest, up into the sky. After all, very few of us really have anyone to give our hearts too – so why not get rid of it completely? Imagine how much lighter you'll feel without a heart. Open up that chest and if you want, you can reach in and pluck the heart out yourself. Raise it up and let the sky take it. Very nice.'

Erica knew this was a bit weird, but she was loving it.

'Now did anyone remember the name of this pose? It's called 'Corpse Pose.' You all make very pretty corpses. Stunning, in fact. Any man would be lucky to embalm you.'

'You again!!'
Alas, the spell was broken. A smash of sandalwood and the dropping of a tray, fifteen sweaty bodies burst out of their cocoons. Erica's eyes snapped open – so *that's* why the voice sounded different – at the front of the class, The Man On The Rock had snuck in, become an imposter, and delivered his suicidal sermon – at the back of the class, the real yoga instructor had only just returned, with a now dropped tray of lemon water. The sight was so ostentatious she clapped a hand over her mouth not to burst into guffaws and giggles, noticing that wow, her wrists were in fact closed. How close she had been to believing her mind could make a mess of her mat.
'I'm calling security! You, how *dare* you take over my class! Everyone, I am so sorry. Did he try and project his vile little suicide trance again? Don't worry, security will be here this instant.'
'I'm going, I'm going,' the man mumbled. He was dressed in the same grey tracksuit as always, must be too hot, only his skinny, wiry ankles poking out. His dirty feet assaulted each mat as they went – prints in the foam like scorpions in the sand. The class stared at him, baffled and disgusted, as though he was a character wandering out of a snuff film and into their morning meditation.
He had called her a pretty corpse, how had he known that would be the words that would stir something in her, after all this time? How would he know that feeling her wrists open would be what opened her mind, that stopped today from being the same as the others? He would not be just footprints on her mat – she grabbed her towel and fled the studio, following him.

Piles could hear the footsteps behind him, as he wound through the lush palm trees of the hotel, the smooth ground too kind on his bare feet. It had gone exactly to plan; a moment of metallic humiliation. But now he wanted more.
Chase me, chase me, get me, pin me to the ground.
It was when he moved this quick that he felt weak, reminded of how empty he was inside. But as soon as the footsteps got closer, he knew he had to be rapid. Because these were the footsteps of a female.
'Hey!' A female voice called. '*Wait*! I'm not angry … that was funny. I actually feel more relaxed than ever.'
Whatever you do, do not turn around. Do not let her see your face.
'Will you *stop*? I just want to know why you did it! It was interesting! Hey! Stop! Can I … buy you a smoothie?'
He went faster, spurred on by the offer of kindness, the antidote to all he stood for. Finally she seemed to stop following him.
'See you on your rock, then.'
He froze. And then he ran.

He was on his rock. He had to be here, in case somebody *did* drown today. He was *not* waiting for her – whoever she was.

The sea was calm and safe, and he was bored.
Eventually, from the corner of his eye, came a swish of long hair, more energy in it than all the waves before him.
He jumped up to move, before he could see her properly.
'Hey, hey, *hey* – stop running, will you? It's annoying. And exhausting. You *know* I'm going to keep following you. You might as well save your energy.'
Piles stopped then. There was something about the way she was speaking that made him believe her. And where would he go, anyway? This rock was a dead end.
'Is it true you call yourself Piles? See, I know things. I know it's important to go after what you want. That's what this holiday is about for me, and I want to know why you are the way you are. So come on. Come here. Talk to me.'
Walk away, Piles. Turn around, Piles. Don't look it into her eyes, Piles.
Piles turned to face her. OH. Fuck.
He had seen her before. Who hadn't? Not just last night, laughing in the bar while he'd been watching the ocean for drunken skinny-dippers - no, he had seen her face on the news, six weeks ago, while he lay in that hospital like a grease stain. She had looked out at the screen imploringly, begging the question; 'How could anybody let this happen to me?' But when his eyes had strayed to her last night, she had emanated a whole different energy. *That* girl seemed to say you could do anything to her.
She patted the sand next to her and he sat, making sure he landed on the hottest part of rock. For the first time, his skinny thighs didn't flinch at the heat, so he made himself flinch anyway, just to look extra pathetic.
He had to say one thing.
'I shouldn't be doing this.'
'Who says, huh? Just … tell me why you sit on this rock all the time.'
He was going to tell her. He could feel it.
'These seas are rough. Untrustworthy. I just think it's important someone be here.'
Erica smiled mockingly.
'That's very nice of you.'
'No it isn't.'
'No it isn't.'
Her eyes glittered. She was too close, close enough to give him a jovial nudge. He moved away just in time.
'Shiver me timbers. Don't sell me to the sharks.' She picked up a shell between them. 'Reckon you could scoop your eyes out with this shell?'
Piles took it from her, turning it over in his hands. He made sure their skin didn't make contact.
Erica continued. 'I'm Erica, by the way. So why do you do it then? You just … love the thought of being a hero? You just love swimming? People watching?'
Piles nodded. 'Yeah. That's it. All the above.'

Erica shook her head.
'No, no that's not it. You do realise I'm not blind, don't you?'
Piles looked her over. 'Neither am I'.
That was flirting. He shouldn't do that. Now he had to take another scalding shower when he got home.
Erica. 'When you've seen the look of guilt, it never goes away. I saw deep guilt in a man's eyes for years, a look I thought I'd never see again … and I haven't. Yours is worse. Why? Why are you so alone? Why, Myles?'
'Don't call me that.'
For the first time in six weeks, her stomach jittered. That was anger in his voice. She kind of missed anger.
Piles spoke again. 'Please just go. There's nothing you're gonna get out of this. Just go.'
'I want to know why. Tell me a secret. You don't think I can handle it?'
Maybe, just maybe, it would feel good to say it. Maybe someone would stop stirring scorpions into his brain if, if, *if* he just let it out. Even if it scared her, even if it got him arrested, maybe these were just words *and they needed to be said.* Maybe this is what would get her to leave him.
Piles looked at her. 'I killed two people.' Nah. Sorry boy, that's not enough.
'*And I stepped on a snail.*'
There wasn't enough salt in the ocean to pour into the size of the wounds he felt as the words left his mouth and it came crashing back again that he, Piles, was a murderer, taker of two lives, two bodies greedily dissolved into him, twice the flesh and three times the bone of others. And everything was crusty again.
But **she** was still there. She wasn't going anywhere. Her arms wrapped around her knees and she nodded, taking it in, like she'd expected as much.
After a moment, she spoke. 'Okay.' Her voice was husky, her eyes wide. 'That's okay, Myles.' A gulp and then a smile. 'It's fine.'
She nodded, processing it, folding the information inside her. 'Don't worry. I - I get it. I understand now.' She granted him a smile. 'Thank you for telling me.'
'Why haven't you left? Why aren't you running away?' Piles asked. 'You should be scared!'
'So you did a bad thing. Or two. It happens. So you took some lives. So you broke some hearts. Doesn't mean I can't talk to you.'
'You should go. I don't want people around me.'
And then …
'Go before I hurt you.'
Even though he knew that was the last thing he'd do.
'Oh really? You big beast.' She leaned into him coyly - he shuffled away before their bodies could connect. 'I bet you can tear this rock in two.'
'Go.'
'Such a beast. Can you show me your horns? Go on, I'll show you my hooves.' She giggled, her toes wiggling.

'You need to go.'
'Why? It's not like you did it to *me*. You haven't done anything to me.' She tossed her hair. 'Not even once.'
'Just go. Please.'
'Okay. I'll go. I'll go if you do one thing for me.' Her voice lilted.
'What's that?' Piles wiped his brow, the sun stinging.
'Kiss me.
Come on.
Kiss me properly.
Kiss me like … like you're trying to forget you killed someone.'
As he looked at her thin but beautiful lips, he wandered, could he? Would it actually work? Could he kiss this girl so hard he would feel the wires being pulled from his brain, could he smash his lips against hers hard enough that the memory would smash too? It almost seemed like he could. If he just tried …
'You need to get away from me.' He looked down.
Erica rolled her eyes. 'Oh come *on*! I'm so bored nowadays. I want to be kissed by a killer.'
'Fuck off, fuck off!' Piles whacked his cheek like he was swatting a fly. How dare he swear at a woman. After everything. But he had to scare her away.
'I'm not scared of you. What could you possibly do to me that hasn't been done already? You think I'll dissolve from one little kiss? Think I can't handle it? I'm not scared of you, whatever your name is, and I never will be.'
Something sung in his spine.
'Okay. I'm sorry. But you don't understand. I haven't been touched in six months and I've sworn to myself I won't ever be touched or touch anyone again. Not until I finally touch the body of someone in those waves, when I rescue them from drowning.'
Erica's eyes met his. She was grinning. She went to give him a conspiratorial nudge and he launched away, making sure there was space in between them.
She laughed. 'You're funny.'
'It's not a joke.'
'You deserve to be laughed at. Not for what you did to your victims, but for how much time you're wasting now.' She rolled onto her knees and leaned in close to him, stopping only when he looked at her lips. 'All you have is this moment. Why not *do* something with it?'
'I can't.'
'But you're making me sad.' She pouted.
'I'm sorry.'
She sighed, shrugged. 'Very well. I'm gonna go get a drink. I presume you're still letting yourself drink, right?'
'Water only.'
'Aw, aren't you good. Well then. You can come get some water with me.'

She left. And, breaking every rule in his heart, like he wanted to break every bone in his body, Piles got up and followed her.

All the way to her hotel room.
He hadn't meant to, but she'd begun telling the story of how she'd got to this place, of where she'd been a few weeks ago, of what it had been like the day she'd escaped. For the first time, something else could fill his brain - it was almost biological, the way his body grabbed onto another kind of stimulation. The story had been so captivating, he'd walked all the way to her hotel, and when she'd invited him over the threshold, he'd stepped.
'So,' Piles poured Erica a glass of water. 'It was only six weeks ago. When do you have to go back?'
'We're going to stay here for as long as we want.' She watched him from her bed, swinging her legs.
'But for... the trial. Is there a first court date yet?'
'Trial?'
He sat opposite her. 'Yes...'
'There can't be a trial if they haven't caught him.'
'Oh. Jesus, I'm sorry. Wow. He's ...he's on the run?'
'No. They have no leads. Everything they look at leads back to an empty result. They'll never find him.'
'Jesus.'
'It wasn't Jesus, no. There's a good reason they won't find him.'
'Why?'
'I gave them all the wrong information. About where I was, what happened, his name – even what he looked like.' She tiptoed her fingers across the bedsheets. 'I told them to go to the left, when I know he's all the way to the right.' She drew her finger the other way. 'They may as well be looking for a woman.'
'You don't mean ... on purpose?'
She tossed her hair, waves of it falling. 'That's exactly what I mean.'
'*Why?*'
'Because he dropped his keys. Not by accident. He chose to drop them. For me. He knew what he was doing.
To this day I wonder why he suddenly didn't want to keep me anymore.
He did that for me, so I'm doing this for him. I could still be there if it wasn't for him. And even if I'd escaped purely on my own accord, I have no interest in putting someone in a cage.' Her eyes clouded suddenly. 'I just wish I knew why I stopped being enough for him.' She flung her hand over her head dramatically. 'I'm chopped liver! I'm old news!' She knocked back her water, eyes narrowing at him. 'But I look so *good* in a cage, Myles. He'll never replace me.'

The sun went down, and still he hadn't left. It had taken a few hours, but he had joined her on the bed. Sat crossed legged opposite each other. Every few seconds that went by, one of them thought the other was about to touch them.
'And so which of us do you think has had the worst luck?' Erica nudged the air beside him. 'Whose had the worst time of it?' Up close, she could see how mangled his leg really was; no wonder he walked with a limp.
'Well there's no question. It has to be you. Of course. I threw my life away in seventy two hours and I've been suffering for six weeks. You – you had years. Years where someone controlled your world.'
'Yes, yes, it's true, but you know what – it's not me. It's you.'
'Why's that?'
'Because - *I* still have my mother. And you don't.'
He backed away. He had told her that, along with everything that he'd done to Taylor and Rose - he'd finally found the space to share his grief too. He'd never believed anyone could know what he did, what he'd taken from others, and yet still acknowledge his own grief. But here she was.
'I wouldn't swap with you, but I bet you'd swap with me. Cos of my mother.'
Piles gulped. 'That doesn't mean my luck is worse than yours. Having your mother doesn't counteract what happened to you.'
'Yes it does. Yes it can. *Stop* stepping on yourself like you don't deserve to feel. I'm not going to drown you like you drown yourself. Well, only if you ask me.' She winked.
And she meant those words, every one of them, from the sympathy of the mother to the suggestion of seduction that maybe, to feel whole again, she needed to kill someone. The thought had niggled at her since she'd escaped the underground, been compounded by her first swim in the ocean; that someone from the footsteps above her, who'd splashed about in her tears, owed themselves to her, their lives to her. That as no one had tried to save her, perhaps one of them had to pay a debt for all the others, and let themselves be killed by her. That then and only then could she forgive everyone. But she bit on it because right now she wanted to just enjoy herself, and get to know this oil spill of a man – about who he was before, about who he might be without the guilt. Then she'd decide whether or not he was the one she would kill.
'Maybe Gravity doesn't exist.' Erica said suddenly. 'After all, there's no proof – we can't see it, can't talk to it, can't even feel it. Maybe what roots us to the earth is guilt. Maybe if you let go of the guilt, you can fly.'
Piles shook his head. 'Nah. I'll never fly. But maybe,' he shivered. 'There'll come a day when I can float. As long as I don't kill again.' His eyes drifted to her body, looking it up and down.
'*Oh*. Oh I see. *That.* Don't worry, Myles,' she giggled. 'I think twice was enough for you.'
'But - but what if I do? Or what if … if … what if I do something worse?'

Her eyes lit up. '*Worse*? Wow. Someone's got an imagination.' She edged closer to him but he scraped backwards. 'Imagine. And then little Erica Ash will be no more. Too scared to tell anyone what you did.'

His nails dug into the sheets. 'I need to be stopped. Snuffed out.'

'Stamped on.'

'Exactly.'

'Turned into an insect.'

'Worse.'

'Into dirt.'

'Worse.'

'Into a plague.'

'Worse.'

'Into me.' Erica lip's parted. 'Would you like that?'

And he was just about to ask her to kill him, when they heard her mother's key in the lock. Lucky for him they were on the ground floor, and her sliding door to the grounds outside was already open.

'Don't go – ' she started to whisper, but like the sun, the man was already gone.

Chapter Eight

Oh Erica. Just couldn't keep her hands to herself.

When she escaped, she thought she'd never feel fear again. She didn't understand how the world, with all its colour and sound, could haunt her. But now, without Myles, she felt it.

She sat in the hotel parlour, looked at the other guests, and felt the fear come. She was afraid of never seeing him again. Afraid of a life of boredom. Afraid of a life without the passion only he or her captor had ever inspired in her.

Or … maybe it wasn't that. Maybe it was the fact that everybody was discussing the same thing, clutching the same phones with the same look of dread on their faces, reading the same story that had just broken in the UK.

A sleepover. Six thirteen year old girls had been invited, seven including the host. Only five had woken up the next day. Not through an accident or natural causes … the case was being hailed 'the serial sleepover', where two unpopular, inferior girls had been invited by their 'friends' so that their lives could be taken.

There was a chill in the air, at how such cruelty could permeate, could become concrete, at such a young age. A chill as they hunted for the inexplicable why, for the explanation about what their country was becoming.

Even though they all knew.

Erica curled her hands into each other as she listened to them say it. 'This is what happens to a country when it legalises murder. The value of life decreases, until it becomes worthless.' Erica bit her lip, willing them not to say what she knew was next. '*This is just the start.*'

And Erica's eyes drifted, across the frangipani and the trays of dragon fruit, to the mirror that hung in the centre of the lobby. She could take in her face, glowing with health now, or the amazing shade of gold her skin had gone, or the way her new seashell necklace sat so nicely between her collarbones, or the gorgeous waves her hair had dried into after her swim. But instead she looked into her eyes and let the question come.

If killing was legal in her country, and murder was becoming more acceptable, then would there be more cases like the sleepover - and should she be one of them? Should she be one of the first? She felt a taste on her tongue and knew it was a taste for just that.

Could she do it? Should she do it? Did he need it? Did he deserve better, did he deserve worse? Did she want it? What would she be if she did it?

Should she kill Myles?

Her mother slid open the door to their balcony where she bathed.

'Hey darling! I was thinking dinner at eight. Just the two of us, at first, anyway. Want to try the sushi place?'

'Sure mum. I'll meet you in your room. Give me half an hour. I'm just gonna braid my hair first.'
As she sat before her mirror, fingers groaning as they continued their dexterous work through the smug strands of her hair, she wondered just why the ground had opened up and let her out. She was reminded of the vote and the chaos it was causing back in her home country, the country that had changed just as she'd come back into it - even more than society was scared of murder, they were scared of how many healthy people were now trying to end their lives. She laughed at her reflection; could there ever be more of an example of life being worth living? Of holding on through the hard times, because there's always a chance of tomorrow? One look at her and they'd all change their minds about giving up. She smirked, a strand snapping in her fist.
Just try and get through what I did. Just try.
Erica looked at her fist. It uncurled without her instruction. She gulped. It was trying to tell her something.

Piles knew what needed to happen, really. It was simple. The reason he was still alive.
He needed to be murdered by women.
One woman, or a hive of them. It didn't matter really. But murdered, by the bare hands of a woman, with their womanly touch and their womanly voices. Not a girl. A woman. In some kind of way that was so inherently 'female' no male would show their face at his funeral. It would be held by a female priest, attended by only women dressed in black lace. Pew after pew of laughing women. And the reliance on female roles would mean no one would be strong enough to dig enough earth up for his grave.
What would they choke him with?
What would cause the expression of confusion on the pathologist's face, as they pulled a strange foreign object from his throat? No bigger than a thimble, pure and white as soap, soft and harmless. A lost blue thread asking to be pulled out of this male cavern. 'Looks like … a tampon,' the pathologist would say. 'Choked to death by a tampon.'
Murdered in a feminine way, the kind only females can. First of all, they will shave me. Then, they will coat me in hot wax only to tear it off in strips. Next, they will pluck me. Finally, they will bleach me. They will tighten me and loosen me as they see fit, spear me but then scold me for opening up so easily. Tighter, young man, *tighter.*
He needed to be murdered by women. By a home cooked meal. A poison for the first course, force feeding for the second, his own teeth for desert. Dainty fingerprints on the knife.
Rose, Taylor, and he bet the snail was female too.

They'd buy *him* flowers, use the thorns to drain him, then scatter them over his grave. His gravestone written in lipstick 'Here lies the man who didn't know what he was up against.'
This was why he had met her. Erica.
What was she waiting for?

Sharkshimi hovered over the edge of a clifftop. It had a bar made of coral, and seats shaped like shark mouths. Plates lolled by on the top of the revolving bar, and every portion seemed to get smaller. But nothing felt smaller than Erica's heart – it was the size of an edamame bean. The runt of the litter.
Her and her mother talked back and forth about their plans for the next few days. They both wanted to go bungee jumping, and Erica wanted to go white water rafting afterwards while her mother was less keen. They couldn't decide between Bellini or Cosmopolitan cocktails, so they ordered both and then the white chocolate peach Bellini cake too. 'For starters?' grinned the waiter in surprise. 'For starters!' they high fived. The manager joined them to get their names for a guest list to a party later.
Just as they were about to pay the bill, their waiter approached them. 'Hey girls,' he grinned. 'I hope my service wasn't off earlier. I'd been having a terrible migraine all day but it's all cleared up.'
A chill went through Erica.
She threw him a grin, nodded him goodbye and then turned to her mother– she could hold it in no longer.
'I have to tell you something – ' she began.
'Me first.' Her mother said. And then she blurted it out, so quickly flecks of ginger and chives came out too. 'Just before you escaped, I went to the doctor.'
Oh no.
'With a lump.'
Oh god no.
'In my breast.'
No.
'I felt it in the shower one morning.'
Oh.
'They said it was probably nothing but they better run some tests.'
Bet they did.
'It was cancer.'
Bet it was.
They were both crying. Tears splashing into soy sauce.
Erica knew it. She'd felt it, all the time she was down there: her mother was ill.
Her knee hit the table in fury and the miniature plates bounced against each other.
Her mother took her hand. *Listen.*

'No, darling, here's the thing. I didn't want to tell you, or worry you - truth is once I saw you in the police station I pretty much forgot. How could I worry about anything once I had you?

But just before coming on our holiday, I had to visit the hospital, to choose a course of treatment. And guess what?'

'What?' Erica squeezed her napkin. How long? How long would she have her for? How long could she nurse her for? How long before everything was ruined?

'He looked and looked for it. Last time I went it was the size of a pork chop. But he ran every test he could, and Erica …'

'Yes?'

'The lump has gone.'

Erica gulped.

'All gone.' Her mother said. 'One moment with you and I was better.'

Erica gulped. She looked from her mother to the waiter and back again.

A shudder went through her.

All that mattered, that should matter, was what had just been said. That the woman sitting in front of her wasn't just a dream she was being forced to wake from, but something real – looking at her, sipping on a straw, liquid flowing through her. All that should be happening inside her was the rumblings of an avalanche of relief.

So why did she rip her hand from her mother's, leap up, knocking her seat over as she did, turn away from the restaurant and run?

Erica stared into her ensuite mirror for ten minutes, before she raised her hands from her sides and pressed them against the mirror.

What were they trying to tell her?

Her hands were still, but she knew they were moving somehow, as though her body was shutting down, or maybe only just waking up. Beneath the skin, foreign objects blossomed; patches of frog spawn popped and bubble wrap floated. The feeling these were not quite hands, but bear traps, waiting to catch a prey or a prize. Creepy hands, full of suspense. Illegal hands asking to be cut off, as though they were infected.

These hands demanded not to be ignored. There were pearls trying to be born through her fingertips. Secret daggers developed, foetal in the depths of her palm.

She held them to the mirror. Normal hands. Eight fingers and two thumbs. Ten fingerprints. Bitten nails. Should she have continued to bite?

She stood there, her fingers splayed, legs parted, back arched, head tilted back. She wanted someone to enter and see her like this. Someone who could make her forget. Or someone who could explain.

What it was that was going on in her hands.

Because as she looked at her body in the mirror, that toned, tanned, taut body, she knew it was a body that wasn't the same as others. And as she felt her arms start to ache, and she thought about what she had just been told by her mother , and about what had been happening since she'd got here, she knew – there was something wrong in her body. Or something all too right.
Please. Please. Don't let it be what I think it is.

It wasn't mentioned again, Erica's outburst. It was believed to be 'normal'; the psychologist's had warned of moments like this, that a holiday might be too much and could trigger moments where you had to flee.
The next morning they went for a sunbathe, holding hands. They set themselves up right next to Wendy's Watermelon shack; a tiny bamboo stall selling the most popular, fresh, party-pink watermelon juice, straight out of the bulbs themselves, and coconut water and fresh mangoes, too, if you'd like. They got there early before the queues started; even helped Wendy set up. Wendy was a mother too; her son Abel, who was about thirty seven. Years ago he had been in a brutal vespa accident, one that had meddled with his body and brain. He now spent his days in the cool of the shade, on his favourite chair, sipping on watermelons and knowing this was a kind of paradise.

'So did you kill your mother, Myles?'
She appeared on the rock next to him; he didn't need to look up to know it was her. Erica. Her arms curled around her lithe legs, and she stared out at the horizon. 'It's ok if you did. I just think you should tell someone. You say you owe three lives to this world – Rose, Taylor … and then a snail. That's the part that doesn't make sense. I don't believe, deep down, you could feel that guilty about a snail. So just tell me, while no one's around; did you kill your mother?'
He breathed again, heaving the wet white claws of his bones. He was losing weight but his skeleton was getting heavier. How exhausted he was, of drowning in the air. He so wanted her to hold her hand.
'If I tell you, you have to answer me honestly, too.'
'Okay.'
'Do you want to kill me?
After everything you went through, everything someone did to you, I wouldn't blame you. I'm your free pass into the dark – if you want to, you can do it.' He pressed a finger to his lips. 'Shh. Do it silently, before you can talk yourself out of it.'
'Okay,' she looked at him, smiling, light and sun catching him. 'Yes. Sometimes I think about doing that. You make it so *easy*, you want it so badly. There was a point a few days ago when
I thought I would.' She held out her hand, splaying the fingers, distracted by some thought locked into them. 'But then I keep seeing the news. The stories.'
'What stories? I don't have a phone any more, I don't see a lot of it.'

'Our country is changing, Myles. You know about the euthanasia bill.'
'Yeah.'
'Ever since then, people are throwing their lives away. And I really thought about it … it really made sense, the idea of taking their lives. If they're going to be ungrateful for what they have, perhaps they deserve that.' She sighed lightly. 'But … whatever Hell they're in, I was in Hell too. Down there, underground, for eight years, I went through things a human shouldn't have to go. Sight, sound, smell, taste, touch that no one should have to experience. And I …' She tailed off.
Intrigued, he leaned into her, only remembering just in time not to let his skin make contact. 'What?'
'*I* held on. *I* got through. I pushed, and I dug, and I barreled through my brain until I got stronger. Strong enough to hold on until one day he dropped his keys, and strong enough to dislocate my own hip so I could reach them.
Now I get to see everything life has to offer. A carnival of colour and sound. Now I bleed pleasure. There's nothing good I don't get to feel, no memory I don't get to make. All because I held on. And I think other people should too.'
As soon as she said it, the words stopped feeling real, as though they were something she'd been instructed to say. She sat on her hands and looked at Myles, who was staring ahead, and breathing deep. 'Are you angry?'
'No. I just think people should be able to end their suffering.'
Erica nodded. 'I get it. I get it. That's why it's a debate, right?'
'Yeah,' he laughed softly, then remembered he was forbidden from laughing.
Erica rose her face to the sun. 'Now you have to tell me the truth. Did you kill your mother, Myles?'
'It's Piles.' He corrected her.
'Piles. Tell me the truth.'
Every time he opened his mouth he opened Pandora's Box – his tongue heavier than mahogany as he tried to speak.
But he could speak this, just this once; the truth.
He knew it seemed that way. Like he'd done it. That it would be the perfect twist in the tale, for him to say, Yes, that he was bad all along. But it wasn't true. He could say No. To this one, he could be innocent. He could remember who he was before.
'No.' He shrugged. 'No, I didn't kill my mother.'
Erica laughed.
'If you feel that guilty about killing a snail, imagine how I'd feel about killing you.' Erica shrugged. She wiped sand off her hands. 'Guess I can't do it.'
'No, no, that's where you're wrong,' Piles even felt guilty engaging in conversation. Sparring, if you like. Edging into flirting. He took the sing-song out of his voice, inserted a nasally, off putting tone. 'That snail was so much more deserving of a place in the world than me. If you killed me, you'd be doing it for the women I hurt. It would be an act of – '

'Oh shut – **up**!' Erica threw her head back in an exasperated cackle. Her hair moved violently through the air. 'Seriously shut up or I'll … give you a big hug and then you'll have to do a full day without water or something! God, *Piles*. You're the saddest man in the world and you wear that title with pride. Like it's relaxing to just not have to try anymore.' She pushed herself up from the sand, dusting it off her skin. 'It's not right to stop trying. We have to keep experiencing..' She jumped to her feet. A wave of spontaneity hit her. 'I feel so restless today. You know what - I'm going for a jog.' She turned without a goodbye and began bounding away, her hair bouncing behind her in an endless ponytail.
'Oi, come back. You haven't killed me yet!' He called after her, then clapped his hand over his mouth. *Flirting*. No.
She sputtered to a stop, turned around, let the sun fall around her like a halo. She let him look at her, knowing he couldn't control his eyes unless he plucked them out; let them fall over her face, her glowing skin, up her legs and over the smooth plane of her lower stomach. Only when his eyes made their way back to her mouth did she speak.
'Yes I have.
I'm doing it slowly.'
She turned again, and continued to run. Kicking sand into his eyes as she fled.

Chapter Nine

'*Everything is blue these days. My eyes, my bikini, my bruises. I don't go two minutes without seeing the colour blue.*'
And she was right. Everything was blue. The sea in front of him, the shell he trod on, the dolphin lilo blowing his way.
And his balls.
His blues were so, so, so very blue. Ever since he met her.
'I'm doing it slowly.' She whispered and they swelled again.
What if *this* was how he would die? If after all the attempts – Gerry's heavy hands, an indulgent supply of pills, a slash of metal in an open bath, thirty feet of gravity – this was how he would go? Burst open with longing, spilling blue on the beach.
Come on, he willed them. A perfect way to die.
They bucked back at him, reluctant at their empty, indefinite sentence.
'Just tell us how long we have to wait before we touch her.' If they knew that, they could count it down, play games with the numbers, and perform mental gymnastics to get them from one hour to the next, until it was over. But it was the lack of answers, the open ended silence, the suggestion of eternity, that made every second without her twist and thump.
Poor Mr Piles and his burning, boiling, baking brain. And poor old Mr Piles and his blue balls.
When he saw her laughing, cartwheeling down the beach in her blue bikini, he saw berries.
Every time he thought about popping one in his mouth he was reminded of what he'd done.
There it came, that good old flaming Fahrenheit, foaming out of both ends. That's right, he was a fussy fissure of a man and the foam came so quickly it hit a G spot. G is for Guilt. Oh boy, he was starting to enjoy the shame.

He'd passed her again this morning, both of them alone on the street. He was making his way to his bedsit and she was making her way to the beach. She'd smirked when she'd seen him, slowed down to a stop.
'Ah, it's the Kilf.' She said.
He trundled to a weak stop. 'The what?'
She swung into the air, her arm lightly clutching a lamppost. 'You're a KILF. A Killer I'd Like To. Fuck.'
He couldn't help it. He laughed. He laughed hard, his abs seizing with the shock. And it slips into the cavity where the heart used to be. And it's not quite jelly and not quite juice but he knows it's wrong, wrong, wrong. When he opened his eyes to recover from the laughter, he was alone in the street, and the cruel sun was rising, in cahoots with the bacteria that rose acne up from his skin.

He sighed, and made his way to the rock. Today was going to be a hot day. He could feel his blisters getting blisters. Good.

He walked along the beach, training himself to not enjoy the cool sand under his feet. He limped up the rock, and sat, tucking his knees beneath him, and looking out across the landscape again. A couple frolicked in the sea. A towel floated by him.
Same sea, same rock, same temperature, same tourists.
None of these buoyant bastards ever seemed able to drown.
He looked across the beach.
There it was. Wendy's shack with her fresh watermelon juice. She was opening it up, laying out the coconut bowls and setting the juice free. A hot pink mirage of girly freedom, tipping into cups. Wendy garnished the bulbs, with handfuls of ice and slices of lime. Her son Abel watched, smiling in the shade.
Nothing was stopping him. Strictly speaking, he could walk over and order one. Imagine how it would feel. His lips around the straw, the flavour on his tongue. A cool commercial cup of sunshine. Just one sip, to pass the time, while he watched the sea.
He could go and do that.
He adjusted. He stood up. He looked at the shack. His mouth watered. He considered it. For once, forgetting all the punishment, and indulging instead. And Piles will never know if he would have gone ahead and broken his pact with himself, by going and ordering that cup of watermelon juice from Wendy. Because the moment he stood, he saw something in the distance. *Somebody.*
Somebody in the water.
Somebody struggling to swim.
Somebody was drowning.

He didn't jump into the sea, he fell.
He'd be damned if he'd let two bodies go down.
He began to swim, cutting through the waves, a knife all of a sudden.
Closer, closer.
Come on Piles.
Come on.
He could see as he closed the distance it was a man, twenty something, thrashing and fighting the power of the liquid.
Don't let him sink.
The snail, Taylor, Rose.
Rose.
Taylor.
The snail.
3. 2. 1.
3. 6. 5.

Three was enough, it was the limit. There would never be number four.
A gleaming trophy, filling with water.
All that cement in his head and all that decay in his muscles, and now here it was at last – the chance to take some of it away.
In the water he did not have to feel his shameful skin. Even the taste of all the salt, bucking into his mouth, sterilised the shame. Salt water was crisp and cruel and it forced him to shut his eyes.
And nobody could see him, and he couldn't see himself, and as if it couldn't get any better, he was coming closer and closer to the body. The functioning hunk of another human; he didn't care for their name, what they had done, what their darkest thought had ever been; they were human like him and he was going to save them.
He was going to take them back onto the land and erase the idea of wetness from their very existence. Yes he was, yes he was, because he was Piles not Myles and this was Pile's destiny.
This leap into the ocean was his first bath in days.
Piles apologised, gagging on the water, as he got closer to the floating body - all he could do was be grateful, grateful for the opportunity like an unpaid intern, to feel the heaviness of a bloated body and commence the workout of taking it back to the shore.
I'm coming for you. I like to swim. I like the salt in my eyes. I like it when it drags me down. I like feeling my calves twist. I'm coming, it's okay, you'll be breathing in a minute. Turn your lips to the surface and if you can, suck on the sky.
He got a metre from the body. No, he hadn't forgotten.
In his pocket he had been keeping gloves for this moment. Call him a perfectionist, but it had to be done. Because he still did not deserve to be touched, or to touch. Bobbing in the water, delaying the rescue, he slipped them on.
It was now or never. Four more strides and he had reached the body.
Looping the man's heavy, unconscious arm over his neck, he began careering his way back to shore. Waves and salt competed to take him down, but the shark inside him was born, he grew fins and fangs. After all, what was the point of being a monster if he couldn't swim like a beast?
On the run, on the run, running again, running away, but this time it was back to shore. Chunky, cold water came for him generously, swilling him at every angle. He remembered, through gritted teeth and grinding bones, to keep the man's face, mainly the nostrils and mouth, above the surface.
It had all come to this, to the only thing he craved now; a life to save. He stuck a fork in the blubbery body and twisted it up like pasta puttanesca.
The swim was hard, but every stroke got easier, the water parting like butter for him. The shore was a magnet. Every salty gulp made it count.

He pushed into the blue, summoning everything in his brain and his balls, giving himself into the ink of it … until the shore was only a few feet away. He could stand.

When the sand hit his feet he saw the crowd. Tanned bodies and colourful trunks, inflatables and ice creams sealed to the sand as they watched The Man On The Rock pull himself to his feet, and take the last few steps, the body now bobbing agreeably along. He threw both of them onto the beach, finally allowing others to take the weight and drag the man into the circle.

He allowed himself a few illegal moments; flinging himself onto the sand, spreading his arms out comfortably, infusing his throat happily with fresh air, warmly watching his heart come down. Nobody was paying attention anyway; they were all focused on the man.

When Piles finally rolled, embalmed in the sand, he was able to see what they were seeing. The man was just a body, and the body was still.

Another person was on their knees, trying, bent double over performing mouth to mouth resuscitation. They gave up and another tried, another pair of lips clamping down. The body remained flat and another took over. The crowd's confidence drained a little more each time.

Chest-pumping-lip-sucking-sun-drenching-foot-trembling work, but none of it was enough. The man was not saved, and Piles was not free.

For such a small girl, she cast a long shadow, darker than the others. **Erica.** She joined the circle, her mother nowhere to be seen. Today she wore a suede bikini, the colour of rust, cupping her perfectly. She had clearly just been baking in the sun herself, her suncream turning to greasy and seductive strings running down her back. She shielded her eyes and was calm when she knelt to the body. The position formed two perfect dimples in her lower back, daring you to hook your thumbs into them. She cat stretched over the body, her back arching; from this angle her new curves were obvious.

She kissed the corpse.

Carbicide, genocide, suicide, it's all the same … any minute now …

The body began to glitter.

Cough, cough, shock, shock, splutter, splutter.

A spark moving through him.

Cough, cough, shock, shock, glug, gasp.

The chest was spiking. And then it was rising.

And … he was breathing.

The man was breathing.

The man had lived.

Erica took her lips away.

'Well done,' the words came like she knew they would. 'You saved him.'

'Oh my god! That's my husband! Oh darlin! Oh thank God, are you okay?'

Cough, cough. 'I think so.' Cough, cough.

A hand on her shoulder, the gentle rub of admiration, or was it wonder, or was it love.
The crowd was getting bigger around her. None of them knew. Yet.
But every grain of sand knew. Grains of glass, bitter beneath her. Every grain of sand on the beach could have told her what she was.
How would you feel after you saved someone's life? You, no one else. Your hands, your lips, wet from their spit. They spit harder than they hit.
It shouldn't feel like this.
It should feel much, much greater than this.
It shouldn't be turning your blood to ice. It shouldn't be causing a ringing in your ear. It shouldn't be making you feel the kind of terror you thought you weren't capable of feeling any more
It should feel good. You should feel proud. It should feel right.
Erica stood before the next thank you could reach her. Before another grateful word could be said, she had to get away. She turned and made them part for her. Blood in her belly, she darted through the first gap she could see.
As the man sat up, Erica was gone. 'Who was that?' she heard them say.

Erica walked, a slash of colour up the beach, ocean salt and the rescued man's spit dripping off her as she went. She walked away from the crowd, the commotion, til the sand got too hot for her feet. She found herself walking in the direction of Wendy's Watermelon Shack, where the bulbs waited, the outrageously pink juice glinting with ice and still promising to be cold in this heat.
Wendy wasn't there, but Abel was. Chilling on his chair, he looked up and grinned.
There was no queue. No one around.
She smiled and waved, continuing her way across the sand. Once she got in the shade she hoped the strange tension in her would evaporate but – no – no – it was bigger than ever.
'Hi Abel,' she smiled.
His hands wiggled and he murmured something back through a bent mouth. Abel had worked alongside his mother for years; though it took him a little longer, he could make a great juice. 'What would you like,' the sounds fought their way out. 'Watermel or co – ca – coco*nut*?' He managed. He held the stall as he attempted to stand. The watermelons wobbled, threatening to spill off the table. Then one actually did. Erica quickly stopped it with her foot.
'Actually I'm fine,' Erica blurted, picking up the watermelon and putting it back gently. 'You relax. I just wanted to … here, let me help you back into your chair.'
Abel smiled and nodded. She slipped her arm beneath his elbow, rested her palm on his back and lowered him down. Flashes of the Vespa accident his

mother had told her about, ground under Erica's hand, setting fire to her fingertips as she helped him take his seat.
Then she closed her eyes, and she waited. She counted up to 7, but by 3 she had to open her eyes.
Through the flicker of them she saw his hands. They were laying flat in a place they'd once curled. She shut her eyes again, let one of them prise open slightly – to see a face that could form a full smile, with cheekbones that were no longer crushed. On a neck that did not stoop. With a jaw that no longer jutted.
Squeezing them tight, she spoke. 'Abel? Are you ok?'
A clear voice came back. Not even a stutter. 'Never felt better.'
That's when she ran.

A stitch, hot sand, a confession.
The choking man on the plane.
Sprinting, ducking, passing through paradise.
The way the peanut shot straight out of his throat.
Running, racing, rippling back through the memories.
Sam's sunburn.
Could it really be true, could it really be *this*?
Cleared up the next day.
The hands, the hands, her hands.
The stray cat with the scabs.
Running to a different beach, swimming in lactic.
It was the same cat.
Feet crashing into sand castles. Itchy blotches on her chest.
The masseuse! The 'mute' masseuse!
Running into the water, so fresh, so clean, but crimson in the sunset.
The waiter's migraines. And of course the lump.
Cancer.
Just like that.
Gone.
She doused her head under, unda-da-sea, every synapse grateful for its creamy crystal massage. If she touched a jellyfish now, would she still get stung?
Abel and his accident.
She swirled in the water, letting it touch her. Nothing sculpted your body like an elaborate swim.
And before that – before he got me – what else, what else? At college, at school, as a kid – anything? Anything at all?
Nothing. Nothing until he let me go. Something happened, in that place.
She realised she'd been underwater for minutes. She punched into the air, people turning to look as her hair pendulum swung, and she sucked in the oxygen, blissful for a moment –

Oh fuck. Relief. That's how ending pain feels. Relief, the underrated secret. I'm gonna have to end all the pain.

Walking out of the water, born again. Eyes soaked her in, all the natural beach bliss she symbolised, probably imagining, wishfully thinking about touching those abs or caressing that ass. Little did they know what might happen if she –

If she t –

If she t –

She gulped. Couldn't say it. Had to do it. Do it first. Then think.

Abel. Abel. He must have been faking. Right? Yes. No. Never a no again. Me.

So. She raised her face and looked directly into the sun, and it went a kind of angry red and rolled behind a cloud.

I'm not meant to kill them. That's not why I came back.

I might be here to do something else entirely.

So. There was only one way to test it.

So. Where was he?

Chapter Ten

Erica

My hands are no longer hands.
They are grubby paws.
Paws of a bear, spooning into honey; a bear that would tear into a bee's nest to get just one lick.
My grubby, hairy paws have an appetite for one thing only: Myles.
They must touch Myles.
It might be a tickle, a scratch, or a stroke – but in some way, they must lay their bare hands on that man. Myles, who is not too hot, not too cold, but just right. The meatiest, hairiest-knuckled, most calloused fleshed hands have nothing on my big paws, clenching open and closed as they picture grabbing him. A small girl like me should not have hands this big, but they multiply as they envisage possessing him. Welts appear where he should be and the fingerprints tingle, singed with longing.
I will touch him. I will know how he feels. We will be flesh pressed onto flesh before he even knows it.
I remember where his bedsit is. It's a ten minute walk. It'll take me five.

'Myles? Myles, are you in here? It's me.'
'Hey, are you ok? Why did you run from the beach?' He opens the door to his bedsit. There he is.
I enter. I reach for him but he moves backward.
'I – I need to tell you something. Oh god, I think, I think … this is going to sound crazy. But … I think I … something's happening to me. That drowned man was gone, right? You saw him. Three people tried and nothing happened. But then I touched him and … he was okay. Just like that, the water came shooting out of him. Not even any complications; he was sitting up straight with a smile.'
'Well, you just knew how to do it right, I guess.'
'No. I don't. I don't know anything. Myles, I think there might be something wrong with me. I think there's something going on, inside my hands. Something weird.'
'Like you can …'
'Don't say it. Let me show you.'
I take a step towards him and he darts from me, sprinkling breadcrumbs for me. This room has four walls, one ceiling, one floor, three chairs, a large sofa, a table and a TV. That's it. It doesn't matter how fast or agile he is – he's not getting away from me. I'll touch him til he screams, I'll touch him til he moans, either or both, but I'll touch him.

'There's no point hiding,' I say, and I am creepy and I do not care. 'I'm gonna touch ya.'
'How? Where?'
'Your leg. Your injury. Let me touch you, Myles.'
A gusp of longing. 'No.'
'Please! Please, I have to know. I have to know what's happening to me. Just let me touch your leg, just once, then I'll never touch you again.'
Red salt in his eyes.
'I'm sorry. But I can't.'
'Oh but you can. And you will.' I tease, I play, slicing up the dark.
'I can't be touched, ever, anywhere. No. No. No. Get out. Please, Erica, go. Go before you regret it.'
I take a step towards him.
'Make me.'
'What?'
'I'm not leaving. So you're gonna have to make me get out of here.' My teeth glint. My eyes flash. I'm ten feet tall and I can't be stopped.
'No. Fine. You can stay, I'll go. I'm not being touched. Not ever.'
Oh but he is.
'Who are you to say that? I thought you were a monster. Last time I checked, monsters can't say no. Your legs belong to me, Myles. I could juggle all your limbs if I wanted.' Mine. Fee fi fo fum. That flesh belongs to me. 'Go on. Slide it into my palm. Let's touch.'
'Please get out of here. Please stop saying it.'
'Myles, if - '
'That's not my name! PILES, PILES, is my name, you've gotta use it!'
'Fine. Piles. If you're all about being so good, then won't you do this for me? Won't you? You can pretend my hand is yours. Just once then you can forget.'
'Never. Ever.'
'What if you get to touch me anywhere you want afterwards?'
'Stop it!' He's panicking. Easier to catch. One little slip and he'll be mine. 'Get back!'
'Oh Piles. Don't you wanna make my day?' How dare he. Gimme that candy. Oh my god I'm so creepy. 'One little touch.'
'I said no.'
'Well I can't hear anything. I guess I'm going deaf.'
'NO!'
'Besides, monsters can't speak.'
'GET OUT!'
'Come on! Come on!'
I dive for him, he ducks. He runs, I chase. He dives away, I launch for him. He spins into the corridor, I follow. He turns into his bathroom but he doesn't get

the door shut soon enough; I jam my foot in and barge through the crack. Now I shut the door.
Nowhere to hide.

Chapter Eleven

If she reached out she just might get him. Piles tried to become one with the wall.

'Let me touch you.'

'*No,*' he could barely whisper it. He wanted it so badly.

'Yes. It'll be quick I promise.'

'No,' he hated himself for the way he whimpered.

'Come on. For me. *One time, I promise.*'

Weakened, he slumped to the ground. His knees up, his head down. He couldn't say it, and he couldn't escape her.

She slid down too, a smile on her face. 'Nowhere to turn.' It came out as a croak. 'This could help people. You get that? If it works. I just need to know. Okay?'

How could he, how could he, how could he, what would Rose say …

'Okay.'

'*Thank you,*' she sighed. 'Roll up your jeans.'

Reluctantly, he rolled them up. Past dirty feet and bruised ankle and sore bone, til his shin was exposed, til his knee was right there.

She reached forward. He closed his eyes.

And then she put her hand on his calf.

Finally, his world sighed, *finally*.

Fuck. I forgot.

A ripple from his legs to his lung. It had been so long since flesh. So long since he'd been real.

Her palm was there and then it was gone. But it took some part of him with it. His eyes snapped open.

He looked at her, meeting her eyes as they tried to sense how he was feeling. He saw her notice, saw her nod, at how a little bit of grey drained from his skin, and a little bit of tension left his shoulders.

'Does it still hurt?' She asked. He couldn't speak. 'Try and bend it.' She commanded.

Of everything he had done, of how thoroughly he'd signed his life away, it had all come down to this. This attempt to bend his leg.

He counted to three, and then he tried, and it bent like it hadn't for months, in a perfect ninety degree angle as simple as the lid closing on a coffin. He sighed with relief, with fear, forcing himself into the wall.

'Does it hurt?' she asked again. Tender this time.

He thought about lying, about dying, about crying. 'It's gone.' He wheezed.

Her eyes gleamed. 'What's gone?' All of a sudden she was nervous.

He gave her what she needed. 'The pain.'

'It's stopped?'

He nodded. 'It's not there anymore.' The leg started to twitch. 'Erica, what have you done with my pain?'
Black feathers falling in her eyes. It was real and there was no going back. The bathroom floor felt like it was cracking beneath them. The drain gurgled in the corner. Erica rolled up onto her knees. He pulled away in fear, curling into a ball.
She was still a decent foot away. *Don't come closer. Back away. Be gone, little one.* They breathed calmly, surrendering to their personal space, their eyes meeting in respect of their one-time pact.
They kissed.
And just like that, Piles became Myles again.
They weren't sure who launched first. The floor was about to split and they had to grab each other before one fell through.
He grabbed her hands, ripping her away from the lava, throwing her onto his lap in a straddle. He realised for the first time how hard he was. His hands locked into her silky hair as her hands locked round his neck. Their lips played a trick and as soon as they touched their skulls were swivelling on their spines and and together they kissed a kiss that would open the moon's mind.
Her body was a bullet. Her lips were a trigger. And he was the gun. Ready, aim, fire.
Smack, crack, into the wall they went, the tiny bathroom tiles not standing a chance as they crumbled open; was his jaw broken, had she kissed him that hard? Inside their mouths were two people who had been buried alive this whole time and were now fighting their way through the rubble to get to the top. The kiss brought him to his feet with her still wrapped around him.
He slammed her into a pipe.
She slammed him into the sink.
He spun her round.
She wrapped around him.
She would shatter his jaw before she stopped kissing him, she was wet with fury that he hadn't ripped off her top yet, and when he did she was surprised her skin didn't come off too.
Violent, violent Myles, all those stories he'd told her, now Erica could see why, could see how it wasn't safe to be in the hands of this man, how you needed to break yourself into little tiny Erica's in the hope of satisfying each part of him.
'You're so big,' she whispered. 'You'll break me in half. I think you'll kill me if I let you inside me, and then that'll be four lives you've taken.'
And just like she predicted, the words turned him on more.
'This is who you are, Myles,' she said. 'Show me why I should be scared, why I should have stayed away from you this whole time.'
He sealed a hand over her mouth. Her eyes widened, gooey, with lust. He grew another inch in her hand.

'I told you to keep your hands off me, and you didn't listen, did you? Now you've gotta pay.' Her skirt was torn. Plaster fell from the ceiling. She slipped her waist into his grip, eyes fusing with his as she did.

He turned her round, kicking her ankles apart with his foot. 'What have you got to say for yourself?'

'I'm sorry,' she croaked, looking into the mirror as he cupped her throat.

'You think you're magical. Special. A fairy, an angel, an elf. Think you've got some power over all of us. Over me. Well you don't. You never could. *And you should run.*'

'Should I?' her voice was breathless, tingling, as the tingles on their skin turned to smoke, an incense that filled with tiny bathroom with its scent.

'You should run far, far away from me girl and never look back.'

'I know. I should.'

'Hide so I can never find you.'

'I should.'

'I'll count to ten. In fact, not even ten. Seven. I'll give you seven seconds to get away from me.' He closed his eyes. '1…2…'

Her underwear was ripped off and she was sitting on the sink.

'3 ….'

His belt was on the floor.

'4 …'

His cock drove through the air.

'5 …'

Her thighs were pushed apart.

'6 …'

And he was inside.

'7.'

Inside.

Inside.

Inside.

Both of them went to that place.

Inside the place you can only leave when your body can't come any more. But over and over again, they came.

Chapter Twelve

After.
After.
Oh, after.
Erica decided to make a phone call.
Or perhaps not decided. This was a must. This was something she had to do. It was written in scripture.
Being an escaped captive comes with its clout. Let's just say it puts you on certain people's radars. Amongst the headlines, and the celebrations, there comes the connections - the powerful people who want to take credit for your happy ending, who promise you all kinds of gifts and indulgences if you send some of that collective glee their way.
And that was even before she became a Healer. Ha. What wouldn't someone do for her once they knew she could do that?
Erica hadn't wanted to milk those connections until now. She hadn't wanted to wade into that influence, that information, the thrilluminati of it all, until now.
But looking at Myles, the first man she had given herself to since her release, she knew she needed to do this.
So she took out her phone, and she made a call. A call that would give her answers.

Chapter Thirteen

Cupid

To the humans,

You do know I can see all your hearts, don't you? I'm looking at them right now. Sometimes I sleep inside of them.
For example, right now I'm looking at the heart of Johnny Bead. Thirty two, a record producer and keen marathon runner. In fact, that's exactly what he's doing right now. Pounding the pavements of the Chicago marathon.
His heart is huge. He's blown it up with all this cardio. Made it bigger than I ever wanted it to be. A thick, hanging shaft of a heart.
I can see, deep in the top left pocket, Johnny has reserved all his heart for a woman, Lana. She is his fiancé, a cute blonde who stretches him every night. She is but a mile away, waiting to jump into his arms and be spun around by a man who finished in the top 20% of competitors.
Ever so slowly, I am just going to apply pressure, at the top of one of the valves, just so that the oxygen is slightly obstructed. Hey, if he has to work a little harder, that's what a marathon is for right?
He keeps running.
Now I am just slightly going to rub the centre of it, a nice little massage to relax it. Let those muscles slow down.
Let me tell you a little more about the host of this heart. The runner is a lot of fun. He dated Lana for a year at university but they went their separate ways once he got a summer internship in Canada. Six years later they met again at a mutual friend's charity brunch – the moment they looked eyes over the pastry tarts, it was obvious they would end up together.
Now I'm just going to add some pressure on the aorta, so it has to work a bit harder.
I have to say, he is doing very well. He's breathing at a lovely steady pace as he cruises through the last mile, gaining energy as he gets closer to the finish line. Wanna know a secret? He has a ring in his pocket. He's going to propose to Lana, right on the finish line, a photo op sure to go viral. She has baked him a cake to indulge in when it's finished, and has on her best underwear for his 'special' massage later. She's going to say yes.
Lana used to run these marathons with him but she's gone off it. Will he still love you the lazier you get, Lana?

I focus my attention back on Johnny. He's picking up pace with every step, breezing past his competitors. He's sweating. Damn, he's only 200m from the finish line. This is gonna be his personal best.
Lana sees him. 'Jon!' She cries out. 'Yes, go on babe! Smashing it!'
Jonny sees her, and that's when I do it.
I close off the valve, and I tell the left ventricle it's time to stop. Not slow down, stop. It's worked too hard. It's time to rest. Same for the right ventricle, which I seal off too. No more oxygen, no more blood, time to rest. Wading through treacle, go on, just try and pump. It can't.
'Jon! Oh my god, JON! That's my fiancée!' Lana is the first to notice, of course. Jonny has ground to a stop, just fifty metres from the line, looking around in confusion and holding his chest. As he gets overtaken, he starts to melt into the ground.
'Jon! Help him!' Lana points, but nobody is stopping. She pushes someone out the way, to get to the barrier. I like that.
'No!' Now that is a cry. I haven't heard one like that in years. She jumps the barrier. She's running upstream through the race.
Even now, Johnny is trying to answer her, trying to calm her. He must be in a world of pain right now, he must be so confused, yet he is still trying to talk to her.
'He runs all the time ... you need to help him, please! No, no, no! *Johnny*!' She reaches him just as he hits the ground.
'Somebody stop! Somebody help us!' She cradles the head of her flustered, fading man, trying to catch his eyes as they roll back into his head.
Everything is slowing down now.
She really does love him.
I could fix this. I could make his heart work again.
I picture his heart again, lying stagnant and still. All I have to do is tell it to move. One flutter and they'll be back together.
'Babe! Wake up! Come ON!'
But I don't. I bring the heart to a stand still, and I hover above the marathon, watching as her screams drown out the cheers of the crowd.
I could do this all day. There's nothing like this power. I will do it over and over again, simply because I can. And now, so can you.

Yours ever,
Cupid.

London

Scott threw the letter down. It had arrived this morning, to his home address this time. Unlike Cupid's other letters, this one gave him a chill, churning a frozen margarita through his veins. He knew what it was saying, what it was accusing him of: it was the same line that had been gently parroted in the media, from panels on chat shows to interviews on the street.

To them, euthanasia was no more than murder, no more than the callous cauterising of another person's heart. To them, you could never consent to murder, and this was a violation of the highest order. And to them, he was disgusting, as disgusting as an evil angel who flew above marathons, stopping the competitors' hearts, just because it could.

And maybe he was. After all, he had known the power he would be unleashing if he pushed the vote through. You give people the right to take life; you don't know what that power does to them. How it's not enough to play God just once. How, maybe, just maybe, like God, they stop following the rules. And take and take and take, whenever they needed to feel good, to feel proud, to feel free. To feel anything.

Fine. Let them. As long as nobody had to take pain.

The thought hit Scott with a satisfying thud: the bill still meant what he had wanted it to mean - the end of pain. So make them feel anything, as long as it's not pain.

Scott let the letter fall to the floor, shrugging as it landed amongst the crumbs. Let them write to him. Let them hate him. Let them come for him. *As long as there wasn't pain.*

He picked out another letter from the pile. This was one of the first ones he had read, and it was one of his favourites. The one about the nuts.

To the humans,
I want to show you a trick.

I am on a bus. How boring you all are, won't one of you at least perform a hand job or something?

I look from couple to friend to family. Which ones do I want to make fall in love? Or more importantly, out of?

Their pale faces, their backpacks, their packed lunches. They don't deserve my powers.

'Ladies and gentlemen,' comes the announcement. 'We have been informed one of our passengers has a severe nut allergy, particularly to pecans. It can actually be fatal so if anyone has any nuts on board, please refrain from opening them until you are *off* the bus.'

'Ah,' I hear a voice coming from the seats in front. I lean forward, look through the gap. A wife is zipping up a box of Tupperware. 'Good job they mentioned it, Peter, I packed those honey roasted ones you like.' Her husband nods, and his stomach grumbles. He unfolds some headphones, sticking them on and closing his eyes.

Oh Peter.

Peter, Peter, Peter.

Today, I am going to make you love something.

Head over heels. Can't live without you baby. You are going to fall in love with your nuts.

It'll start in a few minutes; he won't be able to understand why his palms are sweating. He's eaten before getting on the coach and he won't be able to explain why a hole has opened his tongue, a hole begging to be filled with something brassy yet sweet. He'll try the banana, the chicken sandwich, his wife frowning at the speed with which he devours, but those things don't go *crunch*. Not even sixty seconds later and his stomach'll be gaping apart pitifully. His eyes will be sore, almost like he's allergic to being nutless.

He doesn't have time to hate himself as his hands are reaching, reaching for the shiny foil, reaching just to hear that satisfying *slash* into the aluminium – his wife slaps his hand away 'Peter! Not on the bus, remember!' and he looks at her with half an apology, half rage, as she tries to keep him just as unsatisfied as she does in the bedroom. Is it because she's jealous – can she tell he's feeling more love for these nuts than he has in twenty two years of marriage for her? So he turns away, and sits on his hands, and looks out the window, and thinks – he can't possibly give in to this craving. He *can't* possibly eat them now. He just has to wait til the coach ride is over.

Three hours.

He can do it.

Yet they niggle and nestle, the tinkling sirens, calling to him from their secret case. How many are in there, he can't help but think? Are they big or small? Round, perfectly formed or each one unique? What are their names? How long can he make them last?

The good news for Peter, is his wife always sleeps on long journeys. Going cold turkey, his ears ringing, his head bursting, his balls blue, he manages, somehow, to make it another minute. She is drifting off, distracted, her grip slipping from the Tupperware box. He reaches in, undoing the zipper, seducing them from the bag.

Survival of the fittest, he thinks. If a nut can kill you, should you really even be here?
He releases them, so excited they spill, scattering down the aisle. A few people turn, surprise and dread dawning on their faces.
He throws one in the air.
Crunch.
Three rows back, a girl of sixteen goes into anaphylactic shock. Just like they told him she would. And as the taste hits his tongue, it dawns on Peter what he has done.

See? I told you.
My name is Cupid. Don't fuck with me.

Chapter Fourteen

London

Eli traced the brail of his newspaper, his hand shaking as it searched for his coffee. A few months ago he had written for this newspaper; his words quoted across it, for every household and every commuter to savour. His words were irrelevant now, locked into an opinion and a country of the past.
But that wasn't what raised the bitter bile in his throat, as his fingers laced across the brail; that wasn't what broke his brain today. It was the information that the brail gave way to, that had him tracing it backwards, willing it to rescramble, willing it to change.
Sunset Clinic was due to be opened next month.
Even in the days after the blinding, when all he had seen was the white hot truth of pain, he had fought it: the result of the vote. He couldn't see it, so it couldn't be real. Even when he'd heard it - the senses in his ears now heightened deliriously - he'd shut out the truth of the vote that he hadn't been able to make. Maybe they'd change their mind, maybe they'd go back on it, maybe they wouldn't dare to do it. Maybe they'd just leave it there, as one crazy vote that happened one day - it didn't have to become penetrable, it didn't have to become real.
And then he'd traced the brail. And everything had changed.
Now they were storming ahead with it; the UK's version of Dignitas, its very own centre dedicated to death.
Sunset Clinic, it was going to be called. And the Sun would set indeed.
Eli traced the brutal brail, reading the details that were even worse than he imagined. It was to be a cold, dome shaped metropolis, opening in the heart of the capital - not even in the countryside like in Switzerland. At least it knew what it was - it was pollution, and it would open surrounded by pollution, ensconced in the fumes of the toxic and the traffic of the ungrateful. It would even have glass walls - did it have no shame? Even abattoirs had the grace to keep their murders concealed. Did they have no *remorse*?
The brail boiled his blood as he read about the length of the waitlist, about the slate of high profile clients that had signed up to it already - about how even the US President was considering a visit. 'I'm very proud of the UK,' the paper quoted him as saying. 'This is what a free and fair society is all about.'
Bitter, brutal, broken brail, brail of a battered, beaten, broken nation, brail of a bovine cow on her way to the slaughterhouse.
He traced the words over and over again.
Free and fair.
Free and fair.
Free and fair,.
The President *was* right. He *was* in a free and fair society.

As the milk swilled in his coffee, an idea swilled in his mind. He could do anything.
If they could open a clinic, so could he.
If they could change the country, so could he.
If they were allowed to kill, he was allowed to … revive. Rescue. Save. *Prolong.*
And just like that, Eli could see through the darkness. Just like that, Eli knew - all he had to do was create a clinic too.
But it wouldn't be a clinic. It would be a *retreat.* It would be Eden. A haven, an escape, the very antithesis of everything that was happening in the capital. People could get on the underground and slug their way to Sunset Clinic, or they could take a long, comfy drive to him, roof down, breeze in their hair, and settle into his retreat. He'd let them stay as long as they wanted. He'd give them anything they wanted. Anything they asked for, just so long as they didn't leave him.
They could come to Sunset to end their lives, or they could come to him for Hope.
They could choose to take their final breath, for the final image they see to be a needle, for the final thing they hear to be the sobs of their family … or they could choose to keep seeing, to keep feeling, to keep living.
All they needed was for someone to say it. To show them. That just because you could give up, you didn't have to. That the world hadn't ended when the vote did.
In fact, it had only just begun.
You may wonder how he was able to hope so hard, to stay so strong in his vision when others couldn't. You see, that's not for nothing. Eli knew something.
He had a secret. And soon he would share that secret with the rest of them, and Sunset would be a thing of the past.
For the first time in months, Eli was smiling. For the first time, he was hungry again, energised again, driven again.
He reached across the table, fingers fluttering in the darkness, until they closed around an apple.
And just like that: he even had a name for his retreat.

Chapter Fifteen

Hawaii

'Erica.'

That word. It meant something different now, even though it was still her name. Erica was standing in front of the mirror of the most luxurious suite in the whole island. They had moved in yesterday, a surprise from the hotel after her triumph on the beach.

'Erica.' Her mother said it again but she did not turn round. Because there were no rules any more, and if she wanted to admire herself, she could.

So she did. She was glowing. Her skin was a life-affirming golden, set off by a purple corset and purple jewels. Her hair bounded abundantly around her, as free as she was.

Her mother appeared behind her, and she knew she too was marvelling at her beauty. Missing girls weren't meant to come back like this. Weren't the years without sunlight meant to take things from their skin, their eyes, crumple their bones so they couldn't stand tall? But not her girl. No. Erica was only getting better.

'You look amazing,' she said. 'Ridiculous.'

'Better be careful I don't get taken again.' Erica joked. Her mother flinched but she ignored it, and stabbed two purple earrings through her ears. 'Listen, darling, I need to talk to you about something.'

'Yes?' Erica replied.

'It's about that man you're hanging around with.'

Erica speared another earring through her lobe. 'You mean Myles?'

Her mother sighed. She knew what was coming.

'Listen, darling. I think I've been pretty understanding, pretty accommodating, since we were reunited. There are a lot of mothers who, after what you went through, wouldn't want you anywhere but at home, ever again.

I didn't have to agree to come here with you. I could have spoken to your therapists, could have stopped this. You do remember that it isn't *normal* for a mother to party with her daughter like this. I even got my bloody nipple pierced with you! So you could feel good, so you could feel free, so you could have all the experiences you were craving.

I get it, and I know how lucky I am to have a daughter so … vibrant.

But don't think I haven't been terrified. Terrified of what could happen to you again. These atmospheres you're in, the way you are with everyone, the daring in you, the spontaneity … it's beautiful but it's radical and I'm scared.

And you must realise how stupid I feel. Going on double dates with you by my side. I look ridiculous. I look pitiful. Have you not seen the way people look at me?

But I don't care about any of that. I'll take that a hundred times over if it makes you happy.
I just also need you to be safe.
And I thought maybe you could be until … that man.
Myles.'
She took a deep breath, as she saw him in her mind
'That man. Erica. The way he looks at you. The way he *is*. What he's been doing here. How he is even here. He's hiding from something. He's going to - to - find what he's lost, and he's finding it in you. I promise you darling, I can see it. I know violence when I see it and I see it in him.' There was a tear now, a tear she'd sworn she wouldn't let Erica see.
'Darling. I will never ask you for anything. I will never tell you to do anything. If you just do this, for me.
You have to stop seeing him.'
Erica threw back her hair, cackling. She flopped onto the bed, held out her hands in a swan dive and rolled with the mirth. *You can't be serious.*
She rolled and rolled until she went over the edge. Landed hard on the expensive marble and laughed even more. *You can't be serious.*
She was kicking her feet with glee.
'Erica. You're not well.' Her mother grabbed her suitcase from the wardrobe, and started throwing things inside it. 'Please. Let's go back to London.'
The word London made her raise up. Up and away, and back to him.
As if she was incense, Erica drifted to the door. 'Not yet. I love you, mum, but you can't make me go before I'm ready. Haven't I missed out on enough?'

Myles drove her to the hospital, or maybe she drove him; it was hard to remember anything other than what happened once they were there. This was something she had to do - but she had to be subtle. Erica hadn't claimed the recovery of Abel on the beach - right now half the island interpreted it as a miracle, the other half were accusing him and his mother of an elaborate fraud. Not ready to step into the truth of what she was, but desperate to explore it, she had asked Myles to bring her here. And he couldn't refuse.
With very little security, it was easy to drift up, up, up into the more serious of wings. The chronic, the critical, the terminal. The moment Erica stepped onto the parquet, she knew what to do.
She made her way to the first bed, where a man lay, his body forced to form a letter; not quite an I, not quite a T, and perhaps that made him feel like an It - but Erica would show him he wasn't, that he was a human and he was about to feel human again. His face turned to his pillow; perhaps imagining the white fibres were a cloud he was part of, made this easier. 'Dominic' was tagged to his bed.
His fingers turned as though he'd been casting a spell when the stroke had struck, like the spell had gone wrong and turned on him.

First she touched the rail of his bed, then the duvet. Trepidation for a second, but then certain; she closed her eyes and grabbed his calf.
And all across the world, the fingers unfurled, puckering out of limbo. A hundred ice sculptures melted and a thousand poisoned jellies failed to set in their moulds. They were free. Like cakes, they rose.
With an unnatural strength, Dominic pulled himself up .
'My wife!' He said. 'Somebody call my wife.'
'We will.' Myles whispered.
Erica spun from Dominic, to the bed opposite, where a woman of about forty lay, her bed tagged with 'Isabelle', her head shaved to make way for a bandage. With a flick of her wrist, Erica ran her hand along the bandage.
'Don't touch my sister!' She hadn't realised, in the darkness, a man had been sitting, watching. 'What do you think you're doing? She's in a coma!'
'Marcus?'
The man's voice collapsed. 'Izzy? *Izzy.* I thought you'd never wake up.' He looked up from his smiling sister to Erica. 'Wh-who are you?'
Before she could answer, her hand was in Myle's, and they were running, laughing, slipping on the linoleum and out into the night.

He grabbed her, walked her into an underpass. Pressed her against the wall. The words he spoke should not have seduced her. 'Imagine if I'd met you last year,' he said, turning her against the metal. He ran a finger along a lip he could dip in. 'You could have saved Rose.' He pushed his lips against hers, drawing a picture with their mouths. He came up for air, a churn of engines punctuating his lust. 'I don't know why I wasn't looking for you, missing girl. I should have saved you then, before you had to save yourself.' He grabbed her hands, kissed them, pawed them into his shirt. 'These hands,' he groaned. 'Touch me. Find out what's wrong with me and make me worthy.' He was slipping her thong to the side. 'Make me worthy, I'll make you worthless.' Enter. Open. Sigh. *Fuck*, it was more than love.

Each night she asked him to come to her. And he couldn't say no but he couldn't stop the guilt after. With every yes his follicles widened, filling up with more fumes, each one lasting longer. He couldn't forgive himself but he couldn't resist Erica. Each time the shame was a little worse, but every time she tasted even better.

One time she took him to her hotel room. 'Your mother could be back any second.'
'That's why we're going on the balcony,' she led him through the doors into the refreshing night.
He leaned back against the rails. 'Don't throw me over just yet, girl.'
She threw herself into him. 'Don't kill me just yet, boy.'

He spun her round. 'You're planning to throw me off, I can tell.'
She wrapped her hands around his neck. 'I better hold on a little longer before you do it.'
He picked her up, sat her on the railings. Precarious. Careless. But lust won.
'One last time before you push me,' He drove her legs apart. Slippery. 'Let me feel this.'

Myles went through her with all the shame and trepidation of someone tampering with evidence. Every time he let himself have it, he had to walk the beach, up and down, til his feet bled from the glass in the sand.
He saw it again. Rose bleeding out on the boat. The fact she had not been wearing knickers.
I'd rather accidentally have killed her than have purposefully hurt her. Or would I? No – I'd rather attack on purpose than have a life on my hands. But that means I'm evil, violent and vile – I'd rather kill by accident and know I wasn't an abuser. Except imagine a life where I don't owe someone theirs – maybe I could let myself abuse someone just once.
Rose's ghosts appeared, just before he joined Erica, 'Lucky for you Myles, you don't have to make that choice.' She pulled up her skirt and she was still wearing no knickers.

He had to tell her that they had to stop.
He found her on the beach, her hair in a French plait, her bikini tie dye and printed with sand.
He opened his mouth but she was already speaking. 'Myles. I've found someone.'
'Someone else?' he barked it quickly but it came out weak.
She gazed at him, nose crinkled with amused surprise. '*No*, Mr. Someone to … someone to heal.'
'Okay. You want me to come with you, keep an eye on them?'
'Yes. I do. But here's the thing. They're in London.'
She gripped his face tight so he couldn't look away. 'I have to go. I have to do this. My mother and I … we know it's time to go home. To go back. So … come with me. Come back to London.'
He tried to look down but she held him up.
'Myles! I need you with me when I do it. Please. Help me do it, and then if you want, you can turn yourself in. Why not just try, or are you going to sit on that rock forever?
Because that's not you. You're more than that. You can tell yourself you aren't but you are.
We both know it.'
Her voice was desperate, scratching at his skin. She stood up, bright on the beach. 'Our flight's tonight. Are you coming?'

Myles looked at her. For the first time since he kissed her, he told her no.

As she always did, Erica found herself a moment - a moment where she could be alone, where there was nothing but her and the sun.
She tucked herself away from him, around the corner of the Love Shack Tiki Bar, and took out her phone.
As promised, a number was ringing her, 5pm on the dot as she'd asked for.
She checked nobody was listening, and then she answered.
'Hello?'
A stiff, stilted voice spoke back to her. She pushed the phone deep into her ear, just in case anyone was hiding, and listened.
Her spine became a slope as the call confirmed what she had asked them to do.
'Yes,' she replied to their questions. 'Yes, Myles King is who I mean ... yes, Rose is the name of the woman he killed. Rose Markham.'
'Okay,' they said. 'Now we've got something we want to ask you.'
A black butter churned in her as the request came through. She backed up further, separating herself from the beauty of the beach. Even nodding felt like an abomination that wasn't for its eyes.
'Yes.' She gulped. 'Yes. I can do that.'

Chapter Sixteen

London

To the humans,

I can take you to a place.
Inside of a bone china teacup, there is a cake stand made of frosted glass.
At the top, there is a meringue, the smallest meringue in the world.
I can take you inside the meringue. We will tip toe through the turrets made of frosted flake. At the highest point of the turret, we will find a macaroon. The smallest, pinkest macaroon in the world.
We can jump into the macaroon. Crashing through the perfect roof until we are floating in the fondant. As our bodies are carried to the creamiest point of the cream, we will discover a secret.
Inside of the macaroon is a city called Paris.
And within Paris, tucked along a little cobbled street on which you can still smell the seine, there is a brothel only a few people in the world know exists.
I can take you there.

A figure in a black cloak greets the clients, and leads them up a winding stone staircase, past arches and stained glass windows and pillars, until we reach the office of the brothel's pimp, Louis.
'The best part is the choosing,' he tells today's client, a scientist who flew in from Beirut.
Surrounded by six silhouettes, he offers the options. 'This is Jessenia. The lake, the water, the quench. Hydrating. Keira. The storm. Wild, free, swept off the streets. Davina, the softest, the silk, the silence. Sasha, the clown, the one who can make you laugh, Esme, born with two throats, and of course Colette, the one whose legs don't end. Make your choice.'
He chooses three. Jessenia, Davina and Colette.

He is taken to a boudoir, a place of sunken beds and marble ceilings, and a ceremony begins. Each client is given a ritual, a performance tailored to their tastes; he asked for Paris, so Paris is what they will give him. Three different versions of Marie Antionette approach him.

What they do to him is philanthropic in its pursuit of pleasure. They feed him strawberries, dark chocolate, white chocolate, slipping them in places he didn't know he had. Most of all, he cannot take his eyes off the blonde. She has the biggest eyes, the widest gap in her teeth, the fullest frame just how he likes. He trails his gaze to meet her eyes and let her know she's his favourite.

And that's when she says; 'Daddy?' She's looking right at him, her voice cracking. 'Dad? What are you doing here?'

He jumps up, feathers falling off him, chocolate dripping down him. No. It can't be. His daughter is in Toulouse, studying to be a lawyer, and she is three inches taller than this girl. Isn't she?! Isn't she?! So then why she is she looking at him with such conviction?

Now she is rising too. 'Get away from me! Don't come anywhere near me! How could you! *Dad*?'

That word again. Everything inside him bucks at it. No. No. No. It's not. Could it be? Every pore in him fills with shame.

The hookers rise around him, looking at him in a way he's never known. He's shrivelled inside so much he can't remember why he's here.

'I - I - I promise you I'm not who you think I am! *Please*!'

She backs away. Sadness falls across her like a veil. He knows not to take another step.

And then, suddenly, 'Sorry.' Her eyes are clear and her voice is sweet again.

'My mistake.

We all make mistakes.

This was yours.'

He sees the blade just in time. He spins away from her, but Jessenia is waiting. Their knives meet for a kiss in his kidneys.

He gasps, trying to breathe through fishnet lungs, dropping to the floor as his blood is acquitted. They take his hand. 'Look into your eyes as you leave us.'

A shadow falls across the room. The three women leave him, dropping his hand to flock to the shadow, to their pimp, Louis, the man who built this brothel. They slip into his arms, two on his left, one on his right, his hands dropping down to cup the buttocks that belonged to him. And when the scientist whispers, 'Why?', truth be told, Louis has no answer. All he knows

is it feels good, to saturate in the succulence of the moment they've worked for: watching a man die.
And then it's done. Just as it had been done so many times, ever since Louis opened this brothel five years ago and filled it with his happy little homicide hookers, putting the 'ass' in assasin, draining the city of its desires so long as they can drink its blood too.

What you have just seen, where I have just taken you, is The Brothel Of Blood. And no one must ever know how to find it.

Yours ever,
Cupid.

-

Scott threw the letter down. He really should stop reading these. He had a clinic to build. The pile glowed, tingled, on his coffee table. A red envelope caught his eye. Oh, go on, he deserved it.
After a long day working on Sunset Clinic's opening, Scott loved nothing more than the opportunity to relax, put his feet up with a beer, and do some reading. He needed to bask, to really savour, in It, because he hadn't done that yet. It being the fact that Euthanasia was now legal in the UK. And it was him that made it so. In the end, it had been easy. He'd been able to practically stroll over the finish line, that morning back in February.
The final debate had been won so breezily, light work as his cool friends liked to say. And the vote had melted in his hands, those on the fences swaying easily to Scott's side. By the time they were casting their ballots, everybody had been persuaded.
Especially as Eli hadn't been able to make it. Poor thing. He'd been in too much pain. There was even footage of him trying to make his way out of the hospital, when he'd to give up. After Scott's team created a couple of accounts and posted the footage, it was trending on Twitter, along with comments such as, 'See! Life can take a turn for the worst at any time. Why shouldn't we be able to set ourselves free? Are we gonna throw away this chance?' With the wind in his hair, with Eli's influence out of the room, Scott had sealed the deal. Assisted dying was legal.
Now all he had to do was create the clinic that did it. He hadn't anticipated *quite* how much work that would be. The papers were making it look like he was a lot further along than he was. So, again: a beer.
As he cracked open the Heineken and scrolled his phone, he found himself coming across the story he'd been trying to ignore all day. The doctor who had, the day after the vote, switched off a patient's life support machine 'too soon' -

vindicating every sensationalist headline that had warned Scott's bill would give certain MD's a taste for murder. Headlines such as these dampened the energy around Scott's bill spectacularly, even though Scott felt the prosecution were just out to make a trigger-happy example of somebody here. Suspicion could do that to people, and there was no place more suspicious than the UK right now. He couldn't be bothered with that feeling, not tonight. He knew what would take it away, what would distract him. *Just one more. Last one.*
He put his feet up and unravelled one of Cupid's letters, slipping it from its red envelope before he stalled when he noticed.
It was addressing him by name.

Dear Scott,

No, it's not Cupid. Not any more. Though you'd love that, wouldn't you? I'm afraid it's someone far less radical. It's Eli.
What colour eyes does this Cupid of yours have? Brown, green, grey – they get boring after a while. What about a sort of marbled brew, of deep red and amethyst purple, shot through with a dirty yellow and flecked with remnants of sky blue, their original colour?
Because that's what my eyes look like now, so I'm told. That's how they look, after what you did to me.
I know it was you. Not you directly of course, but you who organised it, you who set it up. The blinding of Eli Jones, maybe one day you'll write a song about it.
Hey, as a competitor I've gotta respect you. It was a great idea. My whole argument was built on being able to thrive no matter what life throws at you, so you took away my most important sense. I can see – ha, ironic – but I can see now, how it all played out just how you wanted it. Me missing the vote, the crucial one, so my deputy had to stand in and enact a pale imitation of my influence that was never going to convince parliament like I could. The photos of me – injured, nervous, as half the man I was. The rumours, half-true, of me pulling away from life, pulling away from my work with Samaritans. The inevitable undermining of my own argument. And just the sheer, obvious proof; that at any moment your life can turn for the worse, so 'let's take back ultimate control, by being able to end it on our terms.' Smart. No chance you'd have got the vote through if you hadn't done that.
Who was it that you got to do it for you? He disappeared so quickly afterwards. You should give him a pay rise cos he really went for it. If you're wondering if, in the deepest moment of the attack, at the height of the pain, if I ever came round to your way of thinking, the answer is no.

You've made me stronger. Take away one sense and the others grow. You've made me sharper. Admittedly, I wasn't quite myself after the attack; I needed a while, to understand life, in the dark.
And then it took a while to gather the evidence.
You see, you fell into the most obvious of traps. You know me as a man who wants to stop his country from murdering, a man who is kind and altruistic. And predictably, you think that makes me weak.
And so I'll answer my own question: that man you got to blind me was called Jed Brittle. You found him in a homeless shelter. You knew you needed someone like that to do your dirty work, so you cleaned him up and got him into your debt, all for the day when you might want to utilise him. And you utilised him to blind me.
But what you don't realise is, I found him. It only took three weeks. And Jed's resolve is brittle indeed.
You see, he spoke. He spoke and he spoke and he spoke and he confessed everything the two of you did together. And I told him I wouldn't turn him in just so long as he said it all again while I recorded. So he did.
Mate, I've even got the CCTV of the day you met him.
But that's all over now. Once I got one bit of evidence, the others came. Slippery slope and all that. You'd be surprised how willing people are to talk. You'd be surprised how little people are really, truly on your side. Shall I start with the tax evasion, Scott? Or perhaps the fraud it took for you to have enough money to campaign for your seat? Or maybe I should tell everybody about the restraining order you earned back at university, the one you managed to pull enough strings to expunge from all legal records. All legal records, but not the ones I can access, Scott. I don't think you have any idea quite whose sight you were taking - quite how many connections I have and quite how many strings they are willing to pull. And if you don't want me to talk about any of this, Scott, then I'll just talk about the other accusations - the ones that have happened yet, but I can make them real. You may as well put your name in a hat and pick out what I'll get people to accuse you of. Nothing is off limits, Scott. Not for me. I've got the money. I dedicated my life to campaigning, you feel, because I've got the resources to do it. How did you not think about that?
And I have friends. After all, someone must be writing this letter for me. I could end you. Your whole career. Your reputation. Your whole damn life. Do you know what they do to politicians in prison?
So here's what you're gonna do, Scott. First of all, you're going to burn this letter. Then you'll burn Cupid's letters too, the ones that 'inspired' you, that made your ethos quite so drastic. You're going to meet with my assistant and give her the ashes. The two of you are going to go over

some documents. Then you're going to release a statement – that after a meeting with executives at Core Retreat, you've uncovered a way our two brands, our two institutions, can align, to create the best and fairest possible outcome for those suffering. Sunset's membership won't understand your statement and they won't respect it, but that won't matter. That inconsistency is just what we need. Slowly, you're going to pull away from your more radical partners. Slowly, you're going to dilute the passion in your message.

And then, my man, we're going to work together. As long as you don't tell anyone what we're doing at Core. That place needs to be kept pure.

Not so bad, is it? I mean, I could have you in handcuffs right now. I could have you just about anywhere I want. I'm being pretty forgiving.

Looks like I'm the merciful one, after all.

Yours ever,
Eli

Chapter Seventeen

Hawaii

A drink for my man

After the healing and after the sex, they watched a little TV. They went to Myle's place this time.

On the news they saw the opening of Sunset Clinic, the UK's answer to Dignitas. The founder handed Scott Luther, the politician who'd championed the assisted dying bill, a pair of scissors. Scott cut a ribbon and smiled. To their surprise, things seemed a little subdued - there wasn't the fanfare you would have expected. A smaller crowd, not as many press as had been anticipated, and a slightly dry, slightly morose atmosphere in the air - a sticky fingered feeling that the ribbon was being cut too soon. The press hadn't been covering this as enthusiastically as they had previously, and some big name celebrities had dropped out of the opening.

As the ribbon fell, Eli Jones stepped forward, surprising the crowd. *Very* diplomatic for him to be here. It seemed a truce had been called between the two men. Myles looked at them; he used to admire influential people like this, before he'd given up his right to influence. He couldn't help but feel jealousy, unlocking his joints.

'Do you think he can see anything?' Myles said. It had taken him a moment to even remember that Eli had been attacked; his eyes had a brightness to them despite the blindness - maybe because of it. 'Sometimes it seems like he can. Like he's looking at something. Look, he's looking into the camera now. Don't you think?'

Erica did not respond. The TV had her in a glaze of submission, a cat's claw hooked out of the screen and into her face. She was rigid until the segment on Sunset was over. Only then, did she look at Myles, and speak.

'I know you wish you were one of them. One of the first people lucky enough to be at Sunset.' She smiled at him and shrugged with clinical charisma. 'And I've just realised something, Myles. If you want to die, you should.' She stood up and made her way to the tiny kitchenette at the back of the bedsit. 'So how about a drink? *A drink for my man.*'

Myles brain swelled and rippled with longing, with fear, with confusion, and he knew Erica was fully aware of the state she was putting him in as she began marching around his kitchenette. 'A love potion for my love.'

She was almost trancelike, possessed by purpose, opening cupboards until she found a glass. She slammed it onto the counter, so hard it should have broken but in her hands, it didn't.

'You see Myles,' she reached into her vest. 'When we went into hospital something came over me. I couldn't resist swiping the medicine that would give you what you've always wanted.' From her bra she plucked a packet of pharmaceuticals, smiling at them with pride. 'Swipe, swipe, I went. When you want something enough it's easy.'

Myles clenched his fists, his knuckles going white. *Don't dare to dream. Don't deserve to dream.*

'Hot cocoa and a cyanide pill.' She whispered. 'Well, almost. I wish I could make it that delicious for you, Myles. Codeine and tap water will have to do for now.' Her soft hands were getting to work, popping the pills from their foil crates, laying them in single file on the counter. With confidence, as though she'd done it before, she picked up the glass and settled it across the pills, blending them with its base. She moved with such agile assertiveness Myles didn't want to do anything but watch her.

She brushed the deathly dust from the counter and into the glass. With a flick of her wrist, turned on the tap and let the water chug into the rim. 'Arsenic and absinthe. I'm quite the mixologist tonight.' She turned off the tap and gave the concoction a swill. Drifted back towards the couch where he sat, and slammed it down again, this time on the coffee table before him. 'This one's on the house.' She winked.

Instead of joining him on the couch, she folded herself into the trifle of the armchair opposite him. It was wedgy and foamy and thick, and her tiny body was consumed by it, all angles and bones, her elbows and knees making pins in the cushions. A real life voodoo doll.

She smiled, rested her chin on her palm, and watched him. He wasn't sure what was more confronting - the expression on her face, or the white dust whirling on the face of the glass of water. When the intensity of one was too much, he would look into the face of the other, each one a different beast.

'Go on then, baby.' She dared. 'If you wanna die right now, you can. If you really believe you've got nothing to live for. If you really believe there's nothing worth staying awake for.' Her voice was sharpening, the water seeming to twist on the whim of her words. 'If there's nothing you've found in this paradise. If there's nothing you've found in the healing. If there's nothing you've found in my hands. If there's nothing you've found in *me*.' There it was; the crack in her voice she'd been trying to hide, the one cut she couldn't heal. 'Then you can do it. You can take it.'

The ball in Myle's fist tightened, tantric with longing. *I don't deserve it, I don't deserve it, not yet, not yet, I have two more lives to save.*

'If you really, *truly* don't want anything else than this, then I give you permission to do this. I give you permission to drink.' Erica's eyes were searching for him now, bending beneath his brow to find him, but he was drifting away. He didn't even notice the tear splashing down her cheek and into the codeine cocktail she had brewed him.

'Cross your heart and hope to die?' He rasped.

She winced. The tiniest but most potent of angers as he confirmed his choice.
'*Stick a needle in my eye.*'
His hand lunged forward and closed around the glass.
Erica nodded, to herself not to him. As he accepted death, she would have to accept this: that she was not special enough for him to live for. 'Drink for me, Myles.'
The rim of the glass pressed to his lips. Now surely the doubt would come? Once his olfactory system was doused in the liquid chalky fumes, surely the fear would set in, and he'd put the glass down?
Yes, yes, yes, he was pausing. Pulling the glass back from his lips, and choosing to speak. 'Thank you, Erica. Thank you for this. Thank you for everything.'
She tried to deny the deflation of her soul, as he brought the glass back to his lips.
'Go on, then. Drink for me, Myles.'
No hesitation this time. *He drank.*
Glug, glug, glug. He knocked it back. Tears lacing his face as he drank. As the poison went in, the tears went out.
It took effect immediately. He should have given Erica one last look, one last word, one last moment, but the death craved him as much as he craved it, and all he could do was submit. His body dissolving just as the pills did in the water. He was ink and oil and sleep and silence, putting on a show for Erica that no healer should ever have to see.
As the glass dropped from his tranquilised hand, Erica heard the first of the footsteps she'd been expecting.
Here it was.
There was a subtle knock at the door. Erica smirked. It was happening. Quick now. She needed his eyes to shut completely first.
'Die for me, Myles.'
On command, his lids floated down to meet his lash line. His head rolled backwards. His limbs slumped, at one with the sofa. Just at the right time, his consciousness cut out, just before he could hear The Others arriving.
Just before he could hear them coming up the stairwell.
Just before he could hear them filing into the hallway.
Just before he could register it was his door they were outside.
Just before they started their knocking.
Just before Erica answered them.
She sashayed to the door, opening it, trying not to be too triumphant just yet.
Four men who worked at the hotel, large and brawny from days of labour, looked down at her.
You didn't believe their story was over, did you? As if she'd let go of him that easily.
'He here?' they asked.

She nodded.
'He's asleep?'
She nodded again. 'You've got the car? Think he'll fit in the boot?'
'Definitely,' they replied. They marched towards him, lifting him - he became a sack of cement in their arms.
For such a tortured man, Myles looked very cute when he slept.
As Erica watched him drift, not into the death she had promised, but the coma she needed him to be in for the next twelve hours, it turned out that betrayal was a lubricant. This treachery she was pulling off had made her wetter than all the tears she'd cried as a captive. So *this* was who she was.

Chapter Eighteen

Look at this. Look at this. How do you bring yourself to break the jaw of a butterfly?

Brutal butterflies of sickly light and abrasive sound fluttered into Myle's eyes and ears, sifting him out of layers of the creamy crutch of sleep he had been churning in.

He knew it as soon as he woke up. He woke up somewhere too loud to be Heaven and too cold to be Hell. He had lived. Again, he had lived.

Where was he?

Messages marched into his brain as he tried to figure it out. The leather beneath his legs. The tight elastic across his torso. The plastic mould all around him. And the height - he was high. Not top floor of a building kind of high, not even skyscraper kind of high. This was the sky kind of high.

He was in the sky, but he wasn't in Heaven, and he was inside something, but it was moving. What the fuck was going on?

His brain pulled him back into the depths, but his vision pulled him back into the space he was in - there was somebody opposite him, on a yellow leather chair that matched his.

Erica.

Look at this. Look at her. Who was she?

'Shh,' she whispered, her hands running alongside the side of the yellow leather. A cabin. A cabin was what he was in. A cabin in the sky. She was her same playful, powerful self. 'Don't worry. Don't worry and I'm sorry. Ooh, that rhymes.' She giggled, and Myles began to feel a little less like dust and a little more like a man, a man who understood where he was, but not why. 'I knew I would never get you to come with me if I asked you. If you wouldn't leave the rock, how could I get you to leave the country? I knew the only way to get you on this plane was to drug you, not to dare you.'

An air hostess walked down the small aisle between them. She was the only other person Myles could see on the plane, but, his senses obliterated, he couldn't be sure they were alone.

'See, sometimes it's not enough just to know someone who owns a private jet,' she said. 'You need to know someone who won't ask any questions when you load an unconscious man onto that jet.' She picked up a tiny aluminium can and slurped the last drops. 'I found your passport under your mattress. Your journey has begun, Myles.'

'Where are we going?' He wasn't sure if the words came out right; he was wading through syrup to speak them, his brain begging him to switch off again, the deepest and darkest of cotton blending with his consciousness. If he

accepted the sleep, he would be spared the dread that was climbing up inside his body.
'No, Myles. No questions. No fear, not yet. Don't swallow your soul just yet - I need it for when we arrive.' She was pushing a tiny plastic cup towards him, ice dancing in the black liquid he recognised from earlier. 'And why fear when you can drink?'
The glass danced closer to him. Maybe it was the fear, the thirst, or the altitude, that made him lunge for it.
'Exactly, Myles. Let's not ruin our journey.'
His lips closed around the rim.
'Don't fear. Just drink. That's it. Drink for me. And, Myles, *sleep.* Sleep for me.'
So he did.

Chapter Nineteen

London

One pill too many?
He was taking a while to wake up. Longer than Erica had estimated. But he would.
A broth of pleasure and nerves swilled in her stomach. Not long now.
It was late now, and it was snowing outside. Everything was just perfect.

As soon as Myles woke up, he felt the air. This was the air he'd tried to die in. And the sounds. These were the sounds of the cars he'd tried to run in front of, screeching along the gridlocked icy road that had lied to him with its promise of shattering him. These were London sounds; visceral and glassy.
And they were mixed with something else too … the bubbling, brewing sound of a party.
Myles never got invited to parties anymore. Myles didn't exist in a world where people partied. He didn't exist in a place of laughter.
Information seeded through to him; he was lying against something, slumped up against something that felt like a bookcase.
Was he back in the Bishopsgate library? But then why would the library be throwing a party? A murder mystery event, perhaps?
His hands traced the darkness - everything around him was too soft to be part of a library. It wasn't a bookshelf he was up against, but shelves of something. They were not full of books, but … clothes. Cashmere clothes, even. He remembered cashmere, remembered its smell. He fumbled through the darkness, further, further, something about the angles and the edges in this specific space speaking to him. He had an agility in here, a coordination in here, like he'd been here before. His fingers toyed with more cashmere until they felt the brush of expensive leather. Black leather. Dior. A belt.
Not a belt. The belt.
The one he had swung from, in the beams of his penthouse.
If this belt was what he thought it was, then he knew where he was - everything clicked now, the carpet beneath him, the corners around him. This was a walk in closet, one he knew very well. This was *his* closet, in *his* penthouse. How the hell was he back here? Was he alone?
None of that mattered but this: he had to get out.
'You're not alone.'
That was Erica's voice. That was Erica's laugh.
And Erica meant safety. Erica meant healing. Erica meant help. Erica was bandages and kindness and miracles and hands.
She laughed again. It carved out of her mouth and into the air.
His stomach dropped.

A switch was flicked, and the lights came on. This *was* his walk in closet. He recognised the racks of the shoes, the perfect charcoal colour he had picked out for the design. It used to be neater than this - there was the sense it had been touched, stretched, by somebody else.
'Myles,' Erica moved into the light, kicking a dressing gown as she went. Her lips were painted black.
'Erica! Erica … is this … are we … are we in London?'
'Welcome home.' She smiled. 'I guess you're wondering what you're doing, in your old closet. I knew you wouldn't come if I asked you, so I bought you here. I've learnt a lot of things about you recently. Things you didn't even know about yourself.'
He felt a trembling rumble in his body, but he couldn't bring himself to answer to it, to let even more dread in. He cocked back his head and calmly listened. What had he done now?

'Let's start with … the building you jumped from,' she smiled. 'The library of the concrete, what was it?'
'The Bishopsgate Library,' he mumbled.
'Ah yes, that's it, Bishopsgate. A few things you never told me about it – how central it was, how it's surrounded by residential flats.'
'What's that got to do with anything?'
'Well, a lot of people can see it, can see you. And you say it was about 9am when you jumped – not exactly a very nice thing for them to wake up to. Do you know if any of them saw you?'
'No. I don't think so.'
'Right, because if they saw you, someone would have probably tried to stop you. Or maybe call the police. But you know what the world is like these days, what with the internet, the shock factor, the desire for clicks, for views. Someone could have filmed you. I know you haven't been on the internet since the day you killed Rose – ' It was the first time she'd said those words, so clearly and casually, her cold voice dipping its finger into the butter of his brain. 'Because you've been too scared, about who's looking for you, about what they're saying about you. But the other day, I did. Guess what I googled.'
She pulled her phone out of her pocket, and flipped it open. She opened it up, and her fingers made pretty little sounds as she typed into the search engine 'Man jumps off Bishopsgate Library, February 13th.'
Sure enough, a video came up on the page, primed and plump, ready to be watched.
Erica clicked on it, pausing it just as the box opened up. But it was too late – Piles recognised the sounds, the specific wind that had blown that day, each car that had gone by, the birds that had sung to him. He was back in the most taunting, bittersweet hour of his life, back in the lengthy, tantric suicide unique to him.

Erica clicked play.
The video was shot from a lowish angle, of somebody maybe on the second floor of the building opposite. Sure enough, like a star on top of a Christmas Tree, it was him up there. Dillying, dallying, pacing back and forth, flirting coyly with the edge. It was infuriating even to watch – *just do it*, his mystery videographer must have been thinking. He was dithering like an old lady trying to choose between lavender and patchouli perfume. He looked watery up there, a man who wasn't made of the metal to launch him over the edge.
The video swayed between him and the ground, the people walking by, oblivious to the burden above them.
And then something happened on the screen that made Myles want to Jump right there and then. It made him hate himself so much he could have launched himself to the ground with such force he would go right through. Even though he was sitting on carpet, just falling a few inches would have made a right old mess of himself.
It was Taylor. For the first time, he saw her. The long blonde hair, the popular girl swagger, the tight jeans. Walking down the street. On her phone. Just like her father said.
A girl walks down the street. Spring in her step, hope in her heart.
His shadow waited, ten feet away, to spoon her into it. And she didn't realise that thirty feet above her, it was all about to be over. Everything she wanted and waited to do, was about to come to an end. Thirty feet above her, where the sky could fall on her. Everything is too heavy when your heart is that light.
Walk slower, he willed as his eyes welled. *Or walk faster. Or stop. Or turn around. Slow down, speed up, just get out my way,* he begged.
He launched forward in his seat and hit pause.
'Don't make me watch this,' he begged Erica. And then stronger, 'I'm not going to watch this.'
'What, watch the moment you crushed a girl to death?' Again, that casual coldness in her voice. The words slipping out like it was all a joke. 'You said yourself you never had to face the consequences of that day. Don't you at least owe her this? Shouldn't you at least appreciate how she,' her voice twisted with sarcasm. ' "Cushioned your fall?" '
Piles sat back. He looked at the girl on the screen. Whole, solid, functioning. And he knew in a few seconds on the screen it would be *him* that revealed all the bits that made her like that; all the blots of tissue and the bundles of nerves, wrung out on the pavement. Taylor was a girl whose looks were so important to her – perhaps Myles duty had been to reveal to everyone if her beauty was internal too. Perhaps that's what she got, for caring more about what was on the outside than the inside; she got burst open so everyone could see how she really looked. She probably had lovely pink kidneys.
Erica pressed play and the whole room gulped.

Another step. Taylor stopped and half-spun, leaning into her phone with laughter, the kind you do when you want people to know what a good time you're having. Myles was backing up, ready for the jump.
Pulses popped up all over him, wings of insects fluttering in his shoulder blades and ears. This was the kind of thing people were trained for years to be able to watch. How did Erica look so calm?
Another step.
And then big, fat, hairy Myles came running over the edge, and jumped.

The first thing he noticed was how wide his leap had been. An overarching soar over the edge, that seemed wider than the pavement.
The second thing was that Taylor had not taken another step.
The third thing was that people noticed him falling. Not **landing**, *falling*. There were screams and a clearing and a definite switch in *everyone's* attention, to the thing coming out of the sky.
Erica hit pause again, with an urgency to stop it at the right moment, and captured a freeze frame of him flying in mid air.
His body was a grey blur on the screen. He was five feet from the ground, **nothing beneath him.** And Taylor, Taylor was still five feet **away from him.**
Erica was smiling at him. 'When you described this to me, you said you landed with a 'CRACK'. If your fall had been cushioned, wouldn't you have gone 'Splat'? A sound a little softer, something with a little more … *give*?'
Myles was frozen to the spot. His eyes flickered from her lips to her finger. She understood he didn't want to wait any longer, and she pressed play for the final time, to watch him fall.
His grey body.
February's grey air.
The grey pavement.
There was no fourth element, nothing else.
It went … one … two … three …
His body in the air …
The air carrying his body …
And then his body kissed the pavement.
Unprotected, raw dog, no sandwich in the filling, no butter on the bread. **It was the pavement, it had always been the pavement.**
Bones + air + pavement = Jump.
And Taylor was still five feet away.
He had not landed on her.
She did, however, start to scream with shock; the whole hearted, functional scream of a young girl still alive.
Beneath him, beneath the closet, beneath the video, the bass of the music brewed. The carpet vibrated on its request. Myles had never known anybody in his building to throw a party like this, one that could be heard from up here.

Erica launched her face into his, her hands on either side of his knees. Was that love in her eyes?

'Do you see what I'm seeing? Do you? You – didn't – land – on – her. On anyone. She was just *there*. She's the one who calls the ambulance, because she had her phone, see. In a few minutes you see her talking to them, and she gives them her details. I imagine that's where somebody got the idea you might have seen her, that it would be more realistic if they built the story around her.'

'The story?'

'Of Taylor. I mean what even is her real name? Or Doctor Harrison's. The trick had to be believable …'

'But why?'

'Keep listening to me. There's more.'

A champagne cork was heard popping from below. Followed by an army of others, bulleting the building below them.

Erica wandered to a rack of his designer shirts, running her hand along the silk. They had been rearranged, no longer ranked by colour. 'When I found this out I thought you might have lied to me, but then I saw how quickly you took the pills last night and I knew, someone actually convinced you you did this. Stay calm, because it'd be ironic if all this shock made your heart give out now. Here, have some water.'

She passed him a bottle and he took it, to squeeze instead of to sip. 'What's going on?'

'When I realised Taylor was just a story you'd been told, I realised someone must have had a reason to tell you that story. To convince you of something that would make you want to vanish. And if they could tell you a story like that, what else could they tell you?' She circled the island in the middle of the closet, her eyes stopping to scour the Rolex watches, and the hush of quiet luxury suede they were embedded into. She nodded, things making sense to her too.

'So I decided to look into it. Being an infamous, escaped captive gets you a lot of connections, a lot of people that are fascinated by you and will do anything to be in your orbit. At first I was going to talk to the detective on my case, but then I realised nobody would do the trick like the internet sleuths who've been contacting me. Trust me, Myles, nobody can pull off what they can - give them a few more clues and they probably would have tracked me down in that dungeon. They wish they could have. They'd have loved to have saved the day. So I gave them a task,' She held up her phone again. 'A task to do some hacking. And they did.'

She paused for a second to look at Myles, to check that he was still with her.

'I'm going to read you some of the screenshots they sent to me. It would take us weeks to get through all of them, but here are the highlights. These are Whatsapp messages that were sent between a man and a woman, from last December to this February. You ready?'

Myles nodded. Erica cleared her throat and began to read -

' "His mother was his only real friend ... nobody will notice if he disappears. They won't even visit if he gets sectioned." ' Her throat filled up for a second, but she brushed over it. ' "Did you get it?" "Yes." "How does it work again?" "It's like a stronger version of rohypnol." ' Myles heart thumped as Erica continued. ' "Listen, he deserves this. He takes credit for everything I've achieved, even though he doesn't even know what field I work in: prosthetics not pyrotechnics. He's never respected me." "You're right; I'm just a trophy to him." ... "Oh my god baby, you did it!" "Yep. Ring on my finger and he's signing the documents tomorrow. I'm gonna be his next of kin - inherit everything in the event of death, serious illness, serious accident, body not found or incarceration." "Baby, we're ready to go. You ready to do it? On Sunday like we promised?" "Of course. And one thing, baby ... we should do it on his boat." ' With triumph, Erica put the phone down, simultaneously pulling open a drawer where he used to keep his ties in the closet. From it, she pulled a thick wedge of paper. 'And you did sign the documents, didn't you?' She passed the envelope to Myles, hoping the paper would make it real. 'Signing everything over to her. The only thing left was to get you out of the way.' Her face paled as she saw the trauma she was unleashing. 'Myles, drink your water.' It was easier to ignore what was going on in his body. He unscrewed the water obediently, and drank.
She tapped on the phone quickly, before turning around to expose the screen to him. Another screenshot loomed before him, his eyes widening as he saw the name at the bottom. 'This is a receipt for a drug that I can't pronounce, but one quick Google and I learnt it's used to cause blackouts after severe injury - blackouts that hit you in an instant. It's orally administered, meaning it can be stirred into your coffee, into your soup, into anything you can consume. Anyone can get it to you, as long as they're happy to cook for you. And, guess what? It feels like a memory gap when you wake up.' She pulled up another photo. An order for a pharmacy's worth of something flashed at him, green. 'But *this* drug. This one's basically a steroid. The kind that makes you angry. Now this can induce a hormonal rage so intense ... it can cause blackouts.' Her imp's eyes flashed, daring him to process this. 'But back to the screenshots,' She brushed through the phone again; Myles saw the glimpse of an icon he might recognise, but she turned the screen back to herself too quickly for him to check. ' "We've found him. A great actor, you should have seen his audition. He's willing to do it for 500." ' Triumphantly, Erica flipped the phone to him again. He was looking at a professional headshot, of the sinister man he had come to know as Dr Harrison; who was now, presumably, actually an actor called Ian.
The closet throbbed with the ever increasing music. More champagne corks became bullets. Now there was a wave of laughter, and that's when Myles realised this had to be a joke. But before he could interrupt her, Erica continued. 'I don't know if he was actually going to hurt you or not, if he was going to do the things he said he would to you. Probably not, I hope not.' She pressed her

fingers into the suede, frustrated all of a sudden. 'I've looked for a long, long time for the missing piece. The nurse. Valentina, you said her name was? I thought she must have been an actress too. I was hoping she could explain what was going to happen to you if you hadn't taken her up on her offer and run away, but, when it comes to Valentina, there's no paper trail. No record of anyone working at the hospital with that description either. It seems like you weren't meant to run away. You were going to be sectioned. And that's what everyone at this party thinks has happened to you.'

She took a breath, stopping for a second, knowing that one more ingredient and this brew would burn. She looked at Myles to see how he was handling it, and was surprised by the anger that was waiting on his face.

'Erica. Why are you doing this? Why are you joking, why are you lying, why are you teasing me like this? Why are you giving me this gimp's glimpse of what my life could be if I hadn't killed her?'

'I'm not!' As surprised as he was angry. 'Listen to me -'

'No, you listen to *me.* Erica, I saw her body. Did I not tell you this? I saw her blackberry blood bleed across my deck that night. I saw the colour she went, I saw the angles her body was bent at, I saw the chest that didn't move and would never move again. I saw it, I saw it, and I know what I've done!'

'But did you touch it?' Playful. Coy. Brutal.

'*What*?'

Erica sighed languidly and began scrolling the phone again, her thumb dancing speedily to its destination. 'You weren't listening, were you? There was a clue in one of the screenshots. This one - ' She cleared her throat and read out loud. ' "*Prosthetics not pyrotechnics.*" He was working in the *prosthetics* department of the arthouse horror film. And she was in the make up department, remember. They must have had access to all kinds of trickery.'

Beneath the door to the closet, dry ice oozed. A dark and dirty bass punctuated Erica's every line.

'See, if you'd touched it, you would have found out what her skin was made of. Now, where is it ... I'm sure I saw it earlier ...' Erica marched across to another rack of clothes and for the first time Myles let it register that there were dresses hanging in his closet now. Some sequinned, some satin, most of them in red.

'Ah yes,' Erica kicked the dresses apart, letting them spray. 'Here it is.' Her foot fumbled into the back of the wardrobe, bringing something loose. 'This is the one.'

There was a doughy, frumpy sound, and then something was sucked forward, falling with an unctious thwack onto the carpet.

What fell was something Myles never could have imagined. In all his wildest dreams and nightmares, he never could have imagined.

It was Rose's dead body. The blood glueing her hair down. The white night dress ridden up around her waist. The ghostly gaze lying over her eyes.

He screamed, his vocals blending into the base, as he scrambled deeper into the closet he knew so well, the closet he couldn't ever escape. This was Hell, he'd been dragged to Hell, and this was not Erica but the Devil.
'No, no, no! What is this, get it out of here, get me out of here, what, what, what have you DONE!'
'Myles. Myles. Myles. Look. Look. *Think.*'
'No, no, no, get me out, get it out, MAKE IT END!'
'Myles. Think. *It's been months.*'
She was right, it had been months, and, and, and - he fought for the words, for the feeling, for the logic, for the space - dead bodies didn't look like that. But Rose was so perfect that she did.
Exasperated, Erica kicked the body towards him. It made the same frumpy sound, too light, too lax, and the logic fought for Myles again: that it wasn't moving the way a body, dead or alive, would.
'Touch it. Just once. This is the last thing I'll ever ask you to touch. Just touch it.'
It was only a few inches away, the perfectly preserved Rose. Just enough logic, just enough hope, allowed Myles to press his finger into it.
Erica sighed with relief. 'See? See?'
It did not feel like a body.
It was not a body.
This was a doll.
A lifesize doll. A waxwork. A Barbie.
And I'm gonna put that Barbie in a blender, I'm gonna watch that Barbie burn, I'm gonna make that Barbie blister, I'm gonna break that Barbie, I'll put that bubbling Barbie in a broth and now I'll watch her brew.
Erica was turning the doll over, explaining how it worked, casually confident, ignoring the expressions running across Myle's face as he contended with the thoughts that were summoned now he knew, or was beginning to know, what Rose had done to him.
'A hole made here and here and here.'
'To pump the fake blood.'
'A tube to funnel it through.'
'They even built in eyelids. You can even shut the eyes.'
'Extremely lifelike, but the texture feels nothing like a body.'
'Horse hair for the wig, I think. You can see where they glued it to the scalp.'
'That's why he offered to deal with it. So you couldn't touch her.'
Erica was whispering in his ear. 'It makes sense. You 'blacked out' when you did it. Jack was the one who 'buried' her. She was never reported missing because she was right here. No mob ever came after you because there was nothing to come for - no crime was committed.' Everything oozed into him, reality gnashed through him, his teeth grew teeth. 'They gaslit you. You never had dissociative fugue, not until they started drugging you. That's why you

never had one in Hawaii. They created your condition, and they took advantage of your bereavement.'

Myles pushed her off. 'No, no, no - *this* is the trick! You've faked the body, you've faked the screenshots, the documents! You're the one gaslighting me, reinventing me! I DID MURDER HER! I DO OWE HER! I AM THE KILLER!'

Erica leaned back languidly. She'd been predicting this. 'Could be,' she shrugged. 'Don't blame you for being suspicious. I don't expect you to have a strong sense of trust any more.' She held out her hand. 'But you'd like to find out for sure, wouldn't you?' She pulled him to his feet. 'Come with me.'

Mind mashing, Myles accepted her hand and let her lead him, moving through his closet like she owned it. She kicked it open - sure enough, she was correct, the party *was* being held in his penthouse. Everything was an assault to his eyes and an even bigger assault to his memory - Erica and him were standing in his bedroom, empty but it had been used, the bed not made from earlier that day. Takeaway containers peppered the bed - he'd never eaten in his room.

Now out of the closet, the music swallowed them, called for them, a hypnotic base begging them to enter its cult. All the action was going on beyond the bedroom door.

Erica oozed through the room, owning every inch of it, as if she'd been here before, and kicked open his bedroom door. They stepped out onto the gallery that gave them the perfect view of the penthouse: an atrium surrounding an open plan space made entirely of frosted glass. A glass heart cracked open, was how the design team had described their vision.

The only thing different than the day he had tried to die in here, was that he was not alone. It was full of people; from those cavorting on the steps to those swinging from the beams, to those chopping lines on the counter and those surrounding the DJ booth, desperate for the next puff of dry ice or blast of lasers; like ants, they partied, filling his space. But they hadn't noticed him yet.

'Nice taste, Myles,' she whispered. 'More chic than I imagined. Come.'

He descended the spiral staircase, on shaky legs. Every step felt like a jump. Every image was a whip to his eyes - the pop art he'd chosen for the walls, the marble he'd had imported for the counter, the ultra modern kitchen with every high tech appliance installed. All of it coming back to him, calling to him, the shock of feeling it could belong to him, that he hadn't had to give it all up.

Erica's finger stroked the centre of his hand as she lead him down, through the froth of people enjoying his penthouse.

As they entered the crowd, something subtle happened, a parting within the people. It wasn't enough to turn the party into a hunt - there were not quite enough people here that Myles knew, not enough from his old life, to cause complete chaos. But there were just enough to stir an unease, to blend into the mixture of neon, strobe, laser and sound, a rumour. A rumour that would shake the walls even more than the bass could.

They took the last step and saw it at the same time it saw them. For that was all he was, an It. Ian The Actor, formerly known as Dr Harrison. He was sitting on a table, halfway to lighting a blunt, when all the light left his eyes. His fingers sizzling with shame, the blunt slipped from his lips.

'Don't even give him the time.' Erica whispered. 'Keep going. I want to show you something.'

As they moved into the depths of the dance floor, Myles noted what had been done with his place. He was even impressed with some of the choices - ice sculptures for vodka to drizzle down, giant ice cube podiums for the guests to groove on, the sunken living room now transformed into a dedicated hookah lounge, so even more smoke could billow and blossom through the room, making tonight even more obscured, even more surreal. There were giant champagne bottles stacked in buckets of glitter, and a parade of models body painted to look like fawns - he only knew one person who could body paint with that kind of skill. Or did he, did he, maybe that was wishful thinking. There was a monochrome chess board plastered across the centre, and that chess board had become the dance floor.

And then there was the booth.

The booth in which Jack danced. Shirt open, cigar in his lips, star-shaped sunglasses falling across his eyes. He was surrounded by people. And oh, how he danced, oh how he laughed.

His arm was around someone. Or something. A petite blonde. She wiggled, then whooped as the song changed.

'That's *it*,' Erica hissed into the space, at the blonde. 'Go on, girl. Turn around.'

The DJ plunged the room into a shower of strobes, and Erica instructed the slender back of the shimmering blonde head again:

'Come on. Come on. *Turn around.*'

Right on cue, the blonde turned, spinning into Jack to look up at him with an indulgent beam.

JESUS.

No, not Jesus, he died for our sins.

But you know who was still alive? Rose.

Rose.

He saw her through the smoke.

Not a Violet or a Daisy or a Poppy. But a Rose.

Alive and arrogant with life. He'd never realised how *full* she was. Look at those big bones, keeping her up, keeping her dancing, keeping her alive. He'd never realised how much flesh she had, and how beige that flesh was

Heart beating, blood pumping, moving, hearing, seeing, smelling, living in all the ways she'd pretended she wasn't.

'They had nothing. They are nothing. So they came for your money.'

He couldn't stop watching her. She twirled into Jack's arms now, leaning back with a lazy smile, big eyes fixed up on him.

Rose. His ghost. His corpse. His perfect dead girl.
Erica felt his hand slip from hers. She turned around to see Myles – but he wasn't there, at least not in her eye line. He had fallen to a heap on the ground, as it had finally hit him.
He was innocent.

Chapter Twenty

And what was once a brain so burning and broken, scattered with shards of glass and mottled in white yeast … slowly, slowly, all across the world, became a brain unfurled, open and cleansed in gasps of creamy, cool air, brushing amongst the barley, a brain basking in the porridge that once boiled it, a brain not too hot, not too cold, but just right..

And this brain that had gorged itself on every nightmare til it had become obese with fear, became a brain so gooey, and a brain so open, until there was nothing but relief, nothing but refreshment, and nothing, nothing but space.

The brain buckled and bucked behind Myle's eyes, with such joyful violence it popped out tears, tears that came out as weapons, came out like bullets – hurdled into the world like rocks used to stone a witch, collaborating together to *release everything, release it all, release him.*

And for the first time in so many days, Myles had something beginning with F. He had a future. A future without the flagellation.

He almost collapsed when he remembered just how many things you can do with your LIFE, choice dissolving into choice osmosing into options - he could be a pop star, an athlete, he could go on reality TV - he could show the world who he was, stand up straight and shout, 'I'm Myles, I'm Myles, I'm Myles, and there's nothing you can do about it, and I don't have to hide no more.'

He could fill every day with pleasure, party, play, dance and if he ever from this moment on *chose to sleep* – you had his permission to douse him in cold water or, for he would never sleep again til he'd experienced every emotion, everything life had to offer – and then and only then, when his feet were blistered from a night all up dancing, when he'd lost his voice from laughing, when he'd forgotten what time was because all he did was marry the moment, then and only then could he let sleep in, and he could tell – he was going to *sleep good.*

How many times can one man melt? Just how many times can he turn to liquid in one moment? He thawed sixty times a second, every time he realised anew that he was innocent.

He looked across the room again, just to check that the nightmare was over.

Rose.

I thought I buried you once. Your mouth should be still, your eyes should be closed. You're meant to be lying flat, in something white, not that tight black bodycon thing. Your arms should be folded across your chest. You should be ten feet deep.

People should be praying for you.

Maybe they will be. By the time I'm done with you.

Chapter Twenty One

Well.
This called for a celebration. Did it deserve a countdown?
Erica and Myles held hands, and they ran towards the booth. Now the people parted - now all of a sudden they remembered him.
'Myles!'
'Is that Myles?'
Make confetti out of her.
Turn her blood into streamers.
Pop her like a balloon.
Someone shouted Myles loud enough that the booth heard. Sharp, Rose turned.
Blow her out for good.
Champagne blood, sequin bone.
Cutting into cake, cutting into you.
Erica leaned on him. 'Yes!!! Champagne bath!'
Rose's eyes flashed to Erica. She gripped Jack's arm. She'd seen him. More champagne was passed to her.
Stiletto's flying through the air, piercing what they find.
Careful the chandelier don't fall on you.
Feathers from your boa, hair from your head.
A bottle was passed to Myles. He popped it seamlessly - still got it - turning the world golden, because he was so *goddamn innocent.*
Through the drunken spell, people were starting to recognise him, confusion on their faces; wasn't he in a coma? Out of the corner of his eye he could see Erica grabbing people, pulling their ears to her lips, and explaining, shouting, accusing, her words getting whipped up in their inebriation. There would be time for that later, for the explaining, for the undoing.
Right now, all he wanted was to look those two cretins in the eye.
A cocktail of sorry and shame. Sip, sip.
All the best parties have one thing.
A piñata.
Let's turn her into a piñata.
Jack and Rose. Rose and Jack. They were shrinking by the second, but he was ten feet tall. Through the blur of inebriation and hedonism, Erica's words were getting through; his old friends were turning, from Rose and to him, gradually starting to process how, why, he was there.
Sparklers in their eyes.
Fireworks down their throat.
Even before it made sense to Myles, it made sense to them. 'Jack wanted his money!' Erica screamed again. The crowd parted, swelled, swilled around him, everyone watching what he'd do next. He grew another three feet tall.
He started walking up to Jack and Rose, aware of Erica watching. He got close.

Pinata. Hit them, split them and see what comes pouring out.
Word had whipped around the dancefloor, each lie a laceration, spiking into the blurred brains of the drunken, sunken, confused people. Myles King wasn't in a coma. Myles King had never been in a coma. Myles King had been tricked. And Myles King had a reason to be very, very cross.
Sparklers in their eyes. Fireworks down their throats.
Rose looked him in the eye. Blonde ringlets, almond eyes, nothing had changed, except she dripped with jewels now. She slammed her hand to the side, spilling other people's drinks as she did.
Myles laced through the crowd, making his way to the booth. Every moment they peeled apart more tenderly, letting him pass. As he looked around, he saw not one of his old acquaintances had taken their eyes off him - stunned at his stealth, at his return - and he realised with glee that it was *him,* not Rose, who was the ghost. And what a grisly, gritty ghost he was going to be.
Erica's hand ran down his back. 'It's ok,' she said. 'You got this. *Revenge.*'
Revenge. Revenge. Myles couldn't believe how everything had flipped, how the alphabet went backwards - how on earth could he now be the one who was owed a revenge? That was a word he'd only imagined coming to claim him, to be inflicted on him, a hundred horrific daydreams about how it would be done. After all, there was nothing more creative than revenge.
Tonight, a black butter would be churned. Churned out of Jack and Rose.
Where did he even start?
Heads, shoulders, knees and toes, knees and toes. Would he start with the body, like a surgeon?
Would he start with the mind, like a psychologist?
Would he start with the soul, like a Devil? After all, look what they'd done to *his* soul.
Veet in your conditioner. Itching powder in your bed. Laxative in your coffee. Sugar in your slimming pills. Rust in your razor. Glue in your toothpaste. Mould in your mouthwash. Bleach in your morning milk. Corrosives in your contacts. Just what oh what creepy, cheeky revenge would they choose to inflict on Jack and Rose?
He had reached the booth, and now an old friend pulled him up. At the same time, an old friend hit the back of Jack's head, docking him at the neck and winking at Myles. Oh, they were gonna wish they hadn't invited so many guests. Erica ran her hand down his back and watched him take his place up there.
Finally on their level. No longer below them, stitched into the fibres of the carpet they stepped on. *Go on baby. Give them Hell.*
Up there, he glowed.
All the colour had come back to his face. He no longer stood with a stoop. He no longer winced every time he swallowed. He no longer had to carry the

ceiling, or the sky. The permanent gurn that had lived in his body had finally up and left. At last, his veins weren't flowing the wrong way.
She'd wanted this for him. As much as she wanted it for herself - she'd wanted to do it for her man.
The crowd was pulsing behind her - the few people who hadn't been on the dancefloor had made their way to it now, wrestling for space at the altar of the annihilation of Jack and Rose. The rumours had spread but still they gawped, still they couldn't believe Myles had returned. Her lips still lacquered black, she whispered in more ears, spreading the information, filling the room with the truth of what they'd done.
'I - I needed money.' He was nothing at all. He was so simple. He was so basic. He was a sponge in the shower.
'Jack,' Myles said. Ooh, that voice. That confidence again.
Jack, unlike Rose, believed he could find the words. 'Mate -' Already he'd chosen the wrong word, the worst one. The crowd booed. 'We looked for you - '
Erica watched him wither, realising what it was to be the one who deserved no empathy, no restraint, no relief.
Grinning coldly, Myles instructed him. 'Stand on one leg.'
'What?'
'Obey him! Do it!' The crowd jeered.
Jack found himself on one leg, bobbing as though he was still on the boat.
'Do a hop.' Myles instructed.
An eternal cringe pressed down on Jack, and he hopped into it.
'Now do a spin.'
For him, he spun.
'Sit on the floor.'
For him, he sat.
'On your knees.'
For him, he knelt.
'Now spit.'
For him, he spat.
'Now lick it up.'
Oh yes, Erica's heart sung as she watched, *Very good. Humiliation is a healthy revenge.*
'Stand up.'
For him, he stood.
'Put your hand on your head.'
For him, he did.
'Pat your stomach. Big boy.'
For him, he pat.
'Faster.'
For him, he sped.
'Faster. Go on, Big Chin Betty.'

Oh how the crowd crackled.
'Can't you go faster?'
Faster, faster, faster, oh how the crowd loved it.
'Now slap Rose.'
Dizzy, too dizzy, Jack spun to a stop, begging Myles with his eyes but his hand already rearing backwards, building momentum. Rose closed her eyes and braced herself.
'Jack!' Faux outrage fed Myle's throat as he launched between them. 'What are you doing? How could you? You weren't about to hit a *woman*, were you?'
Just like that, Jack became nothing, spiralling with space. In one move, Myles showed the whole room but more importantly his whole soul, he was a million times the man Jack ever was.
Now he turned his attention to Rose.
And Erica couldn't help the fact she was angry Jack hadn't hit her. She'd wanted to see her bleed.
'Hey, dead girl.' He was speaking to her now, his words tracing her perfect pout. 'I thought I buried you once.'
Erica felt something strange go over her bones. *I did this for us.*
Was the 'us' they had created already over, now he was about to look into the eyes of Rose? His Rose?
His eyes were bright, but now they were glowing a little more, glowing a little too much.
I dug her up. I did this. Because he had to know. But still ... I made her real. But his eyes are glowing in a way they shouldn't be after this kind of shock.
Rose knew him well, and she knew better than to apologise. She let her eyes widen, ready to take whatever words would come.
And then she cried the most beautiful, delicate of tears.
Oh god. Oh god. What have I done?
Why the fuck did I bring her back?
Rose was really crying now. Erica was willing her nipples to disappear - they were too erect, too obvious in her dress in this light. Any sharper and Myles would forgive her.
Oh god.
How is this happening?
She was the most stunning crier, the kind they could write songs about - she made tears into pearls, made the snail trail of a tear an elixir, made water into liquid crystal. Her eyes were perfect and they perfected crying now, made anguish into an art, quenched a thirst that all other liquid had failed to quench.
Oh my god. Oh my god.
What if he chooses her?
The whole room seemed to have gone silent, watching her cry, her sobs matching the crescendo of the music. Just like the best and deepest of house could, her crying could take the room to another plane.

I did this. I dug her up. I rose her up out of the ground.
Not this. Not like this. Not for this. Anything but this.
A nightmare blasted like plaster into Erica's mind, as the impossible happened - Myles was reaching for Rose's hand.
How could she? How could he? How could she come out on top, now she'd exposed all the dark dust inside of her?
I should have left her in his mind. I should have left her with the worms.
Rose took it, curled it, the whole room soothed with the gesture. The DJ turned the room purple, a hail storm of colours now coming up the glass, all of London streaking the skyline. You could hang it in a gallery - the girl who cried and the man who lost his mind.
'Rose,' the room hung on his every word. 'I want to thank you.'
No. No. NOT LIKE THIS.
Why did I bring her back to him?
Rose wiped her tears tenderly, brushing them from the ooze of her lips. Erica would set those lips on fire.
'In fact, I *have* to thank you.' He pulled her body towards him. Her pout sparkled. Who could blame him if he kissed her now? 'If you hadn't done what you'd done to me, I would have stayed the same. I never would have changed. And I never would have met this girl. Erica. I never would have met Erica. And she never would have rocked my world.'
He dropped Rose's hand. Suddenly her tears became snuffles, embarrassing, immature.
'I didn't know what happiness was until I met her. Didn't know what fun was. Didn't know what lust was. Trust me, if you knew what she is … you'd understand. I'd take all that agony, all over again, everything you did to me I'd let you do twice … if it would lead me to her.'
Oh my god he's looking at me. Oh my god he's holding out his hand.
'Erica is worth everything. Erica *is* everything.'
Oh my god. My man.
'So thank you, Rose, for bringing me to her.'
Erica took her hand and now she was pulled up onto the booth too. The drunken crowd swilled, delighted to look at two women so perfect; one evil, one ethereal.
Within a split second, she was being bent back. The crowd roared up the walls as they cheered at the kiss.
Myles flipped her back up again, spinning her in his arms. In the wild way that only a party can deliver, hedonism and helium, Erica found herself wrapping her legs around him
Erica's pupils dilated. 'Oh god … Myles, I thought you were going to choose her.'
'Choose *her*?' He was genuinely baffled. 'Erica, look at her. Look how … normal she is. Then look at you.'

Erica giggled. Burn baby burn. She looked over his shoulder to watch what his humiliation was doing to Rose; soak, douse, drench. A soggy Rose indeed. She was pleased to see her just standing there, taking it.

She bit Myles ear. 'So what are you gonna do to her? What you gonna do about her?'

Myles nodded into her eyes.

He let her slide down his body, and then addressed the captivated cognac crowd. 'Now you all know what Rose and Jack have done. What they have done, and what they have given me: Erica.

And that's why I will not lay a hand on them. I will not sue them. I will not pursue them. Rose and Jack, you are free to go.'

Brash and brazen, the crowd booed with confusion.

'I'm serious.' Suddenly he'd ripped his shirt in two. 'I know what it is to suffer. I know about what it's like in the depths.' He threw out his arms as though trying to create space for all the thoughts that he needed to process. 'Why would I spend a second doing that to anyone else?' The decision licked through him, impossibly liberating, the words choosing him before he could choose anything else. 'Why would I waste my time bringing anyone down? Man, I'm finally free; all I wanna do is feel *good*!'

Erica was in front of him. 'Wait, baby, no. What are you doing? You can't just let them get away with it.'

He ran his hand down her cheek. 'Oh but I can. Cos I can do whatever I want.' As casually as his next breath, he pushed Jack off the booth, into the crowd that wouldn't catch him. 'And all I wanna do is feel good.'

Erica turned just in time to see Rose scampering off the platform and joining Jack. She reached for his hand but he didn't take it. Desperate, they split, trying to make their way through the guests who now despised them. Champagne was poured over her head, glueing her hair down like she'd wanted her blood to do to her doll.

'You hear me?' Myles said. He was processing it properly now: his decision to forgive. To flaunt forgiveness in the face of fun. 'No matter what we've done, we never deserve to suffer.' Jack was jostled by the crowd, hitting the ground. Myles ignored it, too focused on whipping up the room. 'All we deserve to feel is good! All we deserve to do is dance! All we should ever, ever feel is freedom, so let's feel it!'

A glass was smashed. Rose was disappearing from view. Myles was too busy in his speech to notice Erica jumping down onto the dance floor.

Small and agile enough, she managed to lace her way through the thriving, throbbing bodies; she sailed on the slick of their sweat. This may be a party but for her, it was a hunt. Prey for me.

She was all elbows and angles, guests slipping their hands around her waist, pretending to dance with others, anything to make it easy to get through.

She reached the ripples of blonde hair just as it was about to get out of the mass, the mass that was two twists away from becoming a mob. The only way to reach her was to grab a tendril of that hair and pull her back in.

Rose screamed as Erica seized her, but nobody heard or nobody cared. She whipped around to see who was holding her hair, and Erica let go - no hands here - then perfectly coordinated pressing her up against the wall. *Let's show her real terror.*

'Listen to me, Rose. Or do you prefer bitch?' She hissed through her teeth, watching the imp's eyes widen. 'I know what you are. You're the girl who cried death, now I hope you live forever. And I just might be able to make that happen for you,' Her lips pressed into her ear. Her pout was not as wide or as juicy as Rose's, but oh what she could do with the words that came out of it.

'I'm a healer. I can heal people. I can bring them back. And maybe, just maybe, I can make them last.' Rose was shaking beneath her, her sternum straining, her neck twisting so as not to hear. 'If I made you last, where'd you like me to put you? Inside a tank? All alone? And what if I filled that tank with oil? What if I filled that tank with venom? What if I made *that* your forever?' She laughed.

'You'll be the last person in the world. You'll be so damn lonely. You're gonna age so damn fast. And you're gonna look so fucking old. No one's gonna touch you but you'll live, girl, you'll live as you do now, as you let a man break on the promise of your death - now you'll live, so go on girl, breathe, breathe, breathe, all the air in the world, breathe with what's left of you, breathe until you break, breathe, breathe, *breathe for me.*' Now, at last, Rose screamed a real scream and she cried real tears. She ripped herself from Erica's arms but not before Erica's nails drew real blood - only then, finally, did she let her go.

Calm now, she made her way back to the booth.

Someone had thrust a mic into Myle's hands.

His voice drowned out the music now. The DJ saluted him as he spoke.

'Guess I'm a murderer after all.'

Erica's teeth chattered. '...What?'

The crowd echoed her, their energy splintering. 'What?'

Myles smirked. 'Cos I just killed those two with kindness, silly. And now … now I need you to kill me with something.'

Not knowing if he was serious, the crowd 'With what?'

Myles scooped Erica up. With one final gush of euphoria, he raised the mic to his lips.

'You're going to kill me with kinkiness.'

He unleashed a refreshing glee the room didn't know was possible. Myles raised his fist into the air as he felt them rouse for him, the main man, the party planner, just like they used to.

'Do this for me! Dance for me! On an icy night, up against a black sky, we will die on the dancefloor!

No abstinence! No celibacy! No responsibility! No modesty!

Nothing, nothing, nothing but VIBES.
Can you do that for me?'
His anarchic ants, his hedonistic hornets, his lairy loyal lotuses, looked up at him. Of course they would.
Now, at last, with the trash taken out: the party could begin.

Erica spun and spun and spun, light lace spilling out of her, she spun as the black night finally became a blue dawn, as the guests finally became only Myle's closest friends, hugging their pal with relief, and she kept spinning as even that crowd thinned, kept spinning even as the DJ packed away, kept spinning as the snow stopped falling, kept spinning as Big Ben chimed, and she was still spinning, when at last, it was only the two of them, in the penthouse they would now live in together.
And she wouldn't stop, or maybe she couldn't stop, and suddenly Myles was spinning too. And despite all the dizziness and the fizziness, he had to ask.
'Erica, Erica, wait, wait. *Stop.*'
With a pivot, with a ballerina's control, she at last came to a halt, her mouth perfectly pitched in an 'O' to inquire why: why they couldn't just keep dancing.
'I - I - there's something I need to know.'
She blinked up at him imploringly. 'Go ahead.'
He took a deep, desperate breath. He was about to do something every synapse in his body was telling him not to do. In fact, every person in the world would tell him not to do this. *Why upset yourself? Why ruin it for yourself? Ignorance is bliss. Stop, Myles. Don't ask the question.*
The air was raw inside him. 'I'm only gonna ask you this once.' He sighed. 'This is the only time I will ever say this.'
Her eyes glittered. 'Go on then.'
He had to close his eyes to do it, to get the words out. 'What happened tonight … it doesn't feel real. It doesn't feel right. It doesn't make sense in my body. It hasn't clicked into place - that I didn't actually kill her.
So I have to know, Erica, I have to ask … did you bring her back?'
Erica blinked, something like a splutter finding its way out of her lips. 'What? Babe, what?'
Myles pressed on, his eyes charcoal with intensity. 'Did I do it … and then did you take it away?
I know it sounds mad, I know it sounds crazy, but *you are crazy*, Erica. You're unreal, you're not of this Earth, I've seen you do things thought impossible before.
So … did you do this?'
Did you - did you - I can't believe I'm saying it but - *did you resurrect Rose*?'
At the risk of turning his catharsis carcinogenic, Myles forced himself to ask again.
'Did you give her back her life?

Or did you go back in time, and stop me from taking it?
And Taylor too? The blonde girl they told me I jumped on? Did you bring her back as well?
And then did you - you - you controlled them, *you altered them,* with voodoo or magic or science - you got inside their bodies and their minds and you warped reality and you made it so they were the ones who owed me something?
Erica, if you did it, tell me. I need to know.
Did you change the laws of time and space so *I could be innocent again*?'
Erica was like a hallucination, like a mirage, the way she came towards him with such a quiet, amused confidence, such a playful power dancing across her face.
She closed both her hands around his jaw to steady his face, to steer his eyes into hers as she answered him.
'Myles,' she said. 'I can only heal people. I can't resurrect people.' Her chest curved into his torso. She looked at the mad man who even now, after everything he'd been through, couldn't accept happiness, and she promised herself there and then she would change that for him. 'And if I *could* ... ' she pitched the words playfully ... 'You'd think I'd waste that resurrection on the one other woman that you might love?'
There it was. In every colour of the rainbow, there it was. The end of the nightmare. The last bit of doubt died in Myles, and he knew: Erica was telling him the truth.
Now she snaked even deeper into him, as though winding herself into his skin. 'You're not a murderer. Ooh, look,' she turned him towards the panoramic glass and pointed to the people on the ground, London's early risers now scurrying to start their day. She picked out a female jogger, ant size beneath them. 'Didn't murder her, did you?' Her finger danced to the security guard outside their building. 'Or him. Ooh, or him, or her, or her. Looks like you didn't murder anybody. Looks like you are *inn-o-cent.* As innocent as the rest of them, and now you can laugh like the rest of them, laugh a little harder because you're owed just a little bit more than everyone else, because of what was taken from you.' Her lips brushed his. 'The nightmare is over. The dream begins.'
He blinked, world whirling, world overwhelming, world washing him inside and out til he was clean again. 'You've given me my life back.'
Her eyes locked onto his. 'Yes. So *live,* Myles. Now let's live.'

Chapter Twenty Two

After that, life got good.
It was as rewarding as your country winning the world cup.
No. More.
It was scoring the winning goal for your country.
Nope. More.
It was being the goalie and getting your country to the final without conceding a signal goal *and* the final being won on penalties
Nah. Not even close. **MORE.**
It was as rewarding as being a regular bloke but you're drafted for the world cup last minute, and somehow you're the goalie in the final, and the game goes to penalties and you don't let a goal through but neither do the opposing team, so it's settled by sudden death, and eventually it's up to each goalie to take a penalty, and you as the goalie scores the only goal in the final, and *that's* what wins your country the world cup.
Nah. That was just the beginning of this feeling. **MORE.**
Ah screw it. There weren't words. This was beyond words. This was beyond sound. This was beyond feeling. This, this, **THIS.**
His guilt Rubix cubed into something so light an anorexic fairy would be jealous. And so she should be - flying had nothing on this feeling.
As you can see, life was so good that Myles didn't always know how to comprehend it. How to put it all back together again, that he was no longer 'a bad one'. And yet he couldn't leave the other 'bad ones' behind. All the other ones, the other ones who'd removed the mirrors from their house and the nails from their cuticles. Did he just forget them, now that he was lazily, luckily, lucidly innocent?
He would write in his diary, trying to understand it.
This is for all the other people who've had their lives stolen, who one minute were sipping warm tea then the next minute drowning in its sour milk. I'm sorry that it took me having my own life torn, tendon from cuticle, to notice you – and even then still took a while for me to care about you.
Even now, as I write these words, I wonder if it's because I'm afraid to say them out loud. After what happened to me I don't think I'm afraid of anything, but maybe I'm still afraid of you. Of being you.
Because it really could happen to anyone, and yet I only felt its icky urgency when it happened to me. Still everybody else divides themselves into victims and villains, can't stretch their empathy wide enough, beyond their acne and into you. Did they let you have one last smile before they removed your teeth?

Because if I wasn't bad, then neither are you. What if you are innocent too? You need to be wrapped up in pastry, embedded in the stickiest of iced buns. You need to be laid out in a warm, golden, crispy cinnamon roll, or protected in the most delectable and sweet Cherry Bakewell tart, dusted with the icing sugar of kindness and love

Flick back to a few days ago and I was right there with you – I know you wish you could be the one being kind. You used to be so great at comforting, you used to be so great at advice.

Don't think I have forgotten about you. I remember all the others who've had their lives stolen, in the brisk flip of a mistake – I went all the way there and only Erica brought me back.

For you, I'll live. And I guess I'll live a little for myself, too.

That week Myles threw himself a party. It wasn't his birthday but he christened it as his 69th, a joke he'd loved to make since school. That's what was emblazoned on the invitations and what hung in balloons from the ceiling. The number 69. Oh, how his friends had missed him. He forgave them all for not looking for him - there was too much laughing to do.

Four days later, he threw another party. The theme for this one was 'Adult Playground'. There were slides, ball pits, mazes and of course, games. A game was invented pretty quick; the girls had to throw hoops and the men's erections had to catch them. That was the normal part of the night - you wouldn't believe me if I told you about the other games they played.

The following Monday, he threw another soiree. The theme for this one was 'Under The Sea'. Now that he had all his money back from Jack, he was able to rent out the London aquarium. The bass thumped against the glass and the fish danced. Costumes were incredible, every girl a more beautiful mermaid than the last. He chose to paint his body blue.

The next night, he hosted a mystery tour. He stacked a bus with his wildest and most adventurous friends, and didn't tell them where they were going. It went on for three days. They scaled the breadth of the country and came back covered in mud and memories.

Of course, for all these parties, Erica was invited. Sometimes she was late, but she always came. Erica Ash, the one who had given him everything.

The only thing he didn't like about his new life was the question.

The question that Erica asked him, over and over again.

'So are you gonna hurt her?

Are you gonna harm her? Are you gonna hurt her? Are you gonna get her? And … can I watch?'

See, Erica didn't understand, nor did she respect, his forgiveness, his acceptance, of what Rose had done to him. Having not been in his position, she

couldn't understand the depths of despair and fear that being a 'perpetrator' had put him through, and now that he was out of it, he would never inflict that on somebody else, not even the person who'd done it to him.
But Erica didn't get it. And she didn't accept it. And she didn't like it.
She wanted to see a revenge in him, an anger in him, a brutal taste for retribution that danced on the tip of her tongue. Truth be told, she seemed to hate Rose more than him, and she relished in the vivid fantasies of what the two of them could do to her - knowing that Rose didn't deserve any better, knowing that she'd asked for it, knowing that any punishment was justice and would come without guilt. It was fair. It was right. She wanted to collect her love rival's tears, no matter how many times Myles told her there was no rivalry to speak of.
And every day she asked him the question, as though hoping his mind had changed. And Myles lived in fear that it would.
So he started to ask a question back - the only question he had ever seen make her uncomfortable. One evening, he'd seen her the Youtube app on her phone recommending her a video - it was an interview with the still revered Eli Jones, a simple but serious piece checking in on how he was adapting to his new life without sight.
So Myles had asked a simple question. An obvious one really.
'What about healing him?'
I mean, why not? It made perfect sense. Heal a man who had campaigned for everybody else to be healed too. Even though his values didn't align with Myles, Myles could respect the hard work and effort that had gone into his campaign, and it was certainly impressive that he was persevering with his own retreat despite the challenges he now faced.
But too quickly, an expression had appeared on her face that had never appeared before, Erica had snapped, 'No.'
And so now when she asked 'When are you gonna hurt her?'
He would respond, 'When are you gonna heal him?'
And back and forth they went, back and forth, tossing the question between each other like a fight. Neither one of them yielding first.
Bit by bit, they could feel the tension brewing. They could feel they were stirring, summoning, something neither of them wanted to summon. And yet neither of them could stop.
He was the butter. She was the knife.

Myles continued to throw his parties, unleashing all the ideas he hadn't been able to access when he'd been scalding himself in Hawaii's heat.
There was the one set at an old train station, where he transported his guests back to the 1930s, buried them in brandy and brulee. There was the one in the maze, where you had to solve a series of riddles to get the rave beneath the soil. And there was the one on the boat, yes, on his boat, because he'd be damned if

Jack and Rose would stop him from taking it back. He remembered the moment he'd got the keys to it again. He'd shouted 'ahoy sailors!' and erected a foam cannon there and then. The boat party began on a Friday in Vauxhall and ended on a Monday, somewhere in the Cotswolds.

He loved playing these games with his guests, loved having all his old comrades to cavort with, but he'd have to have been deluded not to know it was just that; games. They'd never cared about him. Only one person cared, only one person had saved him, and he was heading back to her right now. *Erica.*

Erica was the one who had yanked him from the depths his former lover and friend had taken him to. Try as he did to become the old him, the man who turned time into a broth of sensation, too busy making memories to ever remember them, he couldn't deny who he was now. As the weeks went by, party by party, the alcohol and the celebration still felt good, but it stopped mattering. As the truth of the exoneration she'd given him became so rock solid, so undeniable, so irreversible, he found himself drawn away from the club and back to her. She hadn't just given him breath; she'd *turned* him into a breath, into one big exhale of relief who didn't have to feel ever feel shame again. Now he only wanted to feel one thing. *Her.*

If she could do this for him, what else could his transcendent Healer do? Where could they transcend to together? He had to find out.

She wrapped her arms around him; she was a scarf, a python, a collar all in one. *You wanted a noose, you got one.*

'So are you gonna hurt her?'

Myles didn't waste a second. 'So are you gonna heal him?'

'Maybe if you hurt her.'

'I will if you heal him.'

Over and over again, back and forth, they tossed the question, the game, between each other, and time after time, they never got an answer. Neither of them budged. Myles didn't understand why she wouldn't stop. And he tried to ignore, how it made him feel - about her, about her cruelty, about the potential streak inside her - that there was someone she refused to heal, just because she could. That she bathed in someone else's blindness. That she was letting Eli wallow, just to throb with her own power. Who knows what else she would do with that power?

He still didn't trust women. When she asked that question, he didn't trust Erica. But Erica wouldn't have trusted him either, if she knew what he was thinking about.

There was one question he would never say out loud. But he would ask it himself, over and over.

Who is Valentina?

Valentina, was that even her name? He woke up at night with dreams of her dying, of her hanging off cliffs that he never got to in time. He dreamt of her with pink hair, blue hair, no hair at all. Valentina, she walked through him, the lyric that hadn't been there in songs he loved before.

Maybe she was called Veronica, or Vanessa, or Clarissa, or Amanda. He called the hospital, six times til he was told to stop calling again, asking them to look through their records for any member of staff who fitted her description. He recalled staring into the eyes of Rose, Jack and Ian the actor, looking for a clue when he'd said 'Who is Valentina?' but there was nothing. They truly seemed mystified by the concept of another. Yet she was the one who had stuck up for him that day.

He hadn't told Erica about this, about the three little words embedded in his mouth, 'Who is Valentina?' If he wasn't saying them he was thinking them. And all the tentacles of confusion that came with it; who was she, what did she know, what were her intentions, did she do that often or just for him, where was she now? He just wanted to see her again, maybe just one more time, to tell her he was grateful.

Otherwise he had to face the inevitable. Any psychologist would tell him he'd dreamed her up. They'd be wrong.

When he threw a party he told himself he'd invited her. Waited at the door for her to appear. Muttered the words under his breath.

'Where are you, Valentina? Show yourself. What's it gonna take?'

She could hide all she wanted, but he would find her.

Over coffee and croissants, Myles and Erica entered a pattern: of ignoring the stories that broke each day. More and more regular, til it was not a question of them breaking every day, but how many would be there each morning: about what was happening to their society, now that euthanasia was legal.

There was the son found guilty of killing his father, in a bid to tap into his inheritance sooner.

There was the man found guilty of killing his brother, in a bid to get to his hands on the sister in law he'd been having an affair with for years.

At first the stories like this were about 'speeding along' someone who was terminally ill ... then they just became cold, ice murders, of people taking what they wanted under the guise that this was what their 'victim wanted'. After all, if you could want death, what mattered when it came, or how it came, or who it came from?

But it wasn't those stories that shocked the people, or that caused Myles and Erica to turn the page a little quicker. Those weren't the stories that were, let's say, uprooting the country.

It was the story of the woman who'd been turned down for liposuction, and as she couldn't have the fat sucked out of her, she had the air sucked out of her instead. She couldn't have her dream body, so she couldn't have her dream life,

and so why have a life at all? Why should she have to when she didn't have to, when there was another way?
After her, there were others. The teenager who got a spot the day of her first school dance. She had never gone to the dance, and she had never woken up again - she'd raided her parents' medicine cabinet and that had been that.
There was the banker with the gambling addiction, who was passed over for a promotion. The bride who was jilted at the aisle. The woman who reached thirty. 'Most women would die at thirty if they could be beautiful in their twenties anyway,' said the note she left.
All or nothing.
Quality over quantity. Every. Fucking. Time.
Slowly, hour by hour, the hope was halving, splintering into little hunks and chunks that scattered across the country, breadcrumbs of what was to come.
And slowly, bit by bit, the truth was coming for Myles and Erica, blending into their breakfast a little more each morning. The country needed something now, needed one thing that would get them to fight instead of give up: it needed hope.
And all of Hell's hot, haunted hope came down to one thing: one thing that could grant the country the second chance it needed.
Not luck, not dreams, not reason, not science or ethics or theology or fate.
But her. *Erica.* Who needed euthanasia if they had her?
'They need me.' She crunched into her toast. 'Will you let me heal them?'
Myles sat up straight. 'You don't ever have to ask.
Go, baby, go.'

Chapter Twenty Three

Michelle

'Just one more round, Rocco.'

Michelle sighed with only the kind of sweaty bliss only ninety minutes of practice can bring. She slid her hand along the satisfying sweat that lay across her abs, fiddling with her belly piercing as she went. The quiet of the studio poured into her for a moment, before she pressed play, put her hands to the pole, and swung into another practice of her salacious, outrageous routine.

Six months now she'd been running through ideas, chopping and changing, mixing music to get the act that she believed could win her Miss Pole North-East. Coming second last year had been thrilling, flattering – and started a fire. In a few weeks she'd show the whole country she was the sexiest, cleverest woman to ever put her thighs around metal.

Bounding down to the varnished wood, she began the beginning of her routine – the floor work. Her Boston terrier Rocco, who was waiting obediently in the corner, loved this bit. He cocked his head then ran over, curiously pawing at her as she grinded to the ground and slammed her legs from the air to over her shoulders, in a favourite move she called 'Straddle Bangs.' She didn't mind when Rocco came over – it was a hit with the practice videos she uploaded daily on Instagram to her eighty thousand followers.

Though she loved writhing on the floor, she believed she was born to be airborne, especially after the months she'd spent perfecting the following tricks: her Russian Splits, her Scorpion, her Dolphin, not to mention the top secret moves she was sure she had invented and even surer nobody else could accomplish.

She kissed Rocco on the nose then flipped her body over, using her biceps to hover over the ground where she bicycle-kicked her legs, then came down to the ground in low, deliberate thrusts. It had taken her forever to get her hips to move like that; she'd seen a belly dancer do it at a show in Beirut and had known she had to master it too. Rocco barked at her, his paws skidding on the varnished floor, loving playing with her at the level. He jumped up on her butt – who could blame him, the countless daily exercises made it the perfect shelf – and tried to settle.

'In a minute, bud,' she grinned, wiggling him off and spinning up to sit in front of the pole. She stretched both hands over her head and held onto the silvery girth she'd come to know so well. Time to fly.

Holding on with just one ankle, she created her own little fairground for herself, her spins accelerating faster every time. She remembered she had a date tonight then dropped herself down, a death-defying move that was sure to draw horrified gasps from the crowd, even after she'd caught herself with her face a wasp's whisper from the ground.

Detaching herself from the sleek shaft, she finally took a breath and admired herself in the mirror. She loved this little outfit, custom made for her; a pink and black set with two white 'handprints' slapped over her butt cheeks. She plucked the shorts out of her sweat, and then went running at the pole.

This was her move – the one that made her feel like a warrior princess. She caught the pole six feet up, then began climbing, effortlessly inching her way all twenty feet up til she was at the top. Rocco gazed up at her, an encouraging smile seen from a million miles away. Now at the top, she got herself into a pistol split. The only thing keeping her on the pole was the delicate position of her strong Kegel-honed crotch, a crotch that basically let her levitate.

Now, like all the best pole artists, she had mastered her pistol split on both sides. A 1, 2, 3 and she would jump, swapping legs and landing in a mirror image of her previous pose.

Can you guess what happened next?

Maybe it was the sweat she'd just brushed off her body and onto her hands.

Maybe somebody else had forgotten to talc it up after practising.

Maybe it was Rocco's tail, wagging too enthusiastically out of the corner of her eye, distracting her.

Maybe the first two times she'd landed it had all been luck.

Maybe it was meant to be.

But oh fuck. Either way, the fall happened.

One minute she was working on her dream, the next she was living a nightmare.. Everybody's nightmare, but particularly Michelle's. To not be able to dance again.

'Ro – Ro – Rocco – get someone …'

Rocco did not get anyone. He stayed at his owner's body, sniffing around her, his wet nose the only comfort to the shattered senses she felt. Unfortunately, Rocco didn't understand what had happened, and her whimpers didn't stop him from trotting over her; cruelly, one of life's simple pleasures, the nostalgic simplicity of his leathery paws padding on her, became a further nihilistic hell, as his light-but-not-light-enough body ground her bones furthered down and sunk her further into the floor.

It must have been nearly morning, as the studio was being filled with blue light, when Rocco gave a growl as he had heard fresh footsteps. Michelle thought it would be the cleaner, but when they entered the room, they didn't give the shocked, normal reaction a cleaner would have. Instead they stayed still and stared down at her. She couldn't turn her head to look up, to see who it was. Rocco bounced and spun at their heels, and she found herself insatiably jealous of her dog's limber ease of movement.

'Call … call an ambulance ….' She croaked.

'It's alright,' the voice spoke at last. 'I know a place where they'll put you back together again. Better than before.

You're going to come with us.'

Chapter Twenty Four

'So are you gonna hurt her?'
'I will if you heal him.'
'Never.'
'Fine.'
'Fine. I'm going out. I'll be back late. Don't wait up.'

Nobody ever asked Erica how it felt. To be the one.
She would write it in her diary, to try to understand.
So it turns out that I'm the one. Who would have guessed it?
After spending a third of my life underground – while the rest of the world walked above my head, oblivious of what they were trampling on – I'm the one.
I don't blame them for not knowing that once they dug me from my grave, I'd be able to save them all. Now I fly above them, looking down, choosing which one to touch next.
I hope they understand I can't be in two places at once, or take two planes at once, or even heal two people at once. It has to be one by one, one all the way up to seven billion.
Is it tiring? You know the answer. Of course I'm tired. Of course my hands are sore. Of course a cocktail with a friend sounds good right about now, instead of another hospital. We always knew it was going to be like this: that if there was going to be a healer in the world, she was going to be is tired. Who else is so lucky that they can dissolve pain?
Healer, oh healer, what is your name? We want to call it out and howl it at the moon.
Healer, Healer, how do our tears taste?
The only thing I have to do is not be lazy.
All their soft cells smell so good. And they're all mine
.Healer, I've baked you brownies. Do they taste good? Let them melt in your mouth like my cancer did in your hands.
Healer, I'm a zookeeper and my favourite tiger is dying. Can you make him roar again?
'The Kindest Girl In The World'. That's what they call me. But they're wrong. I know what I am. I'm not kind.
All I know is I know what it's like to be in a cage, and I'll be damned if I'll let someone's body become one.
She fed him a chocolate coated strawberry. He licked the chocolate from her fingertips, and his neck was no longer broken. The vertebrae reattached, positioned his head back where it should be; he was able to swallow the strawberry and her work there was done. He had another lick, this time of her little finger and thumb clasping a white chocolate cherry, and the mole on the side of his ear began to fade.

'Don't say thank you,' she said. 'Don't waste your first fresh words on me.' She kissed him on the cheek. He would never see her again.

She got in her car and couldn't drive soon enough. It had been a four hour drive to this house, when she'd heard about this ... what would she call them, the people she healed? This 'case'. This 'client.' Shut up, Erica, they're none of those things. They're people. People suffering. *Help* them. Go go go, buckle up baby, get it done, be productive, be perfect, be painless.

She rubbed her eyes, simultaneously turning on music in her car. She was tired. The call had come through at 4am in the night. She'd jumped straight up and drove.

She switched on the radio. Every now and then, a scandalous euthanasia story was interrupted by a story about 'Core Retreat', the counteractive centre of healing and hope that Eli Jones was spearheading. Unlike Sunset Clinic, it seemed to be coming together without a hiccup - the world seemed to be moving around it, to bring it together with efficiency. When the radio hosts talked about Core, just for a moment, everything seemed calm again.

Her hands stroked the steering wheel, the way they used to stroke the bars of her cage. Golly jee, would you believe, she wasn't in a cage any more. But other people were. Skeleton cages, fleshy bars, roofs of the mouths dripping mould on their tongues. *Help,* their voices came through the music, *help us.*

She looked at her hand suspiciously. So much healing, so much touching, she wouldn't be surprised if they started to stretch to accommodate her deeds. Her fingers expanding, the bones building on top of each other. Was it possible?

She drove through a forest, a forest overgrown; she was always in these dense, thick forests now. Bodies had become large oak trees with the roots planted in regret and the bark made out of reflexes that couldn't react. They twisted and battled for space, as the lives they'd wanted to live shed, falling like leaves all around their stiff, overgrown bodies. There were too many of these trees, stuck in the same place, stooping over because they've been there too long, unable to hack away the bushes that itched them, berries bursting with memories they never got to make.

But now, now these bodies, these people, had Erica. Erica who could chop this forest down or set fire to it or turn it into paradise with a flick of her wrist. And until she did, she couldn't rest.

She cruised along, through country roads, into the cool calm of a summer afternoon. Birds flying high, they knew how she felt. Head back, arm on the dashboard, the road cutting through another forest. The music made her go faster – not a soul joined her on the road.

Why not look for one? Why not find someone? Why not be the sweetest, the kindest, why not turn around and look for someone else to heal, why not go into the forest and find an injured deer, or even a –

She slammed on the gearstick, snapping to a stop. Had she just heard what she thought she'd heard on the radio?
The music had cut out, and a sombre news bulletin was being read.
'We come to you this afternoon with some very sad news. We're being told that the MP for Lewisham, Scott Luther, was found unconscious at home this morning and pronounced dead at the scene. Scott Luther of course became a household name this year through his support for parliament's Assisted Dying Bill.'
Erica coursed through the trees. She willed the music to start again.
'The cause of death is being reported as an overdose. Scott Luther leaves behind his two sisters, Emma and Rebecca. He was just 36 years old.'
Fuck! Erica scrunched to a stop.
Why did she have to hear that? Why couldn't she just have the peace she was giving everybody else?
She kicked the car door open, letting in the air, hoping it would take the tears away.
She looked down at her body. Most girls were just happy to have a body like this. That was their contribution to the world. Why did she have to give so much more, why did she have to do so much more?
Then ever so gently, she started to cry. She cried for those she had saved and those she hadn't saved yet. Cried for those she didn't get to in time and those she wasn't sure she ever would. Really, it just felt good to cry, to expel your own warm honey into your hands, drain all those abscesses inside you no doctor could reach.
She cried into her hands, opulent drops, one, two, three big gulps, then looked up, her eyes readjusting to the grey.

Driving back, Erica thought about all the people who'd made great medical inventions; Frank Patridge with the defibrillator, Fredrich Serturner with morphine, Paul Elrich with chemotherapy.
And then, of course, there is him. My captor, his face fading from my memory. The one who made me.
What did he do to me down there?
I wouldn't be surprised if I walked into a copyright office to find he's already patented me. Under his name. Under his eye.
Maybe I should copyright myself. Somehow.
At that, her car's phone rang. She tapped it, answering. It was Myles.
'Hey babe,' she said.
'Hey darlin'. It go okay?'
'Fine, yeah. All done.'
'Did you hear the news? About Scott Luther?'
Erica sighed. 'Yeah. Yeah, I did.'

She could hear Myles wincing down the phone. 'That's terrible, isn't it. They're saying the overdose was deliberate, that he'd been struggling for a while now. As if people needed even more reason not to trust Sunset Clinic. Things are starting to feel real shaky out there, aren't they?'

Erica leaned back. His voice, somehow, was making her feel good. 'Yeah. I know. I know. But it's okay. They've got me.'

'*Nice*. Listen, I've scratched tonight. I've found someone who needs you. Someone special. You good to go again?'

The healer did what healers do. 'Sure thing,' she lied. 'I'll be there in an hour.'

Chapter Twenty Five

Rhonda

'*Now* she's gonna break. Trust me – she's about to cry.'
'Nah, I don't think so. The ice queen hasn't melted yet.'
'Want a bet?'
The two security guards watched her carefully. It was their job to watch all the accused closely, but if they were honest with themselves, they were watching her a little too closely. For a lady her age, she was an enigma. It was all about the confidence, even after where she'd just been and what had just been said about her.
She sauntered into the holding cell, her lawyer walking meekly behind her. Even he seemed to be checking out her legs. In her Armani suit which she'd been advised not to wear because it would be too isolating to the jury, she sat on the little wooden bench in her cell like she was here to collect a prize. She put down her handbag, opened up her compact mirror and started applying lipstick. Cherry red; her son's favourite colour.
And the guards were wrong. Still no tears.
'*Rhonda*,' her lawyer, Tom, said in exasperation. 'I know this is a lot to deal with. But please listen to me. This is your last chance. The judge needs to see that you are remorseful.'
She didn't acknowledge him, continuing to focus on painting her lips. Tom slid across the bench next to her. 'You know I know you. I know why you did what you did. But if you don't want to be prosecuted, you need to play the game. You need them to think you are sorry.'
She smacked her lips together, admiring herself in the small mirror. Finally she closed the compact with a solid click and looked at Tom with the same withering look she'd been giving him the whole trial. 'You shouldn't even *be* here,' he continued. 'No one's denying how unlucky you are. But it's the video, Rhonda. Right now, that's all you are to the jury. Just a woman holding a pillow over her son's face in a French hospital.'
She rolled her eyes, annoyed that Tom kept bringing up the video like it was a bad thing. She would have done the same thing even if she'd known the cameras were there. She never would have left her son like that.
'We're lucky this trial is in England. You can speak in your own language to the jury. But if you really don't want to speak, can you not just cry?'
They'd love that, wouldn't they? Rhonda's toes curled in her patent black heels. They really expected her to stand up there and apologise for loving someone that much. They'd have to beg her for that.
It shouldn't have been this way. Most people understood why she'd done what she'd done. She'd met people in the street who clasped her hands and told her, 'I'd do the same.' However, the perfect storm of everything – the debate, Scott's

win, the attack on Eli Jones - had made things out there, let's just say, tense. And now she was the perfect person to punish, for her cocktail of a mother's love and a shot of bravery.

They were just jealous nobody loved them like that.

'I'm not going to cry.' She looked Tom directly in the face. 'If you can't get them to understand, then there was no point in this trial. They should have mobbed me in the streets back in France.'

Frustrated, Tom rose his voice. 'Rhonda! I don't want to see you go down for this! Haven't you already been through enough?'

'Then why isn't working?!' she blurted out, emotion snatching through. 'Why can't they see what you see, and just leave me alone?' Though to be honest, she did appreciate the distraction. If, after France, she'd had to contend with the full face of her grief, she didn't know what would become of her.

'You haven't been listening, have you?' Tom looked at her in exasperated awe. 'It's the prosecution. He's got some good arguments.'

'What?!' she snapped.

Tom shuffled awkwardly. 'Well, first, it's the image he paints of you. That you may not have had the most merciful intentions.

Prosecutions got quite carried away creating this character around you. This "monster mother". Black widow, spider eats her young, etc. They say your son was a fantastic skier – '

'He was.'

'Exactly. Looked into his life out there and when you add up his prize money, his sponsorships – he was looking to be quite rich. They're saying you could have been interested in getting your hands on that money yourself.'

She rolled her eyes. 'But no one *believes* that, right? All you have to do is look into our relationship to see it was great. He would have spoiled me with that money *anyway*.'

'Okay maybe don't say spoil – '

'Who seriously believes I could be so driven by money? I'd – you'd have to have a history, of violence or fraud or - '

'There's something else.' Tom gulped.

'What?!'

Resentfully, he sat down, trying to choose the words. 'They have a statement from the doctor. There's a suggestion – that your son – he could have made a full recovery.'

'No.' Rhonda's world went a little colder.

'It's not guaranteed -'

'I *saw* him.' There it was, the crack in her voice. 'I'm the one that had to look into his eyes. He was in agony, Tom.'

'Look, it's probably not true -'

'*Probably*?!' Her voice was shrill. 'But if it is - if it's true -' Her neck snapped around, the hair finally spraying loose from the impossibly tight bun she had

worn the whole trial; it was no match for her grief now. 'Th-th-th-then I took away his chance - ' She looked for something to smack and found she was smacking herself. 'Then - then - you're telling me he could still be here?!'
'Rhonda. Please. Calm down!'
Slowly, she was sinking to the floor. One guard nodded at the other, *'Told ya she could cry.'*
Rhonda looked into Tom's eyes, anger biting through her lashes. A hive of a rash was making its way down her neck, and a ladder was marching its way up her tights. Chaos and the body that couldn't contain it. 'If that's true, if there's any chance that that's true, then – punish me. Send me away.' She gulped and gripped for her forehead, more hair coming loose in her hands. The lines on her face seemed to deepen there and then. 'I'm serious. This is it, Tom. Lock me up.'
Tom groaned. 'Look, there is one other option.'
She looked up, confused. 'What?'
'Give me a minute.'
He left her then, for seven minutes of hell, to sit and wait and think about what she may have done. A mother's instinct? She laughed at the thought.
Eventually, Tom returned. But he was not alone.
Eli Jones was with him.
His face was just as kind and handsome as it was on the television. He had the same air of calm, the same subtle thing within him that made you trust him. Even the eyes still sparkled.
He sat opposite her, gently.
'Eli is prepared to offer you refuge at Core Retreat,' Tom continued. 'He's launching a rehabilitation programme; there's already a few criminals transferred there, but you'd be the most high profile. Eli is hoping that through showing you the work they do; always giving people a second chance at life, never giving up, trusting in revolutionary medical interventions – that it'll be the ideal rehabilitation for you. The deal's already on the table, I've spoken to the judge. What do you say?'
Rhonda looked up, through greasy and wet eyes, staring between the two men. 'And why do you want me there?'
Eli smiled warmly, pleased with the question. He came closer and closer so she could see into those famous eyes, knowing in that moment he could see all of her. Then he gave her his answer, an answer that made her blood run the other way. 'I need someone to make an example of.'

Chapter Twenty Six

In front of Erica was a blind man.

Was it wrong for her to fantasise about what she could do to him?

She wouldn't laugh. Not just yet. She could take this slow. Walk around him in circles. He would think she was to his left then all of a sudden she would be to his right. All he could do was wait, patiently, to be touched.

Myles beamed; 'It's a *blind* man. You've never healed anyone blind, have you?'

No, she had not.

Erica felt beautiful tonight.

To be honest, she felt more beautiful every day. Her hair shone and swung, her skin sparkled and bloomed, her eyes got wider, her breasts got firmer, she smelt better, she was more flexible. She was a girl everyone wanted to be touched by. And the man before her couldn't see it. He had no idea just how hot the healer was.

Wouldn't he like to know? Where in the room was she standing? Which part of him was she looking at? Was she behind or in front of him? She found pleasure in her footsteps, walking around him heel to toe, each floorboard squealing with delight at her footprint. She stopped before him. She looked with fascination at the eyes that never blinked.

'You're not angry with me, are you?' Myles finally broached the question. 'I'm sorry. I know you … I know you had your doubts.' He whispered, looking at the man in front of them. The man who'd been on their minds for weeks now. Eli Jones.

'No,' she said. 'I like that you've gone against my wishes. I mean it,' she hurried before he could think she was being sarcastic. 'I like the dominance.'

'You sure?' Every moment that went by, Myles was starting to doubt himself and his decision. He had, after all, gone behind her back in doing this. He'd contacted Eli's people and volunteered her services, and he'd brought her here without telling her who she was going to be healing. It was, for all intents and purposes, a presumptuous and outrageous act, a suggestion that he didn't respect or care for her autonomy. It was the first moment he was edging into feeling like a pimp for The Healer.

But it *wasn't* that, and it would never be that. He would never respect anybody more than he respected her. He would never take anything from her, never make her do anything she didn't want to do; he'd value everything she'd ever say or ever do for the rest of her life.

So why was he making her do this? Or not making her, but putting her in this position? Because after the Scott Luther tragedy, he didn't want to waste her for a moment - he didn't want to be too late for Eli, as someone had been too late for Scott. Perhaps Myles, a man who believed deeply in Scott and *not* Eli's cause, would redress the balance through providing this act of charity towards the aforementioned Eli.

So he had pledged Erica's services for tonight. He would only ever do this once. And it seemed, to his relief, he had made the right choice. If she had given him a reason why she didn't want to heal Eli, he wouldn't have done this. But she never did - not one bad word about him - as though deep down, she wanted to do it really. He'd gambled their love on this, and it seemed he was right to do so. By the sizzling, sparkling amusement with which she was looking at Eli, by the reptilian way she was watching him, he could tell she was enjoying this.
All is well.
'His eyes are so … milky,' she folded her arms. 'Don't you think Myles?'
Myles looked at her in surprise.
'Look, come next to me,' she said. 'They look like a sort of blue cream. A cream with mould mixed in.'
Myles mouth made an awkward little O. He typed out quickly on his phone;
babe, he can still hear.
She grinned and snatched the phone from him, *But he can't see*, and she splayed her hand atop of Myles crotch. Myles grinned, shocked, grabbing her hand and playfully wrestling her away. She spun round and grabbed his face, collapsing a kiss on his lips. The blind man would have heard that.
Laughter in the dark.
Myles frowned. He'd never seen this side of her. *Bitchy.* To a blind man, no less. She was full of surprises. Myles didn't have much reverence for others, didn't trust them much any more, but he did have some for this man: a man who had fought so hard for what he believed in, fought to keep his country 'safe', even though he had lost.
'I think I should leave,' he nodded. 'So you can concentrate.'
She reached for him but he drifted out of the door before they did something too twisted.
So Erica was all alone. A one woman show. A private show for the blind man. The lights in the room flickered and then she said six words, each carefully chosen, forbidden words that she wouldn't even have let Myles hear her say.
'I'm going to remove my clothes.'
The eyes curdled.
'First I'm going to take off my jacket.' She peeled it off gently and dropped it on the floor. 'Now I'm going to untie my hair.' She pulled at the bow and felt her hair groan with pleasure as it looped and whirled all over her back. 'Now I'm unzipping my dress.' No word of a lie, she did as she said, the zip drawing a streak of noise into the air. She stood still and let it make a satisfied hush as it fell to the ground. 'I'm in just my underwear now. Guess what colour it is.'
He spoke his word. 'Yellow.' His favourite song, a Coldplay one.
'Pink. Close enough.' She looked back into the milk. It had taken on a pearly, iridescent tone. 'I think I'll unclip my bra now.' The noise of bra unclipping was so much harsher than the rest. Her breasts made their own noise as they bounced through the air.

Then he waited. He exercised a remarkable patience. She said nothing. She did not tell him if she removed her underwear, if she silently and subtlety glided the silk from her centre.
But he felt it. He felt it when the tiny briefs landed on his face and glided in a smooth slide, catching on his lips.
'I'm naked now,' she spoke again. 'I bet you would like to see that. Wouldn't you? Answer me.'
'Yes.'
'You'd like to see inside me.'
'Yes.'
'You can imagine it but it's doing nothing for you. Your fantasies are nothing like the real thing.'
'You speak the truth.'
'And maybe you will one day.'
Enough. Enough of the game.
'Well, you haven't flinched or screamed for help once. At the strange woman who's meant to be helping you, but isn't. So you must recognise my voice. Right?'
The man looked right at her, trying to find her through the glaze. 'Yes, but … I smelt you as soon as you came in. Erica.'
Even without his eyes, he was still as handsome as he'd been before.
'Erica. I bet I make a monster in the dark. Just like you did. Eli. Eli my captor.'
'Erica. My – '
She came closer, her fingers parting her where she creased, opening all the secret bits of Pandora's Box that he could not see. Then she was on her knees before him but he remained blind, still, stuck and sad; could reach for her mouth but he knew he'd miss it. She sat back, palms on the floor, legs open, hoping that some part of him knew what she was showing him.
Who would she be if she didn't heal him? She wasn't sure.
'I'm not yours any more.'
'Okay. That's fine.'
'Wow, never thought I'd hear you say that, Eli. You gave up on me that easy. You really want your sight back, don't you?'
'Yes. I do.'
'What's it like in the darkness? Is it scary? Do you see all the things you've always dreaded?'
'No. The opposite. It's peaceful.'
'But it must be lonely, right?'
'I've been lonely since I let you go. This is no different.'
'Let me go?' Erica felt her voice snap. 'No, Eli. *I escaped you.*'
The blind man laughed, a rich laugh that spoke of the colours he could see that she couldn't. 'Erica. Erica, please. You think after eight years of owning you, one day I would suddenly, spontaneously, accidentally drop my keys? Just oops,

bang, wallop, what a clumsy oaf I am. And then not even notice? Not even check? Come on, Erica. You really think I'm that futile?'
Erica folded her arms. She would let him insult her, for it would be good to build her anger.
'I took you when you were barely twenty. I watched you grow. I knew one day you would rise up. Luckily, you didn't rise up too soon - your bravery came just at the right time, just when I knew I was ready to release you into society.' A sickness unbuckled Erica's intestines as she let him continue to confirm the one thing that would stop her from respecting herself - that she had played into his hands all along. 'To see if you were capable of healing them. How was I ever gonna know whether our experiments worked unless I let you go?' He straightened up his seat, his eggy eyes fighting to find her. 'But Erica. Erica. Look at me when I say this. Are you looking?'
'Yes.'
'I just want you to know this: I regret it. Ever since I dropped the keys, all I've wanted is to get you back.'
She believed him. She had seen it in him; on TV, in articles, through every moment of triumph or failure – seen the longing in his eyes. He'd been watching the debate while she escaped, been blinded the morning she'd reunited with her mother. He'd been in hospital for three days after and would have spent every minute wondering if she'd made it out or not. When he'd finally come home, waited for everybody to leave and been able to slip into his cellar, all he would have wanted was for her to be there waiting for him.
She believed him but *fuck, why did that make her happy*? Why did she still want to impress him?
'So, why should I heal you? Why should I give you your sight back?'
'You know why.'
He still looked the same. Too handsome, too tall, too powerful, too strong for fifty nine. Clipped white hair and ice white teeth glowing where his eyes couldn't.
'Tell me.'
'Because we miss each other.'
If she choked him, slapped him, bit him or pushed him, she'd be healing him. She told herself that was her excuse for not hurting him now.
'Who knows what will happen if I let you see me again?' She giggled. 'Who knows what you'll do? What you'll become?'
'Who knows what I'll become if you don't?'
Erica winced. There was a vase over there she could smash on his face, a spare curtain pole she could drive through his chest, a jar of salt she could sprinkle into his cuts, but like always, deep down, she didn't want to cause him pain.
'Do you think you deserve it?' She got so close to him he would have been able to taste her. If he dared.
'Nah. I kept you in the dark. You can keep me there too.'

'Can you cry through those eyes?' She asked. 'Through those useless, frozen eyes?'
'Yes.'
Laughter in the dark.
'Do they hurt?' Her lips parted.
'Always.'
Fire in the dark.
'Well I don't hurt anywhere, any more. All I feel now is good.'
Lust in the dark.
She spun, bent over, writhed, tossed her hair and slid into the splits. All things he couldn't see, but he would know, by the swish of her hair, was happening.
'And I'm about to feel even better.' She slipped her fingers into herself. His mouth parted; he recognised the sound. 'Oh, you wish you could watch this, don't you?' She slipped her fingers out again. She could make him taste it, but that would heal him. She could kiss him, but that would heal him. She could castrate him, but that would heal him. Do anything to him and he'd get to see her face again. So what should she do? What should she be? What was she now?
'I'm proud of you.' He told her.
'You too.' She said it quickly and couldn't be bothered to regret it. 'After all, you've achieved a lot since we've been apart.'
That was true. She'd lost count of the number of times he'd come down into her cellar and all he'd wanted to do was debate *it*. The E word. She didn't know who he was then, didn't know about his ambitions, his ability to counteract a whole political campaign - after all, to her he was just the creep who wouldn't let her go. But she'd soon understood he was more than that. He had a passion in him; he wanted to will people to live. He believed people could fight for their lives, no matter what it threw at them - he believed in hope.
She enjoyed their debates. They were one of the few things that kept her stimulated, kept her sharp, kept her herself. She'd never known that it was all building the backdrop for him to one day create his own reactionary retreat. Core Retreat, that place that had come together so quickly, but remained so steeped in mystery. So yes, she *was* proud of him, for making it real when so few would have withered.
She ran her hands across her body. Something moved in his eyes. He knew what she was doing.
'Eli my captor. Eli my abuser. Eli my owner.'
'Don't say that. I didn't let you go for you to speak about yourself like that.'
She ignored him. 'Eli my master. Eli my creator.' She looked into his detached retinas and longed to twist them. 'I can make it darker in here, you know.'
'That's why I wanted you to be free. I wanted you to know your potential.' He paused for a second, his voice faltering like there was something he wanted to say.

'Go on. Say what you wanna say.'
'When I released you, I thought you would be more … timid. And when you realised your powers, I thought you would be more servile, that all you would want to do is use them. I didn't expect to release an obnoxious party girl, one who plays tequila games on a plane, not caring how many other passengers she disturbs. You don't think I wasn't keeping tabs on you, did you? My friends have been watching you where I couldn't, Erica. Watching how you've even had time to fall in lust with that man Myles.'
Erica spun just out of reach from his hands, letting him imagine every angle of her. 'So do you regret it?'
'No, my darling.' He shrugged. 'Every drop of disappointment dissolves knowing that you're happy. No anguish would be worth keeping you captive any longer. I wanted this, Erica; I wanted you to be free.'
'But if I give you back your eyes, can I ever be free?'
'I know. I understand. You don't have to. It's up to you.'
She rolled over, arching her back, delighting in knowing he couldn't see an inch of her. 'Tell me; you have a good relationship with Sunset Clinic?' Sunset Clinic, Scott Luther's creation, and only six months old. She looked at the man who'd been the only person she'd known for eight years - being blinded couldn't have changed him that much. Not to support mercy killings. No way. Something else was going on.
There was a reason nobody knew Core's location.
He smiled. 'Everything is perfect now.' A chill ran through her. 'I would just like to be able to see again - '
'Bet you would.'
'But it's up to you.'
'But you're longing for it, aren't you? Your whole body's aching for it. To see me.' She rolled back over. 'To see inside me.'
'Yes.' His voice cracked. 'But I cannot make you. Even if I could, I wouldn't.'
She looked into the milk of his eyes. She wanted to drink it. She could make Myles spit in those eyes. She could do anything she wanted.
'Someone did this to you. Someone blinded you. What did you do to deserve it?'
Eli laughed. 'Some people just can't handle hope. But I was right to hope. I was right to believe.'
'Because of me?'
'Because of you.'
'Maybe I'm a fake. Maybe I'm a liar. Maybe it's all gonna go away one day.'
She did a backbend, Oh, this angle; he really was missing out.
'Nah. That's the old Erica, the one before I took you. The Erica of now is the one who can do anything. Anything she wants.' *Even blind you twice.*
'I could tell them it didn't work. That you're the only man that can't be healed.'
'You could.'

'Maybe I'd seem a little less special to them then, but at least I'd know, at least I'd know you were suffering, aching, missing me every day.'
'You would.'
'And then I'd be happy.'
His eyes closed. Still naked, she gazed at him. He may never know how perfect her body was now it had filled out a little. He may never know how much more vibrant her skin was now it had got some sunlight on it.
And he'd never know what he could become if she gave him back his sight. It was the unspoken truth between them: that she would stunt him forever if she didn't do this. Impressive as he was, and as quickly as he had put Core together, it would always be half of what it was if she didn't touch him right now. If she gave him the electric bolt of sight, it would unlock all of his, and its, potential. The place would become beloved. The place would be revered. The place would be iconic. And it might, just might, be enough. Enough for him to leave her alone.
She tossed her bra at him. It caught across his eyes. A blindfold.
She should get him to talk more about Sunset Clinic, so she could make sense of it, of his connection to it. Or maybe she should leave that as it was - something that could stay as the smirk on his face, and not become anything more, not become real. There are some things the body knows it's not ready to hear.
The bra slipped off his eyes, catching on his nose. He sneezed.
Would he be her first failure? The taunting was too easy to stop. She picked her dress up from the floor and grazed the label across his hand. 'Guess which bit of me you're touching.'
He frowned. 'None of you.' Correct. Clever. She dropped the dress so it slid between his thighs. She fluttered them on his fingertips. 'Still not you.' He knew her. He knew her better than anyone, and that was why he hadn't broken a sweat no matter how much she teased him.
Sighing, she took a step forward.
'You once told me you would make me special. No … what was the word you used?'
'Exquisite.'
'So I'll be exquisite for you now.'
She moved towards him. Picked up her underwear. 'I'll be classy for you now.' She slid it on. Found her bra, clicked that on too. Her dress, her jacket, her shoes. 'I'll be gentle for you now.' She walked towards him.
'Special for you now.'
There was a knock on the door. 'Erica?'
She looked into the face of Eli Jones. 'Brace yourself.'
Swinging her hand back, she slapped him, using every fibre inside her to send his face stinging and swinging over to the side. The sound bounced off the walls. Her palm was a stamp on his skin.
'Come in!' She called to the door.

She turned and Myles entered, followed by Eli's assistant, a studious little woman in striped dungarees, carrying a pile of folders. Nervously, she peered at them. 'H-h-has it worked?'

Erica stood to the side of Eli's chair, calmly grasping his shoulder.

'Well let's ask the man himself.' She smiled. 'Did it work?'

He rose to his feet.

He blinked.

And all the colours in the world came back to him.

With a grin to his assistant. 'You didn't tell me how pretty the Healer was.'

His assistant squealed. They always did; never quite believed it would work for them or the person they knew. 'She did it? You can see?!'

'I can see. Nice dungarees,' he nodded, confirming. She dropped her folder with glee.

'Oh my god! Yes! Yes! Eli! Is it too bright? Shall we turn out the lights?'

'No,' Eli smiled sombrely. 'It's just right.'

His assistant flung herself into his arms. 'This is going to change *everything*!' she squealed joyfully. With every blink, Eli's eyes returned to their original blue. 'Erica, come!' She pulled her into the hug. 'Myles, you too!'

The four of them delivered the most warm, baked good hug any of them had ever experienced. Wholesome and healthy as they celebrated a miracle.

And they all lived happily ever after. If only forever hadn't been so long.

Erica thought about telling Myles. After all, all she had to do it was say it. Tell him that that had been him. Her captor. The one who had kept her, all that time, was Eli Jones, entrepreneur turned political campaigner whose profile had skyrocketed in leading the 'No' campaign about Euthanasia. A man who had been mysteriously attacked, left for dead and blinded, but had proceeded to double down on his efforts to make 'Core Retreat', a place where anyone in doubt about their commitment to living, could come. So far it had been nothing but a success. If she wasn't an angel, Eli sure was.

All she had to do was open her mouth. Open it and tell Myles who he was. Let the truth fall and see what happened.

But one truth stood strong. He had let her go. Eli hadn't had to drop his keys outside her cage, in reaching distance of her toes, and he had. And for that, she would let him be free. For that, she would let him fill the world with the hope he lived so hard for, by telling them no one could throw their lives away when any day now, they could be healed. She would be a legend, a myth, a miracle for him, all because he dropped his keys for her. And because he was the one person in the world she could say anything to.

'Everything ok?' Myles said, arm sliding round her neck.

She rolled into him. 'Perfect.'

'Great. Let's go get dinner. I know a place.'

Chapter Twenty Seven

Darren

The father's cancer had waited for him, down in somewhere deeper than the bowels of his bowels. It had waited patiently behind all the charisma, all the success, all the other perfect muscles, until it revealed itself as a 52nd birthday surprise.

Too good for boring symptoms like fatigue, weight loss or vivid flamenco footprints on the toilet paper – he had simply gone for his yearly screening. Of course a man of his importance got the results back the same day. And just like that, he had cancer. Not chewing at his brain, not munching down his back, not swallowing his balls, but *lurking* – shadowy, secretly, soft – two inches above his rectum.

He knew straight away what had caused it, even though his doctor said he was 'the pinnacle of health and very unlucky'. He knew something the doctor didn't. He could hear their voices; *See. That look in our eyes was real. You won't get away with this.* It was his hunts, his quarterly trophy hunts from Zimbabwe to Alaska; him and his Yale buddies found zebra's in January, brown bears in May, hyenas in July and buffalos in October. Or, more specifically, it was what he and his chef Joe did with them. Joe was a magician; all eight of his kids responded with the same awe to his silkiest of wolf stews; and an invite to Darren's summer 'Triple B' (beer and buffalo barbeque) was coveted for the sheer thrill of biting into the chilli jam and giraffe burger. Have you ever seen a hyena rotating on a spit? Nothing says bacchanalia quite like that.

He was a *man*, and nothing could be more natural and primal than devouring those beneath him on the food chain. Every day. Never a meal without meat. He'd allowed those glorious creatures to live on in him, to never fully digest, their ghosts clinging to his intestines, to form their own jungle and eventually, get their revenge in the most humiliating way of all.

When the doctor first announced it, he saw it as an opportunity. He wouldn't just beat colon cancer – he'd beat it in the best, most inspirational way. In fact, he'd find a cure. He'd host a gala, a ball for his bowels, and auction off an antelope head, for sweet justice. And he wouldn't tell anyone about it, just for now. Let those he loved continue to relax, while he could continue to take care of them, as he should.

Red and white, red and white. Red on the marble, red on the china, red on the silk when he woke up. He could do so many things yet all his body wanted to do was this; Drip.

He said he was at a work retreat when he flew to Toronto for the surgery, and he made the most of his week there, a blur of casinos, motorbikes and a woman who let him record her, too busy performing to notice the specks on the sheets.

But his colon cancer was a devious thing, a mocking, cheeky beast playing hide and seek in the shadows of his body. A life of penetrating others didn't know how to handle something so very internal.

He had silenced critics, rivals, lovers for the past 52 years, sailing through life on the power of personality.

But his colon cancer could not be charmed, seduced or outsmarted. Or perhaps it liked him so much and that's why it wouldn't go away. It danced a merry dance, swinging through his digestion, marvelling at itself from how big it could grow. It drunk from his memories and bathed in his confidence. And when he kept on laughing, it made the laughter hurt.

As the fatigue came for him, and as he started forgetting birthdays, his doctor called him in to tell him about the next round of treatment. 'You may find your balance is affected after so much radiation, and some people find the use of a walking stick aids them in the first couple of years or so. Things to expect; nausea, night sweats, hair loss – '

A challenge, he shrugged. Simply another challenge, for him to prove to everybody, but mainly to himself, what he was capable of. When he got home was going to sign up for a marathon. Maybe an amateur boxing fight. A whole amateur boxing evening! He'd smash the recovery; he'd crack the walking stick in half if they offered it to him. He couldn't wait for the celebratory holiday he would take everyone on once he got the all clear.

'The final thing I have to talk to you about, and this does take some adjustment – '

Don't say it.

'We'll talk you through it, and support you as much as you need, and you'll soon find life can be just the same with the -'

Don't say it.

'The assistance of a stoma.'

'A what?'

Say it then. Say it loud and clear.

'A colostomy bag.'

Every cell in his body felt patronised. He tried to be mature, to accept that a part of his life was over: the part that made it worth living. The part that had given him his ego.

Seventeen. On a beach in Tenerife. Watching disdainfully as his father pulled a tank top over his pink belly. He'd sworn to himself there and then he would never have a torso he couldn't be proud of. Through ice baths and celery and muay thai, he'd achieved it. It was actually him who'd invented that phrase '*You never regret a workout*'. He went through the world with the warm glow of a person in their dream body, because they had the willpower to get there. But not any more.

'You won't believe who's having to have a stoma fitted…'

'*Who*?'

'Darren Thames.'
'No!'
'*Exactly.* The last person you'd imagine to have something like that done.'
'Aww. Poor bloke.'
It was that conversation, whether real or imagined or misinterpreted, and those slightly smug, slightly pitying voices, that had led Darren to his decision.
And also this:
On his hunts, once he had found his prey, he got the job done in one shot. He was meticulous and obsessive about waiting for the perfect angle, the perfect moment, before launching the fatal and final bullet. The sporting prowess this earned him was just an added bonus – he did this because he didn't like to see anything suffer. The blood on his hands never bothered him, but humiliating a great creature would. Sometimes his clumsier friends would fire at the wrong time, unleashing unbearable howls from an animal still breathing, and Darren wouldn't think twice before running over, turning the creature round, fixing his eyes on a vital artery, and putting it out of its misery.
That was how he did things.
Why would he be any different?
He would go out with a bang, pulling his own trigger. Out like the lion he had always been.

Darren's colon cancer had picked the wrong family to mess with. The Thames family had unlimited options. They would never be forced into a humiliating choice. When Darren refused the bag, his condition became terminal. After that, the choice was obvious.
That was why they drove, on that oozing August afternoon, to Sunset Clinic. Father, daddy, dearest, papa, if this is really what you want. Because after everything you've done for us, we can do this to you.
They were in a stretch limo, going out in style. All twenty five of them were in the car; his new wife, his second wife, his first wife (his soulmate), all eight children, ranging from ages fifteen to thirty three, his three brothers, his two best friends, and the staff that had been with him for years.
What kind of family drank champagne while driving to a death? *This* family. Any excuse for a celebration, and yes, this was a celebration, a celebration of a life lived on his terms. This was to be an event. He hadn't known, until now, how much his children *got* him. They had been raised with that all-or-nothing passion of his; it was just a shame this was their way of proving to him that they had just as much fire in them as he did. Maybe more. Today was going to be brutal, but for him that was it. They had to wake up the next day, and the next, and the next. Without him.
As he held their hands and looked into their eyes, it went through him like a shot – how could they not be enough?

Too late. Or was it? The limo drove and the song changed and the bubbles grew on their tongues. And the unspoken sentence between them refused to pop – did they have anything in them, anything at all, to make him want to stay?
But they looked at the serene gloss in each of his eyes, and none of them spoke a word. Even Thomas, his eldest, just silently wished he'd stepped up sooner, taken the pressure off him at work so he'd never gotten ill.
They glided past the golden fields they would be driving past again in three hour's time – all but one of them.
He poured around another round of champagne, his youngest daughter, Mila, watching him. She'd lost a stone since he made this decision - she hoped he noticed, hoped he could see her at her thinnest one last time. She'd wanted to lose more but she'd cracked over a Kit Kat in the fridge. The chocolate was still on her lips when she realised - if she couldn't resist an urge as simple as that KitKat, who was she to tell him not to give into the urge he wanted most of all? Even if it that urge was death.
'How about a game?' He said, passing round glasses.
'Ooh, yeah, Never Have I Ever!' His new wife said.
'Ok, Never Have I Ever …ha, what haven't I done.' He grinned. 'I really did get to do it all.'
'There must be something,' his second wife said. 'And we should do it now.'
He looked out the window again, though it seemed stupid to waste these precious seconds not looking at his family. 'There's nothing. I'm ready.'

'Darren? Welcome. Ooh, this is a big crowd you have with you today! Come, all – let's get you in. Let's make the memories a family like you deserve.'
The final time he saw them was in a grand room, the most expensive room he could have rented at Sunset. There was more champagne, but he noticed less and less of them were drinking it. They wanted a clear memory of their father.
He had a moment alone with each of them. He saw the anger in his brother's eyes- the brother who had always wanted to be him and now wished he could swap places with him. His brother almost left without saying anything, but as he got to the door he turned and said.
'It's a *bag,* D.' He paused and said it again. 'It's a piece of plastic. All you have to do is wear a shirt at the beach.' He looked him up and down, shook his head. 'You're serious about this? You really mean this?'
He left before he could answer.
Finally, lastly, he saw Mila. What could he say, that could make up for the decades she would spend without him?
'Will you be angry if I die like this, too?'
He held her face. 'No. You can do anything you want. Feel anything you want. Feel as much as you can, Mila.'

And finally his doctor arrived. 'It is up to you if you'd like anyone there for the procedure. But we wouldn't recommend it. It can be very difficult for families and dangerous if emotions get too involved.'
'Ah, but you don't understand. My family are not like other families. They're rockstars.' He stroked Mila's cheek, the softest move he'd ever made. 'They can be there if they wish.'
'Let's do this, daddy.'

When his eyes opened, he was serene. His body felt light and supple. He didn't know what day, month or year it was – but it didn't matter. There was a clearness to his eyes he hadn't felt in years. His bones felt tranquil yet strong. Energy coursed through him, patient but passionate. He would have believed he was in heaven, if it wasn't for the pit in his stomach.
The pit was there before his mind could sharpen. He had felt pits before; nerves, guilt, dread, but never anything like this. This was real, weighing on him like it was depending on him to be there. Thick and squidgy and moving when he moved; promising him it would never leave him.
This wasn't Heaven. Heaven would smell sweeter than this.
Was this Purgatory – a place where everything was fine but the pit in your stomach?
He forced his eyes to open further, take in more. Take in the white. He was in a white room, almost like the one he had died in, but different. Higher up, perhaps. A similar size, but bigger. A similar bed, but softer. A similar hum, but louder. Unlike when he had died, there was no one around. Nothing but the pit in his stomach.
Ok, relax, use your brain, like you did on Earth.
Still the pit. Heavy, wrong. His stomach fluttered but the pit stayed strong. Rebelling against his body.
There was a door, a few metres from him. Maybe this was the test; he had to get to the door, open it and walk out onto the clouds.
He swung his legs from the bed. He was still in his hospital gown.
The pit grew. Strange. A pit should feel hollow. This pit was full.
He made his way to the door, cold floor congratulating his feet. He pulled the handle. It was locked.
A turn, a gulp, a jesting feel as the oxygen came for him, coating him, as his nerves trespassed into places they didn't belong. He moved around the room, looking for a key. Find the key and enter heaven, right?
The pit came with him.
He passed the mirror. Looked. Pale skin. An indentation on his arm. A spotted hospital gown.
Something was telling him to lift the gown up.

The pit wobbled as he got the hem of his skirt, and lifted, over his knees, the same strong thighs, the same powerful man hood. His tremendous V lines. He closed his eyes and ripped it up to his chest.

Kept them closed and placed his hands on his stomach.

Wibble, wobble. Plastic and jelly. Wire and bandage.

No, No, No.

He opened them.

It wasn't a pit, making him feel this way. It was something attached to him. It was a plastic nest, coming out of him.

There was no pit, no vat, no grave. This feeling was real, and it was coming from the colostomy bag that had been attached to him in his sleep. Because he had not been euthanised. He had simply been put under, and now he had woken up into a life where nightmares were placed on the outside.

'AAAAAH!'

The door opened. The same nurse from before came in, followed by Eli Jones. Darren recognised the political campaigner immediately.

'Hi Darren,' Eli smiled. 'You're up.'

'What's happening?!' Darren roared.

'Gentle, gentle,' said the nurse. 'Everything is as requested. A box of ashes has been sent to your family with your name on the top.'

'And they will never find you,' Eli chimed in. 'In fact, they will never even look for you. *All they will do is grieve you.* After all, that's what you wanted, Mr Thames.'

Now Darren really backed up in panic, needles and petri dishes falling to the floor with an abrasive clatter as he went. 'Wh-what? WHAT? What is this? Where is this?!'

Eli sat on the hospital bed, patted it for Darren to come next to him. 'Haven't you heard? All suicides go to hell. Welcome.'

Remember Hope?

Hope hard. Hope long. Hope deep. Hope dry.

Hope hot. Hope thick. Hope sweet. Hope strong.

Hope bright. Hope tight. Hope sharp. Hope wet.

Hope for nothing, hope for everything, hope for the end, hope for Heaven, hope for Hell. Hope for the first thing you ever thought of and the last thing you'll think of. Hope for the thing you've always wanted and the thing you've been too afraid to crave. Hope for what you thought would never come and what you knew you'd never deserve.

Because the Hope is coming. I have summoned her, and now she comes. She comes for you, she comes for us. The wait is nearly over my friends.

Close your eyes. Hold out your hands. Open them wide. Feel that? Tonight, she fills your hands.

Tonight, she comes.

Chapter Twenty Eight

'Great. Let's go get dinner. I know a place.'
'Wait.'
Eli had burst back into the room, and he was looking at Myles and Erica with his brand new eyes. He straightened up for a second, embarrassed with which the vigour he had launched himself back into the room. He coughed.
'Please - you two - can I take you for dinner?'
Erica tightened beneath Myles arm, and Myles tried to figure out a way to be polite. Erica had had a long day healing strangers, he'd gone behind her back to organise this, and now, if he knew anything about her, he knew she would just want to rest. To switch off and be Erica, not The Healer.
'I owe you in abundance, for what you've done for me. For giving me back my vision. And there's nothing I'd rather do with it than watch you eat.'
Something about how tall he was standing, reminded Myles of how he'd felt the night Erica had outed Jack and Rose to him - restoring him to full power. Eli was - the tabloids were not wrong - the most handsome fifty nine year old on the market, a man who vibrated with charm. Seeing him fully functional, with the bite back in the blue glow of his eyes, was undeniably uplifting. Uplifting enough for Myles to look at Erica, and cock his head to the side in a silent '*Shall we*?'
Erica shrugged, the way someone does when they give in, or give up. 'Fuck it. I'm starving. Let's eat.'

Erica had made the right choice. Eli Jones had access to all the best places.
'This is gourmet. New Nordic noir. All organic of course.'
With every step he sauntered, leading them into somewhere high end, exclusive and above all, secret, Myles was ever more convinced it had been the right thing to bring Erica to him. Maybe it was the lightness in his step now that he could again admire the ornate decor, or the way he could look the maitre d' in the eye when he clasped his hand, and see the respect with which the maitre d' looked back. Maybe it was the gratitude with which he seemed to soak in every detail, every piece of art, every face. Maybe it was the authoritative thrill he exuded now he could properly lead them, and lead them with the knowledge he was taking them somewhere elite; lead them through a restaurant already packed with recognisable, successful customers; lead them through the gleaming chef's kitchen - *I must get those hobs for our place* - and through a steel door twelve feet tall, to a private dining room.
He had already indulged his sight. Tonight, the three of them would indulge all five senses. And maybe a six sense too.

'What I'm really struggling with is how. How – how – can anything ever be enough, to thank both of you? Myles, you, for finding me. Erica, you, for curing me. I mean, look at this menu, point to anything on it. *Scallops and spaghetti*? *Espresso martini*? I mean, they sound lovely, but that's not going to do it, is it? I should be carving my heart out and frying it on this table for you to eat right now.' The waiter blanched in shock at Eli's words, because he sounded deadly serious. 'Heart sashimi by Chef Eli. Fancy adding it to the menu?' Eli grinned at him. 'But seriously. I should be thinking about all the things I can do again, but all I can think is there *has* to be something you could want. Even the girl who can cure all our problems must want something. Even the man who has her must want something more.'

'Well you're wrong there,' Myles said. 'I don't want anything else.'

'And I believe you. You'd have her, even without her powers.'

'You could cut off her hands and she'd be just as good to me.' Myles winked. Erica winked back.

'But back to the topic, the question at hand. Which is … how can I thank you? What do you want Erica?' Eli smiled.

'I suppose it's obvious, but I can't have what I want, not yet, or not in this life. I'd like to sleep. I'd like to rest. But it's ok. I can't yet. More than anything, I don't want people to be suffering when I could stop it.'

'So what's the answer? Because I suppose they must be suffering right now.' Eli picked up the menu, casually.

'We're going to help them,' Myles interjected. 'One woman cannot be the answer. We're hoping there are others out there like Erica, who just don't know it yet.'

They ordered. Over wine and parmesan, they told Eli the story of what Myles had been through, and what Erica had done for him. When they were done, Eli asked her another question.

'You ever been ill yourself, Erica? Or been in any kind of pain?'

She scooped up forkfuls of linguine before answering. 'Never. The closest was stress induced chronic pain when I was doing my GCSES, but once I learnt what it was, it was gone. Every time a migraine or something tried to come I just said 'you're not real' and it evaporated. Amazing. You can be so lucky sometimes.' She took a gulp of wine.

'You sure can,' Eli smiled. 'And so unlucky other times.
If you listen really hard you can probably hear them.'

'Who?' Erica mumbled through a mouthful of carbs and prawns. She washed it down with wine, wiped her mouth then looked him dead in the eye.

'Them. The Unlucky. Aching. Waiting. Itching. Longing. All of them. People who've heard about you. Who've been looking for you.'

'What are you doing?' Myles said sharply.

Eli ignored him.

'Think about them. Sitting in the spit. It's no way to live, for them or for you.'

Myles pushed back his chair. 'Do *not* put pressure on her. Erica is doing something incredible. She can't get to everyone at once.'

'Maybe she can,' Eli said. 'Will you come with me, Erica?'
Before Erica could answer, she was distracted by the actions of the waiters. Who began closing the doors, and gradually sliding by to take both Myles and Erica's phones. From the restaurant beyond they heard a thump, as if people were banging their glasses on the table and stamping their feet on the ground. Thump. Bang. Splash.
Another waiter entered, only to turn a lock in the door. The nasty click unlocked a memory only she could know - this is what happens before *it* happens.
The door to the Fire Exit swung open. Myles looked in surprise but Erica didn't even need to look.
Slow, seamless, as if filling the room with steam, a dozen or so men - one an oak tree, one a boar, one a stag on two legs - began filing in. Walking with silent sinisterness, the way Dread would walk if it came to life. The trio's table was circular, and it was a circle that these men formed around it, closing them in - perfectly symmetrical, the distance with which they stood apart calculated to a mathematical degree. Just how Eli liked it. The final man - henchman, hitman, thug, brute, something worse? - slammed the Fire Exit shut, and took his place at the head, standing behind Eli in a shield.
'If you won't come, Erica, then what if they took you? What if one of these fine gentlemen took you?'
Imperceptibly, trying not to panic, trying not to feel, Erica's eyes drifted to Eli's. He met her with the perfect vision of the eyes she had restored less than two hours ago, and those eyes said one thing only: *Yes. This is happening.*
Balancing her breath on a beam, she let herself throw a look to Myles, to see if the fear had come for him yet.
Instead, she saw focus - there was a promise in his eyes - to save her, to stop this. He got it. He was ready. He'd been waiting for this. Erica started to hear her breath, coming through the grind of her bright white teeth. But Myles, he was staying calm. Big breaths now.
They'd talked about this, about coming across people who couldn't let the Healer go. It was natural, would have been naive not to assume people could develop an obsession with her. There was so much Myles didn't know, so much she hadn't told him, but maybe what they had was enough - just enough - to get through this moment now. To get through this together.
'Eli. Eli. Listen to me.' Calm. Soft. A focused pitch. Good. Good. Come on. 'Everything will be over for you if you take her.'
She couldn't help it. It came out without warning.
'*If*?'
Erica made that word into a bullet. An insult that could do what a nuclear bomb couldn't.
'*If*?'
She pitched it again. Perfect sound, perfect colour.
'Yes,' Eli swung back, understanding before Myles did. 'If we take you.'

'If. If. If, if, if.'
Gingerly, she stepped up onto the table, olives scattering off her body as she did. '*If* they take me.' She looked down at her captors, crumbs of disdain falling. To her, her captors were the crumbs. 'If they do that to me again … if they actually *think* they can do to me … if they take me back to that place …' A rapture was released inside her. She turned from woman to weather. *This* is why hurricanes are named after women.
'I'll gouge their eyes out. I'll tear their tongues out. I'll rip their hair out from the roots.' Swarming, rousing, she swept above the room. The captors didn't move, didn't speak, all bent in reverence at her speech.
'IF they do this to me, as long as they live I'll come for them, I'll find them, I'll hunt them - '
She was half human, half hive, a colony of hornets releasing with every word she spoke.
'I'll rip their spines out just to twist them - I'll pull their lungs out just to pop them -
And as long as they have blood, I'm gonna drink it -
And as long as they have brains, I'm gonna blend them -
And as long as they have skin, I will flay them - '
She sank to her knees, the centrepiece on the table, looking Eli dead in the eyes she had given them. Her voice was sweet, gentle, like she was learning to speak.
'So do you see? Do you see?
If they do that to me, that's what happens to them.
Do you see now?'
Eli leaned back, his hand closing around the stem of his wine glass. 'I do.'
Relief replaced Erica's ego. For the first time today, she breathed. Now she could decide what she would have for dessert; white chocolate meringue, or the salted caramel bomb.
Eli's shirt was open, his chest wide and masculine. There was a swagger to him now, playing on the salt and pepper stubble. 'Myles, cut off her hands.'
Myles gripped the table cloth. 'What?'
'If you don't want me to take her, then cut off her hands. It's a fair trade - I'll take the hands, stitch them onto someone who's worthy of them.' The maitre d' passed Eli the alpha of all knives, the one you couldn't ignore when you walked through the kitchen. 'You keep the rest of her. Treat her like the slab of meat she is to you.' Eli pushed the knife towards him. 'Go on. If you love her that much, cut off her hands.'
Suddenly Erica was being bent over the table, one thug holding down her wrists, two thugs pressing down her hips.
Instinctively, Myles hand made a cocoon around the blade, sealing it in his palm.
'Go on, Myles. Slashitty-slash. Cut them off and you get the girl.'
'Do it,' Erica hissed. 'You can do it. Just get rid of them.'

Myles rose to his feet. He looked into the thug's eyes, the ones that had the hands on his girl. Oh, he'd missed this kind of anger. Here we go.
Beastlike, he swung for the first one. He drove into him all the rage he had had too much highground to give to Jack that night in his penthouse - he gave it to this thug. Velocity and force, he knocked the thug off of her wrists, sending him sailing to the ceiling and then to the ground.
The two thugs at her hips were smirking - not for long. A hulk of heartbreak, he proudly drove his feet into their faces. He heard a neck make a sound it should never make, and watched the men bash their heads as they sunk to the floor.
Erica shot up, her eyes electric. Across the table was Myles - five feet behind him, was the door. She had done this before. Got through a door before. *One more time.*
'Well then,' Eli said. 'Guess we'll take her whole. Bag her up!'
Myles took Erica's hand. And they tried to fly.
They tried to fly out of that room, to grow wings and take flight, to possess the only power neither of them had ever shown. They would have given anything to be airborne, to be angels - after all, all it meant was hovering a few feet from the ground and shooting through the window. Erica had shown them so many miracles, surely this last one couldn't be that hard? They tried to fly instead of fight, believed that as long as they held onto each other they could rise above the thugs, weave through them or float above them, that despite the kicks, and the lunges, and the knees that came their way, some force in the sky would see how much it meant to them, would take pity on them and feel pride in them, and know that they were owed this: they were owed this escape.
But the pity or the pride never came. Only the screams, only the violence, only the pain.
Just when it was too late, just when they realised they were only humans and they needed to use their limbs not their wannabe wings, just when they accepted it and were ready to fight - it was over. It was done. It was Eli's.
Erica was already bundled into the thug's arms. Five of them, all already clasped along the length of them.
The door to the Exit was already open.
There was already ten feet between them. A small distance but too much for them, too much for now.
Myles was already being held down.
Eli had already won.
Erica was dragged out of the room, and Myles was screwed into the floor. He heard her screams all the way down the fire escape, and then came a sound even worse: silence.
All the love he'd let himself feel turned into loneliness.
'Could do with a healer now, couldn't ya?'
Eli bent down to whisper in his ear.

'At the end of the day, I got the girl. Cos I *understand* the girl. She trusts me, whereas she couldn't even tell you it was me that had her captive all those years.'

He placed his hand over his. Eli's was just that little bit bigger.

'We're meant to be. It's fate.'

He rose to his feet. 'Don't fuck with fate - you haven't got the balls to pull it off.'

At that, Myles looked up.

'I know you *think* you do, but …' Eli had drifted to the door. He chuckled.

'You've had a knife in your hand this whole time and you didn't even realise.'

Stunned, Myles felt the clench of the blade in his palm. Stunned, the truth soaked him.

Eli was right.

'You will never see her again. If you need something to believe in, you can make that your religion.'

Chapter Twenty Nine

This is the story of a girl inside a van.

She would remember this moment forever. When the rear doors closed and she realised what she'd done – or what might be about to be done to her. She would remember the white walls, the cold grey floor, the mundane stickers across the door. The sound of the engine.

In their arms there had still been a struggle, some sort of opportunity for escape. She'd been impressed at how her sheer adrenaline had kicked in. She was a fighter at heart so fight them she did. But the moment the door slammed, girl became wolf and oh-how-she-howled.

It was the MYSTERY of it. Of what they were going to do to her. Of the fact they could do anything to her. Of the fact that every bit of her autonomy had now been peeled from her. What more would they peel?

They were BULLIES. Nothing more than bullies. An eternal bullying played out in front of her. She had not a friend in the world. Facts replaced fairness, and these facts were fierce: she was theirs. New laws were drawn up, for this girl who would now be a vessel. If she found a friend, a small mouse or two in the place they were going to keep her, they were entitled to fry it and feed it to her, then stir scorpions into her eyes til she got the message and if she wanted to see, she had to sing for them and all they would show her was venom.

She opened her eyes and – POW – horror went through her stomach when – ZAP – another bolt came from her chest and she wondered why she had ever been given a body at all.

ZIP — BOING – WOLLOP –

they were trying to fit the whole of the space time continuum inside her petite skull KABOOM! – every tsunami needs a beach and this tsunami had chosen her – CRASH – KABOOM! – the fear went in and out so much, maybe it was trying to stitch her up – WOW! SPLAT –

too much fluid in her spine – WOW!

and – POP! – went her tongue

ZIP – ZAP – SPLAT! SPLAT! SPLAT! – a big black hole opened up behind her head and her organs were transplanted – WOOSH! OUCH!

OOPS!

She was a human. But humans aren't designed to feel this much fear. So she had to, like so many other captives that had come before her, switch off her humanity.

What was she now? Don't answer that.

A great big gurn opened up inside her. Her whole body became a tantrum. How was this happening to her? To her life? Again? *Sometimes a life - a little life - boils down to this. Just this. Just fear.*

CRASH - BANG - WALLOP!

The van was going over speed bumps and lurching round corners at a speed that couldn't possibly be legal. So it was already starting; the breaking, the buckling, not a hand in the space to steady her, she felt the injuries come through the adrenaline. Maybe this would be the worst feeling; if this was the worst, she could handle it. Wait, no, she couldn't! No, no! One was enough, but no more. Don't do this to her! No, she took it all back, no, no!
Not another. NOT AGAIN.
She wished she could be stronger than pain, but right now she wasn't stronger than paper. She'd do anything not to be here, and if that wouldn't work, anything not to be her. She no longer gave a fuck about the face she liked in the mirror and the swagger in her step ...she'd be a boy, she'd be eighty, she'd be a frog so as long as she didn't have to be this. Here. Now. Driving along in the abrasive white brick, not knowing when she would next sleep without needles beneath her -
KABOOM - BANG - BOING!
Suddenly she had sympathy for the spinach, sizzling in the pan. Sympathy for the sock, drowning in the washing machine. But who would have sympathy for her?
This is where rejects go.
She wasn't sure if what she heard next was her own voice speaking, or someone from the front, mocking her *'one time when I was sixteen, I thought I had chronic pain ... turns out it was all just stress and as soon as I knew that it went away ... you won't be so lucky this time...'*
Oh god. She was going to miss everyone so much. They might miss her, but they would find others; she was the one being taken to the darkness, the silence, the stillness. It turned out she wasn't pretty enough to get away with it and not plain enough to ignore. She wasn't going to get away with her life, with her joy – she should have tried to be stillborn when she had the chance. This was it now. BASH - CRASH!
Ooh. Another speed bump. She clanged into the other side of the van. She tasted metallic. Her head was bleeding. Her ankle didn't feel right. Her shoulder was tingling like it never had before. Oh well. Fuck did she care? She was going to a place where she didn't need a body.
KAPOW! ZOING! WALLOP!
She was on her way to meet the Gods of the inanimate. They had chosen her, to be the sentient being they would teach a lesson to. Just please let her be strong, please let the nervous system be a lie, please make it true that you pass out from too much pain, she'll do anything to finally be numb.
ZING! NOT AGAIN NOT AGAIN NOT AGAIN!

She couldn't help but be curious, as she felt the van slowing down, backing up. It was happening, they were pulling into wherever they were going to be keeping her.

The van came to a calm halt. This was it. She heard the passenger door open and slam, the exhaust engine pipe down. Familiar sounds of regular life. She heard footsteps, and then the door opened. A man she didn't recognise held out his hand to her, but his face fell when he realised she was too injured to make it to the door. Suddenly he was in the van, gingerly carrying her out in his arms. He put her down as those to present her.

They were in a courtyard.

Gravel and stone and lavender and scents. A large manor house beamed above her. The stone house formed a U around a lawn, each wall climbing with a different flower or vine. Turrets. Verandas. Balconies. Ivy. Stained glass. Lattices. An oak tree. She saw faces in the window, eyes blinking. And of course, Eli. He stood there, smiling, backed by ten or so matronly women. She winced as her shoulder moved unnaturally. Held her hand to her lip as it split. So this is where it was. Core Retreat. His second creation.

'Erica! Welcome!' Eli raced to her. 'Help hold her up.' Two women took to the side of her, looping her arms round her necks. She yelped and Eli snapped, 'Gentler.'

'Everyone,' he called to the courtyard. 'I know you're watching. So let's welcome her properly. The Healer! And we already have our first task for you. Erica – baby – I know that was a bumpy ride you just endured. But now we can see you work your magic.

Now we can watch you heal.

Heal yourself.'

One of the women began calling out to the courtyard. 'Broken elbow – perforated eye – possibly a dislocated collarbone – bleeding temple, bleeding gums … let's see it. Let's see if she's as good as you say, Eli.'

There was silence in the courtyard, the silence of a ceremony.

Until she spat. 'You IDIOT!'

Eli came closer, every step gentle. 'What is it, darling?'

Her eyes going yellow, her teeth shining, she matched him for every step, coming into the centre of the courtyard with a swirl. *Let them see this.* 'I can't heal myself!' Her teeth bared. She caught the eyes of those in the windows. 'That's the *one fucking thing* a healer can't do, Eli! A healer can't heal their own wounds! The ONE thing!'

Her eyes flashed back to the door of the van, the boot of it she'd been hauled into. For a moment she thought her anger might pierce the metal, too little, too late. 'I'd have thrown myself into the road and escaped if I could do that!'

Uncomfortable, painful energy filled the air. Eli looked around awkwardly … 'You sure?'

Erica spun again, electric in the courtyard, the cold air swirling with her. She didn't care about the blood clots that came from her lips or the sound her joints made as she revolved, a revolver now, for them all. 'Of course I'm sure! It's

ME! Only I *know* how this works!! And - I can't - heal - *myself.* What the fuck have you done?!'
'Shh.... Damn ... I'm sorry. Okay. It's ok.' He nodded warmly. 'We have doctors here, great doctors. They'll fix you up overnight. Nothing a hot bath won't fix.' But his eyes were dim, disappointed; he hadn't imagined her welcome to be like this.
'You are a joke, Eli.' Erica whispered through her grinding teeth, cradling her arm. 'And nobody's laughing.'
Eli couldn't meet her eyes. 'I'll make it up to you. I promise.
Right now, let's get you settled. We have a fantastic attic suite for you.
What do you want for dinner? Or maybe that bath first?'
Erica felt her legs give way. She winced as wires went the wrong way down her spine.
It was becoming clear. Where she had been taken. Why she had been taken.
Now or never, she knew she had to speak, not bite down on the begging inside of her. She held her shoulder in its socket, softened her voice and said,
'Eli ... I wish I wanted to be here as much as you want me here. But I don't. So, please, Eli. What do I have to do for you to let me go?'
Eli shook his head. 'Don't ask me that. It's not fair. Not with those big eyes of yours.
You're going to be happy, Erica. We're going to be happy.'
Behind him, more and more matrons were building. Erica's wounds widened.
'No, Eli. Not again. You have to let me go. You have to let me *choose.'*
'Erica, I already did that once. And it became an obsession. The opposite of healthy. It was giving me migraines. My eyelid wouldn't stop twitching. Until now. Already I'm feeling better.' He cupped her jaw. The whimper came, as did the lightning in her eyes. *Let them see this.* 'Don't worry, darlin'. You're gonna raise us up.'
It was a nod, or it was a shudder. But it was enough: they came for her.
Gentle, gentle hands closed around her upper arms. The doors to the manor house swung open. The tulips and the bluebells bloomed apart for her. An apple fell from the orchard to be near her. An aisle opened up in the gravel for her.
The moon came out to watch.
Eli smiled and the weight of all our blood lifted up off him with his lips.
'Bring her in.'
Erica replaced the sky with her scream. 'This is Hell! You've dragged me to Hell! Let me go!'
Eli's hand ran across her head, lacquering her hair down as though his smugness could soothe her.
'Now. Now. Enough of this.
What did Hell ever do to you?'

Chapter Thirty

Eli

Who knew a smoothie could be so scary?

You will need:
A handful of wheatgrass
A handful of mustard greens
One dandelion root
One thumb of ginger
The zest of a grapefruit
Two teaspoons of spirulina
Two teaspoons of sea moss
Twenty grams of turmeric
Three cups of goji berries
Three dragonflies (alive)

Make 'em live, make em live. Watch 'em breathe, watch 'em breathe.

I put my mother in a blender. The question is, did I turn it on?
Maybe I pressed the button, so over the sound of whirring wheels were the cries of 'Did you pack your gym kit?', 'Let me trim your hair' and 'Never trust boys on motorbikes.' Maybe it swirled up in a mix of elbow and teeth and kitchen gloves, of corduroy and cocoa and umbilical. Maybe the breast milk made the contents run creamy. But maybe the new, hormonal hairs on her chin made the mix sticky and difficult to swallow. Maybe I served her up for a healthy breakfast, topped with slices of strawberries and socks she'd found. Maybe I drunk her unconditionally and loved her whatever the flavour, the way she had loved me. Maybe that's why I'm healthy now.

You still don't want it?
Why?
Why are you so scared of a smoothie?
Oh. Of course. I almost forgot.
You want to pour your life down the drain, like you do my big delicious smoothie. You're ungrateful, reckless, all or nothing - won't take a sip unless it's just how you want it. Won't fight for anything, not even your own health. You're scared of tomorrow; of course you're scared of my smoothie.
Nobody is leaving the table til their glass is crystal clear.'
Make 'em live and watch 'em breathe.

I didn't start off this strict. At first Core Retreat was what I promised it would be. A place those in doubt about living could come and learn the value of life. Where anyone is welcome, even those that can't be forgiven.
That's still true. Core is more successful than ever.
But for that, I had to make rules.
The first thing I did was ban music. Music is a distraction. Once I banned that I started to see the potential of this place. The world outside is full of crime and danger. Core could be *my* world. My world where I kept them all safe. Where nothing bad ever happened. Realistically, to get it to that place, to *really* get it to that place, people had to forget who they were before. About the urges that drove them in the world outside. In Core they would never be dirty again.
Now everybody is clean. Scrubbed and disinfected. Finally, they are pure.

Of course, some argue. Some fight. This isn't what they expected. Some didn't even ask to be here at all, like Darren Thames.
Thank god for the carers. My wonderful assistants, who care so deeply about upholding the world I want to create. It took me a while to find the right girls. I had to do much research to find women who wouldn't report what we are doing here. Women who didn't belong to the harsh world beyond these walls. Women not afraid of hard work; changing, feeding, bandaging. Women with just the right amount of authority to make this place work.
Gradually, my guests come round to my way of thinking. They know this is the one place where they may walk again. Now that I've brought them The Healer.

Let's talk about Scott. I'm sure you're wondering what happened to the most handsome of MPs.
Now, as you know, I'd never sing for any suicide, but I can't say that particular one wasn't useful. I suppose it didn't *hurt* my cause for the man behind Sunset to expose himself as suicidal after all. To reveal himself to be just another mentally unstable soul. It validated everything I ever said about the Assisted Dying Bill, about how it came from some nihilistic place inside ourselves that didn't even deserve airtime, let alone a vote. Since he swung from the ceiling, creating Core has been a buttery kind of easy.
Do you want to know a secret?
I suppose I do champion honesty. Loyalty. Truth. The truth is healthy, and I am all about that Health.
So here goes:
Scott Luther is still alive.

You see, it makes sense, just as has made sense since Core came into my mind. The blackmail trap that Scott so easily walked into, becoming just another politician in my pocket. Oh, if only the people knew what I have done to him; if only they knew how complicit I have made him. You won't hear from him

again. He is too afraid to speak now. He is too afraid to do anything but my bidding.
The submissive little Scott, so terrified of suffering, would do anything to not be a 'politician in prison', and now we share a secret, a secret Darren Thames was the first to sample.
Beneath Sunset Clinic, there our secret lurks.
Close your eyes. I can take you there.
Enter Surgery Room 44. At the back wall, head to the wide iron cupboard. Open the cupboard, step inside, and you'll find another door. Open that door and you'll find a staircase. Walk down six flight of stairs and you'll find yourself in a tunnel, a tunnel that runs 25 miles out of London, wide enough to contain vehicles and with the infrastructure for them to travel on. Follow that tunnel until you finally reach the other staircase, the one made of stone. Ascend the staircase until you start to feel the moss. Wade through the moss, and you will come out and into the gardens of Core Retreat.
You can open your eyes now.
This tunnel is where we take the quitters, the ungrateful, the weak who didn't appreciate the lives they had. They come to Sunset to give up … and wake up in Core, where they are assigned a new life, a very different life indeed. A life that will teach them the meaning of gratitude.
We don't do this to every one of Sunset's clients. Only the ones that ask to be cremated.
It makes such sense, you see, it's just so deliciously *practical,* that we had to do it. They go to live new lives at Core, and their families are none the wiser, able to grieve in peace and move on from those who moved on from them. A box of ashes is sent to said family. They'll never know it's the ash of a willow tree in there instead.
I've never been so grateful for the concept of cremation, something I found rather too untraditional before. These untraditional, ungrateful goons made all this possible.
The ash is the answer. The ash is the answer. The ash is the answer.
And so you see, it's science, it's destiny, it's fate, what happens next. That she with Ash in her name has come to us.
The ash is the answer. Erica Ash is ours.

Remember Hope?
It is I who spoke of Hope, who traded in Hope, who knew when my country legalised assisted dying that it would start to give up on itself. You let people quit when things aren't perfect, you raise a nation who see no value in life, or in each other, who forget all the magic this world has to offer. Before the vote, we always held on, no matter what we went through, always believing better days would be round the corner, always fighting for each other, to give each other the chance to find beauty in a new way of life or even show the ingenuity to

discover an incredible cure - humans have discovered so much before. But then, before we could, came the vote, and then the Death.
But they didn't get rid of Hope. They may have halved it, hacked it, hammered it and called it Hell, but it's people like you who still hoped. You hoped hard and hoped long and hoped deep and then she came. I found her for you. I got her. The cure, the medicine, the fucking vaccine. Sorry, I don't like to curse.
Nobody will ever hurt again. Not now we have Erica.
Erica is hope.
Let's just hope you didn't Hope for *this.*
Let's Hope you didn't happen for what happens next.
And if you did wish for this …
Be prepared for what they'll wish upon you.

Chapter Thirty One

Dr Sunset

They called her Dr Sunset. Sunset Clinic's pride and joy.
It was a strange job, she could admit that. Looking around at her fellow commuters, she wondered what they'd think if they knew she was off to lethally inject people from nine til five today. Would their eyes swell with admiration or should she just tell them she was a Doctor?
Maybe one day she'd tell them about it. Not yet. To them she was either a killer or a doctor; to her, it was a fight for freedom. And nobody understood freedom like her.
You didn't know freedom til you saw a person be rolled in, every hump in the ground another obstacle, every turn of the chair another wince, and the family member that would come in behind them, struggling with the handles like they'd struggled with the guilt of not doing enough, and two eyes that would look up with you with such hope, such fear you would change your mind, as they whispered, '*Thank you thank you thank you. We thought a place like this would never exist.*' She knew freedom so well she felt like she'd invented it.
So she slid her hand into a plastic glove, opened a new syringe, filled it with potassium chloride, found a vein and injected it. Into them. Into them. Mothers, sisters, wives, husbands. Sons, daughters, grandsons. Twins, lovers, soulmates, heroes. She did it from nine til five every day, til the push of a syringe became a reflex.
As she folded a strap around their arm, tightening it – 'last time you're going to have to wince,' she said with a wink – she felt the question seep from her. 'So, are you – are you scared at all, about what's on the other side?'
It was a question designed to test them. If there was any chance of a last minute change of mind, this question would do it. She had to be on the ball for that, for any changes in body language, for any sudden utterances as the needle came closer; they had every opportunity to back out, and she had to facilitate that. People would love to catch her being *negligent.* They wet their pants over the thought of catching her *abusing her position.*
But so far, everybody's case held up the question. Everybody, every day, was ready to go.

Today was different though. Today she was not working at Sunset Clinic, but a guest of Core Retreat. Her boss George, Scott Luther's less radical replacement, had sent her there for two days of meetings - it was important that their two ethos's were seen merging, balancing, to keep calm a Britain that had legalised murder.
She couldn't fault what they were doing here, or what Eli had done. Core Retreat took people, the likes of which she saw in Sunset every day, the

difference being they had hope - and Core used that hope to help them find a reason to live. Some came only for their family, as a gesture - but so far nobody had wanted to leave. Plans were already being drawn up for a sister retreat to be built in Ireland.

Drawing through the gates into the large estate, she buckled with excitement. She couldn't blame them for loving this place. Sunset was in the centre of London, in a simple, clinical building without fuss or favour. *Core*, on the other hand, was deep in the countryside, and on the coast. She'd had to sign multiple NDAs to make sure she never revealed the location. As soon as the driver turned into an epic driveway, she knew she was in for a moment of luxurious, ethical peace. Pink, green, blue flowers popped through resplendent bushes, arches, vines and trees that had grown forty feet tall.

She was lost in the nature, when her attention turned to the house. It was the most glorious country manor she had ever seen; piped like silver icing out of a cake mixer, with wells, fountains, and endless lawns. And the *size* of it – somehow it managed to not be gloating or ostentatious. A doll's house come to life, threatening to shrink back to toy size and not let anyone else in.

When she stepped out the air was like no other. Free from the pollution of London, but it was more than that: rejuvenating and somehow resplendent. As her cases were carried into the house, she heard a faint sound; a buzzing, whirring sound. It continued when she entered the manor, and built as she was led up the wide mahogany staircase and down a wide corridor to her room: a suite of course.

'What's that whirring noise?' she said, passing a door and hearing it again.

'Oh, that's just the blenders,' said the woman showing her to her room. 'You get used to them.'

When she entered her room she saw a canopy bed, a watercolour painting, a vintage dressing table and a threadbare carpet - but most of all she noticed a blender, waiting for her on the window seat. A chopping board, a colouring box of fresh fruit, and a kitchen knife all laid calmly around it.

'Make whatever you want,' the woman said. 'Anything your body needs. Eli will see you in an hour.' She made her way to the window, and her mouth fell open. She could see the sea from here.

Washed, dried and changed, she was ready for her meeting with Eli. She waited, in his impressive yet cosy office, sinking into the velvet sofa. An assistant appeared to her left and without asking, thrust an amber juice into her hand, a bamboo straw sticking out of it. 'Thank you – ' she began when another assistant appeared at her right and lunged a ginormous pitcher of green juice in front of her. 'Thanks,' she looked to and from both and they waited expectantly.

'Try it. While you wait for Eli.'

She sipped on the small juice first.. 'Mmm! A tropical flavour.'

'Now try mine!' The other insisted awkwardly.

She swallowed the amber mouthful, then reached and sipped from the large pitcher. 'Can't quite place it.'
'Its cucumber,' the assistant beamed over enthusiastically. 'Very high water content. Every cell in your body consists of – '
'That's enough for now, girls.'
Here he was Eli. She stood.
In person he held a kind of power she hadn't expected. He was even more good looking, and everything about him radiated good. His eyes were everything people said they were, even brighter now they were born again. She beamed, shook his hand, then as they sat back down she blurted out -
'Why all the juices?'
'Well … what better way to make delicious healthy juice … than to fill this place with Vegetables?'
Then he smirked. His words went through her, threatening to bring up the many juices that were now bloating her stomach. Her smile dripped off her face. 'I really hope you're not joking about the patients you have here, Eli.'
'Patients? *You* have patients, my dear. I have a population.'
Dr Sunset nodded. 'Okay.' Her tone was sharp and bitter - you'd think he would know not to mess with someone who lethally injected for a living. 'Shall we get to it then?' She pulled her briefcase onto her lap and opened it up. 'I made some notes in the car.'
'Did you?' Eli's eyes seemed to glow. 'I thought you'd be playing hangman. The word game. Shall we play it now?'
Dr Sunset cleared her throat. 'Eli, was it not you who emailed us? About combining our efforts? About co-hosting a charity gala? About references for a nurse? Was that not you?'
Eli drummed his finger lightly on the back of the sofa. Her stomach gurgled, embarrassed. 'I'm serious. I want to play Hangman. That's what you do every day, isn't it?'
'What is this? An elaborate ruse to insult me?' Bitterness built in her body.
'I'll make it easy. Two letters. The second one is J. What's the word?'
'I'm not entertaining this - I don't know!'
Eli leant back. Leant back with such confidence, such calm, such control, that Dr Sunset knew all she could do was be silent, breathe slowly, and let him speak. All while looking around the room, keeping alert, keeping her wits about her.
'Dr Sunset, do you like music? I bet you do.
I want you to imagine you are at a musical festival. One of the 'edgy' ones - Creamfields or Burning Man. And your favourite act is about to play. It's dubstep; I know you like that.
You weave your way through the food trucks, catching the smell of grease and onions - you'll go back for that later - past the ferris wheel full of screaming couples, and into the crowd. You can hear the bass all the way from the back,

but it's not enough. You weave your way through the crowd - people part for a person like you.
With every step it gets deeper, and slipperier, but you don't care. You pass a girl performing some kind of sexy show in the mud, because there's no rules at this kind of festival. You keep going. Near the front, the crowd parting, forming a festival tradition called 'The Red Sea', where two halves of the crowd wait to run into each other and 'mosh'. There's women on men's shoulders but the crowd's attention is taken by three lads who've formed a tower, and the skinny girl climbing their way to the top man's shoulders. Stupid, or cool?
Once you've planted yourself deep enough in the hive, the dubstep is getting not just louder, but stronger. Everybody knows the drop is coming. You start to sway, let it take you. Ooh, ew, what's that, it's a missile of beer sent from the other side of the crowd; at least you think it's beer; could be piss, who cares, *this is a festival*, you open your mouth and lap it up anyway.
From just overhead, you can see the DJ, the MC, the front man of the performing act. He tears the mic off its stand and he says,
"*What's up? Whose having a good time?"* Me, me, the crowd cries.
You bunch of muddy filthy sexy fuckers - whose ready to rave? When do we stop raving?" When we're dead, they wail back.
"Damn straight! Now I've seen some good dancing and some beautiful ladies in this crowd, but when the beat drops, we don't want none of that. The name of this track is Headbangers. When the beat drops, all you sloppy horny bastards are going to mosh so hard I want you to break your fucking necks. Got it?"
Woo, woo, the crowd obeys.
"Ready ... 3 ... 2 ... 1 ... break your fucking necks now!"
The beat drops and all risk goes out the window. Skulls turn into zorbing balls, to bowling billiards, to marbles, becoming one with their neighbour. They pull away in surprise from each other - is their nose in a different place to where it was before? Only at a festival would you high five the person who just knocked out your tooth.
It's only at a festival that you wouldn't notice the people who've been knocked all the way out, concussed in one go from one simple headbutt. Only at a festival would the red sea, the two separate walls of people, run together. What about the girl in the middle doing the sexy mud show – only at a festival do they forget, or just not care, or think she'll get out of the way just in time, but she doesn't, and she can't. And she is not the only one – too many people joined the red sea at one moment this time, and as they come together, there are splinters and snaps and stamps, there are bones out where they should be skin and feet where there should be faces and blood where there should be hair, there are so many people it takes their breath away, and by that I mean, literally, people are shouting, 'We can't breathe'.
At this point the DJ's face starts to fall, as he realises he has hosted the kind of rave that they will write about tomorrow as a tragedy.

Only at a festival does the mud underfoot turn to people, only at a festival could you realise it is your fiancé you are standing on, you reach down to grab her but she is pinned down by another six pairs of muddy wellingtons and then you go down too. Last thing you see is the broken bottle.

And only at a festival does that daring, hardcore tower of four ravers start to topple - the bottom man becomes powder, the man above him folds in two, the man standing on him is flung so far you don't see where he lands, and the girl on top - chosen cos she was the lightest - is not light enough not to crush the people she falls down upon, but what will be worse is what happens to her when they catch her. A story she'll never have the strength to tell.

And then there's you. He asked you to break your neck. To become a cautionary tale: of the girl who partied too hard. So hard she broke her brain. In the days after the festival, she forgot her name. Her eye wouldn't stop twitching.

Do you deserve that? Do they deserve that? To be paralysed by partying? To live with the guilt of those they crushed? All because they lived too hard, too reckless, even though I told them not to?

Maybe. Maybe they do. Or maybe not. Maybe they'd deserve a chance to redeem themselves. To save themselves.

But there is one person at that festival who *does* deserve to suffer. One person I know for certain that needs to be punished for that day. It's the DJ, of course.'

Eli turned to his assistants. 'Is he ready?'

Dr Sunset felt her stomach swill as the door behind Eli opened and a young man entered. He had long shaggy hair, wore a tank top and a necklace of neon beads, and he kept his head down as he wheeled something into the room. Dr Sunset realised it was a DJ deck, the buttons still flashing, neon and inane. As he got closer, she realised his hands were not just on the turntables - they had been stapled onto them. Wait. No. Not stapled - *stitched.*

'What is this?!' she said. 'Why is there a DJ here?'

Eli turned to the man, who had stopped for a rest against his desk. 'This is DJ Gangha Ghecko. The man who can turn any night from milky to meaty. The man responsible for so many messy memories, and the man responsible for the deathly stampede at a forest rave in Glasgow last summer. Remember the headlines? Remember the videos? Remember how he kept encouraging them to 'mosh'?'

Eli clasped his arm around the man's shoulders, which were ready to give out any moment. 'If the party never stops, why should he? Ghecko, play us something.' Obediently, the MC started turning the tables. An old piece of classical music came out. 'Never used to play this, did you boy?'

'What is this?!' Doctor Sunset cried. She jumped up and ran to the young man, but he didn't even look up. There was nothing in his eyes. 'You *keep* him here?'

Eli's eyes foamed with excitement. 'Some people would rather die than leave the club. When the beat drops, they hit the floor, hit the pavement, hit the earth -

crack. So long live the DJ! Long live the MC! Long live all the fools who think they can live so short and so shallow. Not any more.'

With a push of his palm, the DJ infused a string symphony into the music, the room elevating with it. Eli threw his head back, oozing into the moment.

'To anyone who's ever taken their health for granted, who thinks they were put on this earth to snort and slop and shag and rave and retch and rampage, let the fate of those forest revellers be a warning to them all. There will be no more of that.' Eli looked proudly at his creation. 'DJ Ghanga Ghecko will show them a new way.'

'Are they keeping you here?' Dr Sunset said, trembling. At the same time she ran back to her briefcase and went to grab her phone - but it was gone.

'Yes,' Eli smiled. 'And we're going to keep you here too, Dr Sunset. Your car has gone off the road. Up in flames, in fact. Earlier today we lost a beloved female member of the Core family. Her fatality will not be in vain. The woman's body will be identified and recorded as yours. So that you can remain here with us. Undetected, unbothered, unobstructed. You will learn our way of life.' He moved towards her as she moved backwards, knocking over a juice as she went. 'A sacrifice for Dr Death herself.' She spun to the door but three stocky women now stood in front of it. She spun back to Eli, her eyes breaking as they begged.

'*Olivia,*' she whispered, desperate. 'My name is Olivia.'

He held out his hand to her. 'This may be the last time you'll hear music for a while. Would you like to dance with me?'

Chapter Thirty Two

The Healer

To Everyone,

Before you read this letter, I want you to look at the photograph I've enclosed of myself. Do you like the dress they chose? Do you like the way they've done my hair? Do you like the colour my eyes have become?
Tell me what comes to mind when you see me. Go on, say it. Don't be scared to say it now, I've heard you say it so many times before. 'I want you.'
Well you can have me. All you gotta do is find me.
You may say you've been trying to already, but you haven't really, have you? If you're honest with yourself you could always be doing more.
If you want me, come find me. I'll be waiting. I'll be waiting, mouth open, legs apart, for you to come take me.
They haven't fed me in days - I promise I'll be light in your arms. I'm light enough to carry, small enough to hide away. And every day I become smaller. It turns out that I can just … *shrink* all the way down to the size of a mint. And I'm silent. 3, 2, 1 and they cut out my tongue. I won't say a word when you come for me.
What's it gonna take for you to come find me? I'm not even underground this time. You wouldn't have let me go when you were inside of me, so don't let go of me now.
Wear black when you come for me, and shoes that don't squeak. Bring something I can fit in. Bring a weapon. Sleep well the night before.
I'll never tell them it was you. As long as you come.

I've been good here, I promise.
I've done what they've wanted. I've healed hundreds of people, of every ailment you can think of.
I haven't slept since I arrived. And I haven't refused once.
Except for the first time.
The first time Eli made me do it, I kicked and screamed. I bit at myself, bit at my own body. I held onto every doorway, every railing, every person, as they dragged me down there. I spat and roared and swore as they carried me, every hand female, down and down. I made it rain, I cast thunder, I made the floor ice but nothing worked.
I looked Eli in the eye as he sat me down, and I spoke the way a scalpel would if it came to life, 'I'm not going to do it.'
The patronising *bugger*, he smirked at me, and nodded mockingly. He went about his business, laying a sheet out on the table in front of him. More and more carers appeared; everybody wanted to watch.

Then they bought her in. The whimperer. Told her she would have to be patient. Told her to squeeze their hand if the longing got too much. We all sat there in silence, the carers sipping tea, me counting how many cobwebs I could see on the walls. You know what, I even got up and went for a walk, a little tour around the room. They couldn't stop me and they couldn't make me. There's no cure for stubborn.
You should have seen the way everyone was looking at me. As I ignored every puffy 'please.'
I looked straight back at Eli. Raised my eyebrows, folded my arms and tried to smirk.
Until my conscience came swinging through like a bollard through plaster. Until I looked down and saw what was wrong with them: burns. It was just too simple, and too easy, and too important: so I healed them. Spring sang in me again as I did it. All the sadistic singes went away. We were happy. *I* was happy. But of course, there were more of them waiting. They'd been vomiting all day and they need somewhere to hide it and then I show up. And I could take it all and hide it inside me and make it all better. So I did.
And still, they come. I hear them coming now.

And then, there was the time I tried to run away. The time I tried to escape.
My third night here, I jumped.
They keep me in a tower, you see. Way above the grounds with a tiny stone window. It took me three days to gear myself up to do it - but at midnight, in the moonlight on my third night here, I threw myself from the window. I jumped.
I landed in the lavender.
I landed in a mass of the purple plant, at least six feet deep. The lavender seemed to go on forever, cradling me in its spiky arms and camphor scent. At first it played with me, tousling and bouncing, before it got annoyed by my yells and tossed me out. Eli was waiting.
I had forgotten that this place was cushioned for falls and jumps like this. There is no window, balcony, roof or turret, that anybody here can jump from and not land in the softest of nature's surfaces. Lavender, moss, wheat, blossom … anywhere you jump, you will be caught.
There is no way out. And definitely not that way.

But I've been good here, I promise. I've worked hard. I've given it my all, and now I'm done. Now I'm spent.
Although there is one other thing I need to tell you about. One other thing you should know about me, so you can make up your mind if I'm worth saving.
You need to know about the night with Dr Sunset.

Eli called it a ceremony.
Some called it a show.

Some called it a mistake.
She called it an experiment.

My nipples formed two perfect circles, much like the circle that was around me now. I knew they wanted me to look up, but I looked down, inspecting every inch of my naked body. I was gaining concave curves, my waist swooping in on itself, its walls getting closer to my abdomen, crunching my organs. I was earning my sternum, the delicate ribs of breastbone leading a trail down my stomach, for their eyes to rest on the smooth plate of my V.
I could hear them coming in, shuffling into their seats, chatter halting like butterflies burning as soon as they saw me.
The girl. In the middle of the room. That they were about to do this to. I could see expensive heels go by, the bottom of tailored suits. One person came close and laid a bouquet of roses beside me.
Candles at the end of every row. Incense burning next to me. Golden light dripping from a glass ceiling, making my skin look flawless.
Eli stepped into the middle of the crowd.
Behind him, somebody else was brought out. A woman, with a bag over her head.
'Ladies and gentlemen as you all know I have been trying to find an elixir. Erica has been helpful in letting me do what I will with her, to find it. But so far, nothing has worked.'
He pushed us together, deeper into the circle.
'So tonight, I have an idea. What if we made the angel of life mate with a doctor of death? I think that just might work.'
He removed the hood from the woman, and revealed her: Dr Sunset.

A message from Erica. A plea, if you will.

Tell me this.
If you were kidnapped, captured, caught, netted, reaped, caged, confined, bound, cuffed, and you were weeping, wailing, drooling, sobbing, snorting, and though you had begged, pleaded, tricked, beaten, bitten, blackmailed your captors, you were still there –
Then tell me this.
If somebody came to you, and they told you they were going to take you to a room, and in that room would be a key out of here, and all you had to was find it, then would you go to that room?
Of course. Now tell me this.
When you got to that room it was an attic, right at the top of the house they were keeping you, and it had been converted into some sort of small, subtle theatre. They said not a word because they were waiting for the show, and the show was you; it was obvious as soon as you entered the room, their heads swivelled to

you so quick that you actually checked the rooftop for a puppeteers strings. Anyway, none of this is important; what happened is what was said to you next. In your ear, your left and then your right, 'Would you like a clue?'

Of course you accepted. 'Yes. Please.'

Five words between you and your freedom. 'The key is inside her.'

Not under a seat, not in a pocket, not sleeping in a nest of spiders. The key was inside her. **Wait. Whose *her*?**

They brought her out then, bag over her head, at the same time they marched you into the middle of the circle, two guards on either side of you, but your mouth fell open and your heart fell out because all you could process was that there was another you. Another one in chains, another one bound, another one who didn't choose if she got to wash. As soon as you saw her you knew she was real, not an actress, and going through this too. It couldn't be faked, you could see it in her eyes.

'Where … where's the key?'

'Inside her. All you have to do is find it.'

This is the dilemma I was presented with, one warm Wednesday night in what should have been my summer. I knew what **inside** meant. How could I not.

Ten seconds went by, then twenty, then thirty. In this time, through the bees in my ear, I heard Eli introduce us; me as a healer, her as a black widow, a doctor of death, something to do with Sunset Clinic. I heard glimpses of his speech, prattling on about the 'mission', the goal, that he felt this would be the only thing that worked. Then I heard 'look into each other's eyes' and I obeyed. Looked up, into her eyes, of her, her, the other me– who had been here longer? She was older than me, by ten years or so; her hair was long too, but stringy. Of course, we were both naked.

I looked into her eyes but she wasn't looking at me. She was looking down, as Eli whispered into her ear, 'The key is inside *her.'* That's when I knew: we had been given the same mission. The same test. The same dilemna.

Eli was still talking. 'This is how it must be … the fusing together of two ideologies … our beloved healer, and a misguided killer … Erica's powers will complete her transformation … and to find what we need to find … we must see them make love.'

And so this is where I ask you, to understand, this is where my plea comes in. I did not turn, run away, refuse, didn't even try to fight it.

And neither did she.

They pushed us both down, not just to our knees but on all fours, mirror images of solid golden flesh facing each other.

Forced to all fours all we could do was crawl. I crawled towards her. Like my reflection had come to life, I was no longer alone.

She touched me first.

We kissed because we *needed* to, had to pour a million messages into each other's mouths to go some way to being nourished.

Then she went looking for my key. Parted my folds and tried to find her way to freedom.
This was the slippery slope they talked about. The one you can't come back from. The one where two people lose themselves. The one where everything changes.. One lick and we would know where the metallic lurked.
But she did not taste metallic. And neither did I. And yet we couldn't stop. And as I have told you before, nothing can compare to that. A tongue is still a tongue and a clit is still a clit.
'Don't fuck,' Eli instructed. 'Make *love*.'
Together we disobeyed him. Together we fucked. We took our captivity and we made it lust.
Because of her. Her. We should have hated each other, we should have killed each other, but somehow, together, we made the moment okay.
It could have gone on for days, the amount of pulses and places we drew out of each other, lost in the perfect moments we could give each other, sweat dripping but lips dripping more. All the things they did to me and yet this was the loudest I screamed. You should have seen Eli's face.
Our hands linked the whole time, I would get her out of this place, if not today then right now, if not with my whole body then with my lips. And she did the same for me.
I never saw her again after that.
Tell me, do you think we were wrong?

That's all. That's it. That's all I have to confess.
After the ceremony, they loved me even more. The powerful circle that Eli built this place for; I took all their influence and I turned it into love.

So will you come for me? Will you save me? Don't you think I deserve it?

Now I eat what I want – yes, salty and fried, you should have seen Eli's face when I ordered it – and I sleep on silk sheets and everywhere I go people wave and embrace. They've put so many cushions on my pillow and layers of silk in my bed I can't feel the floor. They've filled my room with every scent of candle so that I have every option; lemongrass, pumpkin, orchid. I'm the only one here allowed to listen to music and the only one here allowed to watch movies. Every day somebody has knitted me a gown or built me a crown.
I am their princess. Their priestess. Erica Ash, High Priestess of Pleasure.
See, some girls are just born with it. An invisible permission that tells the world it's allowed to hold them down.
We're born for that, but we're not born for the world. We're built to be taken. We're built to be stolen. We're built to be captive.
If Eli didn't take me, somebody else would.
If Core didn't come for me, somewhere else would.

If he let me go, what would I be? Empty. What value would I have? None. What am I if not this? Nothing. What am I if not his?

I've changed my mind. Don't look for me. Don't come for me.
Move on and let me become a memory. A dream that couldn't have been real.
This is where I belong. One day you'll belong somewhere too.

Love,
The Healer

Chapter Thirty Three

'I'm here to look at adopting a cat. A female one. I want to call it Erica.'

'Well ... right this way sir. We have plenty of girls in need of rescue.'

It was the first thought Myles'd had when he opened his eyes and the only one that mattered.

'I have to say, you don't look like the typical cat owner. Not that that's a bad thing.' The assistant said such a thing because Myles had got strong. Really, really strong. To distract himself from losing Erica, he'd built back all the muscle he'd lost fasting in Hawaii - built it back and then some. They didn't usually get his type in animal sanctuaries, and certainly not in the cattery.

She took his name, gave him a form to fill in. Two minutes later and he was handing it in, ready to take his pick.

'It'll be my first cat. But don't worry – I'll give it the best life possible.'

'I'm sure you will. We keep females and males separate as most of them aren't neutered yet. So – just let me get this door for you – and you can get to know our girls.'

She put down her clipboard and led him through a corridor, past a door marked 'Dogs'. She grinned at him. 'Do you know much about cats?'

'Nope,' Myles said. In fact, they'd barely crossed his mind before. He knew nothing about them; all he knew was the strange compulsion, the tug he had been feeling since 6am this morning, intensified when he saw a large wooden door with a sign half-falling from it, saying the word 'Felines (F).'

The door was stiff, and she struggled with it. Myles reached out his arm and it effortlessly gave way. He looked at the floor before looking up at the cats, summoning the confidence he'd had this morning that maybe, maybe this would be the one thing that would make him feel better.

'Mimimi.'

'Raw!'

Raw. It sounded like they were saying the word raw. Shouting it at him.

'Look up,' smiled the assistant. 'They're all trying to get your attention.'

Myles looked up. It was an unpleasant room, basically a corridor of cages, black wire to his left, grey grates to his right. Smelt like burnt biscuits. Wood pellets scattered onto the floor.

'Raw!'

Turning to his left, what was once black bars became a face, learing closer and closer to him out of the shadows. It might have been the most beautiful face he'd ever seen. Inquisitive, curious, open yet judgemental at the same time – wide, dewy, chestnut eyes, peering out of ticked, golden to black fur, above a perfect nose and a perfect smile.

'This is Sophie,' the assistant beamed. 'She's two, and she's the first Bengal we've had in a while. Isn't she gorgeous?'

'Oh, she is! Like a goddess straight out of Egypt.' The words were out of Myles mouth before he'd thought them through. Cats must have this effect on him.
'Give her a stroke. She loves it.'
He reached his hand through the bars, cooing as it landed on the luscious, glittering length of her fur. Sophie slipped into his hands, nuzzling her muzzle happily into the crook between his thumb and finger, delighted to be touched. She rolled over to reveal the colour of her belly – a creamy vanilla. Every bit of her was a work of art.
'Do you want to see Jubilee?'
He did not hear the words; he was wrapped up in the shimmering, soft world he had found through the bars.
'I know, I know, it's hard to tear yourself away. Sometimes you get an instant connection.'
His heart slid a little as he slid his hand back through the bars and away from Sophie. He needed to see them all; one of them was Erica.
'It is! She's gorgeous. Ok, which one's Jubilee?'
She led him past a couple of cages marked 'Reserved.' He had to resist looking in, knowing he could be tempted in any direction. She stopped at a large cage and smiled, 'This is Jubilee the mainecoone. Isn't she impressive?' She unclipped the door to the cage, reached into the abyss. 'You can hold her if you like.'
Reaching into the darkness, she picked her up. 'Raw,' Jubilee grumbled, and then he could see her. Instantly he knew he had to hold her, this half-raccoon, half polar bear, a Neanderthal minx in greys and whites, with alarming, alive green eyes. Her face formed a saucy scowl, as she looked up at him, whiskers sprouting from her brows. The assistant passed her to him and he gave himself up to her weight, the perfect soft thud as she landed in his arms. 'Hello,' he said, his finger sliding over her thunderous fur. 'You gonna come live with me?'
Breaking into applause, she set off her purr; the crumbly, satisfying notes oozing through the room. He had no idea they could purr like that. He wobbled her slightly in his arms, smiling down at her. There was one way to describe this cat and that was 'voluptuous'.
'She's fab,' he grinned. 'I think I'd have a fun life with her.'
'Absolutely! She's got great character. They all do here.'
The assistant spooned her out of his arms and back into her cage. He found himself looking in, to check there was enough water, good food, a decent scratching post.
'Now I have to show you another one. Unnamed, so maybe she can be your Erica. We got her last night. She's something *very* special.'
As she led him to the back of the room, a tender, tinkling meow swiped his ears. Almost enough to make him believe Erica was trapped inside a cat's body.
A sharp, amber tail, a lit poker tong, launched out through the bars of the very top cage, the one he came eye-to-eye with. 'Who's this?' he said.

'This is who I was talking about. She's a … *cinnamon Abyssinian.*'
At the words, the tail swiped back in. 'Hey, come out …' cooed the assistant, her fingers between the bars. 'Come on girl. Hmm. She seems a little shy today. Want to meet some other lovely ladies?'
Myles didn't reply, but pressed his face to the bars. In the darkness he could hear her breathing. 'Hey …' he said. Five shiny claws caught the light, flickered and played on an invisible keyboard. 'Is she shy?' he asked.
'To be honest I'm not sure; I wasn't here last night. Maybe feed her a treat?' She placed a tiny, heart shaped biscuit into his palm. Myles dangled it through the bars.
The claws launched, deft and effortless, but still drawing blood. He dropped the treat and yelped, 'Ouch!' but he was amused. A cat's scratch looked alien in the tawny, thick beef of his forearm. 'You just missed a vein,' he said playfully into the dark.
At the word vein, the unnamed cat began to reveal herself. First she sparked like an ember, revealing the first flash of red in the black, and like all fires, one thing led to another, her presence uncurling one by one. He had never seen a cat like it. All kinds of reds blending and blazing in her fur, slickly wrapped around her body. Oh, what a body. Thin, slender, strong, the dictionary definition of the word agile. Her eyes were the widest, brightest in the room – more like jewels than jewels themselves. Her muzzle was delicate as an egg shell, and her lips painted a powerful black. She looked at him, then she reared up on two legs, turning her body into a silky column. Her paw flickered for a moment and suddenly the latch was lifted, the door swinging open. She wiggled her hind and then launched, a trilling, gospel sound filling the air as she leaped with unforgettable elegance, and landed on Myles shoulder.
'Woah!'
'Oh gosh, sorry. It's Abyssinians – they're crafty. They're the most intelligent cats. She's the first one to actually be able to unlock her cage though. *Very* impressive, little puss. Sorry, shall I take her off you?'
'No, no, it's fine.' Myles grinned, reaching round to stroke her. She stood on his shoulder like a red angel, whispering thoughts. 'She's cool. Aren't you girl?' He looked up at her, her expression smug and mischievous at the same time. 'I wonder what she's thinking.'
The pager at the assistant's waist began to beep, flashing black and blue. 'Oh, sorry Myles, I've got to take this. Something must be happening at reception. Are you okay here on your own for a minute?'
'Yes, I'm more than fine,' Myles smiled, stroking through a smoothness and redness he hadn't felt before. 'Oh wow, do you hear that? She's purring.'
'Excellent. You get to know them. Just as a procedure, I'll have to inform you – there is a security camera in here. Everything you do will be recorded.'
'Ok…'

'Sorry, it's just, some people need to be told that. Right. See you in a minute or two!'
She closed the door, leaving Myles in the maze of meows. At every angle, vibrant colours of fur swiped by the bars, claws, paws and tails all swirling past. He wandered further into the lanes, stepping on biscuits, the unnamed red Abyssinian still on his shoulder. He couldn't choose, he really couldn't choose. Was he going to take four or five home with him?
'I once made a cat purr so hard it had a heart attack.'
The voice came out of nowhere; if anything it sounded like the cats were talking. Myles spun around, confused. It was coming from the other side of the cages, the row behind him. He walked to the end, the voice calling him.
'Suppose I should take it as a compliment. Still got the magic touch.'
He spun round, into the row, his shoes squeaking on the parquet. Ten feet away, at the top of the corridor, there she was - the owner of the voice. She looked a million miles different but he recognised the face.
'*Valentina*?!' he gasped.
There she was. Leaning up against the cages, glimmering with feline abandon - the first person who'd shown him mercy, all those months ago in hospital. *Valentina.*

'Myles. How are you? You look good. You look strong.'
'What are you doing here?'
'I hear you've been looking for me.'
She was leant back against the bars, as elegant, as supple as a cat herself. He started walking towards her. 'Did you miss me?' she smirked.
'Who are you? Who are you?' He marched up the aisle towards her, desperate to get to her before she became a mirage who could dissolve. 'Is your name even Valentina?'
'Sometimes,' she smirked. 'But today, you can call me Cupid.'
Myles had always thought Cupid would be red, but it turned out this one was pink. No longer wearing the bonnet she had worn as a nurse in a hospital, her hair was revealed to be a colony of waist length ringlets, indeed in a perfect shade of pink. And every inch of her got pinker. She could have been meat, blood and rubies, but she'd chosen to be candy, coral and ballet shoes. She was doused in shades from peony to pastel, pink that sings, pink that screams, pink that moans. She'd been rolled in barrels of cranberries and had watermelons smashed open on her skull. The humble, timid nurse was no more.
'No, no, you don't get to do that - you don't get to play with me any more. You need to explain everything to me. Who were you that day in the hospital? Why were you there? How did you know to find me? I've called them a hundred times and nobody can answer me. Sometimes I think I dreamed you up. Dreamt up this girl that got me out of there.'

He was coming closer and closer to her, and with every step he took her gaze got wider, as she drunk him in. She moved her body like he was slipping through each of her joints.
'Are you scared of me?' she asked.
'No.' He replied. 'But I need to know what you are.'
The cat on his shoulder hissed, leapt down, and then began twining through her legs. 'Mm,' she smiled. 'I love it when they do that. So, who am I? It's quite simple: I'm the girl with the kiss of death. But I couldn't quite bring myself to give that kiss of death to you.'
'What?'
'I let you live, Myles, not because I wanted you to suffer - because I knew you could thrive. And thrive you did, thanks to Erica.'
'Wait, wait, wait.' The abyssinian stopped her twirling, her ears alert to the urgency in his voice. 'Just slow down for a second. What do you mean when you say the kiss of -'
'Let me show you.'
They heard the latch to the door turning, and Valentina swept to the side, fitting in between the gap in the cages. There were a lot of skinny girls, but nobody did skinny like Cupid - out of her baggy scrubs, Myles could see that now. If everything else wasn't enough, she was wearing a pink lace dress. The opposite of armour.
'Excuse me, sir?'
The door on the other side had opened, and the assistant had returned. Myles darted back round – 'hey, sorry,' to see the assistant looking very distressed.
'Hi, sorry, I'm afraid we've had a terrible case come in. We've just rescued two dalmatians. Missing half their fur. Completely malnutritioned. A vet's looking at them now; we think he can save them but there's a chance he may want to 'put them out of their misery.''
Myles winced, a clear image of the dalmatians grinding in his mind. 'Aw, god, I'm sorry. Is there anything I can do?'
'Actually … the funny thing is, in the rescue, we got their owner too. He was packing up to go. Had all kinds of drugs stashed in his suitcase. We don't always get the chance to do this, but we bought him in. Police are on their way. We've got him in one of our birthing rooms, where we usually keep mothers about to have their pups and kittens. We're all run off our feet today, and I'm just wondering if you'd come to the adjacent room where you can watch him through a screen, and keep an eye on him?'
Myles flexed his chest. 'Sure. Absolutely. Let me just put the Abyssinian back … actually, I think you should let her roam free. She's not built for a cage.'
He followed the assistant out of the room, not looking back. It was too hard to say goodbye to the cats. And easier to imagine, yet again, that Valentina had just been a dream.

He watched him through the glass. Pathetic man. Nowhere near as many muscles on him as Myles.
What had he got from his cruelty?
The man fidgeted, his jeans scuffed, scars all up his arms. Probably all he was thinking about was his next fix.
Behind Myles, a row of cages throbbed with a sinister purr. This was where they kept the wild cats, the ones not suitable for rescue. Feral, they called them.
The door swung open. Valentina. Cupid.
'Let's see him, then.' She came up to the glass, pressed her perfect nose against it. 'He's perfect,' she said.
'Perfect?'
'Perfect for showing you what I can do. If you want.'
'And what's that?'
'Ever since I can remember, every time I ever kissed someone, pressed my lips to theirs, well … they died. One kiss from me and they're gone. God only knows what would happen if I went to second base.'
The incredulity of the moment hit them both at once, and they found themselves sniggering. 'You serious?' Myles asked, his tongue clicking in his teeth.
Valentina's eyes ran over his triceps. 'You've been hanging with a girl with the touch of life … now you've got a girl with something else.'
'Are you screwing with me?' Myles looked down at her.
'Baby, this is just the start of what I can do. I can stop people's hearts in the middle of marathons; I can make grown men fall in love with poisoned nuts; I can turn brothels into brothels of blood.
But this, this right here is my favourite thing to do. I'll do it right now. If you say yes. What do ya say? Put him out of his misery, put him down like his poor two dogs?'
'No.'
'*No*? But … think of what awaits him. So, so, so much shame.'
Myles looked back through the glass, at the twitching man in his chair. Truth be told, this would be the perfect murder. Even Myles the merciful had no time for animal abusers - and what did this man have to live for anyway?
The man was standing up, shuffling around the room with a wiry impatience.
'Right, what is this? Are the police coming or not, because you can't just keep me here?'
Valentina swung closer towards the glass, her pink hair covering the crime of her lips. She looked at Myles and raised her eyebrow as the man continue to whine.
'Hello? Look, I get you're all animal fanatics here, but it's not up to you what happens to me. And quite frankly I have places to go, so – '
Valentina drummed her fingers on the glass. Was she getting impatient for a kill?

'We'll say he had a heart attack from the fear of arrest. It happens more than you'd think.'
Myles rested his head against the glass, as though perhaps something could pierce through it and into his brain. A loosening of instincts, of reflexes, of standards, moving the goalposts on what was right and what was wrong. He *did* believe in mercy, at all costs, for all people, so perhaps, he could believe in this act, and tell Valentina to do it.
But against the glass, all he felt was one memory, pressing into him - the memory of the night Erica had told him he wasn't a murderer. Despite the thrill that Valentina sent through him, the hatred he felt for the animal abuser, and the pity for what might happen to him in prison, nothing, nothing, could set into him like that night could.
So he met Valentina in the eyes, and he shook his head. 'Not yet.'
Languidly, she rolled against the glass too, her head lolling gently against it. Beyond them, the anger of the man seemed to fizzle away - he became nothing, and they became everything. 'Okay. You're not ready.'
'But I will be,' Myles gulped but grinned. 'You know what? One day, I will be.'
'Oh I know you will.' Valentina bit her lip. 'And the adventure begins now.'
It happened quickly; she was between him and the glass, and then she was pushing him back against the cages that contained the most feral of cats.
'So what do you say, Myles?'
'Say to what?'
'What's it gonna be? The touch of life, or the kiss of death?'
She pressed him up against the cage of two simmering calico beasts, her hands curling around the wires, and practically meowed her words. 'How about you give up all this chasing the girl with the healing hands, and come play with the girl who got the lethal lips?' A cat nuzzled her hands as she spoke, making her fingers sticky with its drool. There was definitely some kind of pheromone going on in here. 'How about it? You and me, two crazy cats, rolling around town and taking the kiss of death to anyone we think deserves it? Getting to them before the mob can. Before the pain can. Vanquishing those who disgust even us. That power, Myles! That power! Piss us off, you get put down. Who needs euthanasia when you've got us? Who needs *Erica* when you've got us?'
She pulled him towards her, his chest now pressing into the wires. He felt the thorny flirt of the feline's fur; one of them seized him in its claws. '*This* could be your life. Not a live subservient to someone you can never compete with. A life on your terms, in your own lane, where you never have to think about rules again. And we'll find out what happens when the girl with the kiss of death fucks someone.
I know a place we can go, a place in Paris, just for the day.
Don't you want to know what it's like? To be mine?
What do you say, Myles?'

Myles gripped the bars, both the cats nuzzling his hands now, their claws rupturing his wrists as though his veins were their scratching post. An impossibly evocative scent bled from Valentina's pores into his, and he saw the future she promised, a future carved from the most forbidden of dreams. Murder, mischief and mercy in a blaze of desire, the lust that could take down the lynchings - *this* was who he was. This is what he was made for.
Their faces came together, her jawline crushed under his. 'Or are you still gonna chase The Healer?'
The Healer. For a moment he bought it - that they were only talking about The Healer, some elusive, magical figure, dismissing him from above with arrogance and superiority. For a moment, The Healer was not Erica, the girl he'd met on a rock one night. But that was only for a moment - her real name rerooted him, and everything else was eclipsed by the fact she was the girl who'd taken the agony of Rose and Taylor's death from him. She'd fought for him when he didn't have the strength to fight for himself. Now she was gone, there was nothing he wouldn't do for her.
'It's just - it's just - ' He realised he had to do this. He had to pull his desire back over the edge, had to end this encounter before he flew away with it..'The escape of Erica means the end of Eli.' Horror, hatred and hope hatched all at once, his heart becoming an egg that couldn't wait to crack. 'And Eli has to end. Once you see what he's done, you'll understand: *Eli has to end.*'
She smiled, and he felt as though he had just passed some kind of invisible test. She leaned closer.
'Oh believe me. I know. I know all about that man.' She let go of the cage, pushing him back slightly. 'Smell me,' she whispered. 'What do I smell of?'
His sinuses were wrapped in luscious layers.
'Peach … '
'That's good … what else?'
'White chocolate … honey …'
'Very good. Want to know what you smell of?'
He didn't, but he waited for her to say.
'Loneliness,' she whispered. 'One minute with you and I know loneliness like I never knew it.' She got closer to him now, her face an inch away. 'You really miss her that much, don't you?'
She ran a finger down his cheek, stopping at his lips. She shook her head, tutting.
'Even with everything else you're capable of … all you can do is miss Erica.' She tossed her hair. 'Do you have any idea where she is?'
'No. Yes. I think she's at the retreat.'
'Have you been to the police?'
'Yes. They won't help. To them she's just another missing adult. I tell them my suspicions about Eli but they won't touch him. They must have checked his retreat at least once but how easy would it be to hide her? I asked everyone I

knew she healed and they all tried to get me into the retreat. But they couldn't – it's too secretive. I can't even find a contact number online.'
Valentina nodded. 'Well that's what the phone number is for.'
'What phone number?'
'Come with me.'

Valentina looked around at the kitsch, Instagrammable cafe she had taken him too, and ordered another hibiscus latte. A pink drink for a pink soul. She sipped it, savouring it as he savoured her.
'I can get you in there. There's a number I call and they come and collect you. I say the words "The Cherry Network" and they know exactly who to send. But you have to have be ill. Sick. Sicker than before.'
'You don't think they've made Erica's sick, do you?'
'You know what happens every time you say her name? Your voice cracks. You can't be like that, Myles. Just because she showed you you were the victim of a gaslit fraud case– '
'How do you *know* all this?'
'Your life never should have been taken from you. You don't owe it to her. You can grant her this rescue, or you can come with me - '
'I can't just leave her there!'
'Ok, fair enough. That's where the sickness comes in.' She smiled and sliced into a strawberry buttercream bar she'd ordered for them. 'When you get in there, you'll see a lot of sick people. You may have to watch some sick things. And you may have to do some sick things too.'
She ran her hand up his bicep. 'Is she worth it?'
The truth kicked him, slumped him, battered him. A great, impossible truth loomed above him. Why couldn't he have just died for her instead?
But still, he nodded at Valentina. Yes, The Healer was worth it.
'And there's something else,' She said, her lips fusing to the fondant on her spoon. She spoke through the crumbs, icing sugar dusting her decollage as it fell. 'This is the hard bit. You're going to need every bit of your body and mind to do it. In fact, we should start practising now.' She turned the spoon towards him. She lifted it to his mouth. 'Open wide.' He obeyed her and she edged the dessert into his mouth. 'Now don't move. Don't do anything. Don't even shut your mouth. Just let it melt.'
He blinked at her. *What was this?*
'Of all the ways to be sick, there is only one sure fire way to be accepted into Core: the physically sick.' The buttercream turned to brine on his tongue, and the drool began to dream in his mouth. Still he obeyed her and stayed still.
'You're going to have to spend every single second of every single day convincing them that you are just that. Every moment is an opportunity to remind yourself you cannot move. Every minute that goes by is a chance to osmose further into the illusion that you cannot speak, cannot stand, cannot

drink without their help. You need to liquefy yourself so utterly into this version of yourself that you're not sure where it ends and you begin.' His mouth became the epitome of everything that had ever been syrup, and ever been shame. 'Oil, lacquer, liquefy for them, boy. You need to make them *want* to heal you. Then, and only then, will you have a chance of meeting her.' She sighed and put the fork down. 'Wipe your mouth.'

It had only been twenty seconds of acquiescing to her wishes, but Myles hand tingled like it never had before.

Valentina opened up his laptop, open on Core Retreat's elusive website. 'You're going to have to comply.' Her tone was stern, her eyes instructing. 'With everything they want, and everything your body does not.'

She stood up. 'Let me get you some water.' She was flustered at the thoughts of letting him do this. 'I need one too.'

Leaving him alone, he was able to glance around the room and take in the details of the cafe. To his surprise, he saw what he had seen on the tube this morning, and what had been on a lamppost on his way to the rescue centre, and what had been posted through his apartment building just last night. A series of posters that had been cropping up more and more across London - the abrasive grey clashing with the pink.

'SIGN THE PETITION' they instructed, 'A NEW VOTE.'

'VISIT GOV.UK,' they declared. 'DEMAND A REFERENDUM.'

'WE DESERVE A 2ND CHANCE.'

Myles had been surprised when he'd seen them, hadn't even paid attention to the fact the temperature out there could be changing. A guerilla call to reverse the decision on assisted dying; something he'd originally assigned to fanatics that would soon be a thing of the past. The fact that they were in here, in a cafe seemingly so playful, so geared towards the youth and detached from anything solemn … that was significant.

His eyes swivelled til they met a girl of about fifteen, sitting at the table next to them and staring right at him.

She flicked a shimmering mass of chestnut hair. 'Sorry,' she said, leaning forward and away from the exam books in front of her. 'I couldn't help but notice you're looking up Core Retreat. Are you thinking of going there?'

He tried to smile but it didn't happen.

'I wish every day we'd sent my Dad there. He went to Sunset instead. Now I get nightmares about both. Last night was a particularly bad one.' It was perhaps his lack of response that diffused her awkwardness, had her lean forward and continue. She chimed on, almost like she was just grateful to have someone to talk to. 'They're so vivid and I … I don't know, seeing you here feels like a sign. To tell you.' She took a quick sip of her water and watched Valentina making her way back. 'Sorry, I know that's weird. It's probably just that I miss him. I better go,' she picked up her books, her hair brushing the table's crumbs. 'I hope that wasn't weird of me – I'm trying to be brave. Confident. Like he was. I'm a Thames. Mila Thames. We don't hold back for anyone.' Valentina was giving her a strange look. Mila grabbed the last of her books and Myles realised she was starting to well up. She waved lilac nails at him and whispered, 'Bye.'

Valentina sat. 'What was that?'

Myles shrugged, shivering. 'I'm not exactly sure. But it's got me thinking: why do I have to pretend to be ill? Why don't you just make me ill? You must have a poison or two on you.'

A sad glaze came over Valentina's eyes, dulling her for the first time. 'No. I thought about that, but no.'

'Why?'

'In that place, you're gonna need to be able to run.'

As the weight of the world went through Myles, Valentina eyed his body, willing the sinews to stoop just a little. He was an Achilles today - at least he'd got to feel how it would feel, one last time. 'So. Better get working on Plan B. Fuse your foot to the floor. Sink into your neck. Then we'll get you in there. There's lots we can do. A certain time of day to call 999, and Eli's team comes. A certain ward in a hospital to end up in, and Eli's team comes. A certain therapist you can see, and Eli's team comes. A certain bridge to stand on, and they'll come.'

Myles looked at the muscles he'd worked so hard to build, the hands that had found sanity in lifting weights and flipping tyres - all for nothing, all for this. He tensed then relaxed his quads, knowing it was the last time he was going to be relaxing anything for quite some time.

'And, Valentina?'

'Yes, Myles?'

'What are we going to say is wrong with me? How are we going to explain what has happened to me?'

Valentina swished in her seat. She was back to her best. 'There's only one explanation that makes sense. The only one they'll believe.' She smiled. 'And we'll do it in your penthouse. Just like you did before.'

Once he was surrounded by the paraphernalia, he gave Valentina a nod.

She dialled the number.

'Hi, my boyfriend, my boyfriend! I'm losing him! Is this The Cherry Network?'

'Yes it is.'

'I found him, raiding my cabinet. I don't know what he's taken. Help, help!'

'Ok ma'am. Try and keep his mouth open and his airways clear. We'll be here for him any minute.'

'Ok, ok, please get here, I think it's critical! He was trying to leave me.'

'That's ok. What's your address? We won't let him get away with it.'

Myles didn't need to look out of the window to see what was coming for him. He wouldn't have believed it if he'd looked directly at it anyway; his brain

wouldn't have been able to take it. That it was finally here, and it was finally happening.
The sound of the engine was enough for him. He'd been dreaming of that engine his whole life. He knew it like he knew his mother. There was no vehicle that bobbed the way that this one bobbed, no vehicle that came with the same sickening swill of pith, and juice, and flesh, and seeds and rind, that this one did. Nothing smelt quite like this van as it came streaking up the street, green stalks bobbing in the window, searching for eyes to prod.
It was The Cherry Tomato Van. And it had come to burst him.

Part Three
The Retreat

Chapter Thirty Four

Core Retreat

People love to debate euthanasia, because they love to debate ethics. What is right or wrong, what is good or bad, what oh-so-ambiguously walks the line.

So you want to talk about ethics? Then talk to me about the ethics of ***this***. The ethics of Core Retreat.

You pride yourself on being a good speaker, on being able to win at debates. So draw up an argument for me, that can justify this place.

But first – let me talk to you about Myles. Myles and the mad, mad thing he was doing with his body.

He liked that show, Survivor, the one that aired in the US but he'd download it to watch in the UK. The contestants were sent to an island and put through all kinds of gruelling challenges – requiring their speed, strength and smarts.

But Myles' favourite type of challenge was always the endurance one. It would be some kind of brutal elimination, where contestants would go against each other to prove they had the stamina the others did not. Hanging from a pole, or remaining on tip toes, or holding a heavy mast above their heads, for as long as they could bear until one of them broke. It was a mental game – the triumph hinged purely on how much they were able to suffer.

Myles had always wanted to try something like that. It was the only way to open himself up and see what was inside. He had a sneaking feeling he would be good at it. So, to find out, he had chosen to embark on the unique physical challenge of pretending to be 'locked in'. He had studied what an overdose had done to people, those who hadn't taken enough but had in some riddle still taken too much, and with that he crafted his creation. He wasn't sure if it had ever been attempted before, not like this, not without breaks. Not with the risk that if he did take a break – and was caught – the response to him exploiting Core's hospitality would be brutal.

He felt crude doing it, even though he wasn't doing it to mock people who were genuinely injured. He felt foolish as he practised – who did he think he was, Daniel Day Lewis in My Left Foot 2? Sometimes it was easy to meditate into it, but even then, it got boring. Meditation only worked so long – there was always another layer of contradiction to go through, in a perfectly healthy body held hostage by an act. While the muscle he'd built made it easy for him to isolate parts of himself, it made him heavy to hold up.

Willpower was an underrated quality. He was going to turn willpower into happiness. He just hoped his nose would stop itching soon, now he had forbidden himself from scratching it.

Now back to ethics. Tell me when you know whether this is right or wrong. That's if you're able to make it through the next part of Myles's story. If he's willing to endure this, then you should be too.

I thought I'd chosen a comfortable position. Seated, in a simple wheelchair. Okay, slightly slumped. The left leg crossed over the right, with the calf angled out in an enduring kick. My right arm folded up protectively around my chest, the hand sentenced to be my permanent claw. My neck has committed to loll slightly forward for infinity. My face, however, has not been affected. I knew I'd need my words for this.
I chose to have some flexibility, for my body to have just enough fluidity to flinch, and react, engage with others and to tremble. More than anything I need to be able to tremble.
Not with fear, but with frustration. As I try and build my own statue before I've ever done anything heroic, multiple messages run through me without warning – run your hand over your thigh, shuffle on your tailbone – I hold them down. And you know what happens with pressure, it only grows and grows. I allow my feet to tingle and I remember the glory days of a time when I could reach for a pen. Requests take over my body - insolent, prosperous messages of movement. They cannot win. If I settle into this long enough surely they will obey.
They must.
And besides, I have a room on my own. At 9pm every night I will unfurl you, body I promise, and I will release you of the wicked pact I made you sign, and I'm not sure what we will feel first, the pleasure or the freedom, as we uncurl and loosen and become supple. The delayed gratification will make it worth it. I've been promised a room on my own. Don't worry, body. Not long now.

At the bottom of the hill he waited.
As promised, a sturdy woman emerged at the top. She began the descent to him, her eyes on him: Showtime.
'Myles? I'm Jill. I will be one of your carers at Core Retreat.' There it was, his first challenge: remember not to shake her hand.
'Thank you.'
Her skin was pink and mottled.
'No, thank *you.* Let's get you accustomed, shall we? I'll show you round, then it's almost time for breakfast, how's that sound?'
He wanted to look her in the eye, but his head wouldn't go up that far. He had to fix his eyes on a button in the centre of her chest.
'Great. Thanks.'

‘Great. Right then. Sorry my palms are a little sweaty – ’
‘Oh don’t worry.’
‘No, you might mind in a minute. You see, chairs can’t really get up this hill.’
‘Not even this old thing?’
‘Not even that. So – I’m going to have to carry you.’
With a strength that didn’t make sense, this woman, over 50 for sure, scooped him up, cradled him, and started their climb, to the large, white manor at the top of the hill. His act had begun.

Chapter Thirty Five

Day One

Breakfast is the most important meal of the day, and at Core, it was positively sacred.

First things first: every knife, and every fork, *must* be plastic. If you wanted to be a good little boy or girl, you would slide the food into neat squares, chew slowly and finish everything on your paper plate. That was imperative; no crumb to be wasted. After all, who didn't want to be a member of the clean plate club?

Then of course you must never ask for more. There was a thin line between appreciation and indulgence, and Core Retreat was a place where you learnt to walk it. The fall from that particular tightrope was a long one … though not too long, not too short, but just right.

Speaking of 'just right', guests of Core Retreat were served porridge to start their day, in a plastic bowl with a plastic spoon. Porridge was a perfect morning food, especially when topped with berries and nuts.

The third and most important rule was to say your pleases and your thank you's, your gratitudes and your platitudes, to the ladies who were the reason you were still able to eat. The Carers. All female, all over fifty, their stocky yet cuddly bodies draped in identical grey corduroy. They didn't stop for a moment; wheeling people in, sitting people down, cutting up apples, lifting spoons, wiping chins. These women worked hard and wanted nothing for it in return, as long as the guests remained good.

It took place in the dining hall and it began at 7am. Sharp.

That morning, a hundred or so of the guests were eating in silence, when one by one, spoons were laid down, heads were raised, oats were swallowed unceremoniously, because who should be being carried in but a new guest. The first thing they noticed was his muscles. He must have been in an accident, and recently too, because there was no way a paralysed man could build muscles like that.

They tried not to stare. Jill wouldn't approve. As chief carer, Jill was the one they all wanted to impress. Jill was the one they knew they had to fear.

Once he had been placed in a chair made just for him, at a table to himself, the eating commenced. From all except one girl.

She slid into the seat opposite, somehow translucent; she was the streak left behind after a tear.

She was carrying a plate of colour.

She couldn't be a day over eighteen. 'Hi, I'm Rebecca,' she didn't smile. 'Why isn't anyone feeding you?'

She grabbed the fork from opposite him. There were so many places she could plunge that fork into; even plastic could do damage. His eye, her neck, flying through the room like a missile; but no, it went into the pile of sweet potato on her plate. Predictable.

'What's the point?' she said. And then, 'Open wide.' And she delved the food into his mouth.

He tried to deal with the heat in his mouth and the coldness in her eyes. Before he could ask, 'The point of what?' she was cutting up her grilled broccoli for him.

'The point of being here,' she said. 'Not here. I mean in the world. If you can't be everything you want to be?'

She then turned the fork on itself, and spooned the food into her mouth. It was then he realised just how thin she was.

Her meal was different to the others. 'I get a special early lunch because it's all I'll tell them I'll eat.' She gestured to the grilled, gourmet vegetables. Myles could have done with some of that.

'My parents sent me here,' she spoke through a textured mouth. 'Because they know unless I'm here, I'll starve myself. They don't want that. But they don't want this, either.' She pulled the aubergine corpse from her teeth, and slopped it back onto his plate. 'A daughter who hates herself – who has the the mindpower to be everything she wants to be - to look like a human Barbie. Yet she has to quash all of that potential and *eat*. Open up,' His lips were still closed when she pressed the fork to them, this time spooned high with gleaming black olives. Sharing forks, how sweet. The plastic was spikier than he expected, and just as he felt the prongs flicker against him, he remembered not to move. 'And you know what the saddest thing is – I think they're prepared for it to not quite work … and I think they're starting to let me go. When I look at them, I see less love in their eyes. They're taking their love away by the day, to make it easier for them. You know what my mum said to me the other day? *It'd be a shame to lose you*. A "shame".' She giggled then, her hand clapped over her mouth, her eyes darting to each of his teeth as they chewed. 'That's the kind of word you use after you mixed up darks in the wash. Shame. Shame. Shame. See? Even she doesn't really want this version of me. Feed me.' She demanded, and sat back, her mouth open. Myles used his good hand and traced the fork tenderly through the sweet, stringy handful of squash. He carried it like he was carrying hundred kilos of gold, but just before the nutrition was about to enter her mouth, she slapped her pixie hand around his wrist, stopping him.

'So I ask you, what's the point? Is it the point of this fork, is it the syringe in an eye, the needle that pierces a nipple, the pinprick of a finger? What's the point, what's the point, what's the POINT?!'

She scooped her other hand into the orange mound. He used to love butternut before he saw it today. 'You should have seen me a few months ago. Nothing could break me. My mind could make me do anything before they got my appetite going – is the butternut good? Tell me the truth. Tell me if the butternut is worth me staying alive, trapped in this body, looking like all the other girls, never getting to express *my* power, my talent, never proving that I don't need food for energy – I get my energy from *me* – sitting in this *walrus suit* because other people can't handle my willpower.' She threw the butternut then, landing in someone's hair opposite. They didn't notice, or they were numb to touch. 'Tell me honestly why I should eat. And if you think I should, then prove it. Let me eat you.'

She loosened her grip on his wrist, looking at him for permission. When it was granted, she opened her mouth and bit him, her sedentary teeth delighted at the exercise. When she came up for air, perfect pink tombstones formed a halo around his most vital artery.

Rebecca knew what she was getting herself into by misbehaving at mealtime; she did it anyway. As expected, the drip, drip, drip as not one carer, not two, but three, made their way down to their table.

'Rebecca, dear,' Myles remembered not to look up, yet the hand on Rebecca's shoulder, the way it gripped her, was enough to make him shiver. 'If you don't want to eat, then you have no need for those teeth.'

The carer bent down and whispered through Rebecca's stringy hair. 'They're lovely and white, from all that abstaining from staining them you've done. Call me the tooth fairy because I'll take as many of them as I can get.'

A bell ringing.

'Ladies and gentlemen,' said the same carer. 'Who's ready to see someone learn their lesson?'

If Myles had been able to let himself run, maybe that's what he'd have done, there and then. Instead, in the frozen frame he had chosen for himself, he found himself whispering a word, a kernel of courage that popped open on his tongue.

'Give her another chance.'

A carer bent down to him then, tactfully remembering to stoop to his level. Her face was wide and filled his plate as she answered. 'This *was* her second chance.'

A hand was already on his chair, wheeling him from the table, and everybody was already standing, filing out of the hall. 'Where are we going?' he spoke through one side of his mouth, hoping the reason he couldn't see Rebecca was because of the angle his head was at, and not because they had already whisked her away.

The answer that came back was simple, laced with the hate of a playground bully. 'It's time for a game.'

Be grateful that you can shut a book. I hope you'll hold a place in your heart for those who can't, who are inside Core, too timid to turn a page again; who had to watch what happened next: the reason for the word 'grisly'. The reason we were given a gut. Somewhere for this memory to churn or to bloat, depending on whose side you're on.

19 Feet High

Eli had once said to Erica, 'If I could make you forget something – anything – I'd make you forget whatever has hurt you. Anything anyone said, anything anyone did, anything you did to yourself – all of it – if I could I'd wipe it from your mind until you forgot cruelty existed.'
'Thank you.'
'How about you? Anything you'd make me forget?'
'I'd like you to forget that the pool was drained empty earlier today. Forget about that, right before you decide to go for a dive.'

If only there was water in the pool.
Just one drop. Enough to dip your finger in – enough to wet your tongue with – enough to float a fly.
Nothing gets everyone involved like a good game, and Core's favourite game was called '19 Feet High', and it took place in the epic, converted barn that housed its indoor pool. Or what had once been an indoor pool and was now just a greedy, dry blue bite into the earth below, a turquoise pit daring you to fill it. Just think of all the feet that could pad over those smooth dry tiles with no chance of slipping.
And like all the best pools, it had diving boards. A little one – 7 metres – a medium one – 10 metres – and a big one – 19 metres.
Because 20 would have been too dangerous, and 18 would have been too safe, or perhaps it was the other way round.
One by one, they filed into the bleachers, taking their seats.
Right now everybody in that barn wished there had never been anything between the numbers 18 and 20. As far as they were concerned, 19 was a cruel, useless figure and it could go to hell.
Everybody except Jill.
'The human body is such a strange thing. Remarkably fragile and remarkably resilient at the same time. People have been known to survive motorway bridges falling on them, while others have snuffed it from the wrong kind of handstand. Who really knows what your own body is capable of? Would it take six days to starve you, or would you thrive until day sixty? The only way to know is to jump.'
Jill was on the 10 metre diving board, a black microphone clutched in her hand. Here was a woman who had never been wet.
'I'm giving you an opportunity.
Every day a different one of you approaches me and asks, no, begs, no, demands, that we let you go. Grant you the release you've been longing for. Well here it is. You can climb to the top of the diving board, and you can jump. We've had the pool specially drained. I can assure you the ground below is far from cushioned. No one will be here to stop you, no one will be here to catch

you. I give you my word. Walk to the top, close your eyes and take that one final step over the edge.'

Still tired from their 6am wake up, the rows of Core's guests looked into the pool and back to each other.

Become the rain. Just fall. If rain isn't scared then why should you be?

'However. One more promise.

No ambulances will be called - we don't want that, do we, anybody *interrupting* you. I'm sure you know what this means:

If your jump is fatal, you're gone for good; fair's fair. You won't be revived.

It also means that if your jump is not a success – then you won't be helped.

Whatever state you might get yourself into, that's your body now.

I never said it would be easy. I said you would have to be brave.'

Everybody can fall. Not everybody can crack.

'You were brave, weren't you, when you left your whole family behind. Brave to throw yourself in front of trains, to give commuter's nightmares for the rest of their lives. Brave to leave to someone else to find you swinging. Brave to swallow a few pills. That *commitment* to that goal, that determination to get what you wanted. Whose feeling that same courage today? Or does it turn out, that what I have in front of me, today, is just a bunch of quitters, after all?'

It was a lovely day for a dip. It really was. In another life, they could be at a summer barbecue now, splashing in a pool, surrounded by people they liked or even loved. Suicide would seem like an ungrateful, greedy concept, something washed far away from their smooth, sun creamed skin. But the choices they had made had led them to this instead; the line between being Sleeping Beauty or Humpty Dumpty.

'Joe is not a quitter. Are you Joe?'

It all happened so fast. Suddenly a man stood up. Raised his hand. A volunteer. A real life brave boy.

'Come to me, Joe.'

He didn't need instructions. Joe had already weaved his way through the bleachers and to the feet of the tallest diving board. His hands slid around the silver. 'I'm brave.'

But quick as he climbed he could not hide the fear on his face.

'Joe believes he can land in exactly the right way, with just enough speed, in exactly the right place. Joe believes in his death – who believes in him?'

A hand or two sprouted through the frozen fear of the room.

'Oh dear. Even less than normal. Well you know what you can do – those who are so worried about the impact this fall may have on him - nothing's stopping you from trying to catch him. Please, come – who doesn't want to experience the feel of being in an empty pool? Shoes off first.

Well? Anyone? Anyone willing to catch him? If there was ever a time to be strong … it's now.' She waited.

'Don't tell me it's true what they call you. Don't tell me our lovely Core Retreat is actually just full of .. *cowards.*' She spoke with mock shock.
Someone was weeping.
'Oh no. Not more tears. It doesn't matter how many tears you cry; you'll never be able to fill up the pool in time for him.'
'What about spit?'
It was Rebecca, that slither of a thing, a carer on either side of her, holding her arms tight as she rose from the end of the bleachers.
'Excuse me?'
'I said spit. You heard me. I bet we could spit enough to fill up this pool.'
Tight, tiny, oh so little and oh so fast, she was scattering herself off the bleachers and up to join Jill on the lower diving board. The next time she spoke, Myles realised she was indeed missing teeth, teeth she'd had twenty minutes ago. He released his first shudder.
'Because if you didn't know how much you disgust all of us already, we could show you now. Here's the first drop.' The spit came, confident and clustered, all over Jill's face.
Jill's response was not to swear, or shout, or punish or push. It was to take the black microphone in her hands and throw it up into the air.
It performed a double tuck, and then it switched into a dive so direct and vertical any aquatic Olympian would have envied it, and then it landed so severely on its bulbous head it could have pierced the floor, but instead it rolled and rattled on its neck, until it detached at the middle, spilling out black, wiry intestines. You had to admit it was the perfect response to a rebel: *this could be you.*
And the noise it made … if an inanimate object could sound like that, just imagine how a human would sound.
'Don't cover your ears! Take it!' Jill's voice was as shrill as the mic. 'Drown something today – drown out your fear. Are you ready for Joe? Joe, are you ready for this? Cheer for Joe. This is his chance. Will he be the one?'
'Wait!'
It was Rebecca again.
'My little bones. Surely they wouldn't survive the jump. Early on-set osteoporosis, god I've been hearing that phrase for years. Why not see if all those warnings are true? Let me jump.' She gestured to the empty pool. 'Down in one.'
'Very well. Rebecca first.'
'Wait! I want to try.'
'Very well.'
'And me.'
'And me.'
Myles watched in awe, as more and more of them volunteered. He could see it in their eyes, how much they wanted to believe that physics was a lie. He would

do anything to help them, to take away the crunch. To make it so they only had to dive once.
'Anyone want to volunteer to break the fall? In other words, to catch your 'friend'? Last chance.'
Myles couldn't do that – he was here for one woman only. Confined to his chair, he could only watch as nobody volunteered, and Jill laughed.

There was no such thing as a 'nice face' any more. Just sick, grey faces, turning and watching as volunteer Number One, a tall woman, climbed. Every time she touched the rail her hand seemed sweatier, and more likely to slip. Every step she ascended the idea of comfort seemed further and further away. The climb was too long, and the room loomed around her, most of the audience looking to the roof and begging it to fall in so she didn't have to do this.
But when she put her hand on the board - that high, thin board that saw what none of them could see - oh man, they wanted her to try.
The skin on her hands was so thin that just touching the board made them bleed. She pulled herself onto it, gingerly planting with her knees, and then - calves shaking - she stood. Jelly in the sky.
'Come on!' A roar sparked in the audience. 'Come on, girl, you can do it!'
'All you gotta do is fly!'
'All you gotta do is die!'
It was true. Come on. How strong, how robust, could one person be? How much space could one person take up? After all, one down meant more resources to go round, so this was the right thing, so it would work.
Juddering, she began her walk.
'You're a pirate on a plank! Go for it, girl!'
'Little bit further!'
Her fist balled up, she rose it up for them, then back down before she lost her balance. Too soon, she had reached the edge. As a little girl she'd always liked sport. This was her Olympics.
A whistle from someone in the crowd seemed to weave around all of them, binding them, with the will of this woman. Nobody could swallow until they knew if she could do it.
And then, no, she was turning around, and then - oh yes, she was edging with her heels over the edge. Clever girl. She would fall backwards, offering up her head, her neck, to the hungry tiles first.
Myles had pins and needles he was desperate to itch. And he would, as soon as he could, but if he couldn't bring himself to sit with an itch, how could someone bring themselves to fall from a great height onto cement? Just saying it out loud was enough. *Stop this.*
But this bold, brave woman was ready. She opened up space between her left foot and the air. Let the gravity pull at her heel. Defying what was natural, she

bounced, and let the other foot come up too. Bunny backwards, she hopped, opening a channel in the air.

The gravity was so fast. So greedy.

The room screamed. In that moment, they were normal; they hated heights, danger, fear, falling. Their lungs and throats took the leap with her, sloshing through their throats.

They bathed in the sweet pause of her falling, the pocket of time where she was airborne and everything could still come up roses.

They covered their ears to muffle the sound of her landing.

And then the fall was over.

But they couldn't muffle the scream when she landed, blending in with the wail of the mic, reminding them that screams were a thing and death, and Heaven, might not be real at all.

For she was split in two, but split in the wrong place, with just enough in one portion of her to keep going. Just as Jill had said. Core 1, people 0.

'No, no, no!' Words warbled around the room, people fighting with each other, with themselves, with logic for another answer but this, anything but this, the reason it's dumb to try, how many times did they have to be told that flying is impossible? 'NO!'

In fact, her legs now formed the shape of a No.

Stop. Stop. Stop. 19 is the scariest number in the world.

A triumphant Jill looked at the audience, at the wave of people who wouldn't look at her. Two men next to Myles were clutching hands so tight he was going numb just watching.

'So whose next?' Jill said serenely, cutting through the noise.

From the pack of volunteers, there was a rustle. The audience didn't want him to, and yet he did: a boy of twenty stepped forward.

'Let me climb.'

Jill parted, revealing the ladder behind him. 'Of course.' She respected him more than those that wouldn't even try, that wanted it easy.

He was healthy. Fit. Perhaps that meant he could jump with enough strength - perhaps that meant his body would be harder to break.

'What a waste, what a waste,' the carers sang as his hands closed around the metal and his feet edged onto the lip of the ladder.

The rails already greased by the former faller's hands, he climbed. He would use her screams of agony to make sure *his* jump wasn't a failure.

The higher he got, the more they longed for a harness. Just to see one. But not him; he liked heights. There he was, nineteen feet up; now all he had to do was get safely from the ladder to the plank.

He got his hands on the board. Launched forward on his belly. It seemed like a bad idea, until he jumped to his feet without a tremble. *Yes!* This one. This one. This would be the one that would work.

He walked to the end. All you needed was for one to work. One to work, and show us how. One. One. One. What we want, we get. Let him die.
He caught somebody's eyes. A guilty face in the bleachers looked up at then away from him. Wimpish, they stood, calling out to Jill.
'I sh-sh-sh -' they trembled. 'I sho- I *should* try to catch him.'
'Oh really?' Jill folded her arms.
Chattering teeth managed to speak, 'Yeah, cos -'
'No.' He cut them off. 'Don't you dare break my fall.' He looked back down to the tiles, making out where one cracked and the other stood strong. He watched this game all the time; he knew things the others didn't. He straightened up, wiggling into his perfect spine.
'Showtime.'
To do it, he had to close his eyes.
Three steps back, two eyelids down, and then a run, a run off the side of the board, a run into the gooey, a run into the slippery, a run into the greasy, a run into floorless, the endless, the lawless, the bottomless; a run into every motion in the universe that had ever gone down, down, down, back too straight, legs too upright, posture too correct, neck too heavy, too much stepping, too much like walking when really he was falling, too much knee, too much ankle, too much toe, too far forward, too little time, too much leg for such a hard floor and too much impact and too many breaks and too many angles and then too much face in too many tiles at too much speed until there was no face at all. Just flatness. And too much breath. Of course, still the breath. Enraged, the crowd watched a malevolent cobra of oxygen ripple through his stomach, keeping him here, arching his back. And they all lived nappily ever after.
'Any more?' Jill asked.
'Yes. Me.' Number 3 stepped forward.
Games here didn't end when it felt like they should. Myles realised this and bit down on it; he could get through this, no matter how long it lasted: he just had to remember one thing - *why he was here.*
'Go on, number 3!'

An experimental artist splatters paint up his studio wall. A toddler throws his supper from his high chair to the kitchen cabinet. At India's Holi Festival, revellers celebrate the beginning of Spring by dousing each other in balloons filled with colour.
And at Core, bodies hit the floor. Crack or splat or just a mush. What a masterpiece. What bright colours. What strange shapes. What a coincidence that it could look so pretty.
Eggs full of red yolk, sizzling on the cool blue. Grisly. The word we use is grisly.
Some of them looked like a puppy who was just learning how to roll. Some looked like a piece of paper that had forgotten how to fold. One or two seemed

to be shedding something, as they creepy crawled to a horizon only they could see.
Here's one thing for sure: nobody was static. Even the littlest of motions could be made out on the sparkling tiles; a wiggle of a finger snapping the hope that one of them had made it out of Core. Oh nineteen. What a clever number you are.
Rebecca was next. They had made her wait.
She stood on the board, looking down at the tapestry below. Bodies turned to stains in seconds. She had only been to this ceremony once before.
So, so damn close to freedom, yet so much to lose if you couldn't fall right. Yes, she could admit it, yes, she was lucky to have a working body, yes, she could have been focusing on what her body could do for her, not how it looked, yes, functionality essentially served you more than fuckability – but she hadn't made that choice, ever, to play it safe, so why would she start now?
If she was as fragile as everyone said she was, this fall should split her in half. She looked around at the crowd, started fluttering her hands, getting them to cheer for her. The atmosphere rising, the carers scowling. Now fall. This may be your only chance to fall in love, girl, so fall – head over heels, heart through the mouth – go.
So she jumped, willing biology to just, you know, take a day off.
You can guess what happened next. Even Jill flinched. It was the worst landing of them all. The shape made on the floor was one that should never have been made at all, let alone by a human. She may as well have snapped into a Swastika, so abominable was the sight. She didn't even bleed – her fall was all bones, or should I say all powder.
Ten seconds went by, and then came the whimper; the confirmation: that she was another one damned to be awake.
As the audience winced around her, getting to the point they always got to where they needed it to stop, a carer, Mo, nudged a broom at the crumpled heap. Meeting no resistance, she caught the eye of Jill. Bonding over their achievement, Mo chortled.
'Least she'll be easier to feed now.'

'Joe! At last. Are you ready?' The first volunteer was always made to watch some of the others. Your bravery couldn't really be tested until you had seen what could happen.
Jill folded her arms; Myles missed being able to let himself do that. The room stared up at the man, waiting for him to change his mind.
He grinned down at her. 'I am. So long, Jill!' Joe was the first one to talk with confidence, and the first one to jump like he meant it.
He ran off the edge, almost reaching the roof.
His fall was the fastest.
And the neatest.

Guess he had been studying the technique; it came down to a game of degrees – the way you launch yourself, the way to angle your body, to control the air. Or maybe he was just lucky that when he jumped, his head hit the board, knocking him out first. That wasn't the only luck – the real luck was that the board fell too. It hit him again, right on the temple, then it came down vertically. It stood upright, just long enough for Joe to impale himself upon it. A suicidal kebab.
It flopped to the floor, taking him with it, grazing Rebecca's skull as they came down.
Even then, the audience waited, tense, for a wiggle of his toes or a mumble from his mouth. But there was nothing. Just peace.
For the first time in months, the game had failed Eli.
The man had done it. And not just done it; Rebecca had stopped moving too. You see, a body so undernourished can't take that much trauma - the final damning graze from the diving board was enough to haemorrhage her skull and lead her to the abyss. The sweet girl's eyes rolled back. Her last words never came.
Joe and Rebecca were … yes. They were dead.
'YES!'
'Fuck, yes, one for us, *they made it*!'
'We knew we could do it!'
'Screw you! Screw this place!'
'They're out!'
Screaming, stampeding, thumping, they cheered. Even the flailing not-quite-corpses seemed to be trying to clap. There *could* be success. There *was* such a thing as freedom. Jill was a sadist but she wasn't a sorcerer; she couldn't keep them all alive.
'Ha! Na-na-na! They're out!'
'Go on buddy! Knew it! Have one on me up there!' More stamping. More thunder. More laughs.
'I feel ELATED! I forgot I could feel this!'
Jill's footsteps filled the pool. She weaved among the bodies til she got to Number 7, nudged his body with her boot. She picked up the mic and with one twist, put it back together again, til it was good as new. It's screaming stopped and the cheering dissipated. 'Oh, good for you. Clap – clap – clap. Do you realise you are clapping a murderer?
That's right.
Not one, not two, but *three* young women are no longer alive because of this thing you clap. Joe was brought here by a detective who caught him trying to hang himself over one of his victim's bodies. The policemen thought he should have to live with what he'd done. But never mind that. Clap away, all of you.'
She ran the mic along her lips. 'I'll see you at dinner.'

Once the game was over and the carers got to cleaning, a calm settled over the barn. People got up – helped each other to their feet – dusted themselves off, and walked out of double doors that led into the garden beyond. Myles watched them brush past him as though it had all just been a dream. Maybe it had. Maybe it was easier that way. Suffer and distract.

A pair of hands touched his wheelchair. Just in time he remembered not to turn around and give away the illusion. He could only listen - to the husky, mellow voice behind him.

'Hi. This is your first day?'

'Yes.'

'What a welcome. Come. You need to come outside. They love it when we go for walks. I'll take you.'

She didn't wait for a response, just wheeled him briskly through the crowd and out of the barn, away from the smell of tiles and blood. Bizarre to think it was only 10am.

'So why didn't you try and catch them?'

'Sorry – '

The garden in front of him cut off the voice in his throat.

He had been expecting something pristine yet basic – to be honest, he'd always thought nature was boring. Maybe it was because of what his eyes had just had to undergo indoors, that as he stepped out into the garden, it took his breath away.

'Don't apologise to me. It's just I could tell you wanted to. I was sitting right opposite you, and I saw how you looked when she asked for volunteers.'

This garden was what they talked about when they talked about Eden. Someone with an eye for fairytales had sculpted every flower, bush, tree or spring to form an lolling landscape of twists and turns, everything bowing beneath archways and avenues made of berries and vines. The butterflies and birds had come, unable to resist this particular atmosphere.

There was even a cherry blossom tree in the middle of it.

Myles tore his eyes from the roses and bushes, to almost look round and see who it was that was wheeling him, before he remembered just in time: his spine had *'been damaged from an overdose'*. He could not move. He was frozen. That wasn't for him.

'You didn't notice me? I couldn't take my eyes off you. I always know when someone wants to be a hero. I'm sure you'd be a great one.'

'Me? A hero? It would help if I could move.'

To his surprise, she squeezed his shoulder. 'Wouldn't it just? Or maybe you're not thinking outside the box.' His neck rippled with the suggestion of a shrug, but he bit down on it, giving into the nothing. The urge would pass. It always did. He distracted himself with his new friend.

'Maybe. Show me what you look like. Will you … turn me round? Please?'

'Of course.'

She moved slowly, gently, some may even say sensually. She whispered, 'Keep your eyes closed,' and he obeyed. He waited patiently until she said, 'And open them.'

He did. He blinked, once, twice, three times, trying to make sense of what he saw.

It was a hybrid, devastation and seduction melded into one. It all began with the tattoo; she had the kind of waist that could pull off a dragon tattoo. Six packs on a woman weren't Myles thing, but she made it work. At least, she did until you got to the right side of her body. That was where the bionic woman began. She was laced and latticed in a metal brace, a corset that aesthetically she didn't need. It reached up to her neck and held her head in place; dangerous black hair formed a ribbon, plaiting her together in a braid of metal and flesh. Diamond eyes flashed at him from the centre of a face that was golden, but not denying the bruises that had baked themselves into permanent blue clouds across her face. One hand was manicured, one eye made up, one side of her lips red – she flashed a white smile and conspiratorial, crooked teeth made their way out too. Her body danced in a place between beautiful and broken; she was the ultimate bad girl, a woman so wild that her cage had to be built into her – it could have been inspirational if it wasn't so tragic. Actually, he took that back; this was nothing but inspiration, so awe-inspiring it put his act to shame. She put her hand on her hip and let him look, even gingerly performed a slow turn for him, showing off one nut cracking arse cheek, its twin shallowly sunken in. It was true what they said – attractiveness is *all* about confidence. Here she was. Organic, bionic, electrical woman.

'Name's Michelle. I was injured in a dancing accident.'

The word 'dance' teased him, trying to pluck some movement out of him. He missed dancing. His foot tingled, a tribe of synapses trying to fight their way up to the surface. 'So you came here.' he said, trying to control his travelling eyes. 'Has it worked, their ethos?'

'I didn't 'come' here.' She shook her head. 'He found me, and he took me.'

'Who?'

'You know who. Eli.'

Shouts launched at them across the garden, distracting them, but Myles didn't let himself jump. Discipline on top of discipline, he gingerly turned his head.

'*Healer, healer, let your hair down*!'

Myles hadn't even noticed the ashy stone tower that had suddenly become the focus of the garden. It was surrounded by rings of people. All looking up, up, to a black window, narrow as a suspicious eye. Surely nothing could be inside a tower, dead and dull as this one.

'Healer! Let your hair down!'

'Just wait.' Michelle whispered. 'Any minute now.'

There was a rustle in the blackness, a flicker of fire in the peace.

It poured out, or did it spit out, a waterfall of hair, cascading from the window. Unmistakeable, but even longer: those were Erica's ringlets, Erica's rivulets, Erica's waves. Nothing couldn't grow like her hair. If they were going to take from her, they had to accept: they would never be as strong as her.

Erica bent her head back, trusting her own body not to break her. She enjoyed this, she could say. Of all the moments forced upon her in her pitiful yet prestigious life, she could say with honesty this was one of the few she enjoyed. A game she had suggested to Eli herself, that she would dangle her incomparable locks from the window, every time having grown at an envious rate, and the people of Core would try to climb it. How they jumped and leapt, hungry, runt kittens, each day believing this would be the day they'd get there. Nobody could ever get high enough. The swish of buttery keratin was constantly out of their reach, a comfort only she could provide for them.
She fantasised about other things she could do, from this window, for those who were oh so desperate to heal, and those who had nothing serious to heal from, but had come for her anyway. She longed to pour green juice over them, the celery stinging their eyes, drowning them in health. She wanted them to come up, sit on her knee as she bandaged them, realising too late she wasn't stopping as the bandages coated their mouths, their noses, layer after layer.
'Ok, guys!' she cooed. 'Give it your very best try.'
She flicked the mass of honey and caramel, imagining how tempting her rippling locks were at the best of times, let alone when they held the promise of a healer's touched.

Myles, coating his rage, let words out of their mouthy cage. 'Who are the people? Trying to climb her?'
'Oh. There's the ones who came here by choice. The ones who came here to 'heal.''
Myles bubbled in his chair, as a man with optimum agility leapt in the air, panted like a puppy and almost caught her hair, the delicate ends just slipping through his fingers. Encouraged, he tapped his friend enthusiastically, a strong, tall man who fell to his knees, and allowed him to climb aboard his shoulders. Together they were ten feet tall, and closer than ever to tangling themselves in the healer's hair. The crowd gathered. Myles continued allowing his chair to baste him, in heat and rage and jealousy. His hands in *her* hair. *That* was how it was meant to be. She was his little flame – no one else's.
Pouring out in front of them, a tequila tumble of hair. . He imagined braiding it, washing it, taking care of it. One look and he knew that none of these 'climbers' were trying to take care of her. As if they would even know how.

Erica longed to turn around, to look down into the faces of those who climbed her. She wanted them to look into the eyes of the girl they were attempting to use. To them, pretty and slender as she was, she wasn't a girl. She was an object. A useful one at that. How many times that phrase has been used by women, indignant voices, palms to their chest, 'Oh, they only see me as an object!' How ungrateful of them. Erica would give anything to be seen as a sexual object now. Instead, she was just a pill, more necessary than paracetamol, more reviled the penicillin, beloved in a way a vitamin could never dream of being, but a pill none the less. Sure, they were grateful, they admired her, but she could just imagine the look on their faces if she said no. They probably didn't even think she was capable of the word.

She could turn around now and stare into the eyes of those grasping for her, but it was one of Eli's firm rules. They were not to see her face until they came to be healed.

The man-made tower swayed, bucked, and then clung; the man on top had caught a lock of Erica's hair. He cooed softly as it wound round his palm.

'I've got her hair!' he shouted.

Myles was surprised to hear someone address Erica as a her. By the looks in the eyes of the crowd that came over, here she was thought of very much as an It. A beloved It, yes, but an It nonetheless.

Michelle wheeled Myles to join the crowd. The man had grasped two locks of her hair now, and was just trying to get his feet in the right position to grip the tower.

'I don't understand,' Myles whispered to Michelle. 'Aren't they worried they'll break her neck?'

'Haven't you heard,' Michelle muttered back, then rolled her eyes. '*She* can't be broken.'

So this is how it would feel, at first anyway, to have your neck snapped. Once again, Erica thought it; *they're brave, those who hang themselves. You've gotta give them that.*

Sometimes they fell to their knees in front of her and begged her to cut off a lock of hair for them, one starting at the top of her scalp. 'Why?' 'Because it's long enough. And strong enough.' 'For what?' 'For a noose.'

A million injections called her to attention, spiking her scalp and launching her neck back further. She gripped the edges of the window. No, this wasn't her own attempt for an easy way out; she knew better than to take risks with the idea of 'easy' anyway – that was one thing everyone here learnt quickly.

She didn't care how brutal this life got – she wasn't done yet. She had held on once before; she could do it again. So she could see her mother again.

And I am Erica Ash and I am destined to die in a fire.

Not to mention that, she found a lot of pleasure in her strange new life. There was still almost nothing that compared with the feeling she got after she healed someone. Seeing them enter her room, their bodies lit by an invisible fire, their eyes daring to hope but really believing they weren't good enough for it to work; inching gingerly down on the bed and looking up into her eyes with the wishes of a thousand wistful seconds. The moment where she chose the part of their body with which to touch, where she ceremoniously went to her sink, washed the hands that Eli moisturised himself, demanding they be the softest touch possible, then went over to them, and, with a wink and smile, said, 'Let's find the real you, shall we?' It was so *easy*; one simple touch and everything oozed back into place, pain evaporating out of them. How could she have this gift and not use it. 24.7, year round. Three. Six. Five.

She just wished they let her sleep more. She wished she didn't have to do what she did at the ceremony with Dr Sunset. And she *wished* he didn't make her be part of that … competition, the one with the graves and the shovels and the choice. That was her least favourite part of all this.

Energy soared through her again, as whoever was below locked themselves deeper into her hair. A male voice – 'I'm coming for you baby!' How long it had been.

Myles couldn't take it. He saw a carer walking in the distance, and yelled out to her, 'They're cheating!'

He wasn't even sure if the man-made tower was, but was relieved to see the stern expression this raised. The guardian came charging over, muddy boots, 'Excuse me! We all know the rules! One can only climb the healer's hair if one has it in them to *jump high enough*.' She pointed to the illegal shoulder stand the two men had formed. 'No cheating.'

The men dismantled, letting go of the hair too suddenly, and all seventy inches of it snapped back into the tower. She was gone, and it burnt everyone's brains, just that little bit, to be without her.

The man looked down at him. Thoughts of how easy it would be to get his own back blazed in him. Myles bathed in the darkest parts of his new enemy's brain. His friend patted him on the shoulder. 'He's just embarrassed he can never make it to her. Deep down he knows he doesn't deserve it. He's a time waster.'

The two men walked off, arms around each other, seemingly as healthy as those outside Core. Did people come here thinking if their bodies were already optimal, who knows what could happen if they were touched by a healer?

'Is that where she stays?' he asked Michelle. 'Always?'

'Oh no,' Michelle said. 'Only occasionally. She has a room somewhere, but we're not sure where – the security must be ridiculous. And then at midnight, they take her somewhere else.

There's theories. But it's probably the basement.

We believe Eli – the founder of this place – we believe he's trying to experiment. Create something out of her. There's been...whispers, hints. He thinks that, together, they could create something that could bring people back to life. At least that's my theory. Some people think it's even weirder.'

'What, exactly?'
'It's all in the name. Eli. He might believe him and her can create an Elixir – '
'You mean …'
'Yes. The ability to live forever.'

While picking flowers, Michelle explained to Myles everything she could about Core. The more she spoke to him, the more the memory of 19 Feet High faded. Everybody else was carrying on as normal, so he did too, and within an hour it was like it had never happened.

Core was basically split into three categories, four if you were being generous, of the 200 residents. There were those who had come here in earnest, who believed it was a retreat simply designed to realign their outlook on life – which it was. Then there were those who had heard about the Healer; that Eli Jones had done it, found a girl that could make them better. Of those who came for the Healer, about half were truly ill, the other half were like the men outside her tower - people who were already well but addicted to the idea of becoming better. Some came with a blind hope, excited to meet this half-angel who'd devoted her life to them. They always started off a little guilty, but the closer they got to her, the more it ebbed away, as the promise of peace came closer.

The other half were people who didn't want to be here. It was in fact the last thing they wanted. Many had checked into Sunset and woken up here – others had been minutes away from the last thrust of the noose when a loved one had found them and called the number they thought would help. And within that group, were a small degree of very bad people, who knew they shouldn't be walking the earth, like Joe, who, as Jill explained, was found by the police and offered to Eli. They carried a guilt and had been given no other choice but to lay it down here.

Every day followed the same menial, boring routine. Obeying the rules of the carers and existing purely to be 'good.' Now and again it was punched with spikes of brutality, like in '19 Feet High', earlier, to teach them to remain in line. Those who chose to come here lived a better life than those who were taken here; constantly punished for their choice, their thought crime, of suicide. But really, everyone was just stringing alone on the same thread; that one day, Eli would choose them.

To meet her.

The Healer.

Even if they didn't know what she might heal, it had to be better than this.

To them she was the answer, the only thing that made it all worth it, and they would do anything to be with her.

Erica was the centre of the world. Surely she would be easy to find?

'So what do we do,' he asked Michelle after lunch. 'How does the time pass?'
Michelle sighed sadly. 'It doesn't.'

Myle's head grew heavier. He had to be strict with himself, not to panic about what his chosen position was doing to his neck. 'We can't do anything? We're not allowed music, film, sport, nothing?'
She wheeled him to a patch of shade. 'Just breathe. It gets easier.'

It's been hours, and nothing has changed about pressure. Pressure only grows, pressure only increases. I wish I was as humble as a balloon that knows when to pop.
When this is over I will move in a million ways but more than anything right now I just want to rest my hand on my thigh.
But for now, what you need to do now, for everyone, for yourself, is simply forget that you could ever move at all.

Bedtime came, exactly at 9pm, as, tingling, it had promised that it would.
He was cleaned, scrubbed and rolled as if he were a child. What a wonder it was to have a mother again.
These carers however, despite their ownership of everything to do with womanhood, had far from a mothering touch. Myles skin was raw, his new outfit too tight, and he was convinced he smelt of bleach.
Then finally it happened. He was alone. The luxury of a room to himself.
No one around. His door closed. Nothing to keep him company but the book and the glass of water by his bed.
So, if he wasn't mistaken, he could scratch his nose. He did it, the rascal. And if he was reading this right, he could wiggle his big toe. And he could –
Oh Hell Yeah. A couple of movements and his dam erupted.
He *knew* he should unfurl his body slowly, but he popped open in one go, dropping the claw, rolling his head, wriggling his shoulders, kicking his legs apart and bouncing up into the air. He bounced once, twice, three times up from the mattress, a rebellious revolution against the laws he had set for himself.
Freedom, body, movement, life!
In one day he had forgotten (and his whole life he had been taking it for granted), what it was like to glide like a well oiled machine, to feed yourself at your pace, etc, etc, etc, etc! For all those hours he had been trying to reason with it, with the feeling, and tell himself it was like meditating, and believe he could overcome the splinters his own body gave him. But now he laughed, oh how wrong he was, as he became his own personal rollercoaster and he let the snakes within his muscles run free.
Within minutes he realised he was tingling. He'd done too much too soon. He lay back down, letting his riveting body settle, breathing slow.
What to do? Far too much energy to sleep.
Maybe there were carers at every corner, waiting to catch him. But maybe not. And even if there were, he knew why he was here. He was here to get her out. He was going to look for The Healer.

Reluctantly, he got back into his chair, though he didn't resume today's position. He had given it his day; he couldn't commit to it for the night too. He opened his door, peeked outside, and began to move.

Not in the drawing room. Not in the dining hall. Not in the garden. Not in the barn. Not in the flower bed. Not up the stairs. He went back to the tower she had flung her hair out of – not there.

Night air blazed into him. Tonight would be the night he saved her.

Wheeling towards a maze, he felt a pair of hands clasp his chair and another hand clasp his mouth.

Any normal man would have got up and run, but he was not any normal man. He was a man with a trick to play and a girl to win. Just in time he remembered that if he pulled off this trick in his body – he just might get her back.

So he remained curled up in his chair, and he let whoever it was, take him.

When he opened his eyes he was in what looked like an abandoned library. In the darkness he could make out hands and feet. Subtly, he tried to slide back into position, remembering the angles and shapes he'd promised himself he would stick to.

A light snapped on. He was looking at a desk, and a man leaning boldly against it. Dressed in nothing but blue jeans, he had a torso that looked like it had once been strong, but had been given up slightly. In the dark Myles could make out something else, on the left hand side, towards the bottom of his waist. Something dark and squidgy and unfamiliar.

'Hi new boy,' said the man. Myles recognised him from dinner earlier. He had the presence Myles liked to think he himself had; strong, charismatic, bold. He held out his hand to let him attempt to shake it. 'I'm Darren. What you doing exploring these walls alone at night?'

Myles couldn't think of a reply. More and more faces edged into view in the darkness, staring at him with curiosity.

'Did you choose to come here, or were you taken?'

Myles muttered a reply. 'I was taken.'

Darren nodded. 'I thought so. So I'm guessing you're looking for a way out?'

Myles sent a shrug through his new body. 'Yeah, kind of. I mean I guess you have to try, don't you?'

Darren smiled. 'Even though everybody here is good at giving up.' The room tittered. 'But when you're made to carry on, strange things can happen. I'll give Eli that credit – he made me see that.' He leaned off the desk, then beckoned to someone in the darkness. Together, silently, they lifted the desk up and moved it back.

'You've heard by now how Eli smuggles some of us in. He has some kind of tunnel, connected all the way to Sunset Clinic. Impressive.

I'm not sure exactly where that tunnel is. I've reason to believe it's round outside the kitchens, but I can't confirm that. Anyway, before it was there; this was Eli's study. He has a new one now – much nicer and shinier than this. But this was his study, and this was where the tunnel was originally going to be.'
Darren bent down to the patch of stone the desk had been covering, and silently lifted one of the stones out of the way. 'It took me a while to figure it out, but I did it. You wouldn't be surprised, not if you knew who I used to be. There was nothing I couldn't pull off back then. The old tunnel is here.' He dipped a hand down into the darkness. 'It's all built. It leads to a port. Run for a mile and you can get out. For others, like you, who can't run, the process is slower, *but*, we can do it. We can work together. Lift, carry, drag, whatever it takes. So far eighteen of us have got out.'
He held out his hand. Through the dark red air, emerged a girl. Half her face was beautiful; the other half was burnt. 'This is Cindy. Cindy was found trying to end her life, and sent here.'
Cindy took his hand. 'Being in this retreat – the silence has driven me mad. I realised I want to get back out there. I want to live again, half my face or not.'
'But Eli won't let you go?' Myles asked. 'Even though you came round to his ethos and value your life now?' She looked at him, mockingly.
'You really believe he'll ever let any of us go? Now he has us here? He has a whole kingdom.'
'How do you explain the missing people?' Myles questioned Darren.
Darren narrowed his eyes. 'There's a cannibal here. One of Eli's first finds; see, Eli does keep society safe, in some way. The cannibal wants to help our cause. So he says he ate them.'
Not sure if he was joking or not, Myles watched Darren effortlessly lower Cindy into the hole. She attached herself to some sort of ladder, then dipped down into the darkness. It was that simple; Darren slid the stone back over the gap.
'So,' Darren said. 'Want to schedule an escape? I'd like to get you out of here. You look too much like me. There's only one Darren, I'm afraid.'
Myles smirked.
'Maybe one day.'
'One day? Why are you really here then, Myles?'
'Why do you think? For a woman.'
'Ah.' Darren clapped him on the back. 'Aren't we all?'

After all the excitement, they had snuck Myles safely back to his room. Now he lay in bed, ever so comfortable, sleeping exactly the way he would choose to sleep. He snuggled into the blanket and happily massaged the point between his shoulder blades which had really been seizing up. At the last minute he remembered to set an alarm for half five, so he could awake and position himself back into his treacherous trick, before anybody came in and caught him

like this – sprawled out in the indulgence of a normal body. He checked the clock; 2am. He lifted his legs to let the blood run vertically.
And as he did his door opened.
I think he got away with it, though he definitely made a noise, slamming back down and curling to his side, recalibrating his body back into the wretched claw. His heart threw pebbles at his chest, as he stared into the white wall, pretending to sleep.
Whoever had come into his room took their time, before sitting gingerly on the end of the bed. *Pretend to sleep and they can't hurt you.*
'Hello, Myles.' A female voice, unfamiliar. 'I thought you might like a bedtime story. It must have been a while since you had one.
I bet you've never heard the story of The Humiliated Hero. His story was told until the narrator's were too ashamed to tell it.
There's nothing brave about being brave, you see. Anyone in their right mind would want to be a hero. It's not easy, no, but it is easy to be admired, and praised, and maybe the easiest thing of all is to be owed. If it came down to it, everybody would risk themselves to save others, or so they like to think.
But to risk never being able to look themselves in the eye again; would they do that?
The Humiliated Hero. He's tall, and he's strong, trained in all kinds of combat, and he welds a sword and has an invisibility cloak. Or he's none of those things; but not because he is above the physical.
The Humiliated Hero takes one part of what it is to be a hero; sacrifice. It's not sacrifice to be strong. It's not sacrifice to be cool. Adoration is not sacrifice, neither is adrenaline or adventure. No. It's sacrifice to be hated. It's sacrifice to humiliated. It's sacrifice to be ugly.' The woman paused, inhaling, tasting the air before speaking again.
'If you really love her, peel off your face.
I'm just warning you. That's what they might make you do, if you really want her back.
If you can't, it's ok. Many have tried and failed.' A hand rustled gently in his hair.
'Goodnight, sweet boy. Sleep well.'
He attempted to roll over.
'Don't. Don't turn, please. I don't want you to see me.'

Chapter Thirty Six

Day Two

Three statements, like three bowls of porridge for Goldilocks to try. Three attempts to deny the ethics of *this*.

1.) They keep us like lab rats.
2.) They treat us like dogs.
3.) If euthanasia is good enough for an animal, how can it not be good enough for us? Put us out of our misery too.

They say if you want to know where you'd have stood on the holocaust, look at where you stand on animals. If you agreed with any of the above, what you are is a *speciest.*

From the pigs to the weasels to the buffalos to the bears, now they all know what you think and now they're all hoping you get what you deserve.

Try again. Try once more to justify the ethics of *this.*

Talking of porridge, it was time for breakfast.

Myles had had the best night's sleep of his life; coincidentally, without actually sleeping. He had spent the hours rolling from one position to the next, revelling in his naughty secret: his body worked. He oozed himself in and out of the sheets, working the silk through his back, stretching and sighing like a cat who'd regained a lost purr.

By the time Jill had knocked on his door, checking he was ready to be dressed, he was a new man. Convinced that it would be easy, now he knew what to expect. That after eight hours of massaging and loosening every part of his body, it would be supple and obedient, eager to slip back into yesterday's sculpture.

Ninety seconds in and he knew he was wrong. Turns out it was even harder, anticipating what was in store for it. *Oh god. Can I really do this for another day?*

He amused himself with his claw, as he dug into porridge. Pretending to drop scoops of hot oats, to muster glances of sympathy and offers of help. The weaker he looked, the closer he would get: to her.

He sat next to Darren, the man from last night, who gave him a conspirator's nod. He was still topless, still proudly brandishing his plastic stomach. He pulled his porridge towards him while it was still steaming.

So much starch. So little sin.

Myles felt the small of his back buckle with the impatient strings of the reflexes he denied. Thawing beneath the ice, tribes of impulses were fighting back. So much so he couldn't help but whisper, 'Don't suppose there's another way out, is there?'

Darren smirked. 'There is one,' he said. 'Just one.'

'What?'
Darren plunged his spoon into his oats, gorging out a large chunk. 'Dig.'

Myles struggled with his straw. This was pissing him off; he was fucking thirsty, and remaining in this position meant he couldn't quite close his lips around it. Could he get away with pretending he was having a tremor, one that shuffled his mouth muscles a little?

As he contemplated, a carer slid into the seat beside him. Had she not been about to help him, he never would have noticed her. Her face was plainer than the bread in front of him. She was puffy and beige, sweltering in her grey suit, but gentle as a dove as she directed the straw to his mouth.

'That better?' he recognised the voice straight away. It was the woman from last night, the one who'd told him the story. Her voice was nice, a delicate husk of smoke that betrayed the frumpy cage it came from. Before he could reply, she whispered, 'One time I rubbed butter on a staircase so people would slip.' She thrust the straw back into his mouth and he took it again, letting her continue.

'So I'm not going to judge you. Whatever you do.' She winked and left too soon, Myle's tongue still searching for more water.

He remembered to put his tongue back in, and saw Darren staring at him. 'Who was that?' he asked.

'That's Ann,' Darren said. 'She's the only carer who started out as a guest.'

'Why is she here?'

'She was sent here.' Darren looked unsure whether to continue, but did. 'Word is she pushed a woman in front of a bus. For no reason. Just did it one day.'

Myles watched the back of her bun, a mouse's grey, moving across the room.

'She was a psychopath. Eli chose her for her cruelty. But then he sanded down her edges, and now he trusts her with all of us, with everything. The only thing he won't do is let her leave.'

After a boring morning activity of 'berry picking' in the garden, where a carer named Gwen talked them through good and bad berries, they were left to wait. For what?

For the next meal of course. Their lives were all about nutrition now. 2000 calories for the women, 3000 for the men. Meeting requirements for protein, for carbs, for fats. Eli didn't want them to be sexy, and what could be less sexy than health?

Myles thought back to his fast in Hawaii, how long he had gone without a single meal. He wished he could show them all, the carers too, that weeks without food was possible – show them what their bodies were capable of. How little sustenance they needed to survive and how much pressure their hearts could handle.

At lunchtime, Myles met a woman who had killed her son.

Rhonda said the words with the first glimmer of true evil he had seen. All the guilt that should have been there was replaced by pride. 'I gave birth to him, I loved him and then twenty eight years later I decided to kill him.'
Did you kill your mother, Myles? Erica's voice walked through him. And the horror at the thought of it.
'No wonder you can't live with yourself,' he said. He didn't mean it as harsh as it sounded.
'I could,' Rhonda said. 'It's just that I wanted to be with him again.'
Screw it, Myles thought, let's have a conversation. There's nothing else to do in this place.
'Do you really think that?' he said, intrigued. 'I used to wonder that about … long story, but about this girl, Rose,' Green grit swam through him, made of trauma, trying to pollinate him, but he pressed on. 'And I wondered, if heaven and angels and everything is real, if she was up there, watching me, waiting to see me. Maybe if she'd even forgiven me.'
He looked at Rhonda again. It is always the ones you think you can trust. She wasn't a caricature of cosiness or frumpiness; wasn't a saccharine, storybook idea of a mother. No, she was solid, a real person, the opposite of something like Rebecca, natural and kind, something you could reach out and touch.
Touch her he did. Only her hand. Caring, like a good son. How old was she? Couldn't be more than fifty five. 'I'm sure he does,' Myles whispered. 'Forgive you.'
She let his hand stay on top of hers til it started to sweat. 'There's nothing to forgive. You think I *wanted* to do it?'
Other people were looking over now, dropping forks and spilling juice. They all had one thing reserved in their eyes for Rhonda; admiration. And maybe a bit of hope.
'My son loved to ski, until the day he couldn't.'
Another row of heads turned, the meals abandoned. The carers started to notice.
Rhonda chuckled. 'See how they all look. You should see how many times a day people pull me aside and ask me to do it to them. Like I could just lift my hands up and place them around their throats and not feel a thing. Every day; notes under the door, threats, people sidling up to me while I'm brushing my teeth. *Please*. They even try and call me mother. Because everybody knows, deep down, that's the only way it works. That it's something only a mother could do for a son.'

Lunch was meant to be over, until it wasn't. Until something strange and cool came over the room.
'Oh fuck *that*,' Michelle, who had joined them, gasped. 'Not again. Are you kidding.' She stared at the doorway and shook her head in revulsion.
'What is it?' Myles asked, remembering not to turn his neck too quickly to look.
Be bent, be broken, be boring.

He didn't need to ask twice. Jill swept into the centre of the room, flanked by three carers on each side, each wheeling large trolleys layered with trays. She loved a ceremony, Myles was starting to realise. He could tell she was gearing up for an announcement.
'Ladies and gentlemen,' she smiled warmly. 'I'm bringing back last week's game.'
She picked up a tray from the trolley. On it lay twenty or so miniscule white pills.
'Let's play: Mints or Morphine.'

Mints Or Morphine

The rules: Every player has ten white pills in front of them. They look identical; small, round and white, because there can never be too much of that bland, safe colour.
At the bell, the players pick one tablet at random, and swallow it, washed down with a glass of water.
That's it. Repeat for ten rounds.
The variable: nobody knows what's on their plate – nine mints to one morphine, or half and half. It's a game of luck.
The goal: To fall asleep. To stop the pain.
Even the pills hope it. Even they worry about what's inside them.

Morphine: Celibate, sensible, calm. Women in white. Without trying, it had become the ultimate tease.
Ring, went the bell, and in the mouths they went.
The prize: To be pain free. To silence the stress. To have a moment without electricity in their veins.
The contestants: those who had not chosen to be here, but had been taken here. Those who needed to come round to Eli's way of thinking.
For most of them, this was the first painkiller they had been given since they were here. As soon as they realised what this place was, a plague of headaches, hot flushes and hives had been released in them. So they would play Jill's game and dance to her tune, and swallow and crunch, to get to where they wanted to be. They were playing for sleep.
And if not sleep, then at least an hour of relief. At least something to distract their synapses – to get them back to their lives before they made the mistake of coming here. Even three or four pills; though that wouldn't do much, it would still give them some brush with kindness.
Of course, after a while, it stopped being a game. At some point when a headache crawls through you, when strange skeletons dance in your teeth, and you just want to stop tasting mint.

Mints: the zingy cousin to morphine. Packed with sarcasm and acerbic wit. Little but fierce.
The mints knew they were the majority.
It took the guests longer to realise, or to accept, that.
'No!'
'ARGH!'
'Not again!'
They knew how it would feel to be tranquil again. But did they deserve it?
'Come *on*!'
Still they tried and they chewed, because who would give up on finally feeling good?
'NO!'
'Where is it?'
'Mine was all mints! Again!'
'Who has morphine? Anyone?!'
'I can't … I can't keep doing this.'
The bell rang and the game continued. The exquisite line between relief and frustration only got thicker.
Because every now and then, someone got lucky. Every now and then someone leant back into a serene state. Looking around the room, one or two were even falling into sleep. There was just enough to believe that could be their fate too.
'Ow. Ow. Ow.'
'Can I say something?' Myles asked. It hurt to speak, to let the menthol revolve through every muscle in his mouth.
'Why, yes,' smiled Ann, looming over his table. 'Most people don't feel much like talking after this.'
'Indeed, the mint makes it hard to talk. What's the one thing you might as well do when you've got a mouthful of mints?' He put his arm over the table and beckoned her closer, conspiratorially.
'What's that, dear?' she said.
He launched forward, pretending it was a flinch.
'Kiss!' he hissed. 'Don't tell me I'm the first to think of it. In a game like this … kiss, kiss, kiss!'
Suddenly he was bending Michelle back, all damsel in distress, and leaning her in the crook of his arm, and kissing her. He turned away, put his hand on the back of her neck. To his left was Rhonda; he put his claw on her neck too and combined the two women over him, leaning back and grinning as their lips, Michelle's three times the size of Rhonda's, tentatively connected. The girls giggled nervously then combined and consumed each other, and the table next to them turned and gawped at the show. Even those who were falling into sleep had something to stay up for.
The women pulled apart, their arctic breath mixing in the air.

'Kiss me,' Myles said determinedly, his eyes flicking between their faces. 'What's the point of all these mints, if not that?'
Not one person in this room had kissed since they'd been here, could remember exactly how it felt to close your eyes and get lost in it. But all of them had missed it.
We've all been three inches from a kiss. Not sure it's going to happen then suddenly it is and your senses are a storm. Little kisses, long kisses, light kisses, deep kisses, kisses that make you fall, kisses that let you fly. Once Myles, Michelle and Rhonda met in a three way kiss, it was impossible to pull away.
'Stop.' It was Ann. 'STOP.'
Even her lips tingled. They'd always been thin, and dry. They were punctuated by thirty or so fine, stubby hairs she'd never known what to do about. The word 'Stop' died on her lips, a word she'd never had to use because she'd never been pursued.
'What's going on?!' It was Jill.
The three of them snapped apart. Michelle bounced off his lap and Rhonda slammed down into her seat. With reflexes so smooth he regretted them instantly, Myles wiped his lips.
The room was silent but for Jill's footsteps as she marched around them. The game was forgotten as everybody watched in fear. People had misbehaved before, but not like this.
'Who was that? Who started it?' she snapped at Ann.
Ann gave a stern shake of her head. 'I didn't see.'
Myle's head snapped at her in surprise – *dammit boy, remember, you can't move that quickly, NO more mistakes from now on* – then he looked back down. Jill came closer; he could smell her breath from here, and it certainly wasn't minty.
'So whose idea was it?' she said.
He kept looking down, his eyes fixed on her stubby ankles.
'Come on. Tell me.'
He shot quick glances at the other two. They were in this together.
'Whoever tells me can have as many melatonins as they want. Dipped in white chocolate if they wish.'
'It was Myles.'
He almost snapped his neck in the voice's direction, til he remembered to twist, very slowly, to see who had said it, though deep down he knew who. It was Michelle, and she was blinking back at him with tears in her eyes.
'I'm sorry,' she muttered. 'Jill, he's new. He doesn't know. He was trying to be ni – '
'You know very well, Michelle, that that wasn't not the act of a nice man.' Jill smirked. 'Ann? Wheel Myles this way. Time for him to learn.'
Ann took the handles of his chair and wheeled him away. Phyllis, the largest and most robust of the carers, joined them. All that was left was for Rhonda to look at Michelle in disgust, wiping her scent off her lips.

And it would be hours later, almost suppertime in fact, when Rhonda would find Michelle again, crouched outside a door, knees pulled up to her chest as much as they could be, snivelling.
'It's okay, Michelle,' the older woman said to the younger. 'He's strong. He'll recover.'
Michelle wiped her eyes. 'Yes, he will. We all do.' Sarcastic. Patronising. Exasperated at her naivety. 'I just … I thought it would be quick.'
'What.' Rhonda's expression jolted and a disquieting sickness slid through her. 'Michelle … what did they do to him?'
'What *did* they do?' She widened her eyes, cocked her head at her, let me be your guide. 'They're not done yet. It's still going on right now.'
'What?!' Bubbles and broths reacted in Rhonda's throat. 'It's been six hours! It's nearly tea-time!'
'I know!' She sighed regretfully. She gestured then to the door behind them. 'He's in there. If you press your ear to the door you can still hear him. At least he still has his tongue.'

In the end, all they did was burn him a little. Not even in the most sensitive spots; just an elbow or a toe or two. They used dripping wax instead of open flame. He was new, and they wanted to give him a chance to thrive here. They even allowed him to ask them a question.
'I just don't understand. Why does Eli do it like this?'
'Like what?'
'Look, I get what he's doing here – you'd have to be an idiot not to. Take suicidal people and change their minds. Show them that no matter how hard things are, life has value. It's beautiful.'
'It is.'
'So … why no music? Why all the rules? Why can't people's families visit? And why the *punishments*?'
The carers mopped the hardened wax from his chest, helping him back into his chair. They'd missed a bit below his eye. 'It is hard to understand at first, but it has a purpose. Maybe we shouldn't tell you this, but … wait a little longer. Sleep on this. He's been planning something for a while now. Tomorrow, you'll understand.'
Myles shuddered as his back complained; it couldn't understand why he was still neglecting it.
A carer blew out the candle. A warning lashed in her eyes as she did.
'You think you can fight him, don't you? Change his mind, persuade him?'
Myles didn't say 'maybe' but you could hear it coming from him, locked into his body. The carers looked at each other. 'We should show him. It's for his own good.'
'Show me what?'

Two hands were on his chair again. 'Come with us.'

And what they showed him was worse than all the punishment. Worse than anywhere they could have burnt him and any flame they could have held him to. To Myles, they revealed their secret. The whisper within these walls. To Myles, they showed them what they had shown so few who came to Core, knowing most couldn't bear it: the secret of Scott Luther.

The formerly relentless, handsome politician was not another victim of suicide - he was very much under the care of Core, sealed within their walls. Scott Luther was the man who lived.

Or did he?

When they revealed him to Myles, Myles wasn't sure. They kept him in something that was almost a room but could have been a cupboard, with only enough space for a bed and a bucket. There were no windows, no light, and there was nothing to do.

But before Myles could roar about the inhumanity of this isolation - roar that he at least needed a book or a radio or something - he looked closer at the man. There was nothing behind Scott's eyes. No hint of the intelligence, the vibrancy or the determination that had become so famous and baked into the culture of the his country. Looking at him, you'd never guess he could change a law, let alone stir up controversy in the way he had done. You were looking at a husk. A husk without opinions, feelings or desires. This was catatonia.

Quite simply, Scott had started to rot.

'Eli gave him the silence he gave to so many,' the carer whispered. Even she seemed afraid to broach the edginess of what they had done.

'How is he like this? What happened to him?'

'A mixture of fear,' the carer explained. 'And pills.' She crept towards Scott and she edged another pill into the willing Scott's morose mouth. 'As many as pills as he can take, to keep him silent, to keep him safe, to keep him satiated.' She gulped. 'This was a warning. This is what happens to those who think they can take on Eli. Nobody wins but him.'

She drifted away, closing the door before the fear did the same thing to Myles.

'Nothing wins but Health. Do you see?'

She loves you like lace. She waits and waits. But you don't come. How long will she wait? Her hands are going numb. She smashes a glass in anger. Still you don't come – and someone else does.

You didn't think they'd let him miss one of his three meals a day, did you? Soon enough it was time for supper, and Myles was released. He looked down as he was wheeled towards the grand hall. Must get those 3,000 calories. Good to end the evening with some veggies, keep you regular for the morning.

Everybody looked as he was wheeled in. Everyone was surprised by how intact he looked, how he kept his head up. They even wheeled him to sit next to his friends, Rhonda and Darren.

None of them said a word til their drinks arrived.

Growing up, Myles could never stomach a smoothie. In adulthood he had learnt a trick; he could get it down him, as long as it had ice.

Now a gleaming jar of nightshade looked up at him. Thousands of tiny ice globes decorated the top, and sunk to the middle of the drink. The clinic had made it just as he liked it, as if they knew.

Myles raised the plastic tumbler of sludge to his lips. 'Cheers,' he muttered.

'WAIT!' Rhonda grabbed his arm, bringing it far from his teeth. 'Is that … *glass* in your smoothie?'

'Glass?!' Myles allowed her to bring his arm down, smiling at her softly. 'Babe, they don't allow glass in this place. The carers even shave me for me. It's crushed ice, which I love, actually. Look.'

He dipped his finger into the green, bringing out a shard to show her.

Both their eyes widened in horror as the tip of his finger opened up and confessed three gleaming red drops of blood.

Myles rolled the ice through his finger and thumb, the object sharpening by the second.

'Ok, it's glass,' he nodded and looked down, the drink simmering with hundreds of the refreshing blades in its creamy abyss. 'Who the fuck put glass in my smoothie?'

'That's not what you should be asking, M.' Rhonda pulled the glass to her, dipped her finger in and stirred. It came out tauntingly, perfectly unharmed.

'This is a threat. For your silence. The question is, why? Anyone got a reason to cut out your tongue?'

He looked from her, to the shards of ice, to her warm face, to the cold glass, back and forth. Not even a documentary on glass could have told him that it had been that that was in his smoothie. 'How did you know, Rhonda? How could you tell it was glass not ice?'

'I didn't do it,' Rhonda smiled, nodding, pleased with herself. 'Maybe Becky? As she hates food so much? Oh wait, Becky's dead. Anyway I like the silencing theory more. Darren is trying to keep his tunnel a secret, after all.'

Darren raised his eyebrows at her, amused, prompting Rhonda to add, 'But he's too subtle for that.'

'Michelle?' Darren suggested.

Myles shook his head, scouring the room for her. 'Nah. Hasn't got it in her.'

Rhonda nodded, stirring her smoothie with a straw. 'The bad bitch with the good heart. Maybe it was a carer.'

'I mean of course. It wouldn't be one of us, would it?'

'Of course not.'

'You trust us. You like us.'

'I do.'
'And why's that? Because you want to save one of us. Just the one though.'
Rhonda sucked on the paper straw in her smoothie. She didn't need ice to get it down. She looked into his eyes as she summoned the sludge into her mouth, not even wincing as it packed into her throat. 'You're looking for someone, aren't you? It's obvious every time we turn a corner. Your eyes dart around desperately hoping that you'll find them. So far, no good, am I right?' She pushed her smoothie away, then looked up at him.
He took her hand. 'So you think it was Eli? That he ordered someone to do it?'
'No,' Rhonda picked out another shard of glass. 'I think it was probably her. Whoever you're looking for. It was probably a message; her way of saying 'hurry up and find me'.'
Myles looked back into the glass. He had to stop himself from licking it up. He'd eat only glass for the rest of his life, if it had come from Erica. Excitement at the thought of her made him want to move, so he changed the subject. 'Darren?' he said.
'Yes mate?' Darren replied.
'I've a question. I know the answer must be obvious, but.' He lowered his voice. 'So you found the tunnel, right? Why don't you ever go through it yourself?'
He tailed off as he saw Darren drenched in a rich, rich sadness at the question. He shouldn't have asked. He cringed from within.
'Darren … ' Myles voice eeked out of him. 'Don't … don't tell me it's because of *that*.' He gestured to the bag, the solemn sack hanging beneath the table. 'Come on man … you can be anything – '
'Myles!' Rhonda snapped. 'Everyone has their own reasons for not wanting to face the world. If even our own start to disrespect that, what hope is there for any of us?'
'Ok.' Myles looked down, nodding. 'I'm sorry.'
'It's not the bag,' Darren shook his head, a wry smile on his face as though he was mocking himself. 'I wish I could say I'd never been stupid enough, to throw my life away over a colostomy bag.' He sighed deeply then continued. 'I'm one of the ones who originally booked into Sunset Clinic'
He hushed quickly as the carers put three plates down in front of them. Rice, so much rice, each one an individual, grainy dagger for their guts. And not just rice; the plates were piled high with seeds, nuts like bullets, every shape of bean. So much food, so much to chew. Rhonda picked up her fork defeatedly.
'Yes I was. I had my whole family around me and yet I didn't … I didn't see them. I hate to say it but it was like love didn't matter to me. Like I was bigger than love. Now I know. Nothing can ever be bigger than love.'
'So why don't you go back to them?' Myles blurted out.
Darren eye's swelled. 'Because I think they sent me here. Deliberately. Out of revenge. There's moments, when I think about the day they brought me to

Sunset; certain looks and gestures that just felt wrong. Moments that could mean nothing, but what if they don't? What if it's the thing I fear - that they chose to send me here? When I close my eyes I see them, all in on it, happy that this is where I'm rotting away. Even my little daughter. And if that's true, I can never face it.'

His eyes started to leak. He had never cried before he came here. He raised his hand and a carer came over. 'Yes?' she smiled.

'May I be excused?' he asked. 'I don't think I can digest this.'

'Hmm. Have you had enough carbs today?'

'Gwen!' Ann called over and joined them. 'Haven't you read his notes? His stomach is much more sensitive than the others, he shouldn't have been served rice anyway. Yes, Mr Thames, you may. I'll escort you to your room.'

'Thank you,' he managed to blubber out before leaping up and, Ann tailing behind, he fled the room, before they could see him sob.

Rhonda and Myles locked eyes, then looked away. Myle's sunk his head into his claw. This place. This fucking place. Where the hell was Eli?

Rhonda sighed. 'Can't believe that's what's become of Darren Thames.'

9pm came. Myles was scrubbed, dressed and rolled into bed. His door shut and then, once again, he was alone.

There was always that fear – look at him, talking like an expert, when this was only day two – but always that fear that he would get stuck in the statue he was so loyally committed to. *If the wind changes you'll stay like that forever.* But as he dared to straighten his legs and arch his back, he sighed with buttery pleasure. It was all still there. He licked his lips with bliss. Delayed gratification, he could write a book on it.

Oh, that feeling. That first illegal roll, the first forbidden stretch. His muscles were music. His bones were white chocolate. Yes, yes, *yes*, he was a lucky boy indeed.

It was the ultimate massage, coming from the inside out, his one slice of happiness in this strange world. If he was inanimate, he was the oven when it gets turned off, the tissue when it stops being crumpled, the onion released from the jar of vinegar. Bounce baby bounce, he could do anything he wanted, and he was suddenly overcome by the urge to do a forward roll. So he did.

Woohoo!

For ten minutes he morphed, into a million different states and frames, turning the grinding into a caress. He ironed out every grumpy ache, slowly reminding his body it was worth it. He threw his head to the ceiling and laughed – he could do anything now – rejoicing in freedom, and the reward he was now getting for his willpower.

It was only when he lay his head on the pillow that he found the note. Handwritten, scrawled in pen.

Come to the bottom of the tower. Michelle will meet you there. You need to see something.

His hand was reaching for the lock when the door opened all by itself.
Michelle. Let's talk about Michelle. Though she couldn't dance, she was dancing for him.
She swung on the edge of the door, one hand clutching a bar of dark chocolate.
'Contraband,' she giggled. He looked up at her and she looked down at him.
The chocolate was melting in her hands.
'What can I do for you?' he almost cocked his head, appraisingly, before he remembered he wasn't able to.
'Are you up for some evening entertainment? I've got a plus one.'
'Where in this place is the *entertainment*?'
Michelle leaned into his chair, drummed the hand with the manicured nails on his chest. 'Eli isn't the only one who can play games.'

Once she had wheeled him down the stone corridor, she let go of his chair and ordered him to drive himself, following her lead. He followed her into a bookless library and through a foodless kitchen, he followed her into a white passageway and he followed her into a black, barbed elevator, and waited for her to pick the button, whether to send them up or down.
She chose down, and as they plunged, Myles realised something.
Myles had been following women all his life. Women he wanted, women who wanted him. Women he loved, women he hated. Every period in his life had revolved around a woman. A mother he adored. A fiancé he killed, then a fiancé who tricked him. The woman in Hawaii who had defined him ever since. He had hurt women. He had been afraid of women. Mother. Rose. Valentina. Erica. Michelle. And all the other satiny sucrose sirens, those queens of aspartame, enslaving his senses. His soul turned to syrup when he thought about doing whatever he wished with a woman, yet his stomach turned to slush when he thought about the Carers doing whatever they wished with him. Now, he was here, risking everything for one woman, and yet trying to deny the urge to pull Michelle, a woman he met yesterday, into his lap and confess everything, about why he was here and show her just how dynamically his body could actually move.
The lift continued to sink. No place should have this many underground floors. He thought about asking her, 'Michelle, where are you taking me?' and then realised how weak that sounded, and that she, like most girls, loved to surprise.
He turned back to his thoughts.
Maybe that was why he wasn't scared of Eli. Not one bit. The person who had kidnapped his lover, not once but twice, had engineered himself to a place of influence and power in society, had survived being blinded, had lost a major vote yet now somehow tricked his rival into running a backstreet, nightmare,

vengeful antidote to Dignitas, didn't scare him one bit. Even the fact that he was going to try to bring him down without moving a muscle, just added to the thrill of the challenge. Man to man, Myles could always believe he'd come out on top. Nobody would be more of a man than him. And especially a man like Eli.

'Myles? We're here.'

'Welcome to the show.'

The last person Myles had been expected to be greeted by was Ann, but there she was. Sternness swam in her watery face.

'Take your seats. Oh, Myles, you're already seated. Can you sit, Michelle? Should I get someone to carry you both?' Each sentence swung from one to the other, mocking them in a way too light and fast to catch.

'We'll be fine,' he said. 'Where do we sit?'

She moved out the way proudly, and that's when he saw it. They were in a circular, dusky room. It was a miniature amphitheatre, the feeling of being in someone's perverted dollhouse never more apparent than now. A row of about five circular, oak benches made a circle out of the stone floor in the middle. A meagre attempt at an audience bristled in the benches. Everybody in here was weak in some way; beaten or burnt by the carers.

Except for the two men everybody was watching. They sat in the middle of the stone floor, their healthy bodies lit by candles.

'Sickest of them all,' someone hissed.

'Hey everyone, what's his illness?' shouted another, pointing to the less chiselled, cuddlier man of the two.

'Obesity!'

Hahaha. How they guffawed.

Ann entered the middle of the circle, her boots playing music on the stone. Not too frightening. At least not yet. She clasped her hands together and a warm smile wiggled its way onto her face. 'So. Welcome, welcome, everyone, to tonight's game. You *are* a very lucky few who get to bear witness to one of our procedures here. I trust you'll tell no one about this.' She began to walk around the circle. 'None of you know what you are about to see, and none of tonight's performers know what they are about to do. Truth is, you only know one thing; at 1pm tomorrow, there will be a healing. Bet you're tired of hearing that word, aren't you? Used to roll off the tongue so easily.'

That was when the excitement became apparent in the two performers' eyes. Just how much they were beaming, buzzing with anticipation to get to this point.

'Let me introduce you to Remi,' she gestured to the chiselled man. 'And Henry. Hailing from America, these are the first two tourists at Core. Their behaviour has been nothing short of exemplary since their arrival. They volunteered to come here, checked themselves in, with the acute awareness of their need to be fixed.

Even if we cannot see it, everyone, in some way, needs to be healed. Remi and Henry are alcoholics. Though they have managed to cleanse themselves during their time at Core, both have been very honest and admit that once back in the temptations of the outside world,' she chuckled. 'The first thing they'd do is head for the pub! Remi thinks maybe he'd last a day … while he waited for the online booze order to arrive!' She slapped her knee. 'It takes a lot of guts to confess something like that about one's self. Let's all give them a big **well done.**'

One voice started it, a strip of salad; 'Well done.'

Another voice, this one a little fleshier, a ripening plum, 'Well done.'

Then all the voices started to come in, unsure and undercooked, 'Well done, well done,' until the voices became a little meatier, 'Well done, congratulations,' and within a minute they were the voices of slaughtered, smoky meat, and baying for their blood, 'Well done, well done! Congratulations, congratulations!' The feet that could tap stomped and the hands that could clap clamped together indulgently. If it wasn't for the unblinking gaze Remi and Henry had for each other, they surely would have started to tremble.

The only voice that remained silent was Myles. He couldn't bring himself to speak. *This* was the kind of person that was coming here? Alcoholics? *This* was what they were using Erica for? Just what the *fuck* were they doing to his girl? Turning her into a commodity, for this? *This?*

He looked at Ann and couldn't help but whisper, 'Bitch.'Witch. He wanted to reach inside her and rip out her ovaries. Give Erica something to really heal.

It was like the word 'Bitch' warmed her up, like she was a wholesome apple pie just waiting to be baked.

But luckily, he did not.

Because Ann went on to explain that although the Healer couldn't wait to meet them, she was a good girl: she'd never take on two men at once.

'One of you is going to get so very clean.'

One of us? One of us? One of us? 'Oh sorry, did you need to hold each other's hands?'

Myles watched the light leave their eyes as Ann explained her game. And that game, like all the best games, would be a fight. A fight for The Healer. A fight to be the one who got to meet her, who got to graze in the fields of her fingers, who got to be the one who knew how it felt and to find out if the rumours were true that you left her with increased clarity, increased metabolism, even increased eyesight.

And all they had to do was - he joined in with Ann as she said it - 'fight to the death.'

'And here's the kicker,' Ann added, laughing as she moved between the two men. 'Remi and Henry are lovers.'

No sympathy, no symphony, no symmetry: Myles didn't care how they felt. They were exploiters, users, abusers, and they had come to make Erica their new addiction.
Now they would show everyone just how weak they really were, just how little they had in them; it was already beginning. Remi, the bigger boyfriend, was already whimpering, begging for another option. Remi didn't want the ghost of his boyfriend twinging inside him. Remi didn't want to live as a murderer.
Henry loved Remi more than Remi loved Henry. For Henry, Remi was the one - he even had a ring in his suitcase to propose with for when they got out of here. Remi had waited all his life for someone like Henry. Remi wanted to raise a child with Henry. Remi didn't mind anything Henry did to him in the bedroom, even when he got a little too rough. His boyfriend had the bigger build, bigger hands, bigger everything - Remi accepted it all.
But he couldn't accept this. The fear. He knew how much Henry wanted to meet The Healer, and the fear plunged through him: he couldn't win this fight.
So he gave it one shot. One leap. One lumping leap into the air, to be on top for once, one great big gulp through the atmosphere that would let him land on Remi's bulk, and drive his head to the floor. He hoped, prayed, that it would bludgeon apart, so he wouldn't have to go into the night of pain that Ann had promised. Two men fighting to the death without weapons takes hours. Not two, not four, not six, but ten. Suddenly he wanted his soulmate's head to crack like a melon.
And it did.
'Congratulations,' Ann beamed at him. 'You will be taken to The Healer tomorrow.'
Myles didn't stay for the celebrations. He pretended to be having a hot flush, and asked Michelle to take him back to bed.
In the lift she had explained; there was a revolution developing beneath Core's first layer of flesh.

Back in bed, he didn't sleep.
Myles had seen Remi's eyes after he left the room, and knew even Erica could not cure that.

And it turned out he would not need to sleep. Because within the hour, there was another knock at the door, and it opened without waiting for him to answer.
At last.
Standing there, in the light, was Eli.
At last. **We meet.**
'Myles,' Eli smiled warmly. 'I bought you something.'
He turned around and wheeled in a trolley. 'More food. You're going to need your energy.'

Eli lifted the spoon to Myles mouth.
Soup. He'd always loved it. That morose, lascivious ravine of nutrition that befriended every muscle in your mouth.
'Eat up,' he smiled. 'I wanted to talk to you about that fast you did in Hawaii. Erica's told me everything, of course. Did you know that all that time, when you were starving yourself, what you were actually doing? You weren't starving – you were healing.
Fasting is one of the most powerful forms of healing. It's an ancient practice, overlooked nowadays, first explored in the bible. These days, in our modern life, we're gorging, all the time. We're not open minded enough. Modern medicine would never be allowed to recommend it. But think about it, we're mammals. Don't see any reason why we can't be like a bear – able to hibernate for months and live off our reserves. The body switches automatically, to be able to use all the stored fuel. We've evolved, those who couldn't do it didn't survive past the tenth century. So all that time, when you were wanting, hoping, waiting to die, turns out you were healing. Fast in French is 'Jeune'; another word for getting younger – you were resting, refreshing, replenishing every single one of your cells. You were keeping yourself alive.
She told me you were so easy to heal. That your body was crying out for it. You're made for her, aren't you? But is she made for you? Surely someone this powerful wouldn't – couldn't belong to just one person? Surely it's only fair that we share her?
You want to be a kind man, and you can be kind now. You need to let her go. I'd say there'll be girls like her in heaven but I can't promise it. Let's find you someone else. Someone who looks fantastic in white.
Oh wait. Let's let you finish your soup. Shall I blow on it to cool it down?'
Myles looked into the bowl. Minestrone, the hottest of soups.
'If you'd wanted to die, you should have stopped drinking. Dehydration kills. You'd get to a week at most. Try and do it. You know, Erica reminds me of water sometimes.'
Myles his eye. 'Why, because she makes you piss yourself?' Eli didn't react but his neck went red.
'With fear?' Myles added for clarification. 'Fear about what she'll do to you the day she escapes?' He thought he heard a giggle in the doorway, but no one was there.
Eli stirred the soup. 'So did you kill your mother, Myles?'
Myles flinched as much as his 'accident' allowed him to. '*What*?!' That question again. Sick and thick, starting to drip.
'It's okay if you did,' Eli continued, melding the spoon through the soup, letting steam escape. 'I just think you should tell someone.' Exactly what Erica had said. That day on the rock. 'It can't be easy to carry a secret like that around.'
'No!' Myles barked. 'No, no, no. I didn't.'
'So what did she die of?'

'I've *been* through this. She died of an illness, it came sudden and quick. One day she was fine and ten weeks later she was gone. That's the truth, that's the truth. *That's* the truth. I didn't kill her, didn't lay a finger on her, wouldn't have touched her.'

Eli nodded. He lifted the spoon again. 'I understand. Now eat.' Myles swallowed the blistering mass on the spoon. Just as the soup hit the middle of his throat, Eli spoke again. 'So you didn't save her?'

He choked. Closed his eyes. Thought about all the ways to phrase the words, '*There was nothing I could have done. It was terminal, beyond my control.*' But instead something else came out. The words;

'What about *your* mother, Eli?'

Eli dropped the spoon. Healthy lava splashed onto Myle's toe; he yelped. 'My – my mother?' Eli replied.

'Well everybody's got one. Where is she now? Bet she's proud of what you've achieved.'

It was Myles turn to lean forward, Eli's turn to lean back in his chair, to let his eyes go hollow and open. 'She's not here anymore.'

'You mean … she's dead?'

Eli gritted his teeth. '*Yes*.'

Myles whistled, teeth chattering. 'Damn. Man that sucks. So how did it happen?'

As expected, Eli's lips remained sealed.

'Was it your fault, Eli? Did you hurt her? Or was she the one person you couldn't save?' Myles came closer, gurning out of his chair, his vegetable breath catching Eli in its clench. 'Tell me. Right now, we're just two boys who lost their mothers too soon. You can speak freely. Tell me anything about her. Anything you've ever thought about her.'

Eli's mouth rippled. There were words in there that had never been said. All it would take was a little trust to coax them out.

'Were you a painful birth? Oh. Maybe that's it. Maybe you never met her. Maybe you lost her then. You took her away just by being born.'

A snap went through Eli. He leaned forward. 'No, that's not it. I was a great birth.'

'*Oh*, were you now? Well I bet I was better. I was out in five hours.'

Eli drummed his hands on the table. 'Three.'

'Oh! Ok, you got me beat there. God, she must have loved that.'

Eli smiled. 'Slipped out like an eel.'

'Barely a stitch.' They grinned. Cheers.

'So which floorboards is she buried under?' Myles jibed.

This time, Eli laughed. 'I'll tell you if you tell me how you did it.'

'You first.' Myles replied, enjoying the dance between them, the line they walked between truth and jest, confession and accusation. 'How did her neck feel in your hands?'

Eli wouldn't let him win. 'Did she fit in the car boot?'
'I bet she was too scared to even scream,' Myles hissed. His heart beat and palms sweat. What were they doing, what were they saying, what was even real? He tried to drag himself back to earth, out of something he was in danger of calling a fantasy. 'There's only one mother killer here, and it's not me.'
The soup steamed between them.
'Was she hot, then?' Myles dared to smirk. 'Milf or not?'
The spoon stopped mid-way to his mouth. A splash of fibrous heat landed on his lap. Fuck off, he told the flinch trying to come out of his thigh. He won, stayed still.
Eli let the spoon wobble, taunting red liquid at the sides, before answering. 'She was gorgeous.' He smiled. 'You should've seen her.'
'Really?' Myles cooed back. 'A blonde, like you?'
He shook his head. 'A red head.'
'Ooh. *Love* redheads.' Myles sighed, and the spoon was jammed into his mouth.
As he swallowed, Eli asked him. 'Yours?'
'Oh,' Myles closed his eyes and tingled with a grin. 'Knockout. Pocket rocket. You'd kill to see her.'
Eli smiled. 'Who do you think made a better son?'
'Maybe you. You are a very good boy. But there's no way you loved her more than I loved mine – not a chance.'
'Oh really? Do you wanna know what I did for mine?'
'If you loved her you'd be able to look me in the eye when you talked about her.'
Eli looked him right in the eye, seering through him. 'You know what? I think I believe you: you didn't kill your mother. So I want you to imagine something. Imagine the day before she became ill, terminal, before you knew you were gonna lose her. Close your eyes and picture it.'
Myles closed them.
'It's cold. It's … morning. Grey and crusty like ice cream left out. Up you get, contact lenses in, body working perfectly like it used to. You check your phone, rub your eyes, brace yourself for when the duvet leaves you. You get out of bed. Feet. Carpet. Bathroom, you think – bathroom now. Walk down the corridor, oh you can't wait for a pee. Push it open. Creak. Swing. But it's not just the door that's swinging. She is too. She's swinging from the ceiling, from the rope. Why. Her feet. The soles of her feet. Surely it can't be her because it's too pale to be her. Back to bed. Start the morning again. Wake up and it's a new day where that hasn't happened yet. Back to the bathroom. Quicker this time. Open the door. Oh no. There she swings. It was real. She left you. Are you picturing it, Myles?'
Myles felt his eyes turn to yolk, running down his cheeks. He nodded, ashamed at taking for granted that he'd never had to have woken up to morning like that.

'You do? And now you understand, why I run a place like this. Why I created a place like this, for mothers who do that to their sons.'
Eli was calm again. Himself again.
'So do you see what I'm doing here now? Everyone thinks I'm trying to end death, that that's the great experiment of my life, but they're wrong. I'm not trying to end death. I'm trying to end *grief.*'
Eli's lips tightened, puckered out then in again. He was warmed by his words.
'Grief, boy. I used to play this game when I was younger – on holiday with my parents, they'd fall asleep on the sun loungers all afternoon. I remember I wanted to play and swim, but I couldn't take my eyes off my mum's breasts. I had to watch them do that gentle pulsate, go up and down, with breath. Sometimes I thought it wasn't happening, and everything inside me began to clench. Then I'd see it again – that beautiful ooze, proof she was still moving. Every time it didn't stop, I promised myself I'd pay the world back for making me so lucky. I trained myself at that age to be the most grateful boy in the world.'
He looked at Myles.
'You used to play that game too, didn't you?'
Myles didn't respond.
'And you see every time you go against this place, you're going *towards* the feeling you've had since you lost your mother. And passing that feeling onto others. This place is full of people like my mother; people who wanted to swing and swallow and not give a damn about the people they'd leave behind. I don't hate them, but I hate what they did. What they almost did before I stopped them. Now it's my job to sharpen them up and clean them out and maybe one day I'll give them back.' He stirred the soup, as slowly as grief stirs into the soul. When the steam subsided, he continued.
'Don't tell anyone this, but when I was seventeen we were in a car accident driving to Italy for a holiday. I woke up to us spinning in a foreign road – I thought we were going off a cliff, though we were actually just skidding on the motorway. We got *so* lucky, we were both fine, the dog too. But I had this thought then that I'd never told anyone. I thought I kind of wished we had both gone then. Together, so I didn't have to lose her.'
Myles swallowed, tasting the soup twice. 'Me too.' He whispered. 'The same thing happened to me. Mine was on a boat, in the south of France.'
Eli shook his head. He played with the spoon, which had sunk too deep into the bowl. 'Grief is underrated, people don't talk about what it can do. It's agile. Opulent.
There should be a rule; give birth and you live forever. Father a child and you never die. *That* should be the elixir. Use your fertility and nothing can kill you. Because nobody should be able to bring someone into the world then leave them. Shout it with me Myles; 'leave me in the womb where I belong! Back off and keep me rotting in these tubes.'

Myles couldn't help it, he joined in. 'If only I wasn't such a fast swimmer.'
The words caught in Eli's eyes, and caused Eli to smile. 'Not an elixir, but the antidote to grief. You understand now, don't you, what we're doing here. You understand, why I need Erica, what I'm doing to her, what I'm making her a part of? You'd do the same.'
He cleared away the soup, knowing he didn't need to say anything else. 'You've had enough food for tonight. I'll see you in the morning. Sleep well but – '
Myles finished his words, 'Not too well; I want you to wake up. I used to say that to my mother.'
Eli chuckled. 'Me too.'
And Eli left, knowing he was leaving a different person to the one before he'd served him the soup.

It was at this point Myles realised he hadn't slept for forty eight hours. At that magic thought, he didn't mind being baked. He became a delicious rhubarb crumble, the blanket baking golden and buttery around him.
His eyelids had a dirty, sweaty, post-coital sensation as they chose to do nothing but close. In the morning, he could get back into the game. Or was it a game? That was for Myles in the morning to decide.
Right now, he could do what all humans, even the very worst ones, were granted to do; Sleep.

Chapter Thirty Seven

Day Three

'Myles. I can see your eyes flickering. Get dressed.'
Eight words that were too bright and hot, forcing lenses made of white iron into his eyes. No, no, no. He had just been about to meet a dream, one he had been waiting for for hours. Now all the soft scents of sleep were turning putrid in his brain. He didn't even care to identify the voice that was trying to wake him up.
'Fuckkk off,' he said.
Words turned to hands. They were strong.
'No,' Myles hissed. 'Haven't. Slept. In. Three. Days. Almost. Just give. Me an. Hour. Or. Ten ha. Ha.'
'Myles.' The voice imitated his staccato speech. 'I've. Chosen you. For. Something very. Important. And this. Is. No way. To thank. An Old. Friend.'
As the voice slid coldly into his brain, coming between him and peace, it became the only voice apart from Erica's that would have coaxed him to open his eye, splitting it with fearless light. The lights in his room hadn't even been switched on – all that alabaster goodness was coming from a man's beaming smile.
'Eli,' he rumbled. 'How'd you get those teeth so white?'
Eli slapped him on the back, playfully. 'Get up and I'll tell you my secret,' he said, rising and tossing the clothes that had been laid out for him over his head. 'And you can tell me how you got *Ann* to like you.' He chuckled. 'I've known her for years and she doesn't even quite like me. Isn't that right, Ann?'
An invisible needle propped open Myles' other eye, to soak in the image of Ann standing in the doorway.
'Ann volunteered to dress you before we go,' Eli winked, the blue of his eyes rivalling the white of his teeth for potency. 'I'll leave you two to it.' He was gone.
Myles pulled himself up, remembering to assemble his position. It was only five, but light trickled in, the whole room conspiring against his plans to be a happy black blob. Ann sat on his bed. 'Don't suppose there's any point asking where we're going,' he croaked. 'We're not leaving the retreat, are we?'
'Don't worry, you'll be back in a couple of hours. It's a road trip I guess.' She pulled back the duvet. She took a long hard look at his pyjama buttons before she began to unbutton him. Every finger was colder than the last. 'Want the good news or the better news?'
'First of all, what kind of wake up is this – where's the morning coffee?' The joke bounced off Ann's long nose. 'Wait, good news?'
'Yes, you heard that right. Good news first I guess? Good news is that it won't hurt a bit.' She removed his shirt and stared at where his heart would be. 'Better news is this just might help you get over that girl.'

Her hand hovered over his waistband. Myles remembered he couldn't reach out and do it for her. He closed his eyes and let her dress him.

It had been years since he'd had that 'school trip feeling'. In fact, the last school trip he'd been on had been one of those rock climbing ones, remember those, the ones where they'd tried to insist he '*belay*' his partner, but he hadn't wanted the fate of another in his hands. Eventually he'd quit rock climbing, and let others climb his rock instead. Now as he rolled over the concrete to a large bus, he felt a colloquial mood come over him. He was up for a road trip.
He was greeted warmly when he reached the bus, a ramp already laid down to rise him up. The smell hadn't changed in years – inky, furry seats, cold plastic, trapped air. A bus driver who may as well be faceless. And others.
Michelle. Rhonda. Rebecca. Others.
'Rebecca?' he blurted out.
She was perfectly intact, even her face. Small as ever. Functional, flexible. She balled into herself in her seat. Jill ran her hands along her shoulders. 'She wasn't quite split in half like we all thought,' Jill said proudly. 'So we took her to The Healer, and she put her back together again.'
They were dotted around the seats, looking as confused as him. He slid into the front of the bus and waited for an explanation. Ann sat next to him. She passed around snacks. Another carer emerged and sat by Michelle.
Eli didn't make them wait long. He swung onto the bus and as it began to drive, he began to speak.
'Today I selected the seven of you to go on a road trip.
Now you may be wondering why I chose you. Did I draw names out of a hat? Maybe.
Here's a clue: I did choose seven for a reason.
Michelle. Rhonda. Alfie. August. Myles. Dominic. Rebecca.
Ten melatonin tablets to whoever can guess where we're going.
Ah, I forgot, Alfie and August can't speak. That's ok. We'll communicate through the raising of hands.
Who thinks we're going to a hospital? August, ok, that's your vote.
Who thinks we're going to a funeral? Rhonda, Michelle, that's a vote for you.
Any other ideas? Suggestions?' Nobody responded, stale in the stale air of the bus.
'We're going to the aftermath of a disaster. When I got the call I just couldn't resist.'

Another twenty minutes of silence followed, taking them over a bridge from the clinic, and into the countryside. Hills, country lanes, horses. And then the smoke.
They waited, silently, til the bus pulled into a village. A village that had been set on fire. Burnt out buildings, trees turned to ash, and a sad truth:

Nobody had survived.

They had no choice but to get off the bus, form a line, and listen to Eli. He had a glassy look in his eye as he gestured to the crusty corpses.
'Count them. How many dead, do you think? Forty? Fifty? But only two of them are responsible for the fire.
An accident, of course, like all these things are, but yet another selfish accident caused by suicide. I'll give you a clue; the two responsible for this were brother and sister. They were drawn together by their burning, burning love. But the town shunned them, the town mocked them, the town denied them. So *they* thought – oh how clever – "we'll kill ourselves and then we'll be together! We'll shame this town for what they made us do."' Eli stopped at two of the corpses, considering whether or not to spit.
'I want to wake these twisted siblings up. I want them to face what they've done.' He swept his hands out.
'And all these other lovely people, they deserve to live too. Today, you, my chosen, my lucky seven, are going to resurrect them.'

Eli spoke with such confidence it all felt real.
He continued. Brewing with excitement.
'Michelle, you will do it by Lust. Don't you laugh. I know it's possible.
Alfie, you will make them so Angry that they will not be able to sleep any more.
Rebecca, of course you will do it with greed.
Myles… you will do it with Pride. To this woman here.'
Eli gestured to another body, slumped on top of a pile of others. She was slim, with long grey hair, splayed over the pile as though she was trying to hug them all. 'Help me turn her over, will you?'
He looked into Eli's eyes as they flung the women around. He refused to look down. He couldn't bear to see the burns.
'Look down. She's not burned. She suffocated in the smoke is all. Her face is still perfect.'
No burns, no fire, no heat, no charring. Why did he feel so hot?
He looked down. Eli was right. The face was perfectly smooth, simply slicked in ash.
And then his own face went on fire.
No.
No.
Wait.
Two eyes, a freckle here, eyebrows plucked like that …
Was that … was that … oh god, oh god!
His mother?
He fell closer, his body convulsing. Mother? MUM?

He looked away and all around and up and down then back again, two faces flashing in his brain, melding together.
Finally he looked down.
No. No. It wasn't her. The nose was different.
Just some ordinary women who looked like her.
Eli rubbed his back gently.
'Make her so proud of you that she wants to live to see you succeed ... make her so proud that you bring her back to life.'
There was no way around it, above it or below it.
If he wanted to feel whole again, he was going to have to bring this woman back to life. And it couldn't be done with a stroke of a finger, it couldn't be done with a brush of her hair, he couldn't wish it into existence. He had to make it happen, without medical background, without knowledge, with nothing but some part of him that believed he could do this. A small, mousy voice that wasn't even allowed in his ear – but had always been there. He, too, could save someone.
Go on. Just once. Think about her.
A thought so sharp it should have been banned, his mushy mind had no defence as it slid into it. He slid to the ground next to her.
Think about her. Picture her face. One last time before you let yourself forget.
His skull tried to protect it, but his brain was defenceless to the requests that kept coming. Some in shards, some as pins, one was a snake's fang, each one had their own way of entering him.
Bravely or stupidly, he decided to remember.
Her lips had been an oval shape, always slightly parted. Like this woman, but with more of an even arch.
Why was the first place he looked, her lips?
Their chins were remarkably similar. Both gentle yet defined, and with freckles. They had the same nose, its serene tip made for someone who should die peacefully.
This dead woman was coated in his mother's skin. Same shade, same lines. It lay over her like a respectful blanket.
'Mum,' the syllable escaped. The rest of the seven looked at him in horror. He tried to stuff the syllable back in but it felt so good to live in a world where he could say mum.
It wasn't her. It wasn't.
He hovered his hand above the face of a woman who wasn't his mother; a woman he'd never met, who had died in a fire, a woman whose smile didn't have half the character of his mother but whose eyes shut in exactly the same way, and when he finally let the hand settle on the flesh, he knew he wanted to bring her back to life.
'Mum,' he said again. It still wasn't her. He had buried his mother. But this woman, this thing below him, had just enough pores for him to speak to as though it was.

Blister to blister, lonely to love.
'I … I don't know what it's like, being dead. I tried so hard to join you but nothing would work. Sometimes I felt like you were happy, other times I felt like you were calling for help. I used to pray there wasn't an afterlife, so there was no risk that you wouldn't be lonely or lost in it. Sometimes when I'm asleep I flinch awake, just before I feel I'm about to see you.' Did she recognise his voice? Could a mum detect her son's voice through the subliminal, much like a dog can smell a sugar cube in a fifty metre swimming pool? Would she do one more thing for him, on top of everything she had already done, and open her eyes?
He wanted to see if this woman's eyes were the same brown as his mothers. A brown that had made him into a chocoholic. He felt if he physically prised her eyelids apart he'd be upsetting some strange balance, somewhere in the universe. He could only do it with his words, and he would not stop until he knew – are these woman's eyes as brown as my mother's?
'I imagine that if there's an afterlife, you couldn't be anywhere else but heaven. There's nowhere else for you to go. I remember a description of heaven once that really resonated with me. That heaven's not a physical place, with trees or rivers or … activity. It's just a feeling. A feeling like floating through honey. A … serenity. Where you know that there's nothing to worry about. That you are perfect. That you can rest. You can stay in this scalp massage-y, sensory, molten, satiated feeling because you know that everyone you left behind is ok.' He hated what he had to say next. 'If I've stopped you from being in that place, I am so, so sorry. I know things haven't been simple for me, since you've gone. I hope you haven't had to watch, I hope you've been able to rest – if heaven's like that.
To be honest though, that version of heaven sounds too boring to me. I like the version of heaven we came up with for that English project of mine, remember? That everybody's heaven is what they want it to be. If you always wanted to be tall, you'll be tall in your heaven; if you wanted to be male, you'll be male in heaven; heaven can look like your favourite painting, heaven can be full of a hybrid of your favourite animals; you can star in your own concert every night in heaven. *That* sounds good to me.' He leaned closer, into her ear. 'Listen, if you're in that place, don't come back. Don't worry about me. But if there's any chance you can show me, just for a second, where you are, how you are, then please – work with me – open this woman's eyes. Come back to life, just for a moment, wake her up, if you can. I just want to see you for one second. I just want to know you can hear me. And if you're not in a good place, then … make her flinch. Make her jerk. Or something. Anything. Let me know, and I'll come and get you out of there. I'd swim down to hell to get you. Just show me.'
'Good, Myles, good,' Eli interrupted. 'But enough sentimentality. With *pride*, I said, remember? Make her feel so much pride it's worth coming back to life for.'

Myles didn't look up; nothing could get his eyes off her face, but he nodded.
'Ok,' he hovered his hand over her cheek. 'Let me tell you what I've been up to, since I left. It starts off strange, but bear with me.'
Over in the corner, Eli turned his attention to Michelle. '*Michellle*,' he sung, clamping his hand around the back of her neck; she couldn't help the shiver that rippled through her spine. 'Come with me.' He led her to the body of a man, his shirt ripped open. 'He may be dead but he's handsome, isn't he? Looks a bit like your ex, the one who left you after the accident.'
'Shut up,' Michelle managed to whisper.
'There was a time when men would die to be near you, wasn't there? And then you fell, and you became this.' He tapped the metal in her leg and it echoed through the field. 'Imagine if you could prove to that girl that you've come back better. That now, a man would come back to life to make you his.' He pushed her closer to the corpse. 'I bet not one woman on this field ever moved for him the way you can. Move for him, Michelle. Move for me. Move for *you*.'
Michelle moved closer to the man. Had he had fun, in his time on earth? Enough fun?
Welcome to the Moulin Rouge.
Her fingers twitched. One hand bionic, the other erotic.
The man on the ground had not even reached thirty yet. Just how many experiences had he missed?
She walked another five steps until she was directly above him.
Pop, squish, sizzle, lipstick.
She swung her hair, in one full 360 through the air. Sharpness streaked down her neck, but it was shocked into obeying; it had missed doing that. The ends of the hair caught his face.
Life is a cabaret old chum.
Her prosthetic hip had set strict rules – the leg was to go no higher than 45 degrees. So it thought.
Technology and physics fought will and lust. Her new leg jerked and her new thigh demanded she stop. But like a strange spider, she found some way, some crooked and kinked way, of getting her leg up to her ear. She held it for two seconds before she fell, but this time she fell in a perfect scissor splits across his stomach. She looked down at the grey face and she gave it a wink.
It had been over a year since she had moved and worked her waist the way she moved it now.
'Michelle, what are you doing? Don't entertain this.' It was Rhonda's voice, but it came from far away.
Michelle winked at her too. 'You don't know it yet, but you're just jealous.'
In the middle of a cold, charred, ashy field, she burned him all over again. She moved her body round like a snake, inventing new ways to coil and uncoil. Grinding, working, whirling, twirling, anything, anything to bring him back.
Make 'em look and let 'em watch.

One person who was watching, was Rebecca. No fire could have warmed Rebecca up. She wore jeans and a puffy blue jacket, hugging herself closer to herself. Her eyes darted between Michelle dancing and Myles whispering, before she had had enough, and approached Eli.

'What was it you said I had to bring them back with again?' She asked him, shivering.

Eli rubbed her shoulders quickly, trying to warm up her up. 'Your lips are blue,' he muttered disapprovingly.

'They always are,' Rebecca replied proudly. 'What was it that you wanted me to do?'

Eli swung his rucksack off his shoulders. He passed it to her with a nod. 'You heard me. Look in the rucksack.'

She prised the zips apart and looked inside.

'Gluttony,' Eli said. 'I've set you the most difficult task; the others get to do things they like. It's because I believe in you.'

Inside the bag was a glossy nightmare; a pit of shiny snakes that made a symphony when they slid past each other. Candy. So much candy.

And then it happened.

Her mouth started to water.

'Come,' Eli smiled. He placed the rucksack on her fragile back but helped hold it up as they made their way to another body. They chose a girl around her age. A large girl. He helped her sit, and watched as her trembling fingers reached in, and picked a yellow bar. She unwrapped it deftly, gently. She waved it under the girl's broad nose, hoping the smell could summon memories, revive her. She broke off a piece and placed it on the corpse's lip. It wouldn't take more than a minute for it to melt. Then she broke off another square, and she bit it herself.

'Come back to us,' she whispered.

Eli looked around the field. To his triumph, Alfie was obeying him, walking in circles from body to body, timidly kicking in an attempt to make them angry.. And August – awkwardly thrusting his handsome face at people, trying to bring them back through envy. He kept laughing at himself, then starting again. And Dominic, who clearly didn't believe in this, but was enjoying stealing money from their pockets, hoping to somehow bring them back through greed.

The only one who remained by the bus, arms folded, eyes cold, was Rhonda.

'What the Hell are you doing?' she spat as he approached. 'Where is the ambulance? You need to call one.'

'Trust you to be the lazy one,' he said. He gripped her hand. 'That's why I picked *sloth* for you!'

'Sloth,' Rhonda rolled her eyes. 'I'll just stay here then. What do you even mean?'

'Well, you put someone to sleep once, didn't you? Your son if I'm not mistaken. So I thought you'd be good at this.' He grabbed her hand again and led her to the first body he saw. He pushed her to the ground. 'Maybe if you sleep, one of them will wake up.' He marched away.

Rhonda lay in the cold mud. She would not let him make her feel guilt. Realising she was next to Myles, she listened.

'So I *did* manage to make up for the snail,' he smiled, finishing explaining about the man he'd saved in the sea. 'And, now I'm here. Don't tell anyone but,' he chuckled and lowered his voice so she had to strain to hear. 'There's not really anything wrong with me. It's all an act. I'm putting myself through this so I can rescue her. And I'm gonna do it. I'm gonna stop them. I'm gonna save her.'

He stroked her hair softly. 'Anyway I imagine you're bored of hearing about me. How are you? Mum? I just want to hear your voice. That croaky funny voice you used to do. So tell me. Come on. I bet you had a secret you never told me, one you took to the grave. Tell me now and you can see how well I deal with it. I'll make you proud by showing you how ... how ... you know, how subtle I can be, how sensitive I can be, whatever it is.' He bent to her ear. 'Whisper it to me now and I won't even react.' He looked back down at the flat, marble face beneath him. 'I want to prove to you I can keep it. Don't you want to know how it feels to unburden yourself? Come on, mum, wake up; *tell me a secret.'*

He swallowed. 'I'll tell you one. I was an idiot all my life. How couldn't I see I was seconds away from being doomed the moment I lost you? Yeah, doomed, I know it's a strong world, but that's what this is.

This otherness, this world where I can't make you proud, where I can't celebrate with you, where nothing really counts. I wish I'd composed a fucking musical to make you proud – don't know what I was doing, putting it off, like I had all the time in the world. Now I'm here and you're ... you're ... you're on the wrong side of the moon.' He stroked the skin. It was getting colder. Yet somehow, he could say things to it he'd never said. 'Come back, mum. Give me another chance. What would have made you prouder? My career? Cooking the Christmas dinner? Children? My character? We can try it all. Because this can't be it.

And I've been just another mindless sheep for accepting that we're born into a world where we *have* to lose the one who brought us into it. Of course that can't be right. Of course that can't be it.

One day they'll look back on this period of history and they'll laugh at us. This is the last part of evolution and I'm gonna get it going; I'm going to remove 'goodbye' from people's vocabulary.

Maybe they've already worked it out somewhere; maybe up in the world's elite, presidents and tech billionaires already know how not to lose the one we love. Lose. Ha! That's the word. Lose you and I became a loser. Well no. Not anymore. I refuse to lose. Let's go on a cruise. Round the Caribbean, your favourite. Mum? Mum? MUM! What's it gonna take?' He realised he was getting a little frantic, so he calmed himself, just like she would have told him to. 'You never used to be shy like this. In fact if I remember correctly you were quite the extrovert. But even if you're shy now, even if you're embarrassed now and you think you're ugly now cos half your face has rotted away in your coffin, I want you to remember this: *remember how much we loved each other. I'll love you no matter what.* Isn't that enough to come back?'

'Myles.'

Eli's voice came across the field. Myles stopped talking, already lighter after being able to actually say the things he would only have said to her. 'What?'

'She's moving.'

He winced, jolted, flinched, shook.

Looked down.

Her toe was wiggling.

Looked back up.

And sure enough, the woman who was not his mother, was breathing.

Her eyes had opened serenely. No flinching, no jolting, no Hell. *Thank you.*

Everybody had stopped what they were doing. The last specs of fire frozen out with shock.

If this was a dream, now would have been the time they woke up.

Michelle spoke first.

'I think … I think you just bought her back.'

As the bus drove back, the seven were silent.

The sun was coming out, and Myles was staring into it. Directly into it. Nothing could blind him now.

Four hours ago, he had sat on this bus, a different man. A man who didn't believe in magic and a man who didn't believe in himself.

Now he was being driven back along the same route, with irises that refused to burn, and he couldn't quite explain what he was feeling within him.

Three lives he had saved, and it had done nothing for him. If only he'd known sooner; what he needed to do was bring someone back.

And every second was a new gift. Because at the front of the bus sat the woman with long grey hair. Just like that – back in the world. Because of him.

He leaned back into his new skin.

This was how Erica felt?

How could she need him, when she felt like this?

He could learn more. He could do more. He could *be*, more.

How long had he been able to do it for? Was it just that one time? Would it only work on Her? Was it even real at all?

He shifted position but did not take his eyes off the sun. He dared it to hurt him – it was too weak for him. Half of it had soared inside his chest.

It danced for him, the idea in his brain, about the man he could be, but more importantly, the man he no longer had to be. Was it really over? A life without magic?

At the front of the bus, Ann flicked on the radio. It began to croak out, Van Morrison's hit, the lyrics smiling at him, '*Days Like This.*'

He closed his eyes and let it hit him. '*When everything falls into place, like the flick of a switch – oh, my mama told me; there'd be days like this.*'

Myles was trying to enjoy his lunch. He was next to Rhonda again, who was helping him scrape the peas onto his spoon. Opposite him sat the seat Darren had been in yesterday, which today was lonely.

For some reason he couldn't focus on anything else. The peas tumbled from his spoon to his lap, rolling gleefully from his chair. Rhonda looked at him in confusion, slamming the spoon down.

'Just tell me if you're not hungry,' she grumbled.

'It's not that,' Myles said. 'I'm starving, actually. I just can't stop thinking about something.'

'What?' she asked.

'Hang on,' he said. 'Let me try and remember. Ooh and erm … could you tuck my hair out of my eyes? It's bothering me.' Rhonda rolled her eyes but did as she said. She moved back to her plate; for once she liked the food, an asparagus and pea risotto without the gluten or oil, but just as good. 'Sorry,' Myles piped up. 'Could ya roll down my sock too? It's itchy.'

As she was under the table rolling it down, it came to him. A word he was sure he'd heard yesterday. Thames. 'That's it!' he exclaimed as much as he'd allow one side of his mouth to.

'What?!' Rhonda popped her head up.

'Yesterday when Darren left, you called him Darren Thames, didn't you?'

'Yep. That's his name.'

'And he mentioned his daughter, didn't he?'

'I think so. He definitely has a daughter.'

Myles breathed in passionately. 'Will you wheel me to see him?'

Rhonda groaned. 'Myles! Can't a woman eat around here?'

'Sorry,' Myles chattered excitedly. 'But please. Just quickly. For him!'

Two minutes later they were standing outside Darren's door, Myles managing to knock with his elbow.

Darren opened up. His eyes were red.

'Hey?'

Rhonda wheeled Myles in. 'Myles has something he wants to say to you.'

'Okay … I've never seen you like this, Myles.'

With great effort, Myles spun his chair round so he was facing Darren. 'Mate. Your daughter. She's about fifteen, right?'

The light left Darren's eyes and he sunk slowly onto the bed. 'Yes. Sixteen in a week. How do you know?'

'And she's a brunette, yes? Red brown, glossy hair, down to about Rhonda's length?'

Darren swiped a glance at Rhonda. His voice came out weak. 'Yes.'

'Is she called Mila?'

Darren leapt up. In a second he was gripping the arms of Myle's chair, his eyes singing into his like denim glued to flesh. 'Is that why you're here? Did you do something to Mila?!'

'No! No man,' Myles calmed again. 'But I met her.'

Darren released his grip on his chair, running a hand through his hair. He always tried not to think of his family, and now this man was here talking to him about his daughter. His stomach did a figure of eight and grew a moustache. *Fuck*, he missed her.

'Just in a café,' Myles continued. 'I was googling this place. She was next to me and she leaned over to tell me what she thought of it. She was *very* passionate.' He remembered the day, the smell of green tea, the eager girl with loss in her voice. 'And then she talked a little about Sunset. How she thought it was amazing that the family had *agreed* to bring her dad there.' Myles tried not to choke up. 'And how much she missed you, but she was happy you had what you wanted. She told me her name, because she was proud of it, being a Thames. She was *genuine*, man. I know what loss looks like and she's wearing it. She - she thinks you're dead.

She meant every word. There's no way they intended you to be here. No way they wouldn't want you back.'

He almost stood up then. The will of his words almost rose him from his chair. 'And you can give them their dad back. You can be with them again.' He shook his head with awe. 'Fuck man. If any of us could be with our family again … we'd … fuck … what are you doing here? Seriously. How are you here?' His foot let out a stomp. Oops. 'I promise you. She didn't know. Even if the others did, she didn't. But I'm feeling pretty optimistic today and something tells me none of them did. They're out there, Darren. More love than could fit in the whole of the Thames. They're right there. *Go.*'

He almost screamed it.

'GO. Go to the tunnel. Get out. Go.'

The words entered Darren through his stomach, like everything did these days. Darren Thames, the all or nothing man. What oh what was he doing?!

Red rusty nails and meat off the bone. Steak and ginger, ale and smoke. Black butter in his eyes. Tick, tock, Darren. It's all possible. Darren. There's a tomorrow after all, big boy.

He'd waited so long for a sign, but he'd never believed it would come. He had turned off his hope, turned off his love, let it all collect within his centre. Now it spilled back into him and his intestines twined.

Love is so fucking *fibrous*. Impossible to digest.
Mila. Time to stop pretending she didn't exist.
Life with claws. Life with jaws. Life outside these walls.
Darren finally remembered: he was a lion. And he needed to get back to his Pride.
He ran to the doorway, checking outside. It was afternoon, still light outside; a terrible time to leave the retreat, they would be expecting him at dinner. But … he could not wait. He *would* not wait.
'Guys, will you distract everyone?'
Myles grinned. 'Any time. Come on Rhonda … go give me a lap dance in the great hall or something.'
'As you wish.'
Darren threw his arm round Rhonda, pulling her in for a hug. Rhonda quickly helped him create a fake lump in his bed, and a barricade for the door. He fist bumped Myles, locking eyes with him, then the three exited his room.
Myles and Rhonda went one way, to create the chaos. 'Send us a postcard.'
Darren ran the other way. The abandoned office was on the same floor, only a five minute jog. He could make it. He could be melting into his family by midnight.
Go boy go.

Luckily, it was Ann on duty, who didn't punish Rhonda for her half-hearted lap dance to Myles.
Great as she looked, nothing could compare to the look he'd seen on Darren's face, when he realised what was waiting for him out there. Wow. That really had been something. Myles had no doubt he would make it.
That look though. If …
If Eli hadn't done what he'd done to him, Darren never would have had that look. He'd never have learnt what he learnt. He'd be six feet under. Mila never would have been reunited with her father.
Myles shifted uncomfortably.
You couldn't deny that moment made an argument for prolonging a life.

Don't leave me now, Myles.
You're a gambler. A risk taker. Don't give up on me now.
Guess what colour underwear I'm wearing and I'll never leave you.
I know I'm hard to find, hard to catch, hard to hold down. I know the thorns hurt when they scratch you and the more you cut them down the more they seem to grow. I know the dragon is scary and you can feel the heat of his fire from here. I know you've been shown another way, and I know that way is hard to resist. I know what you're being asked to do is difficult, so, so fucking difficult. I haven't made it easy. I get it. And I can feel it; you must be getting tired now, winding down, as more and more sand fills your blisters.

So all I can do is ask. Please. One last time
Don't give up on me.
I promise to be light in your arms.

Her door burst open.
Erica turned, almost falling from the window she sat on.
But it was just Jill again, carrying a tray laid with things Eli wanted her to eat.
'Thinking about him again?' Jill asked.
Erica didn't reply, just got up and lay on the silk pink of her bed. Jill edged closer, putting the tray down with a soft thump. When Erica didn't stir she sat on the bed next to her and lightly traced her hands up her calf.
'You do realise he sold you to us, don't you?'

One of the carers who had burnt him yesterday wheeled him to his room. 'So you enjoyed today?'
Myles leaned back. 'I can see what you meant now. When you told me he had something planned.'
'Oh,' she chuckled. 'Actually, we were talking about something different. For tonight. In fact, it's me that's going to get you ready for it. We've a suit waiting in your room.'
'For *what*?'
'Core Retreat is going to throw a ball.'

Once upon a time, there was a King. He was known as the kindest king throughout the land. Unlike other Kings who focused their attention on acquiring riches and throwing lavish parties, this King devoted himself only to deeds that were pure. He helped the poor, he protected the weak, and he always made sure no soul ever went hungry. He even had a Queen who – the whispers were – possessed the kiss of life.
As the years went by, he noticed his kingdom becoming more and more unruly. People made foolish mistakes. They stayed out on the streets, causing riots, behaving hedonistically, drinking into the early hours of the morning. There was adultery, promiscuity; hedonism seemed to prevail above all else. People forgot to eat.
One day, the King decided his kingdom needed to be turned to stone. All his advisors told him not to, trying to get him to see sense – that it would be wrong, it wasn't fair, that they didn't deserve it. His loyalist subjects and even his Queen asked him to find another way. But the King believed he had tried everything, and this was the only way to get them to learn. And so he stepped out onto his balcony and he swept a curse across his kingdom.
One by one, they were turned into immobile stone statues. Some were gargoyles, hunched and low and cretinous. Some were cherubs, adorable in their curls. Some were angels, hovered high, wings too big for their backs. Some had

been caught mid-way through a tantrum, their mouth now set in a permanent scream. Some grew moss the moment they were turned. Some didn't even get to form a shape – the ones he really thought worthless and ungrateful became the jagged edge of an eroding cliff.
The only person he did not touch, did not interfere with, was his Queen. She was the one person he felt he could not improve.
She couldn't look him in the eye after what he'd done, but he swore to her, that once they had learnt their lesson, that once he was sure their price had been paid, he would reverse his curse, let them be free and he would throw them a ball, the greatest and most decadent ball the land had ever seen, a ball that would live on in fairytales, and at this ball, the king would not just let them move.
He would watch them dance.

They thought they were waiting to die, when all along, they had simply been waiting to dance.
Beneath the floors of the clinic, where everybody thought there was a dungeon, Eli had built them a ballroom. The golden doors swung open for them. He'd even invited DJ Ghanja Ghecko. Even unstitched his hands from his decks.
It was the ballroom from the fairytales they'd stopped believing in – arched, panelled walls, an engraved tapestry on the ceiling, a circular marble dance floor shot through with golden veins. At the front of the room, a stage, glittering with the welcoming smiles of a string quartet. In the middle, a fountain. Even the air in the ballroom was different.
All of Core's guests made their way into the room, forming a smooth semi-circle at the foot of the ballroom. Myles saw around two dozen faces he had not seen before, and he realised with a jolt these were the people Core really connected with - those who truly needed The Healer. There was a serene pride in their eyes; these people knew an adversity that put Myle's to shame. He would learn from them, he decided there and then, learn and then … serve them. If he could.
Carers stood tall in every crevice of the room. They wore their same suits, but tonight, they smiled.
A minute passed. Nobody would take a step beyond the circle, into the molten gold of the floor.
It was up to Eli to step forward. Dapper in his tail suit.
'Well, come on then,' he smiled. 'If you won't move for me, then, at least the very least; you can *dance* for me.'
He held out his hand. 'I'm going to count to ten and if nobodies taken my hand by the time I open my eyes, I'll see no reason not to pluck them out.' He closed his eyes and clicked a gloved finger. The quartet began. Gorgeous strokes of symphony, meaning something and everything all at once.

Every set of hands in this room had a different story to tell, a different reason to tremble. There were curled hands which thought they'd never pour their own drinks again – guilty hands bunched into their palms – lonely hands that had forgotten what touch felt like. And all of them had had enough. Enough of the curse. Hands slid into gloved hands. 'Shall we?'

The only man who didn't ask was Myles. As his eyes oozed from Michelle to Rhonda to Rebecca, they settled on Ann. When he spoke, it was a command. 'Dance with me.'

A pretty pink blush began, escaping through the one inch of her ankles that was on show. It hatched out of her neck, her face cringing as it went as feminine as a ballet slipper.

But her pale rose blush was nothing compared to the sangria that drenched the rest of the carers, as they watched her give him a slow, wistful, wilful smile, slide her hand into his – for once it felt small – and, wheeling his own chair, lead her onto the floor.

Parting the crowd, they joined the bodies on the floor. These were dances the guests could be proud of – rheumatoid rumbas, terminal tangos, gliding past fibroid foxtrots and sickle cell sambas. And just like Eli knew it would be, they had never been danced with more meaning. When one partner wobbled or fell, the other was there to steady them, to position their body in a way that the other could rest on.

There would never be a night more poignant than this. A hundred people who had arrived here believing they had no more dances left in them. He had shown them otherwise. What would have been a forgotten flamenco, a dance they would have been too depressed to do, had turned into the moment to commemorate the start of their new lives. Blue, bruised, beaten, broken, there was something to sway for after all. Some had come here believing they couldn't move; he had shown them to be fools, fools who could swing, swerve and even lift. Or attempt to – one couple attempted a catch, a champagne glass dropping between them as they did. They were too busy charlestoning to notice they were stepping on the shattered glass.

When Myles and Ann reached the floor, they knew what dance they wanted to dance. The Viennese Waltz; a dance made of water, one they could glide in and out of. Even confined to a chair, it made sense.

The carer's skin flashed red and blue with strict sirens, the smiles dripping off their faces as they watched Ann. 'Someone needs to stop her,' they muttered. Her outfit wasn't made for dancing; it was restrictive and cloying and beneath it she was already starting to sweat. But in his arms it was a ball gown, taffeta and satin gliding around her. Her masculine jacket may as well have been a bodice, with the way his hands ran around it. She lifted her heels and he swivelled her round him on her toes. He looked into her eyes then he bent her back. Her tight bun came loose and her mousy hair glided across the floor.

When he pulled her into him again, he moved the hair, tenderly to one side of her face, looking at the nape of her neck with the focus of a vampire. Then he arched forward, and he whispered in her ear.
That was her last smile of the night. Her expression fell a mile, hitting the floor. Careful not to step on it.
Men danced past Eli; men who had once felt the painful patience of the people behind them in queues. Now women queued to dance with them.
'That's it!' Eli was on the stage, his arm around the conductor of the band. 'Dance for me, dance for me! All you have is this moment. All you have is tonight. So dance! Show me your moves! Show me how a dying man dances!'
Eli had always wanted to dance with a ghost; light on their feet, not bound by physics, able to disappear and surprise at any moment. He'd thought tonight would be the closest he would get, as he hosted a ball for those he had suspended between life and death, but he never guessed it would feel like this. That a room could be full of so much love. Was this how it felt to be in love with a hundred people at the same time?
The room filled with joyful, playful sax, as easy and cheeky as a wink. The guests had forgotten about music like this and the hazy feeling it gave them as it turned their night gold – and as they hobbled from one foot to the next, they felt their chests pluck apart, as it fell with the feathers of nostalgia.
They had grown up thinking about nights like this. At what point had they forgotten them? All of a sudden they were vibing again.

The band hit a crescendo, and filled the room with glorious jazz, a wink captured in an instrumental. Like Eli knew it would, it caused them all to throw their heads back and smile. Real smiles with no need for teeth. The tenderness of their timid movements slowly poked through into something else that had been in them all along. Sharp over soft, crystal over water, as the butterfly learns to sting, the room rippled, and It started to happen. Forced to dance, the guests of Core were forced to confront their own beliefs.
Just off the dance floor, Myles was alone, having sent Ann away.
He was itchy. And he was thirsty.
He was next to the long trestle table, the champagne glasses were quivering with the energy of the dancing room. He was at an angle where he could only reach a glass if he used his 'paralysed' claw. Usually, he would ask someone to pass him one, but everybody was either grooving to or being serenaded by the band, and he didn't like to interrupt them.
Screw it. Nobody was watching. He whipped out a numb arm and gripped the champagne.
Crisp, electric liquid flowed through him; it was too good to pretend to spill any of it.
'LOOK!'

Eli's voice came booming across the crowd, the mike in his hand. A hundred heads whipped towards Eli, and then to Myles, as Eli approached him.

'Look what Myles just did.' Eli held onto Jill for support. 'Look what's in his hand. His left hand. It's working again.' His voice quivered, and bright streaks of true excitement lit him up. 'The ball … it's working. Myles, would you care to take another sip?'

Faced by an expectant room, unable to think of a response, Myles rose it to his lips and took a gluttonous gulp, punctuated by the gasps of the watching crowd.

'See! See! I knew this would work.' Eli's voice wavered. 'Look at his mouth. It's straight. Myles, would you … would you try and stand for us? Jill, go by his side, for support, if he needs it.'

Jill swept over to him. The faces watching Myles grew in expectation. In unison, hope filled their throats.

So Myles made a choice. Gingerly, he chose to stand.

He felt callous doing it, playing into the dream, but he wasn't doing it to mock them, or for any kind of game. He felt even cruder as when he finally stood straight, everybody burst into applause. He was using his wellness against them, dangling his 'recovery' as bait. It turned his own stomach, but god it felt good to straighten his neck.

He felt crass and embarrassed as Jill shook his hand. 'You did it, son.' They were gawping in awe at his two functioning legs, proud as punch of the way he balanced on both feet. The band had stopped playing, and Eli was wiping a tear from his eye.

'*Muscle memory*,' he was whispering hoarsely. 'I told you.' He spoke to the carers, who nodded in earnest. 'Give them something to work for, and they'll find it in themselves to …'

'Eli.' Myles interrupted.

'Yes, son?'

There Myles stood, finally eye level with Eli, the man keeping the love of his life hostage. In truth now he stood, he was a couple of inches taller than him. He looked for a flicker of jealousy in Eli, his eyes swiping past a defiant Rhonda, the only one who hadn't tried to dance. She raised an eyebrow, asking him what he was asking himself; could he really bring himself to trick the sick?

'Listen, Eli, I – '

Then everything changed. Because across the room, a woman wiped her own saliva off her own chin.

'Idiitoo!' Heads swivelled from Myles to the woman in question. Her name was Hannah, and it was unusual for her to speak – in fact, up until that very second, she had only been able to communicate by blinking.

'I – diddd – it – too.' She sharpened the sentence out of her, and moved her hand again. 'I did it.'

A carer moved to mop her brow, and she pushed them away. 'It's … w-working.'

‘Me – me too.’
This time, Myles did drop the champagne. But nobody noticed, because they were all watching what was happening within the room.
It was as Eli said ‘Muscle memory,’ in unison, encouraged by others in the same situation as you. Moving without judgement or expectation but because it felt right. Moving with music after being deprived of it. And finally the sprinkling of belief; in seeing Myles get better, they believed they could too. It spoke to some physiological part of them that finally found the key to whatever part of them was locked.
It wasn’t a miracle. The room wasn’t suddenly full of pirouettes and backflips. But bit by bit, the energy came.. A toe wiggling there, a back straightening up here, a pair of hips back under their owner’s control; the seeping of symmetry. Those who’d believed themselves to be towed to the ground, who’d started to dance with only their fingers, now had a question asked that their cells could not ignore. Just what step was coming next? How high could they get their leg? Could they do a full spin? Could they lift their partner this high? Could they move their feet in sync to the fastest of beats?
And all across the room, without magic or miracle, the answer was yes, yes, yes. Their cells answered yes, and their muscles did too. In some way, that would take work, that would take time, but they could master it, as they had mastered so much all their lives. For their resilience, for their spirit, for the music they made in their minds - at last, the music served them back. And what a wonder it was to be themselves again, to project their power again, to stop being told they were sick and instead be told they were slick. And they were. Now the ball was really beginning.
‘It worked.’ Eli’s hand was at his mouth, his chest heaving at the sight. ‘It fucking worked.’ He clapped his hand over his lips; he wasn’t meant to swear. ‘Band! Play! Play *Dancing In The Moonlight,* by Toploader, that’s the one for tonight! Play, my people, play!’
He’d taken them to Hell and back, and now they were here.
All the lace and the lemon and verbena in the world couldn’t take them out. Part of a revolution, ten feet tall, ten times round the sun, this was who they were. *Fighters*. Fighters and dancers in the same skeleton.
In a golden room with golden light, they went golden too, as they danced to the nicest song in the world, with the nicest people in the world, travelling both back and forward in time, because they’d thought they had no time, but now they did, and now the world would make time for them. This was the day they took back control, the day that music beat science, and on this day they would celebrate. They were stars allowed to become comets. Together, they built the universe.
Lushness before doubt, it wasn’t just their feet that could not stop; a hand held a face, a thumb stroked a lip, a mouth agreed to say yes to anything. As Toploader

would say, '*It's a supernatural delight, and everybody's dancing in the moonlight.*'

If only they knew how they looked. Smaller than ants, working away, to build a hive for their Queen. She was a lazy queen now, watching from her tower, eating honey from a jar. She wished she could see their faces. She felt like jumping on to them from above .

It all reached her, the lights, the smells, the noise – everything but the human contact. She was too pure even for that.

She let the jar of honey roll off her. The ladle was still stuck to her long hair.

She groaned as she pushed herself off her bed. She stayed on her stomach for a minute, letting bits of her drain into the cold floor.

Then she staggered to her feet. Imagine if they could see her now.

She positioned her feet, perfectly apart. Her elbow raised and her head back. A perfect ballroom hold.

And then she danced. All alone, in her tower, she danced for the air.

Afterwards, exhausted, she decided to read. The only thing worth reading. More of Cupid's letters, given to her as a treat. From her four poster bed, she reached for one of them, but her door opened just before she could, lilting her hand in the air.

She smirked as she saw him in the doorway. Eli. Even on the night his dreams came true, he had come to her.

'How are we?' he said. Admiration in his eyes. 'I was coming to see if you wanted to … to join them. The ball. This wouldn't have happened without you.' He bowed his head.

Slowly, Erica crossed one leg over the other, feeling her thighs catch the light for him. 'No. Not yet. This is your miracle.'

'Don't be silly, darlin -'

'There's only one thing I want, Eli.'

'What's that?'

She arched her back, legs swinging playfully. 'I want you to stop looking at me with such reverence. With such tenderness, with such gentleness. I don't want to feel like medicine anymore. I don't want to feel like something holy - something you're afraid to break, something you're afraid to touch.' The strap of her silk dress dropped down her shoulder. 'I want to feel like the opposite. Won't you let me know how that feels?'

Eli took a step further into the room. Once he had, there was no going back. After what they'd achieved tonight, suppression was impossible. 'As you wish.' He slammed the door. 'You just sealed your fate.'

A spirit rising off her, she rose to her feet. Glee in her eyes and glitter on her lips. 'I've missed you.'

Something broke in the blue of his eyes. 'You have no idea how much.' He sighed. '*Look* at what we've done, Erica. Erica my creation.'
'And we did it all without touching each other.' Lips. His. Hers. At last. The kiss. 'Never again, Eli my creator. Show me who you are.'

Most of the retreat were still at the ball. They would dance until the sun came up. But as Ann had promised Myles, she had wheeled him back to his bedroom at the stroke of midnight.
She had changed him out of his suit, but once they got to his boxers, he had stopped her.
He talked to her with a tone she had never heard before: passion.
'Don't look so down, girl. So you did a bad thing, one time. Who cares? Forget it. There's bigger things to think about. Like what happened today.'
Her eyes snapped up at him. Her complexion was already ruddy, but now it went a bright red. She folded his blanket, calmly, moving it so he could get into bed.
He stopped her, his hand seizing her wrist. She froze and breathed a breath deep and slow.
'You tell me. You saw what happened today; what I did, in that field.
You must know more about how that works. So I'm asking you – no, I'm telling you – tell me. Give me a clue.'
She wriggled her wrist free.
'Because I'm not stupid. And another part of me thinks that might all have been an illusion. An installation filled with actors. I wouldn't put anything past Eli.
If it is, then you have to tell me. But if it's real, I need to know.
Cos I can't give up on Erica over a game.'
He pulled back the covers to his bed. He jumped in, then opened them up. Her eyes widened.
'Tell me what it is, and I'll let you in.' He edged his boxers down, revealing pubic hair she'd never known could be so black. 'You can stay the night while you tell me all about it. Don't deprive yourself, girl. Every time you hold back, someone accidentally slams their car door on their Chihuahua.' She giggled. Her first girly giggle. She wrestled with the awkwardness, with the rules, but most of all, with the way she felt about herself.
'I'm sweaty, Myles, from a long day's work, I probably stink – '
'So which one is it? Let me know, then let me have you.'
For the first time in years, Ann stopped hating herself. She decided to let herself live. She gave him her answer, then she fell into his bed.

Are you the milk, or are you the silk? Are you wet, or are you dry? Do you spill, or do you ripple? Are you the white of snow or the white of an eye? Can you be worn, or can you be drunk? Are you clean? Are your seams all together, or are you running all over the place? Do they need you, or do you need them? Are

you just waiting til the day something softer comes along? Do you smell? Well?
Are you the milk or are you the silk?
Go on then. Prove it.

Chapter Thirty Eight

Day Four

Finally, after a delicious sleep, Ann shook him awake. Oh wait no – that was Jill. And it was only 6am.
'Myles?' she beamed. 'Let's get you dressed. Eli has a proposal for you.'

Drunk on his self-pity, all that was left for Myles to do was be wheeled. Past the rooms of people he was forbidden to know.
'I'm not trying to end death, I'm trying to end grief.'
Like a moth drawn to the light, the universe has been drawn towards grief, over and over, banging its head against it. Every time it got close the wings battered against the heat, and fought to fly away. If it knew how to rip off its own wings, it would have.
He still remembered the day his skin fell off, the first layer of muscle and his tendons too. When he realised he'd lost his mother. His grief couldn't decide what to be; inside or outside, stinging or splintering, celibate or slutty.
Without our parents we are pathetic. Just a hundred unfulfilled goals and gratitudes and an enemy of time.
But … oh baby … if he could learn to take it away …
There had to always be an answer to losing who you loved, and now it seemed the answer might be him.
So. Myles. What was it gonna be?
He wanted Erica; her lips, her body, her hair. But Erica was only passion, all sex and perfume and love; and he didn't need to ask himself the question, if his one desire was enough to black out everyone else's.
Had everything led him to letting her go?
He didn't know. And even if he did, he wouldn't have had a choice about what he did next. Jill was wheeling him through double doors now, into the garden.

One more game. Last one (I promise).
In the garden, two eyes had been shaved, revealing patches of earth equal in width and depth. Two shovels slept above them. At the foot of one patch, was a man equal to Myles in size and weight. The only difference was he was standing.
On the other side of the two patches, was a platform. Standing on it was Ann, and next to her, dead centre, sitting on a large oak chair, was Eli.
Eli gestured to them. 'Come.'
Jill wheeled Myles to the other patch of earth. For a minute he thought she might push him, but instead, she left him there, and joined the platform on the other side of Eli.

Myles spoke into the cold morning air. 'So what is it this time, Eli? What are you gonna make me do?'
Eli drummed his fingers on the oak, seducing the splinters. He grinned coyly at Myle's confidence, and nodded.
'I see you've seized up again overnight.' He said, his eyes streaking his body. 'It's normal. We'll get you in some yoga to continue the recovery. That is, if you decide to stay.'
The words wrapped around the air, and Myles had no reply. 'You're doing well, Myles,' he said. 'So, so well. That's why I'd like to offer you a role here.'
Ann continued for him. 'You know what we're thinking about. You know what you could do, here and only here. It's not every day we get someone like you.'
Jill took the vocal knife next, to continue the buttering. 'But you have competition. This is Seth.' She pointed to the man at the other patch of earth, who waved. 'Seth isn't like you. Seth chose to come here, because … what is wrong with you again Seth?'
'I couldn't do the splits.' Seth shrugged.
A hundred versions of Myles burst out of his chair, but somehow, *somehow*, he managed to keep them all still, despite the fury that came from Seth's words.
'But then I saw the healer. She was wonderful, so welcoming. She gave my groin a little massage and now …' He slid into a perfect box split a cat would have been jealous of.
Myles realised he was in love with a toy. A toy everyone wanted to use.
'Anyways, afterwards,' Jill carried on, eyes glinting. 'Seth didn't want to leave us. He saw what this place was worth.'
'And since then,' Ann spoke enthusiastically. 'He's done great work. Look at me, Myles. Listen to what I'm saying. Life doesn't have to be hard any more.'
'So you see,' Eli stood. 'There is only space for one new team member. One person who I will treat, however they wish to be treated. Anything they want, they will have.'
Something lurched in Myles, and this time he did jolt forward in his seat. What exactly was in the earth?
'You're wondering what's in the earth, aren't you.' Eli smiled. 'Why not find out.'
He didn't know what he was thinking anymore. He didn't even know where he was. Or maybe he did and he just didn't want to admit it to himself, when he opened his mouth and whispered, *'So how do we win?'*
The trio's eyes flashed with triumph. *A convert.*
'Simple. Whoever digs the deepest, earns the new role here at Core.'
Seth, good old flexible Seth, grinned and rolled up his sleeves. For the first time Myles realised; they were putting him against a fully intact, healthy man. Why?
'What am I supposed to do?! Crawl?! Chew my way through it?!'
'Whatever works for you, M. This time, there are no rules.'
'But he – of course he'll win - !'

'Here's your head start. If you win, you'll be free. I wonder will freedom look good on you?'
Though I wonder, do you prefer the look of freedom, or the look of unharmed flesh? Because there's a lot of sharp surprises in that mud.'
'So if I win … I can work for you – or I can walk out of here?'
'Walk?!'
'I mean, be carried out, sorry.'
'Yes. I'm a man of my word. Make the choice, once you win, if you win.'
Myles shook his head in awe. 'You're the meat, Eli. You're the meat of the world.'
'And you're the teeth. Now dig.'

What happened next was just another joke Myles may never get to tell.
Knock, knock.
Who's there?
A well man.
A well man who?
A well man who says he is sick.
It should have been an epic moment; his big reveal. He should have leapt from the chair, into a back flip then a bow, then pointed at them all and laughed 'I did it! I fooled you all!' with such enthusiasm that they would all laugh along. But it came too soon. The moment he decided he could move, his body binged on the freedom, and everything happened at once; neck, legs, claw, all grappling to honour their urges – and he ended up face down in the mud, flies buzzing in and out of his body. At first he just thought he was tingling, but then he realised he was twitching. Not grand or glamorous, but finally: free.
When it calmed, he rolled over from the mud, struck by the liberty to raise his hand and wipe it from his eyes, to see their reactions.
Jill: shock. Disgust.
Ann: pride. But fear. For him.
Eli: satisfaction. 'I had my suspicions,' he nodded. 'But I'm impressed. I like the commitment. That's what we need here.'
One more person was looking. Myles rolled over to catch Seth's eye. Now that was *true* shock. Oh Seth you really had no idea.
Seth snapped out of it. Grabbed his shovel and with a competitor's spirit, began to dig; he wasn't going to lose to a liar.
Thirty seconds later, and Myles was digging too.

It felt great, to use his body in this way. The world turned brown but his heart stayed red.
There were riddles in the mud; he found one every time he scooped up more earth.
What gets bigger the more you take away from it?

That was easy.
A hole.
He forked out another chunk. It was like gorging on the world's biggest cake. So very satisfying because mud never said no.
The riddles were what motivated him. He was forgetting the meaning of lactic, and remembering just how powerful the endorphins that came from a workout were.
He dug a huge pile of mud now, it teetering dangerously on the edge of his shovel.
There was a plane crash. Every single person died. Who survived?
Using all his strength, he threw the mud up. Almost all of it exited the hole, only a little showering back down on his face. Satisfied and sinking deeper, the answer came to him.
Married couples.
Happily, he spooned back into the earth, swirling the shovel round. It parted for him happily.
Who is the loneliest man in the world?
He wasn't sure about that one. He dug three times before his blade hit something sharp, the light from it summoning a wince within him.
Then he realised. He had dug up a mirror.
Because the loneliest man in the world is me.
He was deep now, deep in the walls of the earth. He couldn't see over the rim of the ground, and the dirt was starting to fall in on him. Mud became rain became chocolate became hail … became a massage, the little specs of dirt drumming down his back and soothing the pain he'd locked up in his spine.
There was almost nothing to worry about. For ten minutes, he was almost able to be nothing, just a robot programmed to bend and to scoop. Only two thoughts niggled at him; he didn't want to be chopping worms in half. Sometimes he saw them, wriggling in the latest batch of mud on his shovel, and he was happy they were whole, but then another thought hit him, cold and strict – was he separating them from their family? Dammit. He dropped them back in and the hole filled up again a little.
Another dig. Another riddle, or this time, a question.
Your toddlers, two and three, are playing on their bunk bed. They play too rough and the two year old pushes the three year old, who goes flying into the metal radiator.
They die.
The two year old is too young to file this away as a memory.
It's up to you. One day, will you tell them what happened?
He dug again. The answer was obvious, boringly obvious.
Dig to the left for yes, the right for no.

To the right he went. It would always be a no. He shivered at the thought that some people would choose yes; the shiver made him drop his shovel. He picked it up awkwardly, his back angry at having to bend even further.
Ten seconds later he had forgotten the question, so satisfying it was for him to simply climb down into the earth. It was changing colour now; from juicy brown to a burnt orange. It smelt better and better.
What has a voice but can't consent?
More digging. His back clenched up for a second, overworked, then released itself, the muscles warmed up. He could think of too many answers for any of them to be right.
A pig.
He kept digging. He could really feel his sweat now, a satisfying bath in onion cream.
Why shouldn't you run with scissors?
Erm …
His shovel banged on something. He flinched, forking it out. There were a pair of scissors in the mud.
Because you're about to trip.
Digging again, gingerly this time, he came across a blade. The mud no longer gave way, lax and easy for him – it was starting to reveal to itself that sharp, spiky things were buried in it. He had to be careful now.
Would you rather have no mouth, or ten noses?
Erm … erm … ten noses? His shovel banged again against the sharpness. Wearily, he lowered himself to his knees, laying the shovel to the side. He prayed that Seth's mud was sabotaged too, and then he began to dig with his hands, picking and winding his way around the scalpels, shards and syringes packed tightly into the mud. At least there were no skulls. Yet.
Who framed Roger Rabbit?
He didn't know.
He was getting through more mud this way, but – the first cut appeared, a bright slash in the centre of his palm – he was unable to avoid the blades.
How do you make a girl disappear?
He didn't know.
His hands were so sensitive, nothing tough about them. He groaned as the fingers started to get nicked too.
What hurts more; emotional or physical pain?
Again, he didn't have the answer. Or maybe he did and all he could think of was the fact his cuticles were dividing. *Physical for sure.*
A papercut. His blood-riddled hand closed around another bit of paper. A riddle again; he preferred the riddles to the choices.
The person who built it sold it. The person who bought it never used it. The person who used it never saw it. What is it?

He gathered earth in his hands, and threw it up. He was too deep now for it to reach the surface, and it all came back down, crowning him with it. But through it he smiled because he had the answer.
It's a coffin.
If he couldn't throw the mud over the top of the pit with just his hands, and he could no longer use his shovel to get through the mud, how was he going to get deeper?
He answered his own riddle. He couldn't get it out, but he could get it in. He brought the mud to his mouth, inhaled deeply, and began to eat it.
It tasted different. He was grateful for the newness.
You find a family of four. Each one needs an organ.
You find a hermit, who contributes nothing.
Do you take the hermit's organs, to save four people in need?
He chewed, swallowed, licked it from his teeth.
No. No life is worthless.
He gorged on more mud, the crumbs as shocked to meet his mouth as it was to meet them. It danced on his tongue. He felt like dancing too. If they thought being degraded into eating mud would deter him from the competition, they didn't know him at all. Munch, chew, swallow.
RING! RING!
It was the bell. The game was over.

Myles lay there with exhaustion, his eyes closed, mud still clotting in his throat. He smiled when he heard footsteps, when he felt hands closing round him, gently carrying him up and laying him down. Though he missed the earth, it was good to be back in the grey light of morning. He rolled to his side, opening his eyes to see an equally exhausted, sweating Seth. Seth flopped out his hand to him, and Myles shook it. Around them, more carers had appeared, and were silently measuring the graves they'd dug.
Eventually, panting equal gulps of air, they sat up to face Eli, who was sitting at the chair, smiling at them proudly.
'Excellent effort,' He was a king in his chair, leaning back into its power. 'You both dug very deep graves. Seth, yours was a little wider. But Myles … you dug three feet deeper. A nine foot grave, I didn't think that was possible in the time frame. You're our winner.'
A grappling, grumbling Seth was raised to his feet 'Wait! He cheated!'. Despite his best efforts, the carers carried him away.
'So I won.' Myles voice came out in inaudible croaks, mud descending from his throat as he talked. 'I work for you now?' He noticed his right hand and flinched. Flesh was dangling from the bone, and glass was habituating deep.
'Almost,' Eli said. 'Expect I've one more choice for you to make. Tell me, is she worth living for?'
'Who …' his voice was weakening.

'Every time someone wins this game, we offer them this choice. We offer them their freedom, and the chance to take Her with them. And to their surprise, they never choose her. I guess you're just not enough to keep someone alive, are you? After all, he chose death over you once before.'
Myles knew who he was talking to, but he couldn't see. Gradually, she was being raised up from within the wooden platform, a white sheet over her body. He closed his eyes, counted to three, and just as he opened them, the sheet fell. Erica.

They say there's nothing like sex in the morning. Damn straight, Erica had never looked better. She had stolen the moon and brought it into the dawn. Her hair was fearless, daring to touch the back of her knees. Her eyes were icy and fresh as a polar bear's frappucino. Her skin wasn't just dotted with dew, it was dew. Her neck long, her shoulders slender, her breasts higher than butterflies. They had dressed her in a silk night dress, propped up by nipples sharp enough to be jewellery. She had clearly just woken up, with black eye make up smeared from tears, nightmares or sleep. Her lips parted, just enough to make an O in the middle of their crimson pillows.
Resurrection. The end of grief. His mother. Maybe.
Or her?
'So what do you want, Myles?'
No energy left, Myles managed to croak his answer. Ann hadn't given him a straight answer last night, but there'd been enough, in her eyes, in the way she looked down, moved or rolled over when he pushed for information. What had happened in the field yesterday would only happen once. Eli had timed the moment exactly so it could happen like that, that way, for Myles. He had controlled the variables, playing God like he always did. It was real, but suspended in time and space, it was a phenomenon. A special slice of luck saved for one moment only. It would never happen again. And even if it would ...
'I want her.'
Something struck Eli in his core; he the apple, it the arrow. Glee. This was what he'd hoped would happen.
'And Erica?' Beautiful, young Erica Ash. 'Do you want him? The man who sold you to us?'
Myles battled to crane out more words, what?! sold her?! me, never?! no, erica, believe me! But there was no energy left.
And finally she looked at him. Her. His woman. The one he had sold.
NO. NO. He hadn't. Had he?
His girl. The one that stopped him from sleeping. This reunion had burned in him a million times, as it did between every missing person and their loved ones.
He took his first step towards her. But she stayed still.

Nervous, he went again.
Her face was glass, and he had just put a bullet through it, but the glass was bullet proof, and now a beautiful spiders web spanned out from the centre of her nose, creating veins and capillaries, and below the glass fists were thumping, and now a spider crawled out of her eye, travelling down her cheek, its bristly leg poking at her mouth, and he realised this expression was what they called pure hatred.
The one he had sold.
'There's a mirror in the mud, because the loneliest man in the world is you.'
Up there she looked so high, she looked like a whole new religion. She looked like she was controlling the wind that blew through her hair, turned her skin blue, twisted its hands in her silk nightdress. She looked like there was not one thing you could say to her that could turn her back, from glass to flesh.
He wouldn't be pathetic, not any more, not for her. He stood, one leg shaking, his voice still hatching out words. He looked up into her and did the only thing he remembered how to do; he held out his hand. To her. The one he had lost.
Instead of taking it, she began to shake with anger.
'Uh oh.' Eli said. 'Guess it's not so easy to forgive.'
'I didn't sell you. I didn't I didn't I didn't.' He spoke again and again, but all that came out was crumbs.
She didn't take her eyes off him. This time she was the one who couldn't move. Paralysed with hate, she watched him try.

Erica. Don't you know by now, Erica is not the girl who is afraid of lightning. Right now she was peaceful, as she stood up high and watched the one who had put her here, splutter and beg for her back. Nobody could control her thoughts, and nobody was going to stop her from imagining what she might do to him. So stiller than satin, she let herself imagine.
The baying, braying man beneath her feet, and everyone around her, waiting for her to mock him. She'd never felt more like a queen.
'ididn-'
He mumbled on but it meant nothing. She had made up her mind.
She was about to show them *real* kindness. Real kindness wasn't healing, nursing or loving. Real kindness was seeing someone's fire and walking right into it.
Quite frankly all she wanted was this.
She was just so fucking *bored* of resisting him.
So fed up of obeying her bones.
She could end self respect with one word, and that word was Myles. Besides, where was she going to fit him if not inside her?
She was the only one who really did fall in love. Others stepped into it, or hopped into it, or started to fall then clung to edge. Erica was the only one, the only one without vertigo, the only one who understood gravity.

The crash of a piano made of rocks and ocean salt, she let herself think about starting to go, from the platform, to him.
There were so many different, easy ways with which she could turn him down, and yet it felt so very good to turn him back up.
'*This is how you make a girl disappear.*'
She stepped off the platform.
Egged on by the sun, her face slopped into surrender. The slyest of smiles came softly across her face, and she walked towards him.
He held out his hand. A million voices told her no but her hands told her yes. So she gave him her hand. 'Wanna go for a run?'

At the end of the day, the escape was obvious.
Run rabbit run.
Hop bunny hop.
Run black rabbit.
Black rabbit, white rabbit, red rabbit – any colour rabbit just get away.
Ann had set it up for them. That was what Myle's had whispered in her ear last night, and after a few hours of thinking, she had chosen to help. She knew how to contact the boat, after all.
Go bunny go.
Don't get your paw caught in the trap. Don't get blood in your nice soft fur.
She'd told Myles to look for the tiny little arrows she had carved along the way, pointing him in the right direction. First along the walls of the garden, so the two of them tucked around a corner that led them through a door, back into the house. Trusting the arrows and trusting Ann, they found themselves sweeping through room after room; each would have been deserted if it wasn't for one of Ann's loyalist patients there; holding a door, offering a distraction, preparing to fight Eli and his team as they tried to catch up with them.
Run little rabbit, run cruel rabbit, run run run before they skin you alive. You don't know what they need you for – rabbit soup, rabbit hat, rabbit tests, rabbit sex.
So fast but your paws are getting heavier and your ears are catching on the thorns, remember that time the cat almost got you.
Ann watched them go. After all that work, the escape was nothing really. It was the simple part.
Thump-thump-thump, aren't you worried about a heart attack?
If you really wanted to escape, you could. Anything you wanted to get out of, you could. It reminded her of that morning forty years ago.
Little bunny, why you holding the barrel of the hunter's gun?
When her dad had wanted to escape this world, and leave it of his own free will, it had taken him nothing. He was gone before she could ever say goodbye. She had never seen the body, only heard about it from big, tall adults that didn't love her like he did, bending down to tell her they were sorry.

That was when she remembered becoming bad.
Go, go, go. Burrow, burrow, burrow, you got what it takes.
Sniff out the traps. Twitch, twitch, hold the hand of your bitch.
She watched them from above, pretending to be keeping watch, as they streaked through the air like silk. It was easy for them, though they thought it was hard, though Erica clung to Myle's hand so desperately, throwing glances of terror over her shoulder – if they'd looked deep inside themselves they'd have known they'd already won. Nobody could catch the speed of their love.
Hoppity-hop-hop.
Before they knew it, they were at the foot of the hill, standing on a river bank. Eli and his team's voices could be heard trying to trace them, but they were still a good one hundred metres behind. And in the distance, a boat came closer. A boat that was coming for them. Ann had whispered to him about this boat, about how it was the only way to escape. She had arranged it at great risk, open to the peril that would come if Eli ever knew she had more contact. Organised by some elusive figure who had escaped Core in the last few weeks, they would arrive on the ocean, the only thing Eli didn't own, and wait to collect any escapees that had been lucky enough to hear of their imminent, unexpected arrivals. Very few had ever made it to it.
Gasping with relief, they waved to the vessel. It was only a few feet away – it would reach them in time. They had just enough time to realise one hard fact, solid and true.
They may be escaping, but what about the people they were leaving behind? This would never be over, as long as Eli forced people to sit in their spit and jump til they split; no one would ever be safe.

The boat moored up. A muscular man popped out, held out his hand. Myles helped him haul Erica up. Light as a feather.
He was pulled up next. More comrades came spilling to the deck, their feet on fire as they were ready to help.
His feet grappled, fighting their way over the edge.
'Wait. Not her.'
'What?' the henchman replied.
'Not. Her.'
Myles didn't recognise the voice, but Erica did.
'Dr Sunset!'
It was her face, bold and strong, peering out of a hood.
'Sunset, I didn't even know you escaped!'
'Don't call me that.'
She stood tall and bold between them, and commanded everything in the air.
'Two words: Not. Her.'
The crew shrugged. They knew the rules. Whatever Dr Sunset said went.

With a simple flick of a wrist, Erica was pushed overboard. She came sailing down to the ground, smacking into the sand.
On instinct, Myles let go of the hands that had been helping him. He swooped around Erica, getting to her before the confusion could get to him.
A guttural desperation changed Erica's whole voice; this is how a heartbreak sounds. 'No. No, no, no, no. I've gotta get on this boat. I've got to.'
The woman's teeth crashed as her scorn drove Erica further into the sand. 'Not Her. Drive.'
Blubbery and bloated, it was the ugliest Erica had ever looked as she begged. '*Please.*' Dr Sunset became bile. '*Please.* Don't do this to me, don't do this to me, don't do this to me!'
She grabbed at the railings - on instinct, the rescuing raiders bent back her hands, throwing her to the sand yet again.
'What is this?!' Myles blazed his words across the beach. 'What the fuck is going on?'
Truth to be told, the rest of the crew were confused too. Weren't they here to rescue anyone who wanted it?
'You can come, darling,' Dr Sunset smiled at him. 'But not her. Pull the anchor!'
'Sunset please I'll do anything, anything, anything you can think of I'll do it, please please please don't let them do this to me - ' Wet, warbling, weak, whipping, warped - nothing Erica could say was working.
Dr Sunset acknowledged the stunned expressions of her comrades, their discomfort as Core's carers now began pouring over the dunes.
'How can we leave her behind?' One asked.
'So that she can't ruin our lives. Sails up!' Dr Sunset grew taller as she announced her decision. 'What you are looking at here is not a person. This is Eli's pet. This is Eli's toy. He made her. He rose her up from nothing and she knows it. What he says, she does. When he wants, she gives. When he bleeds, she bleeds. She's a weapon. *His* weapon.
She's the opposite of euthanasia. She's eternity - eternal suffering - Eli plucked it out of our nightmares and he put a pretty bow on it. Agony, to infinity and beyond. That's what you're looking at.'
Erica screamed. 'Oh god I am begging you! You have got this so wrong! I am pro-choice, bitch! I hate everything Eli has ever done! I'll never heal anyone in my life again if I don't have to! I am anti-suffering and so are you but only if you let me come! You cannot, cannot leave me behind!'
Dr Sunset shrugged. 'No bitches on my boat.'
Myles leapt for the head of the boat. A man kicked him back. 'Dr Sunset, what are you doing?' She ignored him. He drew his attention to the rest of the pack. 'You, all of you, do something! You can't do this to her! You can't let him win! COME ON!'
'Like I said, darling,' the doctor's lips danced at him. 'You can come.'

Erica's hair came loose in her hands. 'This is not happening.' She gulped. 'This is not my life.' She hammered on the boat. 'This happens to other girls. Not to me.'
Smug mud went through Dr Sunset's skin. The twist. The snail that gets to break a human's back. She shook her head. 'That's who you are, Healer.' She slammed the engine. 'Go! It's a set up! They'll have warned Eli! This is Eli's object!'
'No! No!' Erica screamed. 'This is not happening, not happening, not real. Take me now! Take all of me! PLEASE.'
She leapt for the boat again, but her face hit it instead. Myles ran around the edge, looking for an entrance, some steps, a rope, any other way in or through: there was nothing. He did a full circle of the boat and came back to Dr Sunset's same smug smile.
'DRIVE!' Dr Sunset demanded, turning the whole world into a smirk. 'If I could get out, you could have too, anytime. You know what side you're on, Healer.'
'I can't go through this again I can't live this I can't live it I can't I can't I can't -'
'How can you do this?' Myles screamed up at Dr Sunset. The rest of the rescue mission tried to hold firm.
'She's playing with us,' Dr Sunset instructed them. 'She's faking this. The Healer loves attention.'
Figures were appearing at the top of the hill. Erica's nails speared the boat.
'NO!' She shrieked shrilly, then somehow, someway, she managed to find her voice. 'You kissed me too.'
Dr Sunset, her hand around the gear stick, froze.
Erica's voice cracked. 'You know you did. You kissed me *first.*'
Myles watched the woman, stunned. Silence spun around them.
'You looked for the key inside me.' Erica continued. 'Just like I did. They made us do it.'
Luminous, symmetrical tears vaulted from both women's eyes.
Sharing a look only they could share.
The anchor was pulled up.
'So *please,*' Erica whispered. 'Believe me. I am not on his side. Help us.'
Shock spun through the air. There were at least ten people within the boat, each one frozen in waiting for the decision of the Sunset.
'What's it gonna be?' the muscular man said, grappling with the ropes. 'Quick!'
Dr Sunset flinched. 'I - shh, Healer -'
'Please,' Erica's voice was nothing. 'I am not his. I am not theirs. I am not anyones. And I am not staying here because we were both abused.'
Something like a tear shone in the doctor's eye.
Erica's voice got smaller. 'He *dehumanised* us. Then he broke what was left. He vaporised us. But that was him, not me.'

Dr Sunset's voice was even smaller. 'Drive.'
'No. Please. Look at me. *Olivia.'* Dr Sunset's real name.
The anchor soared upwards.
Dr Sunset's eyes glazed.
The engine roared. More and more people were spilling over the hill.
Chunks of mud came up from him and into the ground.
Erica wriggled up onto the boat but the man flung her straight back. She landed on her wrist in a way that could only cause a sprain. 'You know what, fuck you. I'm not begging for forgiveness because we were abused.' She grabbed the boat again, nails coming off; the man kicked her back. Myles leapt onto the deck and swung for him; he was on the sand again before he could even connect.
The boat began revving up. Watery waves spat back at them. Erica clung to Myles as they watched their dream begin to chug away.
Who would have thought it would be the ocean that would separate them from freedom?
Dr Sunset stood on the dock, watching the woman she was leaving behind. She watched as The Healer repeated that one word she hadn't heard in months.
'Olivia.'
Behind them, she saw the moment Eli's army came.
Over the hill. All of them. Eli's voice spilling around the atmosphere, 'You can get them! You can stop her!', booming through the trees and the vines. More and more people, stocky, stiff, spilled over the hill for them. For the Healer.
Dr Sunset's eyes rippled as Eli's commands got louder, and more and more carers came.
'There she is! You can get to her!'
Sand crashed down the dunes as his cult came. No end to them, no space between them, robotic as they ran for The Healer.
'Go, go, go! Bring her to me!'
A taunting chant oozed across the beach. It was Jill calling, in that unforgettably ugly voice. 'Come now, Healer,' she sung. 'Enough of this skullduggery. Let's run you a nice warm bath. Fluffy towels and cocoa, how's that sound?'
Waves shot Erica back. Rain was ripped out of the sky. Every cloud went grey. Perhaps this was the apocalypse. Myles wiped his eyes and tried to be ready for it.
The boat pulled out from the shore. The first clot of carers reached the bottom of the hill. Eli appeared on top of a dune. The sun rose a little higher when he came.
That was what it took: for Dr Sunset to see the light.
'Oh god what have I done! Oh god oh god what am I doing!'
The veil of hate lifted, and the human was right there instead. A human now panicking with what she was doing to another.

'I'm sorry I'm sorry I'm sorry!' Trauma shook off her like rain. 'What - what - what the fuck am I doing! *What the hell!'* She raced to the end of the vessel. 'Healer - Erica - both of you - GET ON THE BOAT!'
She held out her hand, torso sloping over the rails. Desperation soared against time.
'Come to me - come on Erica - NOW!'
Myles and Erica ran into the sea bed. The churn of the waves pushed them back. Myles used his momentum to spear Erica forwards. As they swallowed the water, they felt the glory of speed, and their faces smacking hard into the bowl of the boat.
Suddenly there was no limit on the people reaching over the rails for them. Dr Sunset took Erica, somebody took Myles, and, as the vessel shot into the horizon, they discovered freedom tasted of ocean salt, and were yanked to safety of the deck.
'I'm so sorry, Erica,' Dr Sunset was weeping. 'He shattered me.'
'That's okay,' Erica spluttered up water, wiping her eyes at the same time, yet somehow managing to smile. 'Now we get to shatter him.'

Alone on the top deck. At the back. The healer and the hero; so why were they so cold?
Core Retreat was becoming a dot in the distance. The water below them was getting murkier and darker.
They locked eyes. *Finally free.*
Goose pimples popped up around them. At last, a sweet sigh. Oh man had he missed her.
They had been given space, despite a sulking Rose, space to process what had just happened. The sun cracked confidently into the sky. Moss slapped up onto the deck.
As the boat sailed a part of England neither of them had ever seen before, they came together.
Myles tried to speak but Erica pushed him down. He flopped onto the bench on the deck. Nobody around, are you sure?
She answered him with a straddle. Her thighs smaller than ever before, she mounted him.
He closed his hand around her neck. Drove their lips together. Wildly, they kissed, only grazing each other before pulling away, unable to take the sweet swelling inside them.
Pleasure. They had forgotten how it felt, now it came to them, twice as strong, impossible to forget. Myles reached into her night dress. She wasn't wearing knickers.
Myles leaned back and groaned as she did that thing, and then he did that thing to her, the thing that made her half as weak and twice as nice.

He became stone as she stroked him. She reached into his sweatpants, moving as she unravelled the thick, fierce force within, one moment of cold air and then she slid it along her pinkness. Up and down. And then in. *Ah-uh.*

She looked into his eyes, brushing another unforgivable kiss all around his lips, and then started to talk.

'Bet it feels good to be inside me again, doesn't it?'

'Yeah.'

A gaze, swirling between them, managing to be born in a haze of breathless sex.

'We're addicted to this. We're too far gone to ever come back.'

He leaned back just as she arched for him, sweeping his own blood along his shaft. 'I know.'

'Even though you sold me to them,' she whispered lightly.

Now he could talk, he growled into her neck. 'Never, Erica. I'll do whatever it takes to get you to believe me.'

She closed her hand over his lips. 'But you bought me to him, to heal his eyes. Then he just … turned up at dinner with us. It's all a bit of a coincidence, isn't it, Myles?'

'I swear.' He jerked inside her, and she leant back with the pleasure. 'You *will* believe me.'

Tongue licking her lips, she moaned. 'You know what, maybe I do.' She reached under and tickled his balls lightly.

'Yet as I ride you right now, and I look down into your face, I realise what I never thought I'd realise.'

She lurched forward now, squeezing him tight, swerving him to the side.

'I don't love you anymore. Just like that, I've fallen out of love with you.' She kissed him, long and hard, the two of them swirling against each other, her hips creating a circle. Her wetness sloshed down him. 'Even though you saved me. Even though you risked everything for me.' She clawed his back, began to bounce from side to side. He drove deeper up into her in response. 'What a shame. Maybe I just like you.'

'That's not true,' he smiled, and gasped as she clenched.

'Oh isn't it?' she whispered.

'You don't fuck people you just 'like' like this.'

'Unless,' she whispered, and then she did something with her pelvis that slid his world to the side. 'This is the cruellest thing I could do.' Then she went faster, and faster, and he couldn't stop her to beg her to tell him it was a lie, because all his energy had been turned into slippery caramel in the tip and the top of what made him a man.

'And unfortunately for you,' she rose again then slid down, gyrating him, a hand gliding underneath him, everything slippery, petals in his earth. 'I'm not going to heal the glass in your hand. You're going to be left with that pain,' she thrust harder. 'For the rest of your life.'

She rocked and rocked and made cinnamon in his spine. 'But that's not the worst thing I'm going to do to you, Myles.' Her hands glided in places they shouldn't and he forgot which Myles he was. 'Because you'll never see me again after this. I may as well have been a dream.'

She sighed lightly. 'And I may have just ruined your life. You're about to be the saddest you've ever been. Because this right now, what my insides are doing to you, is the best thing you've ever felt …' She rippled, arches of hieroglyphics all up inside her, making him feel every single one. 'And you're never, ever going to feel anything as good as this again. All you're going to do is long for it.' She licked his neck. 'Maybe I should stop.

I can stop now before the memory gets too strong, before it fills you up completely. I can stop now before this is all you can remember. I can stop now while you're still you, still a person, still whole, not a nerve sticking out needing to be tucked back in.' She bit his shoulder as he moaned. 'I can stop now while water still quenches your thirst. I can stop now while sleep still leaves you rested. I can stop now while you still own all the parts of you, before I take them away with me. I can stop now before I leave you forgetting how to speak, forgetting how to breathe, forgetting how to eat. I can stop before you're full of hate for every other woman because

They're

Not Me

Or I can do this.' She dropped backwards in an impossible arch. She crashed back upwards in a wave of electric everything. 'And that's what I've done. *That's* why your life is ruined.'

She gave him one final squeeze then slid off him, almost taking him with her, grazing his chest and falling to her knees.

'Now cum for me over these big eyes you like so much.'

He didn't want to burst but he did, all over her, and she gazed up at him, his whiteness hanging off her lashes like tears, and smiled slow.

Just as they approached a port.

'If you look for me, I'll hurt you.' She kissed his fingertips as they moored into the marina. 'Goodbye.'

Chapter Thirty Nine

3 Weeks Later

Paris

Oh, Paris.
Paris baby.
Say it one more time, slower this time: Pa-*ris.*
Ain't nothing like it. Two hours on the Eurostar, and here Myles was.
It had come to him that morning, like all the best ideas do: *I should go to Paris.*
As he had looked around his carriage, he was sure he wasn't the only one who'd that spontaneous thought had got out of bed that morning; he was sure he wasn't the only one surprised to be staring at the Louvre right now.
For the whole journey, he worked on a document on his laptop. It seemed to write itself.
And the moment he stepped off the train, he knew where he had to go.

When the girls saw him coming, they knew he was coming for them. And so a battle began: a battle for a lipstick. There was only one stick of Cerise No.3 left.
'He's here for me!'
'He'll want me!'
'No, look at the way he walks - I'm what he needs!'
Lucinda launched for it first, but Esme ripped it from her hand, bending her fingers back as she did. She squealed and hunched over, fighting the white hot pain driving down her hand; when she turned around, Esme was already sitting at the dressing table.
Victorious, Esme smiled at herself in the mirror. She plucked the gold tube in half. Cerise No.3 was made for lips in her shape; if the other girls could be honest with themselves they'd admit that. Butterily, it glided across her top lip, summoning raspberry, cherry and a glass of cold rose all in one go. At the same time she felt a cold breeze around her jaw.
She didn't accept it when she felt something silky drop and slide between her toes. She didn't accept it when she looked down and saw what had pooled around her feet. She only accepted it when she looked back up into the mirror and saw Lucinda behind her. Holding a pair of scissors.
A defiant Lucinda hissed, 'Let's see if he chooses you now I've hacked off your hair.'

'Tell me your name.'
'Myles. Myles King.'
'Tell me your age.'
'39. I'm forty soon.'
'Nice. And have you been to a brothel before, Myles?'
'Nope.'

'Is that true? I'll find out if you have.'
'It's true.'
'Tell me what you do for work.'
'I used to be a party planner. And I will be again. How many more questions are there going to be?'
'Well. I don't get a lot of walks in here, Myles. I don't expect people to just wander in off the street; but that's okay, it's happened before; we are not averse to spontaneity in this place. This is just a consultation, to get a sense of your tastes, your preferences, your inclinations. One question left.'
'Okay. Hit me with it.'
'Tell me if you've ever had your heart broken.'
'Yes. Yes I have.'
'Good. Then we can begin. My name is Louis, by the way. Girls, you can come in.'
Louis the pimp sat back, his eyes glinting as he watched Myle's expression change as the parade into his office began. He always enjoyed this, recognising the weakness in other men, the lack of originality in how they all responded to the women. His women.
Atlanta, Colette, Lucinda, Davina, Salina, and Lyanna; a fine selection of enwhorephins, all dressed in silk kimonos he had instructed them to leave open, the silk swooning around their flawless, fearless bodies; taut, firm, bouncing.
'Who will you choose?'
Myles shuffled. 'I'm not very good at … making decisions.'
As delectable as they looked, there was something ominous in the atmosphere. There always was. Louis liked it that way. 'We can help with that. Do you know what colour your blood is?' he continued. 'Can you picture the exact shade?'
Myles squinted, considering the question. 'I … think so, yeah.'
'Atlanta, come here,' he commanded. Atlanta, the girl with the most outrageous lips, glided around his chair, settling on his lap. She looked Myles directly in the eye as Louis held her jaw and kneaded her lips together between his forefinger and thumb. 'As red as these?'
'Maybe a little less.'
'Atlanta, sit on the desk.' She hopped up off his lap, swinging round to the front of the desk and taking a seat in front of Mylses. 'Atlanta, open your legs.' She did as she was told.
'As red as this?'
'Maybe. Maybe a little darker.'
'Girls. Help Myles decide.' Seamlessly, in a dance, the women worked their way in front of the desk. In a variety of poses, they opened their legs, stretching each other out.
Louis walked proudly past the parade of reds and pinks. 'Whose shade of pink, or red, will match your blood the best? Are you maroon, or are you cerise?

Scarlet or peony? Look closely and tell me which of these women is your match. Your equal. Tell me your choice.'
Myles sat in his chair, remaining calm. He let the silence stew in the air as the scents of the six women filled it.
'Surprise me.'
Lucinda twitched. Was the stretch hurting her?
'What?' Louis said.
'I can't decide.' Myles shrugged.
'Seriously?' Louis was disappointed. 'Girls. Close your legs. Return to your positions.' He told the women abruptly. Immediately, they obeyed, forming a line behind him as he settled back into his chair and looked at Myle's curiously. 'Everybody always has a favourite'
'I want them all. You choose for me.'
'That's not what I do.' Louis said. 'And that's not how this process works.'
'Why? Cos you like it when they feel rejection?! I told you, I can't choose.' He crossed his arms defiantly. 'Let fate decide.'
Louis kept his cool. 'I mean, it's not a problem. I can select for you. If you're sure. You don't have a single demand? Not one request? Then so be it.'
'I do actually.'
'A-ha. See, girls, I knew it. So what can I do for Myles, the forty year old virgin? Just kidding.'
Myles leaned forward, pressing his elbows into the table intently. Now was the time to ask. 'I'd like to pitch something.'
Louis rolled his eyes. He hated time wasters. 'I'm afraid that's out of the question. I have international clients arriving all afternoon. There's a meeting with one scheduled as soon as this ends.'
'What about after my … booking?' Myles asked.
'Impossible, I'm afraid.' He began standing up. Davina and Salina gestured for the others to make way for him. 'We have a major ceremony tonight. Was there nothing else?'
'I know what you do here.' Finally, Myles had said it.
Louis stopped. His hand settled over the tiger skull on his desk. 'Oh, do you now?'
'Yes. I know everything'
Louis melted back into his seat. 'You clever boy. Colette, call him Sherlock.'
'Hi Sherlock,' Colette dazzled at him from across the desk, reaching out her fingertips for him to take. He ignored them.
'So what is it then, Sherlock? You think you can stop us? Blackmail me? What do we think, girls?' Their bodies rippled with giggles, their kimonos floating open even more. Louis narrowed his eyes as he looked at Myles anew. 'You know you're not the first person to march into my establishment, eyes dancing with dreams of being a hero who'll bring our unique way of doing business down. If those other heroes could speak now they'd tell you: you're never going

to leave this place. What was your name again? Myles? Dear boy: today is the day you become Caspar the frisky ghost.'
'Oh …Louis, you've got me all wrong. I'm not here to stop you.'
'Then why are you here? Because you want to die?'
Davina's eyes narrowed at him. Her nipples were spikes, ready to impale anyone who said the wrong thing.
'Almost. I'm here for an opportunity.'
Myles watched as Louis the pimp digested his words. 'You want to choose how they kill you? But my girls are so creative. More and more dynamic with every murder.'
'Not quite.' Myles reached into his bag, to pull out the ten page document he had been working on. Along with a bottle of something else. 'I bought you a bottle of scotch. All good business is done over a bottle of scotch, I find.'
'Is this a bid?' Louis cackled. 'A bid for this building? Do you know how much history has happened in these walls? My boy, you couldn't run a tap.'
'It's not a bid. For the building, or the business. It's a proposal.' He opened up the contract, spinning it round to show Louis the first sheet. 'Do you want some scotch or not?'
Louis gestured to the girls. 'First one to pour us two glasses gets to spend the night with me.' Davina slammed two tumblers down and filled it with the amber liquid. Salina, who had just missed out, was juicing with jealousy. Myles took a sip, then launched into a speech that had come to him in a dream.
'You can dress it up in lots of little ways, and intimidate a hundred men like me out of this room, but it doesn't change what I know: you're trying to do something here.' He spun the contract back to himself, to read out a list of names written on page three.
'Anthony Lux. 44. Estonian. Arms dealer. After his visit here, he had a trip booked to Qatar. A trip set to make him millions. He was working on a bioweapon.
Nyle Brine, 38. Head of the Irish cartel. Brought a friend here to blackmail him, but they never left'.'
Myles noticed all the girls were leaning in, listening as though he was telling them a bedtime story. 'Shall I go on?
Hanna Blitz. 30. A Dutch political candidate. Her youth and good looks made her a promising choice for her party. What the population of the Netherlands don't know is just how far right her views really were. Just what she might do to them if she was in power. Or would have done if Atlanta here hadn't poured hot wax into her throat and watched it set.' Atlanta beamed at him, excited to hear her name.
'Vincent DuVagn. A judge based in your very own Paris. The DuVagn name strikes fear into even the toughest of hearts. He's almost infamous in his pursuit of 'justice'. Famous for his brutal, lengthy sentences, and for making them more and more disproportionate each time. Well known for denying appeals and for

speaking against prison reform. If only his penis was as long as the sentences he likes to give, right Colette? Did you keep his penis, after the clamp castrated him? Or did his blood wash it away while he bled to death last Thursday?'
Louis pulled the contract away from him, angrily, thumbing through it quickly to see what other information Myles knew. Pouncing into the moment, Myles continued, swinging his voice to just the right temperature to show Louis: he understood.
'You're trying to do something good. You built The Brothel Of Blood because you believed it could make a difference.
But it's not working, is it? Why doesn't it feel … pure? Why are you kept up all night with guilt? This should feel warm, victorious, satisfying - but it doesn't. Somewhere along the way you got it wrong. Somewhere along the way it became about pain.
How about making it work?
How about knowing, for once, you've made the world a better place than the one you came into?
You know you have it in you. The ability to make life fair.
You're almost there, Louis. You're close. And I know how you can get there. I'll tell you, if you let me, what this place could become. And who The Brothel Of Blood is really for.'
Louis sneered at him. Lucinda snaked into the light, her swarm of endless blonde hair moving with her. He twisted his arm into her waist, squeezing what little there was to squeeze, running it under her buttocks. 'Go on then.'
'There's people who deserve to die.' Myles said. 'Not because of who they are. Because of what life has done to them. To them, death is a gift.
I know of these people. I've seen them.
And it should be so simple to answer their requests. There should be clinics, one in every city, for them. So that when they're ready to take that long sleep, they know it can be done, as easily as shutting your eyes.
But every time a city tries, a wave rises up. A nonsensical wave that puts no value on quality, only on quantity. Most recently Denmark tried to pass a euthanasia bill. It was soundly defeated in parliament. America, the leader of the free world, has never even entertained a congressional debate on it.'
'Don't you have one of these places in your own country?' Louis interrupted, winding his fingers through Lucinda's hair as he did. She nodded, looking at him in admiration.
'Ah. We do. Sunset Clinic. Let me tell you about Sunset.. Sunset is actually Core. Core has conquered it and everything it wanted to be. One day I'll tell you about Core too. Funnily enough, I was there not long ago.'
'You worked there?'
'No. I was a guest of some kind. Anyway. The UK's wishes have been … infiltrated. Overtaken. Warped. Even when it voted for it, it couldn't win. There are beliefs, engraved too deeply in society, that won't let it.

But isn't that the second rule of business? Finding a niche.
You've built the infrastructure. You've got the building. You've got the name. You've got the reputation. All you need are the people. The desperate, suicidal, broken people. And believe me, they will come.'
He looked at Louis, hoping this had worked.
'You mean my clients would be … civilians. People without power, who've never done anything wrong.'
'Yep. Louis, they need to die.'
Louis shook his head, catching the girl's eyes. 'Nah. We like the thrill of taking out high up hypocrites here.' They nodded.
Myles smiled. 'I promise I can send you a hundred horny hypocrites on your first day of opening.'
Louis cackled. 'And why should I serve them?' As he was speaking, something like a woman, but also something like a cheetah, was draping herself across him, impossibly liquid.
'Because of the pain.' Myles replied, simple, abrupt. 'The paralysed are running out of patience for the pain. But the pain is so patient with them. Or maybe because of the boredom. The boredom now they can't do anything they used to do. Or maybe for the dignity they believe they've lost.'
Lyanna, he thought her name was, was crying. He fixed his eyes on Louis. 'But who needs dignity when you can have fun?' He tipped his voice over the edge. 'We'll make their deaths so pleasurable dignity will be the last thing they're asking for.' Colette stroked Lyanna's hair, and Louis stroked them both. 'That's what you do here, isn't it? You deal in pleasure. You've built your life around it, about the sweet moment when a body gives way and nothing matters anymore. That's why I know you're the right person for this. To be my business partner.'
He wasn't sure, but he thought Lyanna might have just nodded at him. He spurred on, 'This would be truly anarchic, Louis. It's punk rock. It's taking the law into our own hands, and their own delicate, slender paws. It's so outside of society; something the conformists could never understand. But one second of suffering and they'll crave us. Even more than they crave Atlanta now. We're doing the one thing society isn't brave enough to do to itself: combine sex with death. But what we're doing, it would be *humane.*'
'Did I ever say I wanted to be humane?'
'No. What you do here is more than that. You deal in fantasy, in ecstasy, in euphoria. In hedonism. Show them that hedonism was the humane choice all along.
Forget dying with dignity. Let them die with desire. Let their last moments be the peak of their life, as opposed to ten years of watching it plateau. Why the fuck not?' He thumped the desk. 'Whose gonna stop us?
No more wiping away the sticky liquid from an old man in a chair's mouth - instead, we will wipe it from a flawless woman's pout!'

Atlanta bent backwards across the desk, locking eyes with Myles, letting him know it was possible. 'I've always liked serving the older gentlemen anyway.' The girls giggled around her. One of them was spraying perfume.

'Boom!' Myles said. 'There we go! Yet another reason for this place. Cos this place is *needed,* or the place I've conjured up in this contract is needed; for the grandmother who's just lost her soulmate, for the teenage boy who's been framed for something he didn't do, for the woman whose face was crushed by something falling out of the sky.

And you strike me as someone who likes money, Louis. I bet you enjoy Paris's strong economy. People talk about how the death penalty would be so much better for the tax payer, but they never talk about how much sweeter it is than life in prison. Wouldn't it be so simple - and so profitable - if the ones who couldn't hack it, could come here. Off the taxpayers hands and into Lucinda's mouth.'

'Not so much cruel and unusual punishment, is it,' Louis said, 'More altruistic and ...'

'Unique.' Myles finished. 'A very unique punishment indeed.'

Louis checked his watch. 'The smarter you show me you are, the more I want you dead.' Colette giggled, her piercings sparkling at him.

'I get it. This is your world. I don't have any right to be here. I lied my way in here. You'd have every right to cut me out of it. You like watching the light leave a man's eyes and these girls like the taste of blood. But maybe, you also like mercy.'

Suddenly Lyanna was leaning across the desk, her eyes rocking back and forth between the two men, swirling them together in a blue of brew. She spoke, with conviction, into Louis's ear. "We'll give them something more than mercy ever could. If you let us.'

'Shh,' Salina hissed back at her. 'It's not up to us! Stop interfering with their meeting.' Annoyed, Lyanna backed up, folding her arms behind her pimp's chair.

Louis started thumbing through the contract, still keeping it at arm's length. Myles risked talking again, 'I've broken it all down. How we'd turn a profit, how we reach out to our desired clientele. It's all there, except the legalities. I'm sure you've got that infrastructure in place. You know more than me about how to avoid ... interference, from those who don't believe in what you're doing here.'

It was always hard to tell who a man who chose to be a pimp truly was; why they were led to this, what they thought about women, whether they did this because their ego was small or because it was big. Truth be told when Myles first heard about Louis he'd been sure it was small, but today he sensed an intelligence, a warmth, a generosity of spirit that only came from winning a few lotteries in life. Ever since he'd been in here he'd felt the spark of hope.

'And you have the angels. You want this place to feel like the gates of heaven: and now it actually can, my man, now it actually can.' They loved compliments; Salina was literally purring.
Louis leaned back, enjoying the challenge of the moment.
'I guess fear would have to be a turn on for them.'
'I guess it would.'
'And violence - they'd have to violence titillating. Pleasurable even.'
'That they would. That can be done.'
Louis shook his head. 'Not enough.' He said. 'Not enough would have the stomach for it. To voluntarily come here, knowing what was gonna happen … nah. We'd have to get rid of all the weapons and turn my nymphos into nurses.'
Colette twitched, the curve of her hip bone a blade in the light. 'I like you, Myles, but you're not telling me what to do with my business.'
'One day you may not be able to choose what to do with your own hands.'
Louis froze.
'One day you might wake up and your body won't let you roll over to see who's beside you. Colette drifts past you, and you reach for her soft skin … but your hand refuses to uncurl. Besides, she's busy; she needs to change you.
One day Lyanna might lean in to kiss you and you can't kiss her back. No matter how much you tell your lips to go, they won't, and then you realise your tongue is hanging out too.
And one day Davina might get tired of nursing you. All that effort you can't thank her for. And you'll need to run from her hands as they beat you, as they bruise your shrinking body again and again. But you can't run. You can't even tell anyone what she's doing to you.' Myles looked down, the image making him icky.
'And you'll wonder why you didn't sign your signature on the piece of paper that could have got you out of that nightmare. Now you'll want to but it'll be too late; your hand can't close around the pen.
You wouldn't be the first to turn this down. Maybe you'll be the last. Maybe some other visionary will come along and do what you couldn't.'
And Myles was done. He had said everything he could think of saying. He had done what he could to convince Louis that true freedom was choosing when you got to die. At least he'd been able to say it out loud. At least he had fought for it. He ran his eyes over Atlanta's body, her hips rocking for him. And then he saw her hand close around a knife.
He remained in his seat. He had to. He had to get an answer. Even with the way she was looking at him as she held the blade up to the light. He focused on Louis, hard, ignoring the silver flashing by his ear.
He needed an answer.
'But of course, I'm just a man with an idea. Just a boy with a vision of a world where no one grows old and gets wrinkles. You're the entrepreneur here. You're

the guy who created all this, the one who took all the risks: every brick in this place belongs to you.'
'And everybody belongs to him too.' Lucinda chimed in.
'Everybody,' a simmering, shimmering Salina repeated.
'And everybody,' Myles echoed back to them. 'And maybe one day … everybody's breath will belong to him too.'
Myles waited, and watched. He had never looked at a man as closely as he looked at the pimp opposite him now. On inspection, Louis was really quite a good looking man; with his sharp nose and sharp, small dark eyes that Myles had always found himself drawn to in other men. He had a suspiciously lean frame, diminutive yet hard, a compact little Bond villain in a crisp white shirt. When he looked at Louis he thought of a shark. If Myles had one instinct left, it was to avert his eyes right now. Louis was going to need time.
'Go on then. I accept.'
Myles looked back up, meeting Louis's eyes to check it was really him that said it.
Nonchalant, the pimp grinned back at him. 'What are we going to call it?'
Atlanta exhaled. She put the knife down.
'Dignitas for the daring?'
The girls grappled, chasing each other out for ideas.
'Dignitas for the depraved?'
Inspiration bubbled in the room.
'Dignitas with desires?'
'Diknitas?'
Louis laughed. 'We'll think of something.' He held his hand out to Myles. His band of merry, merciful minxes swelled behind him, watching. 'Let's do it.'

Chapter Forty

3 Months Later

'Why don't you make your mother a nice warm cup of tea?'

Yes. Why don't I.

Erica turned on the tap, filled the kettle with water, flicked it to boil, fetched a pink china mug from the cupboard. Simple, easy movements, but with every one of them her hands shook.

When the kettle was boiled, the promise of liquid agony confirmed, she poured the ghoulish water into the china cup. She dipped in two expensive British tea bags and allowed them to wilt. 'Sorry,' she whispered into the cup. More than ever right now, she felt the tea bags were alive. She doused them in full fat cream, and sprinkled in crystal, iridescent sugar. She added three ginger biscuits to the side of the saucer. Simple, normal, pleasant, mortal movements. Nothing fixes everything like a good cup of tea. And yet as she carried it to her mother, she resisted the urge to hurl it to the floor.

While her mother drank it, she retreated to her room. She sat in front of the mirror and swept her golden hair in front of her. She picked up the brush with her twitching hands, and began gliding it through her locks. It caught, almost instantly, on a brittle nest of tangles.

Not such a popular girl now, are we.

She put the brush down. She tugged at her hair. She willed it to fall.

What am I, if I'm not this?

'You have to leave it now,' her mother had said. 'You can't risk something like that happening to you again. Not for a third time. You can't risk anybody knowing what you can do.'

And so she was just another girl now. Not even a trained nurse. Free to do with her hands as she pleased. To touch herself all day, if she so wished. Free to manicure them, to dig them into crisps. Leave it to the medics. She was normal now.

Not such a popular, pretty girl any more. Everybody gets their moment to be special. Now it was her moment to be safe.

'They don't need you, anyway,' her mother told her. 'What you were doing there was … unnatural. Let the normal order of things play out.'

And maybe it was true, maybe they didn't need her. But in the dead of night, she needed them.

Perhaps her mother would like another cup of tea. Perhaps she should braid her hair. Or knit a scarf. Be dextrous, and delicate, using her hands in some other way.

Normal now.

Are those red ballet shoes, or feet that have been skinned?

She grabbed her coat, leaving the tangles in her hair to cloy together. Perhaps she'd end up having to shave it off; maybe she deserved that now she had no

purpose. She thought perhaps a walk was what she needed. And if she just so happened to come across somebody who was hurting, then so be it.
She burst into the air and set off, thanking the cold.
She reached the road, and watched the cars glide by. Nobody slowed down to see her. Nobody knew she was an accident.
'*Please hit a deer*,' she whispered after one of them, balling up her hands so they were as small as she felt. 'Please, please, please hit a deer and let me save it.'
Animals. She could heal the animals, because animals would never tell.

She walked for half an hour before she saw it. Before the black and white movie of her life came into colour, and that colour was of course red.
A crash on a country road.
The crash went back, eight cars each way. Each car had spun or flipped to bind with the one behind it. In the middle of the collision two cars were propped up in an N shape over each other, threatening at any moment to collapse. It must have been one of them which caused it.
Around a dozen people circled the accident. The lucky ones who had been a minute too late and had escaped any harm, handling themselves with exquisite care as they crept forward to see the mess. Every car window held a different display. They looked in then looked away quickly, hands diving into pockets to pull out phones, their faces turning into symbols of The Winter They Longed To Forget.
Nothing to see here. She was just a girl on a morning walk. An ambulance had already been called, no doubt.
No point interfering.
She walked, dutifully, respectfully to the side of the road, head down as the have-a-go heroes attempted to undo the calamity that had burst into their morning. She heard talk from men of lifting cars; well she was no way strong enough to do that, so, on she went.
Nah.. What help would she be?
As she got closer, not one person turned to look at her. Her beauty could not compete with this tragedy. Every face was either dipped through a car window, trying to help, or buried snivelling in their puffa jacket, unable to look. She took a few more steps, yet nobody sensed her presence.
Good. Nothing to see. Let them do their jobs. No point making the situation more stressful.
Go home. Make another cup of tea. Sign a petition. Relax.
She took another step, and that's when she heard the first moan. It was a moan of a young woman and it opened up her heart.
A man was helping her from her car, his hand propping her up. Over his shoulder was a boy of around five. The man had his phone glued to his ear and was calmly giving instructions; 'We're gonna need a fire brigade, too.'

Just a few weeks ago, she had been both him and her; the damsel and the stallion. She had been something that hadn't even been imagined before: both the hero and the victim, both the saviour and the slave, both the rescuer and the captive.
And what was she now?
Just a passer-by. Awkwardly trying not to get involved.
She kept herself to herself, her hands locked firmly in her pockets, her head down in the granite. Even natural, human curiosity failed in getting her to look up and into the car windows – at all the bloody patisseries waiting for her. The word 'Help' was no longer made for her; it was just a generalised, pre-conditioned idea etched into them. A useless word which they ought to show more patience before using. She couldn't help them. She wouldn't even let herself smell their blood.
She could hear the siren approaching.
All would be well soon.
But what if they're too late?
What if they move someone wrong?
One clumsy angle and they'll be paralysed
What if to cut them out of their car, they have to cut them out of their body?
One of these people could be falling into an unwakeable coma
An hour in surgery
Waking up
'You'll never walk again, I'm sorry sir,'
Unless
Unless I stop it
One touch
I'll never see them again
One touch and I can make it all ok
But remember what mother said
Then they'll know. They'll know what I am. It's not up to me to save them.
They've failed to save me twice now.
If I never heal again, I'll never feel again.
So be it.
I'm not getting captured.
Head down, she pulled her beanie over her ears, blew on her hands and rubbed them together to warm them up.
What would her mother say now? Her mother would tell her to take a deep breath and count to ten. Her mother would tell her to let things play out, the way nature intended. Her mother would tell her to stop being a slave to sympathy, and to get home and into her arms, where she could feed her up, care for her.
She pulled her scarf tighter around her neck. Who was she now?
Normal. Normal people slow down to look.

That was what she told herself when she reached Car Number Five, that she was simply blending in, simply proving she wasn't callous or empty now that she wasn't magical, as she stopped. She was just looking. She followed the drops of blood along the granite, all the way up the car door, and looked into the window. She had seen worse.

Everyone had gathered on the other side of the collision. Something truly tragic must be going up there.

It would take seconds. The window was already smashed. Scurry up, reach in, tap the driver, flick the passenger, and run back.

A pigeon hopped by, landing on the rear-view mirror. 'You won't tell, will you, Mr Pigeon?' she muttered.

Mr Pigeon's head swivelled, a perfect 180 to hers. His tiny eyes looked her up and down.

He flew to her.

She looked him up and down. Did he need her help? His wings were working perfectly, his legs strong, his feathers smooth. He even seemed well fed.

He landed at her feet. He hopped, and turned, and began waddling into the bushes at the side of the road.

Leaving the cars, she followed him.

The fibrous wall of the bush had been blown apart. All the twigs had been flattened. Some kind of clearing had been freshly made. People would have been looking into it with curiosity if it wasn't for the distractions of everything else.

The pigeon hopped down, down, down, a few feet. She held onto branches as she got her balance and travelled down with him. Everything crunched beneath her; she hoped she hadn't stepped on anything alive. The leaves were wet with dew, with slime and with blood.

Like a brand new sketch, she looked at the blood. It wasn't coming from above. It was coming from below.

Encouraged by Mr Pigeon, she continued to weave her way down.

Then she saw something that made her hush out, breathlessly. '*Clever* pigeon,' she whispered. 'Clever, clever boy. Thank you.'

Turns out there had been nine cars in the crash. And this particular one had been spun all the way down the clearing. It hovered only a couple of feet from the next layer of road below.

Moans. She heard them. Fresh, compliant, obedient moans.

There was only one passenger in this car.

The pigeon flew to the window, gazing in it himself. He looked in and then back to Erica.

She braced herself as she walked to the window, preparing herself for the gristle. She was normal. She could look.

So look she did.

Nothing could have prepared her for what was in there.

It was someone she knew.
Someone she had been wanting to hurt for a very, very long time.

Yet again, Erica's mother waited. It had been an hour now, and her daughter was still gone.

It always starts like this. 'Just going for a walk', 'Just going for dinner with Myles', turned into that extra hour, that extra night where she didn't come home. Her daughter wasn't the type of girl who just went for a walk and came back. If she didn't know that by now, she didn't deserve her.

She moved herself closer to the fire. She thought the heat would help, but it only strengthened the contrast of the chill in her bones.

Where was she?

She knew this was hard for her. To not be able to heal. Despite everything that had been done to her, her daughter still wanted to help people. Why couldn't she have got her mother's selfish side?

She looked out of the window. Still nothing.

There had to be some way to replace what she was sacrificing. Maybe she could retrain as a doctor. An … acupuncturist. That only took three years. And they both believed in the holistic approach. Or maybe she could teach her to be selfish. Teach her not to care. Not her life, not her problem.

Did somebody have her, already? Another man's hands around her? A woman's?

No. Not this time.

You're her mother. She's yours. You're not losing her again.

Jumping up, she grabbed her keys. She didn't turn out the lights or put out the fire. She went to the door, her hands shaking, unlocking it, bursting onto the gravel of their driveway. It was getting dark.

Just as she clicked open her car, she saw a car she didn't recognise, careering down the driveway.

Oh god. The police. *Your daughter has disappeared.* Again.

The car sped into the drive like it was trying to get away. The door opened and to her delight, then her confusion, it was Erica who stepped out.

'Darling!' she ran to her, closed her in her arms, ran her hand down her silky hair. 'What's happened? I don't care, I'm so glad you're back! But – '

Then she saw the body, slumped across the passenger seat. The open face. The blood.

'Darling, *no.*' She held her shoulders, shook her. '*No more healing*! We'll get this person inside and then we'll call an ambulance, okay?'

'It's ok mom,' Erica spoke serenely, light, dreamily. 'I'm not going to touch this person. Not today, not tomorrow, I couldn't bring myself to touch them if I tried. You carry them in for me.'

'Okay …'

Her mother opened the door, confused. ‘It’s ok,’ she said to the wounded. ‘Let’s get you inside.’

Erica was suddenly by her side, looking down at the body. ‘I’ll do what you said, mummy.’ She nodded. ‘I’ll never heal anyone again. You get them inside for me. I’ll make the tea.’ She headed to the door, then turned, as her mother struggled with lifting the bruised, cut body. ‘Mummy? Put them in the basement.’

Chapter Forty One

The sad thing was, if Erica had just kept following the trail of the cars, she would never have come across this person who she hated so very much. Had she taken a few more steps, followed the trail a little further, she would have found the supreme sight of the accident - the main 'crunch' shall we say, of the first two cars to collide.

In one car there was Spencer, the eighteen year old girl who had been so delighted to finally have a licence, she'd jumped in her car at midday without a second thought to the fact she'd taken some mushrooms and dropped some acid at only 7am that morning. Make no mistake, it was her that caused the collusion. As with all these ironies, a sprained wrist and a split lip were Spencer's only trophies from the crash - apart from that, she was unharmed.

And then, in the other, beaten down car, there was a man named Myles. Sober, sane Myles, and the only drug in his system was the determination that had got him to drive down these country roads to see Erica again, to see what she thought about his new venture in Paris. Spencer's car had plunged into his, sending it both up on its back wheels and then onto its side. As with all tragedies, it was Myles whose injuries were catastrophic, and Myles who, in the paramedic's opinion, was not going to make it.

But Erica did not keep following the trail, and Erica *did* find the person she wasn't meant to find. And that's how Erica stopped being a victim, and got a victim all of her own. For the first time, Erica was the captor, not the captive. So let's begin.

Chapter Forty Two

The Basement

'Say it.' Erica looked down upon the squirming, blubbering face of her victim. 'Go on. Say the magic word.'

Her victim ground their gums, one time, two times, three times, before managing to etch out the syllables. 'Please, please, s – st – st – '

'Spit it out,' Erica said. 'Or perhaps I'll leave. Come back later.'

'*Nooo*,' the victim gurned. 'St – st – start.'

Start. That was Erica's power. She was not being begged to stop, but to start.

'I'll do anything,' the victim wailed. 'Just – start. Touch me.'

The tip of Erica's finger swelled. Start. Should she? Would she?

'*Pleeeease*,' came the cry. 'Don't go. I need your touch. Touch me.'

'You want it really bad, huh?'

'Yeah…'

'You want these hands all over you?'

'Yes, yes.'

'You want me to touch you? Everywhere? To never stop, huh?'

'Yes, oh god, yes.'

'I bet you do. I bet.'

Her fingertip, etched with lines, plush, plump, cream, cushioned, hovered in the air. And it didn't move an inch.

Wing 808

A little while away, a handsome man lay dying.

People all around him, a friend clutching his hand and a nurse adjusting his drip, he lay deep in the hospital bed, a place he thought he'd never be again, the smell of flowers and cold soup in the air. His friends adjusted for space on the leather chairs around him, as they all tried to process the news the doctor had just told them.

That there was no hope. The internal bleeding had gone too far. That he had a day left, if that.

'Mate,' his friend looked into his eyes. 'We'll get justice. Believe me, we'll get justice.'

He looked at him though it hurt his neck to move it. 'Who was driving the car?'

'It was a girl. A stupid teenager of around nineteen. Coming from a party. She didn't even know how to drive a car that size.'

He lay there for a minute, his head falling deeper into the pillow.

'Was she hurt?'

'No,' the nurse said as she cleared away his water glass. 'Her boyfriend broke his arm though.'

'So they're here?'
The nurse hesitated. 'Yes… a few corridors down.'
'Bring her to me.'
They all looked to one another with confusion, with nerves, with uncertainty. Eventually the nurse spoke.
'I'm afraid we can't do that … we understand this is hard for you but we need to keep the wing calm.'
His cousin stroked his hand. 'We'll be talking to our lawyers next week.'
He shook his head. 'No you won't.'
With a great surge of elbows and shoulders, he sat up in the bed. If this really was his last day, it would be the opposite of what had gone before, the last time he'd been hospitalised.
'Bring her to me. Right now. Get that girl in here.' Myles looked around at them all. 'I want to forgive her.'

The Basement

Stop, stop, stop. That word: *stop.*
Please stop.
Four letters, one syllable, almost onomatopoeic in its nature. Rhymes with pop, drop, flop.
How many times, do we think, has that word been uttered by a victim to their captor? Over and over again, I am sure. An order – sometimes wailed, sometimes whispered, from split lips and torn tongues. It's the only word a victim knows.
Except Erica's victim.
As she looked down upon them, there was only one word in their whole language, blubbering its way up from their smashed face.
'Start.'
That was their word.
'Say it. Say the word.'
'Please, please, please… start.'
'With these hands?' She wiggled them daintily. 'You mean you want these?'
'Yes… please… yes. *Touch me.*'
'Say it again. The word. Our word.'
'St- st – start.' The body laying on the block below her, cracked and fallen like a half-moulded cast, erupted with the syllables. Erica grinned. 'Go on, one more time; what was that? I didn't quite catch it.'

Wing 808

Oh little darling, how she appeared, so timid, so shy, she could barely begin to get around the door frame, she almost stayed behind the glass, couldn't step any closer to the hospital bed, to live in the truth of what she'd done

He'd made sure all his friends had left and allowed her to bring her mother for support, while a male paramedic stood in the corner of the room to jump in if anything went wrong. It was dark now, about 8pm and the wing was silent but for them, killer and corpse.

Little one when she appeared, just how much had she been crying, all those tears over him, what a waste, the lids swollen and damp and the lashes trying not to drown, little one all grey and diminutive, probably lost ten pounds in the past day.

And she was a blonde, just like he'd expected. Just like Taylor had been.

Myles was sitting up ready for her. To her credit, she met his eyes.

'Hi,' he said. 'Horrible weather, isn't it?'

There was fear in her eyes. Who could blame her? She had no idea, he realised, of his emotions towards her. Of what he wanted to do for her today.

He knew just to get herself into this room had to be the most difficult thing she'd ever done. Every step would have made her ankle twist. He knew it was made worse by the fact she'd got out of the accident unscathed; not one bruise, not one ache, to help munch at some of the remorse that had overtaken her life in these past few hours.

'Do you know who I am?' she managed to whisper.

'Of course,' he nodded. 'Spencer. Nice to meet you. I asked for this. You know you don't need to stand so far away from me. Let's at least shake hands.'

He realised her hand was shaking. He ignored that and looked at her eyes. They were swollen.

'Why you so puffy, Spencer? Why you all inflated? What's gonna happen if I pull you in for a hug? You gonna crumple in on me?

Don't do that, girl, you got things to do. Now come here and shake my hand.'

She took one, two, three, four, five, six steps until she was at his bedside and able to look into his eyes and then she crumbled into a mess of the red and the wet.

'Oh god what have I done!' she howled into sobs, bubbling with grief. 'Oh god, oh god, oh god, please, isn't there a way they can make you recover!'

Her mother rushed over, placing her hands to stroke her slender shoulders, but she shrugged them off and balled into the leather chair next to his bed, the leather splintered and cracked almost as much as her conscience.

It hurt but he pulled himself up further in the bed.

'Shh, shh, enough, enough of that. No more tears. You hear me? I put a ban on crying in this room. You think you can do that for me?'

Through her snorts, through her judders, she attempted a nod.

'Good.' Myles beamed. 'Now I want you to listen to me.'

The Basement

Should she? Would she? Could she?

Start?

Erica's fingers hovered in the air, suspended sixteen inches from the ribcage of her victim. They danced in the dust and were illuminated long and slender, in the light getting through the cracks of her cellar.
Start, start, start. Just touch, touch, touch. Or don't.
She lowered her finger and her victim moaned, before the finger came to a brisk stop, now a mere inch from their sternum. They reached up, straining, greedy to connect with the finger, straining so hard Erica could hear the bones in their back shuffling to close the imperfect gap. But Erica had timed the distance perfectly, and they couldn't reach. Tantalising, insulting, the abyss of air stood strong.
'I just don't know what to do,' Erica sighed. 'I mean, I guess I *could* touch you. Indeed I could.'
Touch. That word seemed holy, spoken at this moment.
'But I just don't know, after what you did. I just don't know if I want to.'
She kept staring down, watching with fascination as her victim's lips contorted into new shapes and made new sounds.
'After what you did. I just don't know if it's the right thing for me.'
'*Please*,' came the wail, even more pitiful than the last. 'Don't go. Don't stop. Start.' The voice was muffled, every syllable a fight. 'I need your hands.'
'What's that?' she mocked. 'You want a glass of water? Something to eat? Why of course.'
With that, she got up and left. Slamming the door. Ignoring the sobs.

Wing 808

'Look at you, with all those red crystals in your eyes, with all that black pelt in your brain.
Trust me when I tell you I'm going to take all that away and I'm going to fill you with nothing but crisp blue oxygen, nothing but cool clean air.
All those salty shards gathering where your lashes should be, all that tangled moss rolling behind your brows. It's done.'
She shuddered. Something in his tone told her he knew exactly what she was feeling - that the man she mangled could see every flagellating thought inside of her.
Little did she know, he was going to take it all away.
'I know you don't believe me and I know you don't have reason to but you might as well get used to it; today, I'm taking all that out and I'm filling you with something so light, something so transparent - that after I'm done with you you'll be able to float.
My words are made of feathers and I was wondering when I would finally get to use them. I wrote them almost a year ago and it turns out you're the one I wrote them for. I feel like you're my child, my little freckled killer, because I know

everything you're feeling and I know how much it hurts and I know it feels like the weight is about to drive you into the ground. But it won't.
I understand I must look weak, mangled, pale, and it's hard to trust a man threaded with tubes, but the words I'm going to speak are words made for you and they're the most important words you'll ever hear in your life: so pass me my water, and let's get started.
You were driving the car, I hear? And it was acid you took, I believe? How much?' Spencer could only answer with nods, with holding up her fingers, three this time. Myles grinned, throat rolling; 'Whoa – that must have been fun. Was it your idea or your friends? Ah, the boyfriends. And what did that pill feel like in your brain – loose, adventurous, nice, I believe, yes? Pretty vibey, pretty giddy, pretty good? I thought so.
I can see it now.
Just a young girl, riding through the night, with wind in her hair and pills on her tongue. I bet you looked wild. I bet those eyes were bluer than they are red right now.
And you look at me now and you *think that I* – as if you know me – that I would look back at you and you think, *little darling*, that I wouldn't want you to fly high?' He shook his head. A flicker of hope landed in her mother's face as he continued, calmly self-deprecating, 'Who am *I* to stop you from flying?'
She still wasn't meeting his eyes. She rubbed her face into the chair, willing herself to wake up from this nightmare.
'I know how you feel, little one. I know you think: that's it. It's done. It's over. I'll never be warm again. I'll never be rested again. There's a before and after and this is the after: this is it: goodbye life, goodbye joy, goodbye Spencer.
Nah.
Look me in the eye when I tell you: this may be 'after' but this is only the 'beginning' of who I want you to become.
This is how you're gonna honour my memory: by letting it become a kind of poison. A poison made specifically for anything you fear. Anything you are too shy to do, anything that makes you hesitate – kill it. Let me kill all those parts of you, it's only fair.'
Somehow, she managed to peel her face off the chair, and meet his eyes.
'That's my wish, Spencer.
Find out just how good a person can feel. Find out just how much pleasure one person can take.
Save those tears for the thousands of boyfriends who'd be lucky to have you. Save your 'sorrys' for the neighbours you keep up from too many nights of partying. Save that lawyer money for a visa lawyer when you spend a year living abroad. Save it and forget me. Forget me, forget today, forget the car. You hear me? Six minutes of spinning around in a car doesn't change the fact that you still matter. You'll never think of me again after today.
You think I'm the kind of man who wants to bury you with me?

Never.' He caught the eyes of her mother, stunned in the corner as she watched him work his spell into the crushed, crumbled carcass of her daughter. Could the girl even process what he was doing?

'Oh, I see, you thought it was time to relax, didn't you?' He teased, putting on her voice, "My name's Spencer and I'll never party again. I must wear black and sit in silence and live in regret and take courses about responsible drinking and maybe one day I'll adopt a child and raise it perfectly to never make the mistakes I did.' Well, let me tell you, Spencer, you don't get to give up that easy.

Baby, baby, baby, stop dripping, stop leaking, stop spilling that saline all over the place, stop gushing, stop soaking, don't bloat; *I want you to float.'*

He pulled at the tubes keeping him bound to the bed, a sterile feeling going up his arm. She looked at him in anguish as some part of the bed buzzed in response.

'Shh. It's ok. I can't bear to see you stand in front of me and cry your life away over a mistake. I want you to be free.'

And as he said that, the beeps of his monitor started to slow.

The Basement

An hour later, Erica returned to her victim.

She did the cruellest thing she could possibly do.

She put on a glove.

It was a thin glove, the thinnest she could find. A white glove for a lady who liked to drink tea and carry a parasol – not a glove for this. It was knitted through with the finest, most dextrous lace found only in India, each thread hand crafted to form the pattern of a butterfly or a vine. The mottled white lines caressed each finger and kept them in a delicate cage, like they were the most precious fingers in the world. Which of course they were.

She almost didn't go through with it. When she saw the hope burn in her victim's eyes, when they thought freedom had finally come, she realised what she hadn't anticipated. They probably thought the gloves were part of the ritual, part of the treatment, that they made everything special.

When her finger landed on the crooked arms and she began tracing and swirling, drawing spirals, letters and figures of eight up and down them, and then when her victim realised that there was nothing, no change, no release, nothing but the lukewarm abrasion of lace across skin, they turned the room dark with doom. Erica let them howl.

She simply watched as scuffs of dead skin and tissue that was now turning old fast, caught and clung to the tips of the gloves. Blood, both the dried black raisins of it and new wells of cranberry juice, ran through the lace, fighting for the cracks, pooling in and finding her hand, til there was no white left.

‘I’m sorry,’ Erica sighed, ‘But I just love lace, don’t you? It’s just … exquisite. So gentle. So feminine. It took me ages to find a glove like this.’ She traced a pattern along her victim’s broken spine, tip toeing her fingers up and down. Even when she applied pressure, the lace still preserved her powers. ‘I feel like the world’s best bride in it. I think whoever asked me to marry them right now, I’d say yes to them.’ Gliding her hand around, she stirred lightly into what was left of their hip bone, the threads catching on their deepest cuts. ‘With a glove like this you can’t be anything but tender, anything but kind, anything but beautiful. Maybe one day you’ll know how it feels to wear a glove like this.’ She lifted her finger but the fine china of their bones clung to one of their threads. She gasped. ‘Oh - careful now - you might unravel them. These gloves are very, very important to me; we wouldn’t want to create a hole, would we?’ Moaning, her captive fought for what little strength they had, to hook into the threads. ‘Oh no, careful now - that’s it, steady as we go -’ Erica flicked her hand up; a thread snapped and a bone snapped too. ‘Alright, there, there, shh, not to worry’ she held her hand up to the light, admiring the glove, still tightly intact. ‘Not too much damage.’

‘Erica. *Please.*’ Their breath bubbled. ‘I’m sorry! I’m so sorry for what I did! I wish I could take it back! But tell me what I have to do now. There has to be something that will make you want to touch me.’

Erica smiled, now using her hand to cup their cheek, the embroidery of the glove a disinfectant that kept their interactions sterile. ‘But I have lace, and lightness, and love, and life. And everybody loves me. What can touching you give me that I don’t already have?’

They wrestled, their cheek grinding into her hand, the lace becoming sandpaper. ‘You can’t just leave me like this. You can’t just let me gnarl and gnarl until I’m a husk. You have to take the pain away, or you have to let me go.’

‘Ah, but that’s where you’re wrong,’ Erica laughed into the dust. ‘I don’t ‘have’ to do anything. Nothing I don’t want to do. Nobodies ever gonna use me again.’

‘Then let me go!’ they whimpered.

‘But, darlin,’ she smiled, moving her hand from them to pick up a pastel box she had brought down with her. ‘I didn’t forget. I got you something to eat.’ Her hand sticky with their blood, she untied the ribbon from the box, closing a red handprint around the lid before pulling it off with a flourish. ‘Mint macaroons,’ she whispered. ‘So naughty. Such an indulgence. What are we like? Come; open wide. You don’t have much strength. I’ll feed you.’

With a deep glare into doom, the captive realised it really might be like this forever. That they would exist in a pain made intricately internal, by the tease of an anaesthesia that would never come.

Obedient, they parted their lips. Erica swarmed over them, ‘ooh, poor thing, let me get that,’ and with the betrayal of her glove, plucked a barely perceptible shard of glass out of their gum. ‘This lace is everything, you know. We can do anything now I’ve found it. We can even kiss. But for now, let’s eat.’ And Erica held the perfectly symmetrical, edible little vessel to their mouth - a cool crisp green, their favourite flavour - 'Bite it.' Into it they bit, their lips collapsing around it, catching her fingertips where their teeth slit the treat in two. They realised too late there *was* a tiny hole, forming in the gloves. And if it hadn't been for the sugar, and the spearmint, and pastry, and cream, all of the pain would have been over there and then.

Wing 808

The beeps were getting further apart and it was getting harder to stay sitting up, but Myles was not deterred from his mission.
He was an expert at this feeling. He had lived it himself. And he knew, looking at Spencer, that she wasn't convinced. She couldn't let the guilt go.
He had to make sure to do this right. He had to give her back her life, with some kind of genius inside himself that could figure out how to defeat her regret for good. Right now she just saw his words as a kindness she wasn't worthy of - he had to change that.
That's when it came to him. He needed to tell her about his mother.
In a hospital room that only got greyer and greyer, an idea formulated in his mind, about how he would turn off the leak in this poor girl's eyes.
He had maybe two hours left, and nothing else mattered but getting his killer to forgive herself.
'Okay,' he said. 'There's one more thing I need to tell you. I didn't want to say it because I don't like to jinx it, but screw it. I'm so close now that I'm not afraid any more. Spencer, come here. Sit on the bed. Hold my hand. Have you ever been in love?'
She shook her head.
'Course not, you're only young. I didn't even really like anyone when I was your age. There is one woman I need to tell you about, though.
My mother. Don't panic, she's not here; I can't deny she'd be a little cross with you, but she'd calm down once she heard this. You wanna know the best thing about her?'
Spencer, grateful to have something to distract her, looked up. Her eyes were stretched wide like she was asking him to pour something in them. Something to blind her so she didn't have to see herself.
'She loved me back. One hundred per cent, unconditional, undiluted love. I couldn't believe I was able to feel this warm, this free, this safe, in someone else's delicious love. I knew I would never let it go.'
Spencer nodded. He was convincing her.
'And then one day, I had to.
It was just a routine check up, just a visit to the GP to get our jabs before I took her abroad. Except it wasn't. Except that was the last day everything was ok. That was the day they found an incurable brain tumour that ravaged her from

the inside out with breakneck speed.' His throat filled up. He paused. *Steady now.*
'She was dead seven months later. Those last months we tried to do everything we loved together, but the disease folded her in two. She couldn't talk much but she did manage to say one thing … "I'll see you on the other side."'
He adjusted, getting more into character. The little blood left in his veins swilled around, bruising him instantly.
'Over a year I've been waiting, Spencer. To be with her again.
Every night when I put my head on the pillow, I'd rather not wake up then have to get up in this cold world without her.
I've been a real mess since she left.'
He held out his hand. To his delight, this time, Spencer took it. Something pressed down on his lungs, but still he managed to speak.
'Little did I know when I woke up today it was finally time.
I'd finally served enough time without her.
Not long to wait now. I can feel it.
And it's you, Spencer, *you* did that for me. You're the reason I get to see her again. It was all you. You've done what God couldn't. You've made my dreams come true. You've bought us back together. This was meant to be.'
Spencer snorted. For the first time, he heard her real voice, a voice with a lilt to it. 'You mean … you mean you're really happy to die?'
'It's not dying. It's reuniting.' A red light began flashing above his head. He ignored it, and he leaned forward, making sure Spencer would ignore it too.
'There's one more thing you must do for me … don't let my legacy be tears, Spencer. Let the last thing I do be lift you up. Let today be the reason you go on to be a person that burns so damn bright. Let me legacy be forgiveness; let my legacy be mercy; let me legacy be passion; you're gonna walk out of this room so you can pass that passion on. You get it?'
Spencer grinned and wiped her eyes. 'I get it.'
He winked. 'Little darling, I never would have let ya stub yourself out.'
She looked at him with a smile, a smile so confused, a smile dried through layers of caramelised tears. 'Okay. Let's do it.'
As her lips finally found their smile, Myles veins finally found their rest. In perfect unison: as Spencer gave up on guilt, oxygen gave up on Myles.

Above The Basement

She was still wearing the hoodies and jeans when she'd returned from her car earlier. Grease was gathering in her plaits and she hadn't showered since getting in with the body. Nor had she eaten. It was only 8pm but it was pitch black outside.
Maybe it was time to have a shower. Or eat. Or both.
But that meant moving from the bed, and getting out of the dark, and removing the onion scent of her sin that she had grown fond of the past few hours, a scent

that suited her and her secret downstairs. She couldn't picture herself going into her kitchen, bustling around with the lights on, cutting a loaf of bread and looking for toppings, while all the while a girl was buried alive beneath her. There was one thing she could do, though. She'd already done it four times today - what was a fifth? All she had to do was roll to her side, pull out her phone and she could do it. She would sign the petition calling for another vote on Assisted Suicide, the one that wanted to reverse the decision, on the website that was building momentum every day. Because once she took that from them, then they'd realise there was only one E word that mattered, only one that they needed, and only one thing that could make everything better: *Erica.*

Wing 808

It was not lost on Myles how symmetrical his final moment was. The worst moment of his life had been when he believed he'd taken the life of Rose - he remembered the agony every day. There was no better reward than knowing he'd been able to take that agony from somebody else before he died.

'Rumble, young girl, rumble.'

And as Myles watched the young girl rise from the chair, back finally straight, eyes finally dry, and take the hand of her amazed mother, he thought about telling them how much she reminded him of the other girl he thought he killed once. Taylor. How the memory used to pop the boils in his mind, how he would go to a place so dark he didn't remember it..

But looking at the glow, listening to the swish in her hair, he realised there was no need for that. And the beeps of his monitor were getting really far apart now. His vision was getting blurry too. He definitely didn't have enough strength in him for another monologue.

So he laughed instead, 'don't you even think about coming to my funeral!' - 'oh don't worry, I'll be sleeping off a hangover!' -, practically singing to her as she went to the door;

'You're Spencer the Cannibal now. Get out there and tear them limb from limb.'

She gave him one final look. One final wink. There's that sparkle. And then she was gone.

Myles flopped back into the bed, blissful. Mission accomplished just as his heart started to burn.

Level completed. Body defeated. Nothing left to do but die.

The Basement

When the victim awoke, all they could think about was Touch.

Would they ever be touched again?

They'd been touched so many times and they'd touched so many. Push, pull, kiss, chase.

In the darkness of the cold cellar, all those touches they'd taken for granted piled up into useless, weak memories that meant nothing. There was only one pair of hands in the world that mattered. And they were upstairs right now.

'Please,' they whispered. Maybe Erica was in the dark, watching them. 'Even just a slap. Just one. Slap me with all you've got, and that way we both win.'

What was it about the bitches hands? Did she take care of them, or did she not need to? Did she cream them at night, working cucumber balm into her cuticles? Did she always wash them after? Did she dip them in petrol? Just what did she do that made those goddamn hands so special?

If the victim ever got the chance, if they ever got out of here, they'd cut them off.

Above The Basement

An antelope fought an ant. The ant won. It became the ant queen and then it was devoured by the clouds. A bigger antelope came back for revenge. It grew horns so big they pierced through ghosts. The antelope danced with the devil on its back. A ballerina leapt over them and an opera singer collapsed to a heap on the ground.

Or maybe this was all just shapes that the flames formed in the fire. The fire that Erica's mother looked into all day before she fell asleep in front of it. The fire that went snap, crackle and pop.

Able to get lost in the performance of the fire, she didn't have to think about what was going on under the floor beneath her. She didn't have to think about what her daughter had been doing, every time she disappeared in the cupboard under the stairs that led to the cellar. She could pretend the screams were coming from what she was throwing into the fire.

Toys. Erica's childhood toys. One by one, she chucked them in and watched them melt. The girl in her house was a child no more.

Her upper lip had been sweating for twenty hours straight. She had never imagined a world where she would feel so disgusting that she wouldn't even want to reach up and wipe it, but today was that day. All she could do was look into the fire, and wait for this to stop.

A noise beside her. It was Erica, placing another cup of tea by her side. Steaming. She couldn't bring herself to admit how much she longed for a cold water instead. Erica was just leaving when she gripped her wrist. Ashy fingerprints.

'Erica,' she hissed, looking into the eyes of a daughter she knew was kind, gentle, loving, perfect. 'I want you to get her out of my house.'

Erica snatched her wrist away.

'Is this my fault?' Her mother asked her. 'I told you not to be you. But I never told you to be … *this*.'

A herd of zebra's galloped past. Apples fell from a tree. The tree dissolved and in its place grew a sea which parted. Concert goers cheered and danced. A bee hive was bombed.

'You're dripping, mother.' Erica replied. 'You need to get out of the heat.'

'Let her go,' she looked at her. Embers sparked out and caught her. She didn't flinch. 'Enough now. I can understand maybe some part of you needed this, or maybe she even deserved some of this, but that's it now. Do you hear me?'

Erica shook her head. 'But mother, every time I help them I get hurt.'

'Let me then. I'll go down. I'll drive her to a hospital, far away. No one will know where she came from.'

'You know that's not safe.'

'What do you suggest we do then? Oh god, what are we going to do?'

Erica shrugged. Her mother sighed a sigh only a mother could sigh. 'Erica. Who is she? Who is the girl in our basement?'

Erica reclined into her own sweat, stretching. Let's see how it felt to say it. 'Her name is Rose. Rose Markham. And - trust me, mummy - she deserves this.'

Erica felt the surprise of satisfaction as she pictured Rose's face, foaming with the fahrenheit of fear, and giggled as she remembered she had her greatest love rival in her basement.

'Erica, nobody deserves this. You must see that.'

Oh but she did. It had to be done. It was written in scripture. You see, ever since that night when she'd taken Myles from Hawaii to London, when she'd revealed what Rose had done to him, the forgiveness and altruism that Myles had shown, had grown a tumour in Erica, an injustice that lingered in her bowls. Despite the happiness they had shared afterwards, despite everything that had happened since, and despite the fact that Rose had technically never done anything to her, she couldn't sift off the feeling: that it wasn't right. That there couldn't be fairness until Rose paid a price.

And if Myles wouldn't make her pay, then Erica would.

'Nobody deserves to be mangled in an accident and then deprived of healing.'

Anger swelled in her mother's eyes. 'And what you are doing to her … the deprivation, the taunting, the manipulation, what you are putting her through … nobody could ever, ever deserve that. You're breaking her body and her mind. Imagine what's happening to her spirit.'

Erica tossed her plaits, curling one around her small hands. 'But she *does*, mummy. You don't get it. And all I'm doing is nothing. Nobody else is healing her either. I'm just like everyone else. I'm not violent, mummy.'

'Was she?' her mother questioned. 'Was she violent with you?'

'No.'

'With anyone?'

'No.'

'Erica!'

'But she was worse than violence. She was trauma. She conjured the worst emotions in the world and she forced someone to take them. She chose emotional pain as her weapon and she won. So it's only fair to reward with her physical pain. Let her wallow in it.'

Wing 808

Moments after Spencer left, Valentina entered his room through the window. She had been watching the whole thing, every moment of Myle's interaction with the crying girl. *That's my man.*

Gently, she pitched herself on his bed, finding his hand. She held it as his breath got weaker.

All he could do was smile. '*That was it*,' he said. 'That's what I needed to do. Not save someone's life. Not resurrect someone. Not kill someone with a kiss. But find someone in the place I was in last year, and take them out of it. Forgive them.'

Valentina kissed his forehead.

'I want to do it again,' he gulped. 'I want more.'

The Basement

'Erica. *Stop.*'

As she descended the staircase, Erica realised her mother was already in here, standing in front of the body. Not just standing in front of, but guarding, Rose. The sharpness in her mother's voice caused her to pause and give a petulant sigh. 'What?'

She hopped down the final steps, smug as ever. When she entered the cellar, Erica realised her mother was holding the letter. 'This came for you this morning,' she said. 'Signed from somebody called Darren Thames.'

A frisson glided over her. She'd heard rumours that Darren Thames had escaped Core the day before she did, but it had never become public knowledge so she'd never quite believed them. If he'd made it out, she'd assumed Eli had found some way to exert a hold over him and silence him. So why was he contacting her now?

Ignoring the groans in the background, she took the letter from her mother and began unravelling it. 'You're sure? *Darren Thames*?'

'Yes,' her mother's voice was sharp, cold, tight. 'And one more thing.'

Erica's hands, usually so superior, were shaking as she read the first line. She could hear his melodic tone from here. *Hello Erica.* 'What?' she flicked the words absentmindedly at her mother.

'A phone call came for you too just now. About Myles. You're listed as his next of kin.'

That worthless word, Myles, bit her heart, nipped around it to expose the core. Forgetting to inhale, she choked out, 'What's happened?'
Her mother paused just long enough to see a tear fall; a tear that let her know her daughter could still feel. And then she said it.
'He's been in an accident.'
'What?' Erica whipped around and the room whipped with her, the ground coming up to meet her. She looked up at the long tall steps of the cellar, separating her from him. 'Myles? You're sure? Which hospital?
Her mother didn't respond.
'I need to get to him.'
Before she could stand, two thick fudgy ankles stood in front of her. Her mother, boring down on her. 'Not until you heal her.'
'What?' The colour ripped out of her. The wind tripped on her tongue.
'Darling, please. Just put an end to this.'
Erica turned to where her mother gestured and for the first time, she saw it. What she had done.
The broken, blubbering, bloated body of the Rose she was letting rot. All the passionate rage she felt for Myles had turned the brown eyed, blonde haired vixen into something unrecognisable. While the rage danced on within her, it was replaced by something she couldn't recognise, an urgency she'd never felt before. Just what did Myles do to her?

All her humanity came back at once.

With a running jump, she launched herself onto the bound body of Rose. Smack, she landed; wrist to wrist, stomach on stomach, knees on knees, flesh to flesh. She raced her hands up and down, touching the calves, shaking the hands, rubbing the face, warming her up like she was a snack.
'I'm so sorry,' She crumbled into her. Red and gross. 'I'm here now. I'm sorry.' She swirled her hands, lay them on her bare flesh. 'We're going to take it all away.'
She ground her, kneaded her, stroked her, choked her, rolled her over and did it all over again. She closed her eyes as she did it. These injuries had been festering, feeding on themselves, forming a colony; it was too many angles to watch come back together at once, too many blisters to watch drain without retching, too many smells to turn into syrup if you couldn't focus.
'No, I'm sorry,' her jaw fixed, Rose could speak again. 'Tell Myles I'm sorry. Erica - go. You have to save him.'
'Don't you worry about that,' her mother chanted from the corner. 'You just focus on getting better.'
Erica winced as she heard a crack. Oh. Wait. That wasn't a crack. That was a moan.
A moan of pleasure, so sharp and strong in the air it sounded like a bone.

Then another, then another. Enough to get Erica to open her eyes.
Rose was in ecstasy. She was writhing in it. All agony sacrificed on the altar of euphoria, the altar of Erica, the only girl who could do this for people.
'Steady now. There's just a few cuts to go.'
'*Whatever you say, Healer. I'm all yours.*'
Erica grinned. And, head back, laughing, she became The Healer one more time.

Chapter Forty Three

Erica ran through the hospital. When she finally reached the room Myles was in, a woman with pink hair leaned on the wall outside, who took one look at her and said, 'Just leave him alone, Erica.'
She slammed Valentina into the wall, but she didn't react, just smirked. 'Ooh, I'm being touched by The Healer. Is it as good as they say?'
Erica looked around desperately. 'Is he in there? Is he ok?'
'So tell me, Erica. What made you come back for him?'
'I heard he was dying. I needed to help him. After everything he's been through …'
'But you left him.'
Erica stepped back, loosening her grip, calming down. 'Who *are* you, anyway? Did Eli send you?!'
'Absolutely not. I have no time for that man.' Valentina started braiding her hair. 'I've been everything yet I've never really been anything.'
'Who are you?! Why are you here?!'
'I want to know if my kiss will kill him.'
'WHAT?!'
'I need to know. Because he seems too good for it but nobody is too good for death. Then again … look at him.'
And look they did, through the glass window. He lay peacefully. He had lost consciousness an hour ago.
'Did he do this on purpose? Did he get hurt because of me, to find me?'
'Oh Erica. Always thinking about yourself. Always making it about yourself.'
'Shut up. You're creepy!'
'Creepy. I like that. It makes a change from pretty.' She ran a hand over Erica's face, tracing the angular, arctic fox features. 'Come in then.'
She opened the door to his room. Erica entered. It took her breath away, seeing him again.
They squared off around the bed.
'You missed it,' Valentina said. 'You missed what he just did. He forgave the person who crashed into him. It was the best thing I've ever seen.' She sighed and sat gingerly on the end of the bed. 'I'm not going to stop you, Erica. I want him to be saved just as much as you.'
'Just try and stop me – '
'He's got about an hour left. Maybe less. The bleeding is internal, and they say he already lost most of his blood.'
'I'll save him. I'll heal him. I'll put him back together, I swear.'
'Do it.
But after that, I think you should leave. He would have done anything to get you back. He would have burned himself alive. You hurt him so much when you left him on the boat, after everything he did for you. See, you're not good for him,

Erica. You drag him down into your mossy, messy world. He should be truly free. I think I should put a scorpion inside you, just to show you how it feels. You can choose how it enters you, ear or eyes or other, but one way or another, it's going in. See, you don't impress me, Erica.'
Erica sat on the bed. 'And you don't scare me.' She made sure not to touch him. Together, they weighed nothing. Their hair swept the floor.
'No?' Teeth burning white, Valentina sneered. 'Would it scare you if I told you that your man IS a murderer? That he did kill Rose, and Taylor?' She clapped her hand over her mouth, eyes wide and mocking. 'And then that I went back in time and erased it all, so you could do your big 'reveal' and he could be happy again? You see, I'm an angel too.' Too much information, too quick, too mean, too true, too false, too much.
Erica looked up slowly. Did it make sense, did it make sense.
The question Myles had asked her immediately after the reveal, the one she'd been able to say no to so completely - could someone else have done that instead?
She gulped. This woman was expecting her to fight, to deny it, but Erica knew better, and she didn't want to know more.
'If that's true, he can never know.'
Valentina smiled. 'It's not.' And then, 'Or maybe it is. Maybe that man you've let love you is a killer all along. Maybe Rose and Jack never did anything wrong until I made them.
Maybe I've got more magic than you.
Maybe all the ecstasy he feels is cos I gave him a second chance; I took away his sin because I knew he needed another chance. So I brought them back. I took it away. I changed the past. I changed the laws of the universe for him. I played with time and space to make him innocent again. And I was right; he deserved it. He is good.'
Maybe.
Maybe she did do that.
'Or maybe I didn't. And this is all a game.'
So many things, so much logic, twisted and unravelled underneath Erica. How had *no one* contacted Myles when he left his life? How had Rose gotten away with taking all his assets? Such blatant framing, such fraud? How would Jack and her have been so sure he wouldn't touch the body, wouldn't discover the doll that night? And ...why didn't Myles fight for more of a comeuppance for them? Not a hint of revenge in him, never? How would he have felt that guilt in his body, with the depth he did, if he hadn't done it? And come to think of it, is it possible that someone can just *stop* getting blackouts? That a vacation could just instantly cure you of dissociative fugue? And Ian the actor - would an actor really risk his career to torment someone he'd never met? And could the relief of being 'innocent' really have dissolved any desire, any at all, for vengeance? Is that possible? Really? *How?*

But then again, maybe this woman, this angel, was just playing with her. Just telling her all this to get her to fall out of love. Ha. If only she knew how far she had fallen. Maybe this was all a ruse to get a rival out of the way. From one rival to the next. But then again. Maybe not.

'He can never know.' She repeated to the woman. '*If* you did do that, you can't take it away from him. He has to be innocent.' She pressed her finger to Valentina's lips, silencing her. 'He can never know.'

Valentina raised an eyebrow. 'Right answer, Healer. Maybe you *do* love him.'

Erica's eyes crisped over, half scab, half snowflake. 'I *do*,' she said, her voice cracking. 'I do, and yet I left him. I left him when he saved me from Eli, and now this happened. You know this accident was half a mile from my house? He was probably on his way to see me - '

Valentina laughed at her. 'Oh, *now* you're crying,' she giggled. 'You've got it all wrong, sweetheart. You've got nothing to worry about. If you love him then he's yours. All I can do is kill him with a kiss. You're the one who can bring him back.' She was at the window again, her leg swinging over it. 'He has to choose one of us eventually. I'm gonna let him choose you.'

Erica wiped her eyes, feeling the heady sadness rush back into her, mopping her around. 'Why?'

'Cos I know a soulmate when I see one.' Valentina's eyes hardened. 'Just don't let the mob get him, Erica. Ever. Promise me.'

'I promise.'

Valentina flicked her hair. 'Kiss him before I change my mind.'

Erica launched over to the bed. Done with waiting, done with hesitating, done with the boredom of breaking her own heart, she bent over at the waist and launched her face into his, and, lucky, so fucking lucky to be able to do this, she kissed him. The man, her man, with the jaw, with the stubble, she had dreamed of kissing all her life, with the lips that made sense around hers, with the only skin she would swap for her own, and as the music of a kiss went through her, she almost buckled to her knees as she realised he had started kissing her back. His hand was gliding into her hair, tightening around the roots, his lips working with hers, his skin warming up beneath her, his hand cupping her jaw and kissing her with the confidence that only he had to send liquid electricity all the way through her. His other hand was even reaching for her thigh, so big it closed around it.

When they pulled apart, Valentina had gone.

'Erica,' he said. Cheeks flushed, voice full, the internal bleeding a mere and stupid memory now.

Erica cut over him before he could continue, 'I'm sorry,' she whispered. 'I'm *so sorry, Myles.* I don't know why I left you like that, but ever since then, I've needed you. Without you, I've become somebody nobody could love.'

'Impossible.'

'Trust me, Myles. I've become a bit of a bitch!'

Myles looked at her for a second before bursting out laughing. 'I see, I see,' he purred. 'Well, I'm gonna have to experience this new spicy side of you soon then.'
'No, you don't understand,' Erica shook her head. 'I just - '
'Erica.' Now Myles interrupted her. 'You think I care? You think I care what you've done? You think we should spend our life apologising, feeling guilty, feeling small? Is that what you basically just resurrected me for? Or was it so we could *live?* Like you said to me the night you took me back to London.' He took her hand. 'Let's live, baby girl. Let's go.'
With a swing of her hair, the guilt went away. Erica grinned at him. His eyes flashed back.
'There's nothing you could do that could make me not love you.'
Erica straddled him on the bed. 'Luckily for you, all I want to do is *this.'*

Finally, when they had done it until they could think of no more ways to do it, when finally they were willing to speak instead of touch, Myles told her about his plans for Paris. Then Erica did what she needed to do.
She took a deep breath, and she showed him the letter Darren had sent her from Core.

'Just before Valentine's Day,' Cupid said to herself. 'They did this to me just before Valentine's Day.'
She saw a plane fly over her head. 'Oh Myles. If only our sex had been creamier.'
She saw a teenage couple on a rollercoaster, kissing. When they tried to pull apart, their lips fused together. They couldn't separate without ripping each other's jaws open. When they finally managed it, they pulled apart just in time to see their carriage, spinning off the tracks and falling through the air.
She saw a man with a crush on a co-worker. The moment he decided he was smitten, he became invisible. Still he followed her, and she ran and she ran, convinced she was being haunted by a ghost. When he realised he was invisible, he cried til she drowned in his tears.
She saw a man propose and his girlfriend say yes. His heart swelled and swelled til his head turned blue and he burst. When the police came, nobody would believe she hadn't done it to him. Because she was sitting on the pavement, eating his heart whole.
She saw a girl who could not give her boyfriend an orgasm, who became possessed with the desperation to try, who tried and tried til she started to age, faster and faster. He opened his blissful eyes and the girl on top of him had the body of a geriatric. He screamed and, heartbroken, she started to rot on top of him.
She could keep going all night. She could do this for hours. This was all she had: the opposite of love.

Chapter Forty Four

Jill was summoned to Eli's office.

'If we want her back, you know what we have to do. We have to give her something to save.'

Jill sipped her tea. 'I agree. And we need to get her attention.'

'I knew you'd understand.' Eli poured her more tea. 'So. Name the worst place for a bomb to go off.'

Jill thought. 'A church? The UN? A … a *nursery*?'

'Good. All true.' Eli leaned forward. 'Now name the best.'

Jill took a guess.

'Very good. Correct answer. That's what you'll do for me. It'll be like it's going off inside you.'

Part Four
The Bomb

Chapter Forty Five

Valentine's Day

Pink turns to black.
Wet turns to burnt.
Consider this a lesson learnt.

There were few worse places to be on February 14th. I mean really – name some, I'll wait. The pallid grey walls, fermented with years of nerves and shame; the squeaky chairs, the annoying TV, the bloated water cooler. And the people. All sitting under the web of some invisible, judgemental God, who were pretty sure their prayers were the kind he didn't like to answer – after all, it was them that had played roulette with their own fate.

This groin of thorns.
This pelvic persecution.
Turns out 'no strings' was all an illusion.
Fuck me, Faust,
Bring me the contract, Mephistopheles.
I'll say anything, sign anything, again I'm on my knees,
If you clear it up,
Do anything for you to heal it up,
You big tease!
Bet you never realised how much fun you could have with the word 'Please'.

The men in jeans, the women … in jeans. You didn't dare wear a short skirt or cute dress in this place, think of how that would look. Everybody tossed a couple of glances at the person opposite or next to them, half of them wondering why the other was there and half of them hoping they weren't giving away why they were. But it passed the time. The chairs took the weight of the rest of the boredom.

There was Cam, for example. It was on a Perspex chair like this one that Cam had been ridden by his sister-in-law. Experiencing the 'naughty younger sister' had been a fantasy of his for years, but he never thought it would actually happen. Until last Tuesday it had. It had been everything he'd hoped for … but he hadn't been able to have a proper piss since. The 'naughty' sister indeed. *Serves you right*, he scribbled on his form.

Or there was Kate. Kate, unlike Cam, was a loyal girl and this was her third time at this particular clinic. Once for a sensible check-up and once for a suspicious yellow coating on her tongue. Both times had been false alarms and she'd walked out feeling sexier than ever. But this time felt different, and she was sure she wouldn't get so lucky. All she could do now was sit here and look forward to getting answers, about why, after the best weekend away of her life, all that electric love was now turning into an electric itch. One thing was for sure though; she'd accept nothing less than an overnight cure, because Kate was 'perfect down there'. She'd been told that since her first time, and she wasn't gonna let that change now.

Even the receptionist had a glum expression on her face, every name she called out sounding grimmer. That is until the double doors to the waiting room swung open for the hundredth time that day, and a man in black stepped through.

'Flowers for … Bella!'

Thirty depressed faces looked up in surprise. For the females, that turned to naïve hope – could it be? Even now? That someone had remembered them, today, but then how would they know they were here –

'Oh, that's me. Thank you!'

Ah, of course. Just another insult that on a day like today, they were here instead of being taken to a rooftop restaurant or receiving a bouquet themselves. The faces dropped to reluctant disdain and they watched every step the delivery man took, as he made his way to the desk and handed the opulent bunch of white roses to Bella the receptionist, whose face had broken into a shy smile as she humbly took the flowers and beamed. The women of the room clocked the men watching – why hadn't they started segregating these places? – checking out the one girl in the room they could still consider a catch. There was no card, but Bella knew who it was from. She breathed them in in one luscious gulp, then looked around awkwardly for somewhere to put them. There was nowhere really but on her desk, front and centre, where they stood, awkwardly rejoicing romance in a place built for shame.

'Who sends white roses on Valentines?' a girl whispered jealously to her friend. 'Should be red.'

'Deffo,' the friend muttered back, whilst turning her form from her friend's vision and ticking a depressed 'Yes' in the box cheerfully asking, 'Any symptoms?'

Turns out I'm the freak of this fairytale, written with a phallic pen,
All that humpin' and suddenly I grew a cauliflower, a mushroom, a pumpkin,
Turns out I'm the curse, from which we must protect all men,
Now let's turn Mingerella back into Cinderella,
And I'll never stay out past midnight again.

To his credit, the delivery man had resisted ogling them with amusement, and exited the room, the doors giving a healthy swing. The patients couldn't help but wonder, who would they be when they exited those doors? The same person as had entered, with just a little more relief, or something else, off for a new life, branded from the inside out? Sealed in this timeless room, they sat beneath posters with brutal statistics, and – perhaps now a statistic themselves – all they could do was hope.

Patients of papillae, learning lessons with lesions,
Does everything – even this – happen for a reason?

Kate shifted grumpily in her chair. Her legs looked fat in these jeans. But she knew that wasn't what was truly bothering her. Something was haunting her, and it wasn't a ghost. It walked all around her, its little footsteps spiky and sticky. Each night she prayed for the feeling to go, but each morning she woke up feeling like she'd lost another layer of skin. A phantom fist burrowed into her, proudly waving her around like a mascot. Sigh. At least she'd manned up and finally taken herself here.

A man took his seat next to her. Kate had no idea who he was, but from his calm confidence, she knew he wasn't like the rest of them. There was always one, of course, every time you were in a place like this. Someone with … it. Something more serious than the others. They had a nobility to them, the kind you hoped you'd never have yourself.

Bella was announcing names with the inappropriate positivity of a prize giver at a school speech day. No medals for this lot. And just when Kate thought they had lost her form, she heard it.

'Kate Silver?'

Live your life to the full,
But all balloons have to burst,
Hey, look at it this way –
Hmm. Guess it couldn't be worse.

'Hi, that's me.'

'Great, come this way.'

Suddenly she was following a slim, young nurse through a previously sealed doorway, down a parquet corridor lined with doors to private rooms. She passed the bathroom. The nurse ignored the squeals coming from it, so she did too.

They say love hurts but they don't tell you how lust tortures.
I guess they just hope this never happens to ***their*** *daughters.*
We took the erotic and made it bubonic.
Now here come the locusts, the larvae, the nests,
Who've been waiting so long to lay their eggs,
Here comes the plague, the maggots, the lice,
Who dug themselves up cos we wouldn't play nice

They had a new system in place now, where you went to the bathroom to do your own swabs. That's where the clinic's oldest patient, Heather, was, plunging three inches of cotton inside her and mixing it all around when she heard the screams.

At first she thought it was coming from her own privates as it admitted to itself what was in them. After all, the thing had been grumbling at her ever since she took it to its first sex party two weeks ago, refusing to get on board with her post-divorce bucket list. The plastic bud broke in her hands and she realised that, nope, the screams were definitely real. She wrenched up her jeans and burst out of the stall to identify them.

Amazingly, such horrid sounds could come from such a gorgeous girl. The screamer was a third of her age, not 'model beautiful' but 'Pop Star hot', and the only person here who dared to wear a crop top. A pocket rocket of five foot two, her long cherry red hair as striking as the tiger tattoo down her back. She was bent over the sink, howling into the water, and clearly hadn't expected somebody else to be in here. She lurched up when she saw Heather, eyes streaming, and without thinking, wailed the question she so desperately needed answers to.

'Why?! Why oh why won't they *go away*?'

We're making naughty nectar, cos we were born for this,
This is a sexorcism, and your kiss goes 6-6-6.
Here come the crawlers, the roaches, the rot,
If only you'd been sensible enough to stop,
Here come the boils, the blisters, the bubbles,
Swelling and swelling til you stop causing trouble.

'I don't get it!' Surrendering to her saliva, she started to sob. 'I'm a *nice* person! I am! I've never cheated on anyone but I've been cheated on! I never bitch about anyone, even though they definitely bitch about me! I'm a singer and you know who I just held a concert for? A bloody *seal* charity! So – why me? Why is this happening? Why won't they leave me alone?'

I don't understand
I've been committed no crime and I've only ever been kind
Seems like I'm being punished just for having a good time

'Right.' Heather knew this was serious, and she had to get to the bottom of it. 'Whose been harassing you?'

'Them!' She sunk to the floor. 'AARGH! It's been eight months. I have Mykonos coming up. Oh god, oh god, I just can't take it. I can't fucking take it.' Through her heaving gulps, sarcastic anger pierced her eyes. 'But of course. Of *course* this would happen to me. I'm a size six, with E cup tits. They had to balance me out somehow. I just didn't think it would be like this.'

'Whose they?'

'My sores! The lumps, the bumps, the sores!!' The words leapt from her, and her eyes bounced desperately up into Heather, then back down even quicker. When she spoke again, her voice was small. 'Every time one goes, two come back.'

Heather knelt down next to her. The motion made her remember the plastic inside her. 'Try not to worry, dear. Look, you're in the right place to get better.'

The girl sighed deeply. 'They freeze me so cold I'm on fire. *My body can't beat it. My body can't beat it. My body can't beat it.*' She wiped her tears then, and this time when she looked in Heather's eyes she didn't look away. 'One day I'm gonna get better, and then I'm gonna leave the life of my dreams. It's gonna take more than ice to melt me.'

Heather nodded. 'What's your name?'

'Jade,' the girl said. 'Cool name, right? I better go back to my appointment. I have to be brave now.'

Follow me Faust, into this salt bath,
Get in here and get a close look if you want a good laugh,
The warm water opened me up good and proper,
A shark could've swum up there and I wouldn't have stopped her.
In a salt bath I am safe,
And finally I am enough,
In a salt bath my body can escape,
And finally I am tough.

Beyond them, in the corridor outside, a young woman was led to the back of the clinic, wheeling her suitcase behind her. She looked up at the doctor leading her, and wasn't sure if she was happy or not that he would be inspecting her today. Because he was *fit*. Even through a level of anxiousness she had never felt before, she could acknowledge that - he was one of the few men that could have seen that many lady parts a day anyway, without having to be a doctor. If she had shaved, maybe she would be asking for the examination straight away, willing to show off. Today though, she had a more pressing issue.

He let her into the room, where she tried not to swoon as every tall, dark and handsome inch of him held the door open for her. To her disappointment, they weren't alone.

'This is Nora,' Great voice he had, too. 'She's a medical student on work experience today. Are you okay if she stays in your session today?' A girl-next-door on a chair in the corner, smiled up at the doc. She was smitten too, it seemed.

Well, she didn't wanna look like a bitch in front of him, so, 'Okay.'

'Great. Thanks. Take a seat. Amber, isn't it?'
As soon as she sat down, she remembered why she was there. That this appointment was, in fact, a fight for her life as she knew it. All comfortable feelings collapsed in favour of pathetic, desperate panic.
'So what can we do –?'
Deep breath. 'Okay, I may sound paranoid, but … I'd like the PRP pill. I mean, the PEP pill.' She wrung her hands and hoped she wasn't going red.
'Ok, well we need to ask some questions first.'
'No, look, I'll answer the questions after, ok, but please just give it to me. I had unprotected sex on Thursday morning, on holiday,' she gestured to her case in the corner of the room. 'About 4am with this random guy and now I think I have something.' She pulled up her top, for once not caring about exposing the embarrassing band of flesh over her hips. 'I got this rash straight away. And I googled and,' Panic spat and crackled through her voice. 'The rash looks like you-know-what.' Oh god, she was going to cry in front of him. 'So,' she squeaked, gesturing at the cupboard behind them. 'Please let me have the pill.' She sat back, acknowledging how exhausted she was, dragging herself here from the airport from the moment she landed.
'Ok, I can see you're distressed,' he said sympathetically. He passed her a tissue, 'But what I can tell you is that rash is more syphilis than anything else. It would be very soon for any other rash to be showing.'
Amber scrambled the tissue, the what-if-what-if motif clenching inside her OCD brain. 'Soon, but, is it possible?'
'It could be, yes.'
'Then I want the pill. The clock is going down.'
The doctor sighed, exchanging glances with Nora. 'But it's my duty to make you aware that if you were to take this pill there would be a *month* of side effects. There's several different things it can do to you throughout that month.'
But nothing more than I've already done to myself, she thought. 'Go on, tell me.' *Scare me, shock me, as if I need any more stress.*
'Well, first of all – headaches. Lots and lots of headaches.'
At that point, Amber experienced the greatest headache of her life, as though something had come swinging into her skull. The last thing she saw was Nora pulling on a cord, and suddenly she couldn't breathe. She heard the Doctor cry out, then everything was muffled, then her world went black.

She's pretty, too pretty, she's nice, too nice,
Time to show her what happens when the lid comes off the spice.
Now cardamom and black pepper is grinding in her eyes,
Now paprika and chilli is dissolving in her thighs,
It's time she learnt what regret is all about,
It's time she let a ***real*** *scream out.*

Back in the waiting room, Cam decided to pour himself a cup of water. He made his way round the corner to the dispenser, passing two friends who were still discussing the roses - 'Getting sent flowers is a turn off anyway. Too metrosexual!' – and picked himself up a cup.

As he filled it his eyes were drawn to a woman taking her seat opposite, and the many freckles on her left arm.

He leaned forward and, trying not to be obvious, started to count them.

If he could count them all before his name was called, that would be a good sign and it would just be a zit he had down there. Just a zit. He had done this many times; count something random like the birds on a bench bus stop before the bus arrived, with a superstitious belief his wish would be granted if he counted it in time. Many times in his life he had directed that wish down there; to be bigger, to have that special curve women talked about. He had never, ever wished for it to be purple, yet he had woken up that morning with exactly that; his very own aubergine. Stalk and everything.

He had counted seventeen freckles so far, and still there were more. She made it easy to count; she hadn't moved a muscle since she'd sat back down. Come to think of it, that was strange – he was sure he'd seen her come *out* of the corridor where the depressing row of examination rooms waited. He'd noticed her because she was the only person not looking when the flowers came in.

Maybe she was waiting for medication. He took his eyes from the freckles on her arm, and decided to dare a glance at her face. Just as he got to it, she started to cry.

Damn, he thought, looking around. They were in their own corner of the room; nobody else had noticed her tears. With each one that came she swayed with it, helplessly wiping it away only to be swung forward by the next. Whatever had happened in that room had done this to her, left her glued to her chair. She needed to get up and go, into the arms of a friend. At the very least she needed a hot chocolate.

Yet she remained in the room like the outside world was scary now. When she went outside she would have to be strong again, but for now she could weep, wetly and redly, in a room full of people who had things to cry about too. Surely she was going to get up now – no, now the tears came harder. A couple of other people looked over. But he was the only one that couldn't look away. For a moment, he was able to forget about his polluted penis.

A subtle snap decision in his chest led him to walk across the room and swing himself into the chair next to hers. She threw him a suspicious glance but he wasn't deterred.

'Are you ok?' Suddenly they were centimetres apart. 'What's wrong?'

She gasped with the shock of emotion that came from being comforted by a stranger. A breath bolted through her, rapidly quickening and gathering speed within her.

'Oh god this is so embarrassing,' a cringe, a plea, a wanton gaze up at him as though he was the stars.
'No, look, it's normal. Obviously you don't need to – you don't need to tell me what's wrong. Whatever it is, screw it. It's not your fault, you don't deserve it, and you'll get through it.' He threw his arm around her shoulder. Spontaneous, but it made sense here.
'Oh god you're so nice,' she cried. 'I am so, so sorry. How cringe.' As soon as she said it, a hiccup escaped her mouth. That shocked her more than him; she clapped a hand over her mouth and winced; another one nipped out.
'You don't have anything to be sorry for. We're all in the same position. Look … I don't think I'll be in there too long, touch wood, shouldn't say that, but, basically, how bout I take you for a coffee afterwards?' He offered her a clumsy tissue. 'And *please*, don't be sorry for crying. Especially when you look as cute as you when you cry.' A sob caught in her throat. 'Wait, sorry, I just went *totally* creepy! Last thing you need in a place like this.'
'No, I'm sorry.'
He laughed. 'Don't be. Crying is healthy.'
'No,' she shook her head, wiped away her tears, shook them off her hand, drank a cup of water next to her that probably wasn't even hers – contagious, contagious, tut, tut. 'I'm not sorry for crying. I'm sorry for *this*.'
He frowned.
'Really, Cam, I'm sorry. I wish there was another way.'
Another dewy tear distracted him as she reached into her handbag, pulled out a paper bag of medication, shook out a large bottle, undid the cap and began spraying it into his eyes.
'Now *you're* crying,' she cooed. 'Now you're crying acid.' She ignored his screams. 'Don't be embarrassed. Crying is healthy.'

So many questions; what am I now?
Am I tragic, am I funny, can I still be horny?
Am I still allowed to look in the mirror and say, 'Poor me'?
But more than that, than the way, the why, the how,
Than not knowing which part of me will be next to howl,
Than the throbbing in my head and the loosening in my bowel,
Is this one question; 'Whose gonna love me now?'

'Ah, yes I can see what this is.'
Kate's nurse said the sinister sentence and then she fiddled with her glove. Was she seriously making her wait? If she didn't scream at her to tell her what it was, she was worried her open privates might leap up and do it for her.
She lay there, glaring at the ceiling, her sexiness wriggling away from her as her feet wriggled in the stirrups.
'Show me where it hurts again.'

'Everywhere.' Kate bit the words out. 'It hurts everywhere.'
Just as she had broken enough sweat to turn the seat into a slide, the nurse, Bea, spoke again.
'I'm afraid you have genital lice.'
Unfortunately for the girl who lay splayed, and splattered, cracked apart, a crab indeed, at the exact moment this sentence was said, it cued the curtain to fall from its rails, and the wall before them to crumble, where she, open as a beetle on its back, greeted the rest of the waiting room with the rubbery revolution between her legs. There was utter silence as thirty people heard the words 'genital lice.'
And then, there was chaos, and her crabs were the least of their worries. Because it was not just her surgery wall that crumbled open. Had they not been distracted by actually seeing real lady parts, up close, wide open, they would have noticed the sound of ticking.
The bomb went off a second later, and the wall to the left of them had its hymen broken, erupting open and ejaculating plaster, chunks of cement, metal pieces of pipe all over the waiting room. Without the wall to support it, the ceiling gaped open, and came for them too.
When finally one patient screamed, his jaw was hit shut by a bed, launching through the air and catching at a right angle above the ground. Its patient was still strapped into it. She hung from the stirrups unconscious, a plastic funnel still wedged inside her.
And when a bomb goes off in a place like this, it's not just walls and plastic and chairs that you have to contend with. All those secretive, shameful, swabs and samples, they all come out to play too; these banished objects become weapons. Even though it's only plastic, only cotton, only a tiny needle, much like it was only once, only oral, only with *him*, isn't that what you said to yourself when you didn't think sex could hurt you, that it wouldn't let you down, that *you* would never be one of *those* people who'd catch something like *this*? I bet you thought you'd never be held hostage at a bombing, either.
And when syringes and buds turn into a tornado, they can really hurt, let alone sweep you away. Even a form – we all know there's nothing worse than a paper cut. Especially a paper cut *there*. And each swab may carry something worse than the bomb and each pre-used bit of cotton can find a way to ruin your life. Better hope you get crushed before you get touched.
Throughout all this, Kate just stared at the ceiling, waiting for it to fall on her. And when ten seconds went by and it still didn't, she sat up. She removed her feet from the stirrups and, like a good girl, she closed her legs. She looked through the desecrated wall into the room beyond. Imagine a fruit and veg stall blown apart, combusting into a million pieces – except there's no rainbow when it's human flesh. Just pallid pale greys longing to call themselves pink. A chair leg there, a real foot there, a million shards of plaster and the writhing, mottled pit of bodies who don't understand why their world is upside down.

She looked to her left. Where was her nurse?
To her relief, Bea was not crushed beneath the wall, but walking to a cupboard still as intact as her. From her white pocket she slipped a key, effortlessly twisting it into the lock. Kate couldn't see into the cupboard, but Bea walked in so calmly Kate thought it must have been a shelter, built specifically for moments like this, for when bombs perforate the walls of STD clinics.
Just when she was about to follow her, the nurse returned, now wheeling a trolley stacked with six shelves, each wobbling with at least ten test tubes of fresh wet blood.
She charged forward, through the makeshift hole in the crumbled wall, with her selection of blackberry syrup and raspberry grenade. She rolled the trolley over what was left of a chair, until she faced the crowd. Then with a flick of her foot, she kicked the trolley upward, sending it launching into the air.
The plasma turned into missiles, ruby rockets launching through smoky air, deciding what or who to land on. Never picking a patch of chair or corner of floor, but always a face, a scalp, that tender point on the back of a neck. And for the first time nobody was afraid of the shattering glass – not the sprinkles, not the shards, not the blades – but of what was *inside it:* the blood of their fellow victims, of the people they clung to now, the ones they were shielding and the ones shielding them. They closed their eyes and begged for plaster and iron to collapse on them instead. But hadn't they learnt by now luck was not on their side; 3, 2, 1 and the tubes combusted and everybody was covered in blood, not just their own blood, but painted in a stranger's blood, cast with a red mark that had the potential to make or break them. The torn posters around them told them there was a 10% chance this blood was infected - but that's in the average person. They were here on Valentine's Day - they were not average.
Who would they be now they licked another hostage's blood from their lips? What better weapon than the weaponised blood of the people around them? And as they looked to each other, broken and bruised, huddled groups sprang apart, clutches and embraces dissolved, as they realised the danger was all around them, in them – even holding hands was wrong.
Just as it should be, just as it should have always been and then there never would have been the need for a place like this, this lesson would never have had to be taught, and the bomb would never have had to have been built. They brought it on themselves.

It was called a cryotherapy gun and it could turn a human into a blister, pick any part of you and make you purple ice. A bloated, threatening vessel packed with an emotion colder than hate: blame. Arctic and angry, you didn't stand a chance. Ouch.
A man was crawling to the door, and they wedged the gun inside his mouth and began to fill him with ice cold liquid nitrogen. Nobody was leaving yet.

Nora, Bea, and the other receptionist, not Bella, but the one you didn't notice, the plain Jane at the back– they slowly revealed themselves to be imposters and implants. And also, sadly, Heather. The humiliation of catching an STD over 60 had converted her to their cause. Now they formed a team, a gang of curmudgeonous captors, ready to hold the promiscuous patients to account.
'Consider this a lesson learned.' Nora told the patients.
That's when the blizzard began. A hail storm of flying plastic bulbs and sticks, glass tubes full of who knows what, plastic cups, discarded tampons, DNA sharing and streaming around the crumbling room. Some grabbed syringes, some grabbed stirrups, and began battle, syringe v stirrup, gouging into eyes or tearing along throats.
Kate watched them all in horror, her knees tucked up in bed. The room was possessed. Nobody knew who to fight or what they were fighting for. Half of them couldn't see, and half of them couldn't hear. Slowly around the room, another three women revealed themselves, rising with an eerie calm and joining the others at the front of the room. What did it matter what their names were? They were the terrorists, and they were in charge.
The conscious were coughing, trying to clear the ash from their lungs, but everytime they did, more of the room fell apart. Even more sadly, the unconscious were waking up.
It was only a matter of time before the shelves began to shake, dispensing bottles and tubes that smashed into the greedy ground. Pills showered the floor so those fighting began to skid. Kate was splashed with a shot of something unknown, a splash caused by a loose toe landing in a half-full cup. A strange feeling came over her and she realised – the toe was her own.
Happy Valentine's Day.

Jade was a gorgeous girl. She even looked good being dragged across the floor. It made sense for chunks of her buttery red hair to be wound tightly in someone else's hands, and for that taut torso of hers to be ground into the glass as she was taken from the bathroom to the main room – 'Bet you wish you covered up now.'
And who was it that dragged her? Somebody who was the opposite of her. Everything she couldn't imagine being, from the thick calves to the tight bun. The one who had organised the attack, the one who had spearheaded this righteous reaction. She was tender for a terrorist, more headmistress than extremist. Jill.
Jill had been planning this for months. Eli had given her other options, but she wanted it to be this. Only this place would do.
'Shh.'
The most soothing shh they had ever heard. At last, the room started to settle – surely, if she wouldn't even show her ankles, she couldn't be that dangerous. 'I would say don't be afraid, but honestly I like seeing you like this.'

First she told them where she was from. Core Retreat, they must have heard of it? A good place.
She introduced them to Nora, Bea and Jane, all carers from Core too. She shook Heather's hand. They were ready.
Kate was the only one that rose to stop them. But a condom machine collapsed on top of her before she could, and she was silenced.
Jill explored the room, nodding warmly at her comrades that had helped her pull this off. Amongst the tubes and the stirrups and the plasters, she saw something worthy of bending down and picking up. An unharmed petal. She inhaled it. Deep. 'Ahh,' she smiled. 'I do love white roses.'
The flowers. Of course. The bomb was in the flowers.
She beamed and clapped her hands. 'Everything's going to be fine, as long as you are patient. A friend of mine is going to be joining us soon. They will make this all better. While we wait, I thought I would teach you a few things.' Jill walked around them, every footstep heavier than the last. 'They shouldn't be long now. I know you might be thinking of escaping, so, just so we're clear on what's happening here: there is more than one bomb in this place and we can set it off at any moment. So it will be easier if everybody stays and is open to learning from me. You got that?'
'Yes.' Came the squeaks. If only, before any of this, they had learnt how to say no.
'Then let's begin.' Jill smiled. Eli believed in her, and she believed in them. 'Form a circle on the floor for me. Eyes, ears, hands: everything where I can see them.
Very good.'
If she saw their eyes cloud over, she signalled to one of her comrades to step on their broken hands. And she would keep doing so until relief would be associated with celibacy.

Time and glass and boredom all blended into one. They had no more energy for battle, and Jill knew it. She walked across the bodies, teaching a lesson she had longed to teach for years.
'You did this to yourselves. You built this bomb. *You* chose it, you smuggled it inside you, I bet you were in the shower when you felt it. This began when you decided to be what you are.
By the end of today you will change. I can tell you're changing already. For example, this little situation of ours is already on the news. There's several TV stations outside, and police trying to negotiate a way in – I've told them what I want, so let's see – and if I do let you go, you're going to be on camera. Even you, Cameron.' She gestured to Cam, who was hiding under a chair, much like the one he had ridden his sister-in-law on. 'What will your wife think when she sees you coming out of here? Or you?' She pointed at a girl, curled in the foetal position. 'How will you explain to your strict parents that you were here? Or

you?' She pointed again to a man missing his ear. 'Haven't you just landed a role presenting Ascot? Can't have this as your image.' She paused, wondering if she would ever, ever understand why they were the way they were. 'So tell me, because I'm curious. Who's gonna come for you? Who's gonna be there for you? Who would you let see you like this? Who's gonna *love you now*?'

Beware the monster beneath the bed,
The monster who won't let you sleep.

Jill told them stories, the worst things she'd ever heard about the bedroom. Though their faces were stone, she could tell when she reached some part of them that related to it, that all had a story like that of their own. Then she told them stories of what happened when you chose celibacy: a life of dough, and bread, and respect, where there was no more danger. And just like the bread, she kneaded it into them, her carer comrades whispering it into their ears as they tended to their wounds. Just like the splinters, their libido was being removed.

Because he will distract you from the real monster,
*Not the one in your **head**,*
*But the one **in** your bed,*
The one between the sheets.

This room was full of monsters.

Clitzilla, Labiasaurus Rex and Frankenvulva – burnt babes all in a row. Even a pyromaniac's privates hadn't seen what they'd seen, and that's why they could handle Jill.

Every corduroy-cruel inch of her. She was little more than a storm in a swab. Easy to fool. They nodded as she explained for them her vision for today: that they were part of something great here. Their hostage situation would birth a new world, a world without debauchery or desire. A world of function over fun. All terrorism is is an attack on a way of life, and there was no way more wild than theirs. All they had to do was convince Jill that they would live her way now.

'I can get you the respect you have denied yourself,' she told them. 'I can show you restraint, elegance, purpose. I can make you whole. All you gotta do is want to be wholesome.' Her knee clicked, and the monsters nodded, and she felt calm: no one would ever be used again.

Let's talk about punishment, that age-old idea,
The cruel and unusual is what you must fear.
The judge gave me a beard, of blisters and burns,
And the executioner with his Zovirax stick,
Before he beheads me, declares, 'Should have never danced on his dick.'

I'll say one last thing through this cruel crust on my lips,
'Bring on the apocalypse.'

'Why's it raining indoors?'
'That's not rain, that's plaster.'
'Plaster is white. These are rain drops.'
'Then why's the rain saying sorry?'
They weren't imagining it. The rain was definitely apologising.
'It's called shedding. Look up.'
The voice came from the ceiling. When they obeyed it and looked up, they realised they were huddled beneath a giant chandelier of flesh. A whole human hung above them, strapped into a bed that was caught between a hole in the ceiling. His hospital gown hung open, revealing him like a confident ulcer. Though he was high up, it was clear something was wrong in the crotch area; the colour of it, the texture. And then, with a racing car's sprint to revulsion, they realised that was where the 'rain' was coming from.
'Shedding. I'm sorry. It happens in an outbreak.'
Light flecks of skin, cascading from him and down onto them. They danced in the light, a brazen brown colour. They felt like butterflies and dissolved like snowflakes. They didn't seem to stop.
'Just when I thought I couldn't be any more disgusted.' Jill stormed to the middle of the room, just close enough to not be caught in his impious embers. 'Today the rain stops.'
'Forgive me! Cut me down, please!'
'What do *you* think we should do?' Jill addressed the whole room. 'It'll take hours to cut him down. He'll be making fresh flakes for us that whole time. Or we could punish him.'
'Punish him?'
'How exactly would we do that?'
'Well – '
Suddenly Jill was face to face, eye to eye, with Jade 'Let us cut him down, you bitch!' screamed the girl.
Shock bit down on the room. But Jade stayed standing, blood trailing down the carve of her waist. A light brown flake made its way down. It seemed to know all the attention was on it and enjoyed taking its time, a woodland truffle with the grace of a rhythmic gymnast. Instead of joining the pile of moth wings in the middle of the room, it playfully landed on the tip of Jade's finger.
She held it out gently. 'Close your eyes and make a wish.' She thrust it towards Jill's mouth. 'Make a wish and blow it away.'
It was Jill's turn to flinch, leap back from her. She whacked Jade's hand away then stared at her own in stunned silence; had she touched the flake? Had it broken into a million tiny pieces and now one of them remained on her?

'I already know what you wish for.' Jade smiled sweetly. 'It's not hard to find out what makes you tick. *This* is your fantasy. This is what gets you up in the morning, what lives between your legs, what you'd split yourself in half over.'
'What are you talking about?' Jill snarled.
'Cut him down, then we'll talk.'
Jill gestured to her comrades to get to work. Workhorses, they began attending to the man made of flakes.
Jade continued. 'Cruelty. Not the most unique of kinks. Our pain is your weakness. Our tears are your lube.'
Jill had regained her composure. 'Believe me, this has nothing to do with desire. Nothing in my life does, which leads me nicely to my next lesson.
I am going to get you back to what you were meant to be, before you gave in to all that immorality, before you were persuaded to be putrid. It's not your fault. It's the society we're in. It's made us a disgrace. Living too hard and loving too wide. But if you trust me, I can make you pure again. White as the rose. It should never have had to come to this, dears.'
'But …' Jade came closer. Jill was nothing she hadn't seen in a dozen teachers and matrons all her life. 'Sex *should* make you scream. Isn't that the whole point of it?' The room watched her, transfixed. 'You did a great job at terrifying us today, but you should hear the kinds of screams I can get men to make. And don't even get me started on what I can do to women.' She winked at her. 'You're a terrorist. We should call you Clitler.'

A miracle happened; the hostages laughed.
'Now,' Jade picked her way over spare body parts and gutted shelves. 'While we wait for your friend to turn up, instead of a lesson, why not a game? Truth or Dare, anyone? Hey, how about Twister?'
Shock held the room in its jaws. Until one man began to rise. Shaky on his feet. Looking at Jade. Their hands were oh so close when –
Jill shook her head. 'Disgraceful. I suppose this is good, though: the quickest way to make them learn is to make an example of one.' She smiled sharply. Signalling to her comrades, the shedding man was forgotten; let the blood build, indeed. 'Once I have my way and all desire is banned, I may – just to make sure – take away self-indulgence too.' From her sweaty grey skirt, she pulled a shiny grey knife. The blade looked laughable in her doughy hands. 'I can start the amputations now.' The group went silent. 'What do you say, people?' Their eyes swivelled to Jade. 'Shall we cut out the mess?' Jade's eyes went wide. Sure enough, the group was turning on her.

A noose around my throat? I love a good choke
Can move my hips so well it's a fucking joke.
5 hours in the stocks? Enjoy the view
I know how I look bent over for you.

Screws through my feet? Mmm, treat me like meat,
Nail me to a cross? Go on, show me whose boss.
As my blood drains and my body gets weaker,
I'll look you in the eyes and I'll ask for it; 'Deeper.'

If it was happening to Jade, then it wasn't happening to them. Let it be her and not them. A brutal bullying began as the patients cursed the redhead, scorning her for standing up. After all, she had risen up, when all they wanted today was for things to go down.

Stretched on a rack? Always wanted to do the splits,
Force fed with grit? Hope it goes to my tits
Hung, drawn and quartered? I've never felt lighter,
Lips sewn together? Sure, I'm no biter,
In fact – I've been looking for ways to get a bit tighter.

'Ok. That's enough.'
The bullying stopped, as easily as it had started.
Jill smiled. 'Now Nora? Bury her.'
Nora tugged a cord, and Jade felt the darkest headache of her life. Suddenly she couldn't see, and she was buried, under ever increasing weight. She felt the floor beneath her give way, and then she let herself sink.

As time went on, the monsters started to talk to one another. Just little conversations, fragile whispers to those they thought might understand.
'She was right though,' Draculabia muttered to Rumpleforeskin, not daring to say Jade's name. 'Doesn't it feel like you're being punished – simply for having a good time? Like even before this. Before the bomb I mean.'
'*Yes*,' Rumpleforeskin replied. 'That's what I was thinking. An hour ago or so, we still had our whole lives ahead of us. Yet we were all staring into our laps, so ashamed – why?'
'Me too,' Draculabia nodded, her voice rising. 'How could something so wonderful be turned into something this rough? What kind of world is that?'
Rumpleforeskin shook his head vigorously, passion swelling in his chest. 'I hate it. I hate it. Is it science, is it fate – '
Jill walked towards them, every grey inch of her. Draculabia saw her – up close, her lips were nice – but Rumpleforeskin didn't.
'What could possibly be the reason?'
When, oh when would they learn? There was no chance to be redeemed, not once you'd been opened at the seams.
'It was me.'
She sunk to the floor, folded her legs and leaned into them conspiratorially, and repeated. 'It was me.'

Everyone, even her comrades, was turning to look at her.
'I did it.' She allowed herself to smile. 'I willed it into the world. One day it wasn't there, then the next it was. It was me. I'm the reason you're scared to look down.'
She smiled and revolved to face the group. They all needed to hear this.
'I knew from an early age that copulation was wrong.. I knew only a sickness could stop it. All I had to do was think it up, and then you all helped me spread it, oh so quickly, all over the world.
I thought of chlamydia first. Simple, silent, subtle chlamydia. She arrived so quickly, without even a hello or a welcome from any of you. She worked well for a while, but she wasn't enough. I decided she needed a sister – a sister for chlamydia, and so gonorrhoea was born. Sharper and smellier than what came before. How proud I was of the way she made you wince.
Still you didn't stop. What would it take? I saw more and more places like this pop up, and still you didn't stop. So I didn't want to do what I did next, but I had to. I knew you needed a real threat, something that couldn't be cured. So I made it. Willed it from my mind and into you. All I had to do was close my eyes and I had my very own plague. You never know until you try.'
She looked through the room, til she saw him. The man with the noble expression, the one who life had toughened long before this. There was always one.
'I would say sorry.
But for some of you, that still wasn't enough, was it. For the vainer among you, you needed to see it. After all what good is a punishment if it can hide inside its victim?
And I was cringing over a period I had never wanted to receive, at a time I truly believed I might finally be pregnant, I thought about something else that could visit people once a month too. So came the blisters, the boils, the burns. Herpes was created.'
'That's not true,' a voice shouted. 'You idiots! The first recorded STD came in the 1400s.'
Jill didn't flinch. 'Who said this was my first life? Maybe it's my third – maybe I've been a ringmaster, a horse, a king.'
Another voice came from the crowd, too quick for her to locate.
'If this is true … I hope this isn't your last life.
I hope in your next life you're a whore. I hope in the one after that, you're a creep. I hope no matter how many lives you live you never find one drop of satisfaction.
I hope you come back over and over again and I hope you suffer a little more every time.'
Jill sighed and stood back up. She could see they were getting cranky.
'I want to share some good news.' She clapped her hands and stood up, trying to awaken her tired, sunken,students. She brushed the residue off her chest and

straightened the creases in her tights. It had come to the point where they needed a morale boost. And lucky for her, she could bring them morale like no other - would you expect anything less from her?
She cleared her throat.
'It's time to tell you what I have asked the police for. What they are working on so hard outside: you deserve to know.
I have asked for a visit from a friend. She is coming to meet you.'
They blinked up at her. Bit by bit, the confusion cleared.
'Guess who my friend is? The one who's on our way because she can't miss this? Can't miss anybody who needs her.
She is coming to take this all away.
I'm sure you'll have heard of her. It's Erica Ash.'

Erica.
The queen of touch.
Of course they had.
The one who could feel them all. Feel and touch, touch and feel, all day long, without consequences. In fact, the opposite of consequences. Only glorious things happened when Erica touched you. She'd ridden over every reiki master and acupuncturist, every quartz crystal, in a blaze of talent and gifts.
Nothing but liquid money in her pores. While it was touch that had got them into all this trouble in the first place, when *their* touch led to them being riddled, branded, changed, there was a girl like her. No girl in the world anybody else would rather be touched by.
She was magic.
But why her? Why her? Why not them?

Jill spoke softly, to the restless crowd.
'Before I entered the building, I made it clear: we want her back. Core Retreat is her home, and she needs to return.
Erica knows what is happening to you. The whole country knows what is happening to you. This is all over the news, images of the hospital collapsing; anyone can imagine the horror of a ceiling falling in on them.
The Healer can't ignore it.
The Healer will not let you suffer. The Healer will not let you be crushed a second longer. She will slip your joints back into your sockets, fix your ribs back to your spine, turn your burns into butter. She is coming.
She has never healed the aftermath of a disaster before, only tackled individuals really. Every time she is given a new challenge, she really pushes her powers - she goes beyond what has gone before. More than most of us would. More than I could.' Jill's voice broke. 'That's why we have to get her back.'

Chapter Forty Six

9 Miles Away

Myles slipped out of their new apartment softly, grinning to himself. He had managed to get out without waking her, which wasn't always the case. Then again, she could be pretending – she loved to let him watch her.

Every morning they woke up together, he liked to do this. Slip out to the coffee stall across the road, which they had conveniently discovered served their favourite coffee in the world. He said 'coffee' – Erica went for the unicorn hot chocolate, a pastel whip of cocoa and cream, scattered with gold marshmallows and speared with turquoise candy canes. Himself, he kept it simple – an iced black coffee, no matter how cold the weather. And this morning was challenging him, a bitter morning with all the chill February could muster.

Because it was February 14th; indeed, it was Valentine's Day. And he wasn't going to waste a second thinking about Valentine's Day last year; every second would be spent making it special for her. He grinned as he thought about his first surprise.

He noticed more of the grey, abrasive posters, the ones calling for a new vote on Euthanasia. If only people knew what he knew, about what that really meant. If only they knew the ideology they were buying into. When was this going to die down? When would the posters go away?

Approaching the stand, he saw a familiar vanilla swish of blonde hair, on a woman barely five foot. As she turned, he recognised for certain his old friend, Gina – an installation artist he had worked with on designing numerous parties. She always looked chic, and today was no different; leather jackets, black jeans, chunky boots. He swung into her view as she turned clutching a steaming coffee.

'Gina!' he beamed. 'How've you been? I guess I should say Happy Valentine's Day.'

Her face fell, like a cat losing its purr.

'M – Myl – ' She stuttered. 'Erm, My-M -' Fear twisted her face and her words. She struggled for the syllables before giving up.

Then she threw the coffee in his face. And her coffee, sadly, was not iced. It came for his flesh, latching to it with the claws of a hundred lobsters. The lobsters were yanking, pulling at it, like they'd been told by someone powerful they'd get everything they wished for if they could just bring them Myles King's face.

'I'm sorry!' Gina yelped, before backing away, turning round, and breaking into a run.

Three minutes later and Myles was in a café that had rushed him in and given him enough cold water to rinse away his face. No real damage done, except to his mind. Why would she have reacted like that?
Tingling with dripping dread, he reached into his pocket, pulled out his phone and googled 'Myles King.'
A video popped up.
He clicked into YouTube.
There he learnt a hospital wing in Paddington was being held hostage, by a frumpy fanatic who had smuggled a bomb into flowers. He recognised her straight away – Jill. She had made a video just before entering the clinic, where she promised to let them all go, if Erica joined her and went with her to Core Retreat. If Erica refused, 'who knows what will happen to the patients'?
Then as the video progressed, she reluctantly offered another ultimatum. If Erica wouldn't come, there was one other way she was willing to let her hostages go. And it involved a certain man.
A man named Myles King – beloved by Erica.
Jill would let them go, if he played his part. He just had to do one thing.
Take. A. Life.
His brain swelled as he wound the video back, the cafe customers recognising him too now. Jill's voice blasted into the room; 'All this horror will be over if Myles King kills someone.'

He burst into the apartment, taking the stairs, dripping with sweat, feeling the burn develop on his face. He had been wrong, optimistic, earlier - damage had been done and the burn was coming now, red floral welts blooming under his skin. He didn't have time to look in a mirror, didn't have time to care. He didn't stop leaping til he had snapped through the door to their new loft space, racing through the oak kitchen, past circular bookcases and a trail of clothes, til he could throw open the door to their bedroom and see her.
'Erica!' he roared, almost falling to the carpet.
But the satin sheets left a ruffled print, and wind blew through the window.
Of course. She was already gone.

Chapter Forty Seven

They saw her on the TV screen, breezing past police and paparazzi once she arrived. She arrived in an Uber, and had thrown on a simple white strap top and camo short shorts – basically the most attractive thing a girl can wear. Her buttery hair leapt down her back, and her face had a serene calm as she made her way to the battered automatic door of the clinic.

There was an instinct, in them, that told them what she was. They had all heard the whispers, the rumours, that Erica Ash had come out of captivity a healer. Some kind of superstition kept them from questioning it, from jinxing it, from losing her; there'd been a silent pact to forget the rumours, to let her carry out her mission in secret.

But when they saw her, they knew: there really was a Healer in their world. Those who hadn't been brave enough to hope now felt the hope launch in them. You could hear the sound of the petition for a new vote being signed: who needed euthanasia, if they had her? What was Mercy if not Erica? She felt their love, oiling her joints as she walked, sacred and synovial.

Every code of conduct told the police to stop her, but none of them did; the thought barely even found them to do so. The doors slid apart when she approached, almost bowing to make way, and she took one more step before turning to face the press.

Cameras who sounded like the crunch of candy, formed a halo around Erica's head.

Committing love instead of crimes, holding hands instead of grudges, ripping seams instead of stitches, Erica smiled, or did she, what was that sexy sweet thing she did with her mouth, had she just invented smiling?

'Please, everyone, relax. It's going to be ok – I know she is not going to hurt me, so I am not afraid, I have no reason to be. But before I go inside, I have something to say. Is this live streaming? Ok. Well then I have a request too. Eli? You watching, baby? You watching me? Good.

I can't do this without you. I want you here. Get to …' She looked around, her eyes settling on the shattered wall in front of her, half a sign hanging from the doorway. 'You know the address of this place, you rascal.' She knew Jill was sacrificing everything for Eli; Eli would play innocent while Jill lured her here, letting his top carer take the blame for the entire attack and knowing she wouldn't out him. While the crowds were distracted with Jill's arrest, Eli would make sure an ulterior team was on hand to bring Erica back to him and back to Core.

Erica could see it playing out like clockwork, and yet something wasn't quite right. He needed to be here. He needed to watch this.

'Get here as soon as you can.' She acknowledged the reporters around her.

'Don't worry guys. Something amazing is gonna happen within these walls. Keep live streaming - you don't wanna miss a moment.'

She skipped up the path. Mints fell from her pocket. She turned back to the cameras. She inhaled the air as insipidly, as alluring, as she could. 'Eli, one more thing. Bring Ann. My old friend Ann. I need to see her.'
She came to the door and it sealed her up, tight as the virgin Eli wished she was.

Chapter Forty Eight

Jill took a long look at them all.
'I'm going to give you the chance to prove me wrong.' She smiled. 'We all are.'
The other carers joined her, flanking her on either side.
'They call you promiscuous, pathetic, hedonistic - they say you give away your value every time you open your legs.' She turned the knife over in her hands.
'But what if that's not true? What if one of you would sacrifice yourself for all the others?'
The carers' eyes bobbed across the waves of the distressed and the debaucherous. The knives seemed to be getting shinier in their grip.
'Come on,' Nora whispered. 'One of you for all of them. We'll make it quick.'
Heather licked her lips.
'For such tender terrorists, we sure know how to chop.' She grinned. 'So come on. Come to us.'
There was a gurgle, a protest, and then the voices came.
'I've never been a Best Man.'
'I haven't met my nephew yet.'
'I need another great romance before I die.'
Jill rolled her eyes, suspicions confirmed.
'A life of nothing but indulgence leads to a selfish final choice. What a surprise.' Her superiority washed over them like water.
And that's when, despite everything, the people began to rise. First a man in the centre, his sideburns grey. Then a woman who'd lost a finger to the bomb. Then a bloke of a guy who hadn't stopped crying since it went off. Up and up again, there was a dance in the room, a dance that can only be done when people are volunteering to save each other. Blink and you missed it: all of them that could stand up had risen to their feet. Holding each other up, they came towards Jill and her crew.
'Take me.' One of them said. 'Take me and let the others go.'
Jill could not let herself be angry. This was what she wanted. To test them and to change them. But the sight of them all in front of her, the rebellious versus the righteous, called for some further humbling. The kind of humbling that can only be done with knives.
Without further ado, she gave the other carers her signal, and together, releasing the same sweat from their armpits, they raised their cleavers into the air.
'If you treat yourself as only flesh, then you'll die as only meat. Meat No More, Meat No More, Meat No More.'
Just as they were about to drive their knives down, something happened.
An incredibly polite knock came from behind the door.
So polite Jill lowered her weapon, smiled, and travelled seamlessly to it. She opened it.
'Erica!'

The Healer entered. Every head spun to look at her. So she was real, and just as sweet as they'd heard. She even smelt of mint.
'Relax, guys,' her voice was soothing. 'Nobody has to sacrifice anything. *I* am the sacrifice. And I love to bleed.'

The touching began – she shook Jill's hand with a warm smile. She had no fear – none of them would risk hurting her: Eli's prize.
'Jill! Long time.' She nodded, hands on hips, looking around at the room, hair swishing at every angle. 'So you want me back, do you? You old goose.'
'You know we do.' Jill cooed. 'And so does Eli. Do you miss him?'
Erica shrugged, lightly. 'I guess I'll know how much when I see him.
He's on his way here.'
Jill swallowed, more nervous now. Eli had told her what he dreamed of seeing Erica do in this place; having it this close made her throat thicken and pulse quicken.
'So can we go?' a woman whispered up at them. 'You said if Erica came, you'd let us go.' Her hands were in prayer.
Jill shook her head. 'My dear, I would, I wasn't lying - however everything changes if Eli comes.
If Eli comes, everything starts over. You'll get a whole second chance. To do life again. Nobody can tell me they don't want that.' Jill stroked her chin. 'Just a little while longer.'
Then she rippled through the air and clutched Erica's arms, her nails pinning her to the wall. 'Is he really coming, Erica? Can you be sure?'
Erica smirked, shaking her off easily. Her teeth had got whiter.
'What else is he gonna do?'

Valentine's Evening was beginning.
Dates were starting all over the city. Girlfriends picked up from work, gas stations rushed into to grab flowers. Parties for singles, Tinder experiencing high traffic. Tiffany boxes opened. Surprises revealed. Blindfolds tied.
In the grit of the clinic, they waited for Eli. They were beginning to get cold.
'So do we know why?' Erica spoke as she moved around the room, tending to their burns, putting teeth back where teeth belonged. 'Has Jill told you why she did this? She could have held any group of people hostage, and she knows I would have come. So why did she choose you?'

Chapter Forty Nine

8 Miles Away

In the meantime, Myles was running.
They had been trying to seal his apartment door, when he'd burst out of it, spiralling into his neighbours, a couple he recognised, one he didn't, all three holding planks of wood and nails they'd been hoping to barricade him in with. Caught in the act, they froze, crouched like gargoyles, faces breaking into panic before collapsing into relief when Myles raced past them and into the lift. He'd joined a woman back from walking her dog. Within seconds she recognised him and began begging, crouching what she could fit of her body behind her medium sized beagle. After one attempt, he didn't even bother to reassure her, just let his body be a magnet for her screams and the canine's growls until he could awkwardly stumble from the lift, out into the street, and run.
He hadn't even realised he had taken his phone until it chimed in his pocket. It was a video, sent from an unknown number. He allowed himself to stop, and open it up. The garden of the retreat came into view, packed with hundreds of patients, probably the whole of Core. The camera was held up and its puppeteer came into view. Eli. Since when had his face been so bloated?
'Come on now Myles, don't look at me like that.'
He watched it and then he wished he hadn't. But time might have already been turned back for him once: it wouldn't happen again.

7 Miles Away

Round and round the sun. 360. Full circle. It was always going to go back to this. To Myles being Piles. To Myles with blood on his hands. To Myles the murderer, Piles the persecuted.
No.
He was going to get to Erica – not do what Eli said.
Piles – *no, no **Myles*** – he was Myles – he was going to get to Erica and sort her out. He knew where she was.
All Piles had to do was – no. no. no. he was Myles. He wasn't going to do it. But Eli's words played, a neat tight circle in the top of his skull.

6 Miles Away

'Good morning all. Thank you for coming; I know some of your bodies are tired. I have an announcement.
So.
Do we remember Myles, our old friend Myles?

He left us. And he took what we loved. He took the one thing that could make us whole. He thought he deserved it, more than all of us.
So I think he should prove it to us. I think he should prove he's willing to do anything to keep The Healer. Prove there's nothing he wouldn't do for her. So what about the one thing he never wanted to do?
One word, four letters, go on, try and guess.
Kiss. Cook. Spit. Bite. Burn. Ride. Poke. Shun. Sing. Jump. Maim. Hang. Kick. Wish.
Oh you wish – how you wish it could be one of those tender verbs.
Do this and you win. Do this and The Healer is yours.'
No matter how fast Myles ran, he could still hear Eli's words.

5 Miles Away

'Kill.
We will give him The Healer. We will concede. We will yield. We will never fight him for her.
As long as, by the end of today, Myles has murdered somebody.
It can be anybody. Man or woman. It cannot be a child. He can do it anyway he wishes – with a weapon, with fire, with acid, with his bare hands, but it cannot be simply through neglect i.e just leaving them somewhere with no food or water. He must hear their final words. He must not close his eyes. He must tell their family it was him that did it.
And one final, obvious thing, as if this even needed saying: Myles, you cannot kill yourself.
Go get them.'
Eli's words were a resurrection. Piles was born once more.

4 Miles Away

They've been making Halloween movies for decades now, and yet in all this time, they've missed out on one dynamite plot. The subversion is too obvious. It's time to admit our darkest fear. Why do we fear the times when we run and hide and tremble and make such pretty victims?
All this time, the **real** fear is this. What is truly scary is to be the thing the people are running from. Imagine it. The main villain in the Halloween movie. The thing that makes children scream.
The Candy Man, leaving footprints in the sugar, sweets clattering out of every pocket, mouth opening to show the rot of his gums. Destroy him – destroy you – and everybody else gets their happy ending.
Was he going to do it? What Eli said? It was one thing to save Erica once; it was another to know she'd be his forever.

Was this who he was always going to be? And all he'd been doing was delaying it? Stopping for a breath, My – Pi – no, no, *Myyyylpyyl* – Piles, Piles, he was Piles again, always the murderous pathetic yet petrifying Piles – Piles looked to the sky and waited for it to swallow him … when it didn't, he did it, the thing he'd tried so hard not to do, the thing that had been in him all this time –

He let the thought of murder come to him. Simmer.

Just one life. One person. Anyone. One time. Could he. Would he. Was he. All along.

The Candy Man.

3 Miles Away

The Candy Man.

If he was in Disneyland, they'd evacuate the premises.

You don't know lonely til it's you they're running from. You don't know lonely til they're locking doors to keep you out. You don't know lonely til your only kiss is from the scalding cup of coffee thrown in your face. You don't lonely til there's a weapon in your hand.

Petrol in his fingertips. Bulletproof vests to serve him water. Even buses were too scared to run him over. You don't know lonely til you know about this. Bricks over hugs. They know you're coming to get them.

You don't lonely til the streets gape. That's when you realise how wide the world really is. When you're seeking in hide and seek but you seek and seek and you still can't find the friends. Why couldn't he find the entrance to Narnia? He promised not to finger the foal again.

Just a lost lion, trying to tell the gazelles he wouldn't hurt them. Jaws too big – every time he said 'Sorry' he broke a neck. He had the face of a villain, smeared with ideas he'd tried to keep inside. Light as a feather, free as a bird.

'Just do it quickly!' One tramp begged. 'Just get it over with!'

'But all I want is to give you change …'

'Help, help, help!'

They knew. They knew he wanted them dead.

They knew. Gingerbread truth dripping out of him as he explored more empty streets.

Not a friend in the world. They knew about the bread he was keeping in his kitchen, fascinated to watch the mould grow. They knew about the eczema on his feet.

You don't know lonely til you're unbreakable. You don't know what you're missing til you have ribs that do not crack.

If they wouldn't come out and play, he would have to play himself.

And just when the Candy Man thought he was crying, he realised that those salty drops were not tears, and they were not coming from his eyes, but his forehead. Because he was sweating. Sweating with excitement.

2 Miles Away

'It must be nice,' says the milkman.
'To not be judged,' says the butcher.
'Not having to hold back,' winks the bus driver.
'I'm all yours,' smiles the neighbour.
They stop cutting their bread to hand him their knives. They wait under his wheels for him to hit the accelerator. They rub his side when he gets a stitch from chasing victims. They lay across the hot coal so he doesn't have to cross it. When he does it, they hope he'll let them watch.
If only.
If only it was like that.

1.5 Miles Away

Least you know how to run, boy.
Myles was running. Sprinting. Coursing and creaming through the air. Laced up by lactic, he ran, brewing a heat in his muscles to match the heat still in his face. He had never run so fast, and he had never covered so much distance, either. He suspected nobody had - it was easy to get far when everyone dived out of your way, when they ducked for cover as you came, when even cars were spinning to the side when they saw you approaching, when the road was empty as you crossed it. He must look really quite monstrous, with a face ripped to red, and no explanation as to why.
A little while back, he'd heard a whimper 'Don't drain *meee,*' as he hurdled over a drain, and since then, nothing. The only company he had, the only voices he could hear, were coming from the TV screens, mounted. Every single one of them had been switched to the news, where from BBC to Sky, they were all reporting on the bomb that had gone off in a hospital. On his run, he'd noticed the subtle shift in reporting style as the story developed. There was a definite twist to the broadcaster's energy as they learnt the bomb had gone off not in the main hospital, but in a separate wing - in its sexual health centre.
Erica. Erica. Erica.
He knew she was on her way.
He had to find her. He had to save her. He had to catch her.
Least you know how to hunt, boy.
He would never stop running.
With every corner he turned, every lamppost he passed, he saw another one of the posters; they seemed to multiply with every stride he took. The city littered in the words and the misguided beliefs of men like Eli. His city papered over with erroneous slogans calling for suffering. The next one he passed, he ripped it down as he went. Ooh, that felt good. He ripped the next. And the next, and

the next; the tearing seemed to give him the speed he needed. With every paper cut, he accelerated.
If he could just get to Erica in time, then maybe, maybe, he could remind her of the plan; the plan that had been sealed inside the letter from Darren Thames. If he could get to her in time, he could show her that it was possible. And he could keep the blood off his hands. All he had to do was be fast - but can anyone be faster than blood?
He rounded a corner, blending the pavement and the air and the walls with his feet. He hopped over a wall and cut through an alleyway, his mind scrambling to figure out the fastest route to the hospital. His body swelled into the atmosphere as he forced his way out of the alleyway, cutting round the next corner, onto a street that clearly hadn't expected him, scattering with predictable panic and ducking behind the stalls of a farmer's market, brewing with freshness. Their silence was spears, their breath nitrous as it crystalised from out of their hiding places, giving them away. Again, the only noise was the news report coming from a TV, suspended over a jolly looking cart offering coffees, mochas and cakes.
Despite himself, Myles read the words, running across the bottom of the screen. Myles realised he *was* going to have to break a promise he'd set to himself. He was going to have to stop before he got to Erica.
Because he had seen the word 'Paris.'
He slowed to a jog as he got closer to the screen, momentum still bouncing through his body, as more words bounced into his eyes.
'Coordinated attack.'
'Duel targets.'
'Another explosion.'
'French authorities.'
After feeling what he had felt on his face this morning, he thought he'd never go near a coffee again. But now he was, carelessly, oozing closer to the screen, the whimper of the usually jolly barista the score to his slow, calculated steps towards the TV. He squinted his eyes, mixing them up with the ears he was using to listen to the female reporter's words, her eyes widening as she echoed what was coming from her earpiece;
'French authorities are reporting on an explosion that also happened at the exact time of 10.12am today - 11.12am in France - on a remote street in the centre of Paris. What's clear right now is that one building was hit, in what was thought to be a deliberate targeting.'
Myles had slowed to a standstill but his heart thumped as if he was still running.
'It's unclear what the building was but it's understood it *was* occupied at the time of the explosion. We've learnt it was worth around 20 million euros due to its location and its size, built in the renaissance era and with an estimated five stories. It's reported the bomb has been found and, in striking resemblance to the attack in the UK, was brought in in a bouquet of white flowers.

According to reports, there were around eighteen casualties.
We are about to show you some images of what is left of the building. I must warn you that you may find the following upsetting.'
Myles balled up his fists, looking into the screen, willing the world to stay what it was before 10.12am this morning.
The reporter dug into her earpiece, trying to catch every last word. 'Okay, we can confirm there were no survivors. No survivors. Unlike in the UK which seems to be a hostage situation, it seems the bomb in this mysterious French building was deployed to destroy everything in it.'
Images began to fold across the screen, of stretchers, of ambulances, and then of nothing but rock. Even though it was a crumbled husk of what it had been when Myles had visited. Myles knew what this place was.
The screen switched to an elderly woman in a red headscarf, clutching a pomeranian in her arms. A microphone was being thrust under her wrinkled lips.
'You were walking your dog this morning when you heard the explosion?'
The question was translated back to her.
'Oui.'
'And you live in the area, yes?'
She mumbled to the translator, who responded, 'Yes, she lives in an apartment block over the river and walks her dog here every morning.'
'Do you have any idea what this building was? Or who might have been in there?'
The translator relayed the words, trying to edge out the demanding tone of the interviewer.
The women nodded, understanding. Her small eyes flicked to the camera as she responded, 'Tout le monde sait.
Cet endroit est un bordel. Une maison de pute.'
Her lip twisted.
'J'ai toujours dit que quelque chose de mal allait leur arriver.'
The translator, unsure if he was allowed, repeated her word for word, '*Everyone knows.*
This place is a brothel. A whore house.
I always said something bad was going to happen to them.'
'Thank you,' the reporter responded. 'Back to the studio.'
'Okay, thank you. Now, we also have an update over at the hostage site in the UK ...'
And Myles knew he had lost. He knew he had failed. He knew the world he'd been trying to build had just gone up in smoke. It was nothing more than a fantasy - he'd been two steps behind all along.
But worse than that, he knew it was his fault. All of them would still be breathing, their bodies still together, if he'd just stayed away.
And worst of all: he knew Eli had beaten him.

Bubbling with rage, he saw the barista was trembling beneath him; looking around him, he saw all of the customers were scrunched up, diving for cover, begging him to look away, to not choose them. Maybe he'd given them something to fear.
Catharsis.
Rage.
Fury. Bulls. Meat. Chain. Blood. Bones. Stampedes.
He hadn't let himself be angry, properly angry, since that night on the boat; his last blackout, his last case of 'dissociative fugue'; so today, he did. He let out a tantrum that would make women long to be barren. He tore the TV from its stand and kicked it in half. He smashed through the glass that had been promising chocolate muffins and banana bread. He aged himself ten years as he sent his blood pressure soaring off the scale, freeing himself to kick, stamp, shatter and rise up all the makings of the market. Everything inanimate, he destroyed, reaching back through the glass to pelt the muffins through the air, ripping a whole lemon cake in half. He was so free from inhibition it almost felt good. For thirty seconds, he was truly himself, could truly see how much they feared him. The fear felt good. Even as he pushed over a barrel of coffee and half of it flicked up his arms, it felt good.
For thirty seconds. Then he was done. He gave a final laugh at the positions the crowd had contorted themselves into to avoid the wrath of the raging beast he had become. Should he put everyone out of their misery, just pick one to kill so the rest knew it was over?
No. Never. Not me.
A voice pounded into his head. A foot thumped into his heart.
Erica.
Turning in the direction of the hospital; he continued to run.

1 Mile Away

A street all to himself. Rain began to fall. A lamppost in the corner.
'I'm *siiiinging* in the rain.'
He spun around. Who said that?
'Just dancing in the rain … what a glorious feeling.'
Valentina. Just like that, it was Valentina. In a pink raincoat and black boots. She was the only person in the world who could handle being in the same street as him.
She held up her hands. No weapons.
'I'm happy again.' He finished the line for her. She spun around the pole. The rain came down harder, soaking her hair and running her mascara like mud. She shivered and yet, she smiled. 'That girl always gets you hurting, doesn't she?' She said. 'Always saving her cos you can't save your own soul.'
Myles approached the lamp post. Why wasn't he running any more?

Valentina caught the rain on her tongue. 'You know Eli's lying to you, don't you? You know he won't let you win, no matter who you kill - he just wants you broken, out of the way, so he can get to her.' *She's right.* 'Deep down you know it; you just don't want to give up on her. You don't have to do it, Myles. You don't owe them anything.' Myles wasn't sure if that was rain or tears he could feel on his cheeks. *She's right.*
He grew ten feet taller. Valentina's tits got rounder. *She's right.*
'Baby, if you really want to bring that man down, if you really want to see your country choose mercy, you can't do it alone. And you can't do it with the Healer.
You don't need the girl with the touch of life. You need the girl with the kiss of death.' She licked the rain off his cheek. She held out her hand. 'Only I can destroy him. So what are you waiting for?'
Myles took her hand. 'Are you able to run?'
She laughed. 'Oh Myles, oh Myles. You have no idea. I do not run. *I fly.*'

Chapter Fifty

Back at the clinic, Erica asked them again. 'So? Does anybody know why Jill chose this place? Why she chose you?'

They were silent. For some it was just enough to bathe in her glow.

'You're starting to respect her, aren't you?' Erica said. 'To think you can trust her.' Now and then she reached out to brush a wrist or a calf of theirs, to fuse it back together where the bomb had got it. 'Well trust me; the woman in front of you is not a good person. She's nothing but pious, not an ounce of ethics. She'd close our legs before she closed Guantanamo Bay. Now – anybody gonna tell me why?'

'It's because of the sex.' Someone piped up from the fleshy floor.

'Yes, duh,' Erica replied. They were in a ring around her, mirroring Jill's lecture earlier. 'But why is she punishing you, just for sex?'

Jill sat calmly in the corner. She gestured to them warmly, indicating she did not mind them responding.

'I think I know,' a voice spoke bravely. 'I think she was abused.'

'No!' A voice bit back sharply. 'Nah. Too obvious. I think she's lonely. So rejected she's turned that rejection into rage.'

Erica turned to Jill. 'So, Jill, which one is it? Speak the truth. They deserve to know why you're doing this to them.'

'Wait – it's neither.'

Another weak voice came from somewhere, muffled. They realised with surprise, that a pile of exploded condoms in the corner, was moving. And from it crawled Kate. They'd thought she'd been killed when they'd dropped the machine on her, but really it had just concussed her, and indeed like all condoms should, protected her. She had been listening for a while now.

Sky dragged herself out, blue and black patches all over, her lemony hair stuck to her head. She gritted her teeth in pain before continuing.

'She said something earlier, did nobody else hear it? *'And I was cringing over a period I had never wanted to receive, at a time I truly believed I might finally be pregnant'* … tell us more, Jill. Tell us about motherhood.'

'No, shut up,' someone snapped at Kate, before bitterly looking up at Jill. 'Tell us why you are punishing us for doing something natural.'

Finally, Jill spoke.

'You're right. Sex *is* natural. In fact it's the most natural thing in the world. Even I can admit that – I wouldn't be here without it. None of us would. Because it has a biological purpose, and that is to make children.

The day after I left school, I found out I was infertile. No procedure out there for me. Just like that my future was gone. What was I if not a mother?

I know we're in a modern world, and not everyone feels this, but for me, that was all I did feel. I wanted children. Four. A girl first, then a boy, then another

two. I didn't care who I had them with, it was all about them for me.. Growing old with them. My whole heart was for them.'
She closed her eyes, sucking in the pain, feeling her mind sharpen inside her.
'Just one. Why couldn't I have just one? It made me feel like the only person in the world. It made me feel so, so wrong. I didn't know what to do next so I tried to ignore it.
But you all made it so, so hard. In this world where sex sells and raunchy reigns. Every day watching you use your bodies, not for your purpose, but for your own pleasure.'
'I hate that line.' Erica shot back. 'What is wrong with pleasure?'
The only time Jill would ever get on her knees was to speak these next words. To her they were a whole new prayer.
'You're right.' She crawled through the floor of flesh, til she got close enough to Jade. 'Jade. Do you know how lucky you are – to be able to have a child of your own?' She reached into
Jades pocket and retrieved the form she had been filling in, eyes scamming it quickly. 'But look at this.' She read it out. "Are you on any birth control? Tick.'She shook her head and then gave her the world's worst paper cut. 'How could you waste that gift? Don't you see how there's something in you, waiting to be loved? Why would you use your body for anything but that?' Tears began to flow, chunky and opulent. 'Why? Somebody tell me! Why all this filth, all this selfish sin, rubbing my face in it – *how could you* – '
'Oh cut it out, Jill.' Erica snapped. Then she kneeled down too. 'We all know why you all *really* want one.' A knife in her voice, her teeth started to tease. 'A child just for your own. No one around. Doors closed. No one stopping you. I bet you can't wait to nurse – '
'No!' screamed Jill. Shock bounced in her eyes. 'That's not it! No! Never!'
'Oh but Jill, look how desperate you are,' Erica crawled closer. 'Blowing up buildings over it; that's not desperation, that's *frustration.* Maybe you don't know it yet, but that's what you want. What you desire. I can see it in your eye – '
'NO! Shut up! I want a child – '
'Yes, yes, you do – '
'To care for – '
'Yes, to care for so very nicely – all to yourself - '
'Stop it!'
'Hey, maybe if you admit this to yourself, you'll find a way. To get what you really want. No more standing between you and that deep, inky dream.'
'Stop, Erica, stop …' Jill was begging. Sealing up her ears to not let the words in.
'Cos it's gonna be deep. Isn't it? It's in the deepest part of your mind - '
'NO!' This time Jill screamed so loud, in a mix of tears and flem, and shrieked so high the walls shook. 'NO, NO, NO!' The only word she knew. It wasn't

true, this humiliatingly cruel assumption, and Erica's dainty words skinned her inside out. More tears came; perforated from a life of disappointment, of jealousy, she was already sterile, now she sterilised herself in her own tears, never more useless, never more wombless.

Now there was something in her eyes that had never been there. Enjoying itself as it condensed on the surface. Can an eye smell of milk? Hers did.

She clicked her fingers at the terrorists guarding the door. 'I'm done.' Calm again.

'Done?' they asked.

'Done waiting for Eli. Done with everyone here.' She nodded, agreeing with herself, sweeping her arms across the room. 'We're not going to wait for Eli. He can catch Erica himself if he wants her.'

Suddenly the room felt extremely hot.

'Hang them.'

Suddenly it was a furnace.

'Every one of them.'

Suddenly the ice was burning.

Erica stepped forward. Suddenly her lips were locusts. 'Jill, what are you doing? Eli won't let you go against his plan.'

'I don't care any more,' Jill snarled. 'You're not worth this, and if he can't see that … hang them. Hang them all.'

'Jill!' Erica rasped. 'Stop it right now. You want him to turn up to corpses?'

Jill shook her off. 'I'm not fighting for those who don't want it. Let alone don't deserve it.'

Suddenly a girl was snatched up. Then a guy, then a girl, then a man then a woman then a bloke. 'All of them.' Jill's team got to work. Suddenly they knew what it was to be white hot.

Suddenly there was nothing but sweat.

Suddenly Erica started to fry. 'Jill, I was just *joking. I'm sorry!'*

'Healers don't make jokes. You're not a healer; you're the princess of pain now. Erica Ash, high priestess of pain; witness this.'

It was happening. Cam and Kate were tossed into the air. Jill pointed to the roof. 'Hang 'em all, so my future child can pluck them down and play with them.'

Nobody knew where the rope had come from – perhaps it had been used to wrap the roses – but the terrorists had plenty of rope, and plenty of strength.

The carcass of the bomb through the ceiling had formed a criss-cross of beams above reception. A pipe here, half a bed there - debris that was just strong enough to hang from.

Looking up for the first time in hours, they saw the man who had been raining on them, still strapped into his stirrups. He seemed to finally have stopped shedding. 'Don't do this!' He cried, as he saw ropes being thrown up towards him, catching on beams and tightening. 'Not this! Let them go!'

The carers were still armed, and it was easy to grab people, pick them out at random. The ones who looked too heavy to hang were thrown into a pile.
First one, then two, then three, then four. After the fourth person they heard the first break of a bone.
'Let them touch.' Jill said with a shrug. 'Let them be close.'
Then five, then six, then seven. Bones popped, singing a chorus 'Sorry.' But it was too late.
'Jill, STOP!' Erica grabbed her. 'Fucking stop! I'm sorry for what I said – I was just teasing, just trying to get under your skin, cos I knew that would be what really hurt you!'
'Well you did, Erica. You got too far under my skin, and I'm going to show you that for once you don't belong. So get out.'
'But it was a joke! A joke! Can't you take a joke?'
'I wasn't born to laugh. I was born for this.' She gestured to her comrades. The first two victims were hoisted up, their throats turned into a spinning wheel on a spine. A brutal brown rope groped their necks. How long would they last? Who would snap the strangest shape before they died?
'No, listen, Jill, please! Eli won't want this! He'll want them alive!'
'Well, I want them dead. And it's all your fault.'
A body was carried past them, kicking, the sound of a rope tightening.
Erica went to grab somebody from Bea, but in a fight, she was weak, whimsical, her hands not cut out for real work. She could have healed them from anything, but she couldn't save them from the carer's strength. 'Think of Eli! Think what he'll do!'
Jill sighed. 'What makes you think he's coming, Erica? How do you know he's even forgiven you for leaving us? You know he hates quitters.'

Chapter Fifty One

On that, Jill was wrong.
Eli was in his car now, looking out the window. He had seen the video of her arriving at the hospital, walking confidently into his destruction. In fact he kept replaying it.
And before he had even seen the video, he had been on his way. Summoned, if you like, by the thought of her.
Ann sat to his left, Phyllis, the largest and most physically robust carer to his right. He had known Jill may need backup and had been bringing them already, before Erica had even asked to see Ann again. Yet another sign that it was he that could give her what she wanted.
Ann's eyes danced as she stared through the windscreen, her corneas splashed with the sights he had kept her from. Her mouth parted with every new image, every new flash of the metropolitan life she had left behind. When she'd arrived at Core, he'd told her she'd never see the outside world again, that it had denounced her. He hoped she was grateful to Erica - only Erica could get him to do this.
All he could think about was what she would think when she saw him - the weight he had put on, the hair he had lost, the yellow tinge his skin had acquired, the way his teeth didn't brush bright enough anymore. All because she had left him. But, by the grease in his feet and the sty in his eye, he was going to get her back.

Eli closed his eyes as Paddington Station came into view. The journey had flown by, milked through mellifluously on the thought of her.
Now he was so close he could taste her. By the end of today, she would be his again. She would understand her purpose again. He knew Jill wouldn't let him down; whatever she was doing in there, it would be enough for Erica to devote herself to a life of service.
He stepped out of the car, enjoying the way the press bubbled when they saw him, how the swell of cameras still came for him. He caught the eyes of the crowd and - *yes, yes, yes, there it was* - he saw the reverence. In a capital that was tired of harbouring death, full of people who were tired of being given up on - a daughter whose mother had quit, a husband whose wife hadn't had the strength, a doctor who'd never got the chance to save his own son - a man like Eli, with an ethos like his, was welcome.
He closed the car door and leant against it.
All he had to do was wait. A few more minutes.
By the bloat in his throat and the cyst in his wrist, she would be in his arms once more.
The ash is the answer.

Chapter Fifty Two

Heather read out their names on their forms.
Four people would be hung first. One of them was the deceiver, the adulterer, Cam.
His toes reached for the ground but he was just too high to plant them in the Earth. Erica had been wrong about Jill, and Jill wanted to show her just how wrong: show her that people *could* die under her watch. She was no longer Eli's accomplice, and Erica was no longer Eli's angel - these twitching bodies would be their own legacy.
The first rope was about to be pulled, Nora's hand closing around it, ready to ring the bell of the bellend, the cheating Cam. He looked down at Erica, in fact they all looked at her – could she do anything for them, now?
There was one thing.
Only one thing left she could try.
'Wait!'
She could tell them a story. The story of Erica Ash.
'My name is Erica Ash, and one day I am going to die in a fire.'
She swept directly under Cam. Nora's hand paused on the rope. Proceedings were paused. Right now, they needed a fairytale; Erica could be that for them. She swallowed. *Let's begin.*
'Erica Ash was born in Sussex, in a cottage, and raised by her mother. Growing up she always had a dog. Her last one was a spaniel, Lexi. She was kind of a lonely child; her personality didn't really come til she was a teen.
She did well at school, but not that well. She realised however that she loved to party. It wasn't always easy, though, to get invited. She lost her virginity at 17, way later than she wanted to. She got 3 Bs at A Level. She got into fashion school, but it bored her. So she quit and travelled for a bit.
When she was twenty she was kidnapped by a man named Eli. He kept her in a 6 foot by 6 foot cage in the basement of his house. He did everything he could think of to her and even things he didn't really want to do; things that had to be done to see his experiments through. And then one day he let her go.
Once she was free she wanted to live. They expected her to be more cautious after captivity, but unfortunately she wanted to feel everything she hadn't felt. Everything they told her not to. Can you feel too much? I don't think so.
Then you all know what happened next. She realised what happened she felt people, when she touched them. She realised she had something in her she couldn't waste. The end of loneliness, the end of pain, trapped within her body. What would her mama say if she didn't use it? So she used it, and she let them use her.
Then Eli took her again. And he made her work. For months she was at his retreat, and she never saw anything but skin.

I can't tell you how good it felt to heal you all. To turn your screams into sighs. You can never be too kind, you can never be too nice, you can never be too good.
But maybe you can be too … pure. Was this who Erica Ash really was? All she was? This angel? Surely there was something more to her. A shot of blood in the morning yolk. So a man named Myles came to get her, and she went with him. To see if she could be something more than a healer.
Turns out she was right. She was more. She had edge. She always knew she was born with spice. Always knew she was a bad girl.
But.
She never knew she was had enough to do … ***this.***
A year after her escape, Erica Ash slit a woman's throat.'
The knife had been waiting in her stockings, pressing into the cream of her thigh. It felt good there, the blade crisp and the tip cold. She pulled up her skirt, revealing both thigh and the blade; as she confidently slid it into her hands, she tossed it from one to the other and then mischievously, impishly, she did as she said. The weapon may have been cold but it went through Jill's throat like a hot knife through butter.
Kinkier than thou, she baptised her with hate.
Eli always told her to be a woman, to bleed like one; 'don't bleed like a girl.'
Well, Jill bled like a bitch.

She was a melting cherry and a raspberry rainstorm and crimson quartzes rolling down a hill. She was crushed velvet and strawberry cyanide and a run over robin and everything Valentines Day tried to deny.
Oh yes, sit on them with the mouth of a ruby.
The world turned a little redder.
The world turned a little wetter.
Captors distracted, Cam the hangman was chopped down. He came for Jill too. They all did.
She had treated them like creatures, so now they crawled. All the patients, strong all of a sudden now they saw Jill could bleed too. They came for her, two by two. The knife danced from Cam to Kate to Amber to Erica and back again. It hit a spot deeper and sweeter than anything sex had been able to reach, and turned their bodies out, capillary by capillary. Replacing one urge with the other, morphing desire into rage – there was nowhere else for their rage to go but Jill. She didn't even bother asking them to stop.
For these patients, these guests, who'd come to this clinic on this day, this was their fate: not to heal, but to kill. And now their fate would be sealed.
If it hadn't been for Jade.

It was Jill's screams that woke the girl up.

From the pile of golden plastic, she emerged, wincing as the impact started to play with her bones. She kept her eyes closed – she didn't want to see where or why the screams were happening. Through the flicker of her eyelids, she saw a flash of thick, pink ankle, writhing around on the floor, and couldn't help but prise her eyes open to check – was that *Jill*?

Both eyes popped open. Like a revenge fantasy, the terrorist was now the one lying on the floor, trembling and squealing. Her clothes had been cut. It was shocking to see, she had bosoms and pubes, just like the rest of them. A pack of attackers surrounded her, finally relenting, finally satisfied.

The sky in Jade's head cleared. That was blood. A lot of blood. It was running loose across the floor, slick and energetic. Blood coming from her face, from her neck, from both her sides, from her upper thighs, from her ankle too.

One thing Jade loved almost as much as sex, was working in a team. Guess that's why she liked foursomes so much.

'Guys!' she was standing, hovering on her feet, looking across the beaten heads of the prisoners around her. 'She's bleeding! She's bleeding out! We need to stop the loss!'

She hopped over fingernails, over needles and clipboards, til she reached Jill. Her own hands were bleeding too – she flashed back to Jill, rubbing them in the glass.

She threw herself to her knees and sealed both her hands over Jill's side, the side that was emptying the most profusely. She pressed her knee down too.

'Guys, come on, *help* me! She can't lose this much blood!' With the same enthusiasm as Jill would have stopped her losing her virginity, she managed to back up the flow from the wound. But this was only one hole. And Jill now had many.

'Come on, guys! Please! This is horrible!' Her voice broke. 'I need you guys to help!'

A man opposite her began to crawl towards her. Though his mercy towards Jill was smaller than Kate's crabs, he wanted to help. A large gash had skin hanging off his forehead, and his nose was broken and bleeding, the bone exposed. He took the other side of Jill's abdomen and began applying pressure. The same pressure with which she had stamped on his hands.

'Good! Thank you! You need to hold down, use everything you can, use your knees. Oh god, her throat! Has anyone got a bandage?'

'Use this.' It was flung at her from the corner. It was a white strip of knickers, ripped open to be able to hold the throat together with ease.

'Thank *you*.' Jade said. 'Someone get her thigh! It could have got the artery up there.'

The same person who had thrown their knickers placed their hands over the thigh, but the gash was too big. She looked around helplessly, but nobody had joined to help. So she straddled her leg, her bare pubic bone brushing the thigh.

Two more people joined, holding Jill's wrists, holding her together. The colour was coming back into her face. Another started checking her wound for glass, their own wounded, glass-chipped arm bleeding profusely too.
Another sticky, slashed hand cradled her head, which was leaking really badly now. If they didn't press tight enough she was probably in danger of brain damage.
'STOP!'
At first Jade couldn't believe who the stop had come from. But then it came again, louder and more desperate. It was from Jill.
'Your blood! All your blood! It's everywhere! It's dripping into me!'
She wasn't wrong. Cut, gash or laceration, drip, splatter or flow – all of it was falling without discrimination, and landing in Jill's many wounds.
'You're all bleeding! Please, stop, stop, I don't know what I might catch! I've seen your forms – and you!' She yelled at the woman straddling her thigh. 'You're going to spread something to me. I can already feel it, something in your skin. Please – please, get off!'
A blistered mouth kissed her on the nose. 'Shh, darling. Stay calm. We're going to help you.'
'But you're wounded! You're bleeding! It's going into mine!'
Indeed it was. Not one drop to be wasted, the blood mingled, a flowing free for all, from the hands that kept her wounds sealed. She was gaining energy, shouting back at them. Jade took her hands from the matronly woman's side to grab her face with them.
'Jill! Listen! We're saving you! We're helping you! Now I'll give you a choice. If we stop, you'll bleed out. You want that? Do you?'
The thrill of her betrayal worn off, she remained radicalised by Eli's ideology: breath at any cost. Jill shook her head.
'Exactly. Okay. So calm down. Breathe. You're not dying today. Not with us.' Jade moved her hands back to her wound. 'You're going to live.'
'Because of you?'
'Because of us.'
Weakened, Jill realised what was happening. That the ones she'd poured blame upon, were the ones now out to save her.
She lay back and felt the weight of the people – always more people – applying pressure and keeping her safe. The horny healers. What kind of joke was this?
'You do realise, Jill, this has been who we are the whole time..' Jade spoke softly, sweat running down her tiger tattoo. 'At any point we could've held you hostage with our skin, with our plasma. But we didn't. So I have to ask you. Are we still worthless, in your eyes?'
Jill looked up to the flickering lights. A reel of images went past her, of the life she had lived and the life she had been too afraid to. Jade. What a nice name, if she'd been able to have a girl. 'No.' Her voice bloomed open with regret and even the faintest beginnings of respect. 'No, you're not.'

'Good,' Jade massaged her side gently. 'So tell us the code, to diffuse the other bomb in here. It's time we let the paramedics' in, don't you agree?'
Jill did. And like a submissive, she spoke. The code was 634, and the other bomb was Bea's hairpin. It was diffused within seconds, and one of the most capable captives was allowed to run, to tell the ambulance they could come. On her instruction, her tender terrorists walked out, hands up, beginning their surrender.
In the corner of the room, Jade caught eyes with Erica. Erica gave her a subtle salute.

And what do ya know –
When the story of this day is told, let it be known, it was the 'slut' that saved the day.
A little whore on horseback, too hot to be a fireman, too busy swallowing swords to wield one of her own, but when it came down to it, she was the one that got them out.
It's been staring you in the face this whole time. There's no one kinder than the slut. They're a giver. They're selfless. And they're all about pleasure.
Long live the slut.

Hands up, they exited the hospital.
The terrorists were expecting to see paramedics, paparazzi and policemen but before all that, they saw Eli. Of course he had been let through first. Ann and Phyllis on either side of him, he stood there in a blaze. Waiting.
They couldn't meet him in his eye as they made their way to the riot police, beginning their surrender. The crowd cat called them, angry at seeing the faces of radical righteousness, at the fanatical fascists that had fought against their freedoms. 'You don't get to tell us how to live!'
Then they waited patiently, to see her. Don't tell them The Healer had died in there.
The paramedics spilled in, and to the crowd's disappointment Jill was the first to be stretchered out, only just breathing. Eli didn't give anything away; it was like he didn't recognise her. She knew it would be this way. If she had the strength she would have called to him, but she only had the strength to regret.
And Eli only had the strength to wait. To stare at the entrance and wait for her. Come on. Not long now.
A throng of hostages spilled out. Another gaggle of people, running into their families arms. The paramedics carrying out more. Straight away it was obvious: their bodies were in a much more uplifting state than what had been expected. The Healer had done her thing.
At last, a final ripple of people spilled free, and at last Eli saw Erica enclosed in its voltran. She almost blended in until he caught her eye, driving her to a stop. One look at her and everything inside him flipped.

'Erica.'
As press swarmed around them and hostages streamed past them, Erica and Eli stood on the pathway, six feet from each other, and all that mattered were each other's eyes.
Calmly, Erica went to him. 'Eli. You came.'
'Of course. I came to get you back.'
Erica giggled. She bounced a little on her heels.
Eli grinned. The yellow pallor was fading already. Even she could admit, she liked him like this; more rugged, more messy, more handsome. More to heal.
'Then follow me to the roof.' Wistful, she began lacing away from him, heading for the back of the building, cutting her calves as she stepped into the shrubbery. Careless, not caring, not careful; just free.
He heard the pathetic sounds of an ambulance in the distance, the nee-nor-nee-nor that couldn't do an inch of what she could do. 'Whatever you say, healer.'
'Wait!' The tug at her shorts came, abrasive and powerful. 'Erica. My – my – '
'Oh, of course!' Erica smiled. 'Your *sores*. For you, Jade, anything.'
She looked back over her shoulder. 'Eli, you can be patient, can't you?' She didn't wait for an answer. She touched Jade on the head, running her hand through the crimson waves.
Looked at the other thirty or so people, huddled around the ambulance, bundled up in blankets. 'Eli, you're going to have to wait a little longer.' She marched towards them.
'Sure thing, baby.' He watched her go and reach the crowd.
She had healed them off their breaks and their burns, but it was time for the cherry on top. Healers don't discriminate, and they certainly don't judge. Kate's itch, Cam's zit, Jade's sore and Amber's rash - there was nothing she wasn't willing to quell. Giddily, they lined up before her.
She was holding a torn, crumpled warning poster from reception in her hand, and she read it out mockingly. ' "It feels good in the moment, but the itch will be with you for life. Live sensible, cos there are some mistakes you can't get rid of".'
Slowly, she ripped the poster. 'Who are they to say that?' She dropped the fragments on the ground. 'Shall we prove them wrong?'

In the twenty minutes it took, the cold came, and there's no cold like a February night. Once her fingers were blue and she couldn't feel them anymore, she was ready for the roof. She met Eli's eyes.
'Let's go.'

Chapter Fifty Three

Vibrant. Kinetic. Airborne.

That's how it felt, as Myles and Valentina reached the clinic, the wind of the world behind them. By some kind of neat trick, the moment their feet touched the ground, they blended into the throng of paparazzi and public all absorbing the result, what seemed like the denouement of the day.

The terrorists had surrendered. The hostages had been released. The paramedics were tending what little wounded there were.

Erica had done it all but the most important thing.

'I told you,' Valentina whispered to him, smug as she watched Myles watch Erica.

He had arrived just in time to see her saunter up to Eli, embedding herself in the smile that lit up his face as he saw her. Bile became his brain as he watched her take his hand, and lead him to the rooftop.

Fuck. Fuck. Fuck. 'She's going to let him get away with it.'

Chapter Fifty Four

Now they were just a man and a woman on a rooftop on Valentine's Day. Just two people, trying to be special.

Cold grey air and a heavy grey sky. Wet gravel beneath them and smooth rails around them. They were just two people, with something to say.

Ten feet between them. Eli in the middle of the rooftop, like a dart in its target. Erica leaning, casual, beautiful, on the railings. Both had goose pimples but only one of them was cold.

'So,' he spoke to the girl, the only girl, he wanted to celebrate today with. 'What's it gonna take to bring you back to Core?'

She rippled at his words, reclining her neck, closing her eyes and breathing it all in. Her hands stroked the bars of the rails.

'I know it's not money. Not adoration; you have enough of that, you'll always have enough of that. Not possessions. I can offer you your freedom – this time, you'd be at the retreat on your terms – but you already have that. So what hope do I have really, except for the belief that you miss doing it?'

The wind whistled and the sky got a little darker. She stared back at him with total poise, relaxed and satisfied as he spoke.

'There is something.' She said finally. 'There's something you can do.'

He stepped closer. 'Anything.'

She moved to the side, her hand running along the railing again. 'I want to touch you in a different way. A way we haven't done before.'

'Go on. Tell me where. Tell me how.'

'I want to push you. I want you to die.' She was braiding her hair, all feminine fingers. 'Then I want to bring you back. Haven't you always wanted to be brought back by me?'

She turned now, her silhouette carved into the sky, fingers tapping lightly on the railings. 'We both stand here, and then I push you.

Let me make you a bird. Let me watch you fly, then bring you back. And this time … I'll make you last forever.

I'm serious. You know I can do it. I'll make you infinite. Eternal. You know I can do it. Of course it has to be you. The man who died so he could never die again. That's you, Eli.

You first, then everyone who's ever left someone behind next. We'll bring back the fathers, the mothers, the sons. The end of grief, remember? Isn't that what this is all for?'

He should have been scared. He should have felt it; his jaw dropping, as in actually coming apart from his skull; his eyes peeling, as in the skin literally taken from the membrane. But he didn't. He felt calm. So calm he joined her at the railings.

'So many people have done it. Jumped, I mean,' she continued calmly. 'Jumped. Myles, your mother, a man named Sam this morning. Look down. It's only gravel down there. I'm gonna push you.' She put her hand on his chest. 'Right here.'

Only gravel. Only gravity.

'You're right.' He said. 'I think we should do it. How high are we?'

She smiled a smile he didn't think she was capable of, an aspartame smile that made his neck pulse. 'Nineteen.' She replied sweetly.

A pause. 'Sorry?'

'Nineteen feet high.' Erica leaned back, her hair swinging over the side.

'You're sure?'

'I am. Because *twenty would be too dangerous, and eighteen would be too safe.* Eli? What's wrong?'

Eli took a step backwards, and even that was difficult, walking away from her. But he had to. 'Erica, please.'

'What?'

'Not nineteen.' A gulp. 'Can't we go lower? Or higher? Let's find another rooftop.'

Erica shook her head. 'Nah. What a waste of time, when we're already up here.' She held out her hand. 'Come on, babe. I'll do it quickly. You'll be down there with the leaves and the chewing gum in no time.'

Eli was starting to sweat, February making the secretion cold and sickly. Though her voice was soft and her expression apple-picking innocent, he knew she knew what he was thinking. 'Erica. Please.'

'What is it, darlin'?'

'Make it thirty. Or forty. But not nineteen.'

'Why?'

'I just can't. I've seen what that number does to people.' He saw his words flash back to him in her eyes, lit up with triumph. It had only been a matter of time.

'What do you mean?'

'You know.'

'Nope, no,' she said casually, turning her back to him and looking out at the sky. 'I don't. Jolt my memory.'

'The game – '

'Ah, of *course*! That game you play at Core Retreat?' Her voice rose. 'The one where people are forced to dive into an empty pool? Of course!' She spoke abundantly, sarcastically, in a teasing performance of everything coming into place in her head. 'I thought you *loved* that game.'

Eli looked to the floor. Waves of something suppressed in his subconscious started to seize its chance. Something ominous and thick lay down in his lungs.

'So come on. You've come all this way. Let's play.'

Eli looked up. He looked to the rails. 'We can play. But.' He tried to be calm. 'Are you sure we can't go higher?'

'As sure as I am that you love me.' Her voice broke. 'So do this for me.'

He paced back and forth. 'I can't.' He wrung his hands together. Could he? 'It's the *number*, Erica. Nineteen. Argh!'
Her eyes gleamed as she saw the confession writhe beneath his teeth. 'Say it. If you want me to come back to Core, say it.'
It walked through his mind but he couldn't say, couldn't even find the words. 'It's – '
'Whatever happens to you, I'll bring you straight back.'
'IMNOTSUREIFIWOULDWANNACOMEBACK!' The words lurched out, sprinkled with shock. He tried to put them back in before more tumbled out. 'Not like that! Not as half of me, as some powdered up version of me! What if I came back without my teeth? What if I came back without my mind? Anything can happen, down there, with that number! I can already see it – the way you'd look at me, the way you'd hold me. And to be like that … *forever*?!' He walked to the edge and looked down, the pavement slopping its way up to meet him. This didn't even classify as a 'bird's eyes view'. 'I can't.'
Erica was next to him, not a bit surprised. She ran a hand up his back. 'It does seem a bit *grisly*.' She looked down too. A squirrel darted past. She squeezed his neck. 'There's no such thing as gruesome any more. There's only you, and this. So fall.'
Eli's hands closed over the rail. His breath was loud in the air. He loved her, he loved her, he loved her.
'Be stronger than your nightmares. Be braver than your dreams.'
He hoisted himself up so he was sat on the railing, still facing her. So this was how it felt. 'Like this?' he said.
'Like that.' she smiled, weaving in between his legs. This was home. 'Where shall I push you?' She placed a hand on his chest. Over his heart. 'I guess there's nowhere else but here.' Her hand warmed into him. 'Want me to countdown?'
The rain answered, starting to splash. He nodded. 'Okay.'
'Here we go. Ten. Nine. Eight. Seven. Six.'
'No!' He pushed her off him, the force sending her flying into the safety behind the railings.
Ears ringing, he slid off the railing, planting his feet back on the rooftop. 'I'm sorry, I'm sorry, I just can't!'
Erica pressed against him, looking up with mock concern, mock shock. 'But you're *Eli*. "Life is a gift, no matter what." *Eli* would live through anything. Any hurdle, any trouble, *Eli* can overcome it. *Eli* can't give up. Right? That's you. That's all you've ever said. *Isn't it*?'
Resentfully, the disappointing, silenced truth began working its way through his muscles, twitching his nose and curling his lip.
To Erica's surprise, he sank to the floor.
She knelt down gently next to him. Her voice was sharpened at the edges; landing as light as butterflies who'd learnt how to sting.

'Remember everything you told everyone at Core. Everything you made them do. All the pain they had to walk through. All the rules you laid down on them. A whole world you created. Now it's up to you.'
He looked up at her. With his beautiful eyes she had healed. They were weak. Wet. Something missing.
'How can they believe in you if you don't do it? Believe, Eli.' Her voice rolled with contempt. 'Don't tell me you don't believe in yourself, when you believe so hard in me.'
He looked into her eyes. The one who had changed it all for him. Then he scrunched up his face into a reluctant sigh, and shook his head. 'I'm not gonna do it, Erica. I can't.' Just to be sure; 'Nineteen is the age I lost my mother. I can't face what's down there.'
At this final relent, liquid flowed through Erica. Scorn flashed in her eyes, and finally she spoke truthfully. She leaned into him, the words barely getting out through her bared teeth. 'Then you were wrong about Core. You were wrong about euthanasia. Everything you've done has been wrong.'
There had never been anything weaker, anything more defeated, anything softer or sadder, than the way he simply nodded.
But she was right. If he couldn't do this, he didn't believe in himself, and that meant everything he'd done had been not only a lie, but a mistake. So he nodded, up and down, in the arms of the girl he'd taken all those years ago. He'd always been her puppet really, she'd never been his.
'Say it.'
'Okay.' He said. 'I was wrong. It's over.'
Coward. He heard it all around him. *Hypocrite.* The first of a thousand slurs coming his way. *Quitter.*
There was a whistle of wind that greeted Ann and Phyllis, as they too descended on the rooftop.
'Ann,' Erica said warmly. 'Did you get that?'
Ann held up the phone, tapped the screen twice. 'It's all on a voice memo.' She smiled. 'Every word.' Eli watched, weak, as the mic of the device flashed red: *recording.*
'Don't worry,' Erica brushed Eli's head; he sighed into her touch. Would this be the last time, the very last time he would feel it? 'It's just insurance. Ann's good at keeping secrets; she's had that phone for a while now.'
'What …' Eli said.
Erica giggled. She had been waiting for this moment all day. Even her dreams had relished it. 'Ann. Come here.' She stood up, leaving Eli on the ground. She beckoned to Ann.
The older woman waddled towards her until she got close. Then closer again. Then closer still. Too close.
Eli gasped.
Closer. A little closer. There we go. Their bodies pressed together.

Erica's sunk to her knees. Her hands came with her, before they made contact with Ann. All he'd ever said about Ann was she was a woman who didn't deserve to be touched, and now she was being touched by an angel.
First they touched her ankles. The corduroy socks.
'Oh yes. A little while ago I received a letter from Darren Thames. He'd worked out an undetectable way to get post in and out of Core. The next thing I knew he had sent me a letter from Ann. Ann asked for a camera..'
Now the hands caressed Ann's calves. Closed around the thermal of her tights.
'And so I sent one.'
Eli's eyes stretched as he watched the hands moving up, further still, higher still.
'I got that camera into your favourite well, and I believe it is Michelle that dived down and smuggled it in.' Erica closed her eyes, remembering when she'd read Darren's plan, her heart swelling as she thought of Michelle hearing that she'd almost pulled it off. 'Isn't that right, Ann?'
'Yes,' Ann whispered.
'And that camera was given to Ann. And Ann has been using that camera for all sorts of things.'
And up went her hands, Erica's body sloping with them as they went. They dared to pass the curmudgeonous knees, dared to push the doughy quads of the woman apart.
And then, and then, they dared to rip into her tights.
Ann moaned as Erica's hands claimed her upper thighs. Upper. Inner. Up, up, up.
'I've heard Ann's quite the videographer, and let's just say, Ann's found the angles. Ann's found all kinds of ways of capturing your games - 19 Feet High, Mints Or Morphine, the one where you burn people just a little. Ann's got such an eye for detail, even the hidden details; the truth of the tunnel, the truth about what you did to Scott Luther, the truth about what's really inside the boxes of ash you send to grieving families. Ann's captured it all.'
Erica's hands had now come to a place that was not leg nor quad nor thigh nor really even flesh; the place concealed behind Ann's grey, threadbare knickers, her skirt hitched around her wench's waist to allow Erica easy access.
'Erica,' Eli spluttered. 'Stop. Stop this. This isn't you.'
'I will let Ann, not you, tell me who I am.' Her fingers danced up and down the cotton, the cotton between good and evil, the cotton dividing their morality in two. She made eye contact with Ann, tilted her head to ask if she could go on. Lips parted, Ann nodded.
Butterscotch fireworks erupted inside Ann as Erica edged her knickers, seam by seam, to the side, and found her way inside her. Moving through the folds, slipping into another kind of seams, the most sensitive of seams, Phyllis and Eli shocked into mutism as they watched Erica's hand disappear inside Ann. Moving and moaning, twisting and turning, opening and altering, an existential exploration until Erica's hand emerged holding the thing she wanted.

The thing Ann had smuggled inside her. For her.
The only reason she had come when Jill had called. The only reason she had done what Jill had asked. For the thing she now held between her forefinger and thumb.
Erica was holding a USB. It glittered as she held it up to a shy February sun.
'This USB contains the contents of everything Ann recorded at Core.' Her voice became honey, molasses in Eli's mind. 'Sixty days of footage, I believe. Very crisp quality indeed. All access. Not a stone unturned. Do you understand, Eli?'
'Yes.' A husk of a man spoke back to her.
'Are you sure? You understand that if you do not close Core today, and you do not denounce your philosophy, these videos will become part of UK history. The whole country will know what actually makes Eli Jones tick. Do you understand?'
'I do.'
'So you'll do what we want?'
'I will.' Eli slumped to the ground. 'You can trust me.'
Erica brushed off her hands and approached the railings, leaving Ann to fold down her skirt and readjust her tights. 'If there's one thing I trust, it's that you wouldn't lie to me.' His eyes became water.
'I wouldn't. I swear.'
She tossed him the USB.
'*That's* how much I trust you,' she said. 'That's how much I trust you'll do this for me.'
Ann baulked at the move, her eyes as ripped as her tights. A stunned Eli closed his hand around the USB, the metal lost in the flesh of his palm.
The air rippled around them, as confused as Ann. She could barely bear to question Erica but she had to.
'Erica, what are you doing?!'
Erica knelt next to Eli, to the man who'd shown her what she is capable of. She ran her hand down his face, dismissing all the logic that had ever came as she saw glimmers of what the two of them could do together. 'He's gonna show everyone he trusts me. You have to hold up your end of the bargain for me to trust you, Eli. Trust is Health. Don't you want to be healthy again?'
A glazed Eli nodded. 'I do.'
Erica winked at him. Truth be told, she still admired the man who'd held the ball where the damaged had danced. 'Then we have a chance.'

Chapter Fifty Five

Valentina and Myles were breathless, restless, panting and pulsating as they pulled into the backdoor of the clinic.

All the fun they'd been having had led them here.

She took his hand and they ran, squealing, down parquet floors that squealed too. He laughed and backed her against the wall, running his hands over her shoulders before closing them round her jaw and kissing her. Over and over again, kissing her, spinning.

Plaster fell around them. Like the world was ending.

They stalked the empty corridors, Valentina on his back, both falling to the ground, new bruises popping up everywhere. He was delirious, drunk on kissing her, letting her drag him by the ankle, further down a corridor whose lights flashed on and off.

It was only when they got to the door that they stopped.

It was a wooden door with a glass eye, you see, and when they peeked through it, they could see Eli.

Pressing her eye to the opposite door, Valentina saw Erica, Ann and Phyllis in another room, waiting to leave too. They were wrapped in blankets.

It seemed Eli had been given VIP treatment, and was waiting in a separate room.

'Fuck.' Myles said. 'They haven't turned him in. They have sixty days worth of footage, and they still haven't turned him in.'

Valentina giggled.

'Watch this,' she whispered to Myles. 'You need to hide'

'What are you gonna do?' he spoke through a voice smoked with lust and fire.

'One last trick.'

In his arms, she went limp. 'Put me somewhere he'll find me,' she managed to whisper as her eyes rolled back. 'In the corridor. Quick. Then *hide*.'

Scooping her up, she was heavy for the first time. Myles crept into the corridor and laid her behind an abandoned cleaning trolley. He caught another glimpse of Eli, pacing beyond the glass.

Suddenly, something clicked in his mind. It was like Eli was translucent - Myles could see right through him.

'Valentina?'

'Yes?'

'He should be holding a USB. If what I think has happened has happened, he'll be holding a USB.'

'Okay …'

'Whatever you do to him, get it off him. *Get it off him.* And give it to me.'

Valentina reclined. 'Your wish is my command. Now quick. Hide. He needs to find me alone.'

Myles paced backwards. 'You sure about this?'

'Trust me. It's gonna be perfect. I've seen this in a dream. Ten seconds time and Eli's gonna come out for a glass of water.'
And he did.

Eli

When I turn the corner, what I see would make any other man call for help.
It's in the corner of the corridor. A dead girl. The paramedics must have missed her.
And there I see my opportunity. To match Erica, my Erica, before we start our new life.
Once a girl, now a corpse. Another stain on the carpet – a splash of feminine death. *Don't cry; react.*
I am not like most men. I do not need backup. I *am* the help. I am Eli the great.
Eli the noble as I creep over. And with each step I take, she doesn't twitch for me, doesn't flinch for me, doesn't even breathe for me. She really is dead – but not for long.
Eli the strong as I bend down. Move the pile of pink hair that hides a neck that could be broken. *Strawberry milkshake, this one.* Reveal the tranquil face. See the closed eyes that keep their colour a secret. Run my hand over the inanimate nostrils and circle my finger round the rigid lips. She's crying out for a kiss of life.
Some might say gagging for it.
Not me. Not Eli the bold.
Eli the gentle as I mount her. Beneath me, she feels even more fragile than she looks. One chest compression and she'd just … snap.
So I kiss her. The lips of Eli the hero prise hers open and then I am filling her up with air. I'll blow her up til they call me a radical.
I can hear them already. **'Legend has it Eli resurrected someone in this spot.'**
One pump, two pumps, three pumps from Eli the martyr. All the same silly thoughts that come with resuscitation spin again now – does my breath smell, do I have a cold sore – as I continue because Eli the kind knows what's best, knows that the brittle body beneath him has more to give, knows she's worth every caress, every cradle, every exhale til he can bring her back.
Another thrust of my intimate air. Nothing will stand between me and her throat.
I know how to bring her back.
'Come on darling,' I whisper.
Nobody could have got here in time but me.
The lips are warming up and the jaw is loosening. They're all the same; it only takes a few pumps and they become easier to enter, if it wasn't already easy enough when all you're entering them with is air. I pump and pulsate and that's when a thought hits me hard; *shouldn't she be awake by now?*

In and out, in and out, I will not deprive the world of a mother, of a lover, of a friend, I want to see her smile, I want to know the colour of her eyes –
I'm not giving up on her.
I'm bringing her back.
Suddenly all that matters is giving this girl the chance she deserves. All that matters is bringing her back. Suddenly it doesn't matter about being Eli the great, Eli the bold; Eli the saviour and Eli the martyr mean nothing to me; I couldn't care less about being Eli the noble, Eli the kind.
Just please don't let me become Eli the erect.
Oh god. It's happening. Why do dead girls do this to me?
I'm Eli the upright, Eli the swollen.
Nobody is around. I could do anything to her. But all I want is to wake her up. And nothing is working and she's getting colder and soon it might be too late. So I open my mouth and for the first time ever I shout that word:
'Help!'
But she is already screaming it for me.
'Help! Help!'
Oh my god. Oh my god. She's awake.
Her waist writhing in my arms. Her hips flailing between my thighs. Her ankles kicking up at my back. So much energy all of a sudden. Almost magical.
'Help! Help me!' she is screaming.
That's when I see them. Where were they before?
A crowd, a crew, some would call it a gang.
Half of them paramedics, half of them policeman - some of them even look like press. A few stragglers from the public. All of them have made their way into the shattered corridor of the hospital, and instead of looking at me with reverence, they're looking at me with rage. And now there's even more of them, and they're all coming.
Coming towards us.
Where were they when she needed them?
'Hey! Get off her!'
Oh. *This* must be how it looks.
A man, in a corner, his body atop a woman. Straddling her, bent over her, her chin grazed from his stubble. His hand on her neck, his knees pinning her to the ground. Not to mention the other thing. He'd never realised before how similar lifesaving looked to something else. He would have laughed before at a molester, raising up their hands and trying the excuse 'I was giving her mouth to mouth!'
I leap off her. Can a person ever do that quickly enough? 'I was just … I was trying to help her!'
'He attacked me!' she screams.
I snap round, look at her.
Blue. Her eyes are the colour blue. And they're crying.

'Careful! He's dangerous!'
One, two, three men, they jump to me, pinning me to the ground. I hear the chaos above my head as they scoop her up in a bundle of distress and accusations.
'Hope that was worth it, son.' They haul me to my feet. My hands are behind my back and I don't where they're taking me. 'Sicko.' They look down and suddenly I realise. Oh god. I'm still Eli the Erect.
'Take him to the van.' They say. 'Keep an eye on him til they come.' Too quickly: my life is changing too quickly.
The grip on me tightens. My grip on my reputation loosens.
They let me turn, let me look into the eyes of the women I ... saved ... attacked ... which one is it? It's hard to believe a minute ago she wasn't breathing. Now she stands, so lit up with hate, and I realise she must have known me all along.
And then she doesn't speak, but I hear her. I hear her voice louder than I've ever heard anything in my life. ' *My name is Cupid. Don't fuck with me.'*
Nobody else heard it but me. But they hear her now. She hisses her next statement, her voice lilting just enough at the tip, '*Lock him up.*'
I lock eyes with Erica through the window on her door. She is watching. Ann is laughing. I am being dragged away. Nobody is stopping it. Erica's hand is on the window. Then it's gone.
And Eli the leader and Eli the tender all float away from me, stripping me down to the one thing I've only ever really been. Eli the creep. Eli the abuser.
Eli the monster.
And now they all know it.

Chapter Fifty Six

What a trick that was. And one only Cupid could pull off.

Myles and Valentina were standing on the fire escape. They climbed up here after the police took Eli, holding onto anything they could touch. Their fingers were bleeding and their faces were flushed.

'So do you have it?' His smile swung, his eyes glazed. 'Did you manage to get it?'

'Come on now Myles. Everything you've seen me do; you don't think I can pick a pocket or two?' She reached into the waves of her hair, and as a ringlet fell, so did the USB. She caught it in her grip, and offered it to him.

He took it. *Thank you, thank you, thank you.*

'Why'd you take me up here?'

Closer he came. The rain was confident now, spilling out the sky. Her pink lips quivered. His lips turned blue.

'I love fire escapes,' the words flashed against the sky. 'Always have, always will.' He moved through the air. 'And I love you. I do, Valentina. You make it easy.'

That body. He watched it wind across the steps, a mockery of all the other women's bodies that came before it. The way she walked, the way she let her hair swing, the legs that carried something sacred at their top.

He touched her waist. So it had all come down to this. To something that could fit in both his hands.

He found himself against the wall, the brick biting his back.

She leant into him and whispered. 'I love you too, Myles. And yet now I'm here, all I can think of doing is – '

'Pushing me?'

'I want to show you what Heaven looks like.'

'I know what Heaven is. It's Erica.' The words were out of his mouth before he could stop himself.

And Valentina was out of his arms before he could stop her.

'You can't do this to me again,' she was crying before he could even register what he'd said, what he'd done, the fact he couldn't take it back. 'You can't break me again. I'd rather break myself.'

She pushed past him, using her strength to get to the top of the fire escape. He pursued her, the slippery rust an issue for him, while she had all the balance of an angel. How had he managed to find and fall in love with two angels? And why was he choosing the one that never chose him?

At one with the rain, Valentina stood on the highest level, heels hovering as she looked down at him.

'*I* am the one who can make you happy, Myles. Make you laugh. Make you free. You'll be saving that girl til your last day on Earth. Or you can come with

me. One kiss from me and we go to Heaven together. I'll give you the death you fought for.
I'll show you how to fly. I'll show you how to win. I'll show you how to rule. I'll give you all the power and all the fire and all the pleasure as long as you just *stay with me.*'
Her lips are lava. Don't fall in.
His mind cracked. His face fell down.. 'I want that, Valentina. I want you! But I can't … I can't let her go …'
'No!' her teeth swung with anger. 'You *can.* You just have to choose.. Choose me.'
He looked at her, all the pinkness, all the candyfloss in the world mixed with all the vengeance in the sky, and suddenly a life with her became clear. *We could do anything.*
Anything.
Anything but heal.
'I'm sorry,' his eyes steamed. 'Not without her.'
A smirk like he'd never seen drove up her face. *She twirls so I can see everything I'm turning down, everything I'm giving up, her heels slipping on the railings as she revolves.* And then lightly, she shrugged and whispered, her voice tiny, 'Guess I'll just have to go flying myself.' *Off she goes.*
He ran to grab her but all he caught was the air as she fell.
Not flew. Fell.
Fell, fell, fell.
And joined the grass on the ground.
And cracked.
As quick as that. As easy as that.
Too many moments in too little time. Why wasn't she flying?
She was not moving. She was no more. But Myles was still here. And he had lost her.

He couldn't cry.
Another loss. Another person out of his life. Grief upon grief until there is nothing left. Would he be the last person in the world? He'd always feared that, specifically that, that maybe he was the only immortal person in the world, set to be alone for eternity. There's no way of knowing if that's not the case. And Valentina dying was proving that irrational, paranoid, little-boy fear right. Cupid had gone, so maybe all the love in the world had gone, too. And he knew just who would get the blame if so.

He couldn't think like that.
The USB in his fist reminded him.
He had things to do.

He stormed down the fire escape. The last bit of strength, the last bit of physicality in him, gets him to the bottom and back to the crowd.
The press were still there. The ambulances were still there. The police were still there. The injured were still there.
Press or police?
Press, he thought, press. He couldn't risk a cover up of Eli's evil.
He saw it. A reporter being interviewed for the BBC - live, live, live. *Let's do this live.*
It took two seconds. Two seconds to crash the interview, to declare to the camera, 'This is the truth about Core Retreat.' Hand the USB to the journalist and then he was gone.
And then all that was left was Her.

The only thing he'd ever wanted to do, and the only thing he'd do now for the rest of his life. *Her.*
Across the car park he saw her.
Erica.
The hair. The eyes. The body. The soul. Erica.
Was he selling his soul, or was he turning his soul into gold? He'd only know once he'd done it.
Erica, watch me swing. Watch me win. I'm coming.
And he was running - or maybe he was finally flying - he got to the other side of the car park, dragged himself across the concrete, crashed through the barrier as she staggered to her feet.
But just as he was about to reach her - just as she saw him - just as they exhaled -
It happened.
A crowd of people closed around her.
A hundred of them at once.
Their circle sealed her in.
The ring of desire.
Myles knew this. He'd smelt this. He'd dreamt of this. He knew these people.
He knew their darkness. *He knew what they were.*
And they'd come for her.

Chapter Fifty Seven

As soon as Erica entered the car park, she felt it. That she had stepped into a moment that was … off.

It came from a crowd, not of people Erica had healed, but of those who had been waiting to see her. If they saw her, they would feel good: they'd been promising themselves that all day.

And yet, when they finally caught sight of her, there was no goodness left to feel. They didn't feel the joy or the love they had been promised they would. They didn't feel the thrill of fear either, or the triumph of the day ending with a rescue.

Something was missing. Maybe it was because Cupid had jumped. Maybe she had left behind a world without love, and Erica was getting the blame.

Maybe it was low blood sugar, or dehydration, or the trauma of the day behind them, but out of the emptiness, all they could feel was anger.

But nothing could explain why what happened next.

Even as she walked towards them, Erica knew something about this moment was wrong. And yet, it was a moment Erica chose to give herself to. As she had given so many times before.

What was once more?

Chapter Fifty Eight

Erica

I'm so lucky; I can't believe people look at me the way they do.
As if there's nothing they'd rather look at. Nothing they'd rather touch.
I think they're about to lift me up. I think they're about to carry me across their hands. I think they're gonna hold me up to the sky and spin me beneath the sun. They love me. I'm so lucky that they love me. *Here they come.*
My skin is already slipping off by the time they surround me.
Twenty of them; it reminds me of the time my mother baked a butterscotch brioche pudding for twenty people's dessert. Buried her secrets in layers of cinnamon and egg. I think she cooked it with love, a little at least, then she made sure to keep it warm and I still remember the 'ooh' sound they made when she brought it out. They grinned as she spooned it out, and with a wink they dived into their bowls. However she didn't touch it. She didn't so much as lick the brown sugar off her finger whilst cooking it; she was one of the first people to realise dairy is unhealthy.
Anyways. Now they are holding the eggs, or what are shaped like eggs but look like rocks.
By the time I realise what's happening, they've already bound my hands. By the time I think about running, my feet are already on fire.
Turns out it is rocks they are holding. Not eggs. But they're cracking something over my head.
And some are holding pills. Tiny, white and round. Golly gee. I think I'm about to be stoned by painkillers.
I always knew it. I always knew they would do this to me.
For as long as human's have skin, we're gonna skin each other alive.
A woman's voice. 'Why can't I feel anything?' She is looking right at me when she says it. She is short and sweaty, and her eyes are dehydrated. 'Why can't I feel something?'
The woman next to her goes to hold her hand. They try, and look at each other, and frown because it just doesn't feel right. 'What did you do?'
A man in a leather jacket is speaking over them, his words charging towards me with confusion. 'Why don't I feel anything? What have you done?'
Love has become lethargic. Slowly, it is replaced with blame.
'Ten minutes ago I was terrified,' yet another one pipes up. 'Now I feel nothing.'
They look around, to try and shake the feeling, to spot someone who is crying fresh tears or trembling fresh shakes. They smell the blood on their hands, in the hopes their stomach might turn. Instead, there is nothing. 'She's taken something from us.'
Even the lightning is lazy now.

'Erica.' They know my name. 'What have you done?'
I sigh deeply as I realise what is happening.
I am not going to ask them to hold in their anger. It would only be my little voice against a hundred of them.
'I always knew she was dangerous,' a girl addresses the whole crowd, and she is talking about me. 'You all love her because you think she can make you live forever. What if forever is inside a tank of oil?' The crowd shudders.
Another girl speaks. She approaches me out of the crowd and I see it in her eyes. Envy. 'You left them,' she gets right in my face to say it. 'You left all those people who needed you, and you weren't going to come back.'
Within this crowd of people, there is an acceptance. An acceptance of what they're going to do to me.
Maybe I should be a vessel, something for them to purge themselves on. That anger has to go somewhere, so maybe I should just let it go to me.
Be angry. Be angry. I want your anger to last a generation. I want what you do to me today to define an era.
I sink to my knees, and then I close my eyes. 'Do it.'
Then I wait.
Pain isn't really real, I tell myself as I kneel, and I want pain anyway. My death will matter. Just you wait. You're gonna make me matter.
My compliance, my submission, infuriates them further. They heat up harder.
And the waiting is over. They begin.
The rocks start to come.
Do *you* still love me?
Scalded and flayed, crushed and crippled, which one is which, nothing matters, it's all the same in the middle of this mob.
My moles cast a map of where for them to go, they just need to follow it. They can't decide what to break first so they break it all.
And they pluck. They're plucking my hair out. Strand by strand.
Come on. Come to me. I never liked salt til now; rub the salt in.
Who's the strongest? Who's the fastest? Who can turn a girl into a tissue?
Do you need a tissue? Because all I am is tissue.
All the gravel in all the playgrounds in the world fills me up. It's playtime.
Show me how to play. Show me who you are.
The group distends and I shrink. Drink me.
No rules for the mob. Penetration flagellation amputation. Why is it all so gooey? Why am I coming apart so easily? Why have they started eating me?
Come on, pig. Don't stop now, cow. Keep up, boar. Why so slow, buffalo?
Feed, piggies, feed. Drink, you sows, drink up.
Stick your snouts in the trough. There's enough to go round. Swallow me whole. Scoff me up. You're dooling. Lick it up. There's a bit in your teeth.
Who has ever loved the lynching?

Until today, until me, until now, until I realised what that lynching could do for me, how their rage could lick me clean.
Today, I lap the lynching up.
You do love me.
'Witch!' I hear it.
I see witches, all the witches in the world, my sisters. All the ones who were stoned to death before me. If I'm really a witch then I should be able to fly out of here away from them, right? I squeeze my eyes shut real tight and I try to fly. Just as my feet leave the ground, the first brick hits, planting me back down. The glass goes right through me and I remember.
I remember.
After mother cooked the brioche pudding, two days passed before the phone calls came in, heaving voices splattering down the phone. 'I've been vomiting all night' – 'Ruby is in an awful way' – 'My wife has come down with semolina!' 'What the hell was in that pudding?' One after the other til all twenty people had rung her up, screaming and asking what she'd put in their gut.
Now this mob will serve me up, in batches of curried kittens. Revenge because my mother's pudding was off, all those years ago.
Another rock bounces off my temple.
Please make it quick, make it kind, make it count.
Little by little, they're starting to feel something again. They had to make my tongue to stop being numb. And now there's a music to the mauling; now they can dance again inside of my screams. I had to scream so they could dance again, and dance they do.
That's the essence of a mob, really, isn't it; if they have anything in them at all, it's hate. Hate is what makes them thrive. Hate is what brings them together. Let this happen to me, as long as it doesn't happen to them.
'You thought you were better than us. You thought we needed you. But you needed this.'
'She's not as pretty as I thought she would be.'
Oh god, this is going to be slow.
Ungratefully, sloppily, they start the snapping.
I am sick with myself and sick with them and I can hear them being sick too; a rush of smooth vomit wipes me front to back – what a bad girl I must be, for this to be the way I'm going to die.
By the hair on my head, I am taken in one direction – by the hair on my chin, I am pulled to another – by the pricking of my thumbs, something wicked this way comes.
I want this. I want pain.
If I had been allowed to grow old I would have grown into an ugly woman.
Maybe it is better this way.
Oh. That hurt too much. Oh.
And that.

That too.
And that.
It's getting quicker now. Domino effect. Some hands are soft. Some nails are bleach.
And there's just this.
Just that.
Just touch.
Just hell.
I think the pavement is parting. I think we're going to the underworld. I think that's my ear in someone's mouth. I think I've been a toy my whole life.
You are gonna feel so guilty when this is done.
'Got them!'
So triumphant. Got what? Why can't I see? Is it my eyes?
'Erica! Erica!' I know that voice. The comfort of it is so strange in a mob.
'ERICA!'
I realise I still have my eyes. They snap open to see Myles, fighting his way through the mob. And if Myles is fighting for me, that means this is gonna be over soon. That means we're only a few minutes away from my death going viral.
What will the world make of a mob that takes on a girl? Not just a girl, an innocent girl. Not just an innocent, but a healer.
If a mob takes The Healer from the world, there will never be another mob again.
Take me. Break me. It was never my body. It was never my mind. It was never my life.
'Get off her! Leave her alone! Get off!' I smile as he shouts. And I reach for him but my fingers are bent backwards -
Hate is a fire.
I am Erica Ash, and this is the fire I will die in.
'Erica! No! Fight for yourself!'
I shake my head.
'Erica, please! I love you, I love you, I LOVE YOU SO FIGHT! FIGHT FOR US!'
Though I didn't want to die like this, I know my death will have a purpose. It is knowing this that gives me the push to look into Myle's eyes. Bat my eyelashes and smile slow. His pupils go wide. Our minds lock.
Let a lifetime of loss lift off him: he knows it too. *My death will have a purpose.* He gets it.
Look what they've done to my hair. Look what they've done to my body. Look what they've done to my eyes.
Look what they've done to my soul.
Look what they've done to my song. Sing it with me.
Sing it to me, Myles.

They drag me towards him. It's time for him to join in. It's his turn, it's only ever been his turn, I've only ever been his.

I close my eyes, wait for his spit. Wait for his chemical kiss. Nothing comes. When I open them, he is gone.

And as my ribs become part of a rack, as my skin accepts it was only held together by luck, as my scalp joins the grit on the ground, I tell them they are the last mob there will ever be. No one will ever go through this again.

Then again. Then again. Think about it. Look at them. This has brought them together. This has given them meaning.

And they're having such fun doing this to me.

Why should the fun have to end?

Epilogue

'So. Give me your verdict.' Darren gave his old friend Myles a playful slap on the back. 'Don't be too harsh now.'

Myles put one firm arm around his neck, his eyes wide with respect. 'Mate. I think it's – '

'Oh, wait! There's one more room I have to show ya.' Darren swung his arm over his shoulders, turning them both to face the grand double doors behind them. 'Open up!'

From behind the doors, two assistants hauled them open, welcoming Darren and Myles into the largest room Myles had ever been in. Apart from its glass, domed ceiling that looked up to the sky, the room was made entirely out of quartz crystal.

'Come on in,' Darren said, sliding his arm off Myles and stepping backwards into the room with a knowing grin. 'This is the ballroom,' Darren gestured wide, to the panels, pillars and archways that made up the colossal space. 'Where we will hold balls. And silent discos. And foam parties. And maybe … wife carrying championships! Basically, any kind of party we can think of.'

Myles looked him in the eye. 'I love it.'

'See, when we spoke to the victims, this is the one story that kept coming up. About the night Eli threw them a ball, and how it was the one thing they are actually grateful for. Something about the energy in the room … fixed them, is that how you'd describe it?'

'Yes. Just a little bit.'

'Yeah. Well that's too good an opportunity to waste. We're going to see if that can happen again, and what else could happen. I'm guessing not being held against their will might aid the recovery a bit,' he laughed dryly. 'I hate to so directly steal one of *that man's* ideas, but this place is all about combining the best of Sunset and Core's philosophies, being what they should have been. So we had to include a dance floor.'

'Of course.' Myles ran a hand across the crystal wall, his flesh celebrating the different textures of smooth marble and glassy granite. 'I *love* what you've done with the architecture. I didn't even think it was possible to have a room made entirely of jewels.'

'Yeah, cost a bomb, but look at it.' Darren grinned proudly. 'And apparently crystals have ancient healing properties. We've got rose quartz, amethyst, citrine … might do fuck all but worth a try.'

'Agreed.' Myles pointed to the ceiling and asked with a slight edge in his voice, 'And what are those for?' He had just noticed the hooks hanging from it.

Darren looked up to where he was pointing. 'Ha, don't panic, mate!' He gave him a wolfish grin. 'Those are just for our aerial acts, to perform from. Michelle suggested it – in fact, she wants to perform too. She's here now. Shall we go have a drink with her, to celebrate?'

'Let's do it.'

It had been the obvious answer, once Sunset Clinic had been shut down, under suspicion of corruption and its links to Core Retreat, now known as a site of shame. To prove the UK could still trust in its humanity, there needed to be a new place for people to go – and this place needed not just to be safe, but to be special.

So the best parts of Core and Sunset had to be combined. It had to deliver swift, dignified, doctor-assisted dying, with a less rigorous screening process than there had been before. It had to offer support for the families, entering them into a programme that would help them accept and move on from what they'd done for their loved ones. And it had to offer good final memories, too - people experienced things here they were too shy to experience in real life, the kind of things saved for a few wild months of backpacking, until now. At the same time, it had to have another option, the option of an extended check in to see if they would give the world another try. During this time they underwent intense physical and spiritual therapy, but most of the time was simply spent doing their favourite things, with their favourite people, to see if that could unlock a restorative placebo within them. The retreat knew how to make the vibes flow; DJ Ghanga Ghecko had a permanent residency. Not to mention it had a whole wing dedicated to scientific breakthroughs. Lessons had been learnt from Eli's mistakes; science beat suffering every time. People came out of here tougher than they went in, their minds clarified and ready for whatever was next. And of course, they had the option to quit at any time.

But best of all, was that the all-or-nothing thinking, the rock and roll spirit that had caused people to euthanise themselves after being turned down for lipo, or girls to sign up to Sunset simply because they were about to turn thirty - many had expected that spirit, the spirit that wouldn't accept anything less than a life of euphoria, to be stamped out - but it hadn't. Somehow, it had carried through. The hedonistic desire for a life of your dreams was no longer something to be shamed for, just as much as it was no longer something to submit to. Now, there was a whole wing here dedicated to the attempt to 'have it all'. A state of the art research laboratory that focused on genetic engineering, on bio-modelling, of being able to conquer what might be, let's say, disappointing or demotivating. By the time the researchers were done, no man would ever be born cursed to live five feet tall, and no woman would ever be cursed to carry a slow metabolism with her through her prime - quite the opposite in fact. And just when you might start to say that was too radical, too vain, the lab announced it would be dedicating its research to more serious ailments also; those terminal or debilitating, early on set dementia for example - the things that drew people to support the Assisted Dying Bill in the first place. Essentially, they would fight for health just as much as they would fight for beauty, and almost as much as they would fight for death.

And who should be heading up that wing? None other than Scott Luther. Myles had persuaded the centre to give him a chance, instead of punishing him for his cronyism with Eli, and despite their doubts, Scott had shone in this role.

This place was the perfect new innovation, and it could only have been pulled off by one man: Darren.

Sitting opposite him in his epic office now, Myles realised Darren was who he'd always wanted to be. Or thought he did.

'Woof!' Rocco barked eagerly from his comfy place on Michelle's lap, to which she ruffled his sleek fur happily in response – they had missed each other.

'It's amazing, isn't it?' Michelle said, pouring the three of them the unhealthiest yet tastiest drink on the planet: the sacrilegious Diet Coke. Imagine if Eli could see them now.

'Thanks babe,' Myles said as she slid the coke across Darren's desk towards him, and took a sparkling sip. 'It sure is. It's fucking incredible.'

They weren't just talking about Darren's new centre.

They were talking about the world. About the changes they were seeing in front of them by the day. About the one billion pounds the government had just assigned towards improving the quality of life, for chronically or terminally ill patients. About the other one billion they had allocated to research into cures for illnesses and conditions that had barely been funded before.

But it wasn't just that that had changed.

Something had transformed, deep within their culture. Not just because they had lost Erica, but because it was because the mob had taken her. That loss, and those images of the crowd tearing into her, had caused an irreversible shift in everybody's psych.

There was just a little more *mercy* in the world now. Suspect's names were now confidential, no longer released to the press. Appeals and retrials were being won at a rapid rate. That morning a video had surfaced of a footballer making sexist comments – nobody was calling for his resignation and his shaming; everybody had 'better things to do now'. Even the people who had done wrong had been given another chance. Like Ann. Myles had wanted to see her today, but she was teaching a yoga class. The new Ann had fallen in love with yoga.

And even when it came to Eli. His trial was starting next week. It was going to be long, and it was going to be intense. He was to take the stands for multiple counts of kidnap, false imprisonment, torture, fraud and even human trafficking.

And yet there were the whispers the judge was considering a somewhat lenient sentence. Because 'there had been enough imprisonment, enough cages, for one lifetime, and where has it got us? If the rules aren't working, change them.'

Needless to say, all the calls for another vote on The E Word had died with Erica.

So yes, there was a lot of mercy now. Some might say too much, but … probably not in front of these three.

'So,' Michelle turned to Darren. 'Have you asked him yet?'

'Nope.'
'Asked me what?' Myles took another gulp of coke. *More* surprises.
'There is *one* – '
'One more thing you have to show me,' he finished for him.
'No, not show you - though I do want to get your opinion on our new saltwater floatation pool, it's going to be incredible for the inflamed - but … ask you. You see, we're working on a final wing for this place. Something you said inspired me to open it. This wing is going to deal with grief.' Darren leaned forward eagerly in his seat. 'Imagine it, Myles. The end of grief. The end of loneliness. The end of pain.'
'Woof!' Rocco added happily.
Myles reached over to stroke the dog. 'So … what's your plan?'
He didn't know what else Darren could come up with. There was even a forgiveness chamber in here. Don't get him started on the plans for the CBD maze. And then there was the moon water water park, designed to drench you in all the sensation it could before you made 'The Decision.'
What else could this man, this brilliant but arrogant man, come up with? There was something, Myles could see him glinting. He decided to listen. In this new world, he could drop his jealousy and admire him. And just like that, Darren Thames was his best friend.
'Well, right now it's, erm, very … mortal. Right now all I've come up with is bereavement counsellors. And I'm talking the very best bereavement counsellors in the world. We're going to create a whole programme – of CBT, of therapy, of … erm … well that's kind of it. But we're wondering … both me and Michelle … if there's something more. Some of the stories that have come out about Core, about Erica, about you and that morning in the field – '
'That wasn't real.' Myles shot back.
'Sure. But … what if it could be? What if it's possible, in some way, to do what Eli was trying to do? In an ethical way of course. To, prolong, or, or resurrect, or, fuck knows, maybe we can build a ladder to heaven, I don't know! But I'd like to think anything might be possible. And …'
'We want you to help us, Myles.' Michelle cut across his speech. 'Look at the life you've lived. Look at everything that happened to you, everything you went through. Is it really a coincidence that it happened to you?
There's something about you, Myles. I think we've all seen it, ever since we met you. It's probably why Erica was drawn to you. It's why Darren wanted to help you escape back then – there's something *in* you. The King of Grief. I look at you and I just know – you could help people. In some way ease the loss in the world. Whether it's a rescue, or protection, or prevention, or building a weapon, or really full blown *resurrection,* or just offering the perfect words of comfort. *You're* the one Myles. We believe you can do it. So what do you think?'
Myles picked up his coke. He swilled it in the glass a little, then downed it one, the aspartame settling into his cells. 'No.'

'No?!' Michelle said.
'No,' he repeated. 'Nope.' Then he looked to and from them, to the shock in their eyes, and spoke in a warmer, softer way. 'You know, I used to think that's who I might be too. A hero. Somebody who saved people. I've been chasing that for as long as I can remember. And yet all it's done is lead me here. To this chair, sitting opposite a man who's done it all for me.
So what am I?
I'm not a saviour, or a protector, or a role model. I'm something else.
And now I need to find out what that is.'
He stood up out of his seat. Energy and confidence rode through him. He didn't want to be here. 'I hope you understand. I've got some exploring to do/'
'I think you're wrong about yourself, Myles,' Darren said sadly, before drumming his hand on his desk. 'But it's not my place to stop you. Go out and find yourself.'
'I will.'
'Not before tonight's gala dinner, though,' Michelle chimed in. 'You are coming, right? We have your suite already for you.'
His eyes glinted at her. 'Of course. I wouldn't miss your performance.'
'And Ann wouldn't miss another dance with *you*.' She winked. 'She's coming.'
Darren stood too; Myles had known he would. Neither man liked to be below the other. They shared a nod.
They shook hands. 'Good luck,' Myles said. 'Oh, do you have a name for this place, by the way?'
'No actually.' Darren said. 'I want something with paws and jaws. Something about lions, about wolves. Something primal, you know.'
'Try Rellik. As in relick, but spelt R-E-L-L-I-K.' It had just come to Myles in that moment. 'Rellik. It's killer, spelt backwards.'

A vengeful rainstorm danced down on the grounds, causing everyone to huddle in its atriums and arches. Except Myles. He walked to his suite, refreshed by the rain.
When he had lost her, he couldn't believe it. Standing outside the hospital thinking, 'Damn. I lost the one I love again.' There was a pond nearby, and he considered walking straight into it. He would continue walking, til his head was submerged by the water, walking onto a river bed, walking until he reached the bottom of the ocean and he never had to lose anyone again.
A series of images had gone through him – paying Gerry to kill him, crying for his mother, pissing himself, forgiving Rose, being unable to cut off her hands, confining himself to a chair, chewing mud, having coffee thrown in his face – and all those images turned around on him, and made him into something else.
He realised he was tired. No, not tired. Bored. Bored of grieving, bored of losing, bored of wanting something he couldn't have.

He remembered who he'd been before he'd lost his mother. Or not who he'd been, but who he wanted to be. He'd wanted to be fearless. He wanted to be *fun.* He'd wanted to live a life not even Casanova could have predicted. And it was now or never.

He didn't ever want to follow someone, apologise, or even forgive, ever again. He just wanted to feel. He wanted to be the man he was meant to be, and take the life he was born to live.

After all, the world was just a woman, just a woman that belonged to him. He could place his thumb in its mouth, run it along its lips before drawing them open and winding his tongue inside.

After all, the world was just a woman, just a woman that belonged to him. He could lift it up, place it on his kitchen counter, before parting its legs and making it beg for more.

After all, the world was just a woman, just a woman that belonged to him. He *would* wrap his hands in its hair, back it up against the wall and slid its underwear to the side.

After all, the world was just a woman, just a woman that belonged to him. He *would* hold its face in both hands, before forcing it to its knees before him. Tell it to open wide and don't forget to swallow. Watch it gag but make sure that it didn't choke.

After all, the world was just a woman, just a woman that belonged to him. He could bend it over, hold it around the waist and thrust.

Bend it over, hold it around the waist and thrust.
Bend them over, hold them round the waist and thrust
Bend them over, hold them round the waist and thrust
Hold them round the waist and thrust
Hold them round the waist and thrust
Make sure they don't choke
Hold them round the waist
Don't let them choke
And thrust
Hang on …

And that, ladies and gentlemen, is how the Heimlich Manoeuvre was invented. Or not quite the Heimlich manoeuvre, for that was already out there, but something better; The Myles Manoeuvre - with a different angle with which to bend them at the waist and a new motion with which to thrust into their side, nobody would ever lose their life to the food in their trachea again. Nobody, not one person, would ever choke again.

As soon as Myles showed them how.

Just like that, he saw it: a new way to prevent people from choking. A way to save lives. So many people lost their loved ones from choking, but not any more. Not if they did this.

A whole horizon glimmered as the move became clear to Myles. Crystal in his mind; how had nobody thought of it before? This would work so much better than before. This would be foolproof. A reel of images spun through him, spawned on the one image of stopping people choking - The Myles Manoeuvre. A revolution. Yes, yes, yes.

His purpose fulfilled, he realised *this* is what Michelle must have been talking about: his contribution to ending grief. He *could* do it.

He needed to tell everyone. He needed to show everyone. They needed to know!

And then there was the envelope.

His eyes went straight to it as he entered his suite. Wide, white, calm, a lone whale lying in wait on his black marble minibar, on top a pile of fishy looking invitations. It had been explained to him that now and then something was sent here for him, by people who suspected he worked here, but only now and then. Most of the fan mail was saved for Darren.

A letter.

Dear Myles,

Hey. I hope the handwriting doesn't freak you out – I know it's similar to hers. It's Erica's mother. Did she ever tell you my name? I'll let you in on it. Electra. Anyway. Do you miss our girl? Maybe that's why I'm writing this letter. Maybe I just need to talk to someone who knew her like I did. Maybe if I write it down in ink, it will ease some of what's going on inside me.

But I didn't write this letter for your pity, or to share in our loss. I didn't even write this letter to see how you were doing.

I'm writing this letter to tell you a secret.

How to say this. Well. She was an amazing girl, wasn't she? Beautiful. I'd like to think I'm beautiful too, but never as beautiful as her. Slender. Funny. I'd like to think I'm witty as well, and I think I am. Kind. I can be kind. And above all, selfless. Now that's one thing I know I'm not. And now I am cursed with wondering, if I had been less selfish, would she still be here?

You know what I mean. You must do, deep down.

If I had told her I was a healer too, would that have stopped her? Perhaps I could have warned her and taught her how to keep herself safe. That's what a parent should do. But I was always too afraid to share my powers, even right up until the last moment, because I knew what could happen, and look what did. Mama knows best.

For all those years I thought it had skipped her, that gene. I thought she was just normal, and she would be safe. Then I lost her anyway. Then I got her back - I knew it as soon as we embraced but I tried to deny it. And when the world came looking for her, I could have – no, I should have – said, 'Take me instead.' A less glamorous, older healer, I was what the world should have been focusing on. Every night I went to bed telling myself I would, then when I woke up in the morning, I was too scared. The words died on my tongue. Maybe I was jealous of her. She was what I could never be, what I was never strong enough to be.

And now she is dead.

Can you guess what I'm going to ask you?

I'm going to ask if you think I should bring her back.

All of her, every bit of her. Ten minutes time and we could have her back in the world. All it would take is one touch and the guts to dig her up. Every time I close my eyes, I see it. I dream of it. I look in the mirror and she looks straight back.

But what if she's happy where she is? What if she's finally at peace? What if I get it wrong?

But how can I go another day without her?

So I thought I would ask you. I thought you would know. If it is the right thing to do.

Because I do know you loved her. My memory is hazy these days, but I know that was real.

Should we let her be at peace, or shall we let her release her chaos?

Come find me, and we will make that choice.

Or maybe it's too late. Maybe by the time you read this, I have already done it.

Who could refuse themselves the chance to bring their dead child back?

Perhaps it's already done.

Come find me.

Thank you for what you did for her.

Love,
Electra.

Myles folded the letter. Then he crumpled it. Then he smoothed it out. Then he tore it up. Then he put it back together.

The old Myles would have drowned in the words, but the new Myles remained calm.

Because this woman had two things he wanted; she was Erica, and she was a mother. How had he never put that together before? A fantasy made flesh.

And he wondered if this was all a test. Just one great big Truman Show style joke. At the moment his true purpose had come to him, now apparently Erica could come back to him. But he knew he needed to focus. To not let himself dissolve, all over again on a tease, a false promise. He had discovered something vital. He had lives to save. But what about bringing back the life he'd let the mob take from him? But that might not be real. The Myles Manoeuvre, saving lives, that was real and that was real purpose. But then again, even if Erica wasn't real, Electra was, and why should he deprive himself of Electra?

Because if he did, nobody would ever choke again.
Was he really going to throw away all that progress, and for what? For love.
Focus! Containment! Purpose! Stay strong! He had something of value to share. He had a mission in life, a place in this retreat, a way of brightening the world now. He couldn't let go of that.
The longing had to end sometime. Tonight was the night he did more than fall in love. Tonight he watched grief burn.
'Darren,' he practised his speech. 'I think I've discovered something …'
He bored his eyes into the mirror, tightening his collar. Save them! Tell them! Show them what you can do! His brown eyes and his black stubble and his strong jaw, defined by a crack in the mirror, or was that his scar from that day digging up Core's gardens?
He went to look closer but it had disappeared.
Myles knew it, as sure as he knew it was oxygen not helium nor carbon nor propane in his lungs: there was only one person in the world who could make a scar disappear like that.
Only one person.
Only fucking one.
And so the floor beneath him became nothing but coals he had to run across, and the suite around him became nothing but walls he had to melt through, til he was in a corridor, then at the end of it, then round a bend looking at a staircase he knew he shouldn't be looking at.
And the stairs in front of him became nothing but a height he had to scale, and the door at the top of the stairs became nothing but a boulder he had to break through.
And when he got through that door, he saw there were more stairs: more and more of them and narrower too, a winding staircase leading up to the top tower of the building, promising to take him somewhere.
And if he'd had no legs, he would have grown new ones, to get to the top of it.
Somebody was waiting for him up there.
Hand on the bannisters, he began his ascent, the stone around him closing on him with every swerve of it he turned. And as he continued the climb, he realised he was limping. He powered up, until he came to a door.
And when he blasted it open, there were more stairs.
He continued the climb. **Is she up there?**
Is she there, is she there, waiting for him?
Another set of stairs. His foot gave out, slipping. He gripped the bannister and continued.
Are you there for me girl? Are you waiting?
More stairs, melting beneath him, the stone no match for the fire in his feet, as he thought about one more moment with her.
If I don't have her, I have her mother. The thought flashed into him before he banned it. But then; **or could I have both?**

Who do I want?
Both. Neither.
No. I want her.
And finally the tower got so narrow he knew this had to be the last few stairs.
He was itching. His ears were ringing with how much he wanted it to be her.
His foot was going numb with how much he wanted it to be her.
Whose it gonna be? Erica or her mother?
And when he reached the door - solid, oak, painted white - he knew this was the last one.
And he knew if he went through this one he was making a decision: to give up. People would never know about the Myles Manoeuvre. He'd be throwing away the chance to heal them, the chance to keep a parent in a person's life and vice versa. If he stepped through that door, all purpose, all power, would pull apart, into a pool of what *he* wanted.
But he could just look. He could just see what was behind it.
If there was nothing behind that door, he would go back. He would help so many people. Stop anyone from ever choking again. He'd burn grief to the ground. But only once he knew.
I want Erica. I want my mother. I want her mother.
He had to know. Wouldn't you?
Lover, mother, lover's mother. It was time to know, to choose, to accept. Whoever was behind this door was worth this. But who was it?
Mother.
Lover.
I want it all.
And as he placed his hand on the door he realised his ears were ringing.
Cupid, is this you? Mama, is that you?
He pushed it apart.
A stone, circular room. Empty. No windows. A white wall facing him. Waiting to close in on him.
Yet, on the wall, he saw words. Three little words. A whole handprint had been used to make them, to smear them across the wall; something was dripping on the floor. He couldn't smell it but only one thing dripped like that; blood. The words were written in blood.
'Look behind you.'
As he turned, the ringing in his ears disappeared.The itching all over stopped. The tingle in his foot went away. Oh baby, was the healing beginning all ready? Oh baby, so much, so soon?
Instead of the ringing, there was silence.
Instead of the tingling, there was numbness.
And - instead of seeing who it was - his vision was starting to blur. Had the limp been a dream?

And despite how hard he tried, he couldn't smell the blood, even as it dripped closer to him, just as his vision got darker and darker around him, til only shapes were moving across his iris, just as sound got further and further away.
'Why can't I hear?
Why can't I see?
Why can't I feel?'
Something moved towards him in the darkness. Two hands closed around his.
Here she was.
Her hands were the last thing he was able to feel. He asked the last thing he would be allowed to ask.
'Why can't I speak?
Why can't I move?
Why can't I cry?'
She laughed. Now he knew for sure who it was.

'Because you're mine.'

Tuula Costelloe studied Drama and Theatre at Trinity College, Dublin, before beginning a career as a 'Scream Queen' in indie horror films. Her passion for exploring daring characters and complex morality reignited her creative writing bug and led to her writing her own scripts. Her script 'Prey For Me' reached the Top 1% of the BBC Writersroom Open Call and her play 'Christmas Is Cancelled' had its debut in London, December 2023.

Mercy is her first novel.

When not writing, she enjoys go-go dancing in Ibiza, and most of all, chilling with cats.

Printed in Great Britain
by Amazon

50315109R00249